Yours or Mine?
No!

YOURS, MINE
& Ours

Take one orphaned baby, a career woman
and a bachelor...
How do you make them a family?
Just add love.

Take an eight-year-old boy and a triangle of would-be
parents and guardians.
How do you make them a family?
Just add love.

Take a thirteen-year-old girl—and the father she knows
vs. a mother who's a stranger.
How do my make them a family?
Just add love!

YOURS, MINE
& Ours

Relive the romance...

Three complete novels by your favorite authors!

About the Authors

PENNY JORDAN
New York Times bestselling author and one of the best-known names in contemporary romance fiction, Penny has over fifty million copies of her books in print. Born in Preston, Lancashire, Penny now lives in a beautiful fourteenth-century house in rural Cheshire, England.

CATHY GILLEN THACKER
This bestselling author has published almost fifty titles. Originally from the Midwest, Cathy now makes her home in North Carolina with her husband and three children.

MARISA CARROLL
Carol Wagner and Marian Scharf, the two sisters who make up the award-winning writing team of Marisa Carroll, have published almost thirty titles. Both Carol and Marian live in Ohio, and they each have two children.

YOURS, MINE
& Ours

Penny Jordan
Cathy Gillen Thacker
Marisa Carroll

Harlequin Books

TORONTO • NEW YORK • LONDON
AMSTERDAM • PARIS • SYDNEY • HAMBURG
STOCKHOLM • ATHENS • TOKYO • MILAN
MADRID • WARSAW • BUDAPEST • AUCKLAND

HARLEQUIN BOOKS

by Request—Yours, Mine & Ours

Copyright © 1997 by Harlequin Books S.A.

ISBN 0-373-20133-8

The publisher acknowledges the copyright holders of the individual works as follows:
EQUAL OPPORTUNITIES
Copyright © 1989 by Penny Jordan
AN UNEXPECTED FAMILY
Copyright © 1991 by Cathy Gillen Thacker
GATHERING PLACE
Copyright © 1988 by Carol I. Wagner and Marian F. Scharf

Printed in U.S.A.

CONTENTS

She'll do anything for her best friend's orphaned son—even hire a male nanny.

He'll do anything for his cousin's son—even pose as that same male nanny!

EQUAL OPPORTUNITIES

Penny Jordan

CHAPTER ONE

'WHAT exactly do you mean, it's too late to claim the child?'

David Wilder glanced apprehensively at his extremely grim client. He had been warned when he joined the prestigious city law firm of Rainer, McTeart and Holston that some of their clients were very demanding indeed, with exacting standards and sometimes very strong and unfortunately erroneous views about their rights under British law.

'Unfortunately we do number among our clients a few who do not yet seem to be aware that there are some things that money just cannot buy,' the senior partner had told him.

The senior partner was also his godfather, which was how he had come to join the practice in the first place; a relationship which he suspected was not going to protect him at all when the full wrath of the man standing opposite him burst upon his head.

He had acted for the best, he reflected miserably. A minor matter was how the senior partner had described the whole affair: something that need not concern their prestigious client, who was, in any event, out of the country on business at the time. Besides, the woman had already made it clear that she would take charge of the child. How was he supposed to know that Garrick Evans would want the child himself?

It was not, after all, as though there was anything other than the most tenuous of blood ties between them; the son of his deceased second cousin.

'What do you mean, it's too late?' Garrick Evans demanded, repeating his earlier question. The lowered volume of his voice in some odd way added to its menace.

He was a tall man, a good two inches over six foot, with a frame that reminded David Wilder of his school days and the torments of the rugby field. He himself was of a much slighter built, and he gave an inward shudder at the very hardness of the other man. Garrick Evans was well into his thirties, and yet there was an air of honed fitness about him that suggested that he did not spend all his time poring over balance sheets and negotiating deals. But to read the financial press one would think that he did.

"One of the most important power brokers of our time," was how the *Financial Times* had described him, and in doing so had coined a new phrase. A power broker was exactly what Garrick Evans was: a man whose skills in assessing the weak points of an institution and then turning them to either his own or his clients' advantage were so notorious that it was said in the city that whole boards quailed at the sound of his name.

A millionaire before he was thirty, he no longer spent his time buying and selling vast corporations, but instead used his skills on a consultancy basis, normally working for governments or very large corporations. He also gave a great deal of his time to ensuring the profitable running of several large charities—time which he gave free of charge, although very few people knew it.

Garrick Evans had learned a very long time ago that to show people a weakness was to invite them to take advantage of it.

David Wilder cleared his throat and looked nervously into the cold grey eyes of his client.

'Well...that is... Well, the fact is that by declaring that you were abdicating from any responsibility toward the child, you have also given up any rights you might have had over him.'

'*I?*' Garrick queried drily. 'Odd... I don't seem to remember making such a momentous decision.'

'Well, no. You were out of the country at the time, in Venezuela, I believe. You may remember you had given strict instructions that you were only to be contacted in an emergency.'

'I see. And you, of course, didn't consider that the death of my cousin and his wife was an emergency. Is that it? Never mind the fact that my cousin has named me as co-guardian of his child.'

'He was only your second cousin,' David muttered helplessly. 'There had been no contact between you as far as we knew.'

He didn't add that the whole office knew of his well-documented loathing of hangers-on of any kind, and it was for that reason that David had assumed that he wouldn't want the child.

'So, there was an error of judgement. Now what we have to do is to correct that error. Have you been in touch with the woman? What's her name?'

'Kate Oakley,' David supplied for him, admitting, 'Well, no, not yet. We weren't sure what your instructions were going to be.' He cleared his throat nervously again. 'You see, it would be very difficult now to reclaim the child. We would have to prove negligence on the part of your co-guardian. And here, the mere fact that she's a woman, and you're a man, would immediately balance these scales in her favour... We could try to negotiate, of course.'

He said it so doubtfully that Garrick frowned.

'How much do you know about her?' he questioned abruptly.

Silently, David Wilder handed him a file.

'Let me read this and then I'll come back to you. In the meantime, don't do anything. If I think it necessary, I'll go and see Miss Oakley myself. It may be that I will be able to persuade her to see the advantages of the child's coming to me,' he said grimly.

A few hours later, when David Wilder was relating the story to his wife while she was preparing dinner, she turned her head and said thoughtfully, 'Buy her off, did he mean?'

David winced, but admitted that it was a strong possibility.

'Well, I hope she turns him down,' Elaine told him roundly. 'That poor baby... What on earth does he want it for, anyway? He doesn't strike me as a man who would want to take on such a responsibility. Heavens, he's never in one place long enough to bring up a child.'

'He wants an heir, I suppose,' David told her.

'Oh, I see, and rather than go to the trouble of finding himself a wife, he's decided he'd prefer to take on a ready-made son without the nuisance of a woman who might make emotional and financial demands on him. Typical! Just the sort of thing I would have expected from a man like him,' she said scathingly.

David patted his wife's hand, and put her outburst down to the fact that she herself was four months pregnant with their first child, a very emotional time for a woman, but of course there was a thread of truth in Elaine's argument.

Despite the fact that over the course of the years Garrick Evans had had several long-standing relationships with women, it was rumoured that he always made it plain to them that they could forget marriage. A hard man. A man it would be very difficult to get to know. A man who wore an air about him of always getting what he wanted. And what he now wanted was a nine-month-old boy, currently living with his guardian; a woman who, according to her file, was an orphan herself, without either wealth or family to support her.

Even if she wanted to keep the child, she would never be able to stand out against Garrick. Feeling rather sorry for her, David Wilder applied himself to his dinner.

Not all that very far away from the elegant terraced house which had been Elaine Wilder's parents' wedding gift to her and her husband, Kate Oakley sat cross-legged on her sitting-room floor, the telephone receiver jammed into the crook of her neck while she painted her nails with her free hand.

Her house, although not in as fashionable part of London as the Wilders', was every bit as elegantly decorated and furnished. As a PR consultant running her own business, Kate was well aware of the importance of creating the right image; hence the nail polish.

She finished one hand and studied the effect with a frown, while listening to her friend exclaiming in amusement.

'Kate…you with a nine-month-old baby! This I have to see. How in the world are you managing?'

'I'm not,' Kate told her firmly. 'That's why I'm ringing you. In the last six weeks I've gone through four supposed nannies, Camilla. It can't go on. I came in tonight all set to go out to dinner with James, only to discover the latest one waiting for me with her bags packed.'

'Good heavens! Is the child so difficult, then?'

'No, not at all. If anything, he's inclined to be too subdued. The shock of losing his parents, poor little thing… No, the problem is me. Three nights this week, I haven't managed to get in until gone ten at night. Everyone the agency has sent me expects to work a regulation seven-hour day; they don't like being alone all the time with Michael; they don't like the fact that I can't provide them with a private sitting-room and a whole host of other luxuries, and as for their salaries—' She gave a groan. 'The agency is starting to do quite well, but not that well.'

She didn't want to tell Camilla what a struggle it had been even for her to afford the new house. Up until the arrival of small Michael into her life, she had lived in a flat, but she had strong views on how a child should live, and those did not include being cooped up with no outside area to play in. The reason she had bought this particular house had been because of its walled-in back garden.

Admittedly it wasn't very large, but it was certainly large enough for a small boy to vent his energy in. Of course, she was looking ahead. Michael was only nine months old, but in another couple of years…

'I see. I sympathise, my dear, but why have you come to me?'

'Oh, come on, Camilla. You know everyone there is to know in London. If anyone can help me, it's you. You must know where I can find a reliable nanny who isn't going to cost me the earth…'

It was so unusual for her friend to sound so exasperated that Camilla frowned and stopped doodling on her notepad.

She had known Kate for almost ten years. In fact, Kate had worked for her when she first came to London. Camilla had sold out her interest in her own PR firm several years ago, and now spent all her time helping her husband in his own business and looking after their twin daughters. She was proud of Kate's success and drive, feeling that she had been the one responsible for recognising and nurturing them, and she sympathised with her in her present dilemma.

She and her husband had only just returned from a six months' working visit to New York, and this was her first real opportunity to catch up with her friend's life.

'I think you'd better start at the beginning and tell me the whole story,' she suggested firmly. 'Apart from a frantic message on my answering machine, I know nothing whatsoever about this baby who suddenly seems to have taken over your life. He's not yours, of course...'

'No,' Kate agreed quietly, adding, 'He's my godson.'

Start at the beginning, Camilla had said, but she didn't want to. She had put those years at the orphanage and all the insecurities that went with them firmly behind her now, hadn't she?

'His parents were killed in a car crash. Neither of them had any close family.'

'No one? But, Kate, surely...'

'Alan has a second cousin, but they rarely met.' She said it in such a clipped voice that, even without seeing her, Camilla could sense her friend's reluctance to discuss what had happened. Kate could be like that at times, erecting fences behind which she quietly disappeared. They had known one another a long time, and yet Kate rarely talked about her past.

Camilla knew better than to press her now, saying merely, 'I see. So there's no question of you—er—handing over the responsibility of this baby to someone else?'

'No!' Kate told her explosively, and then, realising how much she had betrayed, felt obliged to explain reluctantly, 'I can't do that, Camilla...I can't explain it to you, but I feel I owe it to Jennifer, his mother, to bring Michael up myself. You see, I know she'd want him to have all the things that she and I didn't have. A real home life..she and I didn't have. A real home life...family...'

Abruptly Kate stopped. Already she had betrayed too much, revealed too much, and she started to shake a little as she clutched the receiver. This was the reason she hated to discuss the past: it opened up too many vulnerable areas, too many heartaches that had never properly healed.

'I see,' Camilla said compassionately. 'Well, my dear, there's only one way to do that, isn't there? You will have to find yourself a husband.'

There was a short silence, and then Kate said harshly, 'You know my views on marriage, Camilla. I'm a career woman who wants to earn her own security, not to receive it second-hand from a man who would walk out of my life whenever he chose.'

'Oh, Kate.' Camilla could have wept for her. Where did it come from, this deep, abiding fear of depending on anyone other than herself that made Kate so terrified of emotional commitment? Independence was fine, but it could be carried to extremes. 'Kate, marriage needn't be like that,' she protested quietly. 'Husband and wife can be equal partners, each loving and respecting the other...each mutually dependent on the other...'

'Perhaps,' Kate agreed after a long pause. 'But it isn't a risk I want to take.'

'Well, then, your next best alternative is to follow the example of someone like Britt Ekland, and hire a male nanny,' Camilla told her.

'A what?'

'A male nanny,' Camilla repeated patiently. 'They do exist, I promise you, and marvellous they are too, by all accounts. You'd be surprised how many single working mothers employ men to take care of their children, especially when they're boys. Male patterning and all that. And apparently it works.

There's also the added advantage that there's less jealousy between Mum and nanny when she's a he, if you know what I mean. Less feeling that somehow or other someone else is taking your place with the baby.

Look, I know an agency that specialises in finding male nannies. Why don't I give them a ring on your behalf and see what they can come up with?' she suggested.

A *male nanny*! Kate frowned. Did she really want a strange young man sharing her home? And yet the suggestion had its good points. She had been conscious of rather more than mere covert disapproval from a couple of the girls she had been employing, as though they felt that she was somehow not doing her best for Michael by going out to work, and yet what alternative had she? If she didn't work, she could not support herself. She had no money, no family, nothing to fall back on other than her own skills in the workplace.

'Look, give it a try,' Camilla urged her. 'What have you got to lose? I'll give the agency a ring, get them to send someone round, and if you don't like them… Well, there's nothing lost, is there?'

'All right,'' Kate agreed hesitantly. From upstairs she caught the sound of a small, fretful wail. 'I'll have to go. Michael's just woken up.'

'OK. Leave everything to me. I'll sort something out. Oh, and by the way, how *are* you getting on with James?'

James Cameron owned, among other things, a chain of supermarkets spread throughout the country, and through Camilla's good offices Kate had got the opportunity to take over his PR work. The super- markets, for one reason or another, did not have a good image, and if Kate could get the contract to change this it would be a very healthy boost to her profits.

'He's taking me out to dinner next week. I've got to prepare a couple of presentations for him. He wants to start going up-market with the supermarket acquisition.'

'Watch out for him, Kate,' Camilla warned. 'He regards himself as something of a stud.'

'Don't they all?' was Kate's grim response, and Camilla sighed at her tone of voice.

'Some do,' she admitted, 'but there are others. Men who like and respect women as well as desire them. The problem with you is that because you prefer to think that all men are like the Jameses of this world, you deliberately close your eyes to the existence of the other sort. I've often wondered why.'

'It's safer that way,' Kate told her, and then stopped abruptly. She was giving too much away. Betraying more about herself than was wise. Good friend though Camilla was, if she were to learn of Kate's fear of committing herself emotionally to someone, and through that commitment being hurt as she had been hurt as a child, Camilla would, for the very best of reasons, try to change her outlook. And she didn't want her outlook changing. She felt safer with it the way it was.

Their conversation over, she went upstairs and walked into Michael's bedroom, switching on the light. She had purposefully put a soft light in this room, so that no brightness would distress the baby.

Michael had been premature, and was still slightly small for his age. He was wide awake and not crying now that he saw her. As she reached down into the cot, he raised his arms to her.

Kate picked him up, and comforted him automatically. She felt the dampness of his mouth where he sucked her shoulder and her silk shirt. Damn! She normally changed when she got home from work, but tonight, what with the rumpus with the nanny, she hadn't had time.

He had thrown off his blankets and his hands felt cold. She reached down into the cot and picked one up, wrapping him securely in it. Thinking he was going to be put down, he started to cry, his small features puckering.

The social worker who had interviewed her following Alan and Jen's deaths had warned her that for some considerable time Michael was going to feel insecure. So far this insecurity had manifested itself in bouts of tears in the middle of the night which had necessitated Kate getting up to take the baby into her own room, while his nanny slept on, apparently undisturbed by the noise.

Years of living with small children had given Kate an expertise she had not even realised she possessed until Michael came into her life. She was half appalled by her own inherent skill in looking after him, at least physically. Emotionally, she wasn't anything like as sure that she would be able to cope with his needs.

She adjusted her stance to cope with his weight with an expertise that would have astounded most people who knew her, easily rocking her body so that its rhythm soothed his whimpers.

The tears had stopped now, but she knew from experience that the moment she tried to put him back in his cot they would start again; it was all too understandable, really, this defiant bid to claim her attention.

None of the nannies she had had so far had been pleased by her ruling that Michael was to remain upstairs. The house was only small, and the sitting-room and dining-room she had had so carefully furnished sometimes had to double as an extension of her office.

Clients sometimes visited her at home; she entertained them at small, elegant dinner parties, using the recipes she had carefully and meticulously learned at nightschool. She wasn't an inspired cook, but she had the intelligence to realise that every tiny skill she added to her repertoire increased her chances of ultimate success.

A male client, dubious about dealing with one of the new breed of city career woman, could have his fears soothed by the production of a delicious home-cooked meal, thus restoring his innate belief that women, even career women, enjoyed pandering to men. It was because she had to look upon her sitting-room and dining-room as extensions of her office that Michael was barred from them. A scatter of toys and baby things, no matter how domestic, would not serve to enhance the image she was careful to project.

Instead she had given Michael the largest of the three bedrooms, and what was more she had decorated it herself—another learned skill.

Nor could she simply abandon her responsibility to him. Jen had been as close to her as if they were sisters. Closer in some ways. And she owed it to her friend to do the very best she could for Michael.

It would be easier once he was old enough to go to school...once she had her business firmly established. Already it was doing well, but not well enough for her to be able to sit back and relax. She would just have to hope that Camilla came up with someone suitable.

Michael was asleep... Very gently she removed him from her shoulder and walked over to the cot. Before she got there, he was awake, blue eyes regarding her with solemn regard, the baby mouth starting to pucker.

'All right, you win,' Kate told him wryly. They had been through this routine several times before. So often, in fact, that it was beginning to become a habit.

Not that she actually minded. There was something quite soothing about working in Michael's room, at the desk that would one day be his, and he seemed to find her presence a calming influence. He didn't even seem to mind the desk-lamp she used to illuminate her work.

Holding him against her shoulder with one arm, she went downstairs for her briefcase. The final details of the plans she intended to put before James were inside it. It was still four days before their meeting, but she wanted to be sure she had everything right.

Back in Michael's room, she put him in his cot again. This time, as though he knew that he had won and that she would stay, he closed his eyes immediately.

Kate wasn't fooled. She knew the moment she attempted to leave the room they would be open again, and he would start howling—that thin, fretful cry that tore at the nerves and penetrated so tormentingly every barrier raised against it.

She ought to be used to crying babies; after all, there had been enough of them at the children's home.

She opened her briefcase and extracted her papers.

James Cameron's supermarkets were in the main small stores in country towns—often shabby and run-down, from the information she had received. She had driven out to some of them to check on the location and size, as well as reading the reports he had given her, and she was going to suggest to him that, since he could not compete with the huge nationwide retailers, in order to make his image more up-market, he got away from the plate-glass-window image of supermarkets and instead went for something cosier and more countrified.

Bow windows with Georgian panes had been her first thought, as this would immediately give both a more up-market image and have a much warmer appeal to the shopper. At the same time she intended to recommend that, where his own lines of produce were concerned, he had the packaging changed in line with the slightly Victorian, country look of the stores. She had experimented with mock-ups of labels and packagings in a soft gingham check so that she could show him what she had in mind.

A new advertising campaign in line with this would all help to reinforce the new image. TV and radio slots with voice-overs in a warm, male, countrified accent. Posters and magazine ads concentrating on the wholefood appeal of certain lines.

What she had in mind would mean a radical rethink on some of the major lines the stores stocked, but since this would only be in line with the current interest in additive free, more healthy food, Kate thought that the two-pronged attack would have an increased chance of success.

It was gone eleven o'clock when she finished working. Her head was starting to ache, because the lamp she was using was not really strong enough for close work, but she hesitated to illuminate the room too brightly in case it disturbed the sleeping baby.

As she put down her pen, she could hear him making small, snuffly noises in his sleep. Strange how accustomed her senses were to him already after only four weeks; so much so that one night the momentary absence of them had actually woken her and she had rushed into his room to discover he had turned over and was lying with his face pressed into the bedding. There had been no real danger of him suffocating but, nevertheless, she was glad that her senses had alerted her to the hazard.

When Jen had asked her to be his godmother, Kate had never dreamed of what was to come. Poor little boy. She was really no substitute at all for his real mother, but she *was* that mother's choice, and when he was old enough to understand she would make sure that he shared as many of her memories of Jen as he could.

She was only thankful that tomorrow was Saturday. Not that she normally took the day off. It had been her habit to go into the office and go through the week's work. The two girls who worked for her were very good. Conscientious and hardworking, but it was not their business, not their future, not their success or failure. She had enjoyed those oases of time alone in the elegant but minute offices in Knightsbridge that cost her the earth, but that were worth it because of the cachet they gave her business.

Industrialists were snobs when it came to whom they used to sell their products, as she had soon discovered. They liked using agencies with smart upper-class reputations, and Kate had been quick to forge her own contacts with the prestigious advertising agencies.

Camilla had helped her there. Her husband was on the board of one of London's most prestigious agencies, and through Camilla's good offices she had made several strong and very valuable contacts.

Yes Camilla had been a good friend to her, right from the start when she had taken her on fresh from university with nothing but her degree and her determination to recommend her.

She had enjoyed those years with Camilla, but once Camilla had taken the decision to commit herself to Hugo and their family, Kate had known it was only a matter of time before her friend sold out, and rather than become a small cog in what promised to be a very large wheel Kate had taken the decision to set up on her own.

It had been the right decision, she was sure of that. The *only* decision, but as an employee of someone else might she not have been freer to spend more time with Michael?

It wouldn't be for much longer. Another couple of years and she would have successfully established herself. Perhaps she could even then start working from home a couple of days a week. Right now that wasn't feasible. She didn't have a good enough reputation, but if she got this contract from James...

Another valuable introduction Camilla had given her.

Yes, she had much to thank Camilla for, and she would have even more if Camilla found her a suitable nanny, she acknowledged tiredly as she snapped off the light and tiptoed quietly out of the room.

CHAPTER TWO

OLD habits died hard, and it had been a firm rule of the children's home where Kate had been brought up that everyone got up at six-thirty.

Even now, when she could have stayed in bed, she found it impossible, and in consequence, however late her night, she was invariably wide awake at six-thirty the next day.

This Saturday was no exception, and as she lay in bed listening to Michael's burblings on the intercom, she reflected wryly on the days when all she had to do when she first got up in the morning was to organise herself for her pre-breakfast run. Now she didn't run, but what she did do, rain or shine, was to put Michael in his pushchair and walk him to the park, so that they could both enjoy the freshness of the new day.

The park was small and Victorian, with formal flowerbeds and trees. There was a muddy pond in the centre of it, normally deserted in the early morning, apart from one or two moth-eaten ducks, soliciting shamelessly for food.

This morning, as he did every morning, Michael showed his approval of their outing by clapping his hands and laughing happily while Kate zipped him into his ski-suit.

She herself had pulled on jeans and a sweatshirt. She had discovered within the first week of having Michael that her pencil-slim designer skirts and silk shirts were not ideal wear around a very young child, and so she had been forced to go out and comb the chain-stores in search of something more sensible.

Half a dozen pairs of jeans, plus an assortment of sweatshirts, had been the ultimate answer. Knowing Michael's propensity for covering them both in sticky mess, she no longer wondered at most young mothers' apparent uniform of jeans and tops. Running a brush through her hair, she gathered it up in a ponytail and snapped a band round it, before pulling on her anorak.

It wasn't easy to manoeuvre the pushchair down the stone steps, but she had developed a knack for dealing with them now. The street was deserted and quite dark still, but that didn't bother Kate; she liked the solitude of the early morning city, when most of its inhabitants were still in bed.

In the park the ducks quacked in welcome, but she didn't do more than pause to watch them. The object of the exercise was not just fresh air for Michael, but physical exercise for her as well, and that involved pushing the pram briskly ten times round the park and then back home.

Once there, she would put Michael in his high chair and make them both breakfast. Michael would probably throw most of his on the floor, and she would be lucky if she could even manage to drink her coffee before it got cold.

She was a dedicated career woman, with precious little security, a huge mortgage, a very new business to develop and no one to rely on but herself. Add to that the fact that she was solely responsible for a nine-month-old baby, the very last kind of responsibility she had ever wanted, and it seemed incredible to Kate that she should feel so absurdly happy. So happy, in fact, that once they had finished their exercise and she was heading back to the house, she stopped to blow kisses into the pram, causing Michael to laugh delightedly, and the man watching her from the other side of the road to frown.

That must be the nanny, Garrick reflected, watching as Kate skilfully negotiated the steps and unlocked her front door.

He had come here on impulse, a little surprised to discover it was so close to his own apartment.

He had spent the previous evening studying the file David Wilder had given him. On the face of it there was no logical reason why Kate Oakley should refuse to hand the child over to him. She was a career woman first, second and third; that much was plain. The kind of woman who would never willingly saddle herself with a child, and he should know…

His mouth twisted bitterly as he remembered Francesca. He had met her when he was twenty-three, and a very naïve twenty-three he had been, too.

Fresh on the London scene and working for a firm of merchant bankers, he had met Francesca at a disco. They had dated for two months before they slept together. Although they had been the same age, it had disconcerted him to discover that her sexual experience was far greater than his own, but he had accepted it when she told him that she had had a previous long-standing relationship with someone else. A relationship that was now over.

Six months later they were engaged. Six weeks after that Francesca had married someone else.

It had been then that he discovered how much she had lied to him. There hadn't been any long-standing relationship with someone, just a series of very brief affairs with a good many someone elses...men in the main much older and wealthier than Francesca herself.

Calvin Harvey had been one of those previous lovers. A married man now divorced—an extremely wealthy, once married man, who now wanted as his second wife Garrick's fiancée. And Francesca hadn't hesitated.

'But surely you understand, darling,' she had pouted when Garrick, white-faced and disbelieving, had finally realised that she meant what she was saying. 'It was fun with you and me, but marriage... Honestly, darling, can you see me as the wife of a poor man?'

'I wanted you to be the mother of my children,' Garrick had protested despairingly. He could hear her laughter still. Shrill and acid.

'A mother? Oh, my poor dear Garrick, what an idiot you are! I shall *never* have children. Such a bore...and it ruins one's figure. Don't worry, darling, it needn't end between us. Calvin has business interests abroad and he's away an awful lot. I'll ring you.'

And so she had, but only once. By then he had realised the truth about her and he had told her in plain and blistering

English exactly what she could do with her favours and her much-used body. It had given him some temporary relief to his heartache. What a fool man was that he could realise exactly what a woman was with his mind, and yet not stop wanting her with his body. But all that was behind him now.

It had left its scars, though. Hence his determination not to marry, and *his* desire to take charge of his second cousin's child.

He himself had been an only child, but his mother had been baby mad. She had filled the house with the offspring of friends and neighbours. She and his father were retired now. They lived in Cornwall, where his mother painted and his father grew flowers.

He couldn't expect them to bring Michael up for him. He would need to find a reliable nanny. Perhaps even the girl that Kate Oakley employed. To judge from her behaviour, she seemed fond enough of the child. That shouldn't be too difficult... But he was running ahead of himself. First he had to speak with Kate Oakley.

He didn't anticipate having any problems, but he had learned long ago that it was as well to be prepared for all eventualities. If she should refuse to hand over the baby...well, then he would need all the ammunition he could find to prove that she was unfit to have the charge of him.

It had started to rain while he stood in the street, a fine November mizzle that soaked his thick black hair and made it curl. He hunched his shoulders against the damp, and wondered irately what had possessed David Wilder to behave so idiotically. Delegate...delegate...that was what he was always being told, and yet, the moment he did, look what happened!

An early morning cyclist braked to a startled halt as Garrick stepped out into the road in front of him, muttering under his breath.

Apologising grimly to him, Garrick crossed the road. He was thirty-five years old and a millionaire; once that had been said, what else was there to say? The woman who had been sharing his bed for the last three years had announced four months ago that the corporation that employed her was moving her out to New York. She would stay, she had intimated, if Garrick married her. He had told her crisply and incisively that he would not and why. And it had come as a slight shock to discover that he missed her sexually almost as little as he missed her emotionally...which was to say not at all. What was happening to him?

He knew the answer. Life had lost its bite, its savour, its challenge.

He had reached a time in his life when simply to succeed was not enough, and for some reason the thought of having a child, a cause, and perhaps at some later stage a companion as well as a successor, appealed tremendously to him.

Of course, he knew there were any number of women who would be only too pleased to give him a son. But that was not what he wanted. Their children would come with strings attached...demands, both pecuniary and emotional, which he had no wish to bear.

No, this child...this orphan would be ideal. And the child would benefit from their relationship, too. He would see to it. That Oakley woman would probably be all too pleased to give him up.

He now knew all there was to know about Kate Oakley, and he would use that information with all the ruthlessness for which he was so notorious, if he had to.

At eleven o'clock Kate's doorbell rang and she went to answer it, still wearing her sweatshirt and jeans. She and Michael had been building a tower of plastic blocks, and Camilla raised her eyebrows a little when Kate ushered her straight upstairs instead of into the sitting-room.

'Well...so this is the young man who's causing so much disruption, is it?' Camilla asked, swooping down on Michael and picking him up. 'Oh, he's gorgeous, Kate! Makes me feel all maternal inside... Oh, dear,' she laughed as Michael started to pout and turn his face away from her, holding out his arms to Kate.

With her hair in a ponytail and her face free of make-up, she looked closer to twenty than thirty, Camilla reflected, studying her covertly. At twenty-eight, Kate could still look absurdly young at times; watching her cuddle the little boy, Camilla wondered if she realised how expressive her face was. For a dedicated career woman, she was beginning to look surprisingly madonna-like. Wisely Camilla decided not to tell her so. She knew that Kate prided herself on her independence, and it wouldn't be kind to point out to her that that one illuminating smile had betrayed all too clearly how very dependent she already was on the small human body she was holding in her arms.

It was odd how kids got to you. Take her own two... She had vowed she didn't want any, and yet from the moment they were born they had turned her life upside-down and she had let them.

'Good news, I think,' she said cheerfully. 'I've found you a nanny. I got in touch with this friend of mine and she knows the ideal chap. Loads of experience. Adores kids and is especially good with young children. He can start straight away. In fact, the sooner the better. It seems that his previous boss started to get the wrong idea about their relationship, and propositioned him...' She gave a rich chuckle. 'It's good to know that sexual harrassment can work both ways, isn't it?'

Kate sat down, holding Michael on her knee. 'Camilla, I'm not sure about this... Perhaps when Michael's a bit older...'

The truth was that she didn't want to share her home with a man; she found the mere thought slightly intimidating, and yet, after all, what was there to be afraid of? She would be the one in control, she would be the boss...he would simply be her employee.

'Not sexual stereotyping, are we?' Camilla tutted archly, grinning at her. 'Men can take care of babies just as well as women, you know. Besides, I thought that we'd already agreed that a man would be best for you, less of a hassle for you to deal with.'

'Well, yes,' Kate admitted, remembering how much trouble

her friend was going to on her behalf. 'But he'll have to live in.'

There was a small, surprised silence, and then Camilla said briskly, 'Well, you've got a spare room, haven't you?' adding firmly, 'Good heavens, Kate! From what I've heard, this man is more likely to be terrified that *you're* going to rape him, rather than the other way around…if that is what's worrying you.'

'No, of course it isn't,' Kate told her testily. 'It's just… Well, I'm not used to sharing my home with a man.'

'No, you're not, are you?' Camilla agreed drily, and then reminded her, 'One day Michael's going to be a man, Kate, and quite honestly, for his sake…'

'Yes…yes, all right,' she agreed, giving in. 'How old is he, by the way?'

She was acutely conscious of how close she had come to making a fool of herself…of inviting Camilla to ask questions for which she had no answers.

'I'm not sure. Sue described him as mature. She says she can vouch for his references, by the way. In fact, she wanted to know all there was to know about you…which isn't a great deal. Apparently this isn't the first time she's had complaints from the men on her books about the—er—extra-curricular duties demanded by their female employers. It seems that there's more than meets the eye to employing a male nanny,' she added with a grin. 'Anyway, I've managed to convince her that you're not likely to demand your evil way with him, and so she's sending him round for an interview. Some time this weekend, but I'm not sure when. I thought I'd come round and alert you. As well as making this young man's acquaintance…' She paused to tickle Michael, who grinned back at her. 'Oh, and I explained to her that you couldn't afford to provide him with transport, etc., but she said not to worry, he has his own car.'

'Umm… It seems odd, though, don't you think?' Kate commented doubtfully. 'A man caring for a small child?'

'Not at all,' Camilla contradicted robustly. 'I know quite a

few that do. Not professionally, perhaps, but I know a fair
number of couples where it's the wife who has the career and
the husband who's bringing up baby, and very well it works,
too. Kate, do stop worrying,' she instructed kindly. 'If you
don't like the man when you interview him, then simply send
him away and we'll try and find someone else. All I can tell
you is that Sue is very particular about who she has on her
books, and according to her this man is one of her best. Mind
you, you won't be able to look upon him as a permanent
fixture, I'm afraid. She did also say that he's studying some
kind of advanced computer course. Apparently he's worked
abroad for some years and was made redundant. Now he's
trying to re-train himself for the job market and earn himself
a living at the same time. Hence the nannying. Look, I must
go. I've got to collect the girls from their dancing class at one,
and then we're taking them out for lunch. Oh, how about dinner some time next week?'

'I'll give you a ring if I may. After all, unless I get a nanny,
I won't be going anywhere, never mind out to dinner,' Kate
told her drily.

By the time Camilla left, Michael was grizzling for his
lunch. Kate took him downstairs with her while she opened
the fridge and removed the puréed soup she had already made.

Michael, sitting in his high chair, banged demandingly on
the table with his spoon while she heated the soup. Already
in four short weeks she had become dangerously attached to
him; already she could see how he was changing, growing,
and her heart ached for Jen and Alan. They had wanted Michael so much. Loved him so much.

After lunch Michael had a sleep while Kate got changed
and did her hair. She had shopping to do, mainly food, but
she liked to buy things that were as fresh as possible.

The rain had stopped, but the pavements were wet, and the
air damply cold. Pulling on her trench coat, she checked that
the safety harness was secure, and then manoeuvred the pushchair down the steps.

In the high street several men looked at her, admiring the

slenderness of her ankles and the elegance of her high cheek-boned face. Her dark hair gleamed in the light from the shop windows, her immaculate make-up making several other women wonder how on earth she found the time to look so good, when she had a small child to take care of.

Despite the fact that her clothes were probably not much more expensive than those worn by her fellow shoppers, Kate stood out from the crowd. She shopped with the same brisk efficiency she brought to everything she did, quite prepared to haggle when she considered that what she was being offered was not value for money. She had learned in her early days in London to make her money stretch a long way. Not for her expensive and un-nutritious ready-made meals. She preferred to shop economically and make her own soups and stews, to search out the best bargains in fresh fruit and vegetables; frugal habits which she had maintained even though they were no longer strictly necessary.

It was almost five o'clock before she had finished her shopping. The streets were dark and damp. She paused outside a toy shop already decked out for Christmas. This would be Michael's first Christmas. She remembered Christmases at the children's home: busy, noisy affairs with presents bought and donated by various charities; church in the morning; then lunch and then a party at teatime.

Everyone had done their best, but Kate knew she hadn't been the only child there with a cold miserable place in its heart, mourning the Christmases that had once been.

Jen had once told her that she was lucky, because she at least had once had parents. She reached into the pram and touched Michael's face. He smiled back at her, and for a moment tears stung her eyes.

A woman of twenty-eight crying in the street—ridiculous. She straightened up firmly, but at the back of her mind lurked the knowledge that she mustn't fail Jen; she mustn't prove unworthy of the trust Jen had placed in her.

She had bought one of Michael's favourite treats for supper—bananas to which she added just the smallest spoonful of natural yoghurt. It was never too early to start teaching a child good eating habits, although she suspected that there would come a time when, like all children, Michael would insist on living for weeks on something like baked beans or fish fingers. Tea over, it was bathtime, a ritual which they both enjoyed, although it was only at weekends that Kate was able to share it with him.

One grim-faced nanny had complained to Kate that she didn't like little boys who made so much mess, and Kate, who wanted to encourage Michael to have as much enjoyment in life's simple pleasures as possible, had not been sorry to see her go.

This last one had been different; young and warm-hearted, she had seemed almost ideal. However, as she explained to Kate, her boyfriend did not like her having to work so many evenings, and so she had found another job which paid more and carried far less responsibility.

She was just preparing Michael's bath when the doorbell rang. Frowning over the unexpected interruption, Kate picked him off the bedroom floor and carried him downstairs with her.

Shielding him from the cold, she opened the front door. The man standing there was unfamiliar to her, and with the light behind him it was hard to pick out individual features. She saw that he was dressed in casual clothes; the streetlight shone faintly on the softness of a metallic grey leather blouson, and she also saw that he was very tall...tall and broad, with a silent, unmoving stance that was rather intimidating.

'Kate Oakley?' he asked her in a cool, firmly modulated, accentless voice, the words clipped and economical, as though he was a man who disliked waste, of either time or energy.

'Er—yes.' Kate stepped back into the hall automatically, and the man followed her inside, even though she had not invited him to do so.

'Let me introduce myself,' he began, and Kate's slight frown lifted as she realised who he must be.

'Oh, you're from the agency,' she interrupted. 'They did

warn me that you would call round some time this weekend. Please come in... I'm just about to give Michael his bath. Would you like to come upstairs? We can talk up there. I don't like to disturb his routine too much.'

Without waiting for his response, Kate headed for the stairs.

Something about the man disturbed her. One look at those flint-hard grey eyes had sent her stomach churning with nervous tension, and she felt very much as though *she* were the one being interviewed, and not him.

He was older than she had imagined, too. Somewhere in his mid-thirties. Not at all the kind of man she imagined would want to spend his time taking care of a small child. But then, Camilla had warned her that he was simply working as a nanny while retraining for a new career.

She reached the top of the stairs and turned to look back at him. He was half-way up, and from her vantage point she could look down on the thick darkness of his head. His hair was well groomed and clean, his nails on the hand that held on to the banister well kept and shaped, but not the nails of a man who regularly visited a manicurist. His clothes were good and very expensive, she observed, noting the softness of his leather blouson and the way the dark trousers clung to his thighs. Italian and very probably cashmere. He must have bought them while he was working abroad and earning good money, she decided.

'The agency tells me that you're very experienced with small children,' she commented as she waited for him to join her. 'I must say I'm surprised.'

Three steps behind her on the stairs Garrick tensed briefly, glad that she couldn't see his face. What on earth was the woman talking about? And what did she mean—the agency?

Garrick wasn't used to being caught at a disadvantage, and within the space of ten minutes this woman had done so twice, even if she herself was not aware of it.

The first time had been when she opened the door and he had realised that the girl he had mistaken for the nanny was in fact Kate herself. All right, so now she had her hair caught up in an elegant knot, and he could see now that he was face to face with her the air of cool authority she wore. But he could also see how trustingly the child looked at her, and how competently she held him in her arms, as though she was both used and happy with his small weight there.

That knowledge disturbed him, alerting him to a range of possible problems he hadn't anticipated. What he had expected was that after a brief discussion he would offer Kate Oakley a generous sum of money to part with the child, which she would be only too relieved to accept, like the sensible businesswoman he had discovered she was. However, he was already beginning to suspect he had been too sanguine.

And what was this agency she was talking about? No one in the last ten years had ever mistaken Garrick for anything other than what he was: a singularly powerful and sometimes dangerous businessman.

'I know that the agency have vouched in full for your abilities, but I expect you'll appreciate that I'll have to ask you a few questions of my own. Did they explain to you that you'll be in full charge of Michael during the day? I work long hours, I'm afraid, and I don't get home until well into the evening some days, which means that you'll be on duty until I do return. Weekends you will be able to have off in full. I don't have a car, but the agency told me that you had your own transport. I'll show you your room in a moment. All right, Michael, I know you want your bath... I'm sorry about this,' she apologised to Garrick over her shoulder as she hurried into the nursery. 'But Michael loves his bath, and he's apt to get a bit impatient if the fun's delayed.'

She paused just inside the room, and said thoughtfully, 'Look, why don't I let *you* bathe him? As you will be in full charge of Michael, I'm sure you'll realise that it's important for me to feel that you can establish a rapport with him. I must confess when my friend suggested a male nanny, I was rather doubtful. She pointed out to me that Michael would benefit from the male influence in his life, but I feel he's rather young as yet for me to worry about male/female roles.'

Garrick, who had followed her into the room, stared at her back as she bent to put Michael down. Had he gone mad, or did this woman really believe that he had come here to be interviewed as a nanny for the child?

As Kate straightened up and gave him a coolly appraising smile, he realised that he hadn't, and that Kate did seriously believe that was why he was here.

He opened his mouth to correct her misapprehension, and then closed it again. Several times during his life he had been called upon to make split-second and impulsive decisions, and never once had his intuition failed him. This time it was telling him to go along with her self-deception. He was rapidly coming to the belief that there was no way Kate Oakley was going to calmly hand over the child. He could see just by watching her with him how fiercely protective of him she was. That in no way altered his own determination to have sole responsibility for Michael, but what it did alter was the method he would now need to adopt to get legal control of Michael.

David Wilder had warned him that the only way the courts would ever take Michael away from Kate Oakley would be if she could be proved to be an unfit guardian. And what better way to be able to prove that than to live here in the same house with them and to observe at first-hand how she responded to her responsibilities?

One set of facts could be presented in so many different ways, to give a hundred different impressions, Garrick knew that. He wondered what the courts would think of a woman who employed an unknown man to take care of a nine-month-old child without even making any attempt to check his credentials.

When Kate looked at him, he was smiling at her. It was an odd, chilling sort of smile, and for a moment she was tempted to snatch up Michael and tell him to leave.

Control yourself, she commanded inwardly. Just because the man is so much more...male than you anticipated, that's no reason to get in such a state. But, as she watched Garrick remove his jacket and deftly roll up the sleeves of the shirt he was wearing, she couldn't help wishing that she had never listened to Camilla's suggestion that she hire a male nanny to take care of little Michael.

Bathe him, she had said, and Garrick thanked his lucky stars that his mother's preoccupation with infants had ensured that he had observed the bathtime routine often enough as a child and teenager to have retained some knowledge of what ought to be done.

Let's face it, Garrick told himself, Kate Oakley probably didn't have much more idea of how to take care of a small child than he did himself.

A dedicated career woman was how his data described her, and from the information he had been given he had formed the impression that she would be much harder, much, much more abrasive than she was turning out to be. Already he had discerned that there were certain anomalies about her…certain vulnerabilities that she tried desperately hard to conceal.

He took hold of Michael and started to undress him.

Kate watched impassively, but secretly just a little pleased, while Michael kicked and wriggled. The man didn't seem to be too familiar with the poppers on Michael's clothes, but his hands were gentle when he touched and held the little boy, she had to admit that, and she had to turn away from the sight of those male hands struggling with the small clothes. It brought back memories she wanted to suppress…memories of a time when she herself had been a much-loved part of a close family unit. A time before her world had been turned upside-down and her parents had left her…deserted her without any explanation, without any warning.

She noticed the faint grimace the man gave as he removed Michael's wet nappy, and suspected that she was probably right in thinking that he had never taken care of such a very young child before.

All her earlier doubts came sweeping back, and she stepped forward protectively, ready to snatch Michael away from him.

'I'm not sure that this is a good idea,' she said unsteadily. 'Michael is very young…'

She gave him a firmly dismissive smile and reached for her godson, but the man refused to let him go.

'Yes. He is small for his age, isn't he?' he agreed, deliberately misunderstanding her. 'Premature, was he?'

Garrick knew quite well that Michael had been premature, but he saw from Kate's face that his remark had startled her.

'Yes. Yes, he was a little,' she agreed reluctantly.

Without a word Garrick picked Michael up and carried him over to his waiting bath. Once there, he asked Kate over his shoulder, 'And his father...what part does he play in Michael's life?'

There was no harm in turning the screw just a little, he told himself, justifying his underhand actions with his conviction that Michael would be better off with him.

'Michael's parents are dead,' she told him quietly, the pallor of her skin making him feel uncomfortably guilty. He hadn't expected her to show such distress. He knew she had been close to Jennifer. The report had told him that much; they had, after all, grown up together in the children's home, but he had gained the impression from the report that she rather tended to keep people at an emotional distance, and he had formed the opinion that she would look upon the responsibility of Michael as an unwanted one. Now he wondered uneasily if he had been too sanguine in his assumptions.

To cover his own inner disquiet, he said quickly, 'So he isn't really your child, then?'

Not really hers! Kate caught her breath on an unsteady shock of tension, increased by her awareness of just how much she feared and resented the assumption behind the casual words. Michael *was* hers... When she thought of Michael, she thought of him as being her child, she recognised. She loved him, and not just because of Jen.

Panic bit into her...the kind of panic she always experienced at the thought of allowing anyone to come too close to her emotionally, but where Michael was concerned it was already too late.

She heard the man saying calmly, 'I'm sorry, I didn't mean to upset you.'

And she focused on him, her body as taut as a bow string as she fought off the feelings threatening her.

'You didn't,' she denied shortly, hoping he would drop the subject. To her dismay, he didn't.

'You must have been very close to the boy's parents. He doesn't look like you, though,' he added, looking first at her and then at Michael.

Kate drew a sharp breath, aching to simply demand that he leave. He had no right to ask her these questions, to pry into her life. And then she tried to control her reactions and remind herself that he was simply trying to do his job and that it was only natural that he should want to have as much information as possible about Michael.

Taking a deep breath, she said as calmly as she could, 'Michael isn't a blood relative. He's the child of a very close friend. She and her husband were killed in a motorway accident.'

'I'm sorry.' He wasn't looking at her now, whether out of compassion or simply by accident, she wasn't sure. 'It can't be easy for you...a single woman suddenly having a baby thrust into your life. Doesn't he have any family?'

He was probing too deeply now, but there was nothing she could do to stop him without betraying herself. She could feel the old, familiar tension building up inside her stomach. She wanted to tremble with the force of it, but she had long ago learned to control that reaction.

'Not really,' she told him shortly. 'Jen and I are...were both orphans. We grew up together in a children's home. Alan, Jen's husband, was an only child, his parents are dead, and I believe there is a distant family connection...a second cousin.'

'Orphans,' Garrick mused, ignoring the reference to himself. 'I see.'

Here was his chance to subtly undermine her self-confidence by pointing out that as an orphan she was hardly qualified to act as a substitute family to such a young child…to ask her if she didn't think Michael would be better off in the care of someone who could communicate to him through their own experiences, just what it meant to be part of a loving family.

Whatever else he might or might not be…however cynical his views on marriage had become over the years, he could never doubt the happiness that his parents had had…nor dismiss the love and security they had given him as a child.

It would be oh, so easy to make some idle comment that would increase the doubts he could see so clearly shadowing her eyes…to reinforce what he was beginning to suspect was her own private fear that she was not an adequate parent for Michael, but to his own consternation he found that he simply could not do it. He was as amazed by the recognition of his weakness as he would have been to discover that the world had suddenly turned upside-down.

This couldn't be him, deliberately holding back on beginning his campaign to win Michael away from her, simply because he had looked into her eyes and seen the lonely, proud child she must once have been, fighting desperately to pretend that nothing was wrong…that her world hadn't been destroyed…that she wasn't….

He shook his head, wanting to dispel the unwanted images. What was happening to him? What was wrong with him? He must be going soft in the head.

'What's wrong?' Kate demanded suspiciously, her tension increasing as she sensed his hesitancy and knew instinctively that it had something to do with her.

'I was just thinking how very hard it must have been for you as a child,' he said quietly. 'And how much Michael must mean to you.'

Later he would ask himself what on earth had come over him, what on earth he had thought he was doing, but in the moment he said the words he saw the fury and panic fight for supremacy in Kate's eyes, and he reacted instinctively to them, reaching out his hand to touch her in an age-old gesture of comfort.

Even before he touched her, Kate froze, and immediately Garrick realised what he was doing and cursed himself under his breath. What the hell was happening to him? He must be going soft in the head, feeling sorry for her.

A nanny… God, he could just imagine what the press would do to him if they ever found out!

CHAPTER THREE

SEVERAL miles away, Camilla listened anxiously to the telephone call between her husband and his mother.

'Dad's been rushed into hospital with a suspected heart attack,' he told her as he hung up. 'Mum wants us to go down.'

'I'll pack a couple of overnight bags and we can leave straight away.'

Camilla loved her mother-in-law, but knew that she was quite incapable of dealing with an emergency.

It wouldn't be for several hours that she remembered that she had never told Kate that Sue had rung to say Peter Ericson had already accepted a post with someone else. She would do her best to find a suitable alternative, she had promised, but men willing to take charge of small children were not easy to find.

Kate, meanwhile, in blissful ignorance, watched as Garrick bathed Michael. It was true that he was less skilled than the other nannies she had employed, but his lack of expertise was more than made up for in the way that Michael responded to him.

Perhaps she had been wrong, she reflected, watching them, perhaps it was possible, after all, for even such a small baby to miss a male influence in his life. Michael, normally wary with strangers, was laughing and clapping his hands as Garrick bathed him, dunking his toys, and generally behaving as though there was nothing he wanted more than to keep on playing with this man who had come to take care of him.

The bath had its own stand, but Kate preferred to put it on the floor, for reasons of safety. She also normally armed herself with protective clothing, knowing Michael's propensity for soaking everything and everyone around him with water.

41

By the time Garrick had managed to fish Michael's wriggling wet body out of the bath, he was almost as wet as the small child.

As he handed Michael over to Kate, after swaddling him in a warm towel, he asked directly. 'First question. Do I get the job?'

He had removed his watch while he bathed Michael, and observing him strapping it on, Kate noticed that it was an expensive gold model that she knew must have cost several thousand pounds. Rather a luxury for a man who was prepared to work for less than a hundred pounds per week, all found. But then, perhaps he had bought it in better times, when he worked abroad.

She hesitated, and he gave her a frowning look. At that moment Michael managed to free his arms from the towel and stretched out towards him. Kate made up her mind, praying that she wouldn't regret it.

'Yes. Yes…you do,' she agreed firmly, adding, 'What was your next question?'

'Do you have a dryer so that I can dry my shirt, and will it be OK if I bring my computer terminal with me?'

'Your what?' And then Kate remembered that he was re-training. Presumably he wanted to work on the computer in his off-duty time. 'Oh, yes. I don't see why not. There's a desk in the room. I'll show you. Unfortunately, though, it doesn't have its own bathroom. There is a bathroom here off Michael's room, but there's no bath—only a shower. The other bathroom is off my room, and…' She broke off, remembering what Camilla had said about his previous employer.

He had been direct with her, and in the circumstances she felt she was entitled to be direct with him. After all, she was employing him, although, looking at him, she found it very hard to believe that any woman was capable of sexually intimidating him…even when that woman was paying his wages. In fact, the more she studied him, the more astounded she was that any woman would ever dare to make unwanted sexual approaches to him. He struck her as very much the kind of man who wanted to be in control of his own life and everything and everyone in it.

Garrick waited, wondering what on earth it was she wanted to say to him. He wondered if she realised how very illuminating her expression could be, and suspected not.

'I know...I know all about the problems you had with your previous employer,' Kate said at last. 'And I just wanted to assure you that there is no question of them being repeated here.'

Garrick stared at her, wondering what on earth she was talking about. What kind of problems was he supposed to have encountered?

'Which problem in particular are we discussing?' he asked her silkily, surprised to see a dull flood of colour warm her skin. From her file he had assumed there could be little that had the potential to embarrass her, but it seemed he was wrong.

Was he deliberately being obtuse, Kate wondered angrily, or was he simply testing her to make sure he knew where he stood? She had a momentary desire to change her mind and dismiss him, but Michael had taken to him so well. He moved, and she couldn't help noticing the way the wet shirt clung to his chest. He must be anxious to get out of it; she knew from experience that there was nothing more unpleasant. Hastily averting her eyes, she said hurriedly, 'The problem of your ex-employer making...sexual advances to you.' She couldn't look at him, and so missed the stunned look that crossed his face.

Garrick didn't know whether to burst out laughing or pretend outraged male vanity. It happened, of course. He had been the victim of some very subtle forms of it himself, but he had never been in a situation where his livelihood depended on him acquiescing to the sexual favours being demanded of him.

He was looking at her in an extremely odd way, Kate realised as she raised her head, and it occurred to her that it might be that he didn't believe her. He was, after all, an extremely physically compelling man; a very male man...the kind of man, in fact, that many a single woman might fantasise about having as her lover. And many a not so single one as well, she acknowledged, giving him a covert glance.

His body had the kind of male power that promised all kinds of enticement and pleasure, if one was that way inclined, which she thankfully was not, but she didn't like the way he was looking at her, and so she rushed impulsively into an unplanned speech, saying quickly, 'I have no desire to have any kind of relationship, sexual or otherwise, with you or any other man. It's not part of my plan for my life.'

She had his attention now, but oddly he wasn't looking at her in the way that men normally looked at her when she made this statement. Indeed, if she had to define his expression, she would have had to describe it as faintly disapproving.

Garrick did disapprove—his immediate, almost emotional reaction to her statement, so surprising that he found himself forced to question it.

After all, she was perfectly free to live her life however she chose, and it was chauvinistic of him in the extreme to succumb to the wholly male feeling that in denying his sex any place in her life she was wasting the feminine gifts nature had given her. He was also angry with himself for allowing himself to think of her as a person, and not simply as an obstacle in his path.

Kate noticed the way he masked his expression, and a tiny inner voice warned her that here was a man it would never be easy to read.

'I see,' he said smoothly. Too smoothly? she wondered, uneasy without knowing why.

'And Michael... Surely he couldn't have been part of this life plan?'

Kate felt a surge of conflicting emotions. Anger that he had so easily found her weak point, and an uncomfortable, illogical dread that refused to be analysed.

'It can't be easy for you, a career woman, and single, presumably without any previous experience of child rearing, to take on the task of bringing up someone else's child. Wouldn't it have been easier to let the State take charge of him...'

Once again her expression betrayed her, although Kate herself wasn't aware of it. Without being able to stop herself, she said fiercely, 'I couldn't let that happen. Michael's mother was my closest friend. I....'

She broke off, and Garrick, realising that he was pushing too hard for a supposed employee, backed off a little, saying fake casually, 'Obviously nothing would make you give him up?'

'Nothing,' Kate agreed shortly, unaware that she was confirming his grimmest thoughts. 'You know I want to start work as soon as possible, don't you?' she asked him, changing the subject. 'Will that be a problem?'

'No,' he confirmed.

'And I'm afraid I don't seem to have your name as yet...'

'It's G...Rick...Rick Evans,' he told her calmly, watching her closely to see if she recognised the name. There was no reason why she should. Evans was a common enough surname, and there was no reason for her to connect Rick with Garrick, even though it had been his boyhood nickname.

He was right, she didn't. Kate was too busy worrying about whether she had made the right decision to wonder about that brief hesitation before he gave his name.

'I can start on Monday, if that's OK with you. I'll move my stuff in some time tomorrow evening.'

'Yes, that's fine. I'll show you your room. Oh, and your shirt...the dryer is in the kitchen.'

'Right. I'll take this off and put it in, if you don't mind.'

It wouldn't have mattered if she had, he was already removing it to reveal a hard, brown male chest so very powerfully muscled that she wondered where he did his exercising. The faint male scent of his body reached her and she stepped back automatically. Garrick, catching the reaction, was slightly surprised by it. His sexuality was something he had come to take for granted over the years, but it didn't normally elicit that kind of response from women.

Strange how her reaction had piqued his interest, making him aware of himself as a man in a way that he had not been for months. He hadn't missed having a woman in his bed, but that hesitant backward step, that covert look of apprehension laced with shock, that very definite reaction he had seen to her awareness of his male scent, caused him to suddenly become aware of the curves of her body, the narrowness of her waist and the rounded fullness of her breasts, so discreetly and tantalisingly covered by the softness of her silk shirt.

He liked silk on women, but a shirt like that should be worn without a bra underneath it so that...

'The room's this way.'

Grimly he followed her, subduing his wayward thoughts. They were neither timely nor necessary.

The room would have fitted into a small corner of his bedroom in his London apartment, but the desk seemed large enough to house a computer terminal. He was going to have one hell of a lot of work to do in the next twenty-four hours. For starters he was going to have to find a nanny to take charge of the boy during the day so that he could concentrate on his work. He would have to alert his secretary to reroute all his calls through his carphone. Luckily he was pretty clear of appointments. He would organise things so that Gerald didn't make any more... He could just imagine his impassive secretary's face when he announced what he was doing. Fortunately Gerald Oswald was the soul of discretion. He had been with Garrick for eight years and was completely loyal.

As to the rest, the fewer people knew what was going on, the better. It was just as well Kate worked long hours, he reflected grimly; the last thing he wanted was an employer who was going to pop home unexpectedly in the middle of the day. But somehow or other events were going to have to be engineered to prove that she was unfit to have charge of Michael.

None of what he was thinking showed on his face as he followed Kate downstairs, his damp shirt in one hand and his jacket in the other.

Michael was tucked up in his cot, apparently for once quite happy to go straight to sleep.

In the kitchen, while they waited for his shirt to dry, Kate showed him where she kept Michael's things and ran through the typed routine she had prepared for his previous nannies, handing him a copy.

'And if there are any problems?' Garrick asked her.

'In that case you'll have to ring me at my office…but only in the event of an emergency.' She saw his face and said defensively, 'I have a career, Rick. A career which I need in order to support Michael and myself, and so it's important that while I am at work I'm free to concentrate on it. That's why I'm employing you,' she reminded him sharply.

It was hot in the small kitchen with the dryer on, and she was acutely conscious of the bareness of his torso. She wished she could ask him to go and wait in the sitting-room, or to put on his jacket, but he would probably think she was mad if she did so. She still found it almost impossible to picture this man looking after children, but he had proved to her that he was capable of doing so. He had bathed Michael with a tenderness that none of his previous nannies had matched, and instinctively she knew that where Michael was concerned she could trust him implicitly. Where Michael was concerned…so was it then on her own behalf that she felt this vague feeling of disquiet, of…danger almost? And what kind of danger? Not sexual danger, surely?

No. Although he was a very sexual man; she was sure of it. His private life was no concern of hers, she reminded herself, and then her face flamed as it suddenly occurred to her that he might quite reasonably expect to entertain his friends here in her house. After all, her female nannies had expected that privilege.

The thought of him bringing a woman home with him and very probably making love with her aroused the most acute and unpleasant sensations inside Kate. She knew she ought to say something, to tell him that she couldn't permit him to do so, but she found she simply could not say the words. It was a problem she would have to deal with at a later date, she told herself, inwardly praying that the occasion would never arise, but all too aware that it most probably would.

The dryer stopped, buzzing its message of readiness. Before she could do so, Garrick reached behind her and opened the door. She moved in order to get out of his way, and instead found that she was trapped between his body and the dryer.

It was a nerve-racking sensation, although after he had gone and her pulse had returned to normal she wasn't able to understand why. He hadn't menaced her in any way, done anything, said anything to set off that sudden terrifying feminine reaction to his proximity. No...this fear was unique and hitherto completely outside her experience, and it was a fear of herself rather than of him...of her reaction, her arousal, her awareness rather than his.

Instinct aided her, making her lower her eyelashes to shield her eyes, making her tense and breathe shallowly until he had retrieved his shirt and put it on, making her avert her head so that she didn't have to look at him or breathe in his scent.

As she walked with him to the front door, she was half hoping that he would announce that he had changed his mind and had decided against working for her. She didn't want him in her home; he was too male, too challenging. When Camilla had suggested a male nanny, she had envisaged a quiet, much younger man; a man who somehow or other would come across as asexual and unthreatening. In fact, the very last thing she had envisaged was this man, and the more she studied him, the more astounding she found it that he should want to work for her, looking after Michael.

As she opened the door for him, impulse made her ask quickly, 'Are you sure you want this job? It can be very lonely. The others found that...and Michael isn't always as lovable as he was today.'

The hair at the back of Garrick's neck rose warningly. She was having second thoughts. He had felt it in the kitchen, sensed it when she backed off from him so surprisingly.

Quickly he reassured her. 'I'm sure. I like kids. Michael

and I will get along fine…and besides,' he added, with what he hoped passed for sincerity, 'I need the money.'

The car parked outside her small front garden belied that fact. It was an expensive and almost brand-new Ferrari. Kate stared at it in amazement, and Garrick cursed inwardly.

He had forgotten about that, and he could hardly disclaim ownership. If he did, she might even ring the police in order to trace the owner, and then the fat would be in the fire.

'I suppose you bought it while you were working abroad,' Kate said weakly, unwittingly offering him an escape route.

'Yes. That's right,' he agreed with studied nonchalance. 'Of course, it's much older than it looks. It had to be re-registered when I came home. It's surprising what a difference new number-plates make to an old car.'

Kate didn't know all that much about cars, and so she simply accepted what he was saying, although she did inwardly question the wisdom of a man who was apparently in dire financial straits running a car that must surely be heavy on petrol. It was not her concern, she reminded herself. She was employing Rick as a nanny for Michael and nothing more.

She didn't wait to see him drive off, for which Garrick was profoundly thankful. His carphone was bleeping frantically as he unlocked the door, and he spoke into it harshly, answering its imperative summons.

He was going to have one hell of a lot of work to do if he was going to start his new 'job' by Monday morning, and he might as well get started right away.

He finished the call which was from a casual acquaintance inviting him to a 'charity' ball. No doubt hoping for a generous donation from him as a result, he reflected as he gave a cool refusal. He was generous when it came to supporting his chosen charities, but he had no time for the antics of those people who spent almost a hundred thousand pounds in order to make a couple of thousand pounds profit for a specific cause, then thought they were being generous.

He picked up the phone and punched out a number. His

secretary answered, and Garrick gave him several curt instructions.

Gerald Oswald was used to Garrick's terse commands, and to being on call virtually twenty-four hours a day, but the perks of being Garrick Evans' personal assistant far more than outweighed the disadvantages.

As he drove into the private car parking bay attached to the prestigious block that housed his apartment, Garrick was surprised to discover how tired he felt.

His shirt was still slightly damp, and it smelled of baby powder, he recognised in mild disgust as he climbed out of the Ferrari and locked it.

She had smelled of it too, only on her... He frowned, disliking the turn his thoughts were taking and irritated that he should find Kate Oakley even mildly attractive. She wasn't his type. He disliked career women as lovers. When he was involved with a woman, he liked her to be able to fit in with his career demands, not to expect him to fit in with hers. His mouth quirked a little in wryly humorous acknowledgement of his own foibles. He doubted very much that Kate Oakley would be quite as indulgent.

Most mornings she got up at six-thirty, she had told him, adding coolly that he needn't follow suit.

'I enjoy the hour or so I have alone with Michael in the morning,' she had warned him in that controlled voice she had.

Well, at that hour of the morning she was welcome to it. He only hoped it wouldn't be too long before Gerald was able to find him a reliable nanny who could take over his supposed duties from him.

A little to his surprise, he discovered that he was almost looking forward to the challenge of the coming weeks. Of course, there could be no doubt as to the eventual outcome. He would win, and he had no compunction at all about what he planned to do. Fond though she seemed to be of him—surprisingly so, in fact—there was no doubt that it was going to be a struggle for her to bring up the child alone. A struggle from which he was going to free her. One day she would be grateful to him…and if she wasn't…

His mouth compressed. The feelings of Kate Oakley were no concern of his. No concern at all.

CHAPTER FOUR

KATE sighed and replaced the receiver. She had rung Camilla several times to tell her the news about Rick, and also to have her small but unnerving doubts as to the wisdom of what she was doing allayed by her friend's sensible counsel, but every time she dialled Camilla's number the only response she could get was a recorded message to say that Camilla and her husband had been called away indefinitely.

She was sitting in her favourite cross-legged position on the floor of Michael's room, while he crawled energetically around her, picking up building blocks. She was wearing a pair of well-washed jeans and a comfortable top. Since Michael's advent into her life, her weekends had changed dramatically: meals out, visits to the theatre and a variety of gallery and exhibition openings that had previously been a feature of her weekends had now given way to walks in the park, shopping, and if she was lucky half an hour of peace and relaxation on Sunday evening after Michael had gone to sleep and before she started going through her diary for the coming week.

Today it was too wet to spend too much time outside. In the park the leaves had lain in damp clusters on the paths, and it seemed to Kate that the temperature had dropped several degrees almost overnight.

Michael demanded her attention by dropping one of the bricks in her lap. They were brightly coloured wooden blocks that linked together to spell his name, an impulse purchase she hadn't been able to resist, and now she obligingly took the letter from him and painstakingly collected the others. As she linked them together, she was acutely conscious of an unfamiliar tension tautening her muscles, a straining awareness of the fact that she was not really concentrating on what she was doing but listening for the sound of a car outside, footsteps on the path, the ring of the doorbell. All of which could herald the arrival of Rick Evans.

Had she done the right thing? To virtually hand Michael into the care of a stranger... The girls she had previously employed had also been strangers. But that had been different; Rick was a man...

She wriggled uncomfortably, all too aware of the fact that she was being guilty of mental sexual discrimination; something she bitterly resented when it operated against her own sex. There was no reason at all why a man should not be able to take perfectly good care of a small child, and Michael had taken to Rick with an immediacy he had not exhibited towards his other nannies.

No. If she got to the heart of things, her doubts and fears were not just fuelled by concern for Michael, but by her own ambivalent feelings towards Rick Evans.

For one thing, he was so different from what she had imagined. So much more intensely male, carrying about him an aura of power she was familiar with in the heads of large corporations and other successful businessmen, but which she had not expected to find surrounding a male nanny. Because society might consider the task of looking after a child to male nanny. Because society might consider the task of looking after a child to be less meaningful than running a company?

She wriggled again, uncomfortable with her own thoughts and what she recognised as her childhood prejudices and conditioning. Until the importance of the work women did in bringing up children was not just recognised but also respected, there could be no true equality for her sex. Kate knew that, but she also knew that she herself was helping to maintain that lack of equality by her own feeling of ill-ease at the thought of employing a man to take care of Michael.

Halfway through the evening, when Rick Evans had still not returned, Kate decided that he had changed his mind. She was surprised to discover that it wasn't just relief she felt; there was also an odd sense of having won a reprieve. But a reprieve from what? Now she would be put to the trouble of starting her search all over again.

Upstairs, Michael was asleep. Kate had just been going through her diary, checking on her appointments. She already had several small clients, but she desperately needed the security that having a client like James Cameron would give her.

She got out all her meticulously filed data and started checking on it to make sure there was nothing she had missed. The two girls who worked for her had been responsible for putting together the lists of the various local TV and radio stations with the best advertising records. She herself had checked rigorously to discover which packaging companies were most likely to supply the right kind of image for the new look supermarkets, and which magazines it would be best to advertise in. She had also prepared data on which advertising agencies held the best record of success for their campaigns in the same kind of field, and, even though she knew she had already done everything it was possible to do to ensure that she won the contract, she was still unable to put her work away.

A burst of nervous energy was driving her on, a relentless feeling that there was still something she had left to do. She wasn't happy about the thought of working closely with James, she acknowledged, putting down her pen. He made her feel wary and on edge, especially when he paid her sexually loaded compliments.

She had made it clear to him firmly and pleasantly that she was not in the market for a sexual relationship, and he had appeared to accept this with good grace, but something niggled at her: an inner awareness that he was not going to be an easy man to deal with. But she needed the contract.

She was so busy worrying about it that she almost missed the sound her nerves had been stretched tensely to catch all day. It was only the sharp slam of a car door that broke through her concentration, making her half rise from her chair, so that she was on her feet when the front door bell rang.

She went to open it.

'Sorry I'm late,' Garrick apologised tersely. 'My stuff's in the car. Is it all right if I bring it in?'

Gerald, excellent assistant that he was, had managed to keep his face wooden and composed when he had explained to him that for the next few weeks he was going to be virtually incommunicado, and that all his appointments would have to be cancelled.

He had not even said anything when Garrick had added that he was going to need a computer terminal that would allow him to tap into the complex system set up in their main office, and that the only way he, Gerald, would have of reaching him would be either via this terminal or on the carphone, and then only between a certain set of hours.

It was only when Garrick had instructed him to find him a discreet and properly trained nanny to take charge of a nine-month-old child that he had shown any reaction, and even then he had controlled it quickly.

Garrick had had no difficulty in realising that his assistant thought that the child in question was his own, and he had not enlightened him. Time enough for that later, once he had sole guardianship of the boy.

The Ferrari was parked outside; Kate could see the scarlet gleam of its paintwork in the streetlights. Garrick had to make several trips between it and his new quarters. Kate left him to it, not wanting to appear curious about his personal possessions. She stifled a yawn as she tidied up her papers.

She was tired and looking forward to an early night. She heard the car door slam and then the front door close. Garrick knocked briefly on the sitting-room door and then opened it.

'All done. I expect you'll want to run through Michael's routine again with me.' He pushed back the cuff of the same blouson jacket he had worn the previous day. 'Can you give me, say, half an hour to get my stuff unpacked, and then we can discuss it?'

Too startled by his assumption of command to object, Kate could only stare at the closing door. When he came back, she deliberately wouldn't offer him a cup of coffee or a drink. One thing she intended to make very clear to her new employee was that he was exactly that, and that she was the one who gave the commands, although she doubted that she had the flair to deliver them with quite the high-handed insouciance he had just employed.

When he came back downstairs, she was ready for him. As he knocked and walked into the sitting-room, she stood up and handed him a printed list.

'I think this makes everything clear,' she told him calmly. 'I've got an early start tomorrow, so I'm going to bed now. If you want any supper, please help yourself. I think you'll find everything you need in the kitchen.'

With a cool nod of dismissal, she opened the door and went straight upstairs.

Garrick stared after her, frowning, conscious of an odd let-down feeling, which he decided was all too probably caused by the pangs of hunger attacking his stomach.

The last time he had eaten had been lunch time, having been too busy to make the dinner date with friends he had previously arranged. But the thought of making himself something to eat was totally unappealing, as was the notion of going to bed at half-past ten at night.

He wasn't quite sure what Kate Oakley was trying to prove by her actions, but if she thought she was in some way asserting her authority over him by sending him supperless to bed, like a naughty child... Grimly he opened the door, having picked up the set of keys Kate had given him.

She heard the powerful roar of the car as she stepped out of the bath. She walked into her bedroom just in time to see the lights of the Ferrari as it disappeared out of sight. Where was he going?

It was no concern of hers, she told herself sharply. Just as long as he took proper care of Michael, what he chose to do in his own time was his own affair.

Affair perhaps being the operative word. He didn't look like the kind of man who lived the life of a celibate. She wondered who she was, the woman who shared his bed, and was horrified by the immediacy of the images that flashed through her mind.

From where had she got this ability to visualise so precisely the structured grace of his naked body? From what dark corners of her psyche came this unwanted awareness of him as a man? Wherever it came from, it would have to be banished.

Tired as she was, she couldn't sleep; at least not until she heard the Ferrari return, and the comforting click of the front door as Rick locked it behind him. He was back. She fell asleep before she could question just why knowing that had been important enough to keep her awake.

Garrick had been out for a meal which now sat uncomfortably heavily on his stomach. It was gone midnight when he got back, and it took him almost a further two hours to set up the terminal to his satisfaction.

As a consequence he slept through Kate's half-past six alarm, and his first intimation that a new way of life had started came when Kate rapped sharply on his door, having returned from her walk with Michael.

'I'm going to give Michael his breakfast now,' she announced, half opening the door but not walking into the room. 'And then I'll be leaving for the office shortly afterwards. I'll put him in his playpen when I've fed him.'

A judicious move, she had discovered in her early days of looking after him, since it gave her time to get changed into her office clothes without any danger of Michael's sticky fingers coming into contact with them.

Kate was a meticulous timekeeper and worked to a very strict routine. At eight o'clock, she walked into Michael's nursery to kiss him goodbye, as she did every morning. There was as yet no sign of Rick, although she could hear sounds of movement from his room. She called out a brief 'goodbye' to him, as she went downstairs to collect her briefcase.

She arrived at her office at ten to nine and unlocked the door. Soon after, Sara and Harriet, the two girls who worked for her, arrived within minutes of one another. While Harriet made them all a mug of coffee, Kate opened the mail.

It was disappointingly bereft of new business. Times were hard in the city; the euphoria caused by the 'Big Bang' change in the stock-market had died away to be replaced by a new atmosphere of caution. People were not prepared to risk their reputation with a PR agent who was not known to them, and the clients Kate did have were in the main small, struggling businesses like her own.

Camilla had helped as much as she could, and Kate had got some business via that help. If she could just succeed with James...

She dialled Camilla's office number and learned from her husband's secretary that his father had had a heart attack over the weekend and that, although he had returned home, Camilla was staying in the country to help her mother-in-law and would not be returning for some time.

Thanking her for the information, Kate replaced the receiver. She was still uneasy in her mind about the wisdom of employing Rick, but what other option did she have? The agency she had used previously had pointed out rather sharply to her when she rang them that the turnover of nannies in her household was alarmingly high. Their tone had implied that the fault lay not with their girls but with Kate herself, and perhaps it did, she acknowledged. Perhaps she expected too much of people, set standards that were too high; then again, perhaps in other households there were others to share the responsibility of the caring: partners, parents, family. She had no one.

The words seemed to echo dully inside her head, tormenting her, and yet previously she had congratulated herself on her solitary state because it left her free of any emotional ties so that she could pursue her career without any interruptions.

But that had been before Michael...and now, ironically, despite the havoc he had caused in her life, she knew that she could not bear to part with him.

Before, she had never understood what drove some single

women to have a child, especially when they had demanding careers to cope with. She had always assumed that she was lacking in that maternal instinct, but now she was not so sure. Over recent weeks, she had sometimes realised to her horror that Michael had crept into her thoughts when they ought to have been concentrated exclusively on her work. She had even caught herself staring dreamily into space, remembering how he had smiled at her, or some new clever skill he had learned.

Outside in the main office she could hear the two girls talking about their weekends. Harriet had been home to the Cotswolds to stay with her parents. Sara had spent her free time with her fiancé who was on leave from the army. Both girls came from moneyed families and worked for her for a very small salary indeed. They were both Camilla's god-daughters and, fortunately, despite their cushioned backgrounds, hard workers. Kate had never felt the remotest twinge of envy of them, but suddenly, listening to them, she was bleakly conscious of how empty of people her life was. What would happen to Michael if anything befell her?

She could feel an unfamiliar sensation of panic claiming her, swelling and building inside her, a terrifying awareness of Michael's vulnerability. Apart from her, he had no one.

Her phone rang and she picked it up.

'Ah, Kate...how are you this morning?'

'James...I'm fine, and you?'

'Look, I was wondering if I could bring our dinner date forward to Wednesday. I'm going to be rather tied up later in the week—a possible new acquisition.'

Kate's heart sank. She was as sure as she could be that her presentation was good, but she had wanted to discuss it with Camilla before submitting it to him. What was it about having a dependent child to look after that was so damaging to a woman's self-confidence? Perhaps it had something to do with the sleepless nights, she decided grimly, as she acceded to James's request.

'I'll pick you up, shall I? Say eight o'clock...'

Kate thanked him and gave him her address, making a mental note to be ready on time so that she didn't have to invite him in. It would do nothing for the image she was so determined to cultivate for James to discover Michael…or his nanny.

Unless she was lunching with clients, Kate did not have an official lunch hour. It was just gone one when her phone rang. Both girls were out and she picked it up, giving her name absently.

'Michael won't eat his dinner.'

The abrupt comment delivered in an exceedingly irate male voice startled her for a second.

'Kate, are you there?'

Kate? When had she given him permission to use her Christian name? The girls she had employed had all referred to her very correctly as Miss Oakley.

'Yes. Yes, I am here,' she responded crisply. 'What did you give him to eat?'

He told her and she frowned a little, realising he had used one of her emergency standby tins of prepared food, instead of using fresh ingredients and blending them as she preferred.

'That isn't one he likes very much,' she told him. 'Try the banana pudding, he seems to have a weakness for that.'

'Thanks.'

'Oh, and Rick…'

She could almost hear his impatience humming down the telephone wires.

'Yes?' he responded tersely.

'In future, perhaps you would follow my instructions and prepare Michael's food from fresh ingredients, using the blender. I think I did mention to you that I don't like him having convenience meals unless it's absolutely necessary.'

As he replaced the receiver, she thought she heard him mutter, 'It was necessary, believe me,' but the mutter had not been clear enough to be sure.

Her fears for Michael in her own absence, always latent, no matter who was in charge of him, rose to swamp her with guilt, distracting her from concentrating on the presentation she was trying to prepare.

What on earth had she done, allowing a mere man to take charge of Michael? A man who, it seemed, had flagrantly flouted her instructions and fed him tinned baby food. A man who didn't have the sense to read her instructions properly, who rang her up at work and completely destroyed her concentration.

What she needed right now, she recognised was some calming reassurance; the kind of reassurance that Camilla invariably gave her, but Camilla had problems of her own.

The afternoon brought a flurry of telephone calls, and the promise of some additional business from one of her existing clients who was thinking of expanding. In order to make up for the time she had lost worrying about Michael, Kate had to work late. Normally she enjoyed the peace of the office when she had it to herself, but this evening she found it hard to concentrate.

At half-past seven she gave in and called it a day. It took her over an hour to get home due to a problem with the underground, and when she did she was cold and tired.

As she put her key in the lock and opened the door, the house seemed unnaturally silent. Her heart did a somersault, all manner of terrible images flooding her brain. Something had happened to Michael...an accident. Dropping her briefcase, she rushed upstairs. Michael was standing up in his playpen, holding on to the bars. He grinned when he saw her. His rompers were filthy and his bib was generously stained with what looked like tomato purée. The room looked as though a whirlwind had hit it, toys strewn everywhere, and there in the middle of the chaos, dead to the world in the Victorian nursing chair she had bought and re-covered herself, lay Rick Evans—fast asleep.

Kate studied him covertly, noting the way the thick, dark lashes gave him an air of vulnerability. He was wearing jeans, and his shirt, like Michael's rompers, looked decidedly worse for wear.

As he crowed his delight at seeing her, Michael held up his arms to her and promptly sat down on his well-padded bottom. Kate picked him up, frowning as she discovered the odd shapelessness of his nappy. A brief investigation showed her that, whatever else Rick Evans might know about small children, he was not apparently *au fait* with the art of fastening a nappy.

She redid his handiwork to her own and Michael's satisfaction, and then quietly set about restoring order to the untidy nursery while Michael chattered unintelligibly to her, telling her all about his day.

He was a good-natured baby, physically affectionate and responsive, and Kate had been surprised to discover how much she enjoyed holding and cuddling his small body.

The room tidy, she picked him up, enjoying the way he nestled against her, before remembering that she was still wearing her office clothes. Normally the first thing she did when she got in was get changed. Thanks to Rick Evans her routine had been overset, and the result was that Michael was happily chewing on the shoulder of her very expensive Paul Costello suit.

Taking him with her, she went through to her own room, putting Michael down on the floor.

Stripping off her suit and blouse, she was standing in her satin teddy, reaching into her wardrobe for a pair of jeans, when her bedroom door was suddenly thrust open and Rick Evans walked in, calling anxiously, 'Michael? Oh…I didn't realise you were back.'

'Obviously not,' Kate agreed drily.

She wasn't used to men walking into her bedroom, and even though common sense told her that she was as decorously clad as any woman lying on a summer beach, she felt acutely vulnerable and uncomfortable with him standing there, watching her.

'I must have fallen asleep. I had no idea it was so late.' He

yawned as he spoke, stretching so that his shirt clung tautly
to his body.

'Yes,' Kate agreed tersely. She was holding her jeans in
front of her as though they afforded some form of protection.
But against what? He seemed to have no idea that she found
his presence in her bedroom both an intrusion and embarrassment, and to her astonishment, instead of apologising and leaving, he sat down on her bed, picking Michael up and making
the little boy laugh as he tossed him into the air and caught
him again.

'Perhaps you'd like to take Michael and get him ready for
his bath,' she suggested in some exasperation when he made
no move to leave.

He looked at her over the little boy's head, and Kate was
suddenly acutely aware of the way in which the satin fabric
clung to her body. She moved her weight uncomfortably from
one foot to the other.

'Aren't we going to have dinner first?'

Dinner? Kate forgot her embarrassment and frowned.

'I shall be having a light supper when I feel hungry,' she
told him freezingly. 'If you had read my instructions you
would have realised that you should have had *your* meal at
six o'clock, after Michael had had his tea. Look, I don't think
this is going to work,' Kate told him, suddenly exasperated.
'I'm sure you're every bit as good as your agency says, but I
don't think for a child as young as Michael...'

'Michael ate the instructions,' he interrupted her. 'Well, at
least—I left them on the table and he got hold of them, but
by the time I'd realised what had happened it was too late.'

Kate could visualise the scene all too easily. Michael had a
propensity for destruction, unlike anything she had previously
experienced.

'Please give me another chance... I need this job.'

The very fact that he obviously found it very difficult to ask
her softened her reluctance to keep him on. Who knew what
kind of personal problems he might have which she knew
nothing about? If she was honest with herself, it was his male-

ness and not his mistakes that was upsetting her so much. And that, surely, was her problem and not his?

'I'll give you another copy of the instructions,' she told him quietly, 'and tonight, as it's so late…I was only going to have quiche and salad for supper, but you're welcome to share it.'

What on earth was she saying? He looked as surprised as she felt, and she made a hurried attempt to re-establish the right amount of distance between them by saying coolly, 'In future, please don't come into my bedroom. To be honest with you, I find it rather strange that you did, especially in view of your complaints about your last employer.'

He looked almost mystified and she reminded him curtly, 'I was told that your last employer made unwanted advances towards you.'

'Er—yes…but you see, I thought you were out. I woke up and found that Michael had gone and I was in such a panic…'

Kate knew that feeling all too well.

'Yes, it's surprising how far they can travel,' she agreed wryly.

Garrick turned his head and looked at her. Nothing in the day had gone as he had planned. For a start, he had not been able to get hold of a nanny, and, although he had witnessed his mother caring for countless numbers of small children over the years, he had soon discovered that watching someone else do the work was one thing, doing it oneself was quite another.

It had taken him nearly an hour just to change Michael's nappy. For one thing the little boy just wouldn't keep still, and for another he couldn't seem to get the damn thing secure. Then there had been the débâcle of lunch—a meal which he had not been able to consume himself, since by the time he managed to get some of the revolting puréed mixture into Michael and clean up the mess this operation had involved, he had totally lost his appetite.

Gerald, summoned to drive round to the house with a large flask of coffee and some sandwiches at four o'clock in the afternoon, had taken one look at his normally immaculate boss and simply stared at him open-mouthed.

'You breathe one word of this to anyone and you're fired,' Garrick had told him threateningly.

They had gone through the mail together, while Michael played on the floor. Gerald had left promising to do everything he could to expedite the arrival of a properly trained nanny.

'The problem is,' he explained earnestly to Garrick, 'that none of the reputable agencies are keen on allowing one of their girls to work for an unknown man. Well, you can see their point, but you said not to disclose your name...'

'Couldn't you give them yours?' Garrick had demanded testily.

'Well, yes, but you see they wanted to see the house and the baby. It seems that good nannies are in very great demand.'

'I can see why,' Garrick had told him grimly.

After Gerald left it had been time to give Michael his tea. His first attempt to use the blender had resulted in the fiasco which even at this minute still decorated the kitchen, despite his attempts to remove most of the evidence.

It had been after that he had fallen asleep. Now he felt more tired than he had ever done in his life, and that included cross-Atlantic travel and the resultant jet lag.

He was also extremely hungry. So hungry that even quiche and salad made his mouth also extremely hungry. So hungry that even quiche and salad made his mouth water.

As he carried Michael back to his bedroom, he wondered where on earth the day had gone. He had nearly had heart failure when he woke up and found the little boy gone, and in the ten seconds it had taken him to find out, he had wondered what on earth he was going to tell Kate when she demanded an explanation for the baby's absence.

It only struck him as he put Michael down in his playpen how odd it was that his first concern had been for how he was going to tell Kate, rather than the upset Michael's potential disappearance might cause to his own plans.

He frowned heavily. His whole purpose in carrying out this idiotic charade was to collect enough proof to ensure that the legal system would give him sole custody of Michael through the negligence of his present guardian. And yet in his own heart of hearts he knew already that Kate Oakley was devoted to the little boy, and that she would defend and protect him as aggressively as a tigress with her cub.

Kate's feelings for Michael were not his concern, he reminded himself. If she wanted a child so desperately, there was nothing to stop her finding a man and having one of her own. She was an attractive woman, with a surprisingly voluptuous body. Very few men would turn down the opportunity to make love with a woman like her. She could have as many children as she wished.

He resolutely ignored the inner voice that pointed out austerely that so could he. It was different for a man: a man would always be vulnerable to the woman who carried his child. No matter what agreement might have been reached, women were notoriously emotionally unbalanced. He wanted the child without the complications of the mother. He wanted Michael.

Dressed in jeans and a sweater, Kate went through to Michael's bedroom, stopping on the threshold when she saw that Michael was in his playpen while his nanny was standing staring out of the window.

'Perhaps you'd like to go and get changed?' she suggested as he carried the plastic bath into the shower room. She deftly undressed Michael as she waited for the bath to fill. 'Oh, and remind me to show you how to fasten a nappy,' she added drily when Rick turned round to watch her.

She was surprised to see a faint burn of colour darkening his skin.

'All right, I admit it,' he agreed harshly. 'I don't have very much experience with such young children. But I do need this job…more than you can possibly realise, and I give you my word that while Michael's in my care, I'll see to it that he doesn't come to any kind of harm.'

Strangely she found his admission and his promise far more reassuring than she found his original contention that he was fully capable of looking after the small boy. Just for a moment she had seen something human and real in his eyes, something that touched a chord inside her.

She was tired of constantly worrying about the skill and responsibility of whoever was in charge of Michael. She trusted this man at least to display common sense and hard-headedness, even if he might lack a few of the more practical mothering skills. And who knew, perhaps Camilla was right when she said it was never too soon for a child to experience the male as well as the female influence in its life.

For better or worse, Rick Evans was Michael's nanny. For better or worse…odd that she should have picked those words from out of the marriage ceremony.

'Perhaps you'd like to bath Michael?' she said briskly to cover the confusion of her feelings. 'I'll stand and watch.'

'I think that might be a good idea,' Garrick agreed. 'Oh, and by the way, I had a small problem with the blender.'

CHAPTER FIVE

WHO other than the male of the species would dream of filling a blender with hard-boiled eggs and heaven alone knew what else, and then switch it on without the top on? Kate reflected wearily when she had removed the last of the mess from her normally pristine kitchen walls.

It was gone eleven o'clock and she hadn't done a single stroke of office work. What had happened to that interlude of calm quietude she normally enjoyed after her evening meal?

Rick had retired to his room to tamper with his computer, after she had refused his solicitous offer to help with the washing up.

'I have a machine,' she had pointed out drily to him. She was so tired now that her bones ached, but she could hardly leave the mess in the kitchen to be tackled by Mrs Riley who came in once a week to clean for her.

There, at last it was done. What she needed now was a hot, milky drink and an even hotter bath, and then bed. At least the activity of the evening had kept her from worrying about the fact that she hadn't been able to test her presentation out on Camilla.

Rick Evans came into the kitchen just as she was pouring milk into a pan.

'Supper?' he asked her, looking pleased at the prospect.

'No, *not* supper,' she told him coldly. 'Simply a hot drink which I am making for *myself*. *I* don't eat supper, but if you wish to do so, please feel free to make yourself something. Actually, Michael's previous nannies normally preferred to take advantage of the fact that I'm here in the evening to take a few hours off.'

'Meaning that's what you'd prefer me to do?' Garrick asked her shrewdly.

Something in the way he looked at her made Kate feel almost uncomfortable, and she found herself saying hastily, 'No...no, not at all,' which was exactly the opposite of what she meant.

'Do you go out much yourself in the evenings?' he asked her carelessly as he walked behind her to open the fridge door and inspect the contents.

It was a natural enough question, but Kate found she was stiffening slightly, ready to bristle with defensiveness should he indicate either by a look or a comment that he found it odd that a young woman of her age preferred to concentrate on her career rather than go out on dates.

'Sometimes—on business,' she told him coolly, letting her voice indicate that she was not pleased that he should question her on her personal life.

He didn't take the hint, removing a carton of eggs from the fridge, saying approvingly, 'Free range...good. I think I'll make myself an omelette, if that's OK with you,' and then adding before she could say a word, 'So when do you get the chance to let your hair down—meet men?'

Kate turned on him angrily. 'My private life isn't your concern,' she began, her eyes widening in startled shock as he put down the carton of eggs and took hold of her, virtually lifting her off her feet.

As she started to protest, her eyes registering her shock that he should manhandle her in such a way, he put her down, and deftly removed the pan of boiling milk from the hot-plate behind her.

'Sorry about that, but it was going to boil over,' he said easily, leaving her scarlet with mortification and temper.

She was beginning to bitterly regret her soft-headedness in allowing him to stay. It was becoming quite plain to her that he did not have the slightest idea of how a nanny should behave. It was not that Kate expected her employees to be subservient toward her—far from it. But she did expect a quite natural acknowledgement of the fact that their relationship was one in which hers was the more dominant role. Rick Evans seemed to have absolutely no awareness of this fact, and looking at him, standing in her small kitchen, watching her with eyes that held intelligent awareness of her confusion, and something else that was less obvious and harder to define, she found it very hard indeed to believe that this was a man who had been so intimidated by the sexual overtures of his previous employer that he had sought another job.

For all that she had known him only a very short time indeed, she found it hard to imagine that anyone, male or female, might intimidate him.

She reached for the pan of milk, pouring it shakily into her mug.

'I'm going to bed now,' she told him, trying to sound both cool and in control. 'And if you must use the blender, please remember to put the lid on.'

Garrick watched her go. Her back was ramrod stiff, but her eyes had given her away when he touched her. He had seen all too clearly that flash of near panic darken her eyes. Women did not normally panic when he touched them. Far from it. She obviously wasn't used to being touched, either. So she couldn't be involved in a relationship. That was a pity. A woman in love might quite easily tend to neglect the small child in her care in favour of that lover, and he was beginning to suspect that he would need all the ammunition he could find if he was going to succeed in his intention of taking the child away from her. No judge seeing them together could fail to see the relationship which she had already established with Michael.

What he needed now was a thoroughly reliable young woman he could employ as Michael's nanny. Someone who could take charge of him and establish a relationship with him that would eventually oust Kate from his affections. But what woman of that calibre would ever agree to the deception that would be needed for her to be able to work with Michael without Kate's knowledge? And how would he be able to trust a woman who did?

As he ate his omelette, he reflected rather wryly that this evening he should have been attending the premiere of a new film, with supper afterwards at the Ritz. His date for the evening had not been at all pleased at the cancellation of their arrangements, so Gerald had told him.

It struck him as he finished his meal that things weren't going according to plan. It had been a long time since anything had been allowed to disrupt the smooth running of his life, and even longer since that 'anything' had been a woman.

The problem was that he had not taken into account the effect of the enforced intimacy of living in such close contact with another adult human being, especially an adult female human being.

Kate had her hot bath and fell asleep the moment her head touched the pillow. When Michael cried out, she was awake instantly, groping in the dark for the switch to her bedside-light, pulling on her robe even as she registered the fact that it was three o'clock in the morning.

With the central heating off, her bedroom felt chilly and she shivered as she made her way to Michael's room. As she had suspected the moment his cry had woken her, there was no sign of Rick Evans.

Picking Michael up out of his cot, she checked automatically that he was not running a temperature and that there was nothing else obviously wrong with him. He was wet, which she had half expected, and now that he had his favourite adult with him, he was quite happy to stop crying and nuzzle contentedly into her shoulder. Sitting down in the nursing chair with him, Kate studied him severely.

'There's nothing wrong with you at all, is there?' she chided him softly.

He gurgled and grinned, reaching out to tug on her hair.

'You're a fraud, that's what you are,' Kate told him. 'Waking me up in the middle of the night just so that you can have a cuddle.'

Her expression belied the severity of her words, and Kate herself was still half surprised by the tender responsiveness that Michael always managed to arouse within her. By rights she ought to be thoroughly cross at being woken out of her badly needed sleep, but the pleasure of cuddling the soft, warm body...the way Michael smiled and gurgled at her, more than made up for her initial irritation.

Engrossed in the little boy, it was a shock to hear Rick Evans saying softly from the open doorway, 'And who can blame him?'

Instantly Kate was acutely conscious of her untidy hair and shabby dressing-gown. All her life she had fought against appearing vulnerable to others, and now here was this man, a stranger, an employee from whom she ought to have been able to preserve a protective distance, and yet who made her feel acutely conscious of herself and him in a way that made her feel acutely uncomfortable.

For instance, now as he watched her with Michael, she was intensely aware of the drag of her cotton nightdress against her breasts; sensitive to the sensation of the fabric in a way she had never known before.

She was equally conscious of the fact that Rick Evans was wearing a towelling robe beneath the hem of which his legs were bare, suggesting that he had pulled it on to cover his nakedness.

A soft shiver gripped her, convulsing her body on a hot tide of shame. It was both ridiculous and foolish for her to be so aware of him as a man. It suggested a weakness, a vulnerability she had not hitherto realised she possessed.

Anxiety coiled tensely in her stomach, locking her body into rigid watchfulness. She didn't like the way Rick Evans made her feel, she didn't like her unwanted awareness of him as a man, and she liked even less her body's awareness of itself as acutely female. She wasn't used to this kind of experience.

The male sex was a race she had determinedly held at a distance, permitting no intimate place in her life.

It had been desperation which had prompted her to agree to Camilla's suggestion that she hire a male nanny, and a ridiculous and dangerous compassion which had led her into allowing Rick Evans to stay, despite his obvious lack of experience with very young children. She had not given enough thought to the problems that the intimacy of sharing such a small house was bound to cause.

Why not? Normally she was careful and cautious in all that she did, never allowing herself to make a decision until she had explored all the possible results.

She had already given herself the answer. Sheer desperation, plus the anxiety of carrying the sole responsibility of both Michael and the business. Since Michael had come into her life, she had lost some of her armour of confidence. The little boy's vulnerability had transferred itself to her. She no longer only had herself to worry about; she had a small dependent child as well. And, just as Michael had shown her an unexpected vein of love and need within herself, so he had shown her a corresponding vulnerability and uncertainty. She was no longer the cool, controlled woman who believed herself to be invulnerable.

And Camilla had deceived her, she thought bitterly. Oh, not deliberately. No, she was quite sure that her friend had not meant to give her a totally erroneous impression of the kind of man Rick Evans would be. She knew her better than that. No. Her friend had acted in all good faith. It was not her fault that Kate had expected to have to deal with quite a mild-mannered type of man…the type of man who instinctively shied away from the female sex, the type of man one would quite naturally expect to meet on learning of his inability to cope with the sexual advances of a forceful female employer. Instead she had been confronted by a man who seemed the exact opposite of what she had expected.

Michael had gone to sleep. He lay heavily against her. Lost in thought, she wasn't even aware of Rick crossing the room until he gently lifted the sleeping baby from her arms. Her body tensed as his hand brushed accidently against the soft curve of her breast, her face unwittingly betraying her shock.

Garrick saw it and recognised her shock for what it was. The women he knew were sexually experienced and sophisticated. The accidental touch of a man's hand against their body did not cause them to go pale and then flush, their eyes mirroring open bewilderment at the recognition of their awareness of him as a man.

It made him feel both angry and protective at the same time. He didn't want to be aware of Kate's sexual vulnerability. It gave him an unfair advantage over her in this battle she didn't even know had begun.

He frowned as he carried Michael over to his cot, wondering why he should find the idea of taking advantage of her vulnerability so distasteful.

Garrick wasn't used to vulnerable women. The women he knew, knew exactly what life was all about. They would never allow themselves to be woken up in the middle of the night by the cry of a child who wasn't theirs.

Kate focused blindly on his robe-clad back, trying to will away the memory of the fluttering sensation of unfamiliar pleasure she had felt when he touched her. It was so very shaming, that flutter of pleasure; so embarrassingly unwanted and unlooked for, and that knowledge made her clench her muscles painfully and say curtly to Rick Evans, 'It might be a good idea if you invested in a pair of pyjamas. I'm beginning to understand why your previous employer might have thought her advances would be reciprocated.'

'Is that how you see me?' Garrick countered smoothly. 'As sexually available?'

He was on familiar ground now, his expression tinged with faint amusement as he turned from the cot to look at her.

To Kate, his amusement, coming on top of the confusion of her own awareness of his effect on her senses, was like acid thrown on to her skin. She burned with the torment of realising what he thought, immediately getting to her feet and drawing her shabby robe protectively round her body.

'I see you as a nanny who has so far shown an appalling lack of awareness of his duties and responsibility,' she said pointedly. 'In fact, I'm beginning to think—'

She was going to dismiss him, Garrick realised, cursing his own stupidity. Just because her vulnerability had caught him off guard, that had been no reason for him to try to undermine her self-confidence by underlining his awareness of the sexual tension between them.

In some perverse way, he had *wanted* her to react sexually to him, he recognised, almost as though by inviting her to recognise and acknowledge that faint sexual frisson he could free himself of his own guilt in what he was doing. And in attempting to do so he had created a potential hazard to his own ultimate success in proving her unfit to have charge of Michael. If she dismissed him now, it would be ten times harder for him to gather the information he needed.

'No, please…' he interrupted her quickly, and then, gambling desperately on the reality of the sense of humour he suspected she possessed, he added with a smile, 'I promise I'll go out and buy myself a pair of pyjamas first thing in the morning.' Shrewdly he refrained from pointing out that if she dismissed him she would undoubtedly face problems in finding a suitable replacement quickly, sensing that to challenge her would have the opposite effect from what he wanted.

His teasing comment gave Kate time to reflect on her own behaviour. She was over-reacting, there was no doubt about it. If she carried on like this… It was almost as though she were looking for an excuse to get rid of him because she was frightened of her own reaction to him, and that was impossible.

'And a manual on how to take care of a baby,' she suggested wryly, acknowledging that he could stay.

Long after she had gone back to bed, Kate was still awake. As a consequence, she overslept, waking only when she was disturbed by someone shaking her out of her deep sleep.

She opened her eyes reluctantly and focused on Garrick in confusion.

'It's eight o'clock,' he told her. 'I thought you'd want me to wake you up. I've made you a cup of coffee.'

Gone eight? That was impossible. But a quick look at her alarm told her it wasn't! It was the first time in her working life that anything like this had happened. Panic hit her as she realised that she was going to be late.

'Michael's still asleep as well.'

'You should have woken me earlier,' Kate told him fretfully.

'I heard your alarm go off, and I presumed you'd heard it as well. Can I do anything to help?'

'No. Not really.'

The moment he left the room Kate jumped out of bed, showering quickly, and pulling on the first clothes that came to hand. There wasn't time to wind her hair into its normal immaculate chignon, and she was acutely conscious of the heavy mass of her hair as she hurried downstairs.

The rich aroma of freshly brewed coffee filled the kitchen. She was hungry, but there wasn't time for her to have anything to eat. She rushed into the sitting-room, gathered up her papers, mentally calculating how long it was going to take her to reach her office. The girls would wonder what on earth had happened to her. Luckily Sara had a spare set of keys, so they could at least let themselves in.

And it would have to be today, when she had a lot on. Three appointments with prospective clients, and a celebratory lunch she couldn't possibly get out of with a client for whom her PR work had resulted in a twenty per cent increase in business.

There was also the normal paperwork to get through, and then at six she had a cocktail party to attend at a new gallery which had just opened and where she was hoping to persuade the owners to give a 'view' for one of her new clients, an artist who specialised in very delicate and appealing water-colours.

She was just stuffing the last of her papers into her briefcase when Rick walked into the sitting-room.

'Come and have your breakfast. Grapefruit, wholemeal toast and coffee. I hope that's OK.'

Her mouth watered desperately, but she shook her head.

'Thanks, but no. I haven't got time. I'm already running late.'

'You've got ten minutes,' Rick told her inexorably. 'I've ordered you a cab and he won't be here for fifteen minutes. Ten minutes to have your breakfast. Five minutes to clean your teeth and get your coat on.'

A cab? She stared at him in confusion. She wasn't used to someone else taking charge of her life like this, and Rick took advantage of her momentary bewilderment to gently usher her into the kitchen.

Her breakfast had been set out for her on the counter: the wholemeal toast was deliciously warm, the coffee fragrant and strong, just how she liked it, and the grapefruit properly segmented and free of sugar.

'I'll just go up and check on Michael,' she heard him saying, and as he disappeared she wondered if he had guessed that she preferred to eat her breakfast alone and in silence. It was remarkable how efficiently he had taken charge.

She was just applying a fresh coat of lipstick when her taxi arrived. Rick was still upstairs with Michael, and she only realised when she was in the cab that she hadn't told him that she wouldn't be in until late. She would have to ring him from the office.

In the event, she didn't need to. Garrick rang her at four o'clock, his voice terse as he told her that Michael wasn't very well.

'What's wrong with him?' Kate demanded anxiously. 'Have you called the doctor?'

'I don't think it's that serious. He's got a temperature, and he's very fretful. Can you come home?'

Could she go home? Her heart sank. Of course she couldn't. She had a thousand things to do, and then the cocktail party, which it was essential that she attend if she was to persuade the gallery owner to take her client.

She took a deep breath and said quietly and firmly, 'No, Rick, I can't. *You* are Michael's nanny. If you think it's necessary, then you must ring the doctor. The number's on the pad by the phone. Oh, and by the way, I shan't be back until around nine. There's a gallery opening I have to attend.'

As he placed the receiver back, Garrick looked with grim satisfaction at the recorder he had placed next to it. If he had written the words for her himself, he couldn't have chosen anything more damning. A mother who refused to come home when her child needed her. How could that look in court?

He reran the tape, listening to the crisp, incisive tone of Kate's refusal as he watched Michael playing happily with his building blocks. There was nothing wrong with the little boy, and Garrick had already known that Kate would not be able to come home, not after her late start this morning, not with the schedule she had. He had looked in her diary before he woke her, and had been a little startled to see James Cameron's name there. He had had dealings with the man himself and didn't like him. He was a bully and not above asserting unwarranted pressure when he thought he could get away with it. He caught himself wondering if Kate knew about his reputation, and then dismissed the thought angrily, irritated with himself for his momentary weakness.

Kate couldn't concentrate. She put down the presentation she was working on for a potential client and tried to banish from her mind tormenting images of Michael's face. Small children were so vulnerable when they were ill. A high temperature could be nothing at all, or on the other hand...

Her imagination worked overtime, busily fuelled by her guilt. How did other women cope with these situations? she wondered miserably. Common sense told her that Rick Evans was perfectly capable of calling the doctor should the situation necessitate it, but instinct and emotion argued unremittingly that she ought to be with Michael. That it was her responsibility and duty to be with him. She pictured his flushed, uncomfortable little body, heard his plaintive cries, and before she knew what she was doing she had risen from her desk and opened the door to the outer office.

'Sara,' she asked the dark-haired girl bent over a list of local TV and radio stations, 'are you doing anything this evening?'

'I've got a date…but I could cancel it. Why?'

'I wondered if you could go to a gallery opening in my place. Michael isn't well and I have to go home.'

Pleasure and ambition brought a pink flush to her assistant's face, and in her eyes Kate read the message that she considered her foolish to miss the opportunity of making such a good contact simply because of a sick child.

Once she would have shared her view, would have gloated in the presentation of such an opportunity, without giving a thought to the child responsible for it.

'Will you be in tomorrow?' Sara asked her casually as Kate stuffed papers into her briefcase and tried to concentrate on what she was saying. Now that the decision was made, she was in a fever of impatience to get home, to see for herself how Michael was. Manlike, Rick Evans had probably not told her the worst. Feverishly she pulled on her coat, mentally picturing Michael in hospital fighting for his life…

'Tomorrow?'

Kate stared blankly at her as Sara repeated the question, her heart sinking as Sara reminded her, 'It is tomorrow that you're having dinner with James Cameron, isn't it?'

'Yes. Yes…I will be in.'

But would she? Ought she to ring James and rearrange their meeting?

It was an evening meeting, she reminded herself. Even if she had to stay at home with Michael tomorrow, she ought to be able to make it for the meeting.

Two-fold guilt nagged at her as she managed to flag down a taxi. Breathlessly she gave him her address. So much hung on her getting James's business. By rights she ought to be concentrating on making sure that her presentation was as close to perfection as possible. She had meant to do that last night. She ought to be doing it tonight. But if Michael was ill...

She paid off the taxi with fingers that trembled, desperately searching in her handbag for her doorkey, for once her normal powers of organisation deserting her.

The door opened before she found her key.

'Michael? How is he? Is he worse?' she gabbled as Rick stepped back to let her in. She rushed past him, heading for Michael's bedroom.

Garrick followed her. He was still recovering from the shock of her unexpected arrival. Her white face and trembling hands had told their own story and looking at her, he had had to quell an unexpected impulse to reassure her.

Upstairs Michael was sitting in his playpen, contentedly pulling apart the complex interlocking tower Garrick had built from his locking bricks.

He beamed up at Kate when he saw her, so obviously healthy and well that Kate started to shake with relief.

'Here...sit down.'

She was pushed gently into a chair. She subsided into it without a word of protest, saying only, 'He's all right. There's nothing wrong with him.'

'I know,' Garrick admitted. 'I suppose I panicked. He seemed very flushed and hot, and wouldn't eat his lunch.'

Strangely enough, instead of the righteous anger she knew she ought to feel, what she did experience was an almost uncontrollable desire to burst into tears. Shock and reaction, she told herself, absently fighting to control the unfamiliar weakness.

'You should have rung me.' The words lacked conviction, sounding vague and woolly. She felt confusingly weak. 'I'd better get back to the office. I'll be late this evening.'

'A date?' Garrick questioned her, knowing it wasn't. She had gone so white that he had thought she might actually faint. He could see the struggle she was having to stop herself from betraying her emotions, and he felt a sudden surge of self-dislike.

She might not be Michael's natural mother, but there could be no doubts about her love for the little boy. Would he in the same circumstances have dropped everything to rush home to assure himself that the child was all right? He was uncomfortably aware that most probably he would not, and that while it was true that financially he was able to buy the best care there was for Michael, that care could in no way compare with Kate's love for him.

'A gallery opening,' Kate responded briefly, too drained to resent his question. 'I'd better ring the office.'

Sara was going to be very disappointed, she reflected wryly as she went downstairs and picked up the receiver. Now that she was home, she might as well get changed.

She had a couple of discreetly elegant black dresses she kept for such occasions. Neither of them were openly fashionable, but they both came from good designers and enhanced the image she wished to project.

The one she chose was plain black wool crêpe with a neat neckline and long sleeves. The neat waist and discreetly curved skirt skimmed her body rather than clinging to it. It was a business woman's dress that made a very positive statement against sexual availability.

Knowing that it was going to be a cold night, Kate wore a three-quarter-length black velvet jacket over it, that was dressy enough for an evening engagement, and plain high-heeled black shoes.

Two pearl and diamanté clips in her hair were her only concession to vanity. She was perfectly well aware that a physically attractive woman could tease and flatter a man into giving her a good deal, but that was not the way she wanted to do business, because invariably the man would expect to be given something in return.

When she went into the nursery to check on Michael, Rick Evans wasn't there. The little boy's skin felt reassuringly cool, his eyes bright and clear.

Kate kissed him and hurried downstairs, wishing she did not have this increasingly urgent desire to spend more time

with him. If the rest of her sex felt like this the moment a
small child arrived in their lives, then she could only marvel
that so many of them were mothers as well as successful career
women. Perhaps she was more anxious over Michael because
he was not her own...because she felt a duty to him for
Jennifer's sake which nagged at her all the time she was away
from him.

Garrick watched her leave from his bedroom window. She
looked tired and drawn. A mixture of guilt and irritation carried him over to the phone. He dialled the number of his own
office, drumming his fingers impatiently on the the table while
he waited to be connected.

'Gerald, Stephen Hesketh is opening his new gallery tonight. I need to speak to him immediately. Find out where I
can get in touch with him, will you?'

'Hesketh. Didn't you buy the Canalettos through him?'

'Yes,' Garrick agreed tersely, without vouchsafing any further information.

Kate's evening went surprisingly well. Stephen Hesketh had
indicated that he would be more than pleased to repay the
small favour he owed her, by giving her client a private view.

Kate, who had expected to have to work very hard to persuade him to agree to her suggestion, had been caught off
guard by his ready acceptance. He was not a man who was
known for his good nature.

'I'll get my secretary to give you a ring to confirm it, but I
think I'm free for lunch on Friday. We can discuss all the
details then.'

'That's fine,' Kate told him, wondering where she could
take him for a meal. To her astonishment he went on to add,
'We'll eat at the Connaught, shall we? I'll get Elise to book
a table,' indicating that he was going to take her out and more-
over pay the bill.

Concealing her surprise, Kate left the party early, not wanting to push her luck by staying and perhaps running the risk
of him changing his mind.

Having time in hand, instead of going straight home, she rang Edmund Howarth, the artist for whom she had arranged the 'view' from a call box, giving him the good news, and then agreeing to go round and discuss the preliminary arrangements for the 'view' with him.

Edmund was a very gentle and shy man, as evidenced by his paintings. A bad stammer had isolated him as a child and he had turned to painting as an outlet for his feelings. Some of the earlier work he had shown Kate evidenced the violence of his teenage emotions, and he had once told her that he had kept them as a reminder of the depth of his despair during those younger years.

He was now in his early forties and very happily married. His wife was six years his senior and they had met when he was attending a summer school for artists. She had been teaching one of the courses, and it had been she who had first suggested that the best medium for him might not be oils but watercolours.

Kate liked both of them. She had always related better to non-threatening men.

It was gone nine when she left, conscious of the fact that she was both tired and hungry, and yet she knew from experience that once she got in her appetite would have deserted her. Tiredly she got in the taxi Edmund had called for her.

Her evening had been overwhelmingly successful, and yet it struck her as she got in the cab that there was no one with whom she could share her triumph. Camilla was still away, Michael was far too young. There was a small ache of pain inside her which she tried to dismiss. What was happening to her? Her whole focus of attention seemed to be shifting almost daily; the foundations on which she had built her life crumbling away with frightening speed; the goals she had set herself with such confidence and determination no longer anything like as clear as they had once been.

And yet now she needed to succeed more than ever. She needed to succeed to provide security for Michael and herself. She must stop spending so much of her time thinking about the little boy. She must concentrate on her work, on her career. Tiredly she closed her eyes and leaned back in the cab. Her head was starting to ache and she massaged her temple and thought longingly of a hot bath and then bed, knowing that by rights she ought to be out celebrating tonight's success with something like a champagne supper. That was, after all, the public image of a successful PR person. That was how contracts were made and contracts won. How long would it be before she was able to leave Michael in the care of others without this constant nagging sense of guilt, this fear that something would happen to him in her absence? It must be soon, otherwise she was going to tear herself apart with overwork and guilt, and that wouldn't help either of them.

Just for one treacherous second she allowed herself to wonder what it would be like to have someone to share the responsibility with her. Someone like…her heart thumped uncomfortably fast as a name and a face formed within her brain.

Rick Evans. It disturbed her that he should occupy so many of her thoughts. It was just overtiredness, that was all. Overtiredness and reaction to the adjustments she was having to make in taking on a male nanny. This constant and unwanted awareness of him would fade in time. After all, she had never reacted like this before, never experienced such an awareness before. It was bound to fade. It had to fade.

CHAPTER SIX

TENSELY Kate studied the presentation in front of her; she had been through it so many times before, she suspected that she was no longer objective enough to make any useful criticism of it, but nervous energy drove her on, refusing to allow her to relax and let her body recoup itself as she knew she ought.

Tonight she was having dinner with James. By the end of the week the entire future of her young company would be decided. So much hung on James's decision. She had other clients, of course, but none of them were of the financial standing of James.

With James as her client, she would automatically be moving up the status ladder; she would attract larger and wealthier clients; she would be able to expand, to allow herself to relax a little. Success in obtaining James's business meant security for Michael and herself.

She knew her presentation was good. The chain of supermarkets was only a very small part of James's empire, but he had tacitly indicated that success with the supermarkets would lead to the chosen PR company getting the rest of his business. Yes, she knew her presentation was good, but what she didn't know was the strength of her rivals' presentations.

If only Camilla was here. She needed the boost of being able to talk to someone who understood her and who understood her business, but when she had rung her home this morning, she had learned that her father-in-law had suffered a second heart attack and that Camilla was continuing to stay with her mother-in-law.

She put the presentation away carefully with a faint sigh. Given free choice, she would have preferred to discuss her suggestions either here in her own office or in James's.

The idea of having dinner alone with him in his flat did not appeal to her. She knew his reputation, but she felt reasonably sure that she had already convinced him that she was not in the market for a one-night stand or even an affair.

And it was true, as he had pointed out to her when she had originally expressed dislike of his suggested venue, that they would be able to discuss and study her presentation far more easily in the comfort of his flat than in some restaurant.

She had planned to leave the office early, but a sudden rash of telephone calls delayed her, and it was gone six when she eventually hurried breathlessly up to her front door.

By rights she ought to have taken a cab rather than use the underground, but the long years of rigorous self-denial after she had left the children's home had left their mark, and, while she wasn't mean, she was very careful about what she spent on herself.

From the sounds reaching her from upstairs, Rick was obviously giving Michael his bath. Discarding her coat and gloves in her own room, Kate hurried through to the nursery.

Rick had put the bath on the floor on a large towel rather than use its stand. Shirt sleeves rolled up, he was kneeling beside it with his back to her, both he and Michael totally engrossed in a game they were playing.

Watching them, Kate felt a sharp surge of envy. Normally his bathtime was her special time with Michael, and she resented the fact that Rick was taking that from her, even while she recognised that it would hardly be fair to the little boy to disturb his routine to fit in with her own uncertain hours.

Even so, as she heard his laughter and watched the small pink body wriggling delightedly in the water, she had a sudden fierce desire to snatch him up into her arms. So fierce, in fact, that it was almost as though she feared that in some way Rick was going to take Michael from her.

At that moment Rick looked up and saw her, and Kate flushed, wondering what it was he had seen in her eyes that made his own darken fractionally.

'You were late, so I thought I'd give Michael his bath.'

'Yes... Thank you.' She knew that her voice sounded strained, her thanks insincere. 'I'd better go and get ready. I take it Michael has had his supper?'

How shrewish and sharp she sounded, almost as though she wanted to find fault with him.

'At five o'clock,' Rick told her calmly. 'Shall I finish off here, or would you...'

Flushing angrily that he should so easily read the resentment in her eyes and know the cause of it, Kate shook her head and said tersely, 'Yes, if you would. I have to get changed. I'm being picked up at eight.'

'A dinner date?' Rick asked her.

Kate shook her head again.

'Not really. It's business.'

Michael, not happy with the fact that he had lost their attention, splashed noisily in his bath. Rick bent down to lift him out, wrapping him in a warm towel.

Feeling dismissed and shut out, Kate walked unsteadily into her own room. She had an absurd inclination to cry, something to do with the sight of Michael's chubby little arms wrapped so trustingly around the neck of the man holding him.

Once she must have been held like that by her father, but she could not remember it. What she could remember, though, was the pain that had come with knowing that her parents' love had been taken from her, and she had spent the rest of her life determined to make sure that she was never vulnerable to that kind of pain again, never allowing anyone close enough to her to cause her pain when they left her, never allowing herself the indulgence of physical contact with others. Until Michael came into her life. And the worst thing of all was that she didn't know whom she envied the most: Rick for the way Michael nestled so trustingly in his arms, or Michael because he had the sure strength of Rick's arms around him.

All the time she was getting ready, she could hear the soft sounds of Rick getting Michael ready for bed; intimate, tender little sounds that caught at her heart and made it ache dangerously.

She was just stepping into her dress when Rick knocked on her bedroom door.

'What is it?' she called out, realising her mistake the moment he opened the door and walked in.

She saw his eyebrows rise as she struggled frantically to tug her dress on, her face flushed and hot with embarrassment as the fabric stuck over her hips where she had accidentally bunched it, leaving the whole of her upper body bare apart from her lacy bra.

'I didn't mean you to come in,' she told him angrily. 'What is it you want, Rick?'

Fear of her own vulnerability made her voice sharp; she knew she was over-reacting, and she could see that Rick knew it too. He must be able to see how uncomfortable she felt, yet he made no move to leave, and Kate felt a slow burn of colour wash her skin as he quite deliberately looked at her.

Long ago, in her days in the home, when she had been forced to share a large bedroom with other girls, she had no doubt thought nothing of dressing and undressing in front of others. But those others had been members of her own sex and, besides, it had been a long time ago.

Her privacy was something that Kate had guarded very protectively in the years that had followed, and to have someone standing in her bedroom, watching her while she struggled to conceal herself from him, made her shake with a mixture of fear and anger that made it impossible for her to untangle the fabric of her dress.

Close to tears of rage and misery, she cried out sharply, 'Will you please get out of my room? I'm trying to get dressed.'

'And not succeeding very well,' Garrick told her drily, crossing the room. Before she could stop him, he was at her side, saying, 'Here, let me help you.'

Kate couldn't have moved if she'd tried. Her entire body tensed and then shook, as though she was in the grip of a fatal palsy. She felt Rick take hold of her dress and gently ease it up into the curve of her waist so that the bunched fabric could fall free. She felt the silk slither of its lining flow smoothly over her hips and thighs.

Like someone in a trance, she remained mute and obedient as Rick eased the top of her dress upwards and away from her body so that she could slide her arms into the sleeves.

He moved behind her. She felt the coldness of the metal zip and then the warmth of his hands through the fabric as he ran it upwards, closing it.

'A business dinner... Which restaurant is he taking you to?' he asked casually as he fastened the hook and eye at the top of her dress.

The question took several seconds to penetrate. Kate felt almost as though she were drugged and unable to respond to anything with her normal speed. Even though he was no longer touching her she could still feel the imprint of his fingers against her skin.

'We aren't going to a restaurant,' Kate told him huskily. It was oddly difficult to form the words, her throat felt tight and sore.

'He's taking you to his flat?' She saw the hard face tighten, a shrewd, mocking smile curling his mouth. 'I see. So that's how you do business is it, Kate—oiling the wheels of success with a little skilful seduction?'

Kate reacted without thinking, raising her hand and slapping his face hard at the same time as she burst out furiously, 'No, it is not! How dare you suggest such a thing? How...'

The protest died in her throat as he took hold of her, the grey eyes blazing with an anger that threatened to match her own and exceed it, but there was no anger in his voice, as the hard fingers dug into her arms, and his mouth curled in mocking amusement as he told her, 'You're very naïve for a successful business woman, Kate. Don't you know that there's only one effective punishment a man can inflict on a woman who slaps him, and that it's this?'

She cried out as his head blotted out the light, but the sound was smothered under the hard pressure of his mouth.

It was the first time she had been kissed by a man so obviously experienced in the art that, despite her rage and fear, she discovered that her own lips were softening treacherously beneath his skilled assault; and, as though the very fact of their tremulous softness pleased him, he didn't let her go, but used his tongue and his teeth to give her the most explicit and thorough lesson in the art of turning the angry pressure of mouth against mouth into the kind of sensual devastation that rocked her self-confidence on its foundations.

Quite when her eyes closed and she went limp in his arms, allowing him to draw her so close to his body that her breasts were flattened against his chest and she could feel the heavy thud of his heart as though it beat within her own body, she didn't know. It was only the awareness of his voice in her ear as he stopped kissing her that brought her back to reality, her eyes opening slowly, the pupils hugely dark with arousal and bemusement. At some point he had slid his fingers into her hair, and now they massaged the back of her scalp lazily as he looked down into her face.

'Perhaps I owe you an apology, after all,' he told her softly, watching every tiny betraying expression that crossed her face as she realised what had happened. 'But naïveté is no protection against a man like James Cameron, you know, Kate.'

The instant she was free of him, all Kate's mental functions sprang back into action.

'How would you know anything about him?' she demanded belligerently.

Instantly his face hardened as it had done before, and she could see that she had angered him.

'What are you trying to say? That as a humble nanny, I'm hardly likely to be qualified to hold an opinion on a successful businessman like Cameron? I read the papers. He doesn't have a very good reputation.'

His mouth twisted slightly, and Kate had to dismiss the accusation hovering on her lips that he was jealous of James's success.

This was a man who wasn't jealous of anyone, she acknowledged, a little shocked at having to accept that this was so; a humble nanny was how Rick had described himself in a voice dry with some kind of concealed amusement, but there was nothing humble about him at all.

'How did you know it was James Cameron I'm having dinner with?' Kate demanded.

'You told me.' He shrugged powerful shoulders. 'How else could I have known?'

Kate frowned. She was reasonably sure she had not told him, but he was quite right. How *could* he have known, otherwise?

She was only just beginning to recover from the shock of his kiss. She would have to say something to him about it…to make it clear to him that it was an incident that was never to be repeated…to even demand an explanation of why it had happened in the first place, only she suspected she knew. The male sex could never resist an opportunity of reinforcing their superior strength to the female. She had always known that, and Rick had just proved that she was right.

She was torn between an urgent need to tell him that she was going to dismiss him, and her recognition of the fact that she could not do so without first making sure she had someone to replace him.

And then there was Michael to think of, and there was no getting away from the fact that Michael responded far better to Rick than he had done to any of his other nannies. She couldn't dismiss him, she already knew that and so, she suspected, did he… Which left her with only one avenue of self-defence.

Drawing herself up to her full height, she said coldly, 'If this is the way you behaved with your previous employer, I'm not surprised she thought you were sexually available, but let me make one thing clear to you here and now. If I want a lover, I'm perfectly capable of finding myself one.'

'I don't doubt it,' he told her gravely, thoroughly disconcerting her both with his words and the look he gave her. It was almost approaching being tender, and she recoiled from it as though he had hit her.

An unexpected wail from Michael's room disturbed them both.

'I'll go,' Rick told her.

She heard him soothing the wakeful child, and then close the door as he went downstairs. It was half-past seven. If she didn't hurry, she was going to be late.

Her hands trembled as she brushed her hair and put on her make-up. Everything Rick had said and done had reinforced her doubts about going to James's flat, but she had no other option.

It was five to eight when she eventually felt calm enough to go downstairs. She had left her presentation in the sitting-room, and she was stunned to see Rick studying it for all the world as though he had every right to do so.

'Just what do you think you're doing?' she fumed as she swept into the room. 'That is private...'

'Sorry,' he apologised to her with a brief smile. 'I was just interested to see what you were planning.'

'And now that you *have* seen it, are you any the wiser?' she asked sarcastically.

She saw the brief flash of anger darken his eyes, but before he could say anything the doorbell rang.

'That will be James,' Kate told him hurriedly. 'I must go.'

For some reason she didn't want the two men to confront one another. Confront? It was only as she snatched up her papers and dashed to the front door that she wondered at her somewhat Freudian choice of verb.

James drove a silver-grey Porsche. He had parked it next to the Ferrari, and he frowned a little as he ushered her past it and opened the passenger door of his Porsche.

'Wealthy neighbours?' he questioned as Kate thanked him.

She responded with a vague smile, not wishing to tell him the truth and not wanting to fib either, but luckily he seemed to assume that his assumption was right and did not refer to the Ferrari again.

James very obviously enjoyed all the trappings of his suc-cess: the suit he was wearing had not come from one of his

own chain store retailers, Kate acknowledged, and nor had the
expensive cotton shirt. And yet, to the media, James pro-
claimed himself to be very much a man of the people. Not
that there was anything wrong with a successful person enjoying that success, but Kate didn't like the way James sometimes mocked the very people who had been responsible for
his success.

As they drove to his flat he name-dropped continuously,
something else she detested, and she wondered whether he was
actually trying to impress her, or if it had simply become a
habit he was no longer aware he had.

His apartment was in an elegant Georgian terrace of houses
of Eaton Square, with a complicated series of security checks
to be gone through before they could walk into the main hallway that serviced all the apartments.

James's was on the second floor. A square hallway decorated in off-white and black, and to Kate's eyes too stark and
modern for the elegance of the building, gave way to a draw-
ing-room decorated in the same modernistic colours and furnished with a good deal of off-white leather and steel. While
she could appreciate its design, she wondered a little at anyone
choosing it for such an inappropriate setting.

'I've arranged for my staff to leave dinner ready for us. The
bathrooms here are all en suite, I'm afraid. The apartment
doesn't boast a separate cloakroom. If you'd...'

Kate shook her head quickly, her nerve-ends prickling, not
so much at his comment but at the way he was looking at her.

A very prettily arranged cold meal had been left for them
in the dining-room, but Kate was too nervous to eat. Refusing
more than a single glass of wine, she fought down her butter-
flies of impatience while James refilled his several times. Then
he insisted on having an after-dinner brandy, while Kate toyed
with a second cup of coffee she didn't really want.

Over dinner, every time she had tried to discuss her presentation, James had steered the conversation into more personal
channels. Kate wasn't sure she was too happy with the emphasis he seemed to place on his questions about her personal

life, and she was thoroughly on edge by the time the meal was over and they were able to move into his study to discuss her presentation.

Whatever his reputation with her sex might be, he was a very able businessman, Kate reminded herself as she sat down opposite him across the expanse of the stained ash desk.

Like the other rooms she had seen, this one too was very modern in its decoration and furniture. It also struck her as rather cold and clinical, and certainly it was the direct opposite of the illusion she had decided to create for his new chain of supermarkets.

Neither of them spoke as he read through her presentation. Kate because she was too nervous, and James because he was studying the work she had done.

'I'm impressed,' he told her when he had finished. And Kate had the impression that he was not just impressed, but surprised as well; that he had not for some reason expected her to produce something of such a high standard. 'Your suggestions are good…if perhaps a little on the high side cost-wise.'

She opened her mouth to speak, but he forestalled her, saying silkily, 'Kate, you're the kind of woman I admire very much indeed…my kind of woman. Together we could form a very mutually advantageous partnership, don't you think? Whichever agency I eventually recommend to my main board will be getting a very valuable contract indeed…in terms of money and status.

'You remind me of myself twenty years ago. Young, ambitious, clever. Clever enough to know that sometimes in order to succeed we all need to give that little extra something.' He looked at her and smiled lazily, supremely confident that he would get what he wanted.

Kate's heart was bounding. She had no difficulty at all in interpreting his comments. He was telling her that if she wanted the contract she was going to have to sleep with him. This was something she had come up against on only a handful of occasions before, and she had made it plain then as she intended to do now that there was no way she was going to barter sexual favours in return for getting someone's business.

She took a deep, steadying breath and, maintaining eye contact with him, interrupted smoothly before he could go any further, 'I'm glad you like the presentation, and I'm flattered that you should compare my ambition with your own, but I'm afraid when it comes to that "little something extra"—well that's not the way I do business.'

She stood up as she spoke, firmly gathering up her papers, refusing to either hurry or appear to be frightened. It was rather like dealing with an aggressive dog, she told herself mentally; if she didn't betray her panic, everything would be all right.

But James obviously wasn't used to being refused. The lazy smile disappeared, and he looked at her in furious disbelief.

'If you think you can push the price up by doing this, forget it. Come on, Kate. I know how these things are done. You want the contract. I want you.'

'It's not the way I do business,' she told him curtly.

'No, so I've heard.'

And, as she looked at him, Kate wondered how much of his desire for her was fuelled by a need to be able to say to others that he had succeeded where they had failed.

It made her feel sick inside. She knew there were still businessmen like James, but they were getting fewer and fewer as more and more women became successful. She had been warned, though, both by Camilla and by Rick Evans.

She had all her papers together now. She looked across the desk and said quietly, 'I think it's best if I leave. If you should change your mind about the terms of the contract, you know where you can contact me.'

'Change my mind?' he laughed mockingly. 'You'll be the one who'll be doing that, my dear. Face it…you need the contract far more than I need your presentation.'

His arrogance made Kate lose her temper, and without even thinking of the consequences she said furiously, 'There's no contract on earth that's worth the price you're asking.' And too late she realised what she had done as she saw his face change, the gloating expression giving way to one of hot dislike.

'You little bitch,' she heard him saying thickly. 'You're all alike, you so-called businesswomen. Trying to turn men into eunuchs. It's time someone taught you a lesson.'

And as he lunged toward her, trying to grab hold of her, Kate realised her danger. It was not just her he disliked and resented, it was all women like her who dared to invade his male world, who made him feel insecure and threatened.

Just in time she managed to evade his grasp, grabbing her papers from the desk and almost running across the room to tug open the door. She heard him following her; the heavy sound of his breathing like something out of a childhood nightmare.

Luckily the door to the hallway was open and she darted through it, hearing James curse as he tried to cut off her exit and bumped into one of the heavy leather chairs.

Her hands trembled as she unlocked the front door to the apartment and then darted down the stairs rather than ring for the lift.

In her haste to escape she had forgotten the security locks on the massive front door into the street, but as she emerged into the hallway the door opened and, ignoring the startled expressions of the couple coming in, she dashed outside, pausing to catch her breath and steady her heartbeat.

It was only then that she realised she had left both her coat and evening bag in James's apartment.

It was a freezing cold night, something she hadn't realised when he'd driven her here, and her dress was very fine wool. The pavement was damp, and she only realised as she stepped out of the protection of the doorway that it had started to sleet, stinging pellets of icy rain that burned her skin and soaked through her dress.

A taxi sped down the street, sending up a spray of ice-cold water to drench her from the knees down as it pulled sharply into the kerb. She stepped toward it, but the driver flicked on his engaged light.

There was no guarantee that James wouldn't pursue her out into the street, although she thought it was extremely unlikely, but now that her initial panic had eased Kate realised that she had no way of getting home other than walking, since her money was in her evening purse in his flat.

If Camilla had been home she could have rung her and begged for help, but she wasn't. There was only one thing for it, she decided grimly, squaring her shoulders. She would have to walk. At least that way she might be able to keep warm. She didn't. Before she was more than half-way there she was soaked to the skin, or so it felt, the ever increasing sleet now like tiny daggers against her chilled skin.

She slipped once, her flimsy high-heeled shoes sliding on the icy pavement, and the shock of falling made her cry out sharply, but there was no one to hear her. By the time she was on her feet again she was shaking as well as shivering, and in the streetlight she saw the smear of blood on her knee, her flesh white against the ripped black tights she was wearing. She had also scraped her hands, and the palms stung painfully.

Blinking back tears of shock and pain, she tried to walk as quickly as she could. Her ankle ached painfully when she put her full weight on it, but at least it supported her.

She had never been more glad of anything in her life than to reach the familiar turning to her own street. She was limping badly now, and if she had had the energy she suspected she would probably have been crying with exhaustion.

As she reached her own front door, she leaned blissfully against it, automatically reaching out for her handbag and her key. But of course she didn't have either.

It was too much…much, much too much. She leaned her cheek against the door and let the tears flow, beating frustratedly on the smooth painted surface with hands too chilled to ball into fists.

CHAPTER SEVEN

WHEN the solid wood gave way beneath her, Kate was too cold and shocked to realise why or to care, and not even Rick's incredulous, 'Kate! My God, what's happened to you?' really reached her.

She took a step forward and then another, shivering like a soaked cat, wanting only to crawl upstairs and go to bed, but Rick was standing in the way and another step forward brought her up against the solid warmth of his body and somehow or other into his arms.

She made a muffled protest and tried to step backwards, but it was too late. His arms had locked round her, and anyway he was so blissfully warm and comforting to lean on that she really didn't want to move at all. Having had her token protest rejected, she was quite content to let him hold her.

It would be bliss to close her eyes and go to sleep where she stood, supported and warmed by the bulk of that male body, but it seemed that Rick wasn't going to let her.

She gave a faint cry of protest when he moved her away from his warmth so that he could look down into her face.

'What the hell happened to you?' he demanded roughly. 'Is Cameron responsible for this?'

The hard anger in his voice penetrated through the shroud of icy cold numbing her. Kate opened her eyes and focused hazily on him. His mouth was a grim, hard line that indented in a severe and authoritative way she couldn't recognise. Her gaze shifted focus to his eyes. They, too, held an unfamiliar expression. Flat and cold and very, very masculine.

'*Is* he, Kate?' he reiterated curtly.

She shook her head and told him huskily, 'No. At least, not directly... He didn't attack me, if that's what you mean.'

Just those few words exhausted her, and she let her eyes close so that she could blank out the male anger in his face. For some reason that she couldn't find the energy to analyse right there and then, she found it almost comforting that Rick should be so concerned.

It struck her rather vaguely that this was hardly the reaction of the dedicated self-sufficient woman she considered herself to be, but she was too exhausted to dwell on the conundrum of her untypical behaviour too deeply.

'So who did?' Rick persisted, shaking her gently when she squeezed her eyes tightly closed.

'No one,' she told him crossly, when she realised he wasn't going to let her lie down and go to sleep as she so desperately wanted to do until he had got his answer.

'I fell in the street...' She shivered and said plaintively, 'Rick, I'm cold. I want to go to bed. I want to get warm.'

'You're soaked through,' he told her roughly. 'Where's your coat?'

'I left it in James's apartment,' she told him, too exhausted to prevaricate.

Even behind her closed eyelids she could feel the penetrating demand of his concentration. Reluctantly she opened her eyes, obeying his unspoken command.

'All right...we had an argument. He told me he'd give us the contract for his PR work if I went to bed with him.' She grimaced bitterly. 'I told him that isn't the way I do business, and left.'

'Without your coat?'

'Yes!' she admitted bitterly. 'He made a lunge for me and I panicked. I left my coat and my evening bag in his apartment, but at least I brought the presentation back with me.'

She heard Rick curse under his breath, and didn't know whether his savage denunciation was for her or for James.

'I warned you what he was like,' he told her, grim-faced. 'God almighty, call yourself a businesswoman, and yet you walked into his trap like a fly into honey.'

His scorn penetrated the icy miasma of exhaustion and misery surrounding her. Kate jerked back in his arms, her eyes glittering with the onset of fever and tears.

'If you're trying to suggest that I allowed greed to blind me to reality…'

'Not greed,' Rick countered swiftly, 'but if I were to substitute ambition for greed, could you be as quick to deny the charge?'

Kate felt a hot stain spread over her body. His words came too close to home for comfort. She had always had her doubts about the wisdom of dealing with James, about the sense of dining alone with him in his apartment, but her desperate need to secure the contract had forced her to put her doubts to one side. And now to have Rick so accurately pinpoint that fact made her feel both resentful and fiercely defensive.

'Of course you would say that—just because I'm a woman. Ambition in a man is something to be praised and admired, but let a woman evidence the same drive and suddenly the whole world wants to criticise her.

'Is it really so very wrong of me to want to make a success of the agency? Not just for my own sake, either. I've got Michael to think of, the girls I employ—and even if I didn't, I'd still want to succeed,' she told him fiercely. 'And I don't see why I should be ashamed of admitting it… A woman has just as much right to want to achieve as a man.'

'Yes, she has,' Rick agreed sombrely. 'It can also be a lot harder to succeed…or a lot easier…depending on what she's prepared to do, to achieve success.'

Kate ached in every bone in her body. The last thing she wanted was to have an in-depth discussion on moral values here in her hallway, when she was freezing cold and soaking wet. In fact all she wanted was for Rick to open his arms so that she could walk into them and forget everything bar the blissful warmth and protection of his body.

This knowledge of her own weakness shocked her. For the first time in her adult life she wanted something from another human being.

It was Michael who had caused her to develop this weakness. Michael, whose dependence and love had pierced the invulnerable wall she had built around herself, Michael who had destroyed that barrier with his dependence and need and left her vulnerable to emotions she had promised herself she would never feel.

She knew all about the dangers of loving others…the pain of the loss…the loneliness of being part of a close knit unit that had disintegrated. She had experienced it all when she lost her parents and she told herself all through her growing up years that she was never going to experience it again. And the best way to do that was not to allow anyone close to her; not to allow herself to want anyone to be close to her. So why was she now aching for Rick to stop lecturing her and instead to enfold her in his arms and comfort her with tenderness and care?

She couldn't ignore his statement though, nor the challenge it contained. It had to be answered.

She lifted too heavy eyelids and focused on him with difficulty:

'If you're saying that life will always be easier for those women who are prepared to barter sex for favours, then yes, I agree with you that in the past that was the case, but that's changing. Women are no longer prepared to sell themselves short. They no longer need to.' Her head lifted proudly, her eyes glittering with more than the fire of the fever she was holding at bay. 'If you're trying to suggest that I might have at any time considered sleeping with James in order to secure the contract, then you're quite wrong. That isn't the way I do business, and it never will be.'

'No,' Garrick agreed quietly. 'I can see that.'

He ought to be feeling angry; if he could prove that she was the type of woman who slept around, who sold herself to gain business advantages, it would be easier for him to prove her an unfit guardian for Michael, but instead, what he did feel was a rush of satisfaction and relief that his judgement had not been at fault, coupled with an urgent and very masculine desire to seek out James Cameron and make him pay for every second of discomfort and fear Kate had experienced. And there had been fear. He had seen it flash briefly through her eyes, even though she had tried to deny it.

As she closed her eyes again and swayed where she stood, he suddenly became aware of everything that his furious anxiety had made him ignore. She was freezing, her teeth chattering, her wet clothes clinging to her like a second skin, while a thin blue line of extreme cold whitened the flesh round her mouth. He cursed himself for keeping her standing in the small, cold hall when she so desperately needed to get warm and dry.

Her eyes closed, unable to read the contrition and guilt in his eyes, Kate shivered and protested huskily, 'I don't want to talk any more. I'm cold.' She tried to walk past him and head for the stairs, but her fall had damaged her ankle more than she realised, and having stood still for so long the torn muscles had stiffened up and refused to support her, so that the moment she tried to move she fell forward with a sharp cry of panic, remembering how it had felt to land on the hard pavement.

But, blissfully, this time she didn't fall; she was instead scooped up into strong arms. The realisation that she was back in Rick's arms made her give a small betraying murmur of contentment that drew his gaze to her white face and closed eyes. A faint frown touched his forehead. The situation was already difficult enough, without any further complications. It struck him as grimly amusing that he should be able to remain immune to the experienced advances of any amount of worldly and beautiful women, and yet the moment he had Kate in his arms his body refused to respond to a single one of his commands to ignore its sexual response to her. Not even as a teenager had he reacted like this. Sex was an enjoyable experience, but desire had never touched him with such sharp necessity that he could scarcely think beyond making love to the woman in his arms.

As he supported her weight, he fought to inject the right note of calm distance into his voice as he told her, 'Kate, you're soaking. You need to get undressed and have a hot bath. Can you manage to do that?'

With her eyes closed, Kate felt the full force of the message of her other senses; all of them registered Rick's tension, told her of his grim dislike of holding her, and she remembered that he had left his previous employment due to the unwanted sexual advances of the woman whom he worked for.

Was that what he feared now? That she was going to make advances to him, that her exhaustion was simply a ploy to lure him into bed with her? She shivered with distaste at the thought of humiliating herself in such a way.

'Of course I can manage,' she lied. 'Perhaps if you'd put me down, I could prove it to you.'

Something dark and intimidating flashed in his eyes, and he set her down so quickly that her whole body jarred with pain.

'You're always so eager to maintain that distance you keep between yourself and the rest of the world, aren't you, Kate? That fierce independence of yours, that refusal to allow yourself to admit that you are human...that there are occasions when you can't be wholly self-sufficient. Why?' he demanded with unexpected harshness. 'What's happened in your life to make you refuse to admit that you can be vulnerable just like the rest of us... Was it a man?' he hazarded.

His questions, so shockingly intimate and direct, coming on top of her fear and physical exhaustion, somehow or other got through the defences she normally erected against such enquiries. She stared at him blindly, trying to breathe evenly and failing as her body betrayed her.

'No. It wasn't a man,' she told him slowly, and with the words came another kind of pain: the bitter sweetness of memories she had tried to forget for too long. Memories of her early childhood, when she had been happy...loved...when she had never known the harsh reality that life could be.

Rick saw the pain come into her eyes and found he was holding his own breath, willing her to confide in him, to share with him whatever it was that had made her close herself up in defences so tightly cast that in normal circumstances she would allow nothing to breach them.

Tonight he had caught her off guard, had almost trapped her into self-revelation, and as he watched her he fought down the compunction and guilt that threatened to make him back off with his questions unanswered.

'No, it wasn't a man,' she repeated slowly, looking not at him but past him, her eyes huge and shadowed, as though she were focusing something beyond his sight...something only she could see... 'It was my parents.'

He felt the shock bolt through him. Her parents! He didn't understand. According to his reports, they had died when she was a child...and then suddenly he knew. Compassion filled him. He touched her arm, and as though in some way his touch communicated to her his feelings, she turned and looked at him and said gravely, in a childlike way, 'They left me, you see... And I...' Tears flooded her eyes and she pushed half-heartedly at their overflow, much in the way a child might. 'I had to go and live in a children's home. I couldn't understand what had happened at first. I kept on thinking that it was all a mistake. That they weren't dead really, and that they would come for me.' She gave a tense shudder. 'Some days I felt I hated them because they'd left me.'

'They couldn't help it, Kate,' Rick told her gently.

'I know that,' she told him with a trace of impatience. 'I knew it then, but can't you see...even though I knew it wasn't their fault, some part of me couldn't help blaming them for leaving me behind... They should have taken me with them, and then we'd...'

'Kate, no!' Rick interrupted her harshly...so harshly that she focused properly on him, and suddenly realised what she was doing, what she was saying...

'Of course, I didn't really want to die... Not after the first few months, but if it hadn't been for Jen...'

'Michael's mother?' Rick interrupted gently. Her eyes had become soft and unfocused again, as though she was physically looking back into the past and witnessing again its pains.

'Yes. She sort of adopted me at the children's home... mothered me in a way. Without her....' She broke off and looked at him. 'That's why I cherish my independence, Rick...that's why it's so important to me. Because I learned young how vulnerable needing other human beings makes you... They go away and leave you alone...in pain... Loving causes pain.'

'Therefore it's better not to love at all,' Rick supplemented softly for her. 'Better not to care, or to become involved...better not to allow anyone inside that fortress you've built around your heart. There's only one flaw in that argument,' he added softly, and when she looked at him in tense watchfulness he asked, 'What about Michael? And don't tell me you don't love him, Kate.'

'Michael's different,' she told him wildly. 'I owed it to Jen to...'

'Love her son? Ah, I see...so it's all right for you to love where that love is a duty...is that what you're saying?'

Suddenly Kate didn't know what she was saying any more. Or what she was feeling, other than an odd feeling of suddenly having put down an enormous burden.

Her independence, a burden? Her almost ceaseless striving to make her life free of any kind of emotional ties, a burden? It wasn't possible...was it?

'Man does not live by independence alone,' Rick told her drily, deliberately misquoting. 'And neither does woman, or should I say, most especially woman does not.'

'That is one of the most sexist remarks I've ever heard,' Kate snapped at him, glad of something to focus her feelings on, glad to have some excuse to recover from the shock of having confided in him so readily...so almost wantonly gladly, she acknowledged bitterly.

'You misunderstood me,' Rick told her calmly. 'Men and women both have their separate strengths and weaknesses. The male sex has a long way to go before its emotions are as well tuned as the female. Don't deny yourself those emotions, Kate. They're what make...'

'Women so vulnerable!' she snapped at him.

'Men are vulnerable, too,' he told her. 'Not all women are as honest as you, as I discovered the hard way as a young and very naïve man.'

Now it was his turn to look confused and frown, as though bewildered by the way he had confided in her and admitted his vulnerability.

Kate was surprised as well, and—yes, flattered, she acknowledged, while mentally berating herself for being so predictably female.

And yet his confidence had been no male ploy. It had been spontaneous and honest. She had an insane desire to reach out and touch him, and both it and the fear it brought showed briefly on her face. She withdrew from him, half stumbling as she started to move away.

She heard Rick curse, but he made no move to touch her, and that sensitivity to her feelings made her whole body prickle warningly. This man was dangerous to her, dangerous in ways that she was only just beginning to be able to calculate. He drew responses from her, both verbal and physical, she would never normally have dreamed of giving...made her feel things she had no desire to feel...made her see things both about herself and him she had no wish to see...

'I'll go and make you a hot drink,' she heard him saying curtly, and Kate tried to convince herself that she wasn't experiencing a sharp sense of loss as he turned his back on her and walked into the kitchen.

She winced as she limped painfully across the hall, and by the time she had reached the top of the stairs, despite the icy chill in the rest of her body, her ankle felt as though it were on fire, throbbing agonisingly with every step she took.

Once inside her bedroom, she didn't even bother to turn on the light, dragging herself over to the bed and almost falling on to it. She lay there, alternately shivering and sweating, drifting in and out of an awareness that kept urging her to do something important, but she couldn't quite reach out and grasp what it was. Her ankle and calf hurt... She reached down to ease off her shoe to soothe the pain, her mind clouded by the trauma of the evening and the onset of exhaustion, so that she was only half aware of the swelling round the ankle and the hot fire of her skin.

She wanted to get undressed and have a shower, but it was too much of an effort. She was cold and she knew that she ought to remove her wet clothes and get beneath the bed-clothes, but she simply couldn't find the strength, so instead she gave in to the exhaustion numbing her and closed her eyes.

At first when Rick walked into the bedroom he thought she was still in her bathroom, and then in the streetlight that il-luminated the room he saw her lying on the bed, the light streaming in, highlighting her swollen ankle.

He put down the drink he had made and went over to the bed, quickly examining the swollen flesh. Despite his care, Kate muttered and winced, opening pain-hazed eyes.

Rick was looking at her with a mixture of ire and conster-nation. She tried to sit up, instinctively seeking to defend her-self against a pity she didn't want by pretending that she was all right, but the movement jarred her ankle and made her cry out.

I'm going to call your doctor,' Rick announced curtly, step-ping back from the bed.

A doctor was the last thing Kate wanted. All she needed was to be allowed to go to sleep so that she could get warm and forget the traumas of the evening.

'No,' she argued. 'It isn't necessary.'

A violent shivering fit accompanied her denial, her teeth starting to chatter. 'I just want to go to sleep and get warm,' she added under her breath, whimpering slightly as she tried to move and jarred her foot.

Her ankle was sprained and not broken, Rick acknowledged, and she was probably right, warmth and sleep were probably more important to her right now than a doctor.

'All right,' he agreed, giving in. 'Don't try to move. I'll run a bath for you and then come back for you.'

'No!' Kate protested sharply, halting him with the vehemence of her rejection. 'I can manage.'

Garrick looked into her white face and saw the stubborn firming of her chin. She was different from any other woman he had known, her stubborn independence both irritating and unnecessary.

Walking back over to the bed, he leaned over her and said levelly, 'I'm almost tempted to let you try, but we both know you couldn't even get as far as the door on that ankle.'

'If you'd let me come upstairs the moment I got in instead of cross-questioning me, I'd have been perfectly all right,' she fibbed, glaring at him, her defiant stance spoiled by the sudden fit of shivering that convulsed her.

Grim-mouthed, Rick headed for the bathroom door, and she could hear him running water into the bath.

She felt as weak as a kitten, boneless and completely unable to move. She knew she ought to be doing something, taking off her wet clothes perhaps and putting on her robe, but it made her head ache just to think of so much painful activity. It was much, much easier to simply close her eyes and let the sound of the running water soothe her. She imagined herself lying in it, lapped in luxury and warmth, and she gave another shiver, unpleasantly conscious of her damp clothes and cold skin.

'Kate.'

The curt voice so close to her ear made her flinch. Rick had moved so quietly, she hadn't heard him come back in. She opened her eyes and stared at him with confused uncertainty.

'Bath's ready,' he told her in a clipped voice.

She started to sit up and found that her muscles were simply too weak to respond, leaving her to flop inelegantly back on to the mattress.

'Here, drink this,' Rick ordered, lifting a mug to her lips.

A strong smell of brandy assailed her, making her gasp and push the mug away.

'I'm not drinking that.'

'Oh, yes, you are,' Rick retorted grimly. 'It probably smells worse than it tastes; hot milk laced with brandy, that's all it is. It will warm you up and help you sleep.'

'I don't want it,' Kate told him petulantly, gasping with shock when Rick suddenly put the mug down on the table beside her bed, and then hauled her into a sitting position, ignoring her angry protests and then firmly imprisoning both her hands at her sides simply by circling one arm around her, leaving him free to use the other to lift the mug to her lips and say savagely, 'Drink it!'

Sensing that to refuse would only prolong her humiliation, Kate opened her mouth and obediently took a swallow. She gasped as the spirit burned her throat, making her choke and splutter, but Rick ignored her protests and refused to give up until she had almost drained the mug.

She had no idea how much brandy had been in the milk, but already she felt dizzy and light-headed. So much so that she was barely aware of the fact that her arms were free and that Rick was briskly unzipping her dress, until she felt the warmth of the centrally heated air against her cold, damp skin.

As she tensed, as though sensing what she was going to say, Rick told her harshly, 'Both of us know you're in no fit state to do this yourself, Kate, and I hope both of us know that I'm not about to take advantage of the situation.'

He had difficulty steadying his hands as he made that second statement. The truth was that he was already affected far more than was safe, and it didn't matter how much he told himself to be clinical and detached, his body flagrantly ignored his commands to deny its awareness of her.

'No, and *I'm* not your last employer,' Kate muttered breathlessly as he moved her gently so that he could slide the damp dress down over her hips.

'Right,' Rick agreed tonelessly. 'Now that we've both agreed that neither of us is in the least danger of being seduced, perhaps we can get on with the task of getting you bathed and into bed.'

Busy trying to analyse just why the odd roughness that had entered his voice should send such a frisson of sensation spiralling down her spine, Kate didn't realise quite how literally he meant his comment, until she discovered that he was unfastening her bra and peeling the damp silk away from her skin.

She was lying on her front, but even so a hot, fierce surge of heat turned her pale skin scarlet, her head lifting so that she could look over her shoulder at him and hiss frantically, 'That's enough! I can do the rest myself.'

'Is that right? Then how come I found you flat out here still in your wet clothes? I admire your modesty, Kate, but there's a time and place for everything, and this isn't it.' His hands rested loosely on her hips. She could feel their warmth through the thin silk of her panties.

'You don't have anything I haven't seen before, you know,' he told her half mockingly, and as she jerked round to glare furiously at him he took advantage of the movement to grip hold of both her briefs and tights, easing them past the feminine curve of her hips before she realised what was happening.

He had never been an indiscriminate lover, and was accredited with far more partners than there had actually been, but there had certainly been enough for the female body not to be a mystery to him any longer, and yet there was something about Kate's...something about the shadowed mystery of the narrow curve of her waist; the soft swell of her stomach, held taut in nervous dread and quivering just slightly; the gentle mound between her thighs that was clothed in soft shadow; the defensive angling of her body, that moved him almost unbearably.

Tense and watchful, Kate could feel the embarrassed heat spreading through her. She had never paid much attention to her own body, never compared it with those of other women, because there had never been any need. Since she had no intention of loving anyone or sharing her life with them, she had had no need to look at her body in the light of its appeal to a man. Now she wondered whether Rick's stillness was caused by revulsion or amusement.

She started to shake violently and not because she was cold.

'What's wrong?' Rick demanded softly.

'Stop looking at me like that.'

'Like what?' he queried, tensing.

'Like I'm some kind of...of inferior specimen of my species,' Kate said wildly.

His head turned slightly and his glance locked with hers; alert and dangerous. 'Is that what you thought? You couldn't be more wrong. I've never seen anything more perfect in my life.'

And as she started to protest that he was lying, his hands cradled her hips and he bent his head and gently kissed her quivering stomach not just once but several times, until his lips came to rest for the briefest fraction of time just above the soft rise of flesh that protected her womanhood.

'Perfect,' he repeated in a hoarse, unsteady voice, and then he released her and stood up abruptly, picking her up in his arms before she could formulate a single word of protest, saying flatly, 'That bath water's going to be cold.'

It wasn't, but Kate was quite certain that nothing could feel as hot as her skin where his lips had caressed it. What on earth had made him do it? Had he felt sorry for her? Was that it? It must have been, because he certainly didn't desire her.

He refused to leave the bathroom, but at least allowed her to wash herself, and she sank beneath the water in a belated attempt to hide her nudity from him. Unaware that her thoughts were quite clearly visible on her face, she froze as she heard him say, 'You're wrong, you know. I do desire you, and don't even think about looking for proof. The way I feel right now, there's nothing I want more than to take you to bed and make love to you all night and to hell with the consequences.'

Too stupefied to say a word, Kate could only give him the odd covert glance as she struggled to finish her ablutions. Was she dreaming or had Rick just said that he desired her?

She gave him a brief glance from beneath lowered lashes and heard him swear softly. 'Don't push me, Kate,' he warned her harshly. 'The last thing you need right now is me in your bed, but that's exactly what you're going to get if you keep on giving me those curious little looks.'

She glared at him, and he laughed grimly,

'OK, go ahead and glare at me if you wish, but you're looking at me as though you'd love to know what my body would feel like over yours, and if you don't stop it, I promise you you're all too likely to find out.'

Quite how she would have responded, Kate didn't know, but a violent fit of sneezing saved her the trouble, and before she could protest Rick had lifted her out of the water and wrapped her in a huge warm bath towel.

'I think for the sake of my health as well as your own, the sooner you're tucked up in bed, the better,' he told her huskily. 'Can you manage to dry yourself while I go downstairs and fill a hot-water bottle for you?'

Kate nodded. In fact, she felt weaker than ever, but she dared not tell him so in case he thought she was inviting him to make love to her.

But what if she did? Would it really be the end of the world—the end of her self-respect? Wasn't she entitled to relax the tight control she had kept over herself for once in her life? After all, they would not be hurting or harming anyone…neither of them owed any commitment to anyone else, and if she knew that Rick could only be a brief interlude in her life, that didn't stop the fierce ache inside her that his soft warmings had aroused.

She wanted him to make love to her, she recognised on a thrill of shock. For the first time in her life she was experiencing the reckless, heady drive of desire…the need to fulfil her female destiny, the urge to surrender her independence and know the dangerous thrill of loving another human being.

Loving. She tensed, her muscles locking. Rick had been talking about sex, not love. *Love* was what she felt for Michael, and had nothing to do with the fierce clamour in her senses that Rick aroused.

Physical desire could play dangerous tricks on the unwary;

and that was all she felt for Rick—physical desire. There was nothing else. There could not be anything else.

By the time he returned with her hot-water bottle, she had managed to stagger painfully back to bed. She took the hot-water bottle from him with a cool thank you. It was better this way, she assured herself as he left the room. Better, wiser, safer. So why did she wish she had been born a different person? The kind of person who could have subtly and freely indicated that there was no need for them to sleep alone. She would feel better in the morning, she promised herself. She would be glad then that she had acted the way she had.

CHAPTER EIGHT

BUT she wasn't, not really. When she woke up in the morning still drowsy from sleep, Kate wasn't sure what had caused the small ache low down in the pit of her stomach. She rolled instinctively on to her stomach, trying to banish it, and then abruptly turned over and shot upright, a wave of heat crawling over her skin as she realised just exactly what the ache was.

Furious with herself for what she saw as a weakness in her defences, she got out of bed, refusing to wince as her still swollen ankle twinged painfully.

She could walk on it—just about, she told herself grimly as she half hobbled, and half dragged herself to her bathroom.

She dressed in a full, soft wool skirt with which she could wear boots which would both disguise the swelling and give her ankle some much needed support. It was a struggle getting them on, and at the back of her mind lay the knowledge that she was behaving both foolishly and irresponsibly. She would be much wiser simply acknowledging the fact that she had hurt herself and working at home for a couple of days.

But she couldn't do that. Now that they had lost any chance of getting James's contract, she was going to have to work doubly hard just to bring in enough money to cover her commitments. As she checked her make-up, she berated herself mentally for her folly in not handling James better. If she hadn't panicked, if she had used a bit of tact...a bit of flattery...

A brisk rap on her bedroom door stemmed the flood of guilt. She called out coolly, 'Come in,' not wanting to admit even to herself how hard she was having to struggle to suppress the faint fluttering of tension in her stomach.

Rick came in, carrying Michael, and a mug of coffee.

He frowned when he saw that she was dressed and out of bed. He himself was wearing jeans and a soft woollen checked shirt with the sleeves rolled back, revealing the muscled hardness of his forearm.

Michael nestled sleepily in the crook of his arm, obviously more than content to be with him, and she had a sharp pang of dark resentment. She should be the one holding Michael.

She was jealous, she recognised miserably. Jealous of the fact that Michael had settled down so well with his new nanny. Was this how other working mothers felt when the time came to return to their work and leave their child in the care of someone else? The violence of her feelings confused her. She loved Michael, but he was surely incidental to her life? A responsibility she had taken on and would do her best for, yes—but it was her career that was the focal point of her life, surely?

Was it? If it had been, wouldn't she have tried harder last night to placate James? Wouldn't she surely have refused to flinch at his proposition and dealt with it in a far more professional and judicious way?

'I don't believe I'm seeing this,' Rick commented brusquely, interrupting her thoughts. 'Don't tell me you actually mean to go into your office? For God's sake, woman, have you no sense? You're in no fit state.'

How long had it been since anyone had expressed this kind of tough male concern for her? How long had it been since she had experienced a very feminine responsiveness to it? Not since her parents had died, surely? That knowledge frightened her; she felt as though she had suddenly stepped on to very treacherous ground and was quickly being sucked down into the trap of its dangers. Emotionalism was the weakness that always trapped her sex, that deflected it from its course; and it was a weakness which men had exploited callously for their own benefit for hundreds of generations. Well, no one was going to exploit her.

'I think that's for me to decide, don't you?' she told him crisply.

She dared not look at him, no matter how in control she sounded. She was all too conscious of the held-in irritation emanating from him, the very male impatience with what he no doubt considered to be her very feminine stupidity.

'Take Michael downstairs and give him his breakfast, will you, please, Rick?' she requested with crisp efficiency, still refusing to look at him. 'I want to get an early start today. I've rather a lot to do.'

With unerring and very unnerving accuracy, he seemed to read her thoughts, because he didn't move but instead said derisively, 'Like getting in touch with Cameron to apologise for running out on him last night?'

Kate couldn't help it, her skin burned dark red. How had he known that had been in her mind?

The look of contempt in his eyes quite clearly betrayed what he thought of her. She wanted to cry out to him that he didn't understand, that he had no idea of the financial pressure she was under…that he didn't realise how important this contract was to her, and to Michael.

'Is that what you're going to do?' he demanded softly.

She was too taken aback to chastise him for the question. The very intensity of the biting sneer in his voice made her face him, her own head lifting, her eyes bright with challenge.

'I don't think that's any concern of yours, do you?'

'Having second thoughts about those ethics of yours, Kate?'

She flinched beneath the quiet words, hardly noticing the familiar way in which he used her Christian name. Suddenly it had become very important to make him see the justification for what she must do.

'Last night I panicked,' she told him huskily. 'I behaved foolishly, unprofessionally.'

'I see. So this time you're going to handle it differently, is that it? This time you're going to let him blackmail you into going to bed with him, is that it?'

'No!'

His grim mouth relaxed a little as she made the instinctive denial.

'You're deluding yourself if you think he's going to accept anything else,' he told her, and in an illuminating moment of self-awareness Kate realised that he was right. Last night she had dealt a blow to James's pride that only her complete ca-pitulation and humiliation would salve.

Wearily her shoulders sagged, her despair shadowing her eyes as she stared out of the window. Last night she had lost her golden chance. She had panicked and thrown it away as carelessly as an unknowing child, and all because she couldn't bear the thought of James touching her.

'I could have handled it differently.'

She said the words more to herself than to Rick Evans, but he caught them and scoffed. 'How? By letting him think you were going to bed with him and then pulling out at the last minute? Is that how you want to do business, Kate?'

It wasn't and she shivered, not liking the image he was drawing for her.

'I've got to get into the office,' she told him tonelessly, and she knew from the flatness of her voice that he had guessed that what he had said had forced her to abandon her plans for making contact with James. He had made her see all too clearly that there was no way back. She had had her chance and she had blown it. Fate might not be inclined to favour her again. And if it wasn't... If it wasn't, she could lose everything she had worked for, she acknowledged painfully.

She moved abruptly, wincing as her ankle twinged. Now that she was up and dressed she felt oddly weak, and not just because of her ankle, either. There was an ominous tickly sen-sation at the back of her throat, and she kept on having to suppress the urge to shiver.

'I must go,' she announced, and was appalled to discover how hoarse her voice sounded.

A cold was the last thing she needed right now. She saw Rick frown, and for one vulnerable moment she almost wished that he would announce that he wasn't going to let her. She must be hallucinating if she was having thoughts like that, she told herself furiously.

'Has Michael got something that can go in the car?'

The abrupt question startled her, and for a moment she wasn't quite sure what Rick meant.

'A carry cot or something, that will keep him safe while I run you to the office. I'd let you take the Ferrari, but with that foot, I'm damn sure you'd never get it out of first gear.'

Take the Ferrari? Her eyes widened slightly, and then hard on the heels of the realisation of how blissful it would be to simply sit back and let Rick take charge, came the panicky knowledge of how dangerous such a weakness would be. She had not fought for all her adult years to preserve her independence and invulnerability simply to throw it all away now just because her head ached and her ankle throbbed.

'I can get a cab.'

'There's no need. Can you make it downstairs, by the way, or...'

'Of course I can.'

But she wasn't as confident as she sounded, and so to distract him she told him where he could find the carry cot that fastened into the back seat of a car.

A merely adequate driver herself, she was impressed by the sure way Rick handled the powerful Ferrari. He had just that powerful blending of control and flair that could perhaps be described as macho, although Kate hesitated to choose such an over-used description.

She was surprised that Rick seemed to know exactly how to find her office without her having to give him any directions. He stopped the car and then courteously helped her out, and she needed the firm support of his hand beneath her arm, she recognised, as she tried not to shiver when the cold morning air touched her heated skin.

It occurred to her that she might possibly have the beginnings of a slight fever, but she pushed the thought away, not wanting to have to handle yet another burden. She had enough problems as it was, and as though he knew what was in her mind, Rick said firmly, 'When you came home last night, I admired you for the stand you had taken, Kate. Not many people nowadays have such a strong set of values. Don't be deceived into thinking that they don't matter, because they do. You'll be the person who'll suffer the most if you abandon them, because you're one of those rare people whose own good opinion of themselves matters more than any fawning flattery from others.'

What he was saying was quite true, but she was amazed that he had recognised that stubborn pride within her, which she privately resented, and which had kept her aloof and immovable from the code of ethics she had chosen for herself. Ethics which she was slowly beginning to realise it was going to be costly to hold on to.

'The world isn't made up of men like Cameron,' Rick added quietly, almost reassuringly, she recognised, as he continued to hold her arm, firmly supporting her.

'It isn't full of good contracts, either,' she told him crisply, not wanting to give in to the pleasure of letting his concern for her wrap round her like a warm comforter. It was weak to want to cling to his reassurance, to want to cling to him. It was because she wasn't feeling well, because last night had re-opened some of the wounds of the past, because James's touch had made her remember the horror and disgust she had felt as a teenager when one of the boys at the home had tried to molest her. Rick's touch, on the other hand, aroused none of those feelings of disgust and dislike. When Rick touched her...

'There'll be other contracts,' he assured her, holding her gaze with his, as though he was willing her to take courage and believe what he was telling her. 'And they'll be all the better for coming after what you experienced last night, because they'll be contracts from people who respect you for the kind of woman you are.'

'For the kind of *person* I am, don't you mean?' Kate corrected bitterly, not wanting him to know how affected she was by his quiet assurances. 'I don't want any of my business contacts to see me as a woman. I want to be judged on equal terms with them. And as for the other contracts—well, I hope you're right, Rick, otherwise you could well find yourself without a job in a very short space of time indeed.''

It was the first time she had ever allowed anyone bar Camilla to see how much her financial insecurity worried her. She had often heard successful people claiming that the days when they had struggled for success had been among the most pleasurable and challenging of their lives, but that was in retrospect, and often said when they had had a partner, a lover, someone to share the hard times with.

She had no one, and she also had the responsibility of Michael. She had initially enjoyed the challenge of setting up on her own, but now, with the knowledge that she had lost James's contract, she felt sick at heart, chilled to the bones and infinitely weary. So weary that she would have given anything to simply lie down, close her eyes and go to sleep...to forget her cares, and escape from them.

But she couldn't do that, and so, giving Rick a tight little smile, she stepped away from him and toward the building that housed her office.

As he got back in the Ferrari, Garrick checked on Michael, who was staring interestedly around him.

'Well, now,' he told the serious-eyed little boy. 'You and I have work to do.' And, instead of turning the car in the direction of Kate's home, he drove to the prestigious block that housed the headquarters of the Evans Gould Corporation.

John Gould, who had been his partner when he originally bought his first company, had now retired, having sold out his share of the business to Garrick, but Garrick had retained the original title, thinking it less confusing than making a change.

He drove the Ferrari into his personal car parking space, and then lifted Michael out of the back. If the staff thought it odd to see their chairman striding through the building dressed in worn jeans and a shirt instead of his normal Savile Row suits, carrying instead of his briefcase a small brown-haired child, they were far too well trained to betray it.

Only the receptionist on the floor that contained the directors' boardroom and Garrick's personal office widened her eyes in amazement and stared at her august boss in obvious confusion.

'Mr Evans,' she stammered hesitantly, 'Mr Oswald told us that you wouldn't be coming in. Er...shall I get you some coffee?'

'Yes, please, Amanda, and—er...some milk, please, as well. But first I want you to ring through to Gerald and tell him to come up and see me.'

His assistant arrived within five minutes, plainly as surprised as the receptionist to see Garrick, but rather better at concealing it.

Garrick had put Michael down on the floor, and he was enjoying himself crawling about and trying to eat the legs of the very expensive rosewood desk.

'I know we've got a lot on, Gerald,' Garrick told him. 'But I've got an urgent job for you. Something that must be kept completely confidential. I don't want anyone here at Evans Gould to know anything about this. Is that clear?'

When Gerald had nodded in affirmation, he said crisply, 'I want a comprehensive list of all the companies in the group who use or need to use a PR agency. I want details of the agencies used, the performance results and how long the contracts already in existence are due to run.'

He saw that Gerald was looking at him rather curiously. 'I'm thinking of trying a new agency.'

He saw the brief flash of comprehension darken his assistant's eyes, and wondered rather drily if Gerald had the slightest idea what was really in his mind. Probably not...which was just as well.

Michael, bored with the lack of interesting things to play with, turned to look at the two men and started to cry, holding out his arms to Garrick once he had caught his attention.

'Had enough, have you? All right.' And picking up the little boy with easy confidence he apologised to the receptionist as she walked in with a tray of coffee and milk.

'Sorry, Amanda, I haven't time to drink it, after all. Oh,

and I want that information just as soon as you can organise it, Gerald. OK?'

It said a great deal for the respect with which his staff viewed their chairman that, after he had gone, not one of them who had seen him saw any necessity to speculate openly on exactly what was going on.

By lunch time, Kate's head was aching so much she could barely see, never mind think. She was suffering from alternate bouts of shivering fits and hot sweats.

A messenger had arrived half-way through the morning from James, returning her coat and evening bag, and, seeing the speculation in Sara's eyes as she brought the things in to her office, she had felt obliged to let the other girl know that they would not be getting the contract.

Dispirited and exhausted, she was in no condition to fight off what threatened to be an ill-timed bout of 'flu, she recognised as the faint discomfort at the back of her throat gave way to a full-blown jagged mountain past which it felt impossible to swallow.

Almost light-headed with fever, she struggled over the columns of figures she was desperately trying to add up. Her emergency reserves were so pitifully small, scarcely more than a month, two months' outgoings at the most. If she didn't get some new clients very quickly...

She closed her eyes, not wanting to even think the words.

At half-past one her telephone rang. She picked up the receiver shakily and croaked her name into it. There was a brief silence, and then Rick's voice saying drily, 'Obviously I don't need to ask how you're feeling. Why don't you call it a day and come home?'

Beyond her shock that as her employee he should speak to her so arrogantly was a weak longing to either burst into tears or beg him to come and fetch her.

Her eyes felt scratchy and dry; her throat was a fiery torment; her body was weak from the spasmodic bursts of shivers that racked it. She ached from her head to her foot, and her ankle was barely carrying her weight. Add to that the pounding headache that was not just a result of her tussle with her accounts, and she had every reason to feel weak and tearful, logic told her, but she couldn't accept that logic. That need she had just experienced to rely on someone else was like a terrifying pit opening up at her feet, a much feared nightmare suddenly come to life. She must not allow herself to be weak, to be anything other than self-sufficient. She dared not. She had suffered once in her life through losing those she had loved; she couldn't endure that kind of pain again. Some children in the same situation became desperately anxious to replace their lost parents and clung fearfully to any adult they could; she had been the opposite, standing proud and alone, and that was how she intended to live her whole life.

'Kate,' Rick urged her, and she gripped the receiver hard, refusing to give in to what she knew to be the most sensible course of action.

'What was it you wanted?' she asked him hoarsely. 'Is there something wrong with Michael?'

She heard his brief indrawn breath of irritation. 'No,' he told her drily. 'Unlike you, Michael is in perfect health.'

'Then I'm afraid I must go. I'm rather busy.'

She replaced the receiver, dismayed to discover how much she was shaking. So much so, in fact, that she hardly dared let go of the instrument.

She got up and walked blindly toward her office door. A cup of coffee, or better still some hot soup, would revive her. She hadn't had any breakfast, and no dinner last night; it was no wonder she felt so weak.

She opened the office door, intending to ask Sara if she could bring her back a carton of soup from the nearest sandwich bar, only to discover the outer office was empty. Of course, both girls would be having their lunch. She would have to go herself.

Her office was on the fifth floor, and by the time she reached the ground floor via the lift she was beginning to wish she had never left it. Gritting her teeth, she walked uncertainly across the foyer and out into the penetrating cold dampness of the lunch-time streets.

Surely they were not normally as noisy as this? The heightened sound battered against her aching eardrums. She had to blink several times to bring things properly into focus. The sandwich shop seemed unpleasantly hot after the coldness of the street, her head pounded and the rich scent of hot food made her stomach churn sickly.

The queue moved slowly, but at last it was her turn to be served. At first she couldn't remember what she wanted. Those behind her in the queue shuffled impatiently, and miraculously her mind cleared. Soup.

She ordered it, and found she had to hold the carton carefully because she was trembling so much.

Outside again in the street she shivered violently. Was it her imagination or had the temperature dropped several degrees while she had been inside the sandwich bar?

It seemed to take her for ever to hobble back to her office building. Her ankle felt as though it was on fire as it swelled protestingly against the confinement of her leather boot. How on earth she was going to get the thing off she had no idea. The thought of not being able to do so and having to wear it for ever struck her as very funny, and she started to laugh, but her chest went tight and she couldn't breathe. She stopped abruptly and someone cannoned into her, knocking the soup carton out of her hand.

A long, expensive scarlet car drew up at the kerb. Kate didn't notice it. She was too busy mourning the loss of her soup.

A hand gripped her arm, a familiar voice said her name peremptorily, and then fell silent, causing her to lift her head in mute query.

For some reason it didn't strike her as particularly odd that Rick should be there, just when she had been thinking so despairingly of him, and wishing she had not been so stubborn when he had urged her to go home. Had she done so, she could by now have been tucked up in bed, fed and warm.

Half out of her mind with fever, she looked at him without surprise and said piteously, 'I dropped my soup.'

And fresh tears welled.

She heard Rick curse and then, so abruptly that she grabbed hold of him in shock, he picked her up, and carried her over to the car, easing her gently into the passenger seat.

'Don't you dare move,' he warned her. 'Which floor's your office on, Kate?'

'The fifth, but there's no one there.'

He wasn't listening, though. He was already half-way across the pavement. It was sheer bliss to simply lie back in her seat and let someone else take charge; she was even beyond being appalled that she should feel like this. She was beyond everything but giving in to the fever consuming her.

When Garrick returned she was lying with her eyes closed, her pale face stained along the high cheekbones with a brilliant scarlet flush. As he got into the car he checked her pulse and found that it was racing erratically.

She opened her eyes and looked at him, her clear gaze for once glazed and unfocused.

'I'm hot,' she told him in a small, bewildered voice. 'I don't feel well.'

'I think you've got 'flu,' Garrick told her curtly. 'I'm taking you home, Kate, and then I'm going to call your doctor, and if you dare to tell me once again that there's nothing wrong with you, so help me…I'll…'

'Michael—' Kate protested drowsily.

'I've managed to persuade one of your neighbours to keep an eye on him for an hour.'

'How did you know that I needed you?'

Had she been fully in control of herself, there was no way those words would ever have been said, and with her eyes closed she was not aware of the brief betraying look he gave her. She might admit that she needed him now, but were he to remind her of those words when she was well again, he suspected that she was all too likely to deny ever having said them.

What had started out as a simple ploy to gather enough information to make sure that a court would award him full guardianship of Michael had turned into something far, far more complicated.

And the worst of it was that he could see no way free of the tangle of deceit he had wound around himself. As he drove over a rut in the road, Kate gave a small moan and he switched his attention from his contemplation of abstracts to the reality of the woman seated next to him.

CHAPTER NINE

FOR Kate, the next twenty-four hours passed in a haze of confused events: their return home, Rick undressing her and putting her to bed, despite her feverish protests, the arrival of the doctor who agreed with Rick that she was suffering from a severe bout of 'flu. The doctor added to Garrick, although Kate herself wasn't aware of it, that she suspected Kate was also under a considerable amount of strain, which wasn't going to help her recovery.

She woke several times from the heavy sleep that claimed her, each time worrying fretfully about Michael and the office, only to be told by Rick that everything was under control and that she wasn't to worry, but over a whole day elapsed before she was able to ask him for concise details of exactly who was taking care of Michael while he sat at her bedside.

'I got in touch with one of those twenty-four-hour emergency services. They sent round a relief nanny. Oh, and they've also arranged for someone to go into your office and deal with the day-to-day routine stuff while you're off.'

'You've what?' Kate shrieked, sitting bolt upright and then groaning as her head started to pound. 'Have you any idea what those agencies charge?' she protested bitterly. 'Rick, I can't afford to...'

She heard him curse under his breath, his hand cool as he placed it against her burning forehead. She was shivering again now, and desperately weak, only too glad to give in to his firm instruction that she lie down again. It was wonderful to lie there and be cosseted, to have the bedding pulled up and tucked round her as her mother had done when she was a child; to have someone telling her not to worry and that everything would be all right, and her mind, already clouded with fever and fear, readily abandoned its anxieties to Rick, as he soothed her and told her she was not to worry.

Garrick sat with her until she had drifted back to sleep, and then he stood up with a frown. He wouldn't be able to fob her off so easily for very long. She was no fool. The temporary nanny was costing the earth, and of course he was footing the bill himself; as for her office, he had instructed Gerald to send someone suitable there, to take charge of the everyday basic things, so that the two girls would be left free to take over Kate's own workload. He had warned Gerald that whoever he sent must be discreet and capable of holding her tongue, but once Kate was back to normal...

He looked down at her sleeping form, marvelling a little that she should have the power to move him so deeply. The problem was, did she reciprocate his feelings? There was a physical awareness between them, there was no doubt about that, no matter how much Kate might shy away from it, but would she be prepared to change the course of her life, to deviate from the route she had mapped out for herself to include him in her life?

It gave him encouragement and hope that she had done so once—to include Michael. He grimaced faintly to himself. He loved her. He who had always sworn that he would never commit the folly of falling in love had proved to be just as human and vulnerable as his fellow men, and he didn't mind at all.

What he did mind was the fact that he was daily deceiving her, that she had a totally erroneous view of him. How would she react when he told her the truth? He would have to wait until she was well, of course. Patience had never been one of his strong suits and he hesitated in the doorway, reluctant to leave her, and yet knowing that sleep was exactly what she needed to aid her recovery.

It was over a week before Kate, who in the early feverish days of her illness had insisted that she was going straight back to work, felt strong enough to get out of bed for a couple of hours a day, and sit with her feet up, listening to Michael's gurgles and staring lazily into space.

She was now in the recuperative stage of her illness, her doctor informed her, adding severely that it was going to be at least a month before she was anything like fully fit.

'And even then I have my doubts about whether you're going to be strong enough to go back to work. You've been pushing yourself too hard for far too long,' she had added gently. 'It can't go on. If you knew the number of young women who are coming to me with all the hallmarks of tension and stress. I'm all for sexual equality, but I sometimes wonder if we shouldn't concentrate on making the male of the species more like us than vice versa.'

The temporary nanny was no longer required, for which Kate heaved a sigh of relief. Every now and again when she allowed reality to penetrate past the lazy barrier of self-protection engendered by her illness, she was pierced by a sharp and frightening awareness of how perilously close to financial disaster she must be.

And her doctor was right about the strain she was under. She found herself increasingly reluctant to even think about going back to work, and that terrified her. Instead of looking forward to it, she found that she was deliberately pushing it to the back of her mind.

It was as though losing James's contract and then her bout of 'flu had robbed her of all her old ambition. She was quite content to allow Rick to take messages from Sara that all was going well and that she was not to worry; she felt no burning urgency to find out for herself what was happening in her absence, and every now and again, like lightning piercing heavy dark clouds, she was rent by panic as she realised how easy it had become to simply allow herself to drift aimlessly from day to day, allowing Rick to take control and organise her life for her.

When she eventually brought herself to confide these fears to her doctor, the older woman smiled grimly and said, 'As

I've already tried to tell you, too much stress. This is your system's way of telling you that it's had enough.'

'But I must get back to work. I can't simply sit here and drift.'

'If you don't listen to what your body's telling you, you could well find yourself on the verge of either a heart attack or a nervous breakdown within a very short space of time,' her doctor told her bluntly. 'What you're feeling now is just a warning, Kate. I can't force you to heed it, but I can tell you that if you don't, you're all too likely to be far more seriously ill in the long run.'

'But you don't understand,' Kate fretted, and then went silent, knowing that she could not confide her financial fears to her doctor.

After she had gone, she sat tensely in her chair, desperately trying to think of a way out of her problem. When her bedroom door opened and Rick came in with Michael, they brought with them the coldness of the outdoors.

'Five times round the park and we've fed the ducks,' Rick told her with a grin, tossing Michael up in the air, much to the little boy's delight.

There was a bond between them that tugged at Kate's newly tender heart-strings. Watching as Michael trustingly allowed Rick to throw him up again, her own emotional response to the sight of them, the big strong man and the small, vulnerable, trusting child, brought a hard lump of anguish to her throat.

This was how life should be: a traditional family unit, two loving adults bonded together by their care of the child life had entrusted to them.

'What's wrong?'

The quiet words hurt her with her knowledge that they were simply an expression of social concern, with none of the deep-rooted and intensely personal caring she longed for.

The unspoken words tolled through her mind, shocking her into abrupt realisation of the truth.

Somehow…somewhere…she had done the unforgivable and she had allowed herself to become dependent on Rick.

Feverishly she searched her mind, trying to push the unwanted knowledge to one side, trying to convince herself that she was wrong, that it was simply her weakened state that was causing her to have these thoughts, but she knew as she looked at him that when the day came for him to leave them her life would be emptier than she had ever dreamed it was possible for it to be.

Somehow or other her heart had turned traitor on her, and he and Michael had become fused together in it as two permanent features in her life.

He reached out and touched her, concern pleating his forehead into a frown as he put Michael down and turned his attention to her.

'What's wrong, Kate?' he repeated worriedly. 'Aren't you feeling well?'

Her skin burned beneath his touch, her pulses thudding tensely and the knowledge burst upon her like a shower of too bright light.

She loved him.

The knowledge hit her with the appalling severity of a mortal wound. She went pale with the shock of it, the blood draining from her extremities like a death flood, and she stared blankly at him, unable to think logically or say a single coherent word.

'Kate, what is it?'

The rough warmth of his voice was like an abrasive powder ground into too tender skin and she flinched from it, terrified of the swift surge of need within her to cling to it and to him. She went hot and cold and her body shook, and it was a hundred, no, a thousand times worse than the 'flu.

'Kate...'

He was actually touching her now, holding her shoulders, cupping the smooth round joints in the palms of his hands, and it seemed to her in her heightened mood of awareness that his fingers actually caressed the silk of her skin, but she knew she was simply thinking that because she wanted to think it.

She drew a deep gulping breath of air, trying to steady herself. She mustn't let him guess what was wrong with her; she shrank from the fool she would make of herself if he were to realise. She, the dedicated career woman, desperately in love for the first time in her life.

'I'm all right,' she lied.

'No, you're not. What is it? Something the doctor said?'

She seized on the excuse gratefully, nodding.

'She's right, you know,' he told her, shocking her with the realisation that her doctor must have discussed her physical condition with him. 'You have been over-straining yourself. I know how desperate you are to get back to work, but you aren't well enough yet.'

His compassion overwhelmed her. She bent her head to hide the sudden, stupid rush of tears to her eyes and was shocked to hear herself admitting huskily, 'That's just it. I don't want to go back.' She drew a deep, shuddering breath, and tried to move away from his constraining hands. When he touched her she could barely think straight; her whole body yearned toward him, aching wantonly for his touch. She could feel the now shockingly familiar coil of painful need tense her stomach, and she ached to press herself against him, to be wrapped in the hardness of his arms.

She looked past him towards the window and said more to herself than to him, 'What's happening to me? I scarcely recognise myself any more. Why do I feel like this? I ought to be eager to get back to work. Instead...'

'It's called post viral depression,' Rick told her gently. 'A common occurrence with 'flu victims, especially when they've been as ill as you've been. I know that doesn't make it any easier to bear, but it will pass, I promise you.'

'How can you say that? You don't know...'

'Yes, I do,' he contradicted her. 'Three years ago I suffered a similar experience. It was the most demoralising thing I've ever known. But I promise you there is life after 'flu,' he told her teasingly.

Life after 'flu, yes. But life after him—never.

The realisation that she loved him kept her tense and restless when she ought to have been concentrating on recouping her strength. She slept so badly for two nights and looked so frail and drawn on the third night when he brought up her dinner tray, he insisted that she was to drink all of the large glass of rich red wine he had poured for her.

'But I don't like it,' she protested. 'It goes straight to my head, especially red wine.'

'Think of it as medicinal.'

Until she'd realised that she loved him, Kate had been having her evening meal with Rick. Since then she had cravenly insisted on eating alone in her room, and she had seen from the expression in his eyes that her refusal to share the evening with him puzzled him. She shrank from his classing her with his previous employer, the woman whose sexual advances had led him to handing in his notice. How well she could understand that woman now. She shivered, despite the warmth of her bedroom, and Rick frowned.

She was not recovering as fast as she should. He privately considered that she would recuperate far more quickly somewhere warmer. He thought of the villa in Corfu bought half on impulse, half as an investment and now so rarely used, but there was no way he could suggest that she stay there without alerting her suspicions.

Kate watched him as he placed her dinner tray on the small table. In the early days of her recuperation, she had marvelled at the delicacy and variety of the meals he brought her to tempt her appetite, and he had confessed to her that they weren't his creation but had been delivered via a special restaurant service he had found in Yellow Pages.

Kate had winced at the thought of how much it must be costing, but when she had tried to point this out to him he had told her bluntly that his own cooking skills were not such as would tempt the appetite of an invalid.

Tonight there was chicken breast in a delicate cream sauce, flavoured with some sort of spirit, although she couldn't recognise which one, accompanied by delicious new potatoes, no doubt flown in at great expense, and a tempting variety of beautifully cooked and arranged vegetables. For pudding there was a very special egg custard, again beautifully cooked and arranged in a pure fruit sauce to add piquancy to its flavour.

But as she ate it, and reluctantly drank the wine Rick had brought her, Kate knew she was not doing justice to the delicious food.

The double burden, not only of her love for Rick, but also of her growing reluctance to face up to the reality of what the loss of James's contract was going to mean to her business, was haunting her, sapping her strength like an invidious disease, leaving her wan and listless when she ought to have been getting better. Sometimes she even wondered if she was deliberately sabotaging her own recovery, just so that she could bask for a little longer in the warmth of Rick's cocoon. Once she would have scorned such an idea, but now... Now she was no longer sure if she knew herself at all.

When Rick returned with the bottle of wine and insisted on pouring her another glass, she demurred, but he poured it anyway and left it on the table beside her bed, saying that she might feel like it later.

He offered her coffee, but she refused, knowing that even the smallest stimulant was likely to keep her awake into the small hours of the morning as she fought to come to terms with what was happening to her.

She sensed that Rick wanted to stay and talk. On previous evenings, before she had realised what was happening to her emotions, she had enjoyed their discussions, finding in Rick a male companion intelligent enough to challenge her, and at the same time confident enough of himself to accept her fully as his equal. She missed their verbal sparring, but that was nothing to how she was going to feel once he had gone from her life completely.

She fell asleep thinking about him, and then woke up abruptly at two o'clock in the morning to find the covers had slipped off the bed, as she struggled restlessly in her sleep, and she was freezing cold.

Pulling on her robe, she went to check on Michael, wondering if a sound from him had woken her, but the little boy was deeply asleep. She touched his smooth soft face and felt an unfamiliar urge grip her body. What would it be like to conceive the child of a man one loved? To carry that child and eventually give birth to it...the strongest bond there could be between two people who loved.

She was shaken by the tempest of emotion that swept her, leaving her shivering and achingly aware of how barren her life was going to be. She would never sleep now...and she wondered how long she was going to be condemned to spend the hours of darkness tormented by her thoughts of Rick.

She half stumbled back to her own room, and saw the glass of red wine. That should warm her, and help her sleep too. She picked it up and drank it quickly, as though it was medicine, pulling a wry face as the full-bodied claret slid down her throat.

There was more in the glass than she had imagined, and even before she had finished drinking it she was conscious of the sudden burst of warmth heating her stomach. On an empty stomach and in her tense, nervous state, the intoxicating effect of the strong wine was almost immediate.

She could see the room blurring almost in front of her, and when she tried to get into bed, to her bewilderment, the bed seemed to shift hazily in front of her, as though it was a floating mirage and not really material at all.

She clutched hold of the quilt to steady herself, and found to her astonishment that she was sitting on the floor with it. She started to giggle, the whole situation suddenly unbearably funny, but somewhere along the line her giggles changed to tears and she started to cry, uninhibited, wrenching tears of intense pain.

The noise woke Rick, who had learned to sleep lightly in case Michael called out during the night and disturbed Kate. At first he couldn't place the alien sound, and then he realised that it came from Kate's room, not Michael's, and he was on his feet, tugging a robe over his nude body. He hadn't worn pyjamas since he was a child, and although he had attempted to do so to soothe Kate's outrage, he had found them so constricting that he had soon abandoned them.

The sight of Kate huddled on her bedroom floor, clutching her quilt, her face streaked with tears, made him think that she had had an accident. He rushed over to her, demanding quickly, 'Kate, what is it? What's wrong? Is it your ankle?'

Her ankle had healed, the bruised swelling disappearing, but it was still liable to give way at odd moments.

Before she could say a word, he was touching her, his long fingers investigating the delicate bone, one hand supporting the slimness of her calf while the other probed delicately around the ankle itself.

Heat radiated upwards from where his hand touched her skin. Her heart was pounding unevenly, her body gripped by a wanton, urgent need, crying out to her so loudly for satisfaction of that need that it drowned out everything else, including the warning voice that begged her to remember her dignity and her pride.

Rick's head was bent over her ankle as he frowned his concern. Unable to stop herself she reached out and touched him, her fingers trembling as they rested, fluttering against the hard angle of his jaw.

He looked at her.

'I want you to make love to me.'

Too late now to recall the betraying words. Her whole body burned with humiliation and despair. What on earth had made her say them?

'Kate…'

He said her name softly, reaching out to take hold of both her wrists and gently push her away from him. She could see the rejection in his eyes and she flinched from it and from herself, burning with self-mortification. No matter how kindly he rejected her, they would both know that he had done so. Why hadn't she held her tongue? Why had she…?

'I'm sorry. I don't know what made me say that. It must have been the wine,' she gabbled, desperate to ease the tension filling the room. She saw that Rick was about to speak, and,

unable to endure hearing his denial of her, rushed on frantically, 'I didn't mean it, Rick. I know how you feel about
female employers who come on to you. Please forget what I
said. I...'

'Forget it? I can't do that, Kate.'

Something had changed; the deep timbre of his voice told
her that. Where he had been about to gently reject her, where
he had been firmly pushing her away from him, his fingers
were now slowly caressing the thudding pulses in her wrists,
and the dark glow in his eyes was not that of an unaroused
man.

The wine had gone right to her head and she barely knew
what she was saying or doing, he knew that. By rights he
ought to put her to bed and leave her there, but he had seen
in her eyes her belief that he was rejecting her, and he cursed
the ill fortune that had decreed that the man whose place he
had usurped had left his previous employment because of the
sexual harassment of the woman of the house.

He was caught in a double trap and he knew it. If he left
Kate now, she would think he was rejecting her, and he knew
her well enough to know that once she was completely herself
again, she would make sure that there would never be another
opportunity for him to break through her defences. Her pride
would ensure that.

And if he stayed then she would probably accuse him of
taking advantage of her when she was too ill to know what
she was doing. He was damned either way; and if he was
going to be damned, he knew which of the two memories he
would rather take with him.

For too many nights now he had lain in that too narrow and
almost too short single bed, on fire for the feel of her in his
arms, aching with a torment he could remember experiencing
even during his teens, his body pulsing hungrily with its need
for her.

A more sexually experienced woman would have recognised that need and probably exploited it, but Kate seemed to
have no awareness of her effect on him. Hence the look of

anguished rejection in her eyes right now. A look he would give his soul to extinguish. A look he could wipe away simply by taking her in his arms and letting her feel how very wrong she was when she assumed he didn't want her.

'You should be in bed,' he told her huskily.

He stood up, taking her with him, and holding her against his body, securing her there with one arm, while he picked up the quilt with the other. The movement hardened the muscles of his belly, and Kate was pressed so closely to him that she could feel it, her own stomach quivering in arousal at being so close to his strength. Still holding her, he tugged the quilt back on to the bed. Kate found that her head seemed to nestle of its own accord in the curve of his shoulder.

She wasn't sure if Rick was simply remaking the bed for her benefit, or...

'I don't think I'm going to need this, do you?' he whispered against her hair, releasing her briefly to shrug off his robe.

'I forgot my pyjamas again,' he added throatily, sliding her own robe away from her body, and then bending his head to nuzzle the scented skin of her throat as he eased down the shoulder straps of her nightdress.

'Rick,' she protested huskily.

His mouth had reached the curve of her jaw.

'Shush... Don't talk now. Kiss me instead,' he murmured against the corner of her mouth, and the movement of his lips sent wild vibrations of sensation coiling through her.

'Rick—' she protested again, but more weakly this time, wild panic seizing her as his lips slid between her own, parting them and then caressing them with ever-increasing passion.

She didn't know when she started to kiss him back, or when he released her arms from the straps of her nightdress to allow it to slide to the floor so that he could gather her body into his arms and slowly caress the length of her spine as he urged her into the waiting heat of his own flesh. It was all so new, this sensation of flesh against flesh, this closeness, this intimacy, and yet it was also as though part of her had known it since the beginning of time.

She stopped kissing him, drawing back in his embrace to search his face with a fevered gaze. 'Rick, I've never done this before. I don't want to disappoint you...'

'You couldn't,' he told her gently, drawing her back against him and tracing the outline of her mouth with his tongue, distracting her from what she knew she ought to say.

Beneath his breath he muttered rawly, 'If anyone's going to be disappointed, it could be you. I want you too much right now. Feel,' he whispered softly, his hands moving down her spine to hold her against him. 'Feel how much you arouse me, and promise me that no matter what the future holds, you'll never doubt how much I want you...'

Kate hesitated uncertainly, sensing the tension in his words, groping towards understanding what might lie behind them, but Rick demanded urgently, 'Promise me, Kate. Promise me that *no matter what happens*, you won't allow anything to destroy these memories.'

His fingers dug into the tender softness of her bottom, and she sensed that he wasn't even aware of the pressure he was exerting. He breathed deeply and his body moved against her own, sending sharp spirals of desire coiling through her.

'I promise,' she told him unsteadily, marvelling at the darkness of his eyes and the faint tremor of his hand as he brushed her hair off her face. Then, holding her shoulder, he kissed his way along her throat and down over her body until she was arched willingly and wantonly over his arm, as instinct and arousal demanded that she focus his attention, both mental and physical, on the feminine perfection of her breasts and their dark crowns of yearning flesh.

She trembled as his mouth moved moistly on her, caressing the soft swell of pale skin, his hand cupping her other breast. Then his fingers began caressing its taut peak, until she quivered and shook and wondered with agonised impatience why he didn't know how tormenting it was to have his mouth moving so delicately on her smooth, pale skin, when what she wanted...what she needed...

'Rick,' she protested huskily, and immediately he stopped

caressing her, lifting his head so that he could look into her eyes.

'What is it? Don't you like that?'

'Yes. No. Rick, I want…' Her heart thundered and pounded within her chest, the words locking in her throat, her eyes darkening with her need to have his mouth against her flesh.

And then, as though he knew that she could not endure the torment any longer, his gaze dropped to the dark peaks of her breasts, and she felt his breath graze tormentingly against them as he said fiercely, 'Is it this that you want, Kate? Is it?'

And he drew the sensitive nub of flesh into his mouth, caressing it with his tongue, and then, when she cried out, he suckled fiercely first on one and then on the other nipple. As though the soft cries of pleasure muted in her throat drove him beyond the edge of his self-control, his palms cupped the outer curves of both breasts, gently pushing them together, so that his mouth could move swiftly from one pulsing pleasure point to the other with a rhythmic urgency that seemed to flow from his body to her own, so that she was not quite sure when the thrusting hardness of his body's possession was no longer merely her fevered mind's hungry fantasy but actual reality.

The feel of him inside her went beyond any pleasure she could imagine there could be; even the brief locking of her muscles as they felt the thrust that broke the final barrier was in some odd way a painful pleasure, willingly endured for the delights that came after it.

'I'm sorry, my love, but this time I can't be temperate,' she felt Rick whisper against her mouth as the tempo of his possession increased.

He groaned against her mouth and savaged it with biting kisses as passion overcame him. Kate felt the tiny, beginning ripples of it, but as she reached out to capture the sensation Rick cried out and she felt the hot pulse of his climax.

'I'm sorry. It was too soon,' he told her, still holding her in his arms, but strangely she felt no disappointment, only a vague ache and an intense feeling of tiredness. She badly wanted to go to sleep and she curled up against Rick, burrowing into the warmth of his body.

By rights, he ought to go back to his own bed. What had happened already was bad enough, but if he stayed here with her there could be only one outcome to the enticement of her soft, naked flesh against his own.

He was right. Towards dawn Kate was woken by the most delicious of sensations she had ever experienced washing slowly through her body, and by the time she was awake enough to realise that it was caused by the soft caress of Rick's mouth against first her stomach and then her inner thigh, she was too aroused to do anything more than cry out in a torment of shocked pleasure that convulsed her body and turned her weak with sensation as Rick's tongue gently traced the most secret intimacy of her sex. Then his mouth caressed her until she was mindless...lost...adrift in an ocean of pleasure, no longer caring if she sank or swam.

Nothing in her life had prepared her for the explosion of pleasure that shook her, nor for the astounding speed with which Rick was able to make her reach out for that same pinnacle of pleasure again as he told her thickly, 'That was for you. This is for both of us. Something for both of us to cherish.'

In the false dawn she saw a muscle beat in his jaw, and wondered at the bleakness in his eyes. He was as grim as though he was a condemned man, but her body, awash with delight, refused to allow her mind to concentrate on anything other than the physical delight he was giving her.

The quivers of her first climax had barely died away before she felt his mouth on her breasts, teasing the hard nipples into aching points of desire. She felt the arousal of his body, moving urgently against her and then within her so strongly that she felt she would die from the pleasure she was experiencing.

This time the pleasure was stronger, fiercer, the convulsive grip of her muscles locking on Rick's body making him groan and shake with arousal, and then for a few fleeting heartbeats they were no longer human, but immortal, spinning dizzily into space together, and the music of the universe rang in Kate's ears as they heard Rick's harsh cry of fulfilment and she knew that it was her body that had given it to him. The sensation she felt at the knowledge was so primitive, so female, that the force of it shocked her.

CHAPTER TEN

'THERE'S a phone call for you. A Camilla Lancing.'

'Camilla? Oh, lovely, I'll speak to her.' Carefully avoiding looking directly at Rick, Kate picked up the receiver.

It had been three hours now since she had woken up to the realisation that she and Rick had been lovers; three hours, during which she had battled frantically against her panic that he might guess that for her last night had not just been the emotional whim of the moment, but a lifetime commitment.

In the cold light of the dark November day, she was all too aware of how irrationally and idiotically she had behaved. She didn't regret that she and Rick had been lovers; how could she? But what she both dreaded and feared was what she might have betrayed to him through her actions.

Discreetly he left the room while she spoke to her friend.

'Who on earth was that?' Camilla asked her, obviously intrigued, once Kate had asked after her father-in-law and been assured that he was now well on the way to recovery.

'You should know,' Kate responded as light-heartedly as she could. 'You were the one who recommended him. He's Michael's nanny.'

There was a small silence, and then Camilla said, 'Kate, are you well enough to have visitors? I'd like to come round and see you.'

Kate was dressed and sitting in her room. 'Lovely. I've rather a lot to talk to you about.'

Too proud to ask for any direct help, she would nevertheless be grateful for the opportunity to talk over her fears for her business with her friend.

Camilla arrived half an hour later. Rick let her in on his

way to the park with Michael. Kate heard them exchanging 'hellos' as they passed in the hall.

Kate greeted her friend with a smile, but there was no answering smile on Camilla's face as she walked into the room.

'Kate, what's going on?' she demanded without preamble. 'And please, no more fairy-tales. The day Garrick Evans needs to hire himself out as anyone's anything is the day the business world turns topsy-turvy... What *on earth* is he doing here?'

Kate stared at her in shock.

Rick Evans. Garrick Evans. Why on earth hadn't she made the connection? Why on earth hadn't she guessed? Garrick Evans, Alan's remote second cousin. Garrick Evans, who had announced to her via her solicitor that he wanted nothing to do with his second cousin's child.

She sat numbly while Camilla's rueful expressions of remorse went past her unregarded. A feeling of terrified panic, not unlike that experienced during the most traumatising of nightmares, possessed her; she felt as though she had strayed into an unknown world without any signposts to guide her. A feeling of physical sickness engulfed her, and she started to shake as she tried to understand why Garrick Evans was living in her home, pretending to be Michael's nanny.

Michael. Suddenly all her fears coalesced and focused on one thing...Michael. Michael was the key to this. He had to be. Michael was the reason that Garrick Evans was here, that he had lied to her, that he had played a cruel charade with her, that he had inveigled his way into her home, her bed...her life, under totally false pretences.

'You didn't know, did you?' Camilla apologised. 'Oh, Kate, I'm so sorry.'

'Where did he go?' Kate demanded tersely, ignoring her apology. 'I've got to get up. He's got Michael with him. Oh, God, how could I have been so stupid? I've got to find him.'

'Kate, no. You're in no fit state to do anything. Please tell me. What's going on? What's he doing here? How can I help?'

'You can't,' Kate told her dully. 'No one can...'

They both heard the front door open and then close again.

Michael's laughter floated upstairs, accompanied by the deep tones of Garrick's voice.

'Do you want me to stay with you?' Camilla asked, sensing that Kate intended to confront him with the truth.

'No!' She shook her head. 'No, thanks.'

What was going to happen would be painful in the extreme, and she wanted no witnesses to it, no matter how sympathetic and kind. It was bad enough that she had betrayed herself so stupidly, without others witnessing her humiliation.

God, how he must have laughed at her! Garrick Evans...superstud par excellence. No wonder he had known exactly how to... Her mind cut off then, refusing to go any further down such a hurtful path.

'I'll go, then,' Camilla said awkwardly, seeing that Kate was hardly even aware that she was still there. 'I'm sorry, Kate. Perhaps I shouldn't have said anything, but I knew that the man who was supposed to come for the interview had taken another job, and I was worried.'

'No...no. You did the right thing,' Kate told her slowly. 'It's better this way...'

And, seeing the look in her eyes, Camilla did not ask her what it was exactly that was better.

She passed Garrick on the stairs. He had Michael in his arms and stood back to let her pass. He noticed her set face, and the way she avoided his eyes, and the vague feeling that he had met her somewhere before became certainty.

He swore softly under his breath. He had planned to tell Kate the truth today, knowing that he could not allow himself to go on deceiving her now that they had been lovers.

He put Michael in his playpen and then opened Kate's bedroom door. The moment he saw her face, his suspicions were confirmed.

'You know, then,' he asked calmly.

'That you're Garrick Evans?' She gave him a tight, hard smile. 'Yes, I do. I suppose Michael's at the root of this whole charade.'

He had known she was intelligent and keen-witted, but even

so her percipience startled him. It deserved the only honest reply he could give her.

'Yes,' he told her bluntly. 'But, Kate...'

'You've got half an hour to collect your things together and leave. And just to make sure you do, I'm going to call the police.'

She was actually dialling the number, he realised, and he had no doubts that she meant exactly what she said.

'Kate, we have to talk,' he protested, but she wouldn't look at him, fiercely punching out the numbers into the telephone.

He bent down and tugged swiftly on the connecting flex, disconnecting her.

'Let me explain.'

'What?' Kate demanded fiercely. 'Why you lied your way into my home...my...trust...my...my bed?'

She couldn't add 'my heart', but it was what was hurting her the most; that and her fear that somehow or other his presence threatened both her and Michael.

'The deceit was accidental, not calculated. If you cast your mind back, you will remember that *you* were the one to assume that I had come for the job of Michael's nanny.'

'You could have corrected me.'

He acknowledged her comment with a grim frown.

'I could have, but at the time it seemed an ideal opportunity to have a chance to get closer to Michael, to collect the evidence my solicitor told me I would need to get a court to hand him over into my care.'

He saw her go white, and ached to take her in his arms and tell her how he felt about her, but she was like a terrified cat, ready to attack friend and foe alike in her panic.

'So I was right,' she hissed. 'Michael *is* what all this is about. *Why?* Why do you want to take him from me? You had the opportunity to accept your share of responsibility to him when Alan and Jennifer died, but you rejected it. I still have the letter.'

'My solicitor wrote that without my authority while I was

out of the country,' he told her calmly. 'And before you say anything, I can prove it.'

'Just as you can prove that you'd make a far better guardian for him than me? Because you've got more money, more power, more everything… I suppose that's why you went to bed with me, isn't it?' she added in a high voice, her whole body shaking with the force of her emotions. 'So that you could prove to the court how unfit I am morally as well as financially. What did you do, Garrick? Make notes to pass on to your solicitor…record…'

She was working herself up into a state of acute hysteria, and he could hardly blame her. There was only one way to stop it. He walked over to her and yanked her out of her chair, binding her protesting body to his own.

'Stop it, Kate,' he reinforced when she tried to claw at him. Her eyes were wild, like those of a hunted animal, her face pale except where her cheekbones were highlighted by patches of hectic colour.

'You're wrong. Oh, I admit that when I first came here I was hoping to get enough evidence against you to prove that I was more fit to have guardianship of Michael than you. You see, I'd reached that point in my life where it was beginning to come home to me that I've worked myself into the ground for nothing…or rather, for no one…and the thought of an heir, a son…who could be had without the encumbrance of a mother whose role in my life I did not want either outside or inside marriage, was a very alluring prospect indeed!'

He saw her face and smiled grimly.

'I'm paying you the compliment of being totally honest with you, Kate.'

'Isn't it a bit late for that?' she countered bitterly.

'I hope not, but only you can know the answer to that question. You're looking at a man who's been converted to a view of life he's never previously wanted to see. I'm a very successful man, Kate, and without being vain or boastful that success has meant that I've never been short of female company and admiration, but just as someone working in a sweet factory grows to loathe the very sweetness of the confectionery they make, so I found I was rapidly growing very disenchanted with the female sex. Greedy, grasping…shallow.' He saw her face and grimaced. 'Yes. I know how it sounds, but I'm trying to be honest with you. You see, knowing you has opened up a whole new vista to me. I see life and my place in it in a way I never have done before.'

'You mean you've realised that women can be gullible fools, easily convinced by an experienced liar?'

'No! What I mean is that I believe that Michael needs both of us in his life. No one could love him more than you do, Kate, but you must admit that it's difficult for you trying to cope with building up a new company and the day-to-day problems of caring for a small child.'

The very reasonableness of his argument struck a fresh chill in her soul. What was he going to do? Offer her money to part with Michael?

'Kate, we're both people who've made a decision to live our lives alone. Both of us have decided that commitment, permanency…a lifelong partner are not for us. I suggest that we should think again.

'I've learned a lot living here with you. I've learned for instance that it's possible for a man to find a great deal of pleasure in caring for a child…even a small child, and I've also now a much clearer insight into how difficult that kind of caring can be…how tying and at times how tiring. I've also learned that there are women who are vastly different from those with whom I've sometimes shared my life, and I blame myself for the fact that I've only just learned this. Call it a self-defensive practice, if you like, but that's what I believe it was.'

He felt the tension in her body and sensed her desire to break away from him.

'What I'm trying to say, Kate, is that instead of fighting over who should have Michael, why don't we join forces and share the pleasure and responsibility of bringing him up?'

'A week with you and then a week with me, do you mean?' she demanded brittlely. 'Turn and turn about.'

'Not exactly.' His eyes narrowed as he looked down into her angry face. He could feel the stubborn resistance holding her body taut, and he knew that this was going to be far harder than he had hoped. 'What I had in mind was something a little better than that. I want to marry you, Kate.'

Her body suffered the shock of it…the awful pain and despair of being given so much and so little.

'Because of Michael?' she asked him bitterly. 'No, I'm sorry, Garrick. You may be enjoying a different vision of how you see your life progressing, but I'm afraid I don't share it. I want a career, not marriage.'

She broke free of him and walked over to the window, keeping her back to him. She didn't want him to look into her face and see how much she was suffering. She had to convince him that she couldn't marry him. To be married to the man she loved simply for the sake of a child in whom they both had an interest… No, that was something she could not and would not endure. She had her pride.

'I see.'

How silky and menacing his voice sounded.

'A career, you say. Doing what, Kate? Working for someone else? Because that's what's going to happen, isn't it? You barely have enough funds to keep your business going another two months. You badly need new contracts. You…'

'*You've* had my business investigated? How dare you? What were you trying to prove? That I'm financially incompetent? Well, I can soon change that… All it takes is one phone call to James. Of course, I'll have to sleep with him to get his business, but what does that matter now? I…'

'God, Kate, no!' Garrick interrupted her explosively. 'Turn your back on me if you must…hate me even, if you want to…but please don't sell yourself to someone like Cameron. It would destroy you. If the company is so very important to you, I'll give you some business. I've already…'

'Thanks, but no thanks. What is it, Garrick…guilty conscience perhaps? I've gone to bed with you, therefore I have to be paid off, just like your other women?' Kate demanded recklessly.

'Is that what you really think?' His mouth twisted. 'I suppose there is a certain kind of rough justice that you should. Listen to me, Kate, because whatever else you may or may not choose to believe about me, this much is true. I didn't want to make love to you last night. I knew it would only add to my burden of deceit.'

Kate went ashen.

'There's no need to remind me that I was the one to proposition you, Garrick,' she said proudly. 'But...'

'For God's sake woman, will you allow me to finish just one sentence? I didn't want to make love to you because I knew it wasn't the right thing to do, not with all that you didn't know about me, but I couldn't stop myself... I've spent too many nights lying awake, aching for you, to be strong-willed enough to deny my need.'

He reached for her and wordlessly she let him take hold of her. Holding her, he traced the trembling outline of her mouth with his thumb, brushing the soft curves tenderly.

'Is this because you hate me?' he asked her softly, undermining her defences. 'I love you, Kate. I didn't mean to... I certainly didn't want to, but I do, and although you may think it arrogantly male of me, I think you love me too. No woman could make love the way you did last night and not care. I fully intended to tell you the truth today, I promise you... and to ask you to be my wife, and not because of Michael.

'The first time I walked into this house, all I could think of was how convenient it would be to have a child without the inconvenience of its mother. Michael himself meant nothing to me, I admit it. But you changed all that. I love Michael. I can't deny it, but that's not why I'm asking you to marry me.'

'I'm a career woman,' Kate protested huskily. 'I wouldn't make you a good wife, Garrick. Not the kind of wife a successful man like you needs to run his home and bring up his family.'

'Wrong,' he told her forcefully. 'You're exactly the kind of wife I need. The only woman I could ever want as my partner through life. And marriage to me doesn't mean you must abandon your career, Kate. In fact, I wouldn't want you to. It may not be easy at times for either of us, but with luck…with sheer hard work…and most of all with love…we can make it.'

'Can we?' Kate sighed, no longer able to resist him.

'Let me prove it to you.'

She quivered wildly as his mouth touched hers, unable to deny herself the bliss of holding him, of touching him, of letting his mouth convince her of all that he had already said.

A career…a husband…a family. It sounded too good to be true.

As though he knew what she was thinking, as he released her, Garrick said huskily, 'I can't promise you that you'll have it all, as they say in the books. No one does! To imagine that they do is a fallacy. Compromises will have to be made, but I think that any amount of compromising is worth while if it makes it possible for us to be together. I want you as my wife, Kate. I want that more than I've ever wanted anything in my life. We go together, you and I. I know you need and want your career, and I don't want to stop you having those things. Marry me and I'll prove it to you.'

She looked at him and he added rawly, 'I'm not going to beg you to trust me, Kate.'

'You don't have to,' she told him softly.

He was strong, this man of hers; strong enough to allow her to be her own person, to accept that she could not devote her life to living in his shadow. As he had said, it wouldn't be easy, but somehow they would find a way to make it possible, feasible, viable. After all, they had the strongest bond there was. Their love.

'So!'

Kate picked up her telephone and punched out the number of Garrick's private line.

'Are you free for dinner with me tonight?' she asked him once she had heard the familiar tones of his voice.

'In what capacity?' he teased her. 'As my wife…or as the director of my PR agency?'

'Neither,' Kate told him with a smile. 'And don't bother asking any more questions. It's a surprise.'

As she put down the receiver she grinned delightedly to herself. In fact, it was two surprises, and she intended to save the best until last.

Only this morning she and Camilla had agreed the final details of the deal that would make them equal partners in the new PR company they intended to form. With Camilla as her partner, both of them would be able to afford to split the responsibilities of running the business. It was rather like jobsharing with a difference, Kate chuckled, and she was also going to be the first to benefit from the new partnership because in eight months time, just in time for their first wedding anniversary, she would be presenting Garrick with their second child. A brother or sister for Michael.

Was it only just over six months ago that Garrick had cautioned her against expecting to 'have it all'? She smiled again. Her life came as close to perfection as it was possible to come.

The M4 motorway made it possible for them both to commute daily to their offices from the pretty Queen Anne house they had bought just outside Bath.

Michael had settled down well with his new nanny, an older woman who seemed to know just how to deal with children; and he had also taken to his adoptive grandparents in the shape of Garrick's mother and father.

Kate herself was getting to spend more time with him than she ever had before, since she had been able to promote Sara to office manager, and now there was the new partnership with Camilla and their mutual agreement that they would take it in turns to work from home, using the advanced computer technology Kate's recent success had made it possible for her to buy.

Garrick had helped her there, giving her as much of his

many companies' PR work as she could handle. And it wasn't nepotism, he had been quick to assure her. He had been impressed with the presentation she had prepared for James, and he continued to be impressed with the work she did for him.

'The results speak for themselves,' he had told her when she had demurred that other members of his main board might not look too kindly of him giving so much PR work to his wife and a company that was still only just getting established.

But she had proved herself now, and the success of the campaign she had introduced for Garrick's companies had drawn other businesses to her. She and Camilla had agreed that they would keep the business small enough for them both to handle, because, as she had discovered these last six months, there was more to life than mere material achievement, much...much more. And she hugged to herself the knowledge of the pleasure Garrick would take in learning that they were to have a child.

Having it all? Maybe not from the viewpoint of the woman she had once been, whose career had been everything to her, but these last six months had taught her that, if she had to lose everything else, so long as she still retained Garrick's love she would have all that she could ever want.

She glanced at her watch. Another five hours before she met Garrick for dinner. She couldn't wait to see his face when she told him their news.

A woman he's never met has a claim on *his* daughter!

AN UNEXPECTED FAMILY

Cathy Gillen Thacker

Prologue

"Is it going to hurt, Mom?" ten-year-old Melinda Matthews asked.

Laura Matthews swallowed the raw knot of emotion in her throat. What was she supposed to say to that? The whole last week had been a nightmare. The whole last month. It had started with that cold of Melinda's that just wouldn't go away and escalated a little more with the large purple bruises that had begun appearing on her legs and arms for no reason. And it had increased even more when her pediatrician had found the lumps under Melinda's arm and simultaneously discovered that her white blood count was sky-high.

That had been hours ago. Now, at Children's Hospital, an oncologist had recommended yet another battery of tests and exams. Laura took her daughter's trembling hand in hers, clasping it warmly between her palms. "It probably will hurt just a little," she said honestly, "but I'll be here with you the whole time. I promise."

"Mrs. Matthews," a resident behind her whispered, "I don't think you understand how painful a bone marrow test can be. I strongly suggest you wait out in the reception area. We'll handle your daughter."

Laura turned to face him fiercely. "I'm staying with my daughter." Though her voice was calm and even, her eyes flashed a powerful warning.

Reading it, the resident backed off. "All right," he said gruffly, "just as long as you can stay out of our way."

The next few minutes weren't easy. Laura cried right along with Melinda, and when the painful procedure and round of X rays had been finished, she held her in her arms, cradling her much as she had when she was a baby.

Hours later, exhausted, Melinda was asleep in a semiprivate room upstairs, Laura still right beside her.

"Mrs. Matthews?" the pediatric oncologist, a pleasant woman in her mid-forties, said from the doorway. "May I see you for a moment?"

Laura gently released her sleeping daughter's hand and walked unsteadily out into the hallway. Dr. Baker led her into a deserted coffee room. "I've got Melinda's records." She sat down, spread them out over her lap and clicked her ballpoint pen into writing position. "I just want to go over them to make sure there's been no mistake."

"Okay," Laura said slowly, not liking the puzzled look on Dr. Baker's face, or the slightly aggravated note underlying her smooth melodious voice.

"Melinda is your only daughter?" Dr. Baker asked crisply, without looking up.

"Yes," Laura said, feeling more baffled than ever by the near animosity she suddenly felt emanating from the doctor. Dr. Baker hadn't been this way earlier in the day. What had she done to annoy her?

"And your husband—he's deceased?"

"Yes, he died in a car accident several years ago."

Dr. Baker looked up. "Melinda was his biological child?"

"Yes," Laura said, feeling more bewildered than ever.

"And yours?" Dr. Baker queried.

Laura leaned forward in her seat and said firmly, "Yes. I don't understand. What's going on?"

"I'm sorry, Mrs. Matthews, but I'm going to have to be blunt. Melinda is very ill. She's going to need blood transfusions and chemotherapy, perhaps even a bone marrow transplant." Her face softened sympathetically. "I really need for you to tell me the truth about this so we can proceed as quickly and efficiently as possible.''

"I *am* telling you the truth!" Laura railed back.

Dr. Baker sighed, her patience exhausted. "Mrs. Matthews, please. We already know you and your deceased husband both had AB blood. Melinda's blood type is O.''

Laura shrugged. "So?" None of this was making any sense to her.

Dr. Baker studied Laura. "So any child of you and your husband's would have had A, B, or AB type blood. It's scientifically impossible for you and your husband to have sired a child who has type O blood.''

The fear she'd felt all day became unmanageable. Laura was so panicked she could barely breathe. "What are you saying?" she finally choked out.

"That either you're not telling me the truth—" Dr. Baker frowned.

"I am." Laura protested. She'd never been intimate with anyone other than Rob.

Dr. Baker's look turned even grimmer. "—or Melinda isn't your biological child.''

Laura stared at her, the knowledge cutting her like a knife. This couldn't be true, none of it. It was bad enough that Melinda was ill, but for them to imply...no, she knew Melinda was her child, her flesh and blood. The doctors had made a mistake. Somewhere they'd screwed up the records or the tests. That had to be it. Had to be...

Chapter One

"Eric, you're going to be late for school," Laura Matthews called.

"I'm hustling," her sixteen-year-old son shouted as he bounded downstairs. Laura thrust his letter jacket at him. He wouldn't remember to take it unless reminded, no matter how cold it got outside. And today the temperature was in the low forties. "Got your car keys and lunch money?" she demanded, following him toward the front door.

Eric nodded affirmatively. He scooped up the stack of books he'd left heaped haphazardly on the front hall table and crammed them willy-nilly into his Central High athletic bag. "The varsity game starts tonight at seven-thirty, Mom."

"I'll be there with bells on," she promised, ruffling his naturally curly dark brown hair.

"Yeah, well try not to yell too loud," he teased, ducking the goodbye kiss she aimed at his cheek. "It's embarrassing when you tell the ref to get glasses."

"Sometimes they need them!" Laura retorted.

"Hey Gramps!" Eric said, when he opened the front door. "What are you doing here?"

Laura's father smiled. "I came over to talk to your Mom." He glanced at his watch. "Aren't you going to be late?"

Eric sped past. "Nope!" he yelled cheerfully over his shoulder.

"And even if he is he'll probably manage to charm the

attendance clerk out of a tardy slip," Laura said, watching briefly as Eric stuffed his six-three frame into his battered red Mustang. The car roared to life seconds later. His seat belt on, Eric backed carefully out of the driveway. Laura waved and shut the door behind her dad.

"So, what's up?" he asked, already taking off his coat and heading into the kitchen to watch her work. Although he'd retired from the Navy three years prior, he still wore his graying haircut military short. His aging body was trim and fit. Her dad tucked his perfectly ironed flannel shirt into the waistband of his chinos. "You said last night you had something to tell me and asked me to come over—without your mother. You sounded very upset."

"I have been upset," Laura admitted, picking up the pie dough she'd been rolling out. She sighed, not knowing where to start. She'd kept this a secret for so long.

"I'm listening," her dad said gently, after pouring himself a cup of coffee.

She knew if anyone would understand, he would. He could also be trusted to keep a confidence. Trying hard to keep her lower lip from trembling, she said, "You remember three years ago when Melinda first got sick?"

Although momentarily taken aback by the subject, her dad nodded grimly.

"Well, something happened then that I've never talked about," she continued shakily. He watched her in disciplined silence. "Dad, the doctors ran some blood tests and they found out that Melinda couldn't possibly be my biological child."

For long moments, her father was too stunned to speak. Finally he shook his head as if that would clear it. "Honey, are you sure?"

Laura nodded. Tears stung her eyes but she held them back. Realizing she was making a mess of the pie dough she was rolling out, she put it aside, dusted off her hands, and sat down. "Yes."

"Why didn't you say anything then?" her dad asked incredulously.

Laura shrugged, battling an almost overwhelming feeling of helplessness. "I couldn't." She sought his glance, begging for his understanding. "With her sick, it took all my energy to take care of her needs and to see to Eric." In fact, that was all she'd done during those heart-wrenching days. Her home bakery business had been put on hold. Because she'd had no income, she'd gone through the insurance money she'd received upon her husband's death, and she'd incurred sizable other debts as well. Debts she was still paying.

Her father exhaled slowly. He reached over and took her hand. "I know how hard it was to shoulder all that alone."

It *had* been hard, Laura thought. Yet somehow she had managed for two years, meeting both children's needs. And then, after Melinda had died, she'd had her grief to deal with, and Eric's. Now, a year later, their lives were finally getting back to normal. They had accepted Melinda's illness and subsequent death, as they had come to accept the loss of Laura's husband years before.

Restless, edgy, Laura got up to roam the kitchen. With Eric, Laura could still put on a front when she needed to, to protect him, but with her father, there was no need. In his years as a Navy officer, he'd seen and heard everything. And because of that, unlike her mother, he was a very tolerant man. "Dad, I've tried to put this out of my mind," Laura continued. "And for a while I really thought I had." But the nearing anniversary of Melinda's death had brought it all up again—all the emotions, fears, and nagging doubts she'd tried so hard to bury. She knew now they weren't ever going to go away, that she wouldn't have any peace until she had some answers.

Unfortunately there were no easy answers. The news that someone else had also taken the wrong child home from the hospital, and loved and raised her as their natural child for thirteen years would be devastating. And very disruptive.

If Laura's natural child had been sent home with neglectful parents, Laura knew she'd have no choice but to sue for custody. Unfortunately, even gaining custody of her child might not be a solution. The child could resent her. The child might not get along with Eric. Laura might find that after all this time they had nothing in common. Nor would they ever have.

It was also possible that Laura's child had been loved and treasured. If that were the case, Laura knew she couldn't and wouldn't disrupt her natural child's life. She wouldn't have wanted someone to disrupt Melinda's.

Whatever happened, Laura would be causing pain. And that knowledge filled her with remorse and guilt.

"What are you going to do?" her father asked gently.

"I need to contact the hospital." Feeling more restless than ever, she dragged a hand through her short brown hair. "I've got to find out what happened."

Her father drained the last of his coffee in a single, throat-burning draught. "You realize you'd be opening up a Pandora's box, Laura."

"I know." *God help me, I know.*

"And you have Eric to think about, too. What if this is true? What if the hospital did send you home with the wrong child? What then, Laura? I know you must be curious, maybe even heartbroken, but what are you going to do if you're actually able to find this other child?"

She knew that the sensible approach was to forget she'd ever learned what she had, to accept the fact that it was too late and move on. But she couldn't.

"What then?" her father persisted. "How are you going to feel about her when you find her? About yourself? How are *her* parents going to feel?"

Laura shrugged helplessly and this time she couldn't stop the flow of tears, or the guilt and anxiety that surged within her. "I don't know, Dad," she said thickly. She remembered how happy she had been the day her only daughter was born. She'd never suspected that anything could go wrong with that happiness. But it had and now she had to deal with that, too. She twisted a dish towel in her hands. "I just know I have to find out the truth."

He got up slowly to help himself to more coffee. As she had expected, he accepted her decision. He had always treated her like a grown-up, with a capable head on her shoulders. Whereas her mother still thought she couldn't do anything right. "Have you told any of this to your mother?" he asked quietly.

"No," Laura said quickly, panic edging her voice once again. "And I wish you wouldn't, either." She knew they'd only fight about it, the way they did everything else.

"All right, I won't say anything," he promised reluctantly.

"To Eric, either," Laura cautioned protectively.

"Of course not." Her dad paused. As his initial stunned reaction faded, he looked both resigned and as if his heart went out to her. "When are you going to do this?"

"The sooner the better. This morning if possible, while Eric's in school."

"Do you want me to go with you?"

Laura nodded, knowing she needed his support to get through this. She was determined, but she wasn't superhuman. "Please."

"Then let's do it," her dad said.

They got the chief of staff to see them shortly before noon. Once in his office, Laura wasted no time in presenting him with the records she had carefully gathered. Melinda's birth certificate, her hospital identification bracelet, the records of all their blood types, and records from Melinda's illness.

The chief of staff studied the records for a long time. He looked up, disbelief etched in the kind lines of his face. "You're suggesting we gave you the wrong baby?" Clearly he thought she was some sort of nut case.

"Yes," Laura said calmly, having braced herself for exactly this kind of reaction. Her dad reached over and patted her arm reassuringly. She continued in the same matter-of-fact tone, "I'm suggesting some kind of accidental swap occurred." Her voice picked up slightly as she twisted her hands together in her lap. "The hospital was a madhouse that day. There'd been a major wreck on the interstate. I remember they drafted every available person to the ER. There were only two of us in labor at that time, myself and another woman about my age. I don't remember her name but I do remember she also had a baby girl. We delivered within minutes of one another. Then there was a crisis of some sort. I don't know what happened after that.''

The chief of staff cut her off. ''Mrs. Matthews, I understand your loss and I sympathize, but this hospital does not make mistakes of that magnitude. We couldn't have mixed up the two infants, no matter how shorthanded we were.''

Laura challenged openly, ''Then how do you explain Melinda's blood type?''

''I can't.'' He returned quickly, ''Unless—''

''Make no mistake about it,'' Laura stated emphatically, ''My husband was the father of that baby. This is a hospital error we are talking about, not an error of my ways.''

The chief of staff's expression darkened. He looked at the protective expression on Laura's father's face and wisely kept his own counsel. After lengthy silence, he sighed and said, ''Suppose, just suppose, mind you, that this is true. That it really did happen. What good would it do to bring it up now. Thirteen years have passed. You can't wish those years away.''

''I know that,'' Laura said impatiently.

''Then what do you want?''

''Peace of mind,'' she said, sounding a great deal more composed than she felt at this moment. She did wish that this had never happened. She felt her stomach twist into painful knots. ''And an understanding of how this could've happened.'' One could've heard a pin drop in the room. The chief's disapproval was palpable. Laura took a deep, bolstering breath and continued, ''And most importantly, I want to know what happened to my baby. I need to know she is safe, well, and happy.'' Laura hoped she wasn't abused or neglected, that she hadn't been orphaned and put in a foster home.

''And then what?'' the chief of staff replied with pragmatic authority. He leaned forward, elbows on his desk. ''Are you telling me that if I help you, your dealings with this child would stop once you see that she's all right?''

An uneasy silence fell. Laura couldn't make promises like that, and they all knew it. She didn't know what she would do or feel when she found her child. But something deep inside told her she had to go on. And do so soon, before even more precious time had elapsed. She had to make sure that her natural child was safe and loved.

She faced the doctor resolutely. "I'm telling you I'm determined to do this, with or without your help. I need answers and I'm going to get them." She paused slightly, before bringing out her wild card. "I'd rather not bring the courts into this but if you force me to do so, I will."

The doctor studied her face. She could tell he didn't want adverse publicity any more than she did. And if she went to the courts, it would get into the papers and, perhaps, to the television stations. They talked for another hour and argued some more. Laura's father backed her up one hundred percent. Finally the chief of staff gave in. "Wait here," he said, his expression reluctant. "And I'll see what I can find out."

Laura sagged with relief as he left. When the door closed behind him, she turned to her father, worried and heartsick at the way circumstances had forced her to behave. "I think what we did just amounted to blackmail."

Her father nodded grimly, looking just as wrung-out as she felt. "I know, but what choice did we have, if we want to get to the truth?"

None, Laura knew.

After an interminable wait, the chief of staff returned. He handed her a slip of paper with a name, address, and birth date on it. "If you say I gave this to you, I'll deny it, but this child was born within minutes of your daughter and she has AB blood."

The same blood type as Eric's, Laura thought. A blood type compatible with hers and Rob's. She stared at the name on the paper. Janey Lynn Anderson, born to Zach and Maria Anderson. Many thoughts crowded Laura's mind. What would Janey look like? Would she look like Eric, Rob, or herself? Or a mixture of all three? Would Janey be healthy in a way

Melinda had not been? What kind of personality would she have? Would Laura feel an immediate connection with the thirteen-year-old girl? Or would there be nothing there, no spark of recognition, no simpatico, nothing? Would having lived with another family since birth override any genetic traits so that Janey would only act like the Anderson clan? And if that were the case, how would Laura feel about that?

Her legs felt rubbery. Laura rose and, after thanking the doctor for helping her, however illicitly, prepared to go.

He stopped her with these parting words, "Think hard, before you act, Mrs. Matthews. Think very hard." His glance narrowed warningly. "There are some things that are better left alone."

"ZACH, there's a lady here to see you."

Zach looked up from the blueprints that were spread across his desk and at his crew boss, Harry Cole, who stood in the doorway. "If it's the owner again—" Zach warned with a sigh. Normally he enjoyed working with the people who bought his custom homes, but Mrs. Gagglione was not the model client. During the course of building she and her husband's two-million-dollar home, Mrs. Gagglione had had the layout of the kitchen changed seven times. The first three times Zach had humored her and had his architect redesign the wiring and plumbing to fit her whim. The last four times he had calmly explained to Mrs. Gagglione that it was no longer possible to change the basic layout of the kitchen. She could fiddle with the wallpaper, countertop colors, and cabinet styles all she wanted, but not the placement of plumbing fixtures or the location of the stove or dishwasher. Each time she'd said she understood, and each time, she'd returned with yet another "plan."

Zach's crew boss grinned. "It isn't Mrs. Gagglione."

"A prospective client?" Zach asked, already tucking in his denim shirttail.

"I'm not sure. She doesn't look like a member of the Million Dollar Club but it's hard to tell. Should I send her in?"

Zach really didn't have time to spare, yet he couldn't turn away prospective business, either. Why didn't people call first? he wondered. He preferred to meet prospective clients in his plush offices in downtown Fort Worth than on the site of a current project.

"Yeah, sure. Tell her to come on in." He took off his hard hat and ran a hand through his light brown hair, smoothing it in place. Seconds later, the door to his trailer opened. An extraordinarily good-looking woman in her mid-thirties walked in. Tall and slim, she had the most arresting pair of dark brown eyes he'd ever seen. She was dressed attractively, like a suburban housewife on the way to a PTA meeting. And yet there was an aura of informality about her, a hint that she could make anyone feel comfortable with her. Zach didn't come across such warmth very often. The people he built homes for were rich, busy, and very high-strung. Not this woman. She looked remarkably well adjusted, if a tad on the nervous side. Just looking at her, Zach felt a glow of pleasure. Perhaps today wouldn't be so bad after all. Certainly this was a pleasant intrusion.

"Hi," she said, extending an unmanicured hand for a brief, confident handshake that somehow prompted him to look straight into her pretty face. Their gazes met and held. He regarded her, mesmerized. *She wants something,* he thought with a surge of unexpected empathy, *and she's not sure how to ask.* Wanting to put her at ease, he said hospitably, "How may I help you?"

"I'm Laura Matthews." She introduced herself in a husky, melodious tone.

"Zach Anderson." He gestured to a seat, noting the absence of a wedding ring, and her faint but continuing vacillation. Was she shy, maybe? He said softly, "What can I do for you, Ms. Matthews?"

She twined her hands together in her lap. "I have a personal matter I need to discuss with you. It's about your daughter, Janey Lynn Anderson."

The mention of Janey suspended his initial good cheer and

held Zach motionless. Worry crept in, and he hoped nothing was wrong. Not that Janey had ever been one to get in trouble. A father couldn't ask for a better daughter than Janey, even at the difficult age of thirteen, when she teetered back and forth between childhood and her exciting teenage years. Zach focused on Laura curiously. "Are you from her school?"

"No." Laura Matthews bit her lip and hazarded a strange, uncertain glance that was also surprisingly intimate. She sighed with what seemed like heartfelt regret. "I only wish it were that easy."

Frankly puzzled, he looked at her, once again taking full inventory of her neat, pine-green corduroy skirt and matching sweater, the sensible black leather flats, and huge carryall bag she'd placed on her lap. Attractive and smart, she didn't seem like the type to play games. "I don't understand."

She lifted her head another notch. The movement caused her thick, fluffy, dark brown hair to swirl in an expertly cut wedge around her face. "I know. I wish there were an easy way to say this, but there isn't. I had a daughter thirteen years ago, Mr. Anderson, in the same hospital where your wife delivered Janey."

Zach blinked, still having no idea where this was leading. He focused on Laura's wide brown eyes. They were the kind of eyes a man could get lost in. "You knew my wife?"

"N-not exactly." She swallowed, then took a deep breath, as if bracing herself for some nearing catastrophe. "I'm here because I think there was some kind of a mix-up the day our daughters were born. I know this is going to sound crazy, but I think our daughters might accidentally have been switched shortly after they were born or while they were in the hospital nursery."

Zach stared at her, sure this had to be some kind of a gag, played on him by the practical jokers in his construction crew. But she didn't look as if she was joking. She looked scared to death. Uneasiness sifted through him, followed swiftly by anger. He stood, hands on his hips. "What kind of joke is this?" he demanded.

She stood, too. Although she tried to hide it, he could see she was trembling badly.

"It's not a joke."

He stared at her, a muscle starting to twitch in his jaw. He'd never had patience with people who profited from others' pain. Laura Matthews might be beautiful and she might look like an everyday angel, but that wouldn't stop him from throwing her out of his office. No one, absolutely no one, threatened his family. "All right," he said flatly, closing in on her until they stood nearly toe-to-toe. "If it's not a joke, then what kind of a scam is it?" Just exactly what did she hope to gain from this lunacy? Money, maybe?

She looked briefly hurt by his accusation, but recovered just as quickly. "It's not a scam." Holding herself stiffly, she reached into her carryall and withdrew a sheaf of papers. "Here." She thrust them at him.

Zach remained where he was, not the least bit willing to play her game, whatever it was.

Ignoring his refusal to take the papers, she continued softly but seriously, "You can look for yourself. The blood type of my daughter is not compatible with my blood type or my husband's." She paused and bit her lip, momentarily unwilling to hurt him. Her voice dropped another empathetic notch, and her eyes grew luminous with compassion. "I have a feeling your daughter's blood type isn't compatible with yours, either."

Zach stared at her. This was like a bad dream. And yet it was real. All too real. This lady or lunatic, he wasn't sure which yet, really believed what she was saying. Could it be true? he wondered, stunned. God knew *she* seemed to believe what she was saying. Reluctantly he took the papers. They appeared to be official.

"I know this is a shock," she said, gentler now. "I felt just as confused."

That was impossible. He looked up sharply, annoyed by her deliberately soothing tone. He didn't trust himself to continue this discussion without losing his temper. Surely this had to be a hoax, he reassured himself firmly. He advised tersely, "Look, lady, I don't know what your game is or who put you up to it, and I'm not sure I care to know, but I think you'd better leave. Now."

Her oval face whitened to the hue of parchment. She stared at him with a mixture of shock and despair. "Please," she whispered, "at least hear me out."

Feeling there might be some truth to this made him want to run. But for Janey's sake he knew he had to stay. He didn't want this woman anywhere near his daughter and if he didn't discourage her now there was a chance she'd show up at his home. "No," he said firmly, "I think I've heard quite enough."

A tense silence fell between them. She stared at him a second longer, then dipped her head in mute acquiescence, as if deep down she had expected this reaction from him all along. Rummaging through her carryall once again, she produced a small pink business card. "My name and number are on this card," she said wearily. "When you've had a chance to think this through, please call me."

He shook his head in wonderment. Either she was the best, most convincing con artist he had ever seen, or she was as vulnerable and loony as the day was long. Either way, it was best to steer clear of her.

Careful not to brush up against her, he moved toward the screen door of the trailer. He hadn't had much experience dealing with crazy people, but he sensed it would be better not to upset her. At least not until he had figured out what to do. Maybe get her some professional help? He held the door open with an outstretched arm, trying not to let the pity he felt for her show. "I'll look at the information," he promised, knowing it was the only way he could get rid of her. But only to find the flaws in it, he amended silently.

"I'd appreciate it." She looked at him, seeing the doubt in his eyes, the wariness. Disappointment turned the corners of her mouth down. "You don't believe me, do you?" she said quietly, looking very distressed.

Should he? He swore inwardly. What a question! His jaw tensing with the turmoil he felt, he repeated, "Like I said, Mrs. Matthews, I'll look at the papers." And then he would call the police. Or the mental health authorities. Or both.

ZACH ANDERSON hadn't believed her, Laura thought, later that afternoon. She was upstairs in her room, sitting propped up against the headboard of her bed, with an afghan draped over her knees. Her own set of papers were spread out over her lap. It was all there: Janey's and Melinda's birth records, including tiny hand and footprints, and the hospital photos of each little girl.

As newborns, the two little girls had looked very much alike, with their pink faces and sparse hair. Even their weight had been almost identical. It was easy to see how the two babies might have been mixed up when the staff was shorthanded. It was not so easy for Laura to decide what to do next. Zach had refused to listen. Would he ever change his mind? she wondered dejectedly.

Downstairs, the front door slammed. Laura glanced at the clock on her bedside table and was stunned to see it was nearly six. Swiftly she gathered up the papers and stuffed them beneath the afghan. Eric mustn't see, she thought.

"Hey, Mom." Eric said seconds later, doing a double take when he passed by the master suite en route to his own room. Frowning worriedly, he asked, "Are you okay?" He knew it wasn't like her to nap.

"Yes, I'm fine," Laura reassured, although to be perfectly honest the stack of crumpled tissues next to her seemed to belie her declaration.

Book bag still in hand, Eric strode toward her for a closer look. Not one to mince words when he was concerned, he asked warily, "Have you been crying?"

Yes, Laura thought, she had been for what seemed like hours after she had returned from her visit with Zach. She'd made such a mess out of everything. In retrospect, she didn't know what she should have expected. Certainly Zach Anderson couldn't have welcomed the news any more than she did when she was first told. She was probably lucky he hadn't called the police and tried to have her arrested.

Aware Eric was still viewing her with a look of concern, she searched her mind for a plausible excuse. "I watched an old movie on TV this afternoon, one of those four-hankie kinds," she lied. "It kind of got to me." The crying jag had been cathartic really, leaving her physically exhausted and emotionally drained of all the turmoil she had been carrying around, hidden inside her, the last few days.

"Oh," Eric said, relieved. He knew what a sentimental fool she could be and didn't question her further.

"So what's up?"

"Oh, yeah." Jerked back to the present, Eric said, "I wanted to tell you that I need to eat dinner early tonight. I've got to go back to school for a student council meeting at seven. Is that okay? I mean, I could fix myself a sandwich or something—" he offered helpfully.

"No, I want you to have a decent meal," Laura said. "I'll make something in a minute. Go on down and take a look in the freezer. Pick something out. I'll be right down to fix it."

"Okay," Eric said cheerfully. "Thanks." He paused. "You're sure you're all right?"

Laura nodded. "Hormones," she said by way of further explanation, knowing no sixteen-year-old boy would question that. And to her relief, he didn't.

As soon as he was gone, Laura gathered the papers. She opened the first drawer of her bureau, which served as kind of a catchall for her personal papers, mementos, and jewelry, and slid the papers beneath her jewelry box. Satisfied they were safe, she turned away.

Zach seemed like a nice man, very protective and caring. No doubt Janey was fine, she told herself firmly. Even if she didn't have her daughter, she still had Eric. Wonderful, funny Eric. Her chin up, she went downstairs to see about rustling him up a meal.

Chapter Two

"This is going to sound strange but I need you to check on something for me," Zach told his family physician later that day. Briefly he explained about Laura Matthews's visit to the construction site.

Dr. Morris listened intently. He was as concerned as Zach had expected him to be, immediately understanding his dilemma. "You want me to verify yours and Janey's blood types?"

"You have all our blood types on file, don't you?"

Dr. Morris nodded. "Yes. It'll just take me a few minutes."

"I'll wait," Zach said. Dr. Morris left the room. Settling back in his chair, Zach's thoughts returned to Laura Matthews. She hadn't looked crazy, but she obviously was. She had to be, to come to him with a story like that out of the blue.

Not that he believed it for a second, of course. Still, it would help if he could prove that Janey was indeed his biological child.

Dr. Morris returned, looking grim. Trepidation stiffened the back of Zach's neck and made the blood pound in his temples. "What is it?" he asked gruffly.

Dr. Morris frowned, and for a second couldn't quite meet his eyes. "It's not good, Zach." He pointed at the thick manilla folder he held in his hands. "Our records show your wife, Maria, had type O blood. You've also got type O. Janey has type B blood." After a moment of silence, he offered, "I'm sorry. If our records are correct, and at this point I have no reason to think they're not, there's no way Janey could be your child."

There's no way Janey could be your child. There's no way Janey could be your child. The words kept ringing over and over in Zach's head as he drove home. He pulled into the driveway and cut the engine of his Wagoneer. Janey was his. He knew it in his heart. He would've known if she were not his child. He would've felt it. His wife would've felt it.

But they hadn't. And the fact remained, Janey's blood type was incompatible with his. *Incompatible.* He swore silently to himself, his heart aching. What a mess. If only Maria were here to help him handle it, to decide what to do. But she wasn't. He wondered despondently if he were up to handling it. He knew one thing, he wished Laura Matthews had never entered his life.

No sooner was he to the door than Janey had swung it open. In Guess jeans and an oversize New Kids On The Block T-shirt, she was the epitome of the eighth-grade student. Her naturally curly, dark brown, shoulder-length hair, with eyebrow-length bangs, was the same color, the same thick unruly consistency, as Laura Matthews's.

The thought was jarring. Zach pushed it away. That doesn't mean anything, he thought fiercely. Lots of people had hair like Laura's.

"Hi, Daddy!" As genial as usual, Janey stood on her tiptoes to give him a quick kiss before bombarding him with the usual round of after-school questions. "Can I go to the mall after school tomorrow if Chrissy's mom takes us?"

"Tomorrow?" Zach croaked, still feeling as if he was in a daze. He swore inwardly again. As confused as he was, he was lucky he hadn't had a wreck driving home.

"Yeah. After school." She tilted her head sideways and peered at him through dark brown eyes. Eyes that were the same shape and hue as Maria's. "Daddy, are you all right?"

Zach shook off his confused thoughts. He could ruminate

later. Right now, Janey must not know anything was wrong. It would kill her to learn about this.

"I'm okay, just tired. Long day." He forced a smile he couldn't begin to feel. "Mrs. Gagglione was back at her home site again, demanding more changes in the kitchen."

Janey grinned and lifted the lid on the Crockpot. "Bear up, Dad. Her house'll be done before you know it."

Zach groaned. That he was beginning to doubt.

"That's what you always tell me!" Janey defended her exuberant advice energetically.

Normalcy, Zach thought, that was the key to surviving this thing. "What's for dinner?"

Janey wrinkled her nose at the concoction the part-time housekeeper had left for them and quickly replaced the steam-misted lid. "Beef stew again."

Zach put his lunch pail on the counter. "I like beef stew."

"I know. I'm the one who hates all vegetables."

"Vegetables are good for you."

"Maybe. That doesn't mean I have to like them."

"Try harder because they're good for your complexion." He tweaked her nose.

"My complexion is fine," Janey said, checking her reflection in the mirrored side of the toaster.

Zach grinned. Maria's complexion had always been flawless, too. But then so was Laura Matthews's. *Stop it,* he thought.

Across the spacious kitchen, Janey was already peering into the refrigerator. "Great. Mrs. Yaeger left tossed salad and French bread, too." Janey turned to her dad. "Want me to heat up the oven and put the bread in?"

Zach nodded. Still feeling as if he was on automatic pilot, he went to the sink to wash up. After shaking the excess water from his hands, he dried them on a towel. "How was your day at school?"

Janey pirouetted around on her stocking-clad feet. Like all the girls at her school, she had on two pairs of cotton slouch socks, layered one over the other. Today's colors were teal blue and fire-engine red, colors that matched the wording on her T-shirt. "Okay. I had a little trouble on my Earth Science test. But then that's nothing new." Janey got out the salad bowl and dressing.

Zach knew from her tone there was much she wasn't saying. "How much trouble?"

"I don't know." Janey shrugged, avoiding his pinning gaze. "Low A, maybe a B plus. I'll find out by the end of the week."

Janey was a straight A student except when she let her incessant socializing get the better of her. And from time to time this past year he'd had to remind her to hit the books more and talk on the phone less. But tonight his heart wasn't in lecturing her.

Eager to get off the subject of the test she may or may not have aced, Janey continued hurriedly, "Did I tell you we were assigned to make a rock collection? We have to find twelve different kinds of rocks and identify them. The whole project is due at the end of this six weeks grading period."

Zach nodded, not really listening. Instead he was looking at Janey's pretty face and the lively light in her clear brown eyes. What would his life be like without her? he wondered. For as long as he could remember, coming home to her had been the highlight of his day. His whole life had centered around her since the day she'd been born.

And now Laura Matthews and Dr. Morris were trying to tell him a mistake might have been made? That Janey wasn't really his daughter? She was his, in every way that counted, blood tests be damned. No one was going to take her away from him. No one. And the sooner Laura Matthews and everyone else understood that, the better.

At 9:00 A.M. the house was silent except for the soothing sounds of Michael Bolton emanating from the portable stereo in Laura's kitchen. Eric had gone off to school for the day, still beaming about last night's win over Central High's arch rival. Laura had enjoyed the game, too, as much as she was able to anyway. After her meeting with Zach Anderson, it had been hard to really concentrate on anything except Melinda and Janey.

Zach Anderson had thought she was crazy. And maybe she was, bringing this up after so much time had elapsed. If only there was another way, she thought. If only this crazy business had never happened. She had tried shouldering the knowledge alone, and learned it was just too much for one person to bear. Maybe when Zach realized that he would be willing to talk to her again, she thought.

In the meantime, she had Eric. She glanced affectionately at the photographs she kept of him on the decorative shelves on either side of the wide kitchen window.

The doorbell rang. Wiping her hands on her white chef's apron, Laura turned off the stereo and went to answer it.

Zach Anderson was standing there, in a tweed sport coat and slacks. Although he was dressed more formally than he had been at the site, he still had a very rugged aura. A man's man, he was obviously a very hands-on type of guy, not someone who would ever be content to sit behind a desk. He was also physically very daunting. His shoulders and arms bore the corded strength of a man who never shied away from hard, physical work. And he was tall, maybe six-four or so to her five-eight.

He looked very unhappy to be there, but there was no raging disbelief on his face. Worry and fear perhaps, but no expectation of being conned. Her heart pounded erratically. She wondered what he had found out in the past forty-eight hours.

There was no doubt in her mind. She had known the first time she had seen him that he was Melinda's natural father. The resemblance was almost heartbreaking, it was so plain. He had the same genial smile, fair, freckled skin, thick eyelashes, and clear blue eyes. He had the same nose. And the same strong personality.

She was attracted to him; she felt almost bonded to him. Whether that was because he reminded her of Melinda, or because of their situation, or just man-woman chemistry, she didn't know. And she wasn't sure she wanted to know. She only knew that he had the capacity to hurt her as no one else ever had.

"May I come in?" he asked quietly. Evidently he had calmed down a lot since they had last talked.

Still, even a fool could have seen how much he was hurting, how betrayed he felt underneath the composed demeanor. Understanding what that felt like, it was all she could do not to reach out and touch him. But guessing how a gesture like that would be received, she remained motionless. He was right. They needed to talk. But that was all. She nodded her permission. "Sure. Come on in." Wasn't this what she had been hoping for, some sign of compliance on his part? Why then did she feel so self-conscious and edgy?

Holding himself aloof, he moved past her. She understood that. This had been tough on her, too, making her want to withdraw into herself, too. Shutting the door behind him, she gathered her wits and said as hospitably as possible, "We'll have to go back to the kitchen and talk while I work, though. I hope you don't mind."

He looked at her with a questioning lift of his brow. She explained, "I've got to deliver twelve fudge brownie pies to one of my customers by noon today."

Zach's clear blue eyes narrowed. "You do this for a living, then?" he asked with gentle curiosity. She thought she saw a measure of respect in his eyes. Maybe because they were both self-employed, the master of their own professional destinies.

Laura nodded her affirmation, remembering she had given him a card advertising her home-baked goods, which was how he'd known where to find her today. "Can I get you a cup of coffee?" she asked. She resumed her station at the long wooden trestle table that doubled as her professional work station. Under his watchful gaze, she began fluting the edges of a pie crust. It didn't matter, she told herself stalwartly, what he thought of her. But deep inside, she wanted him to like her, nonetheless.

This tension between them aside, he seemed like such a nice

man. Had they met any other way, under any other circumstances, they would have been fast friends, Laura thought. But they hadn't. She was sure he privately wished she had never come into his life.

Zach shook his head. "No, thanks." He stood restlessly on the other side of the table, looking as if he was as upset as she was. "I thought about what you said," he began frankly, in a tension-edged tone, thrusting both his hands into his trouser pockets. His glance lifted and met hers unassailably. "And even if it is true about there being a switch—which, you understand, I'm far from convinced it is—there's no reason for either of us to do anything about it now."

Laura studied him wordlessly, aware her heart was pounding, as much from his proximity to her as from her growing apprehension. This man was running scared, just the way she had when she first heard the news. Her heartbeat slowed a notch as she felt herself miraculously regaining some control of the untenable situation. If Zach had come this far in just two days, maybe they could work something out after all. "Janey's blood tests weren't right, either, were they?" she guessed quietly.

Zach said nothing, either way.

But then, he didn't have to, Laura thought. "I figured as much." She sighed heavily, knowing how devastated he must feel, and also that there was nothing she could do or say that would really ease his pain. He would have to suffer through it the same way she had. One day, one moment at a time. And right now, he looked as if he had all he could handle.

Because concentrating on her work seemed much safer than meeting his penetrating gaze, Laura bent to trim a spare strip of crust here and there. Mindful of her noon deadline and the necessity of meeting it, she kept working on the pies, pouring chocolate batter into the prepared crust, aware that he watched her closely all the while.

"You're handling this well," he noted after a moment, wariness lighting his clear blue eyes.

His eyes were so much like Melinda's that it almost hurt

her to look at them. Here was Melinda's natural father. A man of integrity and strength and a deep capacity for love. A man who would have loved Melinda deeply. Only now he'd never have the chance. She had to live with the guilt that she had denied Zach that opportunity of love.

"On the surface I am handling it," Laura admitted, briefly allowing her own emotion to show as their eyes met and held once again. "But inside, Zach, it's tearing me apart." And it was tearing him apart, too, even if he wouldn't yet admit it.

Turning back to her work, she scraped a bowl clean with a rubber spatula. Taking a deep breath, she continued to explain, "I've had three years to live with it—"

"Three years," he interrupted incredulously, staring at her in wonderment. "And you didn't do anything about it?"

She understood his skepticism. Her heart pounding again, she looked up into his handsome face, this time seeing only Zach, the man, the father and not the spitting image of her Melinda. "I couldn't," she said quietly, understanding his hurt and his desperation and his fear more than he could ever know. She swallowed hard, trying to get rid of the tightness in her throat that occurred whenever she talked about the trauma of the past. "At the time I found out about all this, my daughter was very ill."

Zach's expression changed to one of concern and compassion. Ironically that made it all the harder for Laura to go on.

"When she died last year, I was in no shape to do anything about it, nor if I'm perfectly honest, did I want to. It was enough just dealing with my grief and helping my son Eric deal with his."

He stared at her watchfully, the compassion he felt for her loss etched on his handsome face. "But now that you've recovered?" he asked curtly. "You want your daughter back, and if not her, then you want to claim someone else's?"

He was being deliberately cruel, as his fear rose. Yet she could forgive him that. She had reacted the exact same way when she had first found out about this.

He shook his head disparagingly. "It's as if now that she's gone you have nothing to lose."

And everything to gain, Laura thought, finishing what he had tactfully left unsaid. "I guess you're right," she said, knowing how she must look to him, and knowing that he understood her dilemma.

Silence fell between them, thick and unbridgeable. Zach looked as nonplussed as she felt. Needing to do something to keep her hands from shaking, Laura put another ration of unsweetened chocolate and butter into the microwave and began melting them.

Zach dragged a hand through his thatch of light brown hair, pushing the soft clean strands away from his forehead. "Look," he said, "I'm sorry about what you've gone through, the loss you've experienced. I really am. But this isn't going to bring your daughter back, Laura."

"I know that," Laura said, tears glistening in her eyes. A sob caught in her throat, choking her. "My God, don't you think I know that?" she cried.

He did, but he didn't care. Determined, he moved closer. "I want you to drop this," he said.

If only it were that simple, Laura thought with an anguished sigh. But ever since she had seen that photo of Janey as a newborn, she had yearned to get to know her, to see what she looked like now. And she knew it wasn't an ache that was likely to go away, no matter how much she wished for that to happen. "What if I can't?" she asked, troubled.

He turned away from her for a long moment, glancing at the trees in the backyard. His mind made up, he did an about-face. "You have a son, you said." He inclined his head at the photos of Eric next to the windowsill.

"Yes," Laura said, affection filling her as she thought of Eric.

"Then be happy you still have him," Zach advised.

She could see he sincerely wanted to help her, while still protecting his own. She was grateful for his kindness, but she couldn't accept his advice—and have any lingering peace of mind. Until this moment, she hadn't known what she wanted. She'd told herself it was just the knowledge that her daughter was safe. But she'd been fooling herself. She wanted more. Only how could she ask? "I don't want to hurt your daughter," Laura began carefully.

"Then keep your knowledge—or whatever you think you know—to yourself," Zach countered softly. "Because if even a suspicion of this were ever to get out, it would destroy my daughter. Do you hear me, Laura? It would destroy her."

"WHAT DID YOU EXPECT, honey, that Zach Anderson would welcome news like this?" Laura's father said, later the same morning as he helped her box up the pies one by one.

Feeling more dejected than ever, Laura sighed. "No. I don't know what I expected, Dad. I would've thought he'd at least be curious about Melinda." The same way she was curious about Janey. "But he didn't even ask to see a picture of her."

Her father was silent, thinking, she suspected, about both sides of the picture. His years as a Navy officer had given him a sense of fairness that was very deeply ingrained and unemotional. "He's protecting his own, the same way you protected Melinda all those years," her father said finally.

"I guess so."

"Laura, honey, you know I try not to meddle in your affairs, but after thinking about it long and hard I agree with Zach Anderson on this. As much as it's going to hurt us all, I think you should think of Janey and drop it."

Although she rarely ever cried, Laura felt herself tear up for the second time that day, out of frustration as much as pain. "Dad, I've tried," she explained. "But he has my natural child." *My flesh and blood.*

"You don't know that for sure," her father argued, taping each white cardboard pie box shut.

Don't I? Laura thought. "You didn't see the look on his face this morning, Dad. He's done some checking, too. I'd stake my life on it."

Abruptly her father stopped what he was doing and circled

the table to her side. He put his hands on her shoulders, as he had many times when she was a child. "Laura, even if it did happen as you think, thirteen years have passed. Janey is his child in every way that counts, just like Melinda was your child. You have to face the facts. Whatever happened, happened. It's a shame you ever had to find out about it. I'm sorry you did, truly I am, but it doesn't change anything. You can't go back. You can't do that to Zach, Janey, yourself, or Eric. You lost a daughter, but you still have a son. A son I happen to know loves you very much."

Guilt assailed her. Zach had said this news would destroy Janey, and he was probably right. It would also hurt Eric. She'd been selfish, thinking about what would make her feel better and give her peace of mind.

Before she'd gone to the hospital, she hadn't known what kind of family Janey was with. But she had met Zach now, found out what a decent and kind man he was, what a loving, fiercely protective father. Her gut instincts told her Janey was fine, every bit as fine as Eric.

Ashamed, she buried her face in her hands and struggled to find enough courage to do what she knew in her heart was right. Not for her but for the child. Janey's security was with Zach, the same way Melinda's had been with her. Laura swallowed hard. "You're right, Dad. I'm sorry. This—I guess it's the anniversary of Melinda's death—knowing that it's coming up soon." Pain and despair roughened her voice. "I guess it's made me a little bit crazy."

Her father took her into his arms and hugged her fiercely. "It's hurt us all, honey, but you're going to feel better. You'll see. Time *does* heal all wounds."

"You're right," she said again softly, feeling overcome with disappointment. Her voice hardened derisively, "I've got to be grateful for what I have and stop dwelling on the past. It won't change anything for me or for Zach." One way or another, she was going to have to find a way to put this behind her. For Janey's sake and for Eric's.

Chapter Three

"Mom, where's your calculator?" Eric asked later the same evening.

Laura was at the stove, frying chicken for dinner. Since making her decision to leave well enough alone, she felt as if she had a burden removed from her shoulders. Sending her son a lighthearted smile, she answered his question with one of her own. "Where's yours?"

"At school, I hope." Eric shrugged. "I thought I brought it home with me but it's not in my bag and I need it to do my trig."

"Mine should be on my desk, in the living room." Adjusting the heat on the stove, she turned back to the potatoes on the drain board.

"It's not," Eric said genially. "I already checked."

"You're sure?"

"Yep." Eric shoved both hands into the pockets of his jeans and leaned one shoulder against the frame.

Laura frowned, thinking. "Hmm. Well, maybe I left it upstairs in my room when I was doing the bills."

"Where in your room?" Eric asked over his shoulder, already striding for the front hall stairs.

"On top of the bureau," Laura called. "And Eric—"

"Yeah?" He turned.

"Take the clean laundry up with you."

A teasing grin dimpled his youthful face. "What laundry?"

She knew he had to have seen it when he came in from school. He just had an aversion to chores. "Those two baskets at the foot of the stairs," she said dryly. "Put yours in your room, mine in mine, and the stack of clean towels in the linen closet upstairs."

"Okay." He took off whistling.

She heard him take the stairs two at a time. The footsteps moved to her room. Then back to the top of the stairs. "Mom!" he shouted down with characteristic impatience. "It's not up here!"

Laura put the peeled potatoes on to cook. She hated this yelling back and forth. But as the alternative was running up and down stairs, she decided she could live with it. "Are you sure?" she shouted back, giving the sizzling chicken another turn. It was beginning to brown nicely.

"Positive!" Eric shouted back, sounding a tad frustrated.

"Well, it has to be somewhere," Laura muttered. "It's not down here, Eric," Laura called. "So it must be upstairs. I must've left it up there when I did the bills."

"But I already looked!"

"Well, look again," Laura advised as the phone jangled. She picked up the kitchen receiver. The call was from one of the restaurants where she sold desserts. Business had been slower than usual, the manager reported, so they were reducing tomorrow's order significantly. Disappointed but understanding, Laura made notes on the adjustment and thanked the manager for calling.

Wondering if Eric had found the calculator, she moved to the front stairs. "Eric?"

Laura waited. It wasn't like Eric not to answer her and their house was so small she knew he could hear her. "Eric?" she called again. Her heart rate accelerating, she took to the stairs. At the end of the hall a light shone from the open doorway of the master suite. Frowning, she wondered what was keeping him. And then, without warning, she knew. The papers from the hospital. She raced into the room.

Eric was standing next to the tall bureau, his face ashen.

Her missing calculator was on the bed, and the papers were in his hands. "I thought the calculator might have fallen into the drawer," Eric explained. He paused, his shock at what he'd inadvertently discovered, evident. "What are you doing with someone else's birth certificate and baby footprints, Mom?" he asked suspiciously. "What's going on?"

Frantically Laura searched her mind. "I—"

Eric waved the papers at her. "Is this why you were crying the other day?"

Her thoughts jumbled, Laura sat down on her bed. She could barely get her breath and she didn't have a clue what to say. She should have hidden the papers, she realized with the clarity of hindsight, but she'd never imagined that Eric would open her bureau drawer. If he hadn't been looking for her calculator, at her instruction, he never would have. With effort, she pulled herself together as much as she was able. "It's nothing," she lied finally in a feeble tone.

"Nothing?" Eric echoed with disbelief. He approached her with all the resolute finesse of a prosecuting attorney. "Mom, they don't give you a copy of someone else's birth records for nothing. Now what's going on? Do you know this person?"

"Not exactly—"

"What then?" he demanded tenaciously, not about to give up.

Laura swallowed, still unable to come up with something. Eric's face assumed a hurt, shut-out look similar to the one he had had sometimes when Melinda was ill. She'd known then that he sometimes felt left out, overlooked, and less important. So much of Laura's energy had gone to caring for Melinda. She had promised herself after Melinda died that that would never happen again. She'd devoted the past year to making sure Eric felt very loved. But this was something she couldn't include him in. He knew it and resented it.

"Fine. Don't tell me. I'll just find out for myself." Eric tossed the papers aside. "I'll call the hospital or maybe Gramps—"

No, Laura thought, panicked. I can't lose him, too! He couldn't hear about this from anyone else.

She jumped to her feet, knotting her hands in front of her to still their trembling. "Eric, stop! I'll—I'll tell you, okay? But after dinner."

Studying her, Eric demanded bluntly, "Why not now?"

"It's a long story. And our meal is almost ready."

"Does it have something to do with Melinda?"

"Yes."

He was silent, thinking.

"And in the meantime," Laura advised, desperately buying herself a little more time to figure out how to word what she had to say, "you can do your trig."

"All right," Eric conceded finally, "but we're going to talk right after dinner."

Not surprisingly, the meal lovingly prepared stuck like sawdust in Laura's throat. Eric shoveled the food down with the same lack of enthusiasm. Finished, he pushed his plate aside. Elbows on the table, he faced her and said simply, "Okay, Mom. We've eaten. What gives?"

Her heart in her throat, Laura began to explain in halting tones, starting at the beginning when she had first learned Melinda's blood type and following through to the present. Eric stared at her in confusion. For all his size, Laura thought miserably, he looked like a frightened little boy.

If only she hadn't gone to the hospital for confirmation. If only she hadn't gone to see Zach Anderson. No one would've ever known about this devastating switch but her and Melinda's oncologist. But it was too late to back down now. And they all had to deal with it the best they could. Even Eric.

"All this time you knew and you never said anything?" Eric said, looking at her aghast.

She could see how hurt he was, how confused. Guilt flooded her anew.

"I thought we shared everything, Mom!" He stood, pacing restlessly, his long legs eating up the space in the small cozy room. "I thought you didn't believe in keeping secrets from kids! Isn't that what you said the whole time Melinda was sick, that we could count on you to always tell us the truth?''

"And I have," Laura said thickly, her guilt increasing until it choked her. *Except for this one very hurtful thing.*

Eric stared at her as if he were seeing a stranger. "Like hell you have," he snarled, striding for the hall.

"Eric. Eric, where are you going?" Laura followed him to the back door.

"I don't know," he shouted back. "I just have to get out of here, away from all the lies. Away from you."

Seconds later, the engine of his battered red Mustang sprang to life. With tears in her eyes, Laura watched him drive away. *What have I done?* she asked herself, feeling as if she had suddenly lost everything. *What have I done?*

ACROSS TOWN, Zach was pulling on his gold Lady Tigers basketball shirt, with *Coach* written across the back. He was anxious to get to the game. There was nothing he loved more than coaching the gregarious and energetic group of girls that comprised his daughter's basketball team. He grabbed his sneakers, clipboard, and play chart, and started down the stairs.

Janey was sitting at the bottom lacing up her high tops. "Come on, Dad, we're going to be late," she urged impatiently.

There was no reason, save pregame adrenaline, for them both to be so cranked up. They had over an hour until their game started. "We've got plenty of time, Janey," Zach reminded, slowing his own pace with effort.

"Yeah," Janey concurred as she sprang to her feet with a bounce, "but I want to warm up."

Zach smiled. If anyone had told him years ago that his daughter would be a basketball nut, and that he'd coach a girls' team, he'd have said they were crazy. But from the time Janey was old enough to handle a ball, she had declared it her sport.

"Been working on your foul shots?" he asked, lacing an affectionate arm around her shoulders.

Janey shrugged and leaned into the fatherly embrace. "Some."

They started companionably out the door. Unable to resist, Zach prodded gently, "Gonna remember I'm the coach tonight and not your dad?" They'd had a few fights at the beginning of the season because she didn't want to take direction from him on the court.

"I promise I won't get too mad if you tell me what to do," Janey promised good-humoredly.

As soon as they were en route, Janey imparted casually, "You know what, Dad? I found out there's a place at the mall where you can get your ears pierced for only seven dollars. They numb them and everything, use some sort of surgical gun that just zaps the earrings right in there."

Zach slanted his daughter a glance. They had been through this conversation before. "You also have a permanent hole in your ear."

"Yes, I know, Dad," Janey retorted dryly. "That's kind of the point." She grinned. "It'd be a bummer to get your ears pierced every time you wanted to wear earrings."

Zach sighed his exasperation. "Janey, you're too young—"

"All the girls at my school wear them," she defended herself hotly.

Zach had seen some of the earrings worn by the middle-school kids. Appropriate for a twenty-year-old person, they looked ludicrous on the twelve to fourteen set. "We're not talking about them, we're talking about you."

Janey's lower lip slid out at the finality in his voice. "If you were a mother, instead of a father, you'd understand."

Her remark got him where it hurt. "If you still want your ears pierced when you're eighteen, okay," he conceded finally. "But not until then."

Janey clamped both her arms against her waist. "You're being unfair."

No, he wasn't. But he knew there was no way of persuading her of that. Briefly he wondered what Laura Matthews would think of his decision. He had a hunch the easygoing woman would vote for the earrings. But Janey was his child. And she was too young. If he gave in on this, she'd start hounding him on the eye-makeup issue again, and he wasn't about to let her become a raccoon-eyed clown, like some of her friends. He'd allowed her the use of a light lip gloss and a smidgen of blush and that was all he was going to allow until she was in high school.

Stifling his usual lecture on not trying to grow up too fast, he parked his car next to the middle-school gym. Once Janey began her warm-up drills with the team, she would forget her anger with him.

It had been enough, battling Laura Matthews the past few days. He didn't want to have to fight his daughter, too. Nor did he want to think about Laura, with her cloud of fluffy brown hair and vulnerable dark brown eyes. He knew she was hurting, too, but dammit, that wasn't his fault, either. What was done was done.

As he had expected, the game with the Lady Sharks was a tough one and took all of his powers of concentration. But the girls were terrific. They won in the last twenty seconds when one of Janey's teammates, his foreman Harry Cole's daughter Tabitha, made both her foul shots.

"Great game, wasn't it, Dad!" Janey said afterward, sitting down to pull on her sweats.

"Yes, it was," Zach agreed, glad Janey had forgotten all about the earrings for the moment. If only every battle were as easy to win.

THERE WAS NO REASON for him to feel so selfish, Zach told himself later that evening as he got up around 2:00 a.m. and wandered down to the kitchen for a glass of milk.

Still, he couldn't seem to live with his actions. If the situation had been reversed, he would have been much more aggressive than Laura in seeking out his natural child. Why he should care so much about what Laura felt, he didn't know. He only knew that it bothered him.

He didn't like the uncertainty of the possible baby swap

hanging over him, either. He didn't like the heaviness in his heart or the flash of fear he felt every time he saw someone with Laura's coloring or her hair coming his way.

He didn't like the fact that Janey looked so darn much like Laura, that they had the same fluffy dark hair, expressive dark brown eyes, and oval face. He didn't like the fact that Janey moved with an athletic grace that was similar to Laura's. Or that, according to the photos she had in her kitchen, her son played basketball, just like Janey.

So far, Laura hadn't met his daughter. If she did, he didn't know what would happen. Of course, Zach reassured himself firmly as he drained the last of his milk and put his glass in the sink, all this worrying on his part might be for naught. The resemblances could be coincidental. It could all be a mistake.

But why didn't Janey's blood type match his and Maria's? Why hadn't Melinda's matched Laura and Bob Matthews's?

He had been over and over his copy of the records she had given him the other day. He had even made a visit to talk to the hospital chief of staff. What he had learned had not pleased him.

That doctor felt, privately, a mistake had been made. And also that it was much too late for them to do anything about it now. Zach agreed with that. Apparently Laura did, too, for she had stopped calling him.

But what if she changed her mind sometime in the future? Could he live with this possibility hanging over his head indefinitely and have any kind of peace or happiness? He didn't think so.

And then there was Janey. Didn't she have a right to know that she might have a natural mother who was still alive? Granted, Laura didn't have any custodial rights to Janey after all this time. Nor would he ever permit her to have any. But Janey was almost an adult.

If it were him, whose parentage was in question, he knew he would want to know. He sensed Janey would want to know, too. More importantly still, he sensed she would resent him deeply if she ever found out he had kept the information from her.

So, he had to tell her. And he had to discover the truth. The only question was when. It couldn't be on a school day. That left the weekend. Figuring she'd be able to handle the news better after a good night's sleep, he waited until after they'd done the breakfast dishes Saturday morning. Knowing he had to get it over with, he stopped her before she could run off to listen to her stereo. "Janey, I need to talk to you."

Hearing the apprehension he had tried and failed to keep out of his voice, Janey turned her dark brown eyes to his, looking suddenly so much older than her years. In a canary-yellow sweatshirt and jeans, she looked like Laura.

"I know you've been worried, Daddy," she said softly, "that you haven't been sleeping. Is it something about work? About that awful lady who keeps changing her mind about her house?

"No," Zach answered with a heavy heart. Taking her hand, he led her into the living room and sat down with her on the navy-and-red-plaid sofa. "I only wish it were that simple." In contrast to this, his nonstop problems with Mrs. Gagglione were almost laughable.

Janey shot him a confused look. "Then what is it?"

Zach took a deep breath, wishing with everything he had that this wasn't necessary. Deciding the only way to tell her was straight out, he started with Laura's visit, his second talk with her, and concluded with his own talk with the hospital verifying the truth of everything that had been said. Throughout, Janey sat there in shocked silence, her face growing whiter and whiter. "Do *you* think you got the wrong baby at the hospital?" Janey asked finally in a trembling voice, looking as upset and confused as he felt.

Wrong child? "How could I have," Zach asked thickly, feeling as if his heart was breaking, too, as he took her into his arms, "when I got you?"

Janey pulled away from his enveloping hug. "But do you, Daddy?" she asked, tears running down her face. "Is my blood the wrong type? Does it match with yours or does it match with that lady's?''

Until definitive tests were run now, there was no way to be certain. And that's what Zach wanted, to be certain. Once they were, he was sure they could deal with whatever came. It was the not knowing that was tearing him, Laura, and now Janey apart. "I don't know, honey, that's why I want you and Laura Matthews to have a blood test. So we can find out." He covered both her icy hands with his own.

"And then what?" Janey asked, looking even more frightened.

"Then nothing," Zach said in a gruff protective tone, letting her know she had nothing to fear. He tightened his hands on hers. "Nothing will change. Either way you'll still be my child."

"Then why do we have to have the test?" Janey asked.

"Because we need to know the truth to have any peace of mind," Zach said wearily. "We need to straighten things out formally with Laura, get her to acknowledge legally that despite what may or may not have happened, you will always stay with me because that's where you belong."

Janey looked at him hopefully. "You think you can do that?" she asked, lower lip trembling.

Zach nodded. He had finally figured out a way to end the confusion. All he had to do now was get Laura to agree to it.

Janey stared at him a second longer, then started to cry. "Oh, Daddy, I'm so scared," she sobbed, throwing herself into his arms.

He held her close, wishing he could have spared her this pain.

"I don't want to leave you," Janey continued brokenly.

"Janey, that'll never happen," he soothed in a voice roughened with emotion, holding her tightly. "Not ever."

"But if I—if I'm not—" Janey protested.

He took her by the shoulders and forced her to look at him and listen to what he said. "Janey, you are my child. That's all there is to it." And that was final. To think that the years of loving and nurturing could be undone was ludicrous.

"But if—" Janey continued, almost hysterically.

He shook his head, cutting her off. He had parented Janey in every way that counted, made her his natural child in thought and deed and expectation, and that was all that mattered. "I'm not ever going to let anyone take you away from me," he continued firmly. "Not ever. No matter what the tests reveal. Is that understood?"

Janey nodded and threw herself back into his arms. The sobs she'd been withholding racked her body. Tears of frustration at his own helplessness in this situation flowing down his own cheeks, Zach held her until the storm passed.

MONDAY MORNING, he called Laura and arranged for her to meet him at his downtown office. She agreed readily when he told him it was about Janey. "I've been wanting to talk to you, too," she said after greeting him an hour later.

Zach motioned for her to take one of the comfortable chairs on the other side of his desk, unable to help but note how fresh and pretty she looked—how nervous.

"What about?" he asked quietly, his heart going out to her despite his earlier resolve to stay emotionally uninvolved with her.

"My son, Eric." Her skin lost some of its golden glow as she related unhappily, "He found out inadvertently about Janey and Melinda, the possibility of there being a switch." She sighed heavily and shook her head as if just remembering the incident caused her a great deal of pain and anguish. She pressed her lips together tightly. "He was very upset."

Zach knew how that was firsthand. "So was Janey, when I told her," he admitted.

Her head lifted in surprise at the soft empathy in his voice and her posture relaxed slightly as she studied him skeptically. Clearly she hadn't expected him to tell his daughter the truth. He didn't know whether to be amused or annoyed at the way she had underestimated him.

"Does that mean...?" Her eyes round, she gulped, and let her voice trail off, looking almost afraid to voice her hope.

Zach nodded slowly, still standing solidly behind his decision. "We all deserve to know the truth," he admitted frankly.

Laura bit her lip uncertainly and got up to pace the room, her heels digging soundlessly into the carpet.

As she moved back and forth, her slender legs moved fluidly beneath the full soft skirt of her peach-colored shirtdress. Zach became aware again, albeit unwillingly, of what a pretty figure she had, not too full, not too slim, but just right, with gently curving hips and breasts and a slender waist that was emphasized by a thick woven belt. Under any other circumstances he would have wanted to date her. But these weren't ordinary circumstances, he reminded himself sternly. Right now, judging from her doubtful look, he had an idea what she was thinking. She didn't seem to know if she could weather the strain and deal with her son's grief and confusion, too. But it looked to Zach as if they had no choice. "A simple blood test is all it would take," he continued gently, attempting to put her at ease. "Then we would know for sure."

Laura pivoted to face him, demanding he tell her the truth. "What made you change your mind?"

"Nights," Zach said simply, knowing they needed to be completely honest with each other. "I couldn't sleep. Couldn't stop thinking about it. Couldn't stop thinking about you and how you must feel." He shrugged eloquently. "I figured you probably felt the same."

She nodded slowly and her body relaxed. "You're right about that," she murmured.

Zach regarded her intently. "So you'll agree to have a blood test?" he asked, grateful she was being so calm and cooperative about this.

Laura nodded, looking as if a weight had just been lifted off her shoulders, too. "Yes," she said simply.

"Good." He nodded, satisfied they were doing the only practical thing they could do. Now came the hard part, the part she would resent. The part that would protect his daughter irrevocably. "There's only one condition," he continued in the same even tone.

Laura's head lifted at the forced geniality in his voice. Reading all he sought to hide in his eyes, she looked at him distrustfully, as if she should have known there would be a catch to this generous offer of his. "And what's that?" she asked.

He had never been one to shy away from playing hardball when necessary. "The catch is," he said slowly, "that you agree in writing to legally relinquish all parental rights and never to seek custody of Janey. If and only if you do that," he finished in a calm level voice, "will I ever agree to testing."

Chapter Four

Coming here had been a mistake, Laura thought as she stared at him, barely able to believe what she'd heard. "You can't really expect me to agree to that? If she is my natural child—" Laura sputtered.

"So far, Laura, that's a big if," he pointed out calmly, looking more indomitable than ever, seated behind the gleaming solid oak desk. It was the first time she had seen him in his downtown office. In a navy suit, he looked every bit the sophisticated executive. Like a man who was used to going after what he wanted and getting his own way. Trying to stand up against him would be like trying to stop a steamroller with one's bare hands. But she knew she had to try. She was strong, too. The years after Rob's death had taught her that.

She raised her chin in a posture of courage, letting him know this negotiation wasn't over yet. "I can't just give her up, Zach," she said earnestly. "Not if she is mine," she continued, looking into his clear blue eyes and finding them as mesmerizing and compelling as ever. "Not if we know that for certain."

"Why not?"

For him it was just so easy, Laura thought, on a new wave of despair. "Because you're asking too much of me. To not be sure and walk away from what might be my natural child is one thing. To know for certain and still leave her is something else entirely." He raised a dissenting brow, but she gave him no chance to interrupt her as she continued passionately, "How would that make Janey feel, Zach, knowing she'd been abandoned and rejected? How would she ever get over the loss? Especially at such a vulnerable age. An age where a young girl goes through so many changes."

Her last words seemed to hit a mark, because for a moment Zach did look conscience stricken. But the moment passed and he pushed away from the desk. Standing so close to her she could inhale the brisk woodsy scent of his after-shave, he said, his voice low and intense. "You not only can walk away from my daughter but you will, Laura. You have no choice. No matter what happened years ago, Janey's not yours to keep." He paused a moment, letting that sink in as he scrutinized her upturned face, then continued just as firmly, "Janey is my daughter in heart and soul and mind as surely as Melinda was yours. I thought we had settled that."

She still had Eric, Laura thought, and she loved him more than ever, but having a son wasn't the same as having a daughter. She knew in her heart that nothing would ever fill the emptiness Melinda's death had left.

Zach looked at her kindly, seeming to sense her inner turmoil. Instinctively he knew she had meant him and his daughter no harm. "I've just bargained with you as much as I ever intend to," he said gently. Her eyes met his and for a moment she was drawn in by the need for understanding and acceptance she saw in his eyes, a need that mirrored her own. But that faded as he set about getting his own way. "As far as I'm concerned," he continued with subdued implacability, "you can take it or leave it, but it's my only offer."

She knew from the determined look on his face he meant what he said. She had one chance to find out if Janey was her daughter. And only one. "All right," she said impulsively, giving in to his protectorate conditions.

Turning away from him, she walked to the window that overlooked downtown Fort Worth. Maybe he was right, maybe just knowing what the truth was would bring them both a modicum of peace of mind. Certainly, she thought, the confusion and doubt and guilt she felt couldn't get any worse. "You've got a deal," she conceded softly, turning back around to face him, "but I've got a condition of my own, too. I want the test done right away." Before he had a chance to change his mind, she thought. Before the not knowing drove her any crazier. "Like today."

"Today?" he repeated in open disbelief.

Laura nodded, all too aware of how the sunlight drifting in through the window brought out the gold in his light brown hair, and of how the blue in his suit brought out the blue of his eyes. He reminded her so much of Melinda. "Yes," she said.

He fell silent, gave her a measuring glance, and exhaled a lengthy sigh. Like her, he wasn't one to rail uselessly at the heavens about something that could not be changed. "Fine," he said abruptly, already moving to the phone on his desk. "I'll call my lawyer, get him to draw up the papers."

Soon, I'll know, Laura thought as she watched him flip through his Rolodex. The knowledge filled her with a certain buoyant joy. "I'll call my family doctor and get him to recommend a lab to do the blood tests."

That quickly, it was done.

HOURS LATER, Laura was not so sure she had done the right thing. She turned her attention to Eric, and told him what she had done. Not surprisingly, he was confused and torn about the situation, too, and they were still talking about the pros and cons of her actions early the next morning when her father came over to help her build a portable five-tiered rack for her pie-baking business.

"I know it sounds mean, but I really hope Janey isn't my sister," Eric confided as he sanded the edges of the wood his grandfather had cut. "Because if she is—" his young voice caught and it was a moment before he could go on "—it would mean that Melinda wasn't really my sister, you know? And, well, I find that sorta hard to believe. We were so alike...."

Laura's father nodded as he nailed two more finishing nails into the joints. "I've always thought it was who raised the child that counted, myself. The person who cares for the child is the parent, not the person who gave them life."

"Do you think I did the wrong thing, agreeing to the test?" Laura asked.

Her father shrugged and kept hammering.

She knew his silence meant he was trying to be tactful and not hurt her feelings. But she didn't want to be protected. Plus, if the two of them were to stay close, she and her father had to talk about this, even if it hurt. "Would you have done it?" Laura persisted, needing to know.

Her father straightened slowly. "Probably not," he admitted gently as he gave her an understanding glance, loving her enough to dare to be completely honest with her. "I think this is one of those things I'd just as soon not know. But that's me, Laura. That doesn't mean you shouldn't have agreed to do it. You're a grown woman now. You have to follow your heart. Only you know what's right for you and don't let anyone tell you any differently."

She smiled. "Thanks, Dad."

At the persistent blast of a horn in the driveway, Eric dropped what he was doing and ran toward an idling car. Three boys in Central High letter jackets were inside. Laura recognized them from the basketball team. They talked to Eric. Then he jogged back to Laura's side.

"Mom, can I go now? The guys are going out to lunch and then to see a movie."

"Don't you have a game tonight?"

"Yeah, but we don't have to be over at the high school until six. Please? I'll be home by four at the latest, I swear."

"You haven't finished your work," Laura's father reminded his grandson.

Laura looked back at the newly assembled shelf. All that was left was putting on the stainless-steel racks, where pies would cool, and the rollers on the bottom. There was really nothing she couldn't do herself. "I can help you finish, Dad."

To Eric, she said, "Go on then, but take your jacket with you. Do you have enough money? No? Okay, you can borrow ten from me. My purse is inside."

"Thanks, Mom. Gramps, see ya later." Eric trotted off, and a scant minute later, the boys were off with yet another blast of the deafening horn.

Her father went back to work. Though he said nothing to her, she could tell by the stiff set of his shoulders he thought she was spoiling her son unnecessarily. "Since basketball started, he rarely gets any free time," she explained.

"Well, I think you should've asked him to finish what he started here. He shouldn't have left until the job was done."

Stinging from her father's disapproval, Laura frowned. They rarely quarreled, so it hurt doubly to have him speaking to her this way now. Laura countered, "He has so little time to be a kid, Dad. He's been through so much. I want him to enjoy life while he can. He'll be burdened with adult responsibilities soon enough."

Her father nodded his understanding and said nothing more. Nevertheless, she couldn't shake the feeling that he still disapproved.

"You know something don't you, Daddy? You found out what the blood test said."

Zach looked at Janey, so eager and trusting, and felt his heart break. Why had he ever agreed to the tests? "Honey, come over here and sit down," Zach said, taking her hand and guiding her to the sofa.

She sat down beside him, her face losing some of its color, her voice none of its youthful bravado. "I'm your child, aren't I, Daddy? That's what the tests showed?"

This wasn't getting any easier. Zach swallowed the lump in his throat. "Honey, you know you will always be my child, no one else's. That's why Mrs. Matthews signed that document I showed you."

Janey's expression grew pinched. She looked younger than her thirteen years.

"It would appear," Zach said, "that there was some kind of switch made at birth."

"So I'm not your little girl, not really?" Janey asked, her chin quivering.

Anger burst through Zach, fierce, unquenchable. It was coupled with a feeling of stark unreality. This had to be a bad dream, a nightmare from which he would soon wake. Needing a hug at that moment as much as Janey did, he took her into his arms. "You are my little girl, in every way that counts," he reassured her firmly, silently damning the telltale thickness of his voice. For the umpteenth time since this whole mess had started, Janey began to sob against him as if her heart would break. "And you always will be."

"You swear?" Janey demanded desperately, looking up into his face. "You swear she can't take me away from you?"

"I swear," Zach said seriously, meaning it from the bottom of his heart. "And she signed some legal papers to that effect. No one is going to take you away from me. Not ever."

"Good," Janey sobbed, clinging to him like a lifeline to safety. "Because I don't ever want to leave."

That said, Janey began sobbing with new terror. Knowing words would be useless at that point, until she calmed down enough to be able to listen to him, Zach merely cradled her close, the same way he had when she was an infant. As he did so, he remembered flashes of other times. The day she had learned to walk, and how she had fallen flat on her face. Her first words, which had been not Dada or Mama but "Go bye-bye." The fiercely intent way she looked when she concentrated on something, and the peaceful, angelic expression she wore when she slept.

No one could take those memories away from him, no one could take her. Because of what had happened, Janey was his child, biology be damned. And more importantly, he had the legal contract that Laura had signed. The fact there was no precedent for such a contract, that his lawyer didn't know how well it would hold up in court if put to the test, didn't bother him. From what he knew of Laura, she was an honorable woman. She would keep her promise. They would be able to go on with their lives and forget this had ever happened. When he thought of Melinda, there was some sadness, of course, because she had not lived her life to the normal age. But his was a kind of detached emotion, the kind of emotion you felt for a stranger you heard about on the news. Nothing like what he felt for his real daughter, for Janey.

No, that kind of love was forged only by years and years of closeness, caring, shared experiences. It didn't matter what the blood tests said. Janey was his. Melinda belonged to Laura. And that was the way it would always be.

"I CAME as soon as I heard the news."

"Mother." Laura straightened in surprise. The paintbrush in her hand threatening to splay droplets of varnish everywhere, she hurriedly transferred it to the wooden surface on the cooling rack in front of her and resumed painting, trying hard to hide the unsteadiness of her hands.

To no avail. Her mother had always been able to see through Laura's every defense, and earlier, when she was a child, her every artifice. If Grace had been understanding, or even as fair and open-minded as Laura's father, it might have been okay. But Grace was from the old school of rigid behavior and rigid expectations. Nothing Laura had ever done was good enough to suit Grace. Laura had not been ladylike enough, studious enough, or responsible enough. With her father away at sea a good deal of the time during Laura's childhood, and no siblings to run interference and distract Grace's relentless criticisms, Laura and her mother had been locked in an almost continual battle. For as far back as Laura could remember, her mother had tried to control her, to orchestrate every detail of her life. And, for as far back as Laura could remember, Laura had resisted furiously.

During the years she had been married, she had managed to exert some independence, but there were still times like now, usually the most stressful, when her mother felt it was her duty to interfere.

"Well, what are you going to do now?" her mother demanded.

I don't have to fight with her, Laura told herself firmly. It is not too late for the two of us to be friends. "I don't know," Laura said honestly, meeting her mother's probing gaze. "I still feel numb," she admitted. And sad, and scared, she added mentally.

Her mother stepped closer. Laura could tell she had just been to the beauty shop. Her graying hair was sprayed and teased so firmly into place that not even a gale-force wind could have budged a single strand. "Laura, you can't let someone else raise your child."

Laura could feel her hackles rise. "Believe me, I don't want to—" she began, her guilt at relinquishing all claims to Janey assailing her like a ton of bricks. "But I have no choice."

"Laura, I can see you're upset," Grace said firmly, using the same stiff and grating no-nonsense tone Laura had always dreaded in her youth. "That is understandable. But once the shock wears off—and it will, I assure you—you will realize what you must do. Frankly I think more than enough time has been wasted already." Her forbidding glance narrowed. "You've got to get her back."

If only it were that simple. But people could not go around trying to rearrange everyone else's lives to suit themselves. If they did, they would be as miserable as she was when her mother started in on her. Laura argued back reasonably, "I can't think about my needs here, Mother." Or yours, she thought. "I can't take Janey from the only father she has ever known."

"Nonsense, Laura, she is your flesh and blood. Your natural child. Eric's sister—"

"I lost Janey years ago, while I was still in the hospital with her. As much as we might like to do so, we can't rewrite history." As she finished, a sadness and despair deeper than any she had ever known washed over her.

A stormy silence prevailed between them. Bossy and opinionated, her mother had ruled her with an iron hand all those years her father had been off at sea. And Laura had rebelled and rebelled. If her mother had put her in uncomfortably stiff and outdated starched crinolines before Sunday school, Laura had made sure they were smudged with dirt and ripped beyond repair before the morning was over. When her mother curled her hair in ringlets and sprayed it with as much itchy lacquer as her own, Laura had accidentally on purpose dipped those same stiff curls into the water fountain and destroyed the Pollyanna look. Sweets were forbidden in her house, because they weren't nutritional, so Laura had eschewed fruits and vegetables and sneaked junk food every chance she got. Ditto with trashy novels and popular movies and rock music and anything else the normal teen wanted to enjoy. Their battle of wills had continued right up until the time Laura had married, at eighteen. In fact, it was still continuing to this day.

Laura glanced at her watch. "Mom, I've really got to finish this. Eric's got a game this evening and I haven't even showered yet."

"This matter isn't settled yet, Laura. I've let you make plenty of mistakes in the past, but I will not stand idly by and watch you turn your back on my grandchild."

You have no choice, Laura thought wearily, not about to let her mother start interfering in Janey's life. This is my natural child we're talking about and my decision. She knew she couldn't disrupt her daughter's life, or make this ordeal any worse than it already was. And it had nothing to do with that written promise not to seek custody. It had to do with what was right and wrong for the child. Nonetheless, staring at her mother's set expression, Laura felt a nagging sense of loss and depression.

Chapter Five

"Sorry I'm late, boss," Harry said as he walked into Zach's construction site trailer, turning his hard hat over and over in his hands. "I had to go over to the school. It was about Tabitha." The brawny construction worker had been with Zach since he'd started his company, fifteen years prior. They were not just boss and employee, but friends. Tabitha was in the same school as Janey and played on Zach's basketball team.

"Nothing's wrong, I hope," Zach said.

"Actually," Harry said with weary resignation, slumping down in a seat, "there's a lot wrong. Tabitha is close to failing two of her classes. If she doesn't get with it and bring her grades up, she won't be promoted. She'll have to stay in middle school another year."

"How long has she been having problems?" Zach asked sympathetically. In the past, he knew Tabitha had always been a very good student and in fact had been inducted into the junior honor society the previous year, along with Janey.

"This is the first time she's ever had trouble academically. She's—I don't know—a different kid sometimes. Surly, disrespectful. We've tried talking to her but that doesn't do any good."

Come to think of it, she'd seemed moody to Zach, too, even though she usually was attentive and hardworking during both practice and games. "What did her teacher say?"

"Basically that she's not trying. The school counselor thinks it's just a phase."

"What do you think?"

Harry shrugged. "I don't know. We got Tabitha a tutor. Hopefully that'll help."

Despite his confident words, Harry still seemed worried. Searching for a way he could help, Zach said, "Look, if she needs to drop basketball, so she can pull her grades up, I'll understand."

"No," Harry said, vetoing that idea immediately. "That wouldn't accomplish anything. It isn't that she has too much to do and too little time. The problem is her attitude. Hopefully we'll get her back on track soon."

The door to the trailer opened and Zach's chief carpenter came in. He looked grimmer than Zach and Harry put together. "Sorry to break in, Zach," he said, "but Mrs. Gagglione is going crazy over what she says we've done to her kitchen. Better get in the house and calm her down."

"All right. I'll be there in a minute," Zach sighed.

"And uh Zach?"

"Yeah?"

"You had a phone call from Mrs. Yaeger while you were out to lunch. She said Janey came home from school today, that she's not feeling so hot."

Alarm bells sounded in Zach's head but his years as a parent had taught him not to panic. "Did she say what she thought was wrong?"

"No, only that you should call or go home and she'd stay with Janey until you got there."

"Right. Thanks."

His mind on his daughter, Zach went out to talk to Mrs. Gagglione who had decided the ceiling in the room was too low. Reining in his exasperation, Zach spent the next fifteen minutes explaining why the structure of the home could not be changed to accommodate a higher ceiling. Finished, he told Harry he was leaving for the day and he went home to check on Janey.

"She's upstairs in her bed," Mrs. Yaeger said. In the middle of fixing their dinner, she had been watching her favorite soap on television, but she turned off the set to talk to him.

Zach frowned. It wasn't like Janey to head for her bed, even when she was sick. During the day, she much preferred to lounge around on the living room sofa. "Does she have a fever?"

"No, she told the school nurse something about her time of the month and cramps," Mrs. Yaeger said, an embarrassed flush lighting her cheeks. She turned her eyes to the casserole she was preparing. "I offered her some aspirin but she said she just wanted to climb into bed. I'm sorry if you were worried but, the construction site being all men, I didn't want to leave a more specific message."

"I understand completely. And thanks for staying until I could get here." He paused, worried. The past two weeks, since they had found out the results of the blood tests, Janey hadn't been herself. She seemed depressed. Subdued. Tired all the time. Zach empathized because he felt that way, too. The knowledge they had expected to free them had only increased their doubts.

Slipping off his down vest, Zach headed for the stairs. Janey was in her room, curled up on her side. Ducking to avoid the pink-and-white canopy cover, he saw she wasn't asleep and sat down beside her.

She turned to face him. "I told Mrs. Yaeger not to call you."

"Honey, she had to. Besides, I want to know if you're not feeling well."

At his expression of sympathy, her expressive eyes, so like Laura's, flooded with tears. Embarrassed for him to see, she turned her face back into her pillow and ran her open palm over her eyes.

"Honey, if you're in that much pain, I'll call the doctor," Zach said worriedly, already starting to get up.

Janey shook her head disconsolately. "No, Daddy, it's not that, the cramps aren't that bad."

There was no hurt worse than seeing your own child suffer. His throat thick, he said, "Then what is it?"

Janey swallowed hard and kept her head averted. "I'm just sad," she said in a muffled voice, with her eyes still closed against his searching glance.

"About what?" Zach said softly.

Janey lifted her shoulders eloquently and then released them. "About everything, I guess."

"Want to talk about it?" he inquired gently.

Janey shook her head. "What good would it do?"

"Well, it won't change the facts, if that's what you mean," Zach said, aware there were very few times in his life when he had felt as utterly helpless as he did now. He patted her shoulder tenderly, offering her what comfort he could. "But it might help to make you feel less alone and depressed than you are right now," he pointed out practically.

"I'm okay, Daddy," Janey said, shooting him a look of rebuke that said very clearly she wished to be left alone. But that, Zach wasn't about to do.

"No, you're not okay, and if you won't talk to me then—" Maybe a psychologist, he thought. Taking in a slow breath, he tried again, "Honey, you have to talk to someone. You can't hold everything inside. Are you worried about Laura?"

"Curious, is more like it," Janey interjected finally.

"What do you mean?" Zach said, keeping the edge of panic out of his voice with a great deal of effort.

Janey shrugged. "I just can't stop thinking about her. About everything. Daddy, I have a brother out there. And a mother. And it's all so weird. I—I haven't told you this, but I keep dreaming about her. And—and him. I dream I'm living there with them and I miss you and then I'm back here and then I'm there again, only I never know where their house is exactly or what they look like. I only know that they're like me. A lot. Is that crazy or what?" She sniffed again.

It wasn't crazy. It was something that he should have anticipated perhaps. He had been having the same weird dreams. Only his were mostly of the nightmarish variety, about loss.

"What do you want to do?" he asked softly. He felt she had already figured it out, even if she hadn't yet verbalized her desire to herself or anyone else.

Janey pleated the fabric of her pink-and-white bedspread with her fingers. "I don't know. I guess—" she continued with difficulty, not quite meeting his eyes "—I want to meet them. Just—just one time. So I know what they look like. But then that's all," she said hurriedly.

"Do you think that would help?" he asked gently, wanting only to end her distress and protect her from hurt in whatever way he could.

After a moment, Janey nodded. "I think if I could just see them once," she said slowly, "that I'd stop having these face-less people in my dreams." She looked to him for aid. "I think I'd be able to sleep again."

"ARE YOU SURE this is a good idea? I feel funny about this," Eric said as he got out of the car.

Laura straightened her pink-and-white striped chambray skirt and pink blouse. She'd had her reservations, too, but the more she thought about it, the more she knew Zach was right. Their mutual misery wouldn't end until they confronted their fears face-to-face. And considering how hellish the past two weeks had been, that couldn't happen soon enough. She turned to her son reassuringly. "It's only one meeting, honey. And a very brief one at that. Just enough to satisfy Janey's curiosity about us."

Eric's lower lip shot out glumly. "I don't see why she has to know anything," he muttered under his breath.

Determined not to have this get-together end in a free-for-all, Laura stopped halfway up the walk to Zach's house, and admonished her son firmly. "Eric, I know this is difficult for you. It is for me, too. But I expect you to consider everyone else's feelings today and cooperate to the fullest. It's not going to take long anyway. Zach felt half an hour would be plenty for Janey."

At the mention of his natural sister, Eric's expression became even more apprehensive. She knew how he felt. This was her first meeting with her natural child. She was nervous, too. She wanted it to go well, and was afraid it wouldn't.

But Zach was right. It needed to be done. Otherwise none of them would have any peace of mind. Initially, of course, after the tests had been finished, their results known, she had been so stunned and bewildered she hadn't known what to do. Now her shock was fading. She felt, as Janey did, the need to somehow tie this all up, and then move on. She wanted to get back to a normal life. She knew Eric and Zach and Janey did, too. And this first and last meeting, all in one, was the only way to accomplish that.

Satisfied she had Eric's cooperation, Laura took a deep breath and continued up the walk. Zach opened the door before she had a chance to ring the bell. "Hi. Come on in," Zach greeted them. He glanced at her son, his expression both kind and thoughtful. "I suppose this is Eric?" he asked as he extended his hand.

For a moment, Laura thought her son would not take Zach's hand. Finally he did. Unfortunately for all their mutual comfort, his expression was as reluctant when they finished shaking hands as when they started.

Maybe I'm asking too much of him, she thought worriedly. After all, he is only sixteen. This is a lot for me to handle. But then, what choice did they have? Excluding Eric from this would not make him feel any better. She suspected it would only make him feel worse. And Janey needed to meet both of them.

Laura looked over to see an adolescent girl sitting on the sofa and for a brief second her heart seemed to stop. Transfixed, Laura stared at the athletic-looking, dark-haired preteen with the oval face and dark brown eyes. She's beautiful, Laura thought. And so much like me, with her thick, abundant, naturally curly hair.

She was wearing an aqua and light gray slacks and sweater outfit, and looked, not surprisingly, just as shy as Eric. Something in Laura softened as she realized her two children had their shyness in common.

"Laura, I'd like you to meet my daughter, Janey," Zach said.

To Laura's surprise, the raw, overwhelming emotion she had expected—the burst of instinctive motherly love—didn't come. Despite the child's healthy beauty and the physical resemblance between them, Laura felt no soulful kinship with this child whom she had given birth to. Nor, it was very clear, did Janey feel any innate kinship toward Laura. Janey looked as apprehensive as Eric did.

His expression one of compassion and understanding, Zach looked from her to the children, then said pleasantly, "Why don't we all sit down?"

Unfortunately, despite Zach's graciousness as a host, the getting to know one another was as stiff and unnatural as it was possible to be. Before even five minutes had gone by, Janey was up and out of her chair, bounding restlessly toward the door. "I'm going to go out and shoot baskets, okay, Daddy?"

The way she moved, she didn't expect to be denied. And, Laura suspected as Zach looked at Janey, his expression one of concern, she wasn't going to be. Seeing she'd had all the tension she could bear, he said softly, "Sure," tolerating an action, that under normal circumstances, would have been very rude. And probably, Laura thought, gauging Zach's expectations of his child, unacceptable.

But the situation they were in broke all the rules, and hence, obliterated all normal expectations of accepted social conduct.

Eric looked at Laura, then at Janey disappearing out the door. "I think I'll go, too," he said uncertainly. "If it's okay. Mom?"

Like Zach, she nodded her approval.

Offering her his broad back, Zach crossed over to the bay window overlooking the front yard. From outside, could be heard the rhythmic thumps of bouncing basketballs. "Funny, isn't it, that they both love basketball," he murmured in a low voice laced with surprise as he watched them play.

Laura got up to join him at the window. "Maybe there's more to biology than we know."

"Maybe," he agreed softly, his eyes still on the kids.

That being the case, Laura was amazed at the calm, practical way he had been able to handle all of this. And yet there was something very wrong, she knew. Because not once had he ever appeared to want to know anything about his natural child, the child she had reared and lost. She wondered why.

Giving in to her impulse, she asked inquisitively after a moment, "Aren't you ever even curious about Melinda? What she was like or—"

"No."

His denial was kind but quick, almost too quick to be believed. Studying him, she felt he was holding more inside than any of them. And that this would inevitably hurt him. Softly, wanting to help, she pointed out, "But she was your natural child, just as Janey is mine."

He continued looking out the window, his hands in his pockets, his posture relaxed. Turning to her, he assessed her for a long moment. "I'm not going to dwell on what was or what might have been," he said pragmatically, imprisoning her with his gaze. "We all need to just forget about it and go forward."

Laura sighed. How simple that all sounded, how easy. Only for her, she knew it wasn't quite that easy. And she suspected it wasn't quite that easy for him, either, despite his surprisingly realistic attitude. Wanting to forget something and being able to forget something were two different things. How well she knew that. "And if we can't?" she queried softly.

Zach shrugged expressively. "We don't have a choice. Trust me on this, Laura," he advised candidly, able to see she wasn't persuaded. "The sooner we put this behind us and forget about it, the sooner we'll all be able to go on with our lives."

Laura looked at the kids. It seemed safer than looking up

into Zach's handsome face. Though of differing minds, they were getting along better with every passing moment. And because of that she couldn't help but be aware of him on every level. As a father, he was kind, compassionate, devoted. As a man, he was fair and levelheaded. As a lover, she sensed he would be tender and giving, and yet demanding, too. Patient and insatiable. She pushed the unwelcome thoughts away, reminding herself that they were here today to tie up this chapter of their lives, somehow resolve their conflicts, and move on. She commented, "You said on the phone that Janey's been upset the past few weeks."

Zach nodded, his expression worried as the talk turned again to Janey. "Yes, but she was a lot better once we arranged this meeting. She seemed—" he shrugged expressively as he searched for words "—at peace with everything. I think today will help her to put this behind us."

Behind them.

Was that what she wanted, Laura wondered, her heart aching for no reason she could name, for this to be over? Feeling suddenly as restless as the two kids had been, Laura moved away from Zach so they were no longer standing shoulder to shoulder. She concentrated once more on the activity outside. She watched, pleasantly surprised to see that Janey and Eric were no longer as wary of each other as they had been at the outset. They were talking to each other occasionally, Eric remarking on an easier way to shoot lay-ups, then demonstrating, Janey clumsily attempting to imitate his more experienced aim.

How alike they looked, playing together in the sunlight. How tentatively inquisitive about each other, Laura thought with a wave of optimistic satisfaction. As if now that the first barrier had been broken down the two of them really could be friends. Perhaps even brother and sister one day. Knowing how much Eric had missed having a sibling, and that Janey had never had one, she couldn't help but wish that could happen.

"I have to be honest with you, Zach," she said, sighing

softly as she turned back to him, "This hasn't been as cut-and-dried as I would have wished. Since we found out the truth, I still think about her a lot." And she hungered to know more.

He let out a long uneven breath. "Then stop," he advised, his pointed words softened by the kindness in his eyes, "because no good can come of dwelling on this."

She viewed him with barely concealed exasperation, understanding where he was coming from but unable to agree with his remedy. He really expected this trauma to be over, just because he wanted it to be. He expected them to go on as if nothing had ever happened. That promise seemed as silly as it was idealistic to her. But it was also a typically male response. In her experience, men just simply refused to think about what they couldn't easily change, as if by steadfastly ignoring a problem, it would go away. Her husband had been like that. For the most part, her father still was, although his age had mellowed him somewhat and made him more prone to take emotional risks.

Again she tried, as gently as possible, to get through to Zach and offer him what he'd already offered her, the chance to know his natural child, however cursorily. "If you'd like to know more about Melinda—" she began gently, only to be cut off by the deliberate shake of his head.

"No," he refused her wearily. "I don't see any point in going back. I want this to be over. At least as much as it can be."

And for him that meant not dwelling on his loss. After a moment she carefully supposed that she could understand that. Why pine after someone you could never know? Laura suddenly wished she had come to know Zach some other way, without all this tension between them. She had the feeling they could have been friends. Maybe more than friends.

Glancing at her watch, she saw almost an hour had elapsed. And he had mentioned something earlier, when he had called her to arrange the meeting, about having a basketball practice to coach later on. It was time for her to go, past time. "I better get Eric," she said.

He looked briefly as reluctant for her to leave as she was to go but recovered promptly and moved chivalrously toward the door, offering gently, "I'll walk you out."

Together, they moved outside. "Eric. It's time," she said as she walked down the steps, her full skirt swirling around her legs.

"Okay." Slightly out of breath, he handed the ball to Janey, and then without a word, turned and started for the car.

This is the last time I'll ever see her, Laura thought, and this time she felt the pain of that. The loss. By a twist of fate, she'd been blessed with not one but two daughters, and now she'd lost them both—one to death, one to Zach. There were times, like now, when she felt life was terribly unfair.

Janey backed up, two basketballs cradled to her chest. Unlike Eric, who still looked cool and composed, her oval face was flushed with the heat of exertion. Her dark brown hair was mussed and frizzy, falling in a tumble to her shoulder. Yet facing Laura, her dark brown eyes were wary. "Goodbye, Janey," Laura said. "I enjoyed meeting you."

Janey remained silent.

Zach didn't press her to respond, although Laura felt in any other circumstance he would not have countenanced deliberate rudeness.

"Goodbye, Laura, Eric," Zach said.

It was over that quickly.

"TEN EXTRA PIES?" Laura repeated happily. "Four pecan, two chocolate fudge, three apple, and one blueberry. Sure, I can have them at the restaurant by five." Laura glanced at the clock on the kitchen wall.

It wasn't going to be easy, of course—the three apple pies in particular would take at least an hour and a half to assemble—but business had been slow since the holidays and she needed to increase her income in whatever way she could. Besides, maybe the extra activity would take her mind off

Janey and Zach. Heaven knew she hadn't managed to think about much else while she worked since meeting the pretty teenage girl several weeks prior.

By two-thirty, she was whistling and elbow deep in dishwasher suds. The phone rang. Dripping suds, she grabbed a towel and reached for it.

"Mrs. Matthews? This is Eric's basketball coach, over at Central. I wondered how he's doing."

"Doing?" Laura repeated dumbly.

"Yeah. I know he's sick today and—"

"He is?" she interrupted quizzically.

There was a very brief silence. "You're telling me he isn't?"

Eric had skipped school? Deliberately, Laura pushed away a flash of anger. She had never been one to jump to conclusions before and she wasn't going to start now. Maybe this was all a crazy mistake.

Keeping her voice calm, she reported, "Eric left for school this morning at the normal time." She glanced out the back door at the driveway, and confirmed for herself his car was gone. "I haven't seen nor heard from him since." Oh, no, she thought as the next thought occurred. Please, don't let him have been in an accident. But if he had been, she surely would have been notified.

"Well, he hasn't shown up here at school."

"I imagine if he'd had a flat tire he would've called," Laura said slowly. She frowned, perplexed. Heat flooded her face as the silent seconds ticked by. Embarrassed not to know where her child was, but still wanting to give Eric the benefit of a doubt, she continued, "I can't imagine what could have happened. He's always so dependable."

"Well, that's something else we need to talk about." The coach paused, then went on reluctantly as if picking his way through a mine field, "Mrs. Matthews, is everything okay at home? I only ask because Eric hasn't seemed to be quite with us the past few weeks, during practice or games. In the past he's always been one of our strongest players."

"I know," Laura said. On that score, she was worried, too. In the last two games he had played well below his ability, missing almost every basket he attempted. Afterward, disappointed in his own performance, he had been moody and remote. She had attributed his low mood to his "off games," not considering it might be the other way around.

"Is there anything I can do to help? Anything you'd like me to talk to him about, man-to-man?" the coach persisted. "Any girls in the picture I don't know about? Somebody in the family sick? Anything?"

"No, sorry," Laura confessed, feeling even more mortified and confused. "I don't know any more than you do at the moment."

"Well, please let me know if there's anything I can do. And as for Eric's absence, for his sake, I hope there's a good excuse."

"I'm sure there is," Laura said with more assurance than she felt, "and I promise I'll let you know as soon as I find out what it is."

Feeling further dismayed and dejected, she hung up the phone. This had never happened before. The coach was right. Eric had been acting strangely lately. Distracted, surly, upset. And when he wasn't grumpy, he was too quiet. And he had been that way ever since they'd visited the Andersons.

Well, there was only one way to get to the bottom of this, and that was to talk to him face-to-face. While she waited for the pies to finish baking, she started calling the homes of his friends. To her dismay, no one had seen nor heard from Eric all day. Nor had he contacted her parents.

By the time she was ready to deliver the pies, she was frantic with worry. By five, she had completed her business and began looking for him in earnest.

She found his car in front of a popular video game arcade. Eric was inside, hunched over one of the brightly lit machines. As she looked him over and saw he was physically intact, she didn't know whether to burst into tears or grab him by the edges of his letter jacket and shake him. She did know she'd never been so scared or angry in her life. Marching up to him, she grabbed his arm. "I want to talk to you, young man."

He straightened laconically, for a second looking like a defiant stranger. "Okay, shoot."

"At home," she specified clearly.

His face changed. His jaw hardened and his voice was curt, "Fine. I'll follow you."

"No, Eric, you'll ride with me."

He opened his mouth as if about to protest, took a second harder look at her expression, and saw the extent of her displeasure, then bit down on whatever he'd been about to say.

Unable to control her flaring temper any longer, Laura started in on him the second they marched in the door. "You skipped school today, didn't you?"

He shrugged indifferently. "Yeah, so?"

"So?" She spoke heavily, as if verbally underlining every word. "You could get expelled for that, at the very least kicked off the team."

Eric shrugged disconsolately, his expression dark and rebellious. "Yeah, well, my playing hasn't been worth a damn lately anyway. The coach told me so at practice yesterday, so I didn't think it'd be any great loss to anyone if I wasn't there, know what I mean?"

Her face softened sympathetically, despite her resolve to be every bit as tough on him as his father would have been. When she'd been his age, she had needed understanding, not scolding. But that was all her mother had given her and the resulting distance between them had only made her behave all the more foolishly. Feeling much calmer, she asked gently, "Is that why you skipped?"

Near tears, Eric shrugged in a way that let her know it was much, much more.

Bewildered by the raw emotion she saw on his face, disappointed by the unexpectedly unconscionable way he'd behaved, angry at her own unusual obliviousness to his pain, she fought back a wave of frustrated tears. Tears that had been borne as much from hours of worry as anything else. Moving closer, she took him tenderly by the shoulders, letting him know by her touch that she cared very much what happened to him. "Eric, what is going on with you? You've got to talk to me." He had never behaved this way before, not even after the death of his father.

Silence.

"Is it a girl?"

He gave a sardonic laugh and shook his head in mute aggravation, pulling away from her as if he could no longer bear her maternal touch. "Not the way you mean, no."

"Then what is it?"

He turned back, surly and defiant again without warning. "Can't you guess?" His young face was gilded with challenge.

"No." Laura shouted. "Dammit," she said, massaging her aching temples. "Eric, stop playing games. Stop expecting me to be able to read your mind and just talk to me. Tell me what it is that's eating you alive and prompting you to act this way."

"All right, you want to hear it? You'll hear it." Eric announced, flinging off his jacket and sprawling on the couch. "I'm ticked off at you, Mom."

"Me? Why?" Barely able to get out the single word sentences, she stared at him in shock. "What'd I do?"

"It's more what you didn't do." At her bewildered glance, he said plainly, "It's Janey. I don't get how you can just walk away from her that way. I mean, what if it was me, Mom?" he said, his voice breaking. "What if I had ended up in the wrong home? Would you not have cared? Would you have just walked away? Darn it, you have a responsibility to at least get to know her, especially since she doesn't have a mother. And I have a right to get to know my sister!" Finished, he clamped both arms over his chest and glared at her.

Tears streamed down Laura's face. She felt stunned and hurt. "Eric, listen to me." She held out her hands beseechingly and sat down beside him. "I do care about Janey—"

"Yeah, well, you have a funny way of showing it," he said, his eyes filling with pain and anger.

Laura struggled with her grief, her guilt, and her loss. "But she's not mine, not anymore."

Eric's jaw jutted out. He turned his face away from her and stared at the wall. "Yeah, right."

His hurt cut her to the quick. "What do you want me to do?" she asked in a broken, trembling voice.

He turned back to her, his cheeks flushed with temper. "What do you think?"

Her heart in her throat, Laura forced the words out of numb lips, "Eric, I can't—"

He got up abruptly and strode from the room, his face a mask of impotent rage and frustration. "I don't want to hear anymore. Okay?" He was running by the time he reached the hall stairs. The door to his room slammed behind him, and then echoed in the still, lonely house.

LAURA WAS AWAKE all night. By dawn she knew what she had to do. Go see Zach. She found him at the construction site. In a rough chambray shirt and cords, he had been going over some blueprints while he drank what was probably his first cup of coffee. His hair was clean and soft, brushed back away from his face in short, damp waves, his face freshly shaven. Looking at him, she felt another pang of physical awareness, then pushed it away. No matter how attractive he was, she couldn't get involved with him.

Watching her smile at him uncertainly, his bright-eyed look of welcome faded. He straightened slowly and put down the marking pencil in his hand.

"Hi," she said.

"Hi. I didn't expect to hear from you again."

Didn't want to hear from her was what he meant, she thought, sitting down in one of the upholstered chairs in front of his desk without waiting for an invitation. "I know, but some things have changed." Briefly she told him about her conversation with Eric, keeping her voice as unemotional as possible.

Zach's face softened compassionately while she talked about Eric's unhappiness. He got up to pour her a cup of coffee. "I'm sorry you're having trouble with your son," he said carefully, handing her a cup and a small tray that contained packets of sugar and cream, and little plastic stirrers.

Slowly Laura put her cup down on the edge of his desk. She faced him deliberately, her eyes direct. "I was wrong to think we could just let this go, Zach."

It took a moment for her words to sink in and when they did, he was anything but pleased. "We agreed on one visit, to satisfy everyone's mutual curiosity, and we did that."

"I know," Laura replied, "and it was a success."

"Because we knew going in what the limits were."

"We thought we did," Laura corrected. If he were unnerved by the rather intimate setting of the trailer, he wasn't showing signs of being bothered. "Unfortunately," she continued matter-of-factly, "everything we've tried to predict in this situation has turned out to be wrong. And maybe that should tell us something, Zach. Like we need to forget long-range plans and just play it by ear. Take it one day, one moment at a time." Like she had when Melinda was sick and in other traumatic or difficult times.

He shook his head grimly. "I can't do that. I have to think where all this will lead."

"And I have to think about right now, this moment, about how my son is feeling, and how Janey may be feeling."

He lifted a powerful-looking arm and rubbed at the tension in the back of his neck. "She hasn't said anything to me about wanting any more visits with you."

Laura watched as he dropped that same arm back to the arm of his chair, and tried not to think about how it might feel wrapped around her waist. Why not face it, she thought honestly, she'd never been attracted to any man the way she was attracted to Zach. But she'd never been around anyone as inherently sexy and self-assured as he was, either. There was just something about him, something physical and sensual, that she found alluring. Still, she knew she would never let herself act on those feelings.

Forcing her mind back to the subject at hand, Laura persisted, "You're telling me Janey's completely back to normal?"

Zach was quiet. He took a sip of his coffee and looked at her reflectively over the rim of his cup. "It's hard to get back to normal after all we've been through, Laura. And that doesn't mean we have to jump into something that is only going to complicate the situation more."

"All I know," Laura said tiredly, swallowing the faint catch in her throat, "is that I don't want Janey to feel like Eric does, like I've abandoned her, like I don't care."

The words *World's Best Dad* were printed on his mug. Zach traced them with gentle circular motions. "I don't, either, Laura. I'm just not sure your solution is the right one."

"Then what should we do?" she asked.

He shrugged expressively. "I don't know."

She reached for her coffee. Aware he was watching her every move, she took a sip. "What about Janey? Don't you think she has a right to know her brother, don't you think that she might benefit from some contact with a sibling?"

Zach remained silent.

He's remembering how well the two of them played together, Laura thought. She realized with satisfaction that the way the kids had interacted had touched him. Therefore, he wasn't as immune to feelings as he would like her to think.

Laura leaned forward earnestly in her chair, balancing her mug on her knee. "Talking to Eric, I realized he was right. Suppose, for instance, that you or I had discovered somewhere along the way that we had another brother or sister. Wouldn't you want to get to know him or her? At least find out if you had anything in common? I know I would."

Zach stiffened and set his mug aside. "What you or I would or wouldn't want has nothing to do with Janey's situation."

His eyes lifted to hers and he made a plea straight from the heart. "She's vulnerable, Laura."

So were they all, she thought. Zach included. Not dissuaded in the least, she replied softly, "All the more reason she needs a protective older brother in her life." She paused, appealing to his practical side. "I'm not trying to be her mother, Zach, or separate the two of you. I would never do that. But I do think that we should try to become friends. Because if we don't and Janey one day feels like Eric does now, you're really heading for trouble."

He was silent, thinking. Head lifting, he gave her a neutral look. "If I say no?"

She looked into the depths of his clear blue eyes and feeling him to be a very sympathetic, compassionate individual, predicted gently, "I don't think you will once you think about it, Zach. All I ask is that we have some joint family outings. You and Janey, Eric and me. All I want is for Janey to know that even though fate has thrown us all a curve, that I still care about what happens to her and so does Eric, and so do you. And maybe if their insecurity about all this is addressed, they'll be reassured. Surely there's enough love between us to go around," she finished. "Surely we're adult enough to work this out in a way that will satisfy everyone."

Her reasonableness was getting to him. She could see it in the faint relaxing of his jaw. Zach sighed and ran a hand through his hair, the light brown strands looking like shimmering threads of silk against his work-roughened hands. "All right," he said finally, conceding with obvious reluctance. "But if this request of yours upsets Janey in any way—"

"We'll pull back," Laura promised, satisfied she had accomplished what she had set out to do. Her heart was light with anticipation and relief. The excitement she felt was normal, considering that she was going to spend some time with her long lost daughter. It had nothing to do with the fact Zach would be there, too, she assured herself, nothing at all.

Chapter Six

"Janey, come on," Zach said, rapping on his daughter's closed bedroom door, "we're going to be late!"

"I can't help it. I haven't got anything to wear," Janey said, joining him in the hall.

He stared at her robe in mute stupefaction. "I thought you were already dressed." This wasn't like her. Usually she just put on her Mavericks sweatshirt and they were off.

Telltale spots of color appeared in her face. "I was."

"And?" he prompted gently when nothing else was forthcoming.

She shrugged. "That red sweatshirt didn't look right."

It always looked perfect, Zach thought. And so did she. But she didn't want to hear that from him, not tonight. Tonight she needed a woman's reassurance. She needed her mother. Only that was impossible. He regretted the loss of Maria with all of his heart and soul.

Maybe if she had been here, Janey wouldn't have needed any contact with the Matthewses at all. Maybe she wouldn't have wanted any, he thought with guilt and resentment.

Oblivious to his disparaging thoughts, Janey disappeared into her room again, still explaining why the red sweatshirt wouldn't do at all.

Zach hesitated, then offered a way out. "Honey, look, if you'd rather not go tonight, I understand. I don't really want to go, either."

She whirled to face him. "Dad, you promised we'd be there!" Accusation mixed with the panic on her face.

"This inability to get dressed has nothing to do with second thoughts?" he queried firmly.

Janey rolled her eyes in full-blown teenage despair. "Dad, get real. I like Eric. I like him a lot. I just need to go shopping, that's all. I'll be ready in five minutes. I swear."

Zach let out his breath slowly, noticing she'd said nothing about Laura Matthews, only her newfound brother. Somehow that was less threatening to him. "Better shake a leg, then, because I told the Matthewses we'd meet them at the entrance to Reunion Arena at six-thirty." As sticky as things were, he didn't want the determined Laura Matthews to think they'd deliberately been stood up and then go off half-cocked and do something even more damaging than request time with her biological daughter.

Fortunately, Janey was as good as her word, and a few minutes later they were out the door. "Why couldn't we have gone with them to the game?" Janey asked once they were on their way.

"I thought it'd be easier just to meet there," Zach replied. It would be less awkward. And in case the evening was a total bomb, as he half feared it would be, they wouldn't have to ride home together in the same car.

"Oh." Janey fell silent.

Zach cast her a worried glance. "You don't have to get to know the Matthews family, you know. I, for one, would understand if you didn't."

"I want to get to know Eric," Janey said, her chin taking on that determined tilt that said he couldn't budge her with a crane. "He seems neat. We look a lot alike, you know?"

So much so, Zach thought, that it tore him apart. Wordlessly, he nodded.

"It's like discovering I had a twin or something I never knew about. It's weird, but kind of nice, too."

But so far, Zach objected mentally, very little had happened.

"Don't look so worried, Dad," Janey reassured teasingly after a moment. "I'm a big girl now. I can handle this."

Zach hoped so. He never would've agreed to it at all, if Janey hadn't been having trouble sleeping, if she hadn't had so many questions, and if she hadn't reacted positively to the suggestion the two families get to know one another as friends.

Then he'd known she wanted to get to know Eric, too, but had been afraid to voice the emotion. Probably for fear of hurting him. And her request had hurt and threatened him in some way. Intellectually, of course, he knew it was wrong of him to be so petty. Laura was right. There was enough love to go around. Or at least there should be. But in his heart, he wasn't sure that was at all true, or even if this was going to work out. Well, they'd find out soon enough.

They arrived at the gate to find Laura and Eric already there. She, too, had taken an inordinate amount of care dressing for the occasion. From what he'd seen of her in her home environment, Laura was an extremely casual, very happy-go-lucky person. A messy baker, she seemed to get smudges of flour everywhere, and then not mind at all. Tonight, however, she had dressed with enough care to meet the president. Her thick, naturally curly hair had been coaxed into a disciplined wedge. She was wearing eye makeup, pretty earrings, subtle but sophisticated perfume, a dignified navy-and-red sweater that might have been new, and a trim knee-length skirt. Her leather flats showed off her long slender legs to perfection.

Janey, however, seemed not the least bit impressed. She stayed unusually close to his side. But Zach hadn't expected to be disturbed by Laura's presence, too. In a completely different way. And although he would've liked to chalk up his extraordinary awareness of her to the fact he dated so infrequently, deep down it was more than her fresh, pretty looks.

Laura was just so alive. With all the grief and trauma she'd had in her life, losing first her husband, then her daughter, she could have turned inward, adopted a sour outlook. But she hadn't. Instead she was vivacious and lively. He knew from the fond glances she routinely slanted at her son that she was a very loving woman. She seemed to have a wealth of tenderness within her, just waiting to be released.

And, as he looked at her, he found himself wondering who would be the recipient of all that pent-up passion and zest for life. He found himself fantasizing about the softness of her kiss. And he knew damn well that could never happen.

"Let's go on inside, shall we?" Zach asked abruptly, taking charge.

The next few moments were awkward, with everyone trying a little too hard to please, to appear casual. After some shifting of seats, they finally ended up with Zach on one end, Laura on the other, and Eric and Janey in the middle.

Fortunately, the game was an exciting one, and the Mavericks took an early lead. Janey and Eric talked only occasionally—about the basketball being played. At halftime, they all headed to the concession stands.

Not surprisingly, Zach thought he detected a faint note of resentment on Eric's part toward him. Eric wanted to get to know his sister, but he could have done without Zach's hovering presence during the awkward process. He guessed he couldn't blame Eric. If he were in the kid's shoes, he'd probably feel that way, too.

Maybe it would go easier on all of them, Zach thought, if he could just put him at ease. "So, Eric, what are your plans when you graduate from high school next year?" Zach asked as the line to the concession stand inched forward.

Eric sent him a surprised glance. Although he was just sixteen, he was tall, and on eye level with Zach. "I don't have any."

Yet, Zach thought. "You planning to make your college visits this summer? Or are you going to go into the service like your dad?"

Eric shrugged, bewildered by Zach's interest in a subject he apparently didn't care two bits about himself. "I don't know. I guess I'll figure that out after I graduate."

After he graduated? Zach stared at him, nonplussed. By the time he had been a high school sophomore he had known exactly where he wanted to go to school, and what he wanted to do.

"Dad, look," Janey interrupted, tugging on his sleeve. "They're selling the new style T-shirts over there. Can I go get one, please? I've got enough allowance money saved up."

It wasn't so much a question of money as it was of time. If they stood in yet another long line they'd miss the start of the second half.

"I'll go with her," Eric said. "That is if it's okay with my mom," he amended as an afterthought.

Laura nodded. "It's all right with me, if it's all right with Zach. Just don't go anywhere else."

After getting permission from Zach as well, the two left. An awkward silence fell between Zach and Laura. Casting around for something to break the continuing tension between them, Zach said, "About Eric. One of the men who works for me has a wife who specializes in career counseling, for high school students. She helps them define their goals, identify their talents and interests. If you like, I could give you her name."

"Thanks, but no," Laura said firmly.

Zach didn't bother to hide his surprise.

"I don't want that for Eric unless he wants it for himself and he's just not ready yet."

He wasn't ready, or Laura wasn't ready? Zach wondered.

Reading his disapproval accurately, she continued, "When I was a kid, my mother made me adhere to all sorts of schedules and rules. I hated it. I won't put those same demands on Eric."

Zach saw it was an emotional issue for her, and for that reason he didn't want to push it. On the other hand, what he was suggesting wasn't so out of line. For Eric's sake, someone needed to talk to Laura. "Deciding on a career path is not exactly punishment, Laura," he pointed out mildly, inching slightly closer to the concession stand.

"Maybe not for you," she countered quietly but firmly, "but for Eric it would be."

Zach reached into his back pocket and pulled out his wallet. "Don't you think you're underestimating your son? He seems like a very together kid."

"He is. But he's also been through a lot." She sighed, going on, "Most of Eric's early life, our whole family existence was dictated by the whims of the Navy. It encompassed where we lived, how we lived, how often and even when he saw his dad. Then his dad died and everything was dictated by our precarious financial situation, and the demands that were made on me as I moved us back here, found us a place to live, and got my business going. No sooner had I managed that than Melinda got sick and for the following two years after that, our lives were completely ruled by her illness. Since Melinda died, we've been content to take it day by day, to just appreciate what we have every moment. The way Melinda did during her last days with us. That's how we've coped, the both of us. I'm not going to ask him to change, not even to get ready for college or whatever it is that he chooses to do with the rest of his life." Her chin thrust out stubbornly, her pugnacious expression enhancing rather than detracting from her looks.

Zach couldn't argue with her logic. But if Eric only lived from day to day that could severely limit Eric's choices later on. Well, it wasn't any of his business. So he would have to let it drop.

They reached the concession window. Laura ordered colas and hot dogs. Zach chipped in for ice cream and chips. The two of them were thoroughly loaded down when the kids returned, each with a Mavericks T-shirt in hand.

To Zach's relief, the second half proved even livelier than the first, the lead slipping from one team to the other and back again. The winner wasn't decided until the last two seconds of the game when the Mav's sunk a three-point shot. The crowd was on its feet, roaring with glee as the final buzzer sounded.

"What a game!" Janey cried exuberantly.

Zach glanced at his daughter and caught Laura's wistful

expression as she watched Janey. Guilt stung him briefly, then faded swiftly as he realized he stood to lose Janey, too, if she were to transfer her affections to Laura. "Well, we better get a move on," Zach said, a bit more abruptly than he intended. "Traffic will probably be murder."

None of the other three was as anxious to depart as he. Together, they carried their trash to the receptacle, and then walked shoulder to shoulder toward the exit and out into the bracing night air. Once out on the sidewalk, they drew to a halt. Janey looked at Eric, with all the adoration of a younger sister for her big brother. "I guess I'll see you around sometime," she said.

Eric nodded. "Maybe."

Knowing it wouldn't get any easier, Zach said a polite goodbye and then hustled Janey off in the opposite direction. "That was fun, wasn't it?" she said ebulliently, practically skipping along beside him.

Zach nodded, aware as Laura probably was that although his daughter had been friendly toward her new brother, she hadn't said much more than an emotionally aloof "I like your earrings" to Laura.

Clearly, Janey wasn't that interested in finding a mother. She wanted a sibling, but that was all.

Zach wondered if her feelings would change over time. The crazy way things had been going, he decided there was no telling.

"Mom?" Eric questioned as he pulled her car into the driveway and cut the engine. "Are you okay?"

Laura looked at him, stunned by the concern she heard in his voice. "Yes. Why?"

"You've been so quiet. You hardly said a word on the drive home."

That's because I was still living the evening with Zach and Janey, she thought. She had gone into it with zero expectations, only to find the four of them could have a really good time together. A portent of other times to come? she wondered.

Realizing her son was still waiting for an answer, one corner of her mouth lifted and she favored him with a fond smile. "I was quiet because I didn't want to distract the driver."

He gave her a closer look. "I did all right, didn't I?"

"You did great." She felt she could trust his driving in any situation. "Your reflexes are great. You were patient and courteous. A mother couldn't ask for more."

"Whew! That's a relief!" He pretended to wipe the sweat from his brow. "I thought for a moment, from the look on your face, you were unhappy with my driving again."

"No, not so, not at all," Laura said with a reassuring smile. They'd had a few fights initially, while he was first learning how to drive, mostly because he had tended to go too fast or take corners more out of his lane than in it, but those days were behind them now. He drove with skill and care.

Together, they walked into the house. "Are you hungry?" Laura asked, turning on the kitchen light.

I've got to stop thinking of Zach, of how nice he looked in his dark blue sweater and light blue shirt. His khaki slacks had been perfectly pressed, his shoes shined, his jaw closely shaved and scented with the brisk woodsy after-shave he favored. She'd been proud to be seen with him. And knew from the admiring glances he'd given her when he thought she was watching the game that he approved of the way she had looked, too.

Long used to being independent in the way she was attired, she usually didn't give a second thought to what she wore. But tonight she had worried over her selection, unable to choose between slacks or a skirt. She'd finally selected the skirt, feeling it was more feminine. She was glad she had. And she didn't want to think about what that might mean. She wasn't getting involved with Zach, other than as friends. Their lives were already far too complicated. Nevertheless, for a moment tonight as she'd sat shoulder to shoulder with Zach in the noisy arena, she'd had a flash of what it might be like to be his date. And it had been a good feeling.

"Mom—" Eric said, breaking into her runaway thoughts.

Laura jerked to attention, guilty color warming her cheeks. "What?"

"I said I'm still stuffed. I'm going to bed."

"Oh." Laura leaned forward to kiss his cheek. "Good night, hon."

He shook his head remonstratively. "You were a thousand miles away."

Laura knew that. And her thoughts weren't just happy or ridiculously romantic. Seeing Eric and Janey together had stirred up a wealth of memories. Laura realized that Janey, no matter how sweet and lovable and charming, could never take Melinda's place in her heart.

And she had to face it, that was what she had wanted, subconsciously anyway. To find a way to fill the void left by her daughter's death. For Eric, it seemed to have worked, at least a little. She had known all along he missed having a little sister adoring him and tagging along after him, but it hadn't been until the two of them had been sitting side by side in Reunion Arena, their heads bent together over a program, discussing the players, that she'd begun to appreciate just how lonely he must have been the past year.

She had never had a sister or a brother herself, so she had no idea what it was like to have a sibling there day in and day out. But Eric had known. From the time he was small, he had a sister to entertain and keep him entertained, someone to share confidences and secrets and private jokes and stories. He'd lost all that when Melinda died. Now he had a chance to get some of the familial camaraderie back. She couldn't, wouldn't begrudge him that.

Being with Janey the first time had been an experience full of curiosity and wonder. Being with her the second time, Laura had experienced the sense of loss and bereavement she'd felt at Melinda's death all over again. Only Zach's pleasant companionship had softened the blow.

For Eric, it had been different. And for that, she was glad. She just didn't know how she was going to cope in the days ahead. Would spending time with Janey hurt and disappoint her? And how would she cope if it did?

"MAYBE IT WASN'T so much your interaction with Janey that's bothering you, so much as it is the anniversary of Melinda's death that's coming up," Laura's father suggested several days later over coffee.

Laura looked up and recounted soberly, "You think that's the reason behind my depression."

"My dad died twenty years ago, honey, and I still get depressed every year at that time. Sometimes I don't even know why I'm feeling as blue as I do, and I'll go along for a week or two, wondering what's wrong, and then out of nowhere it'll hit me. I'll realize what my subconscious already knows, that it was this time of year when I lost him. I'll be very sad for a day or so. Then it'll pass and I'll be chipper again."

Laura knew that was true. She'd experienced the same phenomenon after her husband had died. She rested her chin on her hand, feeling more depressed than ever. "Oh, Dad, why is life so hard?"

He shrugged with an acceptance she couldn't begin to feel. "Because it is, honey."

She lifted her coffee to her lips and took another long, enervating draught. "That's no answer."

"I know, but it's the only one I've got." He took an oatmeal cookie from the plate she'd set out. "So, how is Eric doing through all this?"

Laura smiled, thinking of the easy camaraderie that had sprung up between Zach's daughter and her son. "Better than I am, actually. He's seen Janey several times since we all went to the Mavericks game. He dropped by her house one day and shot some hoops."

Unfortunately Eric hadn't realized it would have been best to call first. Unhappy about the unscheduled visit, Zach had telephoned to let her know what was going on. Laura'd apol-

ogized and talked to Eric, instructed him to be sure to call and
ask permission first in the future. Which he had dutifully done.

"But you haven't seen Janey again?" her dad persisted,
looking a little disappointed.

Laura shook her head, guilt flooding over her. "No. Zach
and I have both been very busy with our jobs." But that
wasn't it and she knew it. Part of it was that she felt sad
because she knew no one would ever replace Melinda. And
maybe that was the way it should be, Laura thought pensively.

"I see."

She heard the faint note of censure in his voice and found
herself bristling at it. She reached for the carafe on the table
and freshened both their coffees. Keeping her voice casual
with effort, she continued realistically, "I think one Matthews
is enough for Janey to handle at a time."

Her dad's gaze narrowed. He searched her face carefully for
any sign of emotion. "Is that the only reason you're holding
back?"

Sadly, Laura reported, "She's not Melinda, Dad."

"No, she's not," her father agreed. "But you could still be
close to her," her father said softly.

Swallowing hard, she hung on to her composure with a
thread. "No, Dad, I'm not sure I can be."

Her father's glance softened compassionately, leaving no
evidence of the tough Navy official he had once been. "This
makes what I have to ask all the harder," he said. "It's your
mother, Laura. She wants to meet Janey. And Zach, too."

"No. Dad, that's the last thing I need."

"Janey is her natural granddaughter."

"She's yours, too. I noticed you're not demanding the same
thing."

He gestured obliquely. "I've always been more patient than
your mother. You know that. Laura, she's not going to give
up on this."

After all this time, Grace was still making her miserable.
"No, Dad. The answer is no. And it will remain no. So you
better tell her to give up." He sent her a mildly rebuking

glance, prompting her to add, "Look, even if I wanted to do this—and I assure you I most certainly don't—Zach would never agree to it and Janey would never live through it. You know as well as I how critical Mother can be. Janey's a very sensitive kid. She's been through a lot."

"Your mother is just talking about meeting her, not reforming her."

"To Mother, the two are one and the same," Laura responded dryly. "And the answer is still no, Dad," Laura said, closing the argument. "*N-O*. No."

Chapter Seven

"I know you're busy," Zach began when Laura greeted him at the door on a Monday morning two weeks later. "I promise I won't take much of your time, but I need to talk to you about Eric and Janey."

As he had hoped, she had no objection to that. "Come on in," Laura said, her tone casual and welcoming. Yet her studied politeness had an edge of tension to it. He wasn't sure if they were simply friends or on the brink of something more. He only knew he thought about her a lot. And he suspected from the way she was looking at him that she thought about him, too.

"Can I get you a cup of coffee?" she continued, leading the way back to the coziest room in her entire house, her kitchen.

In the bright sunlight there, she looked unusually pale and tired, as if she hadn't been sleeping. Zach knew how that felt. He hadn't been sleeping well, either. "That'd be nice, thanks," he said.

Looking around, he was surprised to see her kitchen was devoid of the usual baking clutter. "You're not working today?" he asked Laura.

"No." Laura's tone was crisp and purposeful, despite the fragility of her looks.

Zach wanted to tell her she didn't have to pretend to be in

an upbeat mood when she wasn't, but he didn't know how to say the words without sounding too intimate.

"How do you take your coffee?"

"Black."

She handed him a cup and cut straight to the chase. "Has Eric been wearing out his welcome?"

"No, not really. It's Janey." He paused, not sure how to go about this. She already looked so fragile that it was all he could do not to reach out and hold her. Bracing himself for her reaction, he continued gently, "She wants to see one of Eric's basketball games. And she wants me to take her. I didn't know how you would feel about us both being there." It could be awkward. Janey cheering Eric on might cause people to ask questions Laura might not want to answer.

Laura's dark brown eyes lit up thoughtfully. She seemed to be considering all the angles. "How does Eric feel?" she asked finally.

Zach shrugged. "Apparently he'd like her to go. He said something about hitting a midseason slump, but he thinks he's coming out of it."

Laura nodded and smiled, proving, Zach thought, once again what a remarkably adaptable woman she was.

"Well, sure, it'd be fine. I could pick her up if you like." She sighed as the next alternative came to mind. "Or the two of you could meet me at the gym."

The thought of such an outing was very pleasing to Zach, but he knew it wouldn't be to the kids. And it was up to him to tell her so. "Uh, no," he said awkwardly, unable to help but notice how shiny and soft her hair looked in the morning sunlight. He liked the fact it wasn't all sticky with spray. "That's not what they want." Her face fell. He continued, "They both felt it was fun but a little awkward, with the two families together."

Zach stuck his hands into the pockets of his jeans. "Janey wants me to drop her and one of her girlfriends, Chrissy, off at the game and then pick them up when it's over."

A flicker of what appeared to be hurt flashed in Laura's

eyes and was quickly suppressed. She moved around the kitchen restlessly. And again, Zach had the desire to hold her, to give comfort.

"And you don't have any objection to that?" Laura asked.

As a matter of fact, Zach did. And maybe it was time he voiced his suspicions, found out if they were shared. He leaned against the opposite counter and took a sip of the hot delicious coffee. "I think they're trying to deliberately cut the two of us out, in their efforts to establish a brother-sister relationship." On one level, Zach wasn't sure he minded so much. It was easier for him, not being involved, not having to fight his instinctive, involuntary attraction to Laura every time they were together.

On another level, he knew he would miss seeing Laura. And right now, getting the kids together, making them comfortable with all that had happened, was his only excuse to be with her.

At all he had revealed, her listless expression grew even more dejected, so much so that Zach felt guilty for upsetting her. "I see," she said slowly, surreptitiously wiping a tear from the corner of her eye.

Zach watched her helplessly, not knowing what to say or do, only knowing that he couldn't bear to see another human being in so much pain. "If you want to talk to them, or set down some ground rules, try to limit the time they're spending with each other—" he offered.

She shook her head and folded her arms at her waist. "No. I can't and won't deny Eric anything that brings him comfort, and being increasingly close to Janey does circumvent some of his feelings of loss." She swallowed hard. "He's missed not having a sister. It helps him to be close to Janey."

"But what about you?" Zach was surprised to find himself asking before he could think to censure himself. "Obviously this has really upset you."

"It isn't Janey or her request," she said miserably, cutting him off. "It's Melinda." Zach was silent, waiting, sensing there was more. Finally, Laura choked out the words. "Today—it's—she died one year ago today, Zach," she whispered hoarsely, as if each word required maximum effort. "That's why I'm so upset."

The words hit Zach like a blow to the chest. No wonder she looked so drawn and pale. "I'm sorry," he said quietly, not knowing how else to ease her pain.

She studied his sympathetic expression and felt almost resentful of his calm.

He felt angry with her for resenting him and angry with himself for not knowing how to help her. "I'm sorry for you, Laura," he reiterated gently, "but she wasn't my daughter. I didn't even know her. There's just no way I can feel your loss, not now, not ever."

Abruptly the fight went out of Laura. Burying her face in her hands, she began to sob soundlessly, the shaking of her shoulders the only clue to the emotional torment she was in. Again, he wanted to go to her, hold her. But something held him back. If he couldn't feel her pain, she wouldn't want his sympathy.

"I'm sorry," he said again, lamely. "I had no idea what day this was. Or I wouldn't have come over to talk to you." And then feeling more guilty than ever, he fled.

THE DINNER HOUR came and went. Laura turned the oven off and transferred the turkey casserole to the hot plate. By seven, she was frantic. She telephoned the school, found the athletic office empty, then one by one started calling all his friends. Yes, Eric had been at practice, they all said. He'd left to go home at the usual time. No, there was nothing wrong except he'd seemed kind of out of it, down. But he hadn't told anyone why.

Laura knew because she was feeling the crushing grief and despair, too. Looking out at the darkness that had fallen, she wondered where he could be. The two of them had visited Melinda's grave very early that morning. They'd taken flowers out and said a silent prayer.

He'd seemed okay, then, as had she.

But maybe like her his grief had grown more unmanageable as the day lingered on. He wasn't with his friends or her parents. She knew there was only one other person he might turn to to ease that ache. Going back to the phone, she dialed Zach Anderson's number. He answered on the third ring.

To her relief, Zach seemed as concerned as she was. "No, he hasn't been here. Let me go ask Janey if she's seen or heard from him today." He put down the phone.

Her heart pounding, Laura waited. Please, she thought, wherever he is, wherever he's gone, let him be safe.

Zach returned seconds later, his voice crisp and business-like. "Janey said she hasn't heard from him."

Laura's whole body was trembling and so was her voice. "I—maybe he's out at the cemetery then. I—I guess I'll drive out there."

Zach's response was incredulous. "This time of night?"

She said stiffly, "I've got to find him."

"You don't sound like you're in any shape to drive."

"I'll manage," she said tightly. She didn't want to turn this into a crisis of epic proportions, that would only hurt and embarrass Eric all the more. He was obviously hurting enough as it was.

On the other end of the phone line, Zach let out his breath in an exasperated whoosh. "Let me drive you," Zach said.

Was he doing this out of the goodness of his heart, or out of guilt for his lack of feeling? Laura wondered. Did it really matter? What was important now, was finding Eric. Zach could help her. And in the process, he would see Melinda's grave. Maybe that, more than anything, would drive the full extent of their mutual loss home to him. Didn't Melinda deserve at least that much?

"All right," Laura said, knowing Zach was right. Emotionally she was in no shape to drive. Besides, if he were driving, she would be free to look for Eric's battered red Mustang. And they'd find her son all the sooner.

On the other end of the line, one hand partway over the mouthpiece, muffling the sound, Zach was talking to his daughter. "Janey, Eric's mom is looking for him, so if he shows up here while I'm gone, keep him here until I get back, okay?"

"Okay."

"Laura," Zach said, speaking to her once again, "Sit tight. I'll be right over." He hung up before she could protest.

AFTER REASSURING his daughter that everything was going to be fine, Zach drove over to Laura's in record time. He didn't know why he was so frantic, only that he was.

"You didn't have to do this, you know," Laura said in a voice stiff with pride. She got into the car beside him, the long trench coat she wore buttoned to her chin.

"I know," Zach said. It was more than chivalry on his part. It was also a mixture of curiosity and guilt. And he didn't want to run from Laura and her pain, as he had this morning. He had a responsibility to her. He might not share her feelings of grief, but he could at least be compassionate. He could at least see where his biological daughter had been laid to rest.

Over the next few minutes, Laura spoke only to give him directions. "I don't see his Mustang here," Zach murmured as he parked.

The memorial garden was well lit and well tended. Peaceful, pretty, the hillside was dotted with marble and granite monuments.

Laura got out of the car. Her collar drawn up around her face, her hands shoved into the deep pockets of her coat, she led the way. Zach followed, his mood somber and subdued.

"She always liked yellow roses," Laura said, kneeling to arrange the lovely bouquet of flowers in the vase beneath her daughter's name. "So much so that near the end, she asked me if—" Laura's voice broke and it was a half second before she could go on "—if I would see to it that the flowers at her memorial service would all be yellow roses, a blanket of them." Laura's voice hardened and she stood. "She knew from her father's funeral, how much people like to send flowers. His was military, of course." She swallowed again. "Melinda's was a different type of service."

Her composure faltered abruptly. Head down, Laura began to weep.

Zach took her into his arms and held her against him, inhaling the flowering scent of her perfume. For the first time he felt the true depth of her pain, and he hoped never to feel anything like it himself. Laura, he wondered, how did you ever get through it? How could you ever bear to let your child go, knowing you would never see her or talk to her or hold her again? But somehow she had done that and she had recovered. Today was full of sorrow for her, but she would be better tomorrow.

"Mom—how could you?" a tortured voice erupted from behind them.

Laura and Zach turned, her soft body still pressed against his, her arms wreathed around his neck. Eric was standing there, his hands shoved into the pockets of his letter jacket, his face and ears red from the cold. The look of complete disgust on his young face plainly told what he erroneously thought: that there was something licentious going on.

"On Melinda's grave?" Eric said contemptuously, getting more furious with every passing second.

Zach released Laura slowly. "Eric, it's not the way it looks," he said slowly but clearly, giving him a direct look. "I was just comforting your mother."

"Yeah, I saw the way you were comforting her!" Eric shot a fierce look at Zach, then glared at Laura as if she were the worst kind of traitor. "You disgust me," Eric continued vehemently, giving Laura a disdainful look. "You really do." Whirling, he trotted off toward his car.

More concerned than insulted, Zach started to go after Eric. Laura stopped him. "No, don't. He needs time to cool off." Mingled with her hurt was an incredible depth of compassion. "At least I know he's all right now."

Zach studied her, his heart going out to her. "Are you sure

you're all right?'' She seemed very fragile to him, very vulnerable.

"I'm fine," she said wearily, brushing the hair from her eyes. She straightened resolutely. "I just want to go home."

"Are you going to be able to talk to Eric when you get home?" Zach asked.

"I don't know." Laura stared out the window. "The truth is, ever since he found out about the switch, he's harbored this silent resentment toward me." She shrugged helplessly and drew her coat closer to her slender frame. "I don't think there's anything I can say or do that will ever excuse what I did, in his estimation, anyway. He blames me for being stupid enough to accept the wrong child as my own. That made me angry at first. It hurt me. But now, I don't know. Maybe I should have known I had the wrong baby. Maybe I should have guessed—And now I wish I could let go of the way I feel. I wish it were that simple," she said desolately, tears shimmering on her lashes.

"It is that simple," Zach said. "We have each other to help get through this. Eric will forgive you, in time." As he spoke the consoling words, Zach discovered he really believed them.

She shook her head disconsolately. "You say that because Janey hasn't blamed you."

He shrugged, knowing he was lucky on that score. "She's younger, Laura. It hasn't occurred to her yet."

"More forgiving."

"More sensible, maybe," Zach acknowledged matter-of-factly. He looked at Laura, fighting the urge to take her in his arms and hold her, as he would anyone in such pain, until her misery passed. "Eric will come around," he reiterated firmly.

"I hope so," Laura said. "I really hope so."

"DAD?" Janey asked anxiously, the minute he walked in the door. "Did you find Eric?"

"Yes, we did."

"And he's okay?"

Zach hesitated. If he didn't level with her, she might hear

about what happened from another source. He didn't want Eric running to Janey with false stories about Laura and himself. Zach sat down beside her on the sofa. "Actually he was very upset. You see today is the anniversary of his sister's death."

Janey's face fell and she looked at a loss for words. "Oh."

"He misses her a lot, I think."

Janey rubbed at an imaginary spot on her jeans. "He never talks about her, though." She looked up at him, as if wondering what that meant.

"Maybe not to you or me, but I'm sure he and his mom talk about Melinda," Zach said. "They probably have a lot of happy memories."

"And some sad ones, too," Janey added compassionately.

Zach nodded in agreement, knowing it must have been very hard for Laura and Eric to lose Melinda. But he and Janey couldn't dwell on that. It would serve no useful purpose. Especially when he had something more important to tell her. "Honey, when we were out at the cemetery, Mrs. Matthews started to cry. I held her in my arms, you know the way people do when they're trying to comfort each other?"

Janey nodded acceptingly, and Zach continued in the same matter-of-fact tone. "Well, Eric saw us and he misinterpreted what was going on." At Janey's blank look, Zach was forced to elaborate, "He got angry. He thought we were defiling Melinda's grave by having a romance there."

"You and Mrs. Matthews!" Janey said, aghast.

"Yes. Of course there was nothing going on. When Eric calms down, I'm sure he'll realize that but I wanted you to know about it, in case he wants to talk about it."

"Okay." Janey gave her agreement readily, then said, "Daddy, did it make you sad, seeing where Eric's sister was buried?"

Zach said, "I felt sad for Mrs. Matthews. And Eric. And Melinda, too, even though I didn't know her."

Janey frowned and looked depressed. "It seems unfair, her dying so young."

"To me, too."

Janey shook her head in mute sympathy. "Poor Eric," she murmured.

But not poor Mrs. Matthews, Zach thought. Initially, the way Janey cut Laura from her life had been a source of relief to him. Now he wasn't sure it was so good.

"Well, I guess I'll go to bed," Janey said, smothering a yawn with the back of her hand. She looked as relieved as Zach that the immediate crisis was over, even if Eric now had some misconceptions. "And maybe I'll call Eric in the morning or something, just to see how he is."

"Better wait a few more days," Zach advised, taking the cautious view. In the mood Eric was in, there was just no telling how he would react.

LAURA was just getting into bed, hoping her age-old cure of an extra hour or two of sleep would make her feel better after the draining trauma of her day, when the phone rang.

"Hello."

There was a second of silence on the other end, then a low, familiar male voice. "Laura...Zach," he began kindly. "I won't keep you. I just called to see how everything is. Did Eric get home intact?"

Glad it was Zach and not anyone else, Laura nodded. She could use his calm, soothing demeanor right now. Talking to him would make her feel as safe and protected as she had when he'd been holding her in his arms. How she had needed that, she thought, yearningly. "Yes, he got home about half an hour ago," she related with a slightly harried sigh.

"And?" Zach prompted cautiously.

She only wished she had better news. Or that Zach could be there with her, to hold her and tell her everything was going to be all right once again. But he couldn't. And she had to accept that. Sighing, Laura continued, "And I told him that what he saw was no more than a hug between friends."

"Was he okay with that?"

"No, but I think when he has time to calm down, he'll—"
Laura glanced up to see Eric standing in her open doorway,

one arm stretched out and planted against the frame. From the stony look on his face he had obviously surmised who she was talking to. Her spirits plummeted to an even lower depth. Partly because she did feel guilty, at least on some level, about what he'd seen. It was true—she and Zach had been doing nothing wrong when Eric had spied them together—but her thoughts were not as blameless. She had been attracted to the man for a long time, since the day they had met.

"I heard the phone ring," Eric grunted in way of grudging explanation as to why he had come to her room.

Knowing, despite her own private, guilt-filled yearnings, that she had nothing to hide, Laura calmly said "It's Mr. Anderson. He wanted to check and make sure you got home safely."

Eric's mouth curled skeptically at one corner. "Sure." Without further comment, he dropped his arm and stalked away.

Watching his retreating back, Laura sighed. It was obvious Eric didn't want her to become involved with Zach. And she wasn't. Wanting Zach didn't count! If only Eric would stop behaving so irrationally.

"Laura?" Zach said, concern lacing his low tone. "Are you still there?"

Laura cast a glance heavenward and exhaled slowly. "I'm fine. As you probably heard, Eric's still in a surly mood."

On the other end, Zach sighed his frustration. She could guess what he was thinking, that her son probably needed a good scolding, but that wasn't the way she worked. Feelings were allowed in her house, no matter how prickly. It was the suppression of feelings that caused conflict, not the healthy venting or discussion of them.

"Well—" Zach seemed to be searching for something to say. "Is there anything else I can do for you? If you want me to talk to him or—"

His concern for her, his willingness to help, was endearing. "No," she said, "there's nothing you can do. I'll manage. But thanks for offering. And Zach—" Her voice softened gratefully as she continued, "thanks for being there for me to-night." She swallowed around the reflexive tightening of her throat, glad he wasn't there to see her blush. "I know I was really overwrought. I just couldn't help it. But I feel a lot better now. Drained but better."

His reply was soft, sympathetic. "I'm glad."

And suddenly, there was nothing else to say. "Well..." Laura said as the moment drew out even more awkwardly.

"I better let you go."

She gripped the receiver tighter. "Thanks again."

"Good night."

"Good night." Their conversation over, Laura hung up the phone, feeling strangely consoled and feeling strangely bereft. His call was just a polite courtesy, nothing more, the kind one would give any neighbor in trouble. There was no reason to make anything more of it. Or of the way he had held her...

Chapter Eight

"Is Eric home?"

Laura put down her account ledger and pen. "No, he's not," she said carefully, suspecting from the girlish timbre of the speaker's tone, that she was not speaking to one of her son's friends from Central High. "He's still at basketball practice."

"Oh."

Just one syllable, Laura thought, and yet so terribly dejected. Laura recognized the speaker's voice. "Janey? Is there something I can help you with?"

Janey sighed. "No, not really. I was just going to ask Eric if he could go rock hunting with me. I've got this collection due, and I—well, I kind of forgot all about it."

Laura remembered Eric having to do the same thing in eighth grade. It was a required project for the Earth Science classes every year. "Oh, my," she said, sympathizing with Janey's panic. "When's it due?"

"Day after tomorrow. My dad's going to kill me when he finds out I haven't even started it. Plus, I don't even know where to begin to look for the dumb rocks. I have to have twelve, from three different categories."

This really isn't any of my concern, Laura thought. I should just let her call her dad and deal with the consequences. On the other hand, if I were to help her, I'd get to know her a little better. And suddenly she wanted that, very much. She hadn't realized until this moment how shut out she'd been feeling the past few weeks, watching Janey get closer and closer to Eric, all the while holding her deliberately at arm's length. Impulsively Laura offered, "I could help you, Janey. If you want, that is. I know where we ended up getting Eric's rocks. And I imagine they're still there. In fact, we've still got several books upstairs on identifying rocks."

Janey sighed her relief. "Would you? I don't want to impose or anything, but I really need to get this done or I'm going to flunk for sure."

Laura smiled at the drama in the teenager's tone and reassured pleasantly, "I don't mind at all. When do you want to go?" Laura consulted her watch. "We've still got two hours before dark. I could be over there in say, twenty minutes?"

"That'd be great. Thanks, you're saving my life."

"No problem. And Janey? Wear old clothes. Where we're going it can get pretty muddy."

Janey was waiting for Laura on the front stoop. She looked both pretty and raring to go. Laura breathed a silent sigh of relief. As she had driven over, she had wondered if she was doing the right thing, especially when she had realized this impulsive idea of hers could very well backfire on her. What if they didn't get along? What if they didn't find any good rocks and Janey failed, then blamed it on her?

Laura didn't know how she would handle any of that. But so far, so good, she thought, looking at Janey's determined and thoughtful expression as she thumbed through the books on rock collecting Laura had put on the front seat.

Fifteen minutes later, the two of them were hiking down a hillside on the outskirts of town, collecting muddy specimens, big and small. "They all look alike to me," Janey moaned as she tossed yet another rock into the plastic bag Laura had brought.

"That's because all we're seeing is the mud," Laura soothed. "That'll change when we give them a good scrubbing."

Back at Janey's house, that was exactly what they did. Filling a bucket with warm water and soap, they took the rocks onto the back patio, and scrub brushes in hand, went to work.

"STILL NO WORD from Janey, huh?" Harry Cole asked as he nailed wallboard to one of the upstairs bedrooms in the Gagglione mansion.

Zach shook his head, using a trimming knife to cut another sheet. "No. And I've called every ten minutes for the past hour."

"Maybe she went over to a friend's house," Harry suggested hopefully, picking up yet another nail.

Zach shook his head negatively. Finished cutting one piece, he began trimming the next. "She always calls me and lets me know where she's going to be. It's a rule we have."

Harry began to look as worried as Zach felt. "Have you checked your answering service?"

"They haven't heard from her, either."

Harry was silent. "Look, I don't want to say anything to upset you, but the police caught Tabitha hitchhiking last Monday, after school."

"What?" Zach said, shocked.

"Yeah, she and some friends were just trying to get a thrill." Harry stopped hammering and gave Zach another worried look. "Fortunately for the girls, the police picked them up before anyone else could. I only mention it because Janey and Tabitha are in the same class at school. They don't hang around that much there but you know how contagious fads can be. From what little we got out of Tabitha, there's been a lot of peer pressure to prove they're daring, adventurous. I don't want anything similar to happen to Janey."

Neither did he. Quickly, Zach unhooked his tool belt and took off his hard hat and put them aside. "I'm going to knock off a few minutes early and head home," he said brusquely, knowing he could trust Harry to disperse the crew and lock up. "If Janey should call, tell her to meet me there."

"Sure thing," Harry said. "And Zach, I'm sorry if I worried you. I just wanted you to know what's been going on with some of the kids.''

Zach nodded grimly. "I appreciate the warning.''

Janey wouldn't do something that stupid. She's a smart kid, he told himself firmly as he climbed behind the wheel. Janey had been thrown a lot of curves lately. Maybe like Tabitha, she was feeling the pressure to keep up with the so-called cool kids in her class.

The drive home had never taken so long. By the time he reached his house, he was both tense and worried. Janey, where are you? he thought. Why are you worrying me this way? Why are you breaking the rules we set up to keep you safe?

Foot on the brake, he stared at the car parked in his driveway. Laura Matthews? What was she doing here? he wondered, easing in behind her and cutting his engine.

As he strode toward the house, he heard the distinctly feminine sounds of laughter emanating from the backyard. Circling the house, he came upon Laura and Janey. Mud, soap suds, and water streaking her from head to toe, Janey was turning off the garden hose. In jeans, hiking boots, and an old sweatshirt, a mud-streaked Laura was kneeling on the wet cement, busily drying off rocks with paper towels. Even in the dimming daylight, he could see that her short, dark hair was damp and curling wildly around her flushed face. Never, he thought, had he seen her look so animated or quite so beautiful. "Do you think we got enough?" Janey asked excitedly, dashing back to Laura's side the moment the hose was turned off.

Her face whitening, she noticed Zach. "Dad—uh—hi.''

Laura looked up, like a kid who'd just been caught with her hand in the cookie jar. She grinned mischievously. "Uh—hi.'' She glanced at her watch and rose awkwardly to her knees, ineffectually brushing off the dirt, her casual movements drawing the shirt closer to her breasts. "Gosh, I didn't realize it was so late. Eric's probably home, wanting supper.''

"I guess I can take it from here,'' Janey said, smiling adoringly at Laura. In that instant, when Zach saw the two of them standing side by side, he was struck by how much they looked alike. Mother and daughter, it was as clear as the day was long. The knowledge combined with his fear of losing Janey and stabbed him like a knife.

Immediately he wanted to lash out at someone for inflicting this kind of hurt and worry on him. But the practical side of his nature forced him not to overreact. Pulling his thoughts together, he forced himself to forget his fears for a moment and concentrate only on why and how this had happened.

Laura gently touched Janey's shoulder, looking Zach thought resentfully, more maternal and loving than any woman had a right to look. "If you have any trouble," Laura advised Janey softly, "you can call Eric or me. We'd be glad to help you identify them."

Janey lit up like a beacon. "Thanks, Laura."

When had they gotten so close? he wondered. He only knew he felt hurt, excluded. And mad. Janey might have been careless, but Laura knew better. Hadn't she gone through hell just a short time ago when Eric was missing?

"Janey, why don't you take your rock collection and go on in the house and wash up," Zach suggested.

Janey looked at him, the guilty expression on her face telling him she knew full well she'd been remiss in not letting him know where she was. Or who she was with. At least now he understood why she had been so secretive. What else had been going on that he didn't know about? Had Laura been undercutting him like this all along? Was that her intention, to tell him she had no interest in Janey and then go behind his back and court her anyway? He had thought Laura was his friend, that he could trust her. Apparently not.

Reading his expression, Janey said awkwardly, "Laura— Mrs. Matthews—was just helping me with my science project, Dad."

"I can see that." Zach forced the most civilized smile he could manage. From the very beginning of his association with Laura, he had feared a showdown like this. He had never expected it would be tonight. "Would you wash up and set the table please?" he asked.

Recognizing an order when she heard one, Janey nodded and slipped inside, shutting the patio door behind her.

He faced Laura in silence.

"I have an idea how this must look," she began slowly, approaching him as cautiously as she would a wounded bear.

Her wariness only added fuel to the fire burning in his gut. "Do you?" Zach asked. "I had no idea where Janey was tonight. None! I was worried sick, scared something might have happened to her, that she might have been kidnapped." He paused, letting his words sink in, then gave in to his soaring temper and added silkily, "I wasn't far wrong, was I?"

At his thinly veiled insult, Laura advanced on him angrily. "Now wait just a minute. Janey called me, not the other way around. Or rather she called Eric and he wasn't home."

"And you couldn't wait for the chance to step in and see her behind my back, could you?"

Laura's face grew more flushed. She touched a hand to her hair, pushing the tousled strands into place as best she could with her fingers, the reflexive action only serving to make her look even more as if she had just tumbled out of bed. "I admit I welcomed the opportunity to get to know her better, without having to compete with my son."

Her honest words struck a nerve. He knew how hurt she'd been by Janey's previous indifference to her. Obviously, judging by the companionable way the two had been washing the rocks together, this was one hurdle that had been cleared. He saw how much that had meant to Laura, and knowing how much she missed her own daughter, his heart went out to her on that score.

Calming slightly, Zach asked, "Is this the first time anything like this has happened?"

Laura nodded stiffly. "Yes. And I would've told you about it before I took her out rock hunting, had I any idea you didn't know what was going on. Although," Laura sighed with weary regret, "thinking back on it, I should've realized she wouldn't call you. She said something about not wanting you to know she had been remiss in not starting her project." Laura ran a harried hand through her hair, adding informatively, "It's due the day after tomorrow."

That explained a lot. "So you bailed her out," Zach supposed quietly, calming as the misunderstanding between them was gradually but painstakingly cleared up.

"Yes," Laura said, echoing his soft, patient tone, "when Eric wasn't home." Her dark brown eyes beseeched his understanding and forgiveness. She shifted her shoulders expressively and her voice grew choked with emotion, "It was the first time she's ever reached out to me, even a little bit."

For a second he thought she was going to start to cry and then she pulled herself together and finished frankly, "So, yes, Zach, I am guilty as charged. I took the opportunity to be with her, and I enjoyed doing it." She shook her head and said lamely, "Maybe you can't understand that. Maybe you don't have to understand it. Maybe you just need to know that's the way I feel." She reached out and touched his arm.

Her soft hand felt warm even through the layers of his clothes. Zach fell silent, unable to refute her soft earnest words.

She continued genuinely, "I should have made sure she had your permission. I just didn't think."

Nor had he, if he hadn't realized this would happen eventually. Laura was impulsive. She lived moment to moment. Whereas he was not. He liked to plan for everything. He studied her silently. Realizing no real harm had been done, he said finally, "You had a good time with her?"

Laura smiled, the happiness she felt lighting up her face. "Yes. It was fun, traipsing around the canyon, hunting for ordinary rocks as if they were the most precious treasure. It was also the first time she's ever really relaxed around me. She's a lovely girl, Zach. You've done a wonderful job raising her."

But I don't want her to relax around you, Laura, Zach realized with a start, surprised by his own selfishness. He didn't want to lose Janey, not even a tiny bit. And at this point in her life, Janey needed a mother, maybe more than a dad. But he also knew Laura wasn't the kind of woman who would ever try to drive a wedge between him and his child. If she had been, he would have seen evidence of it long before this. She had just been doing what she thought best, helping out. He couldn't fault her for that.

Laura glanced at her watch. "I really do have to go," Laura said, stepping by him.

As she skirted past, he caught the whiff of sunshine and flowers in her hair. He knew it was probably just her perfume, yet it seemed so much like the sunny personality of the woman herself. A woman Janey and he had both started to bond to. Feeling suddenly ashamed at the way he had let himself blow up, he trailed after her. She had just circumvented a school-work-related crisis in Janey's life and all he had done was berate her for it. "Laura, wait."

She turned, lifting her eyes to his.

"I'm sorry if I snapped at you," Zach said penitently.

She reached out and touched his hand. "It's okay. I understand."

And looking into her eyes, he saw she really did.

"DADDY, you aren't mad at Laura, I mean, Mrs. Matthews, are you?" Janey asked as they helped themselves to Mrs. Yaeger's casserole.

"Why didn't you call?"

"I was afraid you'd get mad at me for waiting till the last minute to start my science project. I just forgot about it. There's been so much going on."

That much was true, Zach thought. Under the circumstances, it was a wonder Janey had been able to keep her grades up at all. He knew it was hard for him to concentrate on his work. Deciding Janey had learned her lesson, he extracted this final promise from her. "Just let me know if you're going someplace from now on, agreed?"

"Agreed." Seconds later, she told him what was really on

her mind. "Daddy, you know how we always do something nice for people who've done something nice for us, to show we appreciate what they did? Well, I think we should do something nice for Laura."

Laura, Zach thought a trifle jealously. Not Mrs. Matthews anymore.

"Like what?" he forced himself to ask in a reasonable tone.

"Like I don't know. Maybe—well, we'll think of something," Janey finished airily, the momentary sunniness in her disposition reminding him acutely of Laura.

She wants to keep up the contact, Zach realized with growing clarity, resentment, and confusion. Before today any contact with Laura Matthews was a threat to Janey, now the contact was appealing, necessary almost, for her continued happiness and contentment. If Laura could manage to do all that in only one afternoon, what would she manage in subsequent visits? he wondered. Used to being the only parent in Janey's life, he found the possibilities unsettling.

"May I be excused? I've got a lot of work to do. And if you're not too busy, maybe you could help me identify some of the rocks we collected? Laura lent me some books of Eric's that tell me all about them."

"Sure," Zach said, knowing full well if he didn't, Laura and Eric would be only too happy to do it in his stead.

"HERE ARE THE BOOKS you lent Janey," Zach said two days later. He'd stopped by on his lunch hour, en route from his office to the construction sites where he had crews working.

"Thanks." Laura wiped one flour-covered hand on the tail end of her long white chef's apron and then took the books. "Did she get everything she needed?"

Zach nodded, wondering if Laura knew she had flour smudged on her chin and the uppermost curve of her right cheekbone, or that she was unerringly beautiful even when wearing old jeans and a sweatshirt, with her dark hair all tousled.

In the background, the oven buzzer sounded. Laura sprinted off, her high-topped sneakers thudding on the carpet.

As he entered the sweetly scented kitchen, she was lifting a delicate chocolate soufflé from the oven. She turned, the hot pan cradled between two gloved hands, then saw belatedly that she had nowhere to set it down. She sent him a helpless glance. "Would you mind lifting those two pecan pies, the ones next to the refrigerator, and putting them on the five-tiered rack next to the back door? Thanks." When he'd finished, she slid the perfectly formed soufflé on a neatly folded dish towel to cool.

"Sometimes I think I need about ten hands instead of two," she remarked.

"Ever think about renting space and working out of a professional kitchen?"

Laura smiled wistfully. "I dream about it all the time, but I can't afford it, not now. Although I admit it gets a little crowded in here, especially when I get special orders."

"Special orders?" Zach asked, watching as she bent to put two more pies into the hot oven.

"From neighborhood customers. For bridge parties, luncheons, or whatever." Silence fell between them. Zach knew he should get out of there, but it wasn't so easy to leave such a nice, cozy and warm place. Laura Matthews's kitchen felt like home to him, and everywhere he looked there was a woman's touch, from the embroidered picture on the wall that said *Laura's kitchen* to the fresh flowers growing in the windowsill. He wasn't sure but he thought they were red geraniums. Whatever they were, they were as healthy as could be, and very well tended.

"I hope Janey gets a good grade on her project," Laura said. "I know how important schoolwork is to her."

And to me, Zach thought. Curious, he asked. "What about Eric? Does he get good grades?"

"Oh, yes. Rob and I both were very big on education. Me, because I never finished mine. Rob, because he did. We live by the motto if something is worth doing, it's worth doing well.''

Zach smiled, pleased to find they had that in common. "I live by that, too."

A second buzzer went off. Laura moved to the other oven. Slipping on the oven mitts once again, she lifted an apple pie out of the oven, and again found she had no place to set it.

"What you need is more counter space," Zach said as he moved to clear a spot.

"Tell me about it," she moaned.

Remember how you're always telling me to do something nice for someone who's done something for us? Janey had said. Laura had looked for rocks with his daughter, scrubbed the dirt off them, and lent Janey books, which saved him a trip to the library. Like it or not, he owed her for this and he was a man who always paid his debts.

Zach looked around thoughtfully. "Maybe you should consider having a wall shelf built for your microwave, to get it off the counter, and then another for your cookbooks," Zach said. "That would give you another four feet of counter space, easily."

"I don't have a budget for remodeling," Laura said.

"The materials wouldn't be that expensive," Zach argued. Especially if he got them at wholesale prices for her, he thought.

"It's not that, it's the labor."

Zach offered, "You don't have to bother with hiring someone. I could do it for you." Then they'd be even, he thought, and Janey wouldn't have to get involved.

Laura looked shocked, then intrigued, then disappointed. "Zach, that's sweet of you, but I couldn't possibly—"

"It would only take half a day at most," Zach continued persuasively.

Her dark brown eyes widened speculatively. "You're sure?"

"Positive."

"All right," Laura said finally. "It's a deal."

Chapter Nine

An hour and a half later, Laura sat at the dining-room table, going over her accounts, trying to ignore the electric whine of a power saw just outside her back door. Business had been slow right after Christmas, as was usually the case. Now that February was here, people were beginning to eat out more again. Restaurants were upping their orders, though not with any predictable consistency. Laura never knew from one day to the next whether she was going to be asked to deliver as little as ten pies or cakes, or as had happened more than once during the weekends, as many as thirty. She liked not knowing, though. If her business had been the same day in and day out, she would have been bored stiff.

The back door slammed. Heavy footsteps sounded on her kitchen floor. Zach. If she lived to be one hundred, she would never figure that man out. One minute he looked at her as if she were the most opportunistic, least trustworthy person on earth. And the next he was offering to build her a shelf for her microwave. He'd said he wanted to pay her back for helping Janey with her rock collection for school, but she sensed it was more than that. He both wanted to get close to her and to get rid of her.

In the kitchen, Zach began to hammer in steady, precisely measured intervals. Bucking the urge to go in to see how it was going, Laura picked up a cookbook, paper, and pencil.

Turning to the page she had marked, she used her calculator to begin quadrupling the recipe for Praline Pie.

She was nearly finished when Zach strode into the room, his tool belt jangling on his waist. "Want to come and see what I've done?" he asked. "Tell me what you think?"

"Sure."

Feeling suddenly self-conscious, Laura put her paperwork aside and got to her feet. He waited for her to take the lead. Acutely conscious of his presence behind her, she hurried to where he had been working.

I can't believe he did this so quickly, was her first thought. Her second was that it was a marvelous job.

"The wood needs to be stained to match your cabinets. I'll have my paint crew call and arrange a time to come over. They'll match it precisely for you."

"Thank you. It's wonderful," Laura said, meaning it. She moved forward to touch the additional four-foot square of counter space that had been freed up. "I really need this space."

"I don't see how you do it. Keep track of all the various ingredients, I mean," Zach said casually, as he slid a hammer into one of the loops on his tool belt. "I find it hard just trying to make one dish at a time at home."

She shrugged. Cooking had always come naturally to her, the way building things obviously did to him. She grinned. "Well, then we're even because I have a hard time just hammering a nail in straight."

Their gazes met, locked. He gave a reluctant smile, then realizing the attitude had become almost friendly between them, abruptly stopped smiling. There were a few specks of sawdust on the floor.

He reached for the broom she had in the corner, and began to sweep, the tool belt jangling against his hips as he moved. With effort, she tore her eyes from his lower torso. Realizing she was no longer comfortable with him there, with the two of them alone, she reached for the handle. "Here, let me. You've done enough. Really."

For a second she thought he would protest, but a glance at the clock told him it was almost suppertime. Eric would be home soon. Janey was perhaps already home. "I guess you're right," Zach responded. "I better get going."

He gathered up the rest of his things, and then went outside to retrieve his power saw. Laura carried the scraps of excess wood to his truck. Zach was just loading the last of it in when Laura's mother parked at the curb. Fortunately, Zach backed out of the driveway before her mother trod carefully up the front walk.

"Laura, what's going on? I saw that man's truck here most of the afternoon. That was Zach Anderson, wasn't it?"

"Yes, that was Zach. He built shelves for my microwave and cookbooks, that's all."

Her mother stared at her as if she'd lost her mind. "You hired him to do this?"

Laura couldn't prevent a flush of reaction to her mother's probing voice. "No. He did it in return for a favor I did for him."

Her mother's brows rose. Unable and unwilling to imagine what she must be thinking now, Laura supplied dryly, "I helped his daughter collect rocks for a science project at school."

Her mother's expression turned to one of delight. "You mean you helped your daughter."

Laura felt her irritation grow. "Mom—"

"Laura, when are you going to come to your senses and do something definite about your situation?"

Her face flaming, Laura whirled and started for the house. This wasn't a conversation for the street.

"You've lost so much time already," her mother continued doggedly, her high heels clicking heavily as she followed Laura up the walk.

"Mom, please." Once inside her kitchen, Laura went straight to the sink and began scrubbing a sticky pan she'd left soaking. Was it her imagination or did the room smell of Zach and the heady scent of his cologne?

Her mother continued to grumble as she sat with ladylike precision in one of the kitchen chairs. "In the past, you've never hesitated to go after what is rightfully yours."

Laura rinsed the pan and put it in the drainer next to the sink. She had to stay calm. She did not want to fight with her mother. Turning, Laura reached for a dish towel. She propped herself against the counter. "This is different, Mom." They weren't talking about just any old thing Laura wanted, but a child. "Janey's whole life, her emotional well-being is at stake. I can't and won't destroy that." She wouldn't do it to Zach and she wouldn't do it to Janey.

Grace's eagle gaze grew even sharper as she mulled over Laura's calmly issued statement. "What about your emotional well-being? What about Eric's?"

"Eric knows I love him."

"Does he? I think he's been upset about this."

Guilt assailed her. Eric had been upset, but then that was normal, too. She wouldn't let her mother think it wasn't. "It's going to take time, for all of us. We have a lot to adjust to."

"I see." Her mother sniffed disapprovingly. "And in the meantime, Zach Anderson has your natural daughter, who he is falsely raising as his own."

Her mother spoke as if he were a heinous criminal. Holding on to her soaring temper, Laura said, "First of all, Mom, Janey is his real daughter, in every sense. Secondly, he is a nice man. A very nice man."

"What does that have to do with anything? Why are you protecting him? You're not starting to feel sorry for him, are you? Laura, for heaven's sake! Use your head this once, instead of your heart and think about what you're doing!"

Her mother shook her head, baffled. "What good could cozying up to this man possibly do you?" Her eyes glimmered. "Oh, I get it! You're trying to get friendly with her father first, aren't you, get to know him, and then get Janey back, if not officially, then unofficially?"

Laura's face flamed hotter. This time her mother had gone too far. "That is not true!" she said, outraged.

"Well, then, maybe it should be," her mother said thoughtfully. "Think about it, Laura. You're both single. Both raising one child. It would make sense, the two of you combining your households.

"You're jumping the gun here, Mother," Laura pointed out calmly, hanging on to her composure by a thread.

"Perhaps I am," Grace continued, smoothing the strand of pearls at her neck. "And perhaps, Laura, this is something you should think about. That is, if you haven't already."

Laura fell silent, resenting her mother too much to be able to speak and maintain a civil tongue.

"However, if you can't do that, you might consider doing something else, especially now that the two of you are on friendly terms. Your father and I want to meet Janey, Laura."

"Mom, no!"

"She's our granddaughter. We have rights, too."

"Zach would never agree to it."

"What could be the harm in a simple dinner, with all of us?"

"It's impossible," Laura declared, seething.

"You could at least ask."

"No, Mother, I mean it. I won't ask Zach any such thing. It would only make him furious."

Her mother studied her shrewdly. "You really think so?"

"Yes, now can we drop it?"

Grace shrugged. "You leave me little choice.

Silence fell between the two women. Her emotional energy depleted, Laura said quietly, "I have to get back to work, Mom."

Knowing she'd pushed her welcome to the limit, her mother said a few more words and left. Laura waited until the door clicked shut, then sank onto the closest chair, unspeakably disturbed. What her mother had suggested about her and Zach was completely ludicrous.

First of all, she wasn't interested in any man, period. And if she were, it wouldn't be someone like Zach who was able to separate himself so completely from his emotions, someone who could and would deny the heartbreaking loss of his own natural daughter. She was the kind of person who needed to be in close touch with her emotions, and know that was not only understood but accepted by the man she loved. And by the same token, she wanted to know what her potential partner was thinking and feeling, and she could only do that if her partner was willing to take the time and energy to delve into his own emotions. And Zach just wasn't. Second, that conflict aside, she had enough to do, just running her business and taking care of her son.

She had been in one relationship with a man for all the wrong reasons, to heartbreaking results. She didn't want to go into another for anything less than all-out love. She was sure Zach didn't, either. He was too smart to make a mistake like that.

Then why was he here today on a trumped-up reason of returning the books? she wondered. Why had he insisted on paying her back and building those shelves for her, free of charge? And when he had finished, why had he acted as if he were so ill at ease?

"...SO I BUILT THE SHELF and now it's all taken care of," Zach told his daughter as the two of them popped popcorn before their evening television shows. *Or it will be when my painters finish.*

"But I wanted to do something nice for her, too," Janey protested, giving him a betrayed look as she poured lemonade into tall glasses and then set about searching for the popcorn salt.

"This was from both of us," Zach said, watching the hot-air popper.

"Yes, but I wasn't part of it," Janey said sullenly. "I wasn't there."

"Laura understands."

Janey turned mutinous. "You just don't want me to be around her. You're jealous because I'm starting to like her."

Was he that transparent? He hadn't meant to be. "Honey—"

"Dad," Janey said in a soft, reassuring tone, "you don't have to be scared of her. I'm not, not anymore anyway. She really is nice."

Zach knew that, too, and it was killing him inside. It would have been so much easier if Laura weren't so nice. Then he could have ignored her.

But now—now all he thought about when her name came up was her dark brown eyes and soft brown hair, the gentle, loving way she interacted with her son, the way she gave Janey space, the way she had cried when she'd visited her daughter's final resting place, the fragile way she had felt when he held her in his arms, and the vulnerable look on her face when he had released her. She was a very smart, sensitive woman. And, like it or not, she was Janey's natural mother.

Maybe it was time he admitted his jealousy to himself and dealt with it. He felt guilty for surreptitiously wanting to keep Laura away from Janey, even though on a legal basis he had every right to do so. And he felt threatened by Janey's newfound receptiveness to Laura. Because now Janey wanted to be close to Laura, to get to know her, and to exchange mutual kindnesses.

Perhaps it would've been different if Maria were still alive, if Janey'd already had a mother in her life. But she didn't have that and she was at an age where girls needed a caring, female influence in their lives. So what was he going to do? What *could* he do?

"We could ask them to go out to Granbury Lake, or to the Log Cabin Village near the botanical gardens. Please, Dad," Janey continued urgently as the last kernel popped out of the popper. "You said the four of us could get to know one another."

This is a battle I am not going to win, Zach thought. The more I fight, the more determined she will be. Nothing attracts a kid more than the forbidden. "All right," Zach said reluc-

tantly at last. "I'll get in touch with her tomorrow and see
what she says."

ZACH MADE GOOD on his promise to his daughter. Figuring
he'd just wing it, rather than make a big deal out of it, he
decided to just drop by and make it casual, rather than call
first. As he had expected, Laura was home and in the midst
of icing a tray of chocolate éclairs when he rapped on the
kitchen door.

"Hi." After wiping her hands on her apron, she let him in.
His attention moving to his handiwork, he looked past her, to
the shelves he had built. "I see the painters have been here,"
he remarked with satisfaction, striding over for a closer look.

"Yes, they did a nice job."

Zach frowned, not as pleased as she obviously was. He
stepped back, squinted, then stepped closer once again. He
touched the smooth, glossy finish on the new shelves, admitting, "I was afraid of this. You always run into that problem
when you try to match a new stain to cabinets that are slightly
weathered. There's a slight difference in the stains."

Her expression bewildered, she moved over to stand in the
light. "Zach, I can't see it."

Glancing around her kitchen, he picked up two collapsed
white cake boxes, and held them by both the new painted and
the existing cabinet. "Come here and look."

Her expression still perplexed, she moved closer. He lifted
his arms slightly, and with a nod of his head, directed her
wordlessly to slip beneath them.

Being careful not to touch him, she did. With her slim body
ensconced between the warmth of his body and the cool wood,
she took a closer look. "Oh." Zach knew she was seeing what
he had, that the new stain was a shade darker than the old.

Sighing his disappointment, Zach stepped back. "I'll call
the painters and have them come out again."

"No." Laura stopped him from going to the phone with a
light touch to his arm. The light touch was oddly stimulating,
and he turned to face her in silent, subdued reaction. As if

realizing what she'd done, she dropped her hand. Swallowing hard, she continued, "You and your paint crew have already done a wonderful job. Honest. This is fine."

Zach shot her a measuring look and his mouth tightened in exasperation. He hated anything less than absolute perfection. "It could be better," he warned.

Laura shrugged and smiled. "It's fine, really. See, look. If I slide the books up here, see how pretty they look. Help me put the microwave in place."

Dubious but unresisting, he went for the heavy appliance. She started to help. Not sure what it would feel like to be so close to her again, not sure he wanted to know, he shrugged off her help. "That's okay, Laura. I can lift it alone. Just handle the cord for me, and slip it into the wooden slot."

Careful to keep his eyes on his task and not the sunlight reflected off Laura's hair, he lifted the microwave and slid it onto the sturdy shelf. "Is it centered?"

She was standing behind him, the end of the cord dangling in her hand. "A little to the left. Yeah, you've got it." She stepped back to survey it. "The stain on the shelves is perfect, Zach."

Zach frowned suspiciously. Dissatisfaction stamped on his face, he guided her forward, urging, "Take a closer look."

Shrugging again, she said, "Still perfect."

He gave her a strange look, then peered closely at the wood. "You're right," he said with amazement. "With those books and the microwave on the shelves, you really can't tell."

Looking abruptly aware of his nearness, Laura smiled and attempted a light remark. "Are you this picky about all the houses you build?"

His answer was serious. "When people build a custom home in the half-mil range, Laura, they expect the best."

"And you deliver," she said softly, with approval in her dark brown eyes. Love of one's work was something she could not only respect but identify with.

Feeling closer to her, for the shared value, he said wryly, "I try. I don't always succeed."

She lifted a skeptical brow and crossed both arms beneath the curves of her breasts. "I find that hard to believe."

He shrugged again, feeling suddenly, unexpectedly shy. She was...so nice. He could see why Janey was so drawn to her.

"Could I get you something?" she asked impulsively. "Coffee? An éclair?"

He looked longingly at some golden puffs with chocolate frosting. "Aren't those for your business?"

"Yes, but I always make a few extra, just in case one bakes lopsided." She poured him a cup of coffee and handed it to him. "Black, right?"

He was pleased and surprised she remembered how he liked it. "Right."

Her motions quick and economical, she slid a pastry onto a china plate and handed him a fork.

"I rate the good dishes?"

"Everyone around here does," Laura countered dryly, returning his smile. Pouring herself a cup of coffee, she looked relaxed and content. "I've got a motto I live by. Never put off until tomorrow what you can enjoy today."

He could have guessed that about her, though he wasn't sure he always agreed with that. Sometimes anticipation was as heady as the actual treat. Aware she was watching him and waiting for a reaction, he took a bite and then closed his eyes briefly, savoring the sweet, creamy golden puff pastry. "Heaven," he pronounced.

She frowned, unsure. "There's not too much vanilla in the filling?" she pressed.

He grinned and finished another bite. "Now who's being a perfectionist?"

She shrugged. "It's a new recipe."

"Ah," he said. The counters weren't brimming over with her creations as they usually were. "You don't seem very busy today," he remarked.

"I'm not," Laura admitted ruefully.

His eyes narrowed with concern. "Business lagging?" He hated to think of Laura wanting for anything.

Laura nodded affirmatively. "The usual postholiday doldrums. It'll pick up with spring and get really crazy by summer. People don't want to cook in the heat then."

"Makes sense." He glanced around again, this time as a builder. "Must be hot in here in the summer, baking all day," he said.

"My electric bills for the air-conditioning are horrendous," she agreed. Getting the coffeepot, she freshened both their cups. "But it's a business expense."

"A necessary one, I imagine. Still, a ceiling fan would help."

Her chin jutted out determinedly. "I use two oscillating fans. Works fine."

He nodded and refrained from pointing out the obvious, that the oscillating fans used up valuable counter space in her already-cluttered work area. He carried his plate to the sink. She started to follow him, to take the dish for him, then stopped, apparently not wanting to be that close to him. He understood. He was a little leery of any more physical contact with her, too. He didn't need any more reminders what a vibrant, beautiful woman she was and it was impossible to get close to her and not think about it.

Finished rinsing out his dishes, he turned and looked at her. And in that second, he knew without their even realizing it, that everything had changed. They were beginning to see each other as people, rather than rivals for Janey's affection. She liked him. And he liked her.

She slid off her stool. "I better let you go. I'm sure you have a busy day."

He took the hint and started for the door, then stopped and turned. "Before I forget, one of the reasons I came over here was that Janey wants us all to get together again."

Laura did a double take. He wasn't sure what she was feeling, but it wasn't outright joy. More like reservations. "The four of us?" she croaked.

"I know how you're feeling. When she first brought it up, I was reluctant, too."

"And now?" Laura prompted, wariness in her eyes.

He didn't want her to be afraid of him. "Sitting here with you, I'm beginning to think Janey's right. We do need to spend more time together." Laura would not try to rob him of Janey's love. She was too generous a woman to ever do something like that and if he had looked harder in the beginning and not been so territorial, maybe he would have seen that.

Seeing her reluctance, remembering how Eric felt about him, he realized what a complicated situation he was creating. Understanding and respecting her reservations, he said, "You don't have to give me an answer this minute. I can see you need time to think about it. Just like I did when Janey talked to me. So I'll call you in a few days. Okay?"

Laura nodded. "I'll have to talk to Eric. He's still…rather prickly."

"I know," Zach said. Boy did he know.

"I DON'T GET IT," Janey grumbled to Zach later the following week. "I mean, I know Laura was busy last weekend with Eric's tournament but why can't she do something with us on President's Day? Eric told me she'd taken the day off, because he had the day off. Did you ask her about Monday specifically?"

"Yes," Zach replied patiently.

"And?"

"And she couldn't be sure what her plans were going to be."

"Did she at least agree to ask Eric about the possibility of a foursome?" Janey persisted.

"I didn't ask her." Her attitude had been so reticent he hadn't wanted to push.

"I don't get it," Janey repeated, bewildered.

Zach did. Laura was avoiding him. Perhaps out of consideration for Eric's feelings. Perhaps for other reasons of her own. And it was beginning to be very frustrating. It wasn't as if he made a habit out of going where he wasn't wanted, but dammit, the other morning in her kitchen he'd had the distinct impression she welcomed him there, that she liked his company. She had started to open up to him. And he'd liked what he'd seen. He'd thought she felt the same keen interest in him. And then she'd shied away for no reason. He'd seen the rejection in her eyes. And he'd heard it in her voice every time he'd talked to her since. She was holding him at arm's length, deliberately.

"Maybe she just needs to hear it from me," Janey said. As Zach watched, she picked up the phone and started dialing. He wasn't surprised to see that like him, she now knew the Matthews's phone number by heart.

"Laura, hi," Janey said softly, her face lighting up with pleasure as the two of them began to talk. "It's Janey. Yeah, great. I have something to ask you...." Minutes later, Janey hung up. She faced him, glowing with satisfaction. "It's all set," she crowed triumphantly. "We're meeting them Monday morning at nine."

"How'd you do that?" Zach stared at his daughter in amazement. Why could Laura respond to Janey so readily and not to him? In the past week, he'd phoned her—what—three times? And thought about doing it three times as much.

"It's charm, Dad." Janey winked. "You ought to try it sometime."

Chapter Ten

"Another strike!" Janey moaned dramatically, burying her head in her hands as Laura watched. She turned to Zach, zealously pleading her case, "Dad, this isn't fair! They're going to kill us if they're both on the same team. We've got to switch partners."

Zach looked a little embarrassed, as well he might, Laura thought. His last turn he'd only knocked down one pin. Zach glanced at Eric. "Would you mind?"

"No problem," Eric said curtly. Turning to Janey, he smiled and laced an arm around her shoulders, "I'd be glad to be on Janey's team."

He still resents Zach, Laura thought, disturbed. For reasons she sensed weren't even clear to her son. Knowing that, she'd tried to avoid putting the two males together again, but when Janey had called, insisting the four of them get together she'd found it impossible to say no.

"Would y'all mind if just Janey and I bowled for the next game or two?" Eric asked. "We wouldn't have to keep score or anything. I just want to give her a few pointers."

"Sure," Laura said.

"Okay with me," Zach said. "He's very good with her," Zach said to Laura after a minute.

"And she clearly adores him," Laura added. Just the way Melinda had. At the thought of the daughter she'd lost, sadness imbued her mood.

"Sorry you came?" Zach asked, misunderstanding the reason for the long sigh that preceded her frown.

"No, not at all."

"You weren't anxious to go out with us in the first place, at least not when I asked you. With Janey, it's a different story."

Laura cast an affectionate glance at her natural daughter and deftly skirted the issue. "It's true. I find it difficult to say no to her."

"She knows that, too."

He waited for her to confide in him and when she didn't, he picked up the questioning again. "Have I done something to annoy you? The last time we were together I thought we were getting along pretty well."

"We were." Maybe too well, Laura admitted candidly to herself.

He shrugged, unable to conceal his hurt at the change in her attitude. "So what happened?"

Laura looked down at the hands she had folded in her lap and said defensively, "I had a chance to think about it, that's all."

"And?"

She felt herself flush self-consciously. "I don't think it's a good idea for the two of us to get too close. Our situation is muddled enough already."

"Not seeing each other won't change that, it won't erase what's happened."

"No, it won't. But I don't want the two of us to become friends the way Eric and Janey have simply because fate has thrown us together." She'd had enough have-to's in her marriage to last her a lifetime.

His clear blue eyes narrowed. "Let's get something straight. I don't see anyone I don't want to, not even for Janey's sake. You're right, of course, the first time we went out together as a unit, to the Mavericks game, you had to twist my arm to get me to go. I didn't have the best time once I got there, mainly because I was very suspicious of you. Now, I've started to see you as I probably would have all along if our situation hadn't been so complicated. I liked what I saw, Laura. I thought you liked me, too.''

She lifted her eyes to his and forced herself not to look away. He was being so honest with her. She couldn't cover up her feelings. "I do like you—as—as a person." There. Maybe that would be enough to satisfy him.

Not a chance. Encouraged by her admission, he gave her a one cornered smile. "A person or a friend?"

His eyes held hers, his brows slightly raised. As he waited for her reply, she could feel her throat tightening. She wished he would stop looking at her so knowingly. "A friend." As soon as the words were out, she knew that was an understatement. The surprising truth was she was warming to the man. And he was warming to her. She didn't know where it would lead, but so what? Maybe she should just relax and enjoy it. She could handle tomorrow's problems, tomorrow.

"Okay. So now that's settled, do you think you could find it in your heart to stop avoiding me?"

She smiled shyly, "I guess, yes."

"Mom!" Eric came back to stand before the two of them impatiently, and she could tell by the tone of his voice it wasn't the first time he had called to her. "We're ready to start the game now. That is if you guys are done talking."

There was an unconscionably rude undertone to her son's voice, one she had never heard before. Laura stared at him, stunned. Realizing he'd gone too far, Eric flushed bright red and said nothing more as he waited for her to reply.

Two months ago, Laura would have reprimanded him on the spot for his behavior, albeit in a quiet fashion. Of course, two months ago, it wouldn't have been necessary. But now she couldn't fault him for needing to find a target for his over-wrought emotions. And who else would he blame, but the two of them?

Janey's eyes twinkled merrily and she teased, "If the two of you are done talking, maybe we could play a real game? Please?"

Zach smiled, as susceptible to his daughter's sweetly voiced request as Laura. "Sure," he said, offering Laura a hand up. "Laura? Who wants to go first?"

"I'M HUNGRY," Janey announced as they turned in their bowling shoes. "Can we go for pizza with Laura and Eric? Please?"

Zach looked at Laura. They were having fun. Why not? She nodded her okay, adding, "There's a Pizza Hut right down the street. We could go there."

"Sounds good to me," Zach said, then turned to the younger members of the entourage again. "Kids?"

"Yes!" Janey said enthusiastically.

Eric gave Zach the once-over, then shoved his hands into his pockets and nodded. The tension between the two males was unmistakable.

And it only got worse as they moved on to the restaurant. After they'd placed their order, Eric slid out of the booth. "Come on, Janey. Let's go play video games while we wait."

Zach reached into his pocket for a handful of change. He counted out four quarters and handed them over to his daughter. "That's all you're going to get, so use them wisely."

Janey made a face. Eric gave Zach a contemptuous look. "Don't worry, kid," Laura and Zach both heard him soothe as he walked away with Janey, "I'll lend you some money if you run out."

"Eric," Zach said firmly. Both children turned and he continued in the same no-nonsense tone, "I said one dollar. That's all."

Janey blushed, embarrassed. "Dad—he was just kidding around!"

No, he wasn't, Laura thought, looking at Eric's face.

Eric shrugged uncaringly. "Whatever." His jaw set, he turned back and laconically continued for the video machines in the corner.

"I've always made it a firm policy never to interfere in

other parents' relationships with their children, but I think you should nip this attitude of his in the bud.''

If the situation hadn't been so complicated and emotional, she wouldn't have hesitated to act. "He's never acted this way before. He'll come out of it," she said with the assurance of a mother who knows her child. "We just have to give him time."

"And until then?"

"Ignore his temper and don't pick up any gauntlet he throws down."

For a moment, Zach looked as if he wanted to argue. But to her relief he thought better of it and let the subject drop. "So," he said after a moment, when the waitress had brought their drinks and left again. "How is your week shaping up?"

"It's going to be busy."

"So is mine. Maybe we could do something this weekend?"

Laura nodded. "Maybe."

"Just the two of us?"

I don't know, Laura thought. Considering how Eric still felt was she asking for trouble? Fortunately, she was saved from replying as the two children returned to the table.

ERIC STARTED IN on her the moment they arrived home. "You really like Janey's dad, don't you?" He went to the refrigerator and got out a carton of milk.

Laura tried to be honest. As gently as possible, she said, "All things considered, he's very nice."

Frowning, Eric reached for a glass. "That's not what I mean," he said, still radiating disapproval.

Laura had been afraid of that. Sighing, she sat opposite him at the kitchen table. It was clear from the disgruntled look on her son's face that he considered her budding interest in Zach a form of disloyalty to his father. "I loved your father very much, but I can't bring him back."

"I know that." Eric shifted defensively and reached for the cookie jar on the counter behind him, extracting a handful.

"What is bothering you about this?"

Eric's mouth tightened. He gave her a surly look. "That night, when I saw the two of you hugging or whatever, you told me it didn't mean anything."

"It didn't."

But something *had* started that night.

"What about now?" Eric demanded.

"We're friends."

"Is that all?"

"For the moment," Laura answered cautiously, evading what she hadn't yet had time to figure out for herself.

"But it could be more," Eric pushed. "Couldn't it?"

"Maybe," she admitted cautiously as their gazes meshed and held.

Eric was silent, taking in all she had said.

"What is it, Eric?" Laura asked again, deciding to be just as tenacious as her son. "You've never reacted this way to any man I've been friends with before."

He scowled and got up abruptly to get some more milk, then accused gruffly, "That's because you never looked at any guy the way you look at Zach."

Laura struggled to keep her voice level. "And how is that?"

He scowled, resenting the fact he had to spell it out. "The way you used to look at Dad, like he's some sort of super-hero."

This was dangerous territory. "Does anything else bother you about Zach?" So much depended on his answer.

Eric shrugged, accusing, "I don't think he likes me much."

"You haven't exactly been polite," Laura pointed out.

"Yeah, well, he bosses Janey around too much. He's too strict."

"He's her father. That's his job. You have to remember she's younger than you are."

The challenging set of her son's jaw was back. "Are you going to keep seeing him?" Eric asked finally.

"I don't know," Laura said honestly.

Wordlessly, Eric got up, rinsed his glass and then put it in the dishwasher. "I'm tired," he said gruffly, keeping his back to her as he closed the appliance door. "I'm going to bed."

Laura sighed, exasperated and worried. "Eric—"

Finally remembering to mind his manners, he said, almost shyly, "Thanks for letting us all go bowling. Janey and I had fun."

The vulnerable look on his face made him seem so much younger. Her heart went out to him and the disciplinarian in her faded. "You're welcome," Laura replied softly. There was no use letting the sun go down on their anger, she thought. There would be plenty of time to reprimand Eric later, if it was necessary. She hoped it wouldn't be.

"I DON'T LIKE this color," Mrs. Gagglione said as she stared at the satin paper going up on the entryway walls. "I specifically said salmon."

"It is salmon," Zach said, showing her a color card.

"It's too pink. The salmon I looked at in the wallpaper warehouse was not that color pink. It was rosier."

Stifling a reflexive sigh, he rested his hand on his hip. "What do you want to do?"

Mrs. Gagglione waved her diamond-encrusted fingers at the walls. "Take it all off, of course." She moved her poodle to her other arm. "I guess I'll just have to go back to the warehouse."

"They'll charge you for both papers," Zach warned.

Mrs. Gagglione drew up to her full five-foot-one height. "No, they will not. They sold me the wrong paper. It is their loss, not mine! Come along, Millicent," she said to her squirming dog.

As Mrs. Gagglione stepped outside onto the front porch, Laura walked in. "Hi." She cast a glance from him to his customer. "Is this a bad time?"

"No," Zach said, his gaze lingering on her slim form. In a butter-colored skirt and sweater that made her brown eyes seem all the darker, she looked fresh and pretty. And she smelled great, too, like roses in the rain. "You've come at a great time." In fact, it would be a relief to talk to someone normal. Taking her hand in his, he led her to the bay windows in the formal dining room. "What's up?"

Briefly she told him about the conversation she had had with Eric the night before, ending uncertainly, "I don't know. Maybe we should cool it for a while." Her eyes filled with regret. "Maybe just let the kids see each other."

"Aren't you the one who told me problems don't go away by ignoring them?"

Looking torn, she swallowed hard. "Yes, but—"

"You can't let Eric dictate your life and make the rules. That's the parent's job, not the child's."

Laura bit her lip and looked at him uncertainly. "I can't just ignore Eric's feelings on this, Zach."

"If Eric approved of us seeing each other, the way Janey does, would you continue with the family outings?" Zach asked.

Laura flushed, her reaction an answer in itself. "But he doesn't," she protested.

"If he did."

She frowned and only answered, Zach suspected, because she knew instinctively he wasn't about to let her out of it. "All right, yes, if Eric approved I would...continue," she admitted grudgingly.

"But—?" he prompted when something else still seemed to be disturbing her.

"But I worry about what's going to happen if we continue to see each other as a group and it persists in being uncomfortable between you and Eric. If that occurs, you might want Eric and I both to stop seeing Janey...and now that she's finally starting to accept me, and I'm getting to know her, I don't want that to happen."

"Hmm." Restless, thinking, he walked over to the empty fireplace and rested one booted foot on the brick hearth. "There's only one way around that I know—to have you see Janey, like Eric does sometimes now, without Eric or I being there, too."

"You'd allow that now?" She seemed stunned. And very happy.

Thinking about it, Zach was a little surprised, too. His attitude had come a long way in the past several weeks. "I trust you not to try to abscond with her," he said softly, enjoying the sudden flush of pleasure in her face.

Zach moved closer, wanting, needing to be near her again. "Besides, it seems to be what Janey wants, and I want her to be happy."

"So do I," Laura said, surprising him with a soft, grateful touch of her hand on his. "Thanks, Zach. This means a lot to me."

He knew.

"YOU DON'T SEEM surprised that Zach's letting me see Janey alone," Laura commented to her father who was replacing the washers in the upstairs bathrooms.

"Your mother told me you were seeing a lot of him," her father said diplomatically, removing a faucet handle.

"Did she also tell you she thinks I've got plans to ensnare him so I can get Janey back?"

"It's not true, is it?" he asked, removing a packing nut.

"No!" Laura said, catching a glimpse of her indignant expression in a mirror above the sink.

"Then why let her upset you?"

Laura sighed. "Does she still want me to sue for custody?" Laura had been avoiding her mother like crazy since they had last talked, to stave off any further lectures on this subject.

Her father removed a worn misshapen washer and replaced it with a shiny new one. "She thinks you have a right to your own child. She still stubbornly refuses to think about the years and years the two of you have spent away from each other."

Laura studied her dad's impassive expression. As usual, it gave away nothing. "What about you, Dad? Have you changed your mind?"

He shook his head solemnly and looked her in the eye. "No. I admit I've thought about it, mostly because your mother can't think of anything else. I still think the child you raise is your own, regardless of his or her biological roots. You can't take Janey's past away from her, any more than you could take Melinda's from her. If she were still here with us, honey, I'd bet my last dollar you'd relive the Alamo before you'd let anyone take her away from you."

Laura nodded. "You're right. My home would be my fortress. I probably wouldn't want Zach near her if she were still alive."

"Which is understandable," her father agreed gently. "If you like Zach, you should continue seeing him."

"What about Eric?"

Her father gave her a reassuring pat on the arm. "Eric'll come around, given time. He's a sensible boy. He's just hurting right now, is all. But he'll get past this. We all will."

Her father paused, thinking, the reassembled faucet spindle in hand. "It would be nice, though, wouldn't it? If you and Zach did eventually get together, like your mother keeps hoping, if you had a chance to raise Janey as your own daughter after all, if some good could come from this loss?"

Yes, it would be good, Laura thought. Almost too good to be true, too easy, too perfect. And for that reason, she didn't want to even think about it. Fate had a way of kicking you in the teeth when you least expected it. She couldn't afford to want too much. She'd already lost more than she could bear.

"DADDY, there's an Open House on Tuesday night at school. And I want Laura to come. Is that okay?"

Zach stared at his daughter, not sure what to say. Although he had just yesterday granted Laura permission to see Janey one-on-one, he hadn't even had a chance yet to tell his daughter of that decision. And now she was asking him for this?

"Are you planning to introduce her as your mother?" he asked, careful to put no inflection of prejudgment in his voice.

Janey flushed. "No," she said. "If—if I did that," she stammered, "people would ask too many questions. I just want her to come, you know, and see where I go to school and meet some of my teachers. Like a normal mom would.''

For not the first time in his life, Zach became acutely aware of how much his daughter had missed not having a mother. Still he found himself unexpectedly unwilling to grant her this. And it had nothing to do with the eyebrows people might or might not raise. It was because, prior to this moment, the turf of Janey's parent had been sacred ground, his alone.

It's only one night, and a rather stiff and formal affair at that, he instructed himself practically. It will be no sweat off my back to include Laura in it. ''If it means that much to you, honey, I'll ask her.''

''You don't have to do that,'' Janey said brightly. ''I already did. I—I hope it's okay?'' she said, when she saw the avalanche of hurt her unthinking remark caused.

''Sure, it's fine,'' he said hoarsely after a moment. ''But let me call her to make sure,'' he continued, knowing all the while what he really wanted was to find out how this had all come about.

Laura picked up her phone on the third ring. After catching her up-to-date on his conversation with Janey, he said, ''I think it's probably better if you go with me, rather than alone.''

''Okay.'' Laura paused, then said almost apologetically, ''Zach, I want you to know, I didn't initiate any of this—''

Remembering the eager look on Janey's face, he knew that was true. Still, he couldn't help but feel threatened.

He finally said, a bit more gruffly than he intended, ''I gathered as much. But you didn't say no to her or even wait to discuss it with me first before you gave her an answer. And I admit that did bother me some.''

On the other end, Laura drew in her breath rather suddenly. ''Are you telling me she asked me before she asked you if it was okay?'' She sounded shocked, Zach thought. So she wasn't working to separate them after all. And that was a relief.

"Yes," he answered Laura honestly. "She called you long before she talked to me."

"That's one of the perils of parenthood, I'm afraid. Kids want to make their own decisions and follow through, regardless of what their parents think."

Thinking of Harry Cole and the troubles he'd been having with Tabitha, Zach knew it was true. "You're right." Zach looked at the form Janey had given him detailing the Open House. "I'll pick you up at six-thirty."

"Sounds good," Laura said.

"And, Laura, I think I'll wait to tell Janey the two of you can see each other one-on-one."

Trepidation edged her voice. "You haven't changed your mind, have you?"

"No. But let's get through the Open House first," Zach said.

Chapter Eleven

"Where's Janey?" Laura asked as she met Zach at the front door Tuesday evening.

"Over at school. Members of the honor society were drafted to act as guides, to help parents find their way around. So we'll see her there."

Trying hard to keep her disappointment to herself, Laura announced steadily, "Harry Cole just called. He said to tell you a Mrs. Gagglione called. There's some sort of emergency over at her new-home site. She wants you to meet her there right away."

Zach swore and rolled his eyes. "That woman."

Laura offered gallantly, "Look, if you want to forget about taking me to Open House, I understand."

"No," Zach said, his expression adamant. "I don't skip anything this important to my daughter."

Something else they had in common, Laura thought. A heartfelt devotion to their children.

He frowned and glanced at his watch, adding, "I can stop by the construction site of Mrs. Gagglione's new home on the way, if it's all right with you, and still make Open House long before they close up at nine."

"Sounds great. Let's go." Laura grabbed her wrap and they were off.

The inside and outside of his Wagoneer were immaculate. Knowing how muddy it was around the construction site,

Laura guessed he had washed and vacuumed it before picking her up. Knowing he'd taken such care made her smile.

"You sound like you don't want to deal with this Mrs. Gagglione," Laura said.

He sighed heavily. "I don't."

"You could always hand her off to one of your employees."

"No. They don't deserve that. I'll work with her. I just wish she had better timing, but I guess if she did, she wouldn't be Mrs. Gagglione."

Unfortunately his client was every bit as much a pain as Zach had implied. In a fur coat, with diamonds dripping from her ears, she was pacing back and forth in the foyer, a small white poodle cradled in her arms. She took one look at Zach and nearly burst into tears. "Have you seen the kitchen since they laid the tile?"

Zach shook his head.

"Well, come and see!" She led the way. Pointing, she said, "It doesn't match the granite countertops, not at all!"

She was right, Laura thought. It didn't match. But then, it wasn't supposed to color coordinate precisely. And it looked perfectly lovely against the white ceramic tile on the floor.

"Mrs. Gagglione, you picked out all the tiles and countertop materials yourself," Zach said.

"It was that interior designer you hired," Mrs. Gagglione wailed. "She talked me into these awful color combinations. When my husband sees it he is going to be furious with me." She turned to Laura, "It's our dream house, you see. And it's up to me to make it perfect!"

Zach said quietly, "What would you like to do, Mrs. Gagglione?"

"I don't know!" she sniffed helplessly.

"The countertops are lovely and all the rage," Laura soothed. "If I had a new kitchen, that's exactly what I'd put in it, and I'm a commercial cook."

"Really?"

"Really. But if you're concerned about color, you might

want to change the tile a bit, put in something with just a touch of gray."

"Gray and white alone would be awfully plain, though," Zach cut in.

"I agree," Laura said. Able to see his client needed soothing more than anything else, she said, "Mrs. Gagglione? What do you think? Would you like a tile that has several colors in it, including gray? Or would you prefer to go with the plain white and add color in other ways, with drapes, for instance and rugs."

"I don't know," Mrs. Gagglione said miserably.

"Perhaps you should take a few days and think about it," Zach suggested gently.

Mrs. Gagglione sighed. "All right," she said finally, "I'll think it over. But, considering how this is turning out, you'd better get another designer to work with me."

"I will," Zach promised.

"Is she always this difficult?" Laura said after the client had left.

"Yes, unfortunately."

"How do you stand it."

"Isn't it obvious? I don't." His lips compressed grimly. "I mean I try to be patient, but it's hard. She's caused us so much extra work. Of course the cost overruns are all added to her bill. Still it's not easy telling the men to rip out tile they've just put in."

"Is she that insecure about everything?"

Zach nodded unhappily. "Afraid so."

Laura couldn't understand that. "Why? Is her husband hypercritical or something?"

"Just the opposite. I think it's her friends she's worried about. Mrs. Gagglione wasn't born to money, you see. They acquired it about five years ago, when some oil came in on their west Texas property."

"Oh."

"Since then, they've been very successful. Still she's not secure in her own worth. Hence, the hysteria over the house.

She wants it to be perfect, to be proof that she is a special, competent human being. If it's a success, she'll be a success.''

"I never thought of a house that way," Laura murmured.

Zach smiled. "That's because you have a lot more going for you. You don't have to rely on anyone or anything to elevate you to a position of importance."

"How'd you figure all this out?" Laura said, marveling at his insight. In the distance, the sun was slowly setting, basking them in an intimate, dusky glow.

Shrugging, Zach answered her question matter-of-factly, "My wife, Maria, was very much like Mrs. Gagglione. Maria didn't believe in herself, either. She was beautiful and smart and funny, but deep inside, she was insecure. I didn't know it when I married her but I found out later there were a lot of problems in her family. Neither of her parents had ever had much time for her, her mother because she was working almost constantly, and her father because he drank. She never really believed either of them loved her, and in the end she felt the same way about me."

Laura remembered how much it had hurt when her own marriage had started to go awry. "That must have hurt you."

He affirmed so sadly, adding, "I tried to convince her that I loved her very much, but there was no getting through to her."

Listening to him talk, realizing he'd struggled as she had to build a solid, happy life, her heart went out to him. "I'm sorry."

He shrugged, letting her know he had dealt with it long ago. "Life isn't perfect. I just wish, in retrospect, I could have helped her to believe in herself more."

Deciding a more cheerful topic was in order, Laura turned back to the kitchen. "The tile dilemma aside, Zach, this is going to be beautiful."

"You think so?"

"Oh, yes. What kind of refrigerator is Mrs. Gagglione going to get, do you know?"

"A stainless-steel Traulsen."

Laura groaned with undisguised envy. "I should have guessed. Only the best, hmm?"

He nodded. "Want to see the rest of the house?"

"Would you mind showing me?"

He looked at his watch. "Not at all. Open House runs until nine." And it was only seven.

They ended the tour on the third-floor balcony, overlooking the hills. "They're going to have a wonderful view of the city," Laura said.

"I kind of like the view now," Zach teased, looking at her.

Laura flushed with both pleasure and embarrassment. He wasn't so bad himself. He looked very handsome and very urbane. She was proud to be with him, relaxed and easy at his side. And those feelings of camaraderie surprised her. The heat still warming her cheeks unbearably, she moved away from him.

He stayed his ground with obvious effort. "You don't have to run away from me, you know," he said softly, his gaze still on her.

Afraid things were moving too fast, she ducked her head. "We better get going to Open House."

"I haven't forgotten." Zach stepped closer. Before she could protest, he had his arms around her, an intense, ardent look in his clear blue eyes. Knowing instinctively she'd be lost at the first touch of his lips upon hers, she started to resist but his mouth closed over hers with unapologetic hunger anyway. He took what she wasn't so sure she was ready to give, until her lips had parted and she had that familiar, unmistakable weightless sensation in her middle. Her head fell back, giving him freer access to her mouth and she moaned with disbelief, and joy, and wonder, unsure that this, the forbidden, was really happening, yet ecstatic that it was.

Slowly, inevitably, the tension left her body as his tongue continued to tenderly plunder her open mouth and she curled against him, pressing her thighs to his. With a groan of contentment, he slid his hands down her body to her waist and pulled her more firmly against him. Aware of his fierce desire for her, she felt an answering thrill where he held her cupped against him that soon turned to a white-hot throbbing. Her arms moved to wreathe his neck and she let her fingers tunnel through the silky thickness of his hair. His arms wrapped tightly around her, he continued to kiss her with spellbinding tenderness. How she had missed this closeness, she thought, this feeling of being absolutely, completely alive. Of being a woman. Of being wanted. Of having a life outside the boundaries of work and motherhood.

He may have been the aggressor, but she was more than compliant. As he kissed her, she felt the warmth and tenderness and the excitement that had always been missing from her life. And more: she felt cherished, just for being herself. So much so that she was shaking when they drew apart. This had been coming a long time, Laura realized looking up into his face, the fire within her still raging out of control. And now that it had, she wasn't sure she had the willpower to call a halt if he so much as kissed or touched her again.

To her credit and satisfaction, he didn't look any steadier than she felt. Or any more able to stop if they touched again.

But they were in a house still under construction, she reminded herself firmly. And what felt good tonight, might turn into a living hell tomorrow. She had been reckless once, in her youth, letting her passionate nature rush her into a marriage that had never been destined to last. She couldn't do that again, not with the happiness of both their families at stake.

"I better get you to the Open House," Zach said.

Knowing how close she had come to making love with him, right there and then, she didn't argue. Her heart was a little heavier as she made her way to the car.

"YOU MUST BE LAURA," Mrs. Bauer said the minute they walked in the door to Janey's Language Arts class.

Laura looked up, surprised. Recovering her equilibrium, which wasn't easy after Zach's passionate, unexpected embrace, she smiled and held out a hand. "How did you know who I was?"

Mrs. Bauer smiled. "Just a guess, really. You see, Janey wrote a poem. Maybe I should show it to you." Turning, she directed them to the back of the classroom.

Stunned, Laura moved closer to the feminine script and her heart in her throat, read Janey's poem.

It was entitled, "If I Had A Mom."

> If I had a mom,
> I'd want her to be,
>   just like Laura.
> Bright, cheerful, funny,
>   Kind and sweet,
> Always loving,
>   Always caring,
> Laura.

Tears in her eyes, a happiness she hadn't felt in a long while filling her soul, Laura stared at the handwritten poem. Zach stared at it, too, but he looked more as if he'd been run over by a truck than pleased by the expression of his daughter's sentiments.

Mrs. Bauer beamed at them both, Laura especially. "It was a lovely tribute," she said. "Janey must feel very close to you."

"Closer than I knew," she admitted tremulously, while beside her Zach said something equally inane.

As soon as they could, they left the classroom. How they got through the rest of the night, Laura wasn't sure, only that she and Zach met four more teachers in various classes as well as Janey and several of Janey's friends, who were all stationed strategically at various points around the sprawling four-story middle school. But over and over her mind kept going back to the poem.

"Did you see it?" Janey asked en route home, having opted for the back seat of the jeep, leaving Laura to sit in the front with her dad.

"Yes, Janey, I did," Laura said. "It was very sweet."

Janey grinned, pleased with the heartfelt praise, and leaned forward as much as her fastened seat belt would allow.

"Daddy?" Janey asked.

"Your ability to express yourself has really improved," he said finally. "Listen, I'm going to drop you off first, so you can go ahead and get ready for bed. I'll take Laura home and be right back."

"That's a good idea," Janey said, a worried frown crossing her face as she gathered her purse and several leftover maps of the school.

"I'm sorry," Laura said softly, long moments later when they had reached her driveway. Alone again, she was free to tell him what she'd been feeling since the moment she'd spied Janey's poem. "I had no idea what was in store for us tonight."

"Obviously that's why she wanted you to be there tonight. So you could read the poem." And realize firsthand how much she has always wanted a mother of her very own, Zach thought. A mother she could go to for warmth and tenderness.

"It's not surprising she would have those feelings about me," Laura said, looking down at the house key she held in her hand.

"Isn't it?" he responded.

Laura shrugged expressively. "She wants a mother. All children do." It probably could have been anyone, any woman with a sense of tenderness and concern for her well-being, Laura thought. I shouldn't get carried away, she instructed herself sternly. But she wanted to get carried away. Knowing how Janey was beginning to open up to her, she wanted to fly.

"I guess you're right," Zach said tiredly, deciding he was overreacting, as he had so often these past few weeks, when it came to the subject of Janey and Laura. "After all, Janey's never known a mother. Maria died of a stroke when she was just a baby."

"All the more reason for her to latch on to me." Laura

continued the conversation, thinking, there's no reason for you to be threatened by this, Zach. Janey loves you, too.

His shoulders lifted and fell, and he stared straight ahead. "You're right, of course," he said, but his words sounded dull and lifeless even to his own ears.

"And you're worried," Laura said, hating the anguish she saw in his eyes and wishing she knew some magic way to erase it.

Zach looked at her, for once not trying to hide behind an impassive front. "Wouldn't you be worried in my place?"

Laura wished she could say no, but she wasn't that noble and unselfish of heart, either. "Probably," she conceded with a small frown, hoping this latest action of Janey's wouldn't destroy the closeness she and Zach had begun to forge. Or the ardent desire she had felt in his kiss earlier. Because she had started to count on his friendship. And his support. And if it was too soon, or still unwise for them to make love now, maybe it wouldn't always be....

Again, they lapsed into silence. "You better get back to Janey," she said finally. She wished they could work this out now, but even as she thought it she knew it was foolish. It took a lot more than mutual love for a child to bond a man and woman together, to form a relationship that would last. And after her disastrous first marriage, she would no longer settle for anything less. There was simply too much at stake, for her and Zach especially.

"START, darn you!" Laura said Wednesday afternoon, pumping the gas pedal on her station wagon for the third time. The starter made a faint clicking sound but the engine didn't even begin to turn over.

The battery was dead and she had a three-tiered fiftieth wedding anniversary cake carefully loaded in the rear compartment. The party was due to start in another hour, and the cake was supposed to be there before any of the guests arrived.

Getting out of her car, she went back inside the house. She tried calling her parents, to no avail. The auto club couldn't send anyone for at least another two hours. The party giver's line was busy. And the local taxi service was fresh out of limousines—the only car with doors wide enough to allow her to house the gigantic cake.

She needed someone with a station wagon or a Jeep.

In desperation, she punched out Zach's number. "I wouldn't call unless I were desperate—" she began hesitantly.

He laughed softly. "Well, that's flattering—"

Flushing, she began to explain. Hearing, he said, "No problem. I'll come right over."

"You're sure you don't mind?" she asked cautiously.

"What are friends for?"

The moment she saw him she knew he had also had an incredibly busy day. His blue chambray shirt and jeans were dusted with streaks of white, blue, and mint green. Paint was smeared on his chin. His eyes widened at the huge cake. "I see what you mean about it being unwieldy."

"We're going to have to lift it up into the truck," Laura said frowning.

"No problem."

"It's heavy," she warned.

"I'll be careful."

With some difficulty, they managed to transfer the cake. Only when she was certain the cake was secure, did they shut the back door.

In tandem, she and Zach dashed toward the front of his Wagoneer. "Where to?" he asked genially.

She looked up the address she'd written on the invoice and they were off. "The client is going to be furious with me," Laura moaned as they waited impatiently at the third red traffic light. "I should have had this cake at the reception hall two hours ago. I would have, if everything under the sun hadn't gone wrong."

"Like what?"

"I ran out of bittersweet chocolate and hazelnuts and had to make an emergency trip to the store, then I got caught in traffic on the way back. The two bottom layers took an extra ten minutes to bake. I have no idea why. My stand mixer went on the blink, so I had to use my hand-held electric mixer to make all the frosting. I misplaced one of the parts to my electric food gun so I had to hunt up my pastry bag and put on all the swags and bows the old-fashioned way. Then, when I was putting on the names, as the client suggested, I forgot they spelled Karin with an *i* instead of an *e*, and misspelled her name, so I had to scrape off my error, redo the layer of frosting beneath it, make an extra batch of icing, and spell the name correctly."

Just talking about it made her perspire anew. Zach laughed and shook his head in shared commiseration. "When you have a rotten day, you go all out."

Of course, the worst part of it all was she knew why she'd had so much trouble. The problem was she wasn't concentrating on her work. And the reason she wasn't doing that was Zach. Since he had kissed her, she hadn't been able to think about much else.

"Here we are," Zach said, pulling up in front of the reception hall. No sooner had he cut the engine than a woman came running out. "We thought you'd never get here!"

"Sorry," Laura apologized. "It's a long story."

With Zach's help, she got the cake inside, out of the box, and safely situated on a table. Fortunately it was everything the celebrating couple had wanted in an anniversary cake.

Zach and Laura went back outside. "I owe you for this one," she said, breathing a sigh of relief.

He smiled, liking the idea of that. "Now what about your car?"

She fell into step beside him, glad he was there with her. She shrugged. "I guess I call the auto club again."

He slanted her a thoughtful glance. "Want me to take a look at it?"

Laura thought of the mechanic's fee she could save, if he could locate the problem. "Sure, if you don't mind."

"No problem."

"You may need a new battery," Zach said an hour and a

half later. They had jump-started her car, charged it, then let it sit. When they tried to start it again, it was dead.

Laura sighed, thinking what that would entail: a trip to the shop, a wait, the price of a new battery plus a mechanic's fee.

"If you like, I could put it in for you," Zach said.

Laura looked over at him, amazed. Was there no end to this man's generosity? "I don't want to impose."

"It's no problem," Zach reassured her as Eric drove up and parked on the street.

"What's going on?" Eric asked, joining them. He looked from Zach to Laura.

"Your mother's car needs a new battery. Want to help me replace it for her?" Zach asked.

Eric looked at him, his wariness evident.

Ignoring her son's reticence, Zach continued pleasantly, "That way, you'll know how to replace the battery in your car, if and when it quits," Zach continued.

The opportunity to learn skills that would make him even more self-sufficient was too good to pass up. "Sure," Eric said. "I'll do it for Mom." And not, the unspoken declaration went, because Zach had asked him.

Ignoring Eric's subtle put-down, Laura said, "I'll need to get money for the battery."

Zach caught her wrist before she could depart. "That's not necessary. We'll settle up later."

She smiled. "You're sure this isn't too much trouble?"

"No, not at all. But you might call Janey and tell her I'll be late."

After the men left, Laura decided to do better than that. Rather than have Janey endure an evening alone because Zach was busy at her place, she decided to use Eric's car to go and get Janey and bring her back to her house.

"This car is so cool!" Janey said as the two of them rattled along in the old red Mustang. "I want one just like it when I learn to drive." Janey settled back into her seat with a contented sigh, looking so much like Eric at that moment that Laura thought her heart would break.

"So what's for dinner?" Janey asked, once inside the house. She settled in at the kitchen table with her homework, as Melinda used to do.

Her heart brimming with memories, Laura watched her open her algebra book. Janey was such a sunny child, so sweet and outgoing and giving. As Eric normally was. "What would you like for dinner?"

Janey slid the eraser end of her pencil behind her ear. "Do you know how to fix *fajitas*?"

Laura laughed and teased, "Are you kidding, girl? I'm a native Texan. Chicken or beef?"

"Either one."

Laura opened her freezer, glad it was well stocked. "How about both?"

Janey grinned exuberantly. "Radical."

Extracting two packages of *fajita* meat from the freezer, Laura put it in the microwave to thaw. Janey watched, entranced, as Laura quickly whipped up the marinade. Melinda had loved to watch her cook, too, Laura thought. She had missed having a daughter to talk to while she puttered around putting supper on.

"What's in the sauce?" Janey asked.

"Worcestershire sauce, garlic salt, pepper." Laura began slicing up onions to fry with the meat.

Watching, Janey giggled and shook her head in consternation. "I didn't think people who were dating liked to eat onions. Or garlic." At Laura's surprised look, Janey elaborated, "You know, 'cause if you kiss someone."

Laura flushed. Who did Janey think she was kissing? Had Zach somehow let on about Tuesday night? In an effort to recover, she retorted calmly, "That's true enough, but it's not a problem if the two people who are going to kiss eat the same thing."

"Oh, so it doesn't matter if you and my dad both eat onions and garlic?" Janey asked.

She's fishing, Laura thought triumphantly. And I almost fell for it. "If our respective dates also eat the same thing—" Laura began, returning Janey's too-innocent look.

"If who eats the same thing?" Zach asked, coming in the back door behind Eric.

The two of them were covered with black grime, from fingertips to elbows. "People who are dating," Janey replied. "Hi, Eric." She beamed as she looked at her older brother.

"Hiya kid." Grinning, Eric pretended to bop her on the head with one grease-smeared arm. Janey squealed and ducked.

"There's soap in the guest bath," Laura said.

"I'll show you," Eric said.

Laura noted that although Eric greeted Janey affectionately, he still wasn't all that warm to Zach. On the other hand, they had worked together on her car.

Seconds later, Eric returned. He pulled a cola from the refrigerator, and tossed one to Janey, who barely managed to catch it. "Eric Matthews, if those colas explode you will personally mop up the mess!" Laura warned.

"Relax." Eric grinned, winking at Janey. "I know an old trick. Just tap the top about five or six times, right over the cutout of the pull tab. See? And voilà!" He pulled it open. Nothing, not even a bubble fizzed over the top.

"Now you try it, Janey," Eric encouraged.

To Laura's amazement, hers opened without incident, too. Laura said. "Did you thank Zach for showing you how to change a battery?"

"He did," Zach said from the doorway.

Eric looked at Zach over his shoulder, his feelings of ambivalence simmering close to the surface again. "Come on, Janey," he said, inclining his head toward the door. "Let's go watch TV. There's a game on cable...."

"Can I get you something to drink?" Laura asked Zach.

Zach nodded. "A beer if you have it."

"Coming up."

"Something smells good." He nodded toward the meat simmering in the skillets on top of the stove.

"Janey requested *fajitas*. I hope that's okay."

"One of my favorites."

"Great."

"Anything I can do?" He moved closer, yet retained enough distance to give her elbow room.

"Not really. I just have to set the table." He smelled like soap and man. It was a tantalizing combination and disconcerting to have him so close.

"What was all that about people who date having to eat the same things when I came in?" he asked.

Laura felt herself blush. "She wanted to know why I didn't mind eating garlic and onions. She was under the impression most adults who date don't do that."

"Ah," Zach said, his eyes sparkling in a way that let her know he, too, was remembering their first, and so far only, kiss. His impertinent grin said he was anticipating another.

Her heart thudding with telltale speed, Laura decided she had been on the hot seat long enough. It was time for him to have a turn. "Do you make a habit of not eating garlic and onions—for that reason?" she asked, careful to keep her expression innocent. "Is that where Janey got the idea?"

"I didn't," he admitted, owning up to the fact unabashedly, "until a few weeks ago. I guess since then I've been making more of an effort to have restaurants hold the onion and/or garlic. Mrs. Yaeger, too. I guess Janey noticed."

Suddenly Laura couldn't breathe. The sound of the kids, hooting over a game in the family room, sounded very far away. Attempting to diffuse the tension with levity, she said, "If I didn't know better, I'd think you were trying to tell me something."

His eyes softened tenderly. "Maybe I am," he admitted quietly. She was backed up against the countertop with no place to go, a stack of plates in her hands.

He took them from her, and put them aside.

"Zach—" The word escaped her lips on a breathy sigh.

"I like the way you say my name," he countered, taking her into his arms. His mouth slanted over hers predatorily.

Knowing a kiss was inevitable and that if she was honest with herself she wanted it as much as he, her head tilted back.

"And I like the way you look in that apron," he continued softly.

Anticipating, even welcoming his sweet caress, she linked both hands behind his neck and teased back softly, "I'm a mess."

"You're perfect," he murmured, his lips touching hers once, and then again and again. "And you know it."

And there the testing stopped. He kissed her again, even more passionately, until she was limp and acquiescent in his arms. Only the smell of nearly burning meat woke them up. Laura stared at him, wondering how she had ever gotten along without this man in her life, hoping she would never have to again.

She turned swiftly, avoiding another sensual pass of his mouth. "Dinner's ready," she said. "We need to tell the kids."

He gave her a long, sultry look that let her know he, too, felt they should tell the kids, and not just about dinner, but about the two of them, as well. "I'll get them."

Chapter Twelve

"This is so neat! Thank you for taking me shopping," Janey said as she and Laura walked in the entrance to the mall.

Laura smiled, already having fun. "You're welcome."

"How come Dad didn't come?" Janey asked.

Realizing she still had her car keys in her hand, Laura tucked them into the zipper pocket of her purse. "He thought you could use some girl talk, female bonding and all that." Plus, he was keeping his promise to let her develop a relationship with Janey on her own, so if anything did happen to make family outings impossible, she could continue to see her daughter with the least amount of awkwardness possible.

"Radical," Janey said, giving her highest stamp of approval to the idea of she and Laura doing things like shopping alone. Janey continued confidentially, "Dad doesn't really enjoy shopping anyway. He just wants to go in the store, buy what you need as fast as possible and get out. He doesn't like to look around or just hang out. Know what I mean?"

Laura nodded. "Eric hates shopping, too. Most men are that way, I think. Must be something in their genes."

"Or not." Janey laughed, explaining, "The shopping gene. They don't have it."

Laura laughed, too.

They passed a shop that carried only accessories. "Oh, would you look at those earrings?" Janey breathed, holding on to Laura's shoulder with one hand and pointing with the other. "Aren't they to-die-for? And they're clip-on, too!"

Laura noted Janey didn't have her ears pierced. For someone who adored earrings as she apparently was beginning to, that could pose a problem. The selection of clip-on was usually sparse when compared to the selection of pierced earrings. "They are pretty," Laura admitted.

"But they're seven dollars. I only have five," she said, disappointed.

"I could lend you two dollars. Actually, I'd be glad to buy them for you if you think your dad wouldn't mind me doing so."

Janey's expression was indignant. "Why should he mind? We're friends and friends give each other presents. But... maybe you're right." Janey frowned as if seeing a slight problem. "Maybe I should buy them with my own money."

"Then it's settled." Laura reached into her change purse and counted out two dollars. "This is a loan."

"Thanks, Laura!" Janey cried ebulliently. "Wait till the girls at school see these."

As they had predicted, the earrings looked terrific on Janey. Cute and young. Janey wore them the rest of the day and she still had them on when Laura drove her home.

Zach was working in the yard. His smile faded as Janey got out of the car. "Hi, Daddy!" she said buoyantly.

"Hi." His glance narrowed on her ears, then turned back to Laura. Seeing his obvious displeasure, she felt herself tense.

"Thanks for taking me, Laura," Janey said, moving forward to give Laura an impulsive hug. Affection for the child flowing through her in waves, Laura hugged her back. Withdrawing, Janey said shyly, "I had so much fun. It was neat to be able to do girl-stuff, just the two of us, like my friend Chrissy does with her mom. I wish we could be together all the time like that."

"So do I," Laura admitted, not ashamed of how much the time with her daughter had meant to her.

"I'm going in to call Chrissy," Janey said, dashing for the door. "I can't wait to tell her what I got!"

Janey disappeared, the door slamming behind her. Laura looked back at Zach. His face was a mask of displeasure. "Where'd she get the earrings?" he inquired crisply. His deliberate matter-of-fact tone didn't fool her. Zach was furious.

Trepidation making her legs tremble, Laura answered as serenely as she could, "Janey bought them with her own money plus a two-dollar loan from me."

He was incredulous. "You gave her money for those?"

"Yes."

"Why?"

"She admired them."

He leaned on his hoe and Laura could see he was struggling with his temper. "Did she tell you I've forbidden her to get her ears pierced?"

Laura's smile faltered, as did her equilibrium. "No, but those are clip-on earrings, Zach."

His jaw took on a stubborn edge. "I don't want her wearing those, either. I think she's too young. Janey knows that, Laura."

Embarrassed, she had to work to keep her gaze steady on his. "She didn't tell me that."

Zach sighed, realizing Laura had been hoodwinked. "Knowing how many times we've argued about that in the past, I don't doubt it."

Laura cast around for something to say. This was none of her business, she told herself firmly. Or was it? Janey was her child. And Zach was being unfair and dictatorial. Suddenly, she knew she had to come to Janey's defense. "Zach, they're just earrings. All the girls her age are wearing them."

The corners of his mouth curled downward. "I don't know how to say this without offending you, but those earrings make her look cheap."

Now he was being ridiculous. Laura stiffened her spine. "I disagree."

He shrugged. "Disagree all you want. Janey isn't your child. She's mine."

If he'd meant to hurt her, he had. She gritted her teeth.

Janey was back. She hurled herself into Laura's arms and gave her a heartfelt hug. "I almost forgot to say thank-you for the earrings."

"Janey," Zach interjected in a calm, cautious tone. "About the earrings."

At Zach's firm but weary tone, Janey's countenance turned stormy. "I can't get an infected earlobe from clip-ons, Dad."

"I still don't want you wearing them until you're older."

"Dad, I'm almost in high school—!"

"But you're not in high school," Zach countered.

Guiltily, Laura stepped in. She had made a mess of things here, albeit unknowingly. Never would she have undermined Zach's parental authority deliberately. "Your dad is the boss here, Janey. What he says goes. If he doesn't want you to wear earrings to school, you'll just have to wear them at home."

Janey looked at Laura as if she was a traitor. "I thought you'd be on my side in this," she said in a soft, hurt voice.

Laura felt she was caught between a rock and a hard place, with no way out. "I am."

"Sure you are," Janey mumbled. She turned and ran off.

Zach turned back to Laura, the moment the front door had slammed behind his daughter. "Satisfied?"

"Look," Laura began, "I know how this looks—"

"Like you're trying to start a war between my daughter and me?"

Laura imposed an iron control on her own rising temper and countered softly, reasonably, "I never tried to do that."

His blue eyes clouded with uneasiness, Zach shot back, "Maybe not deliberately, but you're doing a damn good job of it."

"Look," Laura insisted with returning impatience, "just because I happen to think you're unreasonable about this earring business does not mean I am trying to replace you in your daughter's affections!''

Zach swore beneath his breath and clenched his mouth tighter. ''Be honest here, Laura, if not with me, with yourself. Admit it would suit your purposes just fine if you could usurp my role as parent and woo Janey away from me emotionally, become her favorite parent, and let me carry all the burdens of the disciplinarian. You get to take her out and have fun whereas I get to be the guy who stays home with her and makes sure she does her homework and doesn't act older than her age.''

''I never would've permitted Janey to buy the earrings if I had known about your rule at the time,'' Laura said again.

''A lot of good that does me now.''

She breathed an exasperated sigh. She knew he was jealous. She could hardly blame him. ''I care about Janey, Zach. I'll be the first to admit that. I might even be starting to love her, but I have never tried to steal her away from you, and I never would. And if you think that even for an instant, you don't know me at all.''

Zach studied her, his hurt visible. ''Maybe not consciously,'' he said finally. ''But Laura...you have to think about what you've just done.''

''I have. And I have nothing to be sorry for. If anyone is acting like a jerk, Zach, it's you.'' Knowing it would be pointless to discuss this further until he calmed down, she turned on her heel and marched defiantly toward her station wagon.

As she suspected, he did nothing at all to stop her.

EARLY SATURDAY evening, Laura was on her knees, turning over the soil with a spade when a shadow fell over her. Shading her eyes with one hand, she glanced up just as Zach hunkered down beside her. His anger of hours before had faded and he was waving a small white flag, made out of a handkerchief and a small stick.

As their eyes met, he said softly, ''Truce?''

Although a small part of her wanted to hurl herself into his arms then and there and just make all this unpleasantness go away, a larger part of her knew glossing over this bitter misunderstanding wouldn't help. They had to talk it out, as honestly as possible, even if it hurt them both. "Easier said than done," Laura said, digging even more sharply into the dirt.

He watched as she turned over another small row of soil.

"I'm sorry I said what I did. I know you didn't mean to come between me and Janey." At the genuine contrition in his voice, she looked up and met his eyes. They were laced with worry as he continued solemnly, "But you've got to realize that I'm Janey's dad. I have final say over what she does or does not do or wear or buy."

Her anger at his patronizing attitude flaring anew, Laura dug her spade even more sharply into the dirt. "And the fact I'm her mother counts for nothing. Is that it?"

She hadn't meant to say those words, hadn't even known she felt them, until now. As shocked as he was by the revelation of what was in her heart, she let her hand go limp. Her mouth dropped open. Zach was silent, too. Finally she dared a glance deep into his eyes and saw naked fear, the kind she had suffered when she'd first found out Melinda was going to die.

The breath left her lungs in one giant whoosh. Her jaw trembled, so did her hands. Tears welled in her eyes. "I'm sorry," she said softly, shaking her head and dropping her gaze. "I don't know where that came from." Somewhere, in the past few weeks, Laura had come to love Janey fiercely. She realized that now.

Looking stunned, Zach sat back in a patch of grass next to her garden, folding his legs in front of him Indian style. "Maybe we should talk about this," he said slowly.

Laura wasn't sure she agreed. They seemed to be on treacherous ground again. Opening a pack of lettuce seeds, she began sprinkling them one by one into the furrow she had created.

"Is that how you think of Janey?" Zach pressed softly.

"Like she's your daughter?" he finished in a voice full of curiosity and wonder.

Although she wasn't looking at him, Laura could feel his eyes upon her, burning into her, wanting to understand. Feeling near tears, she shrugged with feigned indifference. "She's a lot like Eric—in looks, temperament, interests." And not at all like Melinda had been, she thought.

"That's not what I'm asking." When she continued to drop the seeds into the furrow, one by one, with abnormal concentration, he reached out and caught her wrist, holding it still until she was forced to meet his steady, unwavering gaze. "Do you feel she's your daughter?" he repeated in a husky, strained voice.

Laura gulped. She wanted to lie to him, but she knew she couldn't. One, she'd never get away with it. Two, her guilt would eat her alive if she did. She'd made so many mistakes already. Disavowing the depth of her maternal concern for Janey wasn't something she was willing to add to the list.

"Yes," Laura said, swallowing the knot of emotion in her throat, "I guess I do. I didn't at first," she added quickly, stung into softening her statement by the hurt look on his face. "But, as I've gotten to know her, I've felt a bond with her. I'm not sure I can explain it. I just know when I look at her that she's mine. In here." Laura placed a hand over her heart.

"And what was Melinda to you then?" he countered gruffly, an angry set to his jaw.

"She was mine, too, just the way Janey is yours."

Silence fell between them. Looking weary and emotionally embattled, he let go of her wrist.

"About the earrings," she said sitting back on her heels, "I am sorry about that. I never meant to help Janey have anything that was forbidden to her."

"I surmised that," Zach said. Idly he picked up a package of green bean seeds and turned it over to glance at the instructions on the back. With a flick of his wrist, he dropped them back on top of some other packets. His mouth thinned. "But that doesn't mean you should let it happen again."

Laura didn't want to interfere between Janey and Zach. But neither could she stand idly by and watch Zach repeat some of the mistakes her own mother had made when parenting her. "Zach…"

"What?"

For Janey's sake she knew she had to at least try to talk to him about this. He was setting a precedent here, whether he knew it or not. She took a deep breath and took off her gardening gloves. "There is such a thing as being too strict."

His face changed, his visage becoming most unwelcoming. "I thought you weren't going to interfere anymore. Laura—"

"I'm not. But what can be the harm in earrings? Those earrings are all the rage right now."

"Well, it's a rage she'll have to do without."

Anger flared in Laura. Zach was sounding exactly like her mother. "Zach, you're going to have a lot of battles with Janey over the next few years. Janey needs to assert her independence and decide what she likes, and not just do everything you want her to do, willy-nilly. That's how kids grow up and cut the apron strings."

"It's also how they get into trouble," he prophesied grimly. "Today, it's earrings that are a little too flashy, then it's a skirt that's a tad too short. I know how these things work, too, Laura. Lots of men on my crew have teenagers who have or are getting out of hand. Harry Cole's daughter, Tabitha, was picked up for hitchhiking recently. Her only excuse was she wanted to fit in with the other kids. I'm not going to let that happen to Janey. And this is where it starts, with the little things."

Laura knew his concern was valid, one she shared. But he was going about trying to protect Janey in the wrong way. "You have to give her some breathing room," she persuaded practically.

"I will, but not about the way she looks," Zach said stubbornly.

Laura sighed. "I still think you're being unreasonable about this."

"Fine." His expression remained immobile. "I trust you'll keep your feelings to yourself and not let Janey know how you feel."

Laura knew that Janey was loved, nurtured. Zach was only doing what he felt was appropriate. Just as she did what she knew was right for Eric, even when others, like Zach or her father, thought she was being too lax.

Knowing she couldn't win, she gave in. "I promise I won't interfere."

Relief softened the line of his jaw. The beginnings of a smile curled his lips. "Then we agree to disagree and call a truce?"

Warmed by the new gentleness she saw in his eyes, Laura smiled, too. It seemed they were both as stubborn and opinionated as the day was long, and maybe that wasn't all bad. "All right. Truce."

"Are you going to plant this whole area?" Zach asked, changing the subject. He indicated a fifty-foot by ten-foot plot, partitioned off from the rest of the backyard by railroad ties.

"Yes," Laura said.

His brow furrowed. "And you're going to till all the soil by hand?" When Laura nodded, he asked, "Don't you have a Rototiller?"

"I wish. No, I don't."

"And I don't suppose you want to hire anyone to do it for you."

Shrugging, she admitted, "That seems like a lot of trouble and expense for a job I am perfectly capable of doing myself."

Zach frowned. "You really shouldn't have to work so hard," he murmured.

Wordlessly, she shook her head.

"What?" he prompted.

"I'm just not used to having anyone fuss over me, that's all. I've done it this way for years, Zach."

His brow furrowed. "Your husband never felt it was too much for you? He didn't help at least ready the soil?"

Laura flushed self-consciously. "He was in the Navy, remember? And even when he was here when it was time to plant, it never occurred to him to offer to help me care for the garden."

Zach frowned, looking chivalrous and disapproving again, as if he couldn't understand anyone being there and not helping. "That didn't bother you?" he asked softly.

At the time, Laura hadn't given it much thought. Or at least she had tried not to. Now that Zach brought it up, though, she realized she had harbored resentments about the life they had lived. Shrugging carelessly, she allowed, "We didn't share that much. I mean, how could we? He was always gone, at least half the year. At that time, they spent six months at sea, six months at home. When he was here…well, suffice it to say, the kids were all over him. They missed having a daddy. I didn't want to interfere in that." Suddenly needing the emotional release physical activity provided, she started digging again.

Beside her, Zach picked up a spade too, and began tilling the soil several feet away. "That's understandable," he said.

"Yes, but it wasn't any way to conduct a marriage." Laura sighed. She knew she had to be honest with him about this. She knew if he was ever going to understand her, she had to tell him what she'd not confided in anyone else. "The simple truth of the matter is, had Rob lived, we never would have stayed married. We would have been divorced by now." Zach wasn't the only one who'd had an imperfect marriage and maybe it was time he knew that.

Stunned, Zach momentarily stopped what he was doing and stared at her. "I'm sorry," he said.

Laura shrugged and kept digging. "We married too young, for all the wrong reasons. He wanted to have children, to have something and someone to come home to and I wanted to be on my own, grown-up. And for me, marrying Rob was the fastest way to get away from my mother and live my own life."

"So you married."

"Yes," she reported sadly. "Fancying myself a modern-day Juliet to his Romeo, I eloped with him. Only it wasn't as wildly romantic as I had thought it would be," she admitted, digging hard in the soil again. "When it really came down to it, we didn't have a lot in common and he spent a lot of time out with the guys when he was home."

"That doesn't sound like fun."

She shrugged again, realizing she'd just made Rob sound like an ogre. "It wasn't all bad. I mean the homecomings were very passionate and—" She stopped and blushed self-consciously, realizing what she had just blurted out in her effort to make him understand what her married life had been like.

He grinned. "Makes sense."

Blushing even more, Laura plowed on, explaining, "But his homecomings were always empty, too. We were like strangers. It was hard, getting to know each other again. I was going through a lot of changes while he was gone, growing, and then when the kids came along, it became even more strained between us. I ruled the house. Then he would come home and he would want the final word." She shook her head in regret, remembering how bitterly they had quarreled at times.

"A bit of a power struggle, hmm?"

Laura nodded sadly, admitting, "And then some."

"Is that why you would've divorced?"

Laura nodded. "The sad part is in retrospect I'm not sure I ever did really love him. Still I knew how traumatic it would be for the kids to go through a divorce, so I tried to work through the problems, only to find out the willingness to compromise and change was all on my side. He just didn't think it was necessary. And that's when his ship was sent to the Gulf of Sidra, off the coast of Libya. He was part of the U.S. Navy task force that was conducting exercises there. He was in a plane that was hit by an anti-aircraft missile and he was killed instantly."

"I'm sorry," Zach said softly, covering her gloved hand with his own.

She stared down at their entwined palms, his looking so

solid and strong over her more delicate one. "I never told anyone what I just told you about the problems in my marriage," Laura admitted quietly, unable to help feeling ashamed about her failure. "I never even told my parents."

His hand tightened over hers. "Not to worry, kiddo. Your secret is safe with me."

Looking into his eyes, she knew she could trust him.

Suddenly she felt immensely relieved. As if she had been to confession and received absolution for her sins. Deciding a change of subject was in order, she said lightly, "I don't know about you but my throat is so dry it's killing me. How about a glass of lemonade, maybe a couple of cookies to go with it?" She dusted off her gloved hands. "I'd say with all the activity we've earned a caloric splurge."

"Sounds good to me."

Holding out a hand, he helped her to her feet. "I'm glad you talked to me," he said softly.

"So am I." And she was glad they had stopped fighting about Janey. She didn't want to argue with him. It simply hurt too much.

THE NEXT DAY Zach went to work whistling. Harry Cole was already there, waiting in Zach's office. "You're in early," he remarked, surprised.

"With good reason," Harry admitted in a fatigued voice. "I know I haven't given you any advance notice, Zach, and I apologize for it, but I need a couple of days off."

"Anything wrong?"

Harry nodded sadly. "It's Tabitha again. She and her mother have been fighting all weekend. Mostly about this new bunch of friends Tabitha has. They've got Tabitha saying and doing all sorts of things."

"Worse than the hitchhiking?"

Harry shrugged as if that were hard to decide. "We found her climbing out her window Saturday night, trying to sneak out."

"Tabitha?" Zach did a double take. She was so young, the same age as Janey!

"Yes, anyway, I promised my wife I'd take the next couple days off. We're going to try to figure out what to do with Tabitha. We're thinking of putting her in a private school. There's one in Dallas we're going to drive over and look at. Oh—I know she's missed the last two practices and games, but I promise you she'll be there on Saturday for the last one. Her mother and I are both insisting. We're hoping if she's with a group of clean-cut kids again she'll realize how far off the track she's been."

"Well, if it will help convince her to come, we're playing a tough team. We could really use her," Zach admitted, as worried about Harry as he was about Tabitha.

"I'll tell her," Harry said agreeably. "In the meantime, maybe Tabitha will take her mother and I seriously and stop wearing all that trashy black and purple makeup on her eyes."

Remembering Janey's earrings and how he had successfully nipped that behavior in the bud, Zach asked, "You've told her it's forbidden?"

"Yes." Harry shook his head. "She wears it anyway. Says if her mother doesn't get off her back she'll dye her hair purple, too. Well, I better go. I'll be back Wednesday."

Zach nodded. "Take care of your family." That was the most important thing.

"Thanks, Zach," Harry said gratefully. As he slipped out the trailer door, a woman of regal bearing, in a starched yellow shirtdress and heels, walked in. "Mr. Anderson?" The woman, who looked vaguely familiar to Zach, held out her hand. "I'm Laura Matthews's mother, Grace. I hope you don't mind me dropping in like this?"

"Sit down." Zach said. He hadn't yet had time to make coffee. He searched around, looking for something to offer her, all the while hoping nothing was wrong with Laura or Eric. "Can I get you something to drink? A cola perhaps or a glass of juice?"

"No, nothing, thank you. I'm only here to ask you to dinner

at my home. My husband and I would like to meet our grand-daughter.''

Feeling a little shaken, he regarded his guest cautiously. "Does Laura know you're here?"

Grace shook her head. "No. And I'm sure she'd be furious if she knew. You see, I've been trying to convince her to issue a similar invitation herself for weeks now."

"But she refused?"

"She thought it would be too hard on Janey." Grace fingered her pearls. "I would never want to do anything to harm her but I also think she has a right to get to know her natural grandparents."

Zach was silent. Laura had been right in initially warning Grace off about approaching him. A few weeks ago he would not have warmed to this idea at all, but now, it didn't seem like such a bad idea. Particularly since Janey's own grandparents were living far away, having retired in Florida and Arizona respectively.

"It seems like a fine idea, but my schedule is rather full at the moment. May I call you?" If he was going to do this, he wanted Laura and Eric there, too.

"Certainly." Looking victorious, Grace drew a small notepad and pen from her purse and neatly penned her telephone number. "I'll look forward to hearing from you, Mr. Anderson," Grace said as she rose.

Unhappily, Laura wasn't nearly as receptive when Zach dropped by and she heard what her mother had done. "I specifically told her not to call you!" she said furiously, her fists knotted at her side.

"Well, she didn't call me. She called on me," Zach joked, trying to ease the situation.

"You don't understand, Zach. She always does this to me! She feels she has to control my life!"

"It's just one dinner, Laura."

"It's the principle of the thing, Zach. I specifically told her not to do this and she did it anyway."

He knew how it felt to have someone go over your head.

But he also knew a determined woman when he saw one and Grace was not about to give up. "Maybe you should just humor her, Laura. This once."

Laura continued looking at him as if he was the worst sort of traitor. "She thinks my opinions aren't valid. She thinks she is the only person who ever knows what is right."

"Then make her listen," Zach advised. "And don't stop until she does."

Laura looked up at him, stunned by his reaction. Obviously she had expected him to take her side regardless, but he couldn't do that. "I know how irritating parents can be sometimes, Laura," he said in gentle sympathy. "I've had problems off and on with my own, over the years. But they're not going to be here forever. Remembering that can make it easier to work things out. The bottom line is they love you."

Laura sighed. "Do you have to make so much sense?" she asked plaintively. Making a fist, she batted playfully at his chest.

Zach laughed and caught her hand in his, caressing it lightly. "Only when I'm right."

As Laura glanced up at him, her brown eyes grew velvet soft. Her lips parted slightly. Desire stirred inside him. He wanted to kiss her, but he had the feeling if he did that just now, he might not stop there.

His decision made, he took her by the shoulders, turned her around and pointed her in the direction of the phone. "Now call her. Set this dinner up and then forget about it." Contenting himself, for now, with only cursory contact, he pressed a kiss to the top of her head.

Laura groaned and murmured a reluctant, comical excuse.

"Do it. Because we have much better things to think about." He wrapped his arms around her waist and held her close, cloaking her with his body heat. She relaxed against him, feeling so soft and warm and right. It was all he could do to keep track of what he'd been about to say. "Starting with what we're going to do tonight. Maybe the four of us could go out to dinner."

Zach had sensed a definite softening in Eric's attitude toward him, since he'd showed him how to replace a car battery. And he wanted it to continue. Because only if Eric accepted him, as Janey had already accepted Laura, could he and Laura ever have a future together.

Chapter Thirteen

"I'm so glad you could come!" Janey said as Laura and Eric walked into the gym. "I really wanted you to see my last game."

"We wouldn't have missed it," Laura said, warmly returning Janey's welcoming hug.

"Yeah, and I brought our camera," Eric threw in. "So be sure you turn and smile in my direction as you're scoring all those points."

Janey scoffed at him. "You're crazy. I can't think about pictures when I'm playing a game."

Eric viewed her with mock skepticism. "I don't know why not," he said, his eyes glimmering. "All the girls I know spend every waking moment trying to look good." Seeing the growing outrage on Janey's face, he put up both hands in front of him, as if comically trying to ward off a blow. "Think of it as good practice for when you get older and are desperately trying to land a boyfriend."

"Very funny, big shot." Knowing it was expected of her, Janey landed a teasing blow to his shoulder.

Leaving the two to continue their good-natured bantering, Laura walked over to say hello to Zach. Several feet away, he had been watching the playful exchange between their two children with a look of quiet satisfaction on his face. She knew how he felt. It was good to see them getting along so well.

"Hi," she said shyly.

"Hi." He looked happy to see her, too.

Their increasing closeness left them both silent, searching self-consciously for something to say. "I hope Eric's being here won't distract Janey."

"I wouldn't worry about it," he advised with cheerful authority, looking very capable and handsome in his gold Lady Tigers shirt. "When the action starts, all her attention will be on the floor. The President could be in the stands and Janey would never know."

Laura smiled, feeling blissfully happy and alive. "I know exactly what you mean. Eric's the same way." It was all she could do to stand motionless and not stand on tiptoes to give him a pregame hug for good luck. "I hope you win."

"So do I." His eyes glimmered affectionately as they roved her face. "But either way," he promised, "we'll have fun."

Without warning, there was a commotion at the other end of the gym. Laura turned to see a girl with vivid purple hair and black eyeliner arguing with her father. She had on a gold shirt that identified her as being a member of Zach's team.

"Poor Harry," Zach murmured, concern radiating from his eyes. "He really has his hands full with Tabitha." He sent Laura an apologetic glance. "Since this is the first game she's been to in several weeks, I better go over and say hello."

While Zach walked over to join Harry and his wayward daughter, Janey walked up to Laura. "Can you believe what she's done to her hair?" Janey asked incredulously. "It used to be brown, like mine."

No doubt about it, Laura thought, Tabitha had ruined her hair. That color would probably take a year to grow out, and that was if she sacrificed a good deal of the shoulder-length strands.

Knowing this was the type of touchy situation that needed tactful handling, Laura advised, "I wouldn't say anything about the color to Tabitha, Janey. Just let her know you're glad she's here today and then concentrate on playing a good game."

"I will," Janey promised. "See you later, Laura." She ran off to join her father.

Laura climbed into the stands. With the exception of the purple-haired Tabitha, who remained slumped on a seat at the far end of the Lady Tigers bench, all the girls on Zach's team went through their warm-up drills. When their ten minutes had ended, they all gathered around Zach. Laura watched with a mixture of pride and affection, as Zach's team put their hands together and shouted "Go Tigers!" with a maximum amount of team spirit before running off onto the floor. It was clear, by the adoring way the girls looked at him, and the attentive way they listened to him talk, they all had a lot of respect for their coach. And it was a respect he deserved, she had decided by the end of the first quarter when the Tigers were ahead, 10 to 6.

As was the rule for league games, when the first quarter team came out, the second team went in. Tabitha was among those tapped to play. She left the bench reluctantly while her father glowered at her from the stands. She tromped over to Zach. It looked as though she was telling Zach she did not want to play.

Zach listened quietly while she talked, then put his hand on her shoulder and said something. There was a moment of silence between the two. Then amazingly, Tabitha went in.

The girls on the bench exchanged tense looks. Laura had an idea what they were feeling. As did Eric. "If this Tabitha screws up, the Tigers could lose their lead," he whispered.

"I know. Let's hope she gives it her all," Laura said.

Unfortunately she didn't. And by the time one minute had passed, two rival team players had gotten by her and scored to tie up the game. Zach signaled to his point guard, who called a time out. The girls returned to the huddle. Laura could see there was some fighting going on, as the other teammates, who were rightfully angered by Tabitha's attitude on the court, started in on her. Laura watched as Zach spoke to all of them, and then to Tabitha.

The game resumed. Tabitha did a little better, but because

she was out of shape, she wasn't able to keep up with the others. The other team scored. Fortunately, despite Tabitha's sluggish performance, the Tigers were also able to score. By the half, the teams were tied again.

"Janey's doing great," Eric said as she scored her tenth point at the end of the third quarter.

"You've helped her a lot with her lay-ups," Laura responded.

"Yeah, well she's a great student," Eric said.

Yes, she was, Laura thought. And she had Eric's talent for handling the ball.

The quarter ended with the Tigers ahead by six points. The final quarter began. "I can't believe he's putting Tabitha back in again," Eric moaned.

"It's only fair," Laura whispered back discreetly. "All the other girls are playing two quarters each."

"Yeah, but, to lose now, because of her," Eric muttered.

Unfortunately her son's prophecy was right. The other team quickly took advantage. When the other team took the lead, because of Tabitha's mistake, one of the disgruntled fathers yelled, "Oh, wake up out there, will you?"

Tabitha burst into tears. Almost instantly, Zach was on his feet, calling time out. He jogged out onto the floor, toward Tabitha. Try as he might, he couldn't calm her. When the buzzer sounded, he had no choice but to call another player from the bench to replace her. Still sobbing, Tabitha stalked toward the exit. Her father ran to catch up with her. When he did, Tabitha whirled on him angrily, "I told you I didn't want to play!" she screamed hysterically. "I told you I was no good! But would you listen to me? No! You had to make me play! I hate you! Do you hear me? I hate you!"

She bolted from the gym, her distressed father following closely on her heels.

"Jeez," Eric said. "Was she ever upset!"

Laura silently concurred. Seeing how much pain they were in, her heart went out to both of them. Poor Zach; he'd been put in the middle of it.

Fortunately the game continued without further incident. Zach's team recovered the lead and amidst excited cheering from the parents in the stands, went on to victory. Afterward, the whole team went for pizza. Laura, Eric, and others tagged along. At six, Eric glanced at his watch. "I better go. I've got a date."

"Be home by midnight," Laura warned.

"I will. Bye Mom." He leaned over to kiss her on the cheek. "Zach." He held out his hand. For the first time in weeks, respect glimmered in Eric's eyes. "You were great, coaching the girls today," he said.

Zach beamed. He met Eric's gaze, man-to-man. "I'm glad you were there," he said simply. Eric nodded while a grateful Laura marveled over the peace that had been made.

No sooner had Eric left, than Janey came up to join them. "Chrissy's having a slumber party tonight for the whole team," she said without preamble, looking at Zach for permission. "Can I go?"

"Sure," Zach said. "Just do me a favour and try to get some sleep this time."

"Oh, Dad!" Janey shook her head as if he'd just said the silliest thing in the whole world. "Get real." Zach laughed and Janey continued, "Is it okay if I go home with Chrissy? Her parents said they'd drop by our house and let me run in and get my stuff."

Zach gave his approval. Seconds later, the restaurant had cleared out. "Some day you've had," Laura said, leaning back in her chair. Now that the rest of the guests were gone, the restaurant had a cozy feel to it.

Zach nodded. "Want to go home?"

Laura didn't even have to think about that. Her eyes still holding his, she shook her head. "Do you want me to?"

He shook his head. They both smiled.

His hand covered hers warmly. "So, what'll we do this evening?"

Laura shrugged, aware that both her heartbeat and spirits had picked up immeasurably in one short minute. She hadn't felt this happy or content in a long, long time. And it was all because of Zach. "I'll let you decide."

ZACH DECIDED on a movie. Afterward, still not ready to part company, they went back to his house for coffee. As it started to brew, he went to check his answering machine. "Any messages?" Laura asked, having an idea what was on his mind.

Zach shook his head and didn't try to hide his disappointment. "I was hoping I'd hear from Harry," he confided.

"Why don't you call and check on them?" she urged.

"You wouldn't mind?"

"Not at all." Laura smiled.

Unfortunately, when he came back several minutes later, he didn't seem cheered. Laura was seated at the kitchen table, cup of coffee in hand. "Well?" she prompted immediately, anxious to hear the news, good or bad.

Zach sighed heavily and reached for a mug. "Tabitha's still pretty upset. Harry said she's locked herself in her room."

"I'm sorry."

"I am, too. He's a nice guy." Zach sat down across from her and shook his head in bewilderment. "Tabitha used to be pretty sweet, too. I don't know what's come over her the past few months. Harry says she's been running with a wild crowd."

"Maybe he should ease up on her," Laura suggested.

"That's the problem," Zach disagreed. "I think he's been too easy thus far."

"You don't know that," Laura said quietly.

Zach nodded. "You're right. It's probably pointless to speculate. So let's not talk about them anymore. Let's talk about us."

Us. The word had a wonderful ring to it. Aware her heart was beating very fast as his eyes roamed her hair, her eyes, her mouth, she croaked, "What about us?"

He shrugged, a new and different light coming into his eyes. "Anything. Everything," he said, a possessive sound to his voice.

He was close enough for her to inhale the scent of his cologne, close enough she could see the sprinkling of hair above the open V of his shirt. He had changed into jeans in the locker room after the game, and those jeans, so soft and worn, clung to his thighs as though they were custom-made, revealing taut calves, powerful thighs. His stomach was as flat as a washboard and just as taut and strong-looking as the rest of him. And lower still, the denim was even tighter and more revealing. Shyly, her heart tripping madly in her chest, she forced her eyes away. She didn't need to see that, didn't need to think about it.

He clasped her hand and drew her slowly to her feet.

Although she was laudably inexperienced, having only ever been with one man, her husband, sex or the possibility of it had never scared her. But then, this didn't feel like simple desire. It felt like much more, like commitment, compromise, devotion. All the things she had tried to give before when she had failed.

"What about your coffee?" she asked, panicking ever so slightly as the erotic look in his eyes deepened and grew.

"My coffee can wait," Zach said softly, brushing the dark brown stands of hair from her face.

Whereas he evidently could not, for no sooner had he murmured the soft, decisive words than his mouth was on hers, evoking a sweet response. The dizzying anticipation faded as a languid, sensual weakness stole over her, pushing her doubts aside. It was as if she had waited a lifetime for this moment, to let their feelings for each other grow to fruition, to experience his gentle loving. "You feel good," he murmured, holding her close.

So did he.

His face very close to hers, his blue eyes both searching and intent, he said, "If you want me to take you home, I will." He paused and his voice dropped another emotional note, "But, if not—Laura—"

He didn't finish the sentence. He didn't have to. She knew to stay would be asking him to make love to her. And although there wasn't anything she wanted more in the entire world, her doubts about herself, her fears, were still plaguing her. She didn't want to lose him. And she was afraid. If she didn't measure up—Zach was a man who deserved, who commanded, so much....

Reading her indecision, knowing her personal history and perhaps guessing at the reason why, he gently pressed his mouth to hers, exploring the tender inner flesh with his tongue. His arms holding her possessively, he repeated the tender, evocative caress again and again, each time going a little deeper, a little slower. Never had anyone kissed her so passionately, with just the right amount of pressure and heat. The sharp urgency of desire melded with the wonder of finding themselves together, in this way, at long last. A part of her had known it would happen, almost from the first. She had a suspicion he had known, too.

Realizing the searing depth of her need and his, she pressed closer and gave a tiny moan. As they continued to kiss, sensations splintered through her until every inch of her body cried out with wanting him. But it was more than just simple desire driving her, she realized shakily, exquisite as their ardor was. Cradled in his arms she felt loved. She felt safe. She felt wanted. Important. As if for the first time in her life she was everything she was supposed to be. And more, everything he had ever wanted. And there was a part of her, however selfish, that just didn't want to let that go.

A shudder ran through his body at the completeness of her response. "Oh, Laura," he whispered, burying his lips in her throat. "God. I don't know...if...I can...stop."

That said, he kissed her again, demandingly. Trembling, snuggling closer and closer to the heat and power of his body, she erotically deepened the kiss, tasting him as he had tasted her until he could take no more and had to stop and draw in a ragged breath.

"Laura, my sweet lovely Laura," he whispered as their embrace softened tenderly and they kissed again, this time with gentle, fragile balance. Over and over they touched and caressed until she felt the insistent nudge of his arousal against her, burning and tempting. He skimmed his hands down her breasts. Her hands swept lower to his hips and thighs. And it was all there in an instant, the sensation she was losing control and wanting it that way.

In that second, time froze and the clarity and meaning of the moment struck her. What they were about to do would change their lives forever. And she wanted it that way, she wanted the passion and the sensation of being truly, completely alive for the first time since her daughter and husband had died. She knew she would remember forever the whisper of his clothes against hers, the warmth of his skin emanating through the cloth, the unique male fragrance of his skin and cologne, the gentleness of his touch, and the splendid sight of him, so tall and handsome, so drawn to her.

Finally she was experiencing the total love and adoration of a good man. She wanted to cherish it, draw it out, and make it last. So much of the good in her life had passed in an instant. But not this. This was one moment she was going to savor and hold on to for the rest of her life. "I want you," she whispered, "so much."

His hands captured hers, held them still. He didn't want to be accused later of unfairly seducing her. "You're sure?"

She nodded. "I've never been more sure of anything in my life," she avowed. And she meant it. Yet when he took her by the hand and led her upstairs, to his bedroom, she felt an unsettling and unexpected wave of anxiety. He slanted her an intrigued, compassionate glance. "This is a big step for you, isn't it?"

"Yes."

"And you're frightened," he said, taking her trembling hand in his and pressing a kiss to it.

"Not of you," she swore. But of my own inadequacy, she thought.

He lifted his head, his eyes searching hers. He didn't understand. "Then of what?"

She swallowed. "It's been so long. I'm not sure I—oh, Zach, I don't want you to be disappointed."

"Believe me," he said assuredly, lifting her chin and pressing a light, reverent kiss on her lips, "I won't be."

She lifted her head and saw all the tenderness she had ever wished for reflected in the depths of his blue eyes.

"If we're going to be absolutely honest, this isn't going to be so easy for me, either." He grinned self-consciously and in doing so, drew a smile from her, too. "In case you didn't know, I haven't exactly been hopping from bed to bed the past few years. If you think it's too soon. If you want to wait..."

Melinda's death had taught her to take each moment as it came, to savor the present as if there was no tomorrow. And that was exactly what she planned to do. But now he was the one who needed convincing. She took his mouth, showing him how much she cared about him, how much she had to give. Reassured he wasn't taking unfair advantage, he showed her all there was to discover. About herself, about him.

He kissed her cheeks, her forehead, her chin, then blazed an erotic path down her neck to the soft womanly curves of her breasts. The warmth of his hands followed the slow unbuttoning of her blouse, the unclasping of her bra. He knew how to touch her, how to mold and explore and caress. When his mouth opened hotly over hers again, she found herself clinging, holding nothing in reserve. And though kissing him, holding him, was wonderful, it wasn't nearly enough. Not anymore. She wanted to touch him as he was touching her. Her fingers managed the first button, and then the next, until she had uncovered his sleek-muscled chest with the tufts of light brown hair that arrowed down into the waistband of his jeans.

"I'm not in any hurry," he murmured languidly, looking very pleased as she slipped the cloth from his shoulders and his shirt dropped to the floor to join hers. "You?"

She shook her head and, gasping as his thumb rubbed over her nipple, caught her breath. As she swayed against him, an enervating, sensual weakness stole over her. "As far as I'm concerned, we could do this forever."

The rest of their clothes followed slowly, drifting piece by piece to the floor. When they were free of encumbrances, he buried his face in the fragrant depths of her hair and held her close. The sensation of being held skin to skin with him was electrifying, a hint of the fulfillment to come. Taking her hand, he led her to the wide comfortable bed with the crisp dark green sheets. He followed her down to the mattress and stretched out beside her. Lying side by side, they kissed and touched their fill. She couldn't remember ever feeling so whole. So free. So accepted for who and what she was. "You surprise me," he said as she moved over him.

She glowed with his throatily voiced praise. "I'm surprising myself," she murmured back. "And you know why?" She kissed the flat plain of his abdomen and tasted the salty tang of his skin.

He threaded an idle hand through the silk of her hair. "Tell me."

"Because there's never been—" and never will be, she amended silently "—a night like tonight."

"For me, either," he acknowledged softly. Catching her suddenly beneath the arms, he slid her up and over so she was flat on her back, trapped beneath the sensually pleasurable weight of his body and the mattress.

The time for waiting was past; they both knew it. His tumescent flesh throbbing, he slid between her thighs. She opened herself up to him and then he was inside her, ridding her of the deep, aching emptiness, filling her with pulsing male power, heat, and strength. For the first time in her life she knew what it was like to be loved and accepted completely. Happiness sifted through her as they began their slow, inevitably erotic dance. And then the last thin barrier of reserve was ripped away. She knew only pleasure as they moved together in delicate harmony, tears of release streaming down her face. She felt only the thundering of his heart against her breasts, felt only the love and care in the arms around her, and then all was lost in the consuming, enveloping heat.

LAURA LAY EXHAUSTED, her damp cheek pressed against his shoulder, his body still a part of hers, although he had rolled slightly, relieving her of the bulk of his weight. Delicately his hand dried the dampness on her face. "Why were you crying?"

She shrugged shyly. "For silly reasons." Feminine reasons. "Because it was so good. Because you made me feel so loved. Because I've never felt quite that way before. So abandoned and replete."

"Did I really do all that?" he asked in wonder. His hand cupped her chin, forcing her gaze up and his voice was very soft and very tender. "I'm glad I made you happy, Laura." His voice dropped a husky notch. "I wanted to make you feel loved. Because you should be. You are one hell of a woman, Laura Matthews."

The way he said it, the way he hugged her, made her smile. She pressed a tender kiss to his shoulder. "And you're the nicest, most loving man I've ever met." If only this moment could last forever, she thought, gripping him tighter. If only they could hang on to these feelings of peace and contentment. If only they didn't soon have to face the intruding reality of their everyday lives, with all the attendant frustrations and complications that went with them. But now that the passion had faded, reality had intruded and she was thinking of how complicated their lives were again. And how very much she didn't want to give this up.

"Why the frown?" He traced the furrows between her brows, then lovingly drew his index finger softly along the southernmost curve of her lip.

Laura sighed and cuddled closer, needing to feel his warmth and strength for just a little while longer. The truth wasn't going to be easy to say, but she knew he deserved to hear it. "I don't trust unencumbered happiness," she admitted after a moment, thinking how little of it she'd had in her life. "When something feels this good, I find myself waiting for the next catastrophe to hit."

His eyes darkened compassionately. He reassured her

firmly, "You can trust this, Laura. What we've found with each other is the kind of thing that lasts."

His confidence was catching. Laura smiled. He was right. She was silly to be so wary of the future.

Unfortunately a glance at the clock beside his bed told her it was after ten. Time was passing with alarming speed. She frowned again, not happy about this, either. "I have to be home by twelve, to make sure Eric makes his curfew."

Zach smiled and turned to her, so that she was once again lying on her back, beneath him. "Well, then, Cinderella," he drawled, "I guess we better get started because you're not getting out of here until I show you how I feel, at least one more time...."

Laura was all for that.

Grinning, she smoothed her hands across his shoulders, and promised, "I've got a few things to show you, too."

"YOU AND LAURA have been spending a lot of time together haven't you?" Laura's father said several weeks later as he and Zach worked side by side to install a ceiling fan in Laura's kitchen.

Zach nodded. Since the night he and Laura had made love they'd managed to see each other or talk on the phone every day. "Does that bother you?" he asked as he tightened yet another bolt.

Her father shook his head. "I'm glad the two of you can be friends. Or is it more than that?"

Zach knew these were the kinds of questions her dad should be asking Laura. He also knew as private a person as Laura was, they were exactly the kind of questions she was likely not to answer. "It's more than that," Zach said.

"How much more? Enough to get married?"

Her dad didn't pull any punches. But then he had more or less suspected that about him the first time they'd met. Knowing his directness was prompted by caring, made it tenable. "Maybe," Zach allowed. Probably. They just weren't there yet. It was enough now that they were together, that Eric was beginning to accept him, and that Laura no longer interfered in his parenting of Janey.

"Can you hand me the third blade?"

"Sure." Reaching for it, Zach couldn't help but notice the picture of Melinda on the windowsill. It had been taken when she was still healthy. She was curled up in a chair, a book in her hands, her eyes sparkling merrily, a saucy grin on her face. She looked so happy there. As Laura must have been. What had it been like to lose her? Zach wondered. What had she looked like when she was ill? he thought, and then as soon as the thought came, he pushed it away.

"You don't talk much about Melinda, do you?" her dad asked as Zach handed him the third blade and watched as he screwed it to the rotund brass base.

"Not a lot, no." Her father raised a brow, and Zach found himself adding, somewhat defensively, "There isn't much point, now that she's gone."

"Isn't there?" Laura's dad asked mildly. "Hand me that fourth blade, will you?"

Zach went to get it. Returning, he said, "No, there isn't."

Again her father raised a skeptical brow. "If you want to know Laura, you have to know about that time in her life."

Although normally open to discussion about most anything, Zach found himself resenting the older man's advice. Maybe because it was true and he knew it but didn't want to face it. "That's up to her, what she wants to tell me," he countered gruffly. *And when.*

"I suppose it is. Just bear in mind Laura's a sensitive woman. She knows what makes other people uncomfortable. She usually avoids it."

Her dad's words stayed with him the rest of the day, haunting him, long after he'd said goodbye to Laura and gone back home. By late evening, he knew what he had to do. He'd been putting it off too long.

He called Laura. "Are you busy?"

"No, just sitting here in the kitchen, winding down after a long day, admiring my new ceiling fan."

The pleasure in her low voice made him smile. It took so little to make her happy. "How's Eric?"

"He went to bed early. He was tired."

"So did Janey." Zach paused, knowing he was about to ask a lot of her, but knowing her father was right, it had to be done. "I know it's late, but would you mind coming over, just for a little while?"

Concern radiated in her voice. "What's up?"

Zach found he was clenching the phone cord. "I want to know about Melinda," he said calmly. "I think it's time we talked. Don't you?"

ZACH'S GUT was in knots by the time Laura arrived, a box of old photos in hand. "Are you sure you want to do this?" she asked. She knew how he hated talking about things that hurt. Whatever had prompted his decision, there was no denying it was a major step. One he had needed to make for a long time.

Needing to feel as close to her as possible, Zach laced an arm around Laura's shoulders and walked her into the family room. "I've been avoiding dealing with this a long time," he admitted candidly. He swallowed hard. "Maybe because I just wasn't up to it. But a talk I had with your father this afternoon made me realize I can't go on hiding from it forever." Zach shook his head, knowing how painful an occasional glimpse into Melinda's illness was, knowing he had to somehow find the courage to stop telling himself it didn't matter, and examine his buried feelings. He had to find a way to heal them. He knew, if anyone could help him, it was Laura.

Laura touched his arm, not only able to see his fear, but empathize with it, "Zach," she said softly, "if you want to wait on this, I'll understand."

He shook his head. "No. Sooner or later we have to talk about this, Laura, all of it. If we don't, it will always be between us." And he didn't want anything between them.

Her face clouded with uneasiness as she took his hand in hers and clasped it firmly. "All right. We'll talk," she said determinedly, a mixture of sadness and apprehension in her low voice. "But first we need some coffee because I think it's going to be a long night."

LAURA STAYED in the family room, sorting photos while Zach went to make their coffee. The truth was, she wasn't all that thirsty; she had just needed a moment to herself, to pull herself together.

She had never been able to talk about Melinda's death without breaking down. And being with someone who was sympathetic made it all the worse. Indifference, thoughtlessness, even cruelty she could handle, but kindness always undid her. And if there was one thing Zach was to his very soul, it was kind. And she knew right now, more than anything, he really needed her to be strong.

He returned carrying a tray with a thermal carafe, two mugs, and a plate of homemade chocolate-chip cookies. "Here we go."

Delaying the inevitable as long as possible, Laura picked up a cookie and bit into it. "Let me guess. Your housekeeper made these."

"For that, the lady wins a kiss." He leaned forward to touch his lips lightly to hers. She melted into the tenderness of his embrace. If only they didn't have to go through this, she thought. What if he felt she was to blame for Melinda's death? What if he thought there was something more she could have done, or should have known?

"Laura," he said gently, feeling suddenly like the worst kind of heel for putting her through this. "Are you okay?"

Looking at the strain lines around his eyes, she knew this wasn't any easier on him than it was on her. She took a deep, hitching breath. "Yes," she said, accepting the mug he handed her and curling her hands, with their telltale shakiness, around the fragrant, steaming warmth. "I am. I just don't know where to start, that's all."

"Start at the beginning," he said softly, feeling now that he wanted to hear everything about his natural child whom he had never known. "From the time you took her home from the hospital. What kind of baby was she?" Happy, he hoped.

Laura rooted through the pictures she had brought and found several of Melinda wrapped in baby bunting. "She was a quiet child, from the very first. Maybe it was because Eric was such a bundle of energy at that age, but she seemed content to just watch him running around or giggle at something he said or did. She rarely cried, and then only if she was hungry or wet. She slept through the night...."

As Laura talked, it became easier. Zach found himself relaxing as they covered Melinda's toddler years and went on up into elementary.

"She was ten when she first became ill," Laura said, a quiver in her voice. "We didn't know it was cancer right away, but I knew it was bad, Zach. All I had to do was look at the doctor's faces and know that this wasn't something that was easily fixed." Her throat began to tighten, but knowing how much Zach wanted and needed to hear this, she forced herself to go on. "Melinda, of course, was only concerned with getting through the tests. Some of them were very painful. I remember how she cried and cried, particularly after the bone marrow tests." She shook her head. "I felt so helpless. I wanted to make it easier for her, but I couldn't. All I could do was sit there and hold her hand, and tell her that it was going to be all right."

Zach thought about what that must have been like, knowing her child—his child—was going to die. He didn't know how she had ever gotten through it. And he felt incredible rage against fate, knowing that she had had to get through it. It wasn't fair, dammit, he thought, struggling to hold on to his tenuous control. If Melinda hadn't been stricken, she would be here now. And I would know her the same way Laura knows Janey, he thought. But she wasn't here. And they had to find comfort in whatever way they could.

He reached blindly for Laura. Able to sense how much she was hurting, too, he held her close and said, "I'm sure your being there meant a lot to her.'' His eyes burned as he struggled to hold back the tears.

Laura shook her head, the anger and exhaustion she'd felt then coming back to her with amazing clarity. Withdrawing slightly, she shook her head in helpless uncertainty. And that made Zach angry, too, that she could have doubts about her capacity to love, to help and to heal.

Tears streaming down her face, Laura said, ''I don't know, Zach. Sometimes I think I was more of a hindrance.'' She wiped her eyes and a pain almost too deep to be borne radiated in her low voice, ''You see, she knew she was going to die long before I did. But I wouldn't listen to her. I wouldn't even let her say it. But she tried to help me anyway. She tried to tell me it was going to be okay, that I didn't have to be scared for her because she wasn't afraid. I wouldn't believe it of course, any more than I really believed she had cancer.'' She gestured helplessly.

''It's like there was this part of me deep down that was so angry and so scared, a part of me that just refused to accept that it was all really happening to us. I kept thinking it was a bad dream and I would wake up and everything would be fine again. But I didn't wake up and Melinda kept getting sicker.''

Zach sorted through the pictures in the box, each one tearing his heart out a little more. Melinda in her hospital bed and gown, looking frail and helpless, but doggedly playing a game of Junior Trivial Pursuit with a nurse. Melinda with her headphones on and an IV in her arm. Melinda with hair that was so thin in places you could see her scalp. And another where she had none, and was wearing a funky black-top hat to cover her head.

Seeing him looking at that photo, Laura said sadly, ''She cried when she lost her hair, because she thought she looked so ugly.''

''But she didn't,'' Zach said, really sharing Laura's pain for the very first time, because he knew now—he could see in these pictures—exactly what she and he had both lost.

''She had a beautiful soul,'' Laura said reverently. ''She

was so kind and giving. Always concerned about the other kids at the oncology clinic.''

Zach picked up a photo of Melinda, the surge of protective feelings in him incredibly strong. ''Did she wear the hat because of hair loss?'' Zach asked, looking at the photo again. And loving the way she looked in the hat, bald scalp and all, so brave and saucy and willing to face the next challenge.

''Yes.'' Laura smiled through her tears. ''Being an old stodgy, I felt we could do a little better than that. So I went out and got her all kinds of wigs—blond, red, brown, even brunette. She really didn't want one because she said it was stupid—everyone knew she had lost all her hair anyway, but I persisted and finally got her to try them all on and at one point it was just so silly…because none of them looked like her. I mean we laughed until our sides ached and tears rolled down our faces and then, we ended up in each other's arms, both of us sobbing as uncontrollably as we had laughed.''

Laura's pain transmitted to him in heavy waves. Struggling to maintain his composure, Zach sorted through the pictures. ''Which wig did she pick?'' he asked in a low, unsteady voice.

Laura gave a bleak smile. ''I let her pick out four, one in each color. She wore them all and made a joke of it, telling the nurses she was the only one of them who could have a different color hair every day of the week.''

He stared at her in shock, not understanding the tastelessness of the joke.

''I know, it's pretty dark humor but it got her through the really tough days,'' she said earnestly. ''Sometimes, if you can just find a way to laugh, even for a minute…'' Her voice caught and she couldn't go on.

''Did it help?'' he asked, hauling in a deep, shaky breath.

Laura nodded. ''Some. And then there were times—'' she teared up again, looking so vulnerable that his heart went out to her ''—when nothing could help.''

He gripped her hands tightly. ''How did you ever get through it?'' he whispered, a desolate look in his eyes.

Laura shrugged. The truth was she didn't know. ''I took it

day by day. One minute at a time." That was all she had asked of herself, and all she had continued asking of herself until Zach came into her life. Now, for the first time since she could remember, she was wanting a future again.

As if shutting out the pain he couldn't bear to feel, he closed his eyes, his grasp on her hands becoming almost painful. When he finally spoke again, his voice was so ragged and low it was barely audible. "Did she ever get well again?"

"Yes," Laura said, relaxing a bit as she thought about that happier time. A little of the boundless joy she had felt crept into her voice. "After about a year and a half of therapy she had one remission, a brief one for six months. And it was wonderful." Laura sorted through the pictures and found several photos.

Melinda had looked great, then, Zach thought. Her hair had grown back, she had gained weight, and had some healthy color to her face.

Laura sighed, admitting, "When this photo was taken at the beginning of the school year, we thought we had the whole world by the tail." Slowly Laura lost her smile. Zach's grip on her hand tightened. "But then it hit again, and when it hit the second time, it hit her very hard, physically and emotionally." A ragged, defeated sigh escaped her parted lips. Laura eased a breath past the terrible constriction in her chest and continued in a voice brimming with painful memories. "She lost the will to fight. Eric and I tried to lift her spirits, you'll never know how we tried. But at the end, she just couldn't go on."

Zach tried to imagine what that must have been like and found his heart filled with as much pain as Laura's low voice. He wanted to bring her peace and vanquish the hurt she still felt, but found instead that increasingly, he was the one in need of comforting. Zach suffered a swift irrational pang of guilt for not being there then, not knowing, not helping.

"She went into the hospital again with pneumonia and they did everything they could for her, but—" Laura stopped, her voice breaking, and pressed a hand over her eyes "—it just wasn't enough. Her body had no strength left to fight off the infection and she died two nights later.''

"In the hospital?" Zach asked softly.

Laura nodded, looking both numb and emotionally exhausted as she recounted, "Yes. Eric and I were both with her. I'm thankful for that much. But, I wished we could have had her at home, you know?"

It was foolish for her to berate herself about that, Zach thought. Taking her hand, her said, firmly, "You had no choice but to keep her hospitalized, Laura. After all, there was always a chance, even a slim one, that the hospital might have saved her. At home, she would have had no chance."

She withdrew from his touch, in too much pain to accept his sympathy. "But they didn't save her," she said sadly.

He was silent.

He had no answer for that, no way to aid her. Cursing his own helplessness, he asked, "Was she in much pain?"

"No," Laura said. "At least I don't think so," she said softly, knowing she could ease his mind about this much. "She didn't appear to be. She was drifting in and out of unconsciousness. She just came to a couple of times and when she did—" Laura was unable to help it, she teared up again and began to tremble. Folding her arms tight against her chest, she said, "—I remember her being very concerned about the two of us. She didn't want Eric and I to be sad because she wasn't. She was at peace with her dying." Remembering, Laura shook her head. Even now, her daughter's courage and wisdom amazed her. "But we just kept trying to hold on to her, to urge her back to us." And that had been selfish of her, she knew. Guilt flooded her anew. "And then she was gone, Zach. And a part of me and of Eric died, too."

"It must have been very hard," he commiserated gently, holding her.

Incapable of speech, Laura nodded. Yes, she thought, it had been very hard. And for a brief time, until she had started concentrating on Eric's needs again, she had thought her whole world had ended. She, too, had wanted to die. But her love of her son had pulled her together and made her get through that first day after the funeral and then the next and the next. It was Eric who had saved her. And now there was Zach, sweet, loving Zach....

At a loss for words, Zach stroked her hair and held her fiercely. "It's funny, the things that go through your head at a time like that," Laura said after a moment. "I kept picturing her in heaven with her dad, with Rob. I kept thinking that as long as she was with him it would be okay, that I wouldn't have to worry about her."

Zach could picture her in heaven, too. Happy and free. Well again. With Maria. "If I had only known," he whispered in a strained voice, her trembling confession making him aware of all he had lost and could never recapture. Of all he would give his life to experience. Just for a moment. "I would have been there—I could have held her—I could have helped ease her suffering. I could have done something!" he finished in impotent rage, angry at having been deprived of knowing his child. It angered him, too, that Melinda had never known *him*. For she would have loved him. Just as he now loved her. He was sure of it.

"I wish you had known her," Laura said. Their anguished glances met. Her strength depleted, her voice caught on a sob and she broke down. For several minutes, both of them simply held each other.

"I'm sorry, so sorry you went through that," he said at last, his sorrowful voice muffled against her hair. He felt devastated by the loss. As though a part of him would never get over it. Needing to hold on to something, someone, he embraced Laura tighter. Brokenly he whispered, "It hurts that I'll never know her."

Laura drew back to face him. "You would have loved her."

Zach nodded, his eyes locked with hers, accepting all he had refused to accept for so very long. "I know."

Chapter Fourteen

The alarm went off like a siren, blasting inside his head. Zach reached for it, and then lay there in silence, exhausted but awake. The talk with Laura last night had been cathartic. He never would have guessed how much. For the first time he felt he knew his natural daughter, and he understood the loss they all had suffered.

Unfortunately Janey wasn't in the best of moods. She snapped at him over breakfast and remained strangely sullen and uncommunicative on the way to school. "Everything okay with you this morning?" he asked, stopping her before she could get out of the Wagoneer.

"Why wouldn't it be?"

There was the faintest hint of derision in her tone. Zach shrugged and took a closer look. She looked as though she hadn't slept much and there were puffy circles around her eyes. As though she'd been crying. The last time she had looked that way, he remembered, she had been in a fight with her best friend Chrissy. She hadn't appreciated answering questions then. She wouldn't now. But if she was still this upset when she got home tonight, they would talk.

Deciding it would be wise to change the subject, he said, "Don't forget. We're supposed to go bowling again tonight with Eric and Laura, so try to get your homework done right after school if at all possible. That way, we can leave right after dinner and make an early night of it."

Something flickered in Janey's eyes. She shrugged and grabbed her backpack full of books. "Sure, Dad. See you later."

"Bye." He watched her go, still puzzled over her strange behavior. If he didn't know better, he'd think she was a little miffed at him, but that was impossible. They hadn't argued.

Hormones, he decided. A typical teenage mood swing.

When he got home from work, hours later, Janey wasn't home. There was a note from her on the counter. He picked it up and read it quickly:

Dad,
I went to the mall with Chrissy. Won't be home until late. Go bowling without me.

Janey

Zach frowned. She knew she wasn't supposed to go anywhere without asking permission and that went double when they already had plans. Clamping down on his annoyance—he could read her the riot act when he saw her—he reached for the phone and dialed Chrissy's number. To his surprise, Chrissy answered on the third ring.

"Chrissy?"

"Mr. Anderson."

She didn't sound glad to hear from him, Zach noted, stunned. In fact, contrary to her usual vivacious greeting, her voice was full of dread. Anxiety edging his voice, he asked, "Is Janey there?"

"She's not here, Mr. Anderson."

"I thought the two of you were going to the mall. At least that's what the note she left me said."

"I know," Chrissy evaded politely. "She wanted me to go with her, but I couldn't. Not tonight. My mom wouldn't let me...." Chrissy's voice trailed off reluctantly.

Zach had known Chrissy long enough to realize she was hiding something. His annoyance over his daughter's unexpected wayward behavior turned to worry. What was going on here? Knowing he had no other choice but to put his daughter's friend on the spot, he asked bluntly, "Chrissy, do you know where Janey is now?"

There was a telltale silence on the other end. Zach's sense that his daughter was in trouble increased dramatically.

"Chrissy, please. I'm worried about her." And if Zach was reading Chrissy's unusual unease right, she was worried about Janey, too.

"She might be at the mall."

Zach shook his head in confusion. "At the mall? How did she get there? If your mother didn't take her—" The two of them always went with Chrissy's mom. Another telling silence. Zach's panic began to mount.

Chrissy said, "Look, Mr. Anderson, you're a nice guy and all but please don't ask me any more questions because I don't rat on my friends."

So Janey was up to something shady and stupid. Zach warned firmly, "Chrissy, you either tell me all of what you know, or I come over and tell your parents. And then we'll all talk this out. But one way or another I am going to track my daughter down. If you care about her, if you're really her friend, you'll help me find her and make sure she's all right."

Chrissy sighed then asked hesitantly, "You promise you won't tell Janey how you found out she wasn't with me?"

Zach had no intention of destroying Janey's relationship with her best friend. He just wanted his daughter home, safe and sound. What in the blazes was going on with her? "I promise."

"Well, there are these guys that go to our school and they're kind of radical—"

"Speak English, please."

"Uh—wild. Anyway, they've been after me and Janey for a long time, trying to get us to sneak out with them. Like a date, you know?"

Zach felt sick inside as Chrissy continued to talk.

"...We always tell them no, but this morning when they

asked if we wanted to go to the mall after school Janey said she'd go. I told her she was crazy and she got mad at me. We had a big fight."

"Did you make up later?"

"No. We still weren't speaking after school. I mean, I like to flirt with those guys, too. They're cute. But they're also bad news. You know, always getting into trouble with the teachers and everything. Janey's always had too much sense to run off with them. I don't know what got into her this morning. She was kind of angry, but she didn't tell me why. Did the two of you have a fight or something?"

"No, Chrissy, we didn't, and I don't know what's going on with her, either." He paused. "Do you have any idea how they got to the mall?"

"The city bus."

"And they planned to come home the same way?"

"As far as I know."

"Thanks, Chrissy."

Zach hung up and dialed Laura's number. There was no answer. Glancing at his watch, he realized she was probably still out delivering pies. He left a message on her recorder that because of a crisis at home, bowling was off. He promised to call her later, when he could.

Hanging up, he headed out to his Wagoneer.

Fortunately, Janey was just where she'd told her best friend she was going to be. She was standing in front of an ice-cream shop, surrounded by boys in faded jeans, black T-shirts, and denim jackets. All of them had earrings that looked like fishing flies dangling from one ear. Zach estimated the four boys must have each used a pint of mousse on their spiked hair, which was long on top and sheared very short on the back and sides. One had laced a possessive arm around his daughter's shoulder.

Zach started toward the group. Janey didn't see him until he was right on her. As she turned to look at him, the color left her face. The boy standing next to her realized who Zach was. No fool, he dropped his arm from her shoulders and stepped back.

Her shock over seeing him there fading fast, Janey stared at him with defiance. For a second Janey looked like a stranger. Oh, no, Zach thought. The tumultuous teenage years I've heard everyone else talk about—especially Harry Cole—have just hit me full blast. The more Janey looked at him, the more he was reminded of Tabitha.

"What are you doing here?" Janey asked rebelliously, very much aware she had an enthralled male audience on all sides of her.

"I could ask you the same question," Zach said levelly. Now that he knew she was all right, he wanted to deliver the sternest lecture she'd ever gotten in her life. But that would have to wait. Right now he had to get her out of here. Away from these boys. Who were, from the looks of it, providing support for her newfound truculent behavior.

"How did you know where to find me?" she asked.

"You left me a note, remember?" Remembering his promise to Chrissy, he looked around, "Where's Chrissy and her mom?"

Janey's lower lip slid out and she folded her arms defiantly across her chest. "They didn't come."

Janey continued to regard him contentiously. Zach sighed. This wasn't going to be easy. "Let's go."

Her jaw thrusting out even more, Janey clamped her arms even tighter against her chest and resisted his attempt to put a paternal arm around her. Hurt, confused, Zach let her go. They walked in silence to his Wagoneer.

They didn't speak on the drive home. Janey, because she was afraid—she knew she had been very disobedient and would have to pay for her infraction of the rules. Zach, because he was too careful to risk what was bound to be a heated argument or emotional scene when he was driving. He also wanted to look at her face when they talked. One way or another, he had to find out what was going on here, what was upsetting Janey so. None of this was like her at all.

Once inside the house, Janey headed for the stairs.

"Hold it right there, young lady. We're going to talk about this."

Her shoulders slumped. She sounded tired, defeated. "Do we have to?" Now that the moment of truth had come, she was practically begging for pity. But after what she'd put him through, Zach wasn't of a mind to let her off easily. Besides, if he did, she might think it would be worth it to try something like this again. And that, they simply couldn't have.

"Living room, Janey."

He followed her into the room and watched as she flounced down on the couch, her arms still folded defiantly in front of her. "You have some explaining to do. I suggest you start now. And I warn you, it had better be good."

She shrugged and gave him an unpleasant look. "What's there to explain? I didn't want to go bowling. So I did something else."

Zach stared at her. More confused than ever, he asked, "Since when don't you like spending time with Eric and Laura?"

"Since today," she replied, looking at him with eyes that were filled with hurt and anger. "I didn't feel like it, okay?"

"No, it's not okay," Zach shot back, just as furiously. "You had me worried sick." Realizing it wouldn't help anything if they ended this in a shouting match, Zach calmed himself with effort. "Janey, what is going on with you? What is—" Zach broke off abruptly when Janey turned her head and he saw the flash of silver in her ears. Stepping closer, he saw with shock that she'd had her ears pierced. Silver studs were in both ears.

Knowing he'd seen, she said defensively, "I did it with my own money."

"And without my permission." Was this what her rebellion was all about? he wondered, amazed. Because he had refused to let her wear those stupid earrings Laura had helped her buy?

"Only because you wouldn't give me permission!"

"Which was the same reason you went to the mall with

those boys, because you knew I wouldn't let you do it?'' They were heading into dangerous territory now. Fear that Janey would go off the deep end, the way Tabitha Cole had, made Zach even angrier.

Seeing his response, Janey got even more rebellious. ''Why do you care, anyway?'' she said, jumping up from the sofa. ''It's not like I'm your real daughter anyway!''

Before Zach had a chance to call her back the doorbell rang. Resenting the interruption, he went to get it. His irritation faded when he realized who it was. ''Laura,'' he said in quiet relief.

She looked as panic-stricken as he had felt upon arriving home and finding Janey missing. ''Are you okay? Where's Janey?'' She looked past him, to see Janey. She put her hand over her heart and sagged visibly. ''Oh, thank goodness you're both all right. When I got home and heard that message on the recorder, I thought maybe there'd been an accident or—'' Breaking off, she looked from Zach to Janey and back again. ''What's wrong?''

''Janey went to the mall without permission.''

''Zach is mad at me because I got my ears pierced!'' Janey cut in rebelliously.

Zach? Where had that come from? She'd never called him by his given name before. It had always been Dad or Daddy. Never Zach.

''Oh.'' Laura said heavily, looking as if she'd just backed into a hornet's nest.

''Tell him, Laura,'' Janey insisted. ''Tell him how unreasonable he's being.''

Laura bit her lip, looked at him, concern radiating from her dark brown eyes and then back at his daughter. ''Janey—'' she began in a tentative, soothing voice.

''You're both mean, you know that?'' Janey said, cutting Laura off. She raced up the stairs.

Her bedroom door slammed with a force that shook the house. Zach looked up the stairs after her. Tabitha, too, had demonstrated her temper with aggrandizing force. Whether Janey liked it or not, this was going to have to stop.

"Want to talk?" Laura asked quietly.

He didn't know if that would be a good idea or not. "It hasn't been a very good day."

"I can see that." She held out her hand anyway. Realizing he needed to talk to another adult, and more importantly someone who understood and supported him in this battle with his child, he took Laura's hand, and together they walked into the living room where moments before Janey had been vacillating between defiance and tears. Briefly he explained everything. Laura listened intently. When he had finished, she looked as worried as he felt. She cast a tentative look at the stairs. "Maybe I should talk to her."

"I don't know, Laura. She's awfully upset."

Laura was already on her feet, gently disengaging her hand from his. "At least let me try, Zach. Sometimes a girl her age needs a woman as a sounding board."

Was that all it was? Zach fervently hoped so, even as his every instinct told him it was much, much more.

Laura was upstairs for over an hour. When she came down, she looked grim, worried. "Well?" He was on his feet instantly.

"I still don't know what's going on with her, only that she wants to come home with me, Zach. Just for a couple of days. I said it was okay with me if it was okay with you."

"Without even asking me first?" he asked incredulously.

She blinked. "I'm sorry. I guess I wasn't thinking." Laura held out her hands in a helpless gesture. "She just seemed so upset. I think you're right, Zach, that there is something wrong, something terribly wrong."

"But you don't have even the slightest idea what it is, either, not after talking with her for an hour?"

At his question, Laura ducked her head. And in that instant he knew that Janey had said something to Laura. Reluctantly, Laura repeated, "She said she thinks you're 'unfair and mean' not to let her wear earrings."

He saw the tension in her slender frame, the worry that mirrored his own. "And you agree with her, don't you?" Zach demanded unhappily.

Laura nodded tactfully. "I think in this instance you are going a little overboard. We're just talking about earrings here, Zach. It's something all the girls her age do," Laura continued in the same pragmatic, accepting tone.

Aware this was the first disagreement he'd had with Laura since they'd become lovers, Zach's shoulders tensed. "Not my daughter."

"It's too late for that dictum, Zach. She's already done it and it can't be undone."

Looking at Laura's exasperation with him, he suddenly knew where Janey was getting her ideas. It was all he could do to keep his voice calm. "You encourage this in her, don't you?"

She looked at him in confusion. "What are you talking about?"

His resentment building he spelled it out for her, "The earrings."

"What is the harm in that?"

"I'll tell you what the harm in that is." Unable to stop, he heard himself thundering, "You've been undermining my authority with her from the first."

Laura's eyes flashed. "I have not."

"The hell you haven't."

"How have I been doing that?"

"By telling her I'm too strict!"

"I never said any such thing."

"Not in so many words, no, but the message was clear enough. 'What harm can there be in wearing the earrings around the house, Zach?'" he mimicked furiously in a falsetto voice.

Laura's jaw clenched. Riotous color spread across her cheekbones. "If you will remember," she said in a low, barely controlled but reasonable tone, "I also told her that as her father, your word was law."

"Yes, and indirectly that your word, as her mother, would be so much more lenient than mine."

Her fists knotted at her sides, Laura looked down at the floor, then slowly back up at him. "It probably would be since you are too strict sometimes."

They glared at each other. Realizing this was getting them nowhere, Zach stalked through to the family room, then slid open the patio doors and stepped out into the coolness of the night. It was a moment before he realized Laura had followed him and was behind him. "Please, Zach," she said softly, stepping nearer in the chill darkness of the night, "Let me take Janey home with me."

"Why?" *So you can brainwash her against me even more?*"

"Because I understand what she's going through, even if she doesn't." He lifted a skeptical brow and she continued, even more urgently. "I understand that kind of rebellious behavior because I lived it. I also know there's a reason for it. Maybe it is the earrings, but maybe there's more to it. All I know for sure is that she is talking to me more easily than she is talking to you. If we're to solve this problem with Janey, she needs understanding. And that I have in abundance, Zach."

"You're saying I don't?" he countered stiffly.

Her expression was gentle as she soothed, "Not at all. I'm saying you're confused and angry right now, and that the two of you both need time to cool off."

Zach almost gave in to her request before snapping back to his senses. If he let Janey go now, the damage would be irreparable. No one, absolutely no one, was going to separate him from his daughter at this late stage of the game.

"No," he said calmly. "I won't let you take Janey home with you."

It was Laura's turn to recoil in hurt and surprise. "Why not?"

"Because you're the reason Janey is so upset. You're the problem, Laura." He continued gently, knowing this had to be said even if it hurt her. "I know you care about her, but the truth of the matter is you've been a disruptive force. I won't let you take Janey home with you or drive the two of us apart."

"Is that what you think I'm doing?" The tears streamed down her face.

"I know it is." Maybe she hadn't meant to do this, but she had. It was up to him to find a way to stop it before the damage to his daughter was any more severe. And the first way to fix it would be to re-cement his relationship with Janey, not push her away, as Laura suggested.

But now Laura was angry and disapproving, too. As she faced him, he saw some of that wildness she had claimed to have in her youth. "You don't have any right to stop me, Zach. I am her mother."

"No, you're not. You'd only like to be."

Laura stared at him, unable to believe what he had just said. "Meaning what?" she demanded. "Either I do things your way, or everything else is off? My friendship with Janey, and my relationship with you?"

He hadn't wanted to be quite so blunt, but since she had put it that way, he knew she deserved a truthful answer. "Where my daughter is concerned, yes. There isn't any room for discussion on this, Laura. I am Janey's parent, not you. I will make the decisions that shape her life."

"Even if you're pushing her away from you?" Laura countered.

Her assault on him stung. "You're the only one pushing us apart," he said sadly. Because the truth was, until Laura had come along, he had not had one problem with Janey.

Laura reeled as if he had struck her physically. "I was a fool to think this could ever work out."

"Maybe you were," Zach said disconsolately. But he had been, too. Because he had really thought this would work. How could he have been so naive?

Regaining her strength, Laura said, "I won't let you separate me from my daughter now that I have found her."

"You have no choice," Zach warned, mimicking her tone to annoying perfection.

Laura's jaw jutted forward. "You're wrong about that," she said very quietly, letting him know in that second that it was all over. They were finished, forever. "Dead wrong, Zach." And then she turned and left.

Watching her go, knowing his daughter was still upstairs, and that both she and Laura now detested him, Zach had never felt lonelier or more bereft.

Chapter Fifteen

"What time should I be home, so we can go?" Eric asked as
he grabbed his jacket and prepared to head out the door Saturday morning.

"What do you mean?" Laura looked at him, confused.

"Isn't tonight the night we're supposed to have dinner over
at Grandma's, with Zach and Janey?"

Realizing this was so, it was all Laura could do not to moan.
She'd completely forgotten about that. They'd arranged it several weeks prior. "Yes," Laura answered her son's question,
all the while wondering how she was going to get herself out
of this one. "Tonight was the night we agreed on."

"So, what time?" Eric demanded impatiently, a basketball
cradled under his arm. In Central High sweats, he was anxious
to get over to the gym and work out with the rest of his team.
They only had a few games left as the play-offs approached,
but they were going at them full tilt, hoping to at least win
the district title.

"Be home by six," she decided, still not sure what she was
going to do about dinner at her mom's.

"Okay. See ya."

"See ya." Laura echoed his enthusiastic adieu lamely then
sat in silence after the door had slammed shut.

She hadn't told Eric about the fight she'd had with Zach,
only that the bowling was off because Janey had gone somewhere without permission, and was in hot water with her dad.

Having done a similar thing himself a time or two, Eric didn't question what Laura told him. Even though several days had now passed, memories of her fight with Zach were still raw and painful.

She had hoped that he had just been speaking in anger and hadn't really meant half of what he'd said, but as the third day passed with no word from him, she knew he hadn't relented in the least. He really thought she was a disruptive, damaging influence on his daughter. That alone had been bad enough, but his rigidly dictatorial behavior toward her had been even worse, reminding her of her overbearing mother and the Navy. Both had run her life for so long.

Well, Zach probably wouldn't want to go to dinner, either, she thought. If that was the case, then she would have to tell her mother. If Grace found out about this, she'd probably start harping at Laura to sue for custody of Janey. And right now, Laura just didn't think she could deal with that. Picking up the phone, she dialed Zach's number.

He answered on the fourth ring. "Anderson residence."

"Zach. It's Laura." Not giving him a chance to say anything, she rushed on, "About dinner at my mother's tonight—"

"She called just a little while ago to remind me," he said heavily. "I didn't know what to do. I gathered you hadn't told her we—our relationship—was off."

"No." Laura said, squeezing the words out of her aching throat. "I haven't."

"So, I told her we'd be there," Zach finished.

"Oh." She was so surprised she couldn't think of anything else to say.

"To be blunt, Janey really isn't up to it. Neither am I. But I figured it would be easiest to go. I hope you'll understand if we don't stay long."

His voice was so cool and formal it stung. He hadn't forgiven her, Laura thought, heartbroken, disappointed. Any more than she had forgiven him. But then what had she expected? She knew how different they were in outlook. The

episode with Janey had just made them face it, that was all.
"I agree, leaving early would be best," Laura said.

"Fine, then I'll see you there," Zach said crisply, then hung up the phone.

Unhappily, the evening was every bit as tense as Laura had feared it would be. Zach and Janey arrived well after Laura and Eric. From the way the two distanced themselves physically from each other, Laura could tell they were still fighting. And although her heart went out to any child and parent locked in a dance of pain, she was also aggravated with Zach. If he would have loosened up a bit, and let her help out, the situation would already be back to normal. Instead, everybody was miserable.

"So, Zach," Laura's mother started in on him promptly, the moment Eric and Janey had moved off to nibble hors d'oeuvres and watch a movie in the den, "we understand you and Laura have been dating."

Laura gave her mother a sharp look, warning her off the subject. As always, her mother steadfastly ignored the visual clue.

"We've become acquainted," Zach said evasively.

Her mother persisted cheerily, "What does that mean?"

"It means the subject is off-limits," Laura cut in.

"Laura and I are just friends, although I think in the future, now that we've gotten to know each other, we'll be seeing less of each other."

"Why, for goodness' sake!" her mother retorted, with her customary lack of tact. "I thought the two of you had a romance going."

"That's true," Zach said curtly, rubbing his forehead as if the pain behind his eyes was intense and throbbing. "But people change." Avoiding Grace's searching glance, he looked at Laura, amending, "Or sometimes they don't."

"But what about Janey!" her mother sputtered. "She needs her mother!"

Zach stood abruptly. The subject of Janey's welfare was not

something he was willing to discuss. "I think I need a breath of air. If you'll excuse me—"

Her father stood, too. "The patio is out back, son. Right through those doors over there."

Laura waited until Zach was gone, then turned on her mother. "How could you?" she demanded furiously. Grace had promised her this would be a fun, purely social evening with no demands put on anyone. She should have known better then to believe her.

"I didn't think I was asking anything forbidden," her mother countered defensively. "Of course if anyone around here ever bothered to fill me in on what's going on, it might be a different story!"

"Okay, so now you know," Laura hissed, hating the defensive way her mother always made her feel. "Zach and I have broken up. Is that enough of a news flash for you?"

Her mother's mouth tightened. "I'll get dinner on. And keep your voice down, Laura. Do you want the children to hear?"

No, she didn't. Fortunately, they were so engrossed in a movie on cable that they were oblivious to the activity in the other room.

"I'm sorry if there's a problem between you and Zach," her father said quietly as soon as her mother had disappeared into the kitchen. "But that doesn't give you any excuse to be rude to your mother."

Laura knew that, as nosy as her mother had been, she hadn't helped the situation any. Her curt, aggravated retorts had only made things worse. She took a deep, steadying breath, promising, "I'll try to cool it."

Her father nodded his approval. "Good. Your mother has worked very hard on this meal. For the children's sakes, I'd like it to be a success."

Thankfully the children carried the conversation at the dinner table. Eric and Janey continuously charmed them all as they cheerfully traded stories back and forth, all of them centering on the highs and lows of being a middle school student.

"You'll like the senior high," Eric promised Janey. "There's a lot more freedom when you get to the ninth grade. You can hitch rides with your friends instead of riding the school bus."

Janey sent her dad a brief, aggrieved look. "I don't know if I'll be able to do that."

"Not when you're just a freshman," Zach agreed.

"Why not?" Eric turned to Zach, looking at him as if he had suddenly sprouted two heads. "She'll be in high school."

"Right and she'll be there for four years," Zach replied.

Eric looked at Zach and shook his head in mute remonstration. "That's...stupid," he said.

"No, it's common sense," Laura's mother cut in. "Young girls need to be protected. I often thought if I'd been stricter with your mother, Eric, she wouldn't have married so young."

If Grace had been stricter, she would have suffocated and died, Laura thought.

Zach shot Laura's mother a grateful glance for jumping to his aid.

Seeing the two of them in cahoots on any issue, made Laura all the more certain Zach was out of line. Plus, she couldn't bear the thought of Zach making Janey as forcibly repressed and miserable as she had been at that age, always fighting to be heard, always fighting to maintain something of her own identity despite the crushing demands and restrictions continually put on her.

"Dessert anyone?" Laura said, rising with her plate in hand.

"Good idea," her mother said, also rising. "I've got the most wonderful Mississippi Mud Pie in there just begging to be eaten..."

"I want you to talk to your son," Zach told Laura later, getting her alone.

Visibly uncomfortable, he seemed so at odds with the man she had fallen in love with. But maybe that, too, had been an illusion, Laura thought. Maybe she'd only been seeing what she wanted to see. Because of Janey. Because of everything.

Her heart aching, she faced him apprehensively. "What about?" she asked.

Zach's answering look was filled with both remorse and gentle censure. "Janey doesn't need any more encouragement to rebel."

"Eric didn't mean anything by his remarks, but you're right, he shouldn't have commented." Laura sighed, then caved in reluctantly. "I'll speak to him."

"Thanks."

"But about Janey—" she began, watching him tense up again. "Zach, you can't keep—"

"Laura, I think it'd be better if we didn't discuss this again, and especially not here, in front of your folks. We both know where each of us stands. Nothing's changed."

They faced one another in abject misery. She saw he was blaming her and now Eric, too, for all his troubles with Janey, instead of looking to himself and his own behavior for the answers.

"I shouldn't have come here tonight," he said finally, his expression disconsolate.

No, she thought wearily, considering how everything had worked out, he shouldn't have.

"JANEY TOLD ME what Zach did to her at the mall, embarrassing her in front of all her friends," Eric said as the two of them drove home. He turned sideways to face her, his back lightly grazing the passenger door. "How come you didn't tell me that, Mom? You knew, didn't you?"

"Yes, I knew." Laura signaled for a left turn as she approached the next intersection.

"Well?"

Keeping her eyes on the road, Laura said civilly, "I didn't think it was any of your business." And she had feared if Eric found out about it, he, too, would be upset. He might even try to put himself in the middle of Zach's disciplining of his daughter, as he had at the dinner table tonight.

"Janey is my sister!" Eric said.

Laura sighed. "I know that, honey, but this was a fight between Janey and her dad."

"It's still my business," Eric said defiantly. "You want to know what I think? The guy's a jerk. Not letting her wear earrings—"

Laura wasn't sure why, but she found herself coming to Zach's defense. "Zach thinks they are inappropriate for someone Janey's age. He has a right to his opinion, just like you and I have a right to ours."

"Even when his opinion is dead wrong?" Eric asked. "All the girls wear them," Eric continued. "You know that."

"That doesn't make a bit of difference to Zach. He still doesn't approve of flashy earrings on thirteen-year-old girls."

"What a crock!" Eric shook his head. Settling back against his seat, he ruminated casually, "Janey says she and her dad are barely speaking."

Laura had suspected that might be the case. Seeing how upset her son was, she searched her mind for something positive to say. "They'll work it out in time."

"Not unless he changes his mind," Eric predicted grimly, glancing out the window as Laura turned onto their street.

Their moods quiet, depressed, she and Eric went into the house. Claiming fatigue, Eric went to bed and Laura followed soon afterward. It had been a horrible night, to be sure, a horrible couple of days. Surely it had to get better, didn't it?

IT WAS SHORTLY AFTER 2:00 a.m. when Zach heard the first of the sirens. Loud and blaring, they were close by. Alarmingly close! Swinging his body lithely out of bed, he padded to the window. As he drew the curtain aside, he could see flashing red lights of two police cars down the block, and another fire truck on the way.

Wondering if the noise had awakened Janey, he went down the hall to her bedroom. Her door was shut. He knocked lightly. No answer. He pushed open the door. In the shadowy confines of the room, he could see the outline of her figure in the bed. He was surprised the noise hadn't awakened her, but decided to let her sleep through it if possible. She'd been so tired lately, because of all their fighting. She needed her rest.

Down the block, the sirens increased in number. Zach knew there were several elderly people down the block. Maybe someone needed help. He could go see.

By the time he had dressed the sirens had stopped. He paused to check on his daughter. Janey's form was still immobile. Satisfied she wouldn't awaken, he went downstairs and quietly went outside.

By the time he arrived, quite a crowd had gathered at the corner. Many of the people were standing around in bathrobes and slippers. As he neared, he saw it had been a car wreck of some kind. One of the cars was a big Suburban and in that, the people appeared unhurt. The other was a red sports car. A Mustang.

"Crazy teenagers!" one of Zach's neighbors said. "There's no reason for a crash like this on a suburban street!"

One of the paramedics was ordering the crowd to move back. His heart pounding, filled with a feeling of dread, Zach pushed closer anyway.

LAURA STRODE through the automatic glass doors of the Emergency Room entrance, her heart in her throat, tears in her eyes. Her hands and legs were shaking so badly she could hardly walk. All she could think about was Eric. Her baby. It didn't matter what Eric was doing out driving around at two in the morning. They could sort all that out later. Right now, all she cared about, was that he be all right.

Hurrying over to the admitting desk, Laura told the nurse. "I'm Mrs. Matthews. You called. You said you have my son."

"Yes. He was in a car accident with Janey Anderson."

Laura's heart stilled. Her insides went cold and numb with shock. "Excuse me?"

"Janey Anderson. That was the name of the young girl who was with him at the time of the wreck. Her father's already in the treatment room with her."

"Is she going to be all right?" Laura asked.

"The doctor is still with her," the nurse said in a crisp, professional tone.

"My son—" she croaked.

"Is back there, too. Would you like to be with him?"

Laura nodded, her vision blurred with tears. "Please." The nurse signaled to an aide who'd just walked up. "Show Mrs. Matthews to her son Eric."

"He's in a back bed, over here," the aide said as she led Laura past several curtained beds.

In the next to last curtained area, Laura saw Zach. He was standing next to Janey's bed, tightly holding one of her hands. Hearing her quick intake of breath, the stilled footsteps, he looked accusingly at Laura, then back down at Janey, whose arms were a mass of bandages. A long white bandage ran the length of her forehead. Blood was matted and drying in her hair and there was a large bruise on her cheek.

Laura wanted to say something, but there were no words that could begin to convey what she was feeling. She hurried after the aide and into the curtained area where her son lay.

He looked so small and vulnerable. For the first time, she realized with startling clarity just how young sixteen was. She thought of him as an adult now, so much of the time, but in his heart and mind he was still a child in many ways.

Like Janey, he looked as though he had been through sheer hell. His eyes were closed. His hair was matted with blood. His face was bruised. Two strategically placed butterfly bandages closed the worst of the wounds.

His eyes opened as she moved next to him and took his hand. "Mom." He croaked the word and tears poured from his eyes. "I'm so sorry."

She bent close and squeezed his hand reassuringly, all the love she had for him in her heart flowing into her soft, low voice. "It's all right, honey," she reassured softly, meaning it. "I'm not angry."

"But—"

"We'll talk about how it happened later. I just want you to rest."

"Janey—" Eric whispered, distressed.

Laura squeezed his hands harder. "She's close by. Her dad is with her."

Eric relaxed slightly and shut his eyes briefly. "Is she okay?" he asked in a trembling voice.

Laura had never seen her son look so afraid. "I think so. I'll have to talk to the doctors but she looked stable." Eric sighed in relief.

"Mrs. Matthews? We're going to move him upstairs now. We want to keep him overnight, just to be sure there are no internal injuries."

"Mom?" Eric asked, when she moved back to let the orderlies close enough to work.

"I'll stay with you, honey," she promised, leaning over the gurney.

It was almost five before Eric fell into a deep, exhausted sleep. Her mind full of questions, Laura started for the coffee machine. Farther down the hall, she saw Zach must have had the same thought for he was coming out of a patient room and heading in the same direction.

They met at the coffee machine. He had never looked more alone. Her heart went out to him. She still didn't know what had happened, but she knew he hadn't deserved to suffer though this. None of them had. "Janey asleep?" she asked softly.

"Yes." Zach nodded solemnly. "She's asleep. What about Eric?"

"He's asleep, too." Silence fell between them. Laura took a sip of her coffee and found it bitter. They stared at each other awkwardly. "I'm sorry," Laura said finally, wishing fervently that they had never fought. She would understand if he were furious with her for this. The last couple of hours had given her time to think, to realize that Eric was at fault, both for driving and having Janey out at that time of night. She shrugged helplessly. "I don't know what was going on."

"It's pretty obvious," Zach said, his voice hoarse with a mixture of hurt and disbelief. He sighed heavily, looking as if he had the weight of the world on his shoulders. "She had a suitcase in the back of Eric's car. She'd made up her bed to look as if someone was sleeping there."

Shock held Laura motionless. "Eric was helping her run away?" she gasped, stunned.

Zach nodded and his lips thinned. "The accident happened a little over a block from my house, at the intersection. The driver of the other car said Eric was driving with his lights off. They hit head-on."

"Oh, my God," Laura gasped. They could have both been killed. At the stark realization, all the strength left her. Somehow she managed to right her precariously tilting cup and then groped behind her for a chair and fell weakly into it.

"The Suburban wasn't damaged too badly but Eric's Mustang is totaled. Neither Janey nor Eric were wearing seat belts."

Knowledge of that made Laura furious. "He knows better."

"So does Janey," Zach said.

"Was anyone else hurt?" Laura asked, still feeling too shaky to stand.

Zach's expression remained wearily remote, as if he wanted to keep all his hurt locked deep inside. "No."

He blames me for this. I know it. Distressed, Laura buried her face in her hands, aware she was trembling visibly yet able to do nothing about it. The past week rivaled the worst times of her life. Melinda's final days, the days immediately after Rob's death. She didn't know how much more she could take.

Beside her, Zach was silent, too. He knew this accident was his fault. He should've seen it coming. But he hadn't because he'd been so wrapped up in his feelings for Laura, in trying to figure out if there wasn't some way to surmount all the obstacles in front of them. He wanted to find a way to make their relationship work, instead of giving it up for the lost cause it really was. And because of his self-absorbed attitude, his daughter had almost died. Well, he had his priorities in order now. His love for Janey came first, even if it meant giving up the best time he'd ever had with a woman. He couldn't afford to lose Janey the way Laura had lost Melinda.

Laura heard him move to the window. When she looked up again, he was standing, staring out at the first pearly gray light of dawn on the horizon, a look of grim self-indictment on his face.

Wearily, Laura stood. She wanted to say something. She just didn't know what. Nothing could make things better at this point. Zach didn't speak to her again and she left silently.

"MOM, PLEASE. Do we have to talk about this now?" Eric grumbled as he attacked the breakfast the nurse had brought. He looked even worse than she felt. "My head is killing me."

"I don't wonder," she retorted sarcastically. Now that she knew he was all right, her anger and disappointment in him had reached mammoth proportions. Unable to wait any longer, she demanded, "What were you thinking last night?"

Eric's lip shot out truculently. "She's unhappy there. She wanted to get away. I said I'd help her." Eric put a fork into his scrambled egg, then looking nauseous, pushed the whole plate away.

"With no thought to the trouble you were causing?"

"Causing who?" Eric demanded, just as contentiously. "Zach?" When she flinched, he went on, "I care about Janey, okay? She is my sister. Zach—well—Zach is just going to have to worry about himself. I've got to worry about Janey."

"I see. And were you worried about Janey when you were driving without seat belts and headlights?"

He blinked, severely taken aback by her censuring tone. Recovering, he crossed his arms over his chest, then restlessly disengaged them. "We were trying not to be seen. How was I to know some big car would round the corner?"

"Don't blame this all on the other driver. If you'd had your headlights on, this most likely would not have happened!"

"I said I was sorry."

"Well, in this case sorry isn't enough."

Eric looked at her, distressed. "What do you mean?" he asked apprehensively.

"I mean you're grounded," Laura shot back. And the moment the words were out of her mouth, she knew it was the right thing to do. Having always been a parent who prided herself on not harshly confining her children in any way, she knew the time had come for her to take a stand and let Eric know his behavior had been unconscionable.

"You're kidding." He looked her up and down, with suspiciousness.

"No," Laura enunciated clearly, "I'm not."

Eric's jaw set. Long minutes passed in which neither of them spoke a word. "When am I getting out of here?" he demanded finally.

"By noon, the doctor said last night."

Eric's jaw turned even more rigid. Laura knew it wouldn't be easy taking him home. But then getting a phone call from the hospital in the middle of the night hadn't been easy, either.

She couldn't go through this again, wouldn't go through this again. And somehow, someway, Eric would just have to understand that. And, in the meantime, there were some things Zach would have to understand, too.

"ZACH, can I talk to you?" Laura said, from the doorway of Janey's hospital room. He looked up from his daughter's bedside. Like herself, Zach was still wearing the clothes he had hurriedly pulled on the night before.

Janey had been lying prone against the pillows, but at the sight of Laura she sat up gingerly. "I want to talk to you first, Laura. Please?" She looked at her dad, sensing rightly that he was about to object. "Alone? It'll just take a minute."

Zach sighed and dragged a hand through his hair. "All right. I was about to go down to the business office anyway." He looked at Laura, his eyes direct, but his feelings, whatever they were, successfully hidden from her. "I'll meet you in the lounge down the hall in ten minutes."

"Thank you," Laura said and nodded graciously at him as

he passed her, even though she knew he was only accommodating his daughter because he had nearly lost her.

"Don't be mad at Eric," Janey said. "It wasn't his fault. I asked him to come and get me."

Eric hadn't told her that. Laura let that fact sink in. So, this hadn't been all Eric's idea after all. "Maybe so," Laura countered gently but firmly, "but he knows better than to drive without lights at night. That was incredibly dangerous and foolhardy. The two of you are lucky you're still alive."

Janey hung her head. "Dad says he's going to be taking me home in a little while." She gulped. "Laura, I don't want to go. I want to go to your house. That's where I belong now. Before we didn't know who my real parents were, but now we do and I just think that's where I ought to be."

Laura regarded Janey carefully. There was no doubt in her mind at all the child thought she knew what she was doing. But Laura wasn't convinced. When all this had started Zach and Janey had been so close. Janey had been suspicious of and mistrustful of Laura, friendly only to Eric. She hadn't wanted to be taken away from Zach. Now, suddenly, she did. The fight about the earrings aside, it didn't make sense. More had to be going on here. She sat down on the edge of Janey's bed and took her hand in hers. "Your dad loves you, Janey." More than life.

"But he's not my real dad," Janey sniffed. "Please talk to him."

Sitting on the bed next to Janey, holding her close, the way she had once held Melinda when anything was wrong, Laura felt a surge of maternal affection. And although she had promised ten minutes, it was more like half an hour before Janey was composed enough for Laura to leave her.

Zach was standing at a window. One look at his tense expression told Laura he had seen her holding Janey. Briefly she wondered what else he had seen and heard. "Janey wants me to take her home."

He kept his back to her and responded evenly, "I told you before, that is not an option."

Janey didn't need stubbornness from him, she needed understanding. And so did Laura. "Do you want her to run away again?" Laura queried insistently.

That caught his attention. He whirled on her, doing his best to hide his hurt. "Did she tell you she was going to do that?"

Laura shook her head slowly. "No, but she's done it twice in the past week. Once to the mall, and once with Eric. I'd say that makes her intentions fairly clear."

Zach paced back and forth, his frustration with the situation evident.

Zach had known guiding his daughter to adulthood would be complex, full of ups and downs, but he had never expected it to be this emotionally draining or devastating. Not so very long ago he had been his daughter's hero, confidant, and conscience, all wrapped up into one. He'd been privy to her worst fears and her loftiest dreams. He'd felt so close to her then. He knew in his heart Janey still loved him deeply and always would, but knew they were no longer so close. And that hurt, almost more than he could stand. Still, he hoped her deliberate distance would pass. And be replaced by something deeper yet.

He didn't see how he could let Janey go. If he did, before they worked things out, he feared they might continue this parent-child stalemate indefinitely. "She's upset," Zach said. She's young and impulsive, not thinking things through, but living moment to moment, like Laura.

"Maybe that's true, Zach. Lately her judgment has been off. But that doesn't change the facts. She's still my daughter," Laura said in a soft, persuasive voice. "And she wants to be with me. And because I love her, I can't deny her that, even though I know it means I'm hurting you."

Fear ran through Zach. He felt as though he was living his worst nightmare. He turned, his blue eyes narrowing dangerously as he looked at Laura. "What are you trying to tell me, Laura?" he asked, hanging on to his composure with a thread. "That you want her back?"

Tears filled her eyes and she looked at him with guilt and

indecision. "I never meant to go back on my word—" she began gently.

Considering what was at stake, Zach didn't want her kindness. "But you are now anyway, right?"

"She's unhappy, Zach. Right or wrong, she needs a woman in her life now. She needs me."

He shook his head in abject misery. Janey was young enough to want to go where the grass was greener, but he hadn't expected this from Laura. "This—from the lady whose other, real child just landed mine in the hospital?"

Laura stood firm. "If you love her, Zach, you'll let her go."

He shook his head and moved farther away from her. He thrust his fists into the pockets of his jeans. The loss of Laura and Janey was enough to bring him to his knees permanently. "You don't know what you're asking," he said very low, fighting the tears that threatened.

"Yes," Laura said slowly, "I do."

"You wouldn't turn your back on Eric."

"Yes, I would. If it was the only way to reach him."

"This isn't."

"I think it is. Zach, she almost died last night, trying to get to me. I agree it was stupid and senseless but that's the way kids are at that age. They think with their hearts, not their minds." Her eyes filled with tears. "I can't stand idly by and watch this happen again."

He weighed her plea before responding. "You won't have to," he pronounced calmly. "This time I plan to keep a better eye on her."

Laura took a deep, bracing breath. "What are you going to do? Stand watch over her night and day? Run your home like a prison?"

Zach shrugged, the images Laura was concocting not appealing to him at all. "If I have to," he admitted reluctantly, "until she starts talking to me again, telling me what's going on with her." He would do anything to break the cycle of hurt and alienation that had been started.

Seething with frustration, Laura fell silent.

If she thought Zach's plan would work, she'd be all for it. "At least give me time with her, then," she urged passionately, knowing in her heart she could make a difference, that with time she could reach her.

"I can't," he said in a voice laced with deep regret. "Not when your involvement with her is what started this." Stepping closer he said softly and seriously, "For the time being, I don't want you to see her at all, Laura. Not until her life is back on an even keel again and maybe not even then. It's too confusing for Janey."

"Please reconsider," she whispered, feeling as though her heart was breaking.

"No."

"Zach, please. Don't force me to—"

"To what?" he asked, waiting.

Laura searched vainly for the words that would prompt him to do what she wished. "To take you to you to court." She hadn't meant to say the words, but once they were verbalized, she knew it was the only path.

He stared at her as if seeing a stranger. "You promised me you would never do that," he accused hoarsely in disbelief. He stepped closer. "I have your pledge in writing."

Laura knew that. And if Zach had been reasonable, it never would have been necessary. But looking at his closed expression, she knew that was never going to happen. And as such, he left her no choice. "All contracts can be revoked, Zach," she said firmly, hoping he would buckle under when he saw how serious she was. "Sometimes, like now, circumstances change."

Although her demeanor was calm and matter-of-fact, he was furious, seething. "Don't threaten me, Laura," he warned.

Stubbornly she held his penetrating gaze and refused to give in. "Then don't keep me away from our child." Seeing he was still unreachable, she braved his scorching look, knowing he was no longer going to forgive her for this. But somehow, she had to get to the root of Janey's troubles, so she could mend his relationship with her. "It's been an upsetting week,"

Laura said finally, furious Zach still wouldn't relent. "I'll give you until next Wednesday to reconsider."

"And if I don't reconsider and let you see Janey?" he queried harshly, his face a mask of pain that almost broke her heart.

Only if and when the two were close again, would they ever be happy. And the only way to get that to happen was to get Janey to open up. Even if that meant sacrificing Zach's trust and the possibility of them ever reconciling. She looked at Zach and pressed ahead bravely, because she loved him and Janey, because she had no choice. "Then I'll file suit."

Chapter Sixteen

"Why didn't you tell us what happened?" Laura's mother said, the moment they walked in the door Tuesday evening. "We had to hear about Eric's wreck at the grocery store!"

In the middle of cooking dinner and unable to indefinitely leave the pork chops she had simmering on the stove, Laura led the way back to her kitchen. "I didn't want to worry you until I knew how bad the situation was," she explained.

"You could have called us when you knew he was going to be all right," her mother chided, aggrieved.

"Yes, I guess I could have," Laura said. But frankly, her mind had been so full of Janey and Zach that she hadn't thought of her parents. "I'm sorry," she said.

"It's all right. We understand," her father said, patting her on the shoulder. He stepped back and gave her the kind of thorough once-over a general gave those he was inspecting. "But we are concerned about you and Eric. I hope you understand that."

"I do."

"I also hope you've taken corrective action with your son."

Laura smiled faintly at her father's military way of putting things. Although more sensitive to others' feelings than her mother, he, too, felt the world ran on discipline, and floundered hopelessly without it. "He's grounded. And the matter of whether or not he will get another car is yet to be decided."

Her father nodded approvingly.

"What about Janey?" her mother asked. "How is she doing?"

Laura pretended to busy herself tearing lettuce for salad. "I haven't heard but she was recovering when I left the hospital."

"What did Zach have to say about all this?" her father wanted to know.

He blames me for all of it, Laura thought, depressed. But unable and unwilling to go into that with her parents, she said only, "He was very upset with both of them."

"Was the rumor true?" her mother persisted. "Was Janey trying to run away?"

Wishing she could avoid this question entirely, Laura said, "Yes."

"And?" Grace persisted.

"And obviously she didn't get very far."

"Is that all you're going to say?" her mother prodded, hands on her hips.

"Yes, as a matter of fact, it is." Laura picked up a cucumber and began slicing it in neat quarter-inch rounds.

"Well, it's not all I have to say. I think it's high time you consider doing what I've advised all along—suing for custody," her mother said.

Laura knew her mother's heart was in the right place. She just wanted Laura to have everything that was coming to her. But Janey wasn't a commodity to be bandied about between Zach and herself. Deciding however, the only way to get her mother off her back was to level with her, Laura said, "I thought about it. I even talked to Zach about Janey coming to live with me, just for a little while."

"And?" her mother asked with bated breath, one hand clutching the pearls she wore around her neck.

"And I decided I couldn't do that to her," Laura said in a voice laced with sorrow. "She's already been through so much. I can't put her through a custody battle. I can't let her be dragged into court."

"Even if it's the best thing for her in the long run?" her father asked gently.

Laura sighed. She had thought about this long and hard and had come to the only conclusion she could. "Zach loves her and she loves Zach. They will work things out, given time and opportunity."

"And if they don't?" her mother asked, her eyes narrowed disapprovingly as she broke the heavy silence in the kitchen.

"They will," Laura said firmly, tightening her hands into fists at her sides. She had to believe that or she'd go crazy.

"You're doing it again," her mother exclaimed, upset.

Laura turned to face her mother, aware her face was growing red as she asked, "Doing what?"

Her mother stared at her, tight-lipped, then shook her head in silent disparagement. "Taking the easy way out, that's what. What you have always done from the time you ran away and married that sailor—"

Laura's temper flared at the cruel and inaccurate recitation. "Rob was a Navy officer, Mother."

Ignoring Laura's icy correction, her mother continued accusingly, "I don't know why. Heaven knows I tried to bring you up right, but you never could manage long-range plans."

Nor could I ever manage you, Laura thought. But maybe it was time she started. Gathering her courage, she faced her mother resolutely.

"If you won't sue for custody then we will," her mother declared.

Before her astonished father could reply to that, Laura cut in, "No, you won't, Mother. You'll do nothing of the kind." Her mother's mouth dropped open in mute surprise at the way Laura was suddenly fighting back. Knowing she was doing what she should have done all along, Laura continued, "This is my problem. I'll handle it."

"If only that were true!" her mother asserted, ready and willing to take control of Laura's life once again.

Laura wiped her hands on a dish towel in front of her. She knew she was about to lose her composure, but for the first time in years she didn't care. Some things had to be said. "Mother, I swear to you, if you interfere in this, if you say one word, if you so much as think about picking up that phone to talk to Zach, I'll cut you out of my life. For good.''

Her mother's cheeks grew spotty with color, too. "You have no right to talk to me that way!" Grace swore.

Knowing she had a right to happiness, too, Laura said, "I have every right. I am a grown woman, fully capable of making my own decisions, and living with the consequences. Yet you treat me as if I am incapable of thinking for myself and worse, in constant need of rescuing. This is just not true, Mother. I can stand on my own and I have been doing so for a very long time. You just haven't noticed."

Laura's father grinned at his only child. "Bravo," he said to Laura in an approving undertone, and then to his wife, "Come on. We've done enough damage here. It's time to go home."

"Wait a minute." Grace dug in her heels. "You're going to let her talk to me like that?" In the past, Laura knew, her father had always insisted Laura treat her mother with respect, regardless of what her mother had said or done. But not this time.

Her father shrugged. "Like Laura said, she is a grown woman, perfectly capable of making her own decisions."

Her mother gasped. Outraged, she clamped her lips shut, picked up her coat and purse, and marched from the kitchen.

Her dad paused for one bit of advice. "Follow your heart, hon. It won't steer you wrong." And with that, he, too, was gone.

JANEY CAME DOWN to supper wearing the outrageous earrings Laura had helped her buy at the mall. Because she still wasn't talking to her father, she sat down in silence and began picking at her food.

She didn't look good. Her color was pasty. Her face and right arm still bearing the scars of her battle with the Mustang's windshield. The only time she had spoken to Zach since he had vetoed her going to Laura's and brought her home from the hospital was to ask him to help her wash the blood out of her hair. She wasn't allowed to get the stitches on her forehead wet. He knew if she had been able to keep her forehead dry and wash and rinse her hair alone she would've done so.

In the forty-eight hours since then, she had been totally silent. She went to school, but didn't say a word coming or going. If she had been giving him the silent treatment in overt rebellion, it would have been one thing. But she was just sad. For some reason, Janey had become inexplicably depressed. And he didn't know why. He didn't have so much as one damn clue. He had tried everything, from acting normal, to giving her space, to just being with her. Nothing worked.

"Do you want me to help you wash your hair again tonight?" Zach asked, passing the basket of rolls her way.

Janey nodded, the frivolous earrings bobbing on both earlobes, reminding him of Laura.

She had said she would sue him for custody of Janey if he didn't make arrangements to let her see her daughter by Wednesday. That meant he had twenty-four hours, maybe less.

He wasn't sure what hurt worse, that Laura was going back on her word to him, or that she didn't seem to believe he really loved his daughter. Her doubts were all too reminiscent of what he had suffered with Maria. Always having to prove his love, his goodness, his commitment.

He had promised himself he would never get involved with anyone who couldn't believe in his capacity for love or the worth of his devotion. And yet apparently he had. What kind of fool did that make him? he wondered. What kind of fool did that make Laura?

ZACH WAS STILL in a glum mood when he went to work the following morning. But he wasn't the worst looking guy there. Harry Cole was.

"You okay?" he asked as, blueprints in hand, the other man stepped into his trailer.

"No, as a matter of fact, I'm not," Harry admitted glumly. His eyes filled with tears. "We had to hospitalize Tabitha last night."

For a moment, Zach was too stunned to move. "Damn, Harry. I'm sorry. So sorry." Because Harry looked as if he was about to collapse, Zach pushed him into a chair.

His face devoid of all color, Harry related what had happened in a shocked monotone. "She tried to swallow a bottle of sleeping tablets. She did it in front of one of her friends. The friend called us. We got there. The psychiatrist said because she did it in front of a witness she obviously wasn't trying to kill herself. If was just a cry for help."

"Have you talked to her since?" Zach asked, horrified.

Harry nodded. "Yeah, my wife and I both saw her this morning, briefly." He sighed heavily and related in a hurt, bewildered voice, "She said we haven't been listening to her, Zach, that we haven't heard anything she's had to say. That she's been unhappy for a long time."

Galvanized into action, Zach said, "Whatever the costs are, whatever the insurance doesn't pay, I'll help you."

"Thanks," Harry said, looking relieved about that much.

Zach wished he could have reversed what had happened, or known enough to offer help earlier. Barring that, he suggested, "Why don't you take the day off?"

Harry nodded indicating he would. "I'd like to be with my wife. This has been really hard on her. They don't want us seeing Tabitha for a few days. They think it'd be better if we let the doctors get her settled in."

Zach nodded, listening.

"Then we're supposed to start family therapy." Harry shook his head and swore. "I wish I hadn't let it come to this...."

I wish I hadn't let it come to this.... The words echoed over and over in Zach's ears all day long. It hadn't been that long ago that Tabitha and Harry had been blessed with a happy family relationship. Could what happened to them happen to him and Janey? *I want to go live with Laura, Dad....* Zach pushed the words from his mind. The situations weren't the same. They weren't the same at all. But they could be, given more time and difficulty, and he knew it in his gut.

"HAVE YOU HEARD from Janey?" Eric asked Saturday morning when he sat down to eat the pancakes Laura had set out for them. After breakfast, as arranged with the conditions of his grounding, he was going to clean up the backyard and spend the rest of the afternoon writing to various colleges, asking for information about admission requirements. Never having grounded Eric before, Laura mainly wanted to keep him busy and productive. And she seemed to be doing that with ease.

What surprised her was Eric's attitude. Rather than chafing constantly at the restrictions on him, he had accepted them with equilibrium. Not that he always enjoyed the yard work and cleaning chores she had assigned, but he seemed to know it was only fair.

Reminded of her son's question by his expectant glance, Laura answered. "No, I haven't heard from Janey." Nor had she talked to Zach. That wasn't particularly surprising, either, considering the ultimatum she had flung down the previous Sunday. That had been foolish on her part and ill conceived. Remembering it, she was embarrassed by the shrewish way she had behaved. She still felt she was right, in wanting to see her child, but she also knew Zach and Janey had a lot to work out by themselves too. And as hard as it was for her to admit, she was getting in the way of that. Janey saw Laura as a magic cure-all. Laura had come to love Janey, but she knew her feelings still must pale in comparison to Zach's. Janey needed Zach right now, even if she didn't yet know it.

In the background, the doorbell rang. Laura motioned her son to stay where he was. "I'll get it. You stay and eat."

She was half expecting her mother, even though they hadn't spoken since their fight. She was stunned to see Zach. Janey was beside him, and she had a suitcase in hand. Her heart lodged in her throat, Laura opened the storm door and let them in.

"Hi," Zach said.

Janey's eyes brimmed with tears. "I've come to stay," she

choked out, her voice little more than a hoarse whisper. "If you'll have me."

If she would have her? Her heart brimming over with love and compassion, Laura reacted instinctively and held out her arms. Janey tumbled into them. As Laura held the sobbing teenager, she met Zach's eyes. Like Janey, he was in unspeakable pain. "I thought it over," Zach said thickly. His eyes held hers as if begging for forgiveness. "I decided Janey and you were both right. Maybe she should spend time with you."

Zach must feel as though he is losing Janey forever, Laura thought. With effort, she held back her tears. "I'll take good care of her," she finally managed. "We'll have lots of talks. And do girl-stuff, too."

"Can we go shopping again and maybe cook together?" Janey asked. Despite her bright tone, she looked as miserable as Zach. And yet oddly relieved too.

Laura nodded. "Sure." She helped Janey out of her jacket. "Why don't you go into the kitchen and say hello to Eric? He's been thinking about you a lot. I'll be there in a minute."

"Okay." Janey turned to give Zach a fleeting look, full of misery and hurt, and then went on her way.

"Thanks for the girl-stuff," Zach said with difficulty. "She sure can't get that from me." Even though he wished with all his heart he could give it to her.

But she had gotten that from him, Laura thought guiltily, before I came on the scene. Janey'd had plenty of good times with her dad, plus a sense of closeness that had been almost impenetrable. And now—now they were barely speaking. But hopefully, that wouldn't last, Laura thought determinedly.

Knowing the next part had to be spoken, she said, "Zach about the lawsuit. I—I never would have really done that. I just said it because I thought it might make you see reason. When it didn't, I knew I couldn't tear the two families apart or take this to court and make it a public battle. I love Janey—" And you, she wanted to say, but couldn't, not when he no longer felt the same.

"I love her, too," Zach said with difficulty. "That's why I'm here, because I knew she needed to be with you."

Laura reached out and touched his arm. "I'll take good care of her," she promised finally. At least he understood now that she'd been acting out of love for their child, not because she wanted to hurt him.

"I'd like to say goodbye to her, if I could."

"You can stay a while, can't you? Have some breakfast or a cup of coffee?"

"Maybe some coffee," he agreed reluctantly after a moment. But that's all I'll be able to stand without breaking down. "And then I really have to go."

Swallowing her disappointment, Laura said, "Okay. Coffee it is then."

She led the way into the kitchen. Janey and Eric looked up as she came in.

"Have you had breakfast?" Laura asked her daughter. Janey shook her head, looking shyly at Laura, but avoiding Zach altogether. And though Zach didn't react in the slightest, Laura could sense his hurt. "Well, how about some pancakes?" Laura asked cheerfully, trying to end the tension. "And then when you and Eric both finish," she suggested to Janey, "the two of you can go out and work on the backyard together."

Stilted minutes later, the kids were out back, wrestling with rakes. As Laura watched them go at their mutual chore, her heart filled with the picture they presented. So much love, she thought. If only she and Zach could have shared this, as man and wife.

"You're sure it's all right—Janey staying?" Zach asked, looking as though he wanted to bolt.

Laura studied him, aware that, in his eyes, he had lost his daughter. And Laura was the woman who had stolen her away from him. Collecting herself, she assured him in the levelest voice she could manage, "Yes. I'd love to have Janey with me, however long she needs to be here."

He nodded, his expression relieved and sad. He glanced over at her, his mouth compressed apprehensively. "I won't lie to you. She's in bad shape. She said more to Eric this morning than she has to me all week." He swallowed hard and the confession tore at her heart. "I want her to be happy, Laura. For whatever reason, right now she just isn't when she's with me."

Laura wanted to reach out and cover his hand with her own, but not sure how the gesture would be received, she held herself in check. She said, "I told you before I thought something more was bothering her. Seeing her this morning, the way she burst into tears when she came in, I still think that's true. Maybe she'll open up and tell us what's on her mind."

"I hope so," Zach said. He sighed, not looking convinced.

Silence fell between them. She studied his strained face and the circles around his blue eyes. She wondered if anything else was adding to his pain. "Has my mother called you lately?" Laura asked, hoping not.

To her immense relief, Zach shook his head.

At least they were making progress in one area, she thought. Now if she could only make some headway in others.

"DON'T YOU THINK it's time you told me why you are so angry with your dad?" Laura asked Janey the following evening as the two of them worked together, folding a load of laundry.

"What makes you think I'm angry with him?" Janey evaded, smoothing a washcloth into a neat square.

"Oh, I don't know," Laura said idly as she picked up another towel and shook it out. "Maybe the fact you're here with me."

Janey's back stiffened. "He's too strict," she complained.

Laura's maternal instincts told her this was just a smoke screen, but she decided to play along. "Hmm, back to the earrings again."

Janey's chin took on a stubborn tilt. "He gets mad every time I wear them, even around the house."

Maybe because they remind him of me, Laura thought. How could we have thought the two of us, as different as we are, could have a lasting relationship? No, as much as she loved Zach, they just weren't right for each other. Not when he felt she was too flighty and shortsighted, and when he could never seem to look at anything but the big picture. They would never be happy.

Laura looked at Janey. She was wearing her earrings now. "How long have the earrings been an issue between the two of you?" she asked lightly. "How long have you wanted them?"

"Since I was eight."

"Oh, dear. That long?" Laura asked.

Janey shrugged. "We fought about it off and on every year. It always ended with him saying no. He didn't want to hear any more about it, period."

"But you never ran away before," Laura guessed.

"No." Her expression dejected, Janey looked down at her lap.

"Why did you run away this time?" Laura asked.

Janey was silent a long time. When she looked up again, her eyes were awash with tears. Her bottom lip trembled. "Because h-he was s-sorry he had me."

Laura stared at Janey in bewilderment. "Honey, what are you talking about? Did your dad say something to you, during a fight?" Something Janey had totally misunderstood? She knew Zach. He loved his daughter more than life.

"Not to me." Janey shook her head, looking even more disheartened.

"Then I don't understand."

"To you."

"To me?" Laura splayed a hand over her heart.

"The night you came over with all those pictures of Melinda. I—I overheard the two of you talking. I heard Daddy crying and saying how sorry he was she had died. How sorry he was he'd never known her." She clasped her hands together tightly and said in the softest whisper, "And I knew then that he was sorry he'd gotten me at the hospital instead of her. Because if he hadn't, he would have had her as his daughter."

She finished on a tearful hiccup. Embarrassed, the tears stilled streaming down her face, she pressed a hand to her mouth.

As Laura took in what she'd said, she felt an incredible mixture of emotions. Relief that this was all it was. Compassion for what Janey had needlessly suffered. And aggravation for not having suspected this.

Her brow furrowed as she struggled to put it all together. "The day you went to the mall without permission. Was that the day after your dad and I talked about Melinda?"

Janey nodded mutely, looking more miserable than ever. "Oh, honey." Laura held out her arms and Janey went into them gladly. They rocked together, mother and daughter, for several minutes. Tears slipped down Laura's face. "If we had only known what you'd been thinking and feeling...." Laura said, distressed. She drew back so Janey could look into her eyes and see for herself that Laura spoke the truth. "Don't you know how much we all love you?"

"But—" Janey sputtered in disbelief.

"Your father was just sad about Melinda," Laura reassured her softly but firmly. "That's all. I was sad, too. It helped us to talk about it." Studying Janey's distressed expression, a light bulb went on in Laura's head. Maybe there was a way to help her. "Maybe it would help you to talk about her, too," Laura suggested. Maybe if Janey dealt with this directly, the way Zach had, it would be as cathartic.

"Do you want to do that?" Laura asked softly, wanting the final decision to be Janey's.

Slowly, Janey nodded and wiped at her tears. "Would you mind? I know how upset you get talking about her."

"I don't mind. In fact, talking about things that hurt us with someone we love makes it easier."

"Okay," Janey sniffed. "Let's do it."

"Atta girl," Laura said, rising and taking Janey's hand in hers. She led her toward the living room and the box of photos she kept there.

"Laura," Janey said, her tears fading as they sat down to

look at the pictures. "After we look at the pictures, would you mind very much if we called my dad?"

Laura smiled through her tears, knowing at last their hopes had been answered. "I think Zach would like that very much."

"So ALL THIS wild and crazy behavior was because you thought I didn't love you?" Zach repeated in a shaky voice as he regarded his daughter in astonishment.

Janey nodded. During the past four hours, she hadn't stopped crying for more than a few minutes at a time. Janey's eyes would be swollen tomorrow, Laura thought, but her heart would be freer than it had been in weeks.

"Janey, I will always love you. Always," Zach promised firmly, taking her into his arms. He drew back to look at her. "I have been so miserable the past few weeks, not knowing what to do or say to you, seeing that you were hurt, not knowing how to help. For the longest time, I blamed Laura. I can see now that I was wrong." He looked over at her. "And for that, I'm genuinely sorry," he said softly.

Laura accepted his apology with the same goodwill it had been tendered, soothing, "It's been an upsetting time."

Janey looked at Laura. "Would you mind if I went home with my dad?"

Laura swallowed around the burning lump in her throat, glad she had been able to reunite father and daughter, while at the same time acutely feeling her own loss. "Honey, that's where you belong," she said softly.

"I'll go pack my things." Still wiping her eyes, Janey scampered up the stairs.

Left alone, Laura and Zach stared at each other. So much had happened. But they had worked through the worst of it, she knew. "I don't know how to thank you," he said thickly, looking a bit overcome himself.

Laura shrugged off his kind words. She didn't want his gratitude. She wanted his love. And if she couldn't have that, the rest was just too painful to contemplate. "Just be happy," she advised, keeping a tight rein on her own spiraling emotions. She gulped hard. "Be good to her. And Zach—"

He waited, not moving in the slightest, totally in the dark about what she was going to say.

"—think about those earrings," Laura advised softly, feeling as if her heart was breaking all over again as she prepared to say goodbye to this man one more time. "Maybe you can buy Janey some sedate ones she can wear to school all the time since her ears are already pierced."

Zach nodded, his eyes never leaving hers as he said slowly, softly, "I'll keep it in mind."

Janey was back, having packed in an amazingly short time. "I'm ready to go!" she announced. Zach gave Laura another reluctant look, then thanked her again and followed his daughter out the door. Laura watched them go, glad it had all worked out for father and daughter, wishing it could have worked out for the two of them, too. But that was foolish of her, and not very realistic, and she knew it. Knew it only too well.

"OUR HOME is way behind schedule," Mr. Gagglione complained the moment he stepped into Zach's downtown office. "And I'm tired of all the excuses! I want an explanation!"

Zach looked at the irate businessman, then over at his wife. Mrs. Gagglione had her poodle along with her, as usual, but beneath the layers of rouge and makeup on her face, she was deathly pale. Worse, she seemed to be silently pleading with Zach not to let her husband know the delays were the result of her constantly and irrationally changing her mind.

He swore inwardly. Now what was he supposed to do? Be a gentleman and bail Mrs. G. out? And let the reputation of his business be ruined? Or be a gentleman and take the blame. Perhaps, he could just be diplomatic.

He turned to Mr. Gagglione. "You're right, sir," he said smoothly. "We are way behind on the work. Mrs. Gagglione and I are both aware of that, but it's not for lack of time put in. We've been working very hard to create the home of your dreams."

Mr. Gagglione growled impatiently. "I just want a place I can entertain in. What's so hard about that? Meanwhile, my current place is going to blazes because she is always over here."

"I see where that might be a problem," Zach agreed. The truth was, he could do with less of Mrs. Gagglione.

Ignoring Zach's response, Mr. Gagglione continued his tirade, "The servants need direction! They can't get a thing done! In fact, I think they sit around watching TV all day. Two days ago I walked in with guests. Dinner was a half an hour late, not even the canapés were made!"

"I got caught in traffic on the way home," Mrs. Gagglione interjected weakly.

Listening to the couple argue as if he weren't even in the room, it soon became apparent to Zach what the problem was. The Gaggliones were both perfectionists. That's why they couldn't get anything done. Mrs. Gagglione couldn't make a decision because she feared it would be the wrong one. Mr. Gagglione was staying out of it completely, or trying to, so he wouldn't be to blame for the final product.

Maria had been a perfectionist, too. Expecting a dreamy type of romance instead of marriage, thinking he didn't love her when her vision of what should be failed to jibe with the reality of what was.

Laura, on the other hand, was not a perfectionist. She strove for excellence, loved it, but also knew there'd be plenty of problems along the way. She strove to meet them with equanimity. He'd been so afraid of failure, with Janey and with Laura that he'd been too rigid, too unwilling to compromise. Like Laura's first husband, he had acted as if there was only one way to do things—his. No wonder Laura had given up on him.

A decision made, Zach turned back to the still quarreling Gaggliones. It took some time and effort on his part, but he finally persuaded Mr. Gagglione that he needed to have more input on the house, to relieve Mrs. Gagglione of shouldering the burden alone. And that settled, he turned his attention to his own life.

"SO, THAT'S ALL it was," Eric mused the morning after Janey had returned to Zach's. He downed a glass of orange juice. "Weird, isn't it, how people can jump to the wrong conclusions?"

"Yes," Laura said. It was weird. And sad. Because if it hadn't been for all that jumping to conclusions, if Janey had just told them initially what she had overheard, maybe she and Zach would still be together.

"Gotta go. I'll see you tonight," Eric said. He slammed out the door, just as the school bus roared down the block and came to a brake-squealing halt two houses south of theirs.

Laura went to her calendar and looked at the orders she had today. Mondays were always busy, and today was no exception. She had over a dozen pies to bake, plus four layer cakes. Well, she thought, I still have my business. And Eric's doing well. My mother is at least out of my hair for the moment. I ought to feel good. But she didn't. Couldn't. Life without Zach just wasn't the same.

But it was over, all over. When would she get that through her thick head? And it was then that she heard the sound of footsteps on the back steps and saw Zach. Hoping nothing was wrong with Janey, she waved him into her kitchen.

The back door shut softly behind him and they faced each other awkwardly, the morning sunlight streaming down between them. "You probably want to kick me from here to Arizona," he remarked in a highly reasonable tone.

"I probably should," she agreed slowly, apprehension coursing through her veins.

He stepped closer, the apology in his eyes heartfelt. "But I wish you wouldn't," he confessed softly. Still studying her quietly, he continued, "I was up all night, thinking. About Janey, Melinda. You. Me. We've got one helluva complicated situation on our hands. It seems like it can blow up at any time, and who knows, it probably will again. When we least expect it.''

Laura nodded, unable to stop looking at him, unable to stop wanting to be held in his arms.

''But I love you. And dammit, I know you love me.''

Her heart was pounding and it seemed she had forgotten how to move. She didn't want to misinterpret this. ''What are you saying?'' she asked thickly.

''Well,'' he drawled and looked at her uncertainly. ''You know those earrings you've been encouraging me to buy my daughter? I think it's high time I did that.'' His blue eyes burned into hers. ''So, want to go with me to the jewelry store?''

Laura's heart fell, she'd been hoping for so much more. But at least this was a start. If they couldn't pick up where they had left off, they might be able to work up to that point again. ''It'll have to be after five.''

''That's fine.'' Zach smiled, adding a mysterious stipulation of his own, ''as long as you have time to help me pick out something else, too.''

Laura's heart began beating very fast. ''What?''

''An engagement ring and a pair of wedding bands, the kind that pledges you'll love me forever and I'll love you.'' His voice thickened and he went on, drawing her into his arms, weaving a hand through her hair as he spoke. ''The kind that will bind us together through thick or thin, past or present, and well into the future.'' He tipped her head back, so she was looking deep into his eyes. ''Do you think you can do that?'' he whispered emotionally. ''Do you want to?''

''Well—'' Laura said, as his eyes searched hers.

He tightened his grip on her possessively. ''I promise I'll be less hardheaded in the future.''

She smiled, buoyed by a joy so intense she felt she was on cloud nine. She liked a man who could compromise. And she liked all the love she saw in his eyes. ''That sounds reasonable.'' Knowing it was her turn, she confessed softly, honestly, ''But you aren't the only one who needs to change, Zach. I've realized something, too. I can't go on living moment to moment. It was important when Melinda was dying. We needed to hold on to every precious second and it was too scary then to contemplate the future. But that time in my life has passed. I've got to take a longer view. And—'' this confession came harder ''—I've got to stop calling you a tyrant whenever your opinion is different than mine. Adults can have different views and still get along. Or at least they should be able to when they love each other as much as we do.''

Moving closer still, Laura hugged him tightly. And then looked up at him through her tears of happiness, her gaze sure and steady. Zach took her face in his hands and bent to kiss her. ''You're all I ever wanted,'' he whispered.

''And you're all I want,'' Laura echoed fiercely. In his arms, she felt at last, as if she knew what love was all about. It was about holding on and it was about letting go. Most of all, it was about Zach and her and the love they had found in each other. Everything was going to be all right. She just knew it.

He's falling in love with his young son's *mother*....

GATHERING PLACE

Marisa Carroll

PROLOGUE

TYLER DANIELSON WAITED under the sheltering branches of a huge old live oak tree, a still, silent figure in the soft, expectant hush of a Sunday morning in May. He was on a wide residential street and from where he was standing, he looked across it to a church, his night-blue eyes narrowed against the glare of sunlight filtering through dusty leaves. His lean, rangy body was propped negligently against the tree trunk, his relaxed stance belying his anticipation. That was evident only in the static lines of his right hand, balled into a fist at his side.

Morning services were just ending at St. Matthew's Church, and the caroling voices of three great bronze bells momentarily drowned out the full-bodied tones of the organ and the growing chorus of sound as parishioners began to emerge from the sanctuary.

St. Matthew's was an unpretentious building. It was foursquare and solid, like the residents of the old, established neighborhood of Columbus, Georgia, who worshiped there. Built of red brick and sandstone, it had something of the look of a fortress. Or a prison—if not for the saving glory of its stained glass windows. Tyler could draw that conclusion because he knew something, now, of prisons. For the past nine months he'd looked out at the world from behind steel bars.

A year ago his wife, Allison, had died of the injuries she'd suffered in a car accident for which he'd been held responsible. Tyler had served his sentence. Nine months of physical confinement, a lifetime of remorse. Was that an adequate forfeit to pay for the loss of another's life? The guilt of Allison's death would always be with him. But life went on, and for

Tyler Danielson life meant renewing his relationship with David, his son.

"David." Tyler wasn't aware he'd spoken the child's name
aloud until the vibrations of the joyful sound rang in his ears.
While he'd been lost in his thoughts the congregation had
dispersed with laughter and good wishes. The last notes of the
organ died away on the heavy humid summer air. An older
man, white vestments brilliant in the Sabbath sun, paused at
the top of the steps holding a wiggling eight-year-old boy by
the hand.

No, not eight, Tyler thought dazedly, *eight and a half.* He'd
missed David's birthday while he was in prison. He'd missed
several of the other seven, too. But no more, never again, if
he could help it.

"David." His voice was louder this time, stronger, as he
stepped into the street. His son had grown at least two inches
in the months they'd been apart. His navy-blue dress pants
were almost too short. He needed a haircut, too, Tyler noticed.
His hair stood up in tufts wherever the breeze touched it, soft
and shiny brown like his eyes. So different from either his
own thick, dark hair or Allison's. She had been as blond and
fair as Tyler was dark.

The last small groups of worshipers drifted away. Tyler
found himself moving forward, walking out of the shadows,
crossing the street, still unsure what to say to David, or to the
man beside him—Allison's father, the Reverend Elliot Brandon.

"Hello, Son." Tyler saw the surprise in David's eyes, the
happiness overtaken by shyness. It was that, the hesitancy, the
reserve between them, that he wanted to banish forever. He
owed Allison's memory that much; he loved David that much.

"Daddy." David looked up at the tall, slightly stooped man
beside him. "Is it all right, Granddad?" Tyler flinched inwardly at the question.

A single barrier still stood between Tyler and his plans for
his reunion with David. Elliot Brandon. A stern and just man
who was a caring and forgiving shepherd to his flock. His
advice was eagerly sought by members of the congregation

and the community at large. A man just and fair to every sinner except the man he held responsible for the death of his only daughter.

"Hello, Elliot." Tyler stood quietly, his hands at his sides, waiting. He'd learned to wait these last months. "I want to take David away for a while. To Mackinac." He owned a cottage on the small wooded island commanding the Lake Huron end of the Straits of Mackinac in northern Michigan. Although "cottage" was a misleading name for the many-gabled, gingerbread-trimmed Victorian summer home.

"I don't know if that's wise, Tyler." Elliot's voice was deep and resonant. It resounded into the far corners of the church on Sunday mornings, but now it was lowered, with more than a hint of ice.

"He's my son." Tyler felt the muscles along the line of his jaw tighten with tension. Elliot wouldn't, couldn't, deny him this opportunity to learn to know his son. All their lives had been disrupted by Allison's death. She had died because of his carelessness; that couldn't be altered or undone. But surely Elliot knew how much he loved her child. "We need the time together, Elliot." Time to spend with David, time to put their lives back together, to begin again, to try to find a future for themselves as father and son.

"Do you want to go with your father, David?"

Something of the tension between the two men had communicated itself to the little boy. He nodded solemnly. "Yes, Granddad."

"Then we'd better get Mrs. Walen to pack your things."

With that one quick sentence, the last gate opened. Tyler's parents were retired and living in California. When he'd gone to prison he'd agreed to give Elliot custody of his son in order to avoid the further trauma of uprooting David from school and friends. That arrangement, legally, was still in effect. The simple truth of the matter was that he needed Elliot's permission to take his son away.

Tyler held out his arms. David hesitated one second longer, a second that stretched out toward eternity for Tyler's tightened nerves, then the boy launched himself down the church steps and into his father's embrace.

Tyler folded the child into his arms, unwilling to admit even to himself that he'd been afraid he'd never hold him like that again. He looked up as a shadow passed across the sun, his eyes dazzled by sunlight and tears he wouldn't allow to fall. Elliot stood above him, remote and aloof, his face wiped smooth of any emotion. But his eyes were hard, still edged with bitter grief. Grief so deep and painful it had once led him to brand Tyler his daughter's murderer in David's presence.

Did he still grieve so? Tyler didn't know. He hoped not. But for now, having David with him, safe in his arms, was enough. He would deal with the future when it became the present as he'd learned to do these past months.

David would enjoy the island, with its horse-drawn buggies and bicycles built for two, and its interesting mixture of tourist hoopla and a very real and continuing sense of history. His son would be happy and content there. And perhaps, for himself, there would be some small measure of peace.

CHAPTER ONE

SARAH AUSTIN SLID A CHART into the circular rack on the counter of the second floor nurses' station. There were half a dozen other charts already pushed into the wire spokes. She gave the rack a spin before lifting one long-fingered hand to stroke away a beat of tense pain from her temple. Soft wisps of brown hair escaped from the bun on top of her head. She wasn't wearing her cap. She never did, nor a uniform in the traditional sense.

Instead, she was wearing scrubs, shapeless and much-washed but in a soft and flattering shade of pink. All the nurses in the Neonatal Intensive Care Unit of Holy Family Hospital wore them. They complemented the soft pastel shades that decorated the long room. Even the rocking chairs, where the older, more stable "preemies" were rocked and cuddled, were painted in soft, light shades of yellow and green.

She gave the rack another spin as it slowed its march past her line of vision. Seven. Before her were the records of seven fragile new lives, some held by a thread, some indefinable strength of will that kept them with her, allowed her to use all the skill and care that the well-trained staff of the unit could provide. Others were there merely as a precaution against being admitted a little too early into a world too cold and harsh for their fragile new bodies.

It was a good job, a good life. Sarah was glad she'd come to work at Holy Family three years ago, even if it did mean returning to Chicago and all the memories the city held for her.

But she was tired. She'd been working too hard and she knew it. When her supervisor had told her she had two weeks of sick leave that could be added to her regular vacation time and that she should use it, Sarah had agreed. She hadn't known her destination then, and still wasn't decided today, even though her leave time started at the end of the week.

Would she go to Key West to visit her father? He was happily, if somewhat surprisingly for an ex-Air Force colonel, retired to a life as a charter-boat captain. Or should she go to Mackinac, as her great-aunt, Camilla Weaver, had requested?

Mackinac: cool and green in its setting of pine and maple and cold blue water. And Aunt Camilla. It had been so long since they'd seen each other. Sarah walked toward the window, looking out at a city visible in gaps through the grimy buildings surrounding Holy Family. It would be an awkward visit. Perhaps she should go to see her father after all; Sarah couldn't make up her mind. She raised her hand again to smooth away that niggling dart of pain. Heat rose off the pavement in shimmering waves. It was going to be a long, hot summer.

The insistent beep of a monitor spun Sarah away from the window in the blink of an eye. Another RN, younger than Sarah by three or four years, only recently added to the staff, moved toward the Dudic baby's isolette, her round black face tense and concerned above the pink of her scrubs. She flipped a switch, silencing the warning call of the monitor, but other, less strident warning devices continued to beep and flash on various pieces of equipment.

Sarah hurried to the isolette. A blue tinge spread over the baby's skin, which was still fuzzy with a fine fetal hair called lanugo on his arms, shoulders and forehead. The tiny boy was choking weakly as she hurried forward. Inserting her hands through the two portholes, she elevated the infant's head. The child was so slight, so fragile, no bigger than a doll. His unhealthy color deepened and the gurgling, choking sounds, barely audible through the plastic bubble, increased. Sarah picked up a tiny syringe and quickly cleared the small mouth and nostrils of mucus. The baby's color showed little improvement.

A trembling began somewhere deep inside her, yet Sarah's

movements remained efficient and swift. She couldn't let this little one be taken; he'd fought so hard, come so far. She refused to let him slip away. The wheezing gasps continued. Turning the baby slightly and tapping his back with her fingertip, Sarah worked to clear an airway.

She glanced at the monitors. His pulse was weak, his respirations shallow and rapid. Feeling the furious race of the tiny unfinished heart caused Sarah's own pulse to accelerate in alarm. She felt another stab of fear. Would the increased strain of this near respiratory arrest be too much for the inefficient organ?

The little barrel chest heaved and shuddered with each labored breath. Long thin fingers spread, the newborn's hands flailed the air. Flipping a lever on the isolette, Sarah increased the oxygen supply in the plastic dome. She had no specific order to do so but his survival was imperative. It took precedence over everything—standard operating procedure, hospital policies, everything.

Now the baby no longer fought to breathe. With each inhalation his color improved, fading, changing now from blue to gray to pink. Sarah smiled, biting her lip against a flood tide of emotion as she fitted shades over Josef Robert Dudic's eyes to protect them from the increased oxygen being pumped into his isolette. The last of the warning beeps and flashing lights of the monitors shut off automatically.

Sarah felt painful pressure in her own lungs and wondered how long she'd been holding her breath. Purposefully, she exhaled, trying to push out her tension along with the spent air, patting and crooning to the now quiet infant.

"That's my boy," she whispered softly. "You're going to be fine. You're going to grow up to be big and strong, healthy and happy. I promise."

"How's he doing?" Dr. Emilio Fiori spoke over her shoulder. She glanced up at the middle-aged pediatrician and smiled once more.

"He's doing fine." The gesture softened the austere lines of her well-shaped mouth, accenting the clear, determined line of her jaw, lighting sparks of gold in the violet blue of her eyes. Taking several deep breaths to slow her own hammering heart, she surrendered her place next to the child.

His eyes on the winking monitors, Dr. Fiori completed his examination with quick, sure hands. He nodded his head in agreement. "He's coming around just fine. I think we're over the top with this fine little fellow. We'll keep an extra close eye on him for the next hour or so but I don't think we'll have any more trouble. You've done a superior job, Sarah. I honestly didn't think he'd make it. It seems, sometimes, like you've made him a special project."

"They're all special, Doctor." Sarah made the statement so softly she wasn't certain he'd even heard her speak.

"But for you, boy babies are the most special of all." So he had heard the guarded wistfulness in her voice. Not much escaped Dr. Fiori's practiced eye or intelligent mind.

"I think I am a little prejudiced in their favor." She looked up from the now sleeping infant. Her eyes were shadowed and there were tension lines around her mouth that hadn't been there moments before. It had been eight and a half years since she'd given her baby away. It shouldn't hurt so much anymore. But it did.

The balding physician nodded, respecting her reticence. "I'll bring my notes up to date on his chart," he said, effectively changing the subject.

Sarah nodded absently as he walked away, her attention on the sleeping child. Young Master Dudic would be going home someday soon to his loving parents and excited brother and sisters. She was part of the miracle of medical technology and human caring that would bring that moment to fruition. Her career gave her life purpose and meaning, and for that she was grateful. In some way, did it also make amends for the crime of the heart she had committed when she'd been scarcely more than a child herself?

Sarah glanced down at the sleeping, doll-like figure inside the protective bubble and her heart went out to him. She wanted to scoop him up in her arms, hold him tightly to her breast, tell him that everything was going to be fine and that the future was spread out before him, exciting and full of promise.

She wanted to do the same for her own son. But that was an impossible dream.

Sarah struggled with that ache of wanting every day of her life. On most days she subdued it ruthlessly, uncompromisingly. But on days like today, when her defenses were breached, it was a yearning so deep in her heart and soul that she could feel the need in her bones.

Very soon this baby, so light and fragile, would be whole and strong. He'd be held in his parents' loving arms without the restraining shield of plastic between them. He'd be cuddled and cherished; he would grow to be a man. She'd never held her son, although she had seen him, once. An eight-months baby, small, but far better equipped to face the harsh world outside her womb than this baby was, even now. Yet still so tiny and helpless and so alone. Perhaps if she'd held her baby, if only for a moment, she might have been able to come to terms with her longing. But she had not. She had agreed to give him away. All she had now was a memory, garnered in a moment of defiance to hospital policy, to carry in her heart.

Sarah had chosen this field of nursing to help exorcise her own demons. Instead, she'd found real joy and great satisfaction in helping each little one in his turn. In a small way it made up for not knowing where her baby had gone, what stranger he called mother.

Sarah moved away from the isolette to glance briefly at the monitors standing mechanical sentry over her other small charges. She had done what was best for both of them at the time. She was mature enough and strong enough now to understand and accept that reality. But she'd also wanted to find her son. That's why she'd returned to Chicago, where he'd been born. But too much time had passed. The path was cold and the one man who might have helped, her grandmother's lawyer, the man who had arranged the private adoption, Justin Delano, was dead.

Somehow the thought of him made the woman who'd grown from a heartbroken, pregnant seventeen-year-old girl suddenly decide to go to Mackinac. Sarah was under no illusions that there would be any clue to her child's fate on the small island caught between past and present, even though Justin Delano had spent his summers there. She had accepted the fact, at least for the time being, that her search had reached a dead end. No birth certificate had ever been issued in her name. Justin Delano, a man with power and connections all over the city, had evidently arranged for any records to be destroyed. She wasn't going to give up her search but she needed time to regroup and plan anew.

In her grandmother's will the Mackinac cottage on the east bluff of the island had been left to Camilla and Sarah equally. Now Camilla was home from Europe for the first time since her sister's funeral three years earlier. She wanted Sarah's advice and help in deciding what to do with the cottage and her sister's personal effects. She'd written three times in the past few weeks, each letter more insistent than the last.

It would be far easier to simply write and say she couldn't come, Sarah knew. That would be the easy way out of an awkward situation; it would be the expedient thing to do. How Sarah hated that word. She'd been practical and expedient once before in her life and it had almost broken her heart. This time she would take the steeper path, try to bridge the gap that had opened between her and the woman she'd once thought of almost as a mother. She would confront old ghosts and old hurts and perhaps find a measure of peace in the future because she had done so.

CHAPTER TWO

SUNLIGHT RICOCHETED off the wave tops, sending tiny shards of brilliance dancing back up into the sky, dazzling the eye. Sarah narrowed her vision to lessen the glare as she watched two sailboats racing away from her around the far curve of the island. Behind them, a huge ore freighter moved with ponderous dignity through the channel toward Lake Huron. She leaned forward over the railing at the edge of the high bluff, ignoring the steep drop below her to watch the swift duo retreat out of sight. Twin rainbow-hued sails remained neck and neck as they disappeared.

"I wonder who will win that race?" a light, feminine voice called from behind, lilting across the narrow graveled road that paralleled the east bluff of the island like another soft summer breeze.

Sarah pivoted away from the wooden railing, leaving the vantage point from which she'd watched the impromptu race, turning to face her Great-Aunt Camilla, who was standing at the foot of the cottage steps. "I haven't the slightest idea," she answered with a shrug. She'd been on the island for almost a week and her skin was losing its city pallor, turning a rich golden brown under the warm Michigan sun. Her color was enhanced by the faded aqua-blue cotton shirt she wore over summer slacks.

"What kind of wager do you suppose they have riding on the outcome?" Camilla asked, selecting a sprig of white lilac from a huge bush shading the screened veranda. The first week of June saw bushes of white and purple lilacs blooming all over the island. Below, in the town, the annual Lilac Festival would soon be in full swing.

Camilla Weaver, for she preferred to use her maiden name, was once widowed and twice divorced with no children of her own. Her first husband had been killed in the Korean War; her second and third marriages had ended in divorce. Both of those husbands had been European, and Sarah had met each only once or twice. Her aunt had spent most of the last twenty-five years, except when she'd been living with Sarah and her father, in Paris and London. Her familiarity with the Continent showed in her exquisite taste in clothes and her air of savoir faire.

"Drinks on the porch of the Grand?" Sarah ventured, hooking her thumb over her shoulder in the general direction of the world-famous resort hotel. She was perfectly willing to enter into the spirit of her aunt's lighthearted bantering, although it had never occurred to her more practical turn of mind that the two skippers might have a bet riding on the outcome of their race.

"Or possibly dinner at the Island House," Camilla suggested as she tucked the fragrant sprig of lilac into the brim of her floppy straw hat.

She set it carefully on top of her head and gave Sarah a saucy look from beneath the brim. Camilla was well past her sixtieth birthday, but you'd never know it to look at her, Sarah thought with an envious little pang. She was tall, only an inch shorter than Sarah's five feet seven, and elegantly slim. They wore the same size shoes and dresses. Camilla's hair was even the same rich dark brown, with only a pale frosting of gray. A few tiny wrinkles at the edge of the mouth and the corners of her eyes were at odds with the youthful sparkle of her hazel eyes but to give her credit, she did nothing to hide those small reminders of her true age.

"In any case I can't help thinking how marvelous it would feel to be speeding across the water like that on such a beautiful day. It's perfect for sailing, just enough chop, a good following breeze."

"Haven't you done any sailing since you've been living in Chicago?" Camilla asked, as Sarah opened the gate in the low picket fence and came into the yard. Surprise edged carefully shaped eyebrows up toward the equally carefully styled sweep of brown hair on top of her head. "With the income from your grandmother's trust..."

Camilla halted abruptly when she saw the sudden darkness in Sarah's sapphire eyes. "Never mind." She changed the subject without apology, adjusting the straw hat slightly. "I'm going to play bridge with Madge Benson and two of her friends."

"That's nice." Sarah tried very hard to swallow the irritation she felt with the older woman for mentioning the trust fund Sarah had never touched. Somehow the inheritance seemed too much like blood money, a reward for being reasonable and practical, for giving her baby away without making a fuss.

"Seeing old friends after so many years is always nice," Camilla agreed mildly. She sat on a green painted lawn bench near the steps and placed an elastic band around the narrow leg of her fashionably tailored linen slacks. Evidently she was in no more of a hurry to confront the past than Sarah was. "I've missed this place."

"I have, too," Sarah admitted and was only a little surprised to find she really meant it. "Will you be home in time for dinner?"

With all the grace and aplomb of a duchess entering her Rolls-Royce, Camilla dropped her shoulder bag in the oversize basket attached to the front wheel of her unhandsome, sturdy bicycle and settled onto the seat. "I'll be back by six to help with dinner. I thought perhaps the cold chicken left from Sunday and a salad?"

"That sounds good," Sarah agreed warmly. She wasn't sure how long it would take to feel comfortable around her great-aunt once more. She didn't like to think that they might have grown so far apart that they could never be close again.

Camilla might be her grandmother's youngest sister but she was much closer in age to Sarah's father. In fact she had been so very much like a mother to Sarah, whose own mother had died when she was ten, that she didn't seem old enough to be

a great-aunt at all. They had been very close, until the summer
Sarah had turned seventeen…and become pregnant.

Down that path of recollections lay only heartache and regret, as well she knew. Sarah smiled and shook her head as if
to clear it of all thought beyond the concerns of the moment.
"I'll fix something for dessert," she offered, as Camilla prepared to peddle off. Her great-aunt continued to watch Sarah
from beneath the shadowy brim of her hat.

"Something cool and low-cal." Her tone was determinedly
light.

"But chocolate?" Camilla was trying, too, Sarah realized,
and this time her answering smile was open and free of the
past.

"Yes." Camilla's gurgle of laughter was bright as a young
girl's. "Cool, low-caloried but definitely chocolate. Goodbye,
dear." She wheeled away and Sarah waved her off on her
journey from beneath the towering branches of the copper
beech tree. Camilla was soon out of sight, heading inland toward the Annex, a section of summer cottages not visible from
the shore. If they both continued to work hard at establishing
their old rapport, perhaps before they left the island the past
could be forgotten as well as forgiven.

Sarah skirted the yellow clapboard house as she made her
way toward the backyard, still lost in thought. The path leading to the carriage house was uphill. The building was two-
storied, painted yellow like the cottage, trimmed with ornate
wooden gingerbread and topped by a small cupola. In one
corner the two horses Camilla had leased from their mainland
owner for the summer were stabled. No one could afford to
winter horses on the island.

They were strong, sturdy animals with the ability to pull the
small Amish-style buggy used for errands as well as providing
a chance for Sarah and Camilla to do some riding if they
wished. Sarah enjoyed having the animals around. A handyman came every morning to clean the stalls and put fresh feed
and water in the bins. There was a small fenced area behind
the barn for exercise.

The sound of voices coming from inside the cool darkness

of the building caught her attention. For a moment Sarah thought the handyman might be late at his chores. Then, with a small quickening of her pulses, she realized that what appeared to be several voices echoing in the big open spaces of the barn was in reality only one. And that the single voice belonged to a child. She listened closely a few moments longer. *A boy,* she decided, and smiled a little when she realized he was holding earnest conversation with the horses.

The youngster spoke softly and gently as Sarah stepped into the dusty, fragrant atmosphere. She heard the rasping swish of a scoop being thrust into a sack of grain, then the spiky ring of wheat and barley as it was poured into one of the metal half-bushel tubs the horses ate from.

"Feeding time?" she asked, stepping all the way into the open space below the haymow.

The startled youngster banged the side of the metal bucket with the scoop, spilling the grain he'd been transferring from the storage bins. He spun around, fear and consternation crossing his face simultaneously. "I'm...I'm not hurting them. Honest," he hastened to assure her. "It's just that...my dad and I don't have..."

"Don't have horses of your own." Sarah finished the sentence for him. Did this child belong to the new owners of the Delano cottage next door? She didn't know anything about the couple, although Camilla had learned their names from Meecham, the handyman: Tyler and Allison Danielson. The handyman had never met them, he related, explaining that this was the first time they'd visited their summer home. Sarah herself hadn't seen much activity the past few days and had never suspected there was a child on the premises.

The boy looked down at the half-full scoop of grain guiltily. "I'll pay for what I spilled." His small, determined chin came up and he looked her straight in the eye. "As soon as I get next week's allowance. I...I spent this week's already."

"That isn't necessary." Sarah laughed, she couldn't help herself. He looked so serious, so grown-up and embarrassed. "Just open the stall door a little way and Sugar will be able to eat it right there." She gestured toward the latch. "Go ahead, it's all right. With names like Sugar and Spice you can't afford to be afraid of them. At least, that's what my aunt always says.''

"Okay." He gave her a smile that quickly grew into a full-fledged grin. "Only I sure wouldn't name two swell horses like this Sugar and Spice." His shyness forgotten, he opened the stall with eager fingers. The placid bay mare inside ambled forward to mouth the spilled grain with velvet lips. The boy patted her neck with his free hand.

"What would you call such swell horses?" Sarah asked, leaning her forearms on the top rail of the stall where Spice watched the proceedings without much apparent interest.

"Eagle and Terminator," the young trespasser answered without hesitation. He grinned up at her again.

Sarah inhaled quickly. The shape of his smile, the arch of his eyebrow were hauntingly familiar. Her baby's father had smiled that way at her, at life, once upon a time. Occasionally, over the years, other small children had given her fleeting pangs of recognition. *This is how my son might look as he takes his first step, rides his first bicycle.* She always turned away from the recognition in pain and sorrow. But not today. Today the feeling was stronger than it had ever been before. Today she could not turn away.

"But in the future when you want to visit them, you will come and ask me or my aunt, won't you?" Sarah forced herself to shake off the chill of aching memories that couldn't be changed. She hadn't seen her baby's father in years. In fact, she hadn't even looked at a picture of the spoiled, selfish boy she'd loved so desperately, right up until the moment when he walked out of her life. It was only a trick of light and shadow that gave this small boy his features, his smile.

"I won't come without asking first, ever again. I promise." He held out his hand to seal their bargain.

"My name is Sarah Austin." She took his hand and held it a moment before he pulled away. He couldn't be more than nine, almost exactly her son's age.

"I'm David Brandon Danielson. We live next door, my dad and me...I," he amended hastily. "My dad's name is Tyler

Danielson. He's an engineer. But we're on vacation now." A cloud of sadness much too heavy for a child his age seemed to darken the golden brown of his eyes.

Sarah shook off the uncomfortable thought. "It's nice to meet you, David. I'd like to meet your father someday, too," she added conventionally, although she didn't care about the man that much one way or another. David hadn't mentioned his mother yet. Were his parents divorced? Sarah frowned in consternation. She usually wasn't so interested in strangers. But she was interested in David. "I think the horses might enjoy being curried. Brushed," she explained when he looked a little puzzled. She held out a wide metal-toothed comb.

"I'd like that a lot." David took the currycomb shyly, following her grooming movements from the corner of his eye. "Like this?"

"That's fine," Sarah encouraged. There was a bruise on his forearm, Sarah noted, and both his knees were scraped. An adhesive bandage covered one knobby kneecap. "Did you have a fall?" She gestured downward with her comb. Most males, men or boys, enjoyed talking about their battle scars.

David flushed and looked down at his long skinny legs. "I tripped on the steps when we were moving in. It hurt like fury."

"I bet it did," Sarah answered with due gravity. "Are you staying at Lilac Time?" She gave the old Delano cottage its official title.

"Yeah." David snorted in contempt. "Isn't that a wimpy name for a place that big? I wanted my dad to let me pick a different name, but he said no. He said it had been called Lilac Time for a hundred years. Ever since it was built. He said I'd just have to be satisfied they hadn't painted it purple." David got the last words out with difficulty. "Whoever heard of a purple house? Even on an island like this one, where no one is allowed to have a car? Has your place got a wimpy name, too?"

"It's called Gathering Place," Sarah admitted, her hands busy along Sugar's flank, her mind busy with forbidden yearnings of how much like this boy, David, her son might be.

"Oh." David's reply was noncommittal.

"It's one of the names the Indians gave the island a long time ago." Sarah supplied the information in a very ordinary tone so that it couldn't possibly be misconstrued as a history lesson.

"It's an Indian name, huh?" David perked up, slightly more interested than he'd been.

"Uh-huh. The Indians used the island for a meeting place hundreds of years before the French or British, or the Americans, for that matter, came to Michigan."

"That's neat."

"Have you been to the fort?" Sarah heard herself ask the question and was vaguely surprised. She wasn't at ease around most children. She never had been and she didn't need a psychologist to tell her why. She was probably leaving herself open for more pain but if David smiled that beguiling little-boy smile at her one more time she was going to be totally lost and she knew it.

"No, but I hear the musket fire and the cannon go off every day." He smiled again, touching fire to fuse with the tip of his currycomb and the barrel of a cannon that existed only in his imagination. His imitation of an explosion of shot and powder was vivid and noisy. He laughed out loud and Sarah slid quietly over the edge.

"Perhaps we could go together." It was as though another woman, one not afraid of hurting, of loving, spoke those words.

"Yeah! But I'd have to ask my dad if it would be all right." A frown replaced the sunny gap-toothed smile.

"Of course. Your mother and father will want to take you." Sarah swallowed her disappointment. She couldn't interfere with a family vacation. After all, she didn't know anything about Tyler and Allison Danielson beyond their names and the fact that they had a very charming son. She wondered whether they had known Justin Delano or simply acquired Lilac Time from the lawyer's estate.

"My mom." Something in David's voice drew Sarah's attention back to the moment at hand.

"Are you all here together, David?" Sarah asked quietly, unwilling to pry but responsive to the new tension she heard in the child's voice.

"It's just me and my dad, now. And my granddad—but he's a preacher and he has to stay in Georgia and take care of his church."

"I see." So that accounted for the softening of vowels in his speech.

"I might be a preacher someday. I like to sing. And shake hands," he confided ingenuously. "But I'd like to be an engineer, too, like my dad. Maybe build bridges on the moon!" He eyed Sugar with speculation. "But right now I wish I knew how to ride a horse."

"I think we can do something about that. I could teach you to ride, with your parents' permission."

Again that shadow crossed his features. "Just me and my dad," he repeated soberly, holding out the currycomb. "I'm done," he said abruptly.

"No brothers or sisters?" Sarah couldn't stop herself from prying. She didn't want to see that heartache darken his gold-brown eyes. She wanted to know the reason behind it, to make it go away and never return.

"No. And my mom isn't with us because she's dead." The matter-of-fact words dropped between them with the weight of a stone.

Sarah turned from the anguish in David's eyes because the pain in her chest was so great she couldn't breathe. She wanted more than anything in the world to kneel down in the straw and take him in her arms, comfort him, making everything right in his world again. But she had no such right. None at all. So instead she took the currycomb from his stiff fingers and laid her hand on his thin shoulder.

"I'm very sorry, David." She was at a loss for words. A sound from the open doorway diverted her gaze from David's small, pinched face. She looked into the glare of sunlight to find a tall, dark figure silhouetted against the light. How long had he been there? How much had he heard? There was no doubt in her mind the stranger was David's father, come to find his missing son.

David didn't see the still form in the doorway. "They had an accident with the car." Sarah wasn't looking at the child anymore although she felt the tension in his shoulders and tightened her hand to comfort without words. All her attention was centered on the silent figure in the doorway. "My dad was driving," David went on in a toneless little voice. "He went to jail so I guess that means he killed my mom." Sarah didn't resist the impulse to comfort this time. She pulled the child close but she didn't look down at the brown head nestled against her stomach. She couldn't take her eyes from the dark anguish mirrored in Tyler Danielson's eyes.

CHAPTER THREE

DAVID'S WORDS DID NOT so much echo in the dusty silence of the old barn as they did in Tyler's soul, each one lodging like splinters of shrapnel in his heart. *He went to jail, so I guess that means he killed my mom.* Tyler stood rigid, silent, a moment longer, allowing his sun-dazzled eyes to adjust to the gloomy interior, willing his emotions under control.

His son hadn't seen him yet; his head was pillowed against the softness of a woman's body. Her arms were around David, comforting, soothing, as Tyler longed to do himself but could not. Her eyes, however, were not on the boy. They were watching him with a level measuring gaze that he could not return.

Tyler felt his muscles tense, felt himself drawn forward to ease his son's painful bewilderment, but he did not move. Instead he covered his own pain with the mask of studied nonemotion that had served him well over the past months. It was obvious David had no idea he was anywhere near. And it wasn't the time or the place to speak about Allison's death.

Soon, for the sake of his own peace of mind, as well as David's, he must find the words to tell his son more of the truth than the boy already knew. But not now, not in front of this stranger, no matter how compassionate she might appear to be.

"David." He spoke quietly so as not to startle the child, but he could hear the rough grating edge in his tone and regretted it. "I thought we agreed you wouldn't leave our property without telling me first where you were going." That last sentence, at least, sounded more normal. Tyler stepped forward.

David raised his head and backed away from the comforting circle of Sarah's arms. She wanted to reach out and pull him close again but controlled herself with an effort that was more difficult than she would have believed possible a few minutes earlier.

"I'm sorry, Dad." David hung his head. Tyler Danielson remained silhouetted against the bright sunlight beyond the doorway. He made no effort to touch his son. Sarah felt her ire rise but said nothing. "The horses. I could hear them from my bedroom window." He scuffed his sneaker over the dirt floor. "They sounded hungry," he finished in a rush.

Sarah saw the change come over David's father's strong, chiseled features. Memories of his own boyhood, perhaps? Horses, after all, were a temptation few boys could resist.

"It's all right, Son." Tyler's heart squeezed shut. He longed to reach out and draw David into his arms. But he stayed where he was. Almost all nine-year-old boys were very conscious of their dignity. David probably wouldn't welcome his embrace. "But more importantly, do you have the lady's permission to be here?" Tyler made himself concentrate on the matter at hand. One day at a time. One hour at a time. One minute at a time. That was how you got through endless days in prison. That was how he would handle each unfamiliar new challenge of fatherhood. Of single parenthood.

"It's okay." David looked for confirmation to the woman still standing half hidden in the shadows of the haymow.

"David is welcome to visit Sugar and Spice whenever he has your permission." Sarah stepped forward into the square of light beaming in through the double doors. David's father was an enigma; that much she'd deduced in only a few moments. Hard as steel on the outside, that was plain to see. But what of the man inside the armor? She had glimpsed the anguish David's blunt statement had caused him. Now, just as plainly, she could see his love for his son in the depths of his almost black eyes.

"I told you it was okay," David crowed triumphantly, breaking Sarah's fanciful train of thought, bringing her back to a sense of time and place, making her aware she was seeking knowledge of the man beneath Tyler Danielson's icy veneer. That could be a very dangerous quest. Sarah told herself firmly not to be silly and held out her hand.

"I'm your neighbor, Sarah Austin." She smiled and Tyler felt himself drawn to the warmth of that friendly gesture even as his whole body stiffened in disbelief. It was as though a jolt of current had streaked along his nerve endings, scalding him. *Allison.* He blinked and shook his head a little as though to dispel the illusion of a dead woman suddenly returned to flesh and blood. "You must be Tyler Danielson."

She smiled again and mercifully the spell was broken. This woman wasn't Allison. It had only been some blending of light and shadow, a similarity in height and weight perhaps, that had bemused him. With a second look he could see the differences very clearly.

She had none of Allison's girlish affectations of speech and movement. This woman held her head proudly erect; she looked at the world straight on, not through fluttering lashes. Her tall, softly curved body moved with smooth fluid grace. Sarah Austin had none of Allison's delicacy, her very fragile hold on reality. This woman was self-confident, sure of herself. Even though her dark blue eyes held a hint of sadness, caring and compassion were also visible in their sapphire depths.

She let her hand drop back to her side, resting it against the soft faded denim of her jeans. Tyler came out of his trance with a jerk. "I'm sorry," he said gruffly, extending his own large brown hand. "For a moment...I thought..." He shrugged and brought the explanation to a halt. "You reminded me of someone." For the space of three heartbeats he thought she wasn't going to accept his attempt at an apology but she did. She touched his hand briefly and nodded in acknowledgment.

"That's always a disconcerting experience." She smiled again and Tyler found himself responding to her warmth. She was a very good-looking woman. Her lips were full and creamy pink. Her skin was a pale shade of gold against the dark nut-brown color of her hair. Even pulled back with combs the chestnut waves had a tendency to curl around her face in feathery wisps. As Tyler studied her, he noticed that Sarah's eyes had darkened to the deep shaded violet blue of midnight. She was watching him with interest and more than a hint of wariness.

"David. We have to go." He beckoned to the boy and David came toward him reluctantly. Probably because he didn't want to leave the horses, Tyler reasoned, but in his present unsettled state he couldn't be sure. "David." He spoke more sharply this time and saw a frown cross Sarah's forehead. Did she think he was being too strict with the child? Or did she merely resent his tone of command? *Hell, what man ever knew what a woman was thinking?*

He just didn't have enough practice being a father and, except for his enforced absence the past year, he had no one to blame for the lack but himself. It made him angry; with her, with David, with himself.

"Goodbye, Sarah." David moved past his scowling father with real disappointment pulling at the corners of his mouth.

"You will allow David to come again." She made it a statement to cover her confusion. Why was she involving herself like this? It wasn't like her to meddle in other people's private lives. But David was special—at least to her. "I'd...I'd enjoy his company." She wouldn't blame Tyler Danielson if he told her to go to hell. He certainly looked angry enough to do just that. "I haven't been on the island for years. We could go exploring together." She lifted her hand in a helpless little gesture that was half demand, half entreaty.

"Could I, Dad, please?" David tugged at the sleeves of Tyler's gold and brown plaid shirt. "There's the fort and caves and Indian burial grounds. Everything." He danced from one foot to the other in his attempt to influence his father's decision.

"We'll see, David. If it's convenient for Miss Austin."

So he'd noticed she wasn't wearing a wedding ring. The man was quick, she had to give him that. Sarah lifted her chin to show this haunted, aloof man she wasn't going to be cowed by his remoteness. "It's more than convenient. I'm looking forward to it."

Tyler Danielson only nodded in reply. "Good afternoon, Miss…" Sarah opened her mouth to object but he amended his statement before she could utter a word. "Sarah." The corners of his well-shaped mouth curved into the edges of a brief smile. It transformed the dark, austere planes of his face, touching them briefly with light and warmth. Sarah caught her breath. Even the edges of that reluctant smile heated her blood and caused her pulse to slip into a higher gear. It seemed both generations of the Danielson men had the ability to disarm her with the greatest of ease.

Sarah put her hand out to rest against the rough edge of the barn door. David danced around to skip backward, waving while his other hand was firmly held in his father's strong grip. Sarah waved back as she watched father and son disappear through a gap in the spirea hedge that separated the two properties.

Her thoughts were in a whirl. She didn't usually allow people—men especially—to move her to rash behavior. Today it had happened twice—first with the boy and then the father. The outer shell of tempered steel Tyler Danielson presented to the world was only that, a shell. Of that, Sarah was sure. Inside, he was a man in torment. A man who interested her almost as much as his son.

And that, Sarah decided, as she walked into the dusty aromatic barn to make sure Sugar and Spice were both secure in their stalls, was an impulse she could ill afford to indulge.

"AND THEN THEY WALKED AWAY, through the hedge, and I haven't seen any sign of them since." Sarah concluded her recital of the afternoon's events as they finished the huge chocolate-dipped strawberries she'd walked down to the village to purchase at Camilla's favorite fudge shop.

"Your afternoon was more interesting than mine," the older woman admitted with a wry smile. "Madge Benson and her friends can talk of nothing but stock portfolios and their grandchildren."

"And they probably spent far more time talking about schools and hobbies and summer visits than they did the stock market," Sarah said with a shake of her head. She cradled her coffee cup between strong narrow fingers and smiled across the table. "Poor Camilla."

"You know me and other people's children." Camilla shrugged in an elegant little gesture of dismissal. She'd been thinking entirely too much lately of the grandchildren she'd never have. She made herself pronounce her next words in a lighter tone. "I would have enjoyed myself more if we hadn't gone into such minute detail on how badly Madge's daughter-in-law is potty training her youngest grandson, and how Grace Carmondy's oldest granddaughter is working miracles with the computer Grace and her husband got her for Christmas last year. And imagine, she's only nine." For almost half a century Camilla had convinced everyone she knew that children were of little importance to her. She couldn't very well change her image now.

"I wonder if David is into computers?"

"The little boy you met this afternoon?" Camilla asked, more as a means to reopen the subject than anything else.

"Yes. David Danielson. He must be about nine, too, like Grace's granddaughter." Sarah looked past her for a moment, her eyes traveling over the hodgepodge of late Victorian furnishings in the small breakfast nook that now served as the dining room. She wasn't really seeing anything, Camilla knew. Her thoughts had turned inward toward the child she'd given away when she was little more than a child herself. Camilla longed to tell her great-niece that the pain would lessen, if never completely go away, but of course she could not. The habit of secrecy was too deeply instilled within her to be broken easily now.

"What does he look like?" Camilla asked, tipping her head a little to one side, studying Sarah with quiet intensity. Her relative blinked, looking away from the series of hunting prints that lined the walls. Behind her, sheer white curtains waved gently in the early evening breeze.

Sarah considered for a moment. "He's tall for his age.

Skinny as a rail fence." She lifted her cup to take a sip of cooling coffee. "He has curly brown hair and brown eyes. For a moment he reminded me strongly of Ryan." It was the first time she'd mentioned her baby's father for a long time. It wasn't as hard to say his name aloud as she thought it might be.

"Sarah." Camilla's hand moved in a small soothing gesture. Time, too, would heal that pain. Faces and memories faded with the passing of years. She couldn't quite speak her thoughts aloud. "It's bound to happen occasionally, especially since you've been unable to find out what happened to your baby." Camilla managed to keep her face impassive, but it was an art that had taken her years to master. Her hazel eyes were full of sympathy yet her fingers, where they rested on top of Sarah's, trembled slightly. She withdrew her hand.

"It's all right, really, Aunt Cam." The childhood nickname came easily to Sarah's lips. "David's just such a cute kid. It was something about his smile...the way he held his head."

"I understand." Camilla couldn't help the catch in her voice. *Oh, Sarah, if you only knew how much I really do understand.*

"It doesn't happen often anymore." Sarah realized suddenly that she'd never discussed children, or more particularly her child, with Camilla since the day she'd come home from the clinic without her son. Did Camilla regret never having had a child of her own? Sarah was ashamed to admit that the thought had never occurred to her until this moment. Always before they'd avoided the subject because of her experience...or so she'd always believed. "Aunt Cam..."

"Yes, dear?" Her aunt was smiling again, the shadows gone from her eyes. The moment passed. Camilla stood up and began stacking china to carry into the high-ceilinged, old-fashioned kitchen. "Do you know anything else about David?"

"His father's name is Tyler," Sarah volunteered. "He's some kind of engineer. His mother's name was Allison, if I remember Mr. Meecham's gossip correctly."

"Of course. My memory must be starting to go." Camilla

sounded a little flustered although the sad tone in her voice was gone. "But you spoke of the woman in the past tense."

"Yes." Sarah met her aunt's hazel eyes directly. "Mrs. Danielson is dead. She died in an auto accident for which Tyler Danielson was found responsible. He's just been released from prison. David told me so."

"How terrible," Camilla said and Sarah knew she meant it. "Such a burden for so young a child to bear." She moved toward the cupboard to place her stack of dirty dishes beside the deep enameled sink.

"Terrible for both of them." A fleeting memory of Tyler Danielson's dark eyes seared through Sarah's mind. There were injuries to the soul that left scars as visible as scars on the body.

"Yes." Camilla nodded her understanding of Sarah's unspoken observation. "Still, David sounds like an enterprising young man. Did he truly offer to pay for the spilled grain out of his allowance?" She gave one of her chiming laughs and Sarah joined in.

"Next week's allowance," she reminded her aunt, holding up a soapy hand as warm water swirled into the sink. "He's already spent this week's."

"Buying on credit. The American way." They both laughed again and Sarah felt some of the constraint that had been between them earlier in the day slip away.

"He told me he's been living with his grandfather in Georgia. And that he wants to be a preacher just like him because he likes to sing and shake hands." Sarah smiled. "Or he might be an engineer like his father, only he's going to build bridges over craters on the moon."

"His grandfather is a minister?" Camilla felt a chill of recognition squeeze her heart. *Dear Heaven, it wasn't possible. David Brandon Danielson. Could his grandfather be the Elliot David Brandon she'd known so long ago?* "Did the child mention his grandfather's name to you?"

"No, I don't think so." Sarah frowned thoughtfully as she shut off the tap and lowered a stack of dishes into the water.

"Do you know the man?" Sarah slid a plate into the rinse water and handed it to Camilla to dry.

"I might have once. A very long time ago." Camilla wiped the plate absently. *Could it be?* "In 1942, the summer after Pearl Harbor, I met a young divinity student, a lieutenant just out of Officers' Training School, at one of Justin Delano's lawn parties. His name was Brandon. Elliot David Brandon. And he was from Georgia." *Were the secrets buried so deeply in her own past about to catch up with her?*

"A family connection of some sort would account for how Tyler Danielson might have come to own Lilac Time." Many of the Mackinac cottages never changed hands on the open market, so it was possible that the young minister Camilla had met that summer at the beginning of America's involvement in World War II was David's grandfather.

"Or I could be rambling on about nothing." Camilla spoke sharply to banish the ghosts in the room. "I'm surprised I even remembered him." But she'd never forgotten him, not if she was truthful with herself. "After all, it was nearly half a century ago. A lifetime ago."

"Aunt Camilla, what's wrong?" Sarah was looking at her intently.

"I'm fine." She was. What had happened to her that long-ago summer was ancient history. She hadn't been in love with Elliot Brandon, not completely. "Let's get started on some of those boxes up in the attic tomorrow." Camilla changed the subject abruptly. If she'd told Elliot Brandon her secret that summer he would have grown to hate her. Or even worse, would he have offered to marry her out of pity and compassion? It was better that she'd broken off their relationship the way she had. A neat, clean break for their love affair and for her aching heart.

"It will take days to get through the stuff in the attic."

"Not to mention the boxes in the third bedroom," Camilla reminded her. For the first time, Sarah thought how old her aunt was looking.

"We'll tackle it first thing in the morning," Sarah said with gentle firmness.

Camilla placed the last dish in the cupboard and folded her cotton towel over the edge of the counter. "In the morning. Have I told you how happy I am to have you here, Sarah? I'd forgotten how many memories this cottage held for me. I'm glad I don't have to face them alone."

Sarah gave her aunt a hug. She no longer blamed Camilla for not standing by her in the past. Sometime soon she would tell her so. But not tonight. Camilla looked very fragile still, as if her memories did indeed weigh heavily on her. She needed to rest. Emotional confrontations, whether for good or ill, could wait until morning. "Good night, Aunt Cam. Pleasant dreams."

"Pleasant dreams, Sarah." Camilla stepped through the swinging doors into the main room of the cottage and paused for a moment at the foot of the stairs. She spoke so softly no one else could hear. "But no dreams at all are better still."

[faint show-through text from previous page, illegible]

CHAPTER FOUR

"GOODNESS. Whatever do you have in that box?" Camilla was curled up in the medallion-backed wicker settee on the veranda. Her short-sleeved cotton sweater and slacks were a subdued contrast to the multicolored floral print of the cushions and pleated shades on the window at her back.

Sarah craned her neck to see over the top of the big cardboard box she carried in her arms and gave her aunt a rueful smile. "I thought I'd bring some of these things of Dad's we found in the closet down here. It's getting awfully stuffy upstairs. The windows in that back bedroom are painted shut so tightly I can't get them open even a crack." She looked around the small, cozy sitting area for a convenient place to deposit her burden.

"Put it there," Camilla advised, setting aside her crossword puzzle. She curled her feet up under her and sat up straight, eyeing the carton with disfavor. "I've seen enough old postcards and dance programs in the past two days to last me a lifetime."

Sarah put the box down alongside one of the wicker side chairs that complemented the settee. "I can't imagine how this stuff ended up here at all." That detail had been puzzling her ever since she'd discovered the container of memorabilia marked with her father's name the afternoon before.

"Your grandmother had it brought here after your father asked her to store it for safekeeping, I imagine. My sister had some peculiar notions about this place toward the end, you know. She spent a lot of time here." Camilla looked thoughtful for a moment. "Perhaps this was where she hoped we'd all be together again. I should have visited her more often those last years."

"Dad gave me some of Mother's things before he moved to Key West," Sarah said quietly, filling the awkward silence. She might be ready to start talking about the past but Camilla obviously wasn't. It didn't take an expert in human psychology to read reluctance in the tense frown that marred her smooth skin. "I have their wedding pictures and some jewelry that belonged to Mother. But very few snapshots, no keepsakes like her high-school yearbook or old family albums. I've always assumed Dad gave those to Uncle Mike." Sarah's mother had been very close to her twin brother although Sarah saw her uncle infrequently now that he'd retired to a condo in Arizona.

"There are probably some of her things in there somewhere." Camilla viewed the box dubiously over the rim of her reading glasses. "It's such a lovely day. Do you really want to spend it like this?" There was a very faint hint of pleading in her words. "We could go swimming in the pool at the Grand. Or at least you can. I'll lie in the sun and bake my weary old bones." The public was allowed the use of the hotel's famous Serpentine pool for a small fee. Sarah had swam there often as a small girl, pretending she was Esther Williams because she'd once seen the movie the swimmer had made on the island.

"Your weary old bones look great in a swimsuit and you know it," Sarah pointed out with a smile that brought a faint flush of pleased color to Camilla's cheeks. But as a diversionary tactic the suggestion didn't work. Sarah was far too interested in her unexpected discovery. "Perhaps later this afternoon." She picked up a pair of scissors from the glass-top table where she'd placed them earlier and started to cut the heavy twine holding the box tightly closed.

"I don't think you're going to get very far into that box." Camilla's tone was amused and maybe even a little relieved. Sarah looked up, opening her mouth to protest another delay, only to see her aunt pointing toward the front gate with the eraser end of her pencil. "We have a visitor."

David Danielson was coming up the gravel pathway, swinging a bright neon orange yo-yo from the end of its string. "Your young admirer is coming to pay you a call."

"You mean Sugar and Spice's young admirer, Aunt Cam." David had paused to swing on the gate of the picket fence that fronted the property, proving that little boys hadn't changed very much at all over the years so far as picket fences and swinging gates were concerned. He was wearing a pair of scruffy cutoff jeans and a red and white striped T-shirt. The bandage was gone from his knee but had been replaced by one on his left elbow.

"I stand corrected," Camilla said with a chiming laugh, her good humor restored. Sarah made a little face at her aunt as she stood and dusted a smudge from her peach colored drawstring slacks and matching shirt.

"There hasn't been a woman born who can compete with a horse for an eight-year-old boy's affection," Sarah said with great conviction.

"Even those two plodding nags."

"I think there's a lesson to be learned there somewhere, Aunt Cam," Sarah said with mock seriousness.

"Vanity undone, or some such thing," Camilla agreed with a sanctimonious nod. They both laughed.

"Hello, David," Sarah said, opening the screen door to his knock.

"Hi, Sarah." He stood uncertainly on the step.

"Come in," she urged with a smile. "My aunt and I were just sharing a joke. How are you today?"

"Fine, thank you," he replied, gravely polite. The yo-yo was rewound, dancing up the string in a series of leaps to rest in the curve of his hand. "You have a nice house."

"Thank you," Camilla said from her seat on the settee. "You handle that yo-yo very well, young man."

David ducked his head but looked pleased by the compliment.

"David, this is my great-aunt, Mrs. Weaver." Sarah made the introduction. Did Camilla see the resemblance to Ryan?

"You can call me Aunt Cam if I may call you David,"

Camilla offered with a smile, no sign of special recognition in her eyes.

"Thanks...Aunt Cam." David gave the name a trial run. Apparently he liked the taste of it on his tongue because he broke into a grin. Sarah felt her heart give a little kick just as she had the day they'd met. Only this time, surprisingly, it wasn't because David's smile reminded her of anyone from her past. It was because he was a little boy with a thoroughly engaging grin. "I came to see the horses if that's okay, Sarah."

"I don't see why not," Sarah said without a moment's hesitation. Camilla glanced first at her niece, then at the untouched box on the floor. Her eyebrows rose a fraction of an inch but Sarah pretended not to notice. "I'll be out in a few minutes, David. I have to take this box back upstairs."

"Why don't you just leave it where it is, Sarah?" Camilla suggested. "We aren't going to be entertaining anyone out here. It's protected from the wind and rain. You can go through it later at your leisure."

"You talked me into it." Sarah abandoned her quest with an airy wave of her hand, the past no longer as compelling as the present. "Go on out to the barn, David, I still want to change my shoes." She looked down at her sandals and wiggled peach-tinted toes. "These aren't quite the thing for mucking around in the stable."

"Mine are," David said triumphantly, sticking out one skinny leg that ended in a thick-soled running shoe that looked three sizes bigger than the foot it covered could possibly be.

"You must be a Boy Scout," Camilla said, straight-faced. "You are certainly prepared."

David looked pained for a moment, then grinned when he realized he was being teased. "Nah, but I play second base on our Little League team. And I want to learn how to ride. Are there any saddles around?"

"I don't think there are any," Sarah disclosed on her way into the main room of the cottage. "Maybe I could ask Mr. Meecham if there's a saddle stored someplace in the haymow." Her voice faded as she began to climb the stairs. If

David made an answer, she didn't hear, only the snick of the latch on the wooden screen door as it closed behind him.

David was nowhere to be seen when she entered the barn ten minutes later. Sugar and Spice munched contentedly on the grain in their mangers. "You two seem to spend most of your time doing that," Sarah addressed the pair sternly. "David was right. You need some exercise." She looked around for the youngster. "David, are you here?"

There was no answer, but a flash of movement overhead caught Sarah's eye and she looked up. "I bet I could sail right across the barn on this rope," David announced, leaning precariously over the edge of the mow, one hand holding on to the end of a thick rope suspended from a block and tackle hanging from the main beam. In the old days it had been the means of lifting bales of hay into the loft. As far as Sarah knew it hadn't been used in years.

"I'm not sure that's safe." *Stupid thing to say to a boy,* Sarah chided herself. She just wasn't used to dealing with children.

David yanked on the rope. "Looks safe to me." He backed out of sight and Sarah knew he was getting ready for a running start. "David! Don't!" It was too late. David sailed out over the open space and then out of her line of vision into the loft. He dropped onto the planking with a thud.

"Wow! That was great. I'm going to try it again. This time I'm going all the way across." His voice was taut with excitement and bravado. Sarah was beginning to understand the origin of some of the bandages David sported.

"Wait until I check..." Sarah never finished the sentence as David swept out across the high open space again. Sarah's heart climbed into her throat.

"It's just like flying," David yelled. The old block and tackle squeaked and groaned under the unaccustomed weight. Sarah walked over to the ladder leading to the mow and began to climb.

"Did you find the saddles?" she asked, hoping to keep David from soaring off into the void yet again.

"Nothin' up here," came the quick reply. "I looked first thing."

"Are you sure?" Sarah was clutching at straws and David knew it. He frowned impatiently for a moment when her head appeared above the floor of the loft, then let go of the rope.

"There's only one place they could be up here." David pointed to a low shallow cupboard in the shadows to Sarah's left. It was built against the wall, just beyond the opening for the ladder. David was right. It was the only enclosed space in the loft and it was far too narrow to hold anything as large as a saddle. "I think Mr. Meecham has to go look in some other loft."

"You're probably right," Sarah admitted, climbing the rest of the way into the loft. "If we don't find the saddle soon I'll check with the livery stables about renting a couple. Okay?"

"Okay." David brightened considerably. "I really want to learn how to ride." There was more wistfulness in his tone than he'd ever acknowledge outright. "That way when I get back to school maybe the bigger guys will let... I mean, since I can't be on the Little League team..." He stopped speaking abruptly and looked down at the toes of his running shoes.

"What about the bigger guys, David?" Sarah asked, her throat suddenly tight.

"Nothin'." Sarah was noticing that in moments of stress David's Georgia accent intensified. He turned and walked back to the rope. Sarah decided to alter the subject slightly.

"How long have you been living with your grandfather, David?"

"Two years. My mom and I went there to live when Dad went to Brazil on his last assignment. He builds bridges, you know. Or at least he used to." David frowned, then went on. "Mom hated the jungle." Sarah intuitively knew he was reciting word for word a complaint he must have heard repeated many times. "We live in Columbus. My granddad and I and Michael Parker. He's a preacher, too. Granddad's assistant but a swell guy. He can hit a baseball a mile. We live in the same house my mom grew up in. Have you ever been to Georgia?"

"Only passing through, on my way to Florida," Sarah confessed, trying to file away all the bits and pieces of information David had provided her with in his rambling speech.

"Oh. It's an okay place," David said loyally. "Most of the time."

"Except for those bigger guys?" Sarah probed gently.

"I shouldn't have said it." David swung in an arc, his hands above his head on the thick rope, his feet firmly planted on the plank floor.

"David, you can tell me about it if you like but you don't have to. I won't pry."

His next words came in a rush. "Some of the bigger guys keep callin' my dad a jailbird. I hate it but it's true so what can I do? And besides, my granddad says it's not Christian to punch them out." He looked at Sarah so earnestly that she found it hard to hide her smile although her heart ached for his confusion. "'Course it's not Christian to ride right over the top of them on my horse but that's what I'd like to do if I knew how to ride. And if I had a horse back home," he added.

This time Sarah wasn't able to hide her smile completely but she managed to turn it into a cough. "No, I don't think riding over the top of your classmates would be the thing to do at all—even if you did have a horse of your own. But knowing how to ride would give you something else to talk about when school starts again, wouldn't it?"

"It's better than nothin'. Anyway, the bicycles Dad rented for us are for the birds. Mine's got great big old tires and no gear shift." His expression was pained. "It's a piece of junk."

Sarah was grateful for the chance to comment on something else. Theology wasn't one of her strong subjects and neither was explaining to a child why his father had been in jail, especially when she didn't know all the facts. "Your bike's a beater, all right," she said with a chuckle.

"A beater? It's sure beat up, if that's what you mean." David shook his head in disgust, still swinging in an arc, leaning back against the pull of the rope.

"No. The people on the island call them beaters because they sure beat walking."

"But they don't beat riding a horse." David ended the discussion with that inarguable statement. "I'm taking another swing on the rope," he announced in the next breath.

"Oh, no, you don't. My turn first." If she were busy with the rope at least David wouldn't be flying through the air.

"Aren't you too old to do something like that?" David asked with devastating candor.

"It's been years since I've done it but I'm not that old." It was difficult for Sarah, who had just celebrated her twenty-sixth birthday, to ignore the unthinking challenge in David's words. She gave several sharp tugs on the rope and jumped, putting all her weight on it. "It seems in pretty good shape," she said, scanning the length of hemp to where it disappeared into the gloom at the top of the barn. "Here goes."

With a yell that escalated into a scream as she ran off the end of the hayloft, Sarah swung out over the floor of the barn. Seconds later she came sailing back, her hair streaming behind her, to drop with a plunk a lot closer to the edge of the loft than she would have liked to be.

"Whew. I haven't done anything like that for ages." She sat on the dusty floor because her knees were suddenly too weak to support her. She was a little bit ashamed to find her voice was breathless and shrill.

"My turn." David grabbed at the rope still clutched in Sarah's hand. "I don't believe you did that," he added with an awed shake of his curly brown head. "That was swell flying for a grown-up."

"I don't know if you should…" Sarah stopped to find a better way to phrase her order to cease and desist when her words were interrupted by a harsh male voice from below.

"I don't believe you did that, either, Miss Austin. And you are not going to take a turn, David." Tyler knew he sounded gruff and probably unreasonable but there wasn't any help for it. And maybe he didn't sound all that bad. Maybe he only sounded like a worried parent?

"It's safe, Dad. I've already done it twice," David boasted. "And you saw Sarah yourself. She weighs a lot more than I do and she made it okay."

Sarah was trying to find the best way to rise from her un-dignified sprawl on the dusty planking when David grabbed the rope and backed away for a running start, eager to show off and prove his point at the same time.

Sarah and Tyler spoke simultaneously. But it did no good. David came hurtling toward Sarah, who was still on her hands and knees at the edge of the loft. With an earsplitting screech that raised the short hairs at the nape of her neck, the rope parted company with the block and tackle as David threw his full weight against it on takeoff.

Sarah looked up to see David stumble and try to catch him-self, his mouth a surprised O, his eyes filled with sudden fear, but his forward momentum hurled him toward the edge of the loft. Desperately Sarah flung herself forward and threw out her hands, to knock him backward toward safety. But David was sturdier and heavier than he looked. The collision did indeed keep David from becoming airborne, but it also knocked Sarah completely off balance and sent her rolling helplessly over the edge.

Grabbing for support, her hands caught and held the rough flooring. Two heartbeats later she slid to a stop, dangling twelve feet above the barn floor, her elbows and ribs aching from contact with the unyielding wood.

"Hang on, Sarah. Dad! We need help!" David was crawl-ing toward her, his voice shaking with fear, his brown eyes enormous in his scared little-boy face. He grabbed for her hand, trying to pull Sarah back onto the loft.

"No," she croaked, "don't. I'll pull you over with me." Her legs kicked at thin air. Her arms were blocks of wood, dragging weights suspended from her aching shoulders, and she knew there was no possibility of pulling herself back up.

Sarah looked over her shoulder and closed her eyes against a rush of vertigo. It was a long way to the floor.

"Don't look down again." Tyler's voice below her was calm but stern. "It won't help at all. Can you pull yourself back up into the loft?"

"No." Even though her elbows and forearms rested on the

wooden floor, there was no way to gain enough leverage to heave herself back over the edge.

"I was afraid of that." Tyler looked around him at the cluttered lower level of the barn. Even with something to stand on it was going to be a long stretch up. He dragged a bale of hay across the floor and stepped up, trying to position himself close enough to an upright beam to use it as a possible support if Sarah's weight overbalanced them both.

Endless seconds passed. Sarah felt the strain on her shoulders pulling her closer to the edge. There were slivers in her hands that stung and burned. David was crouched beside her, not touching her but crowding close. She wasn't altogether certain that he wouldn't try to grab her if she started to fall. That frightened her almost as badly as the fear of falling herself. "Go down the ladder, David. Now."

"No," he replied succinctly in a good imitation of his father's gruff, no-nonsense tone.

"Sarah, listen to me."

"Yes." She closed her eyes, surprised even in her disoriented state at how much she liked the way Tyler Danielson said her name. "Ease yourself down." Steely fingers closed around her ankle and calf. "I've got you." He sounded strong, calm, in control. "It's safe to let go."

Was it? Sarah's stubborn common sense took over. "What are you standing on?"

The question didn't seem to bother him. "A bale of hay," Tyler answered calmly.

"How tall are you?" Sarah wasn't about to launch herself into his arms, no matter how much she liked his voice, if they were both going to end up with broken necks.

"Six-one." There was a ghost of a chuckle in his answer. "Are you asking these questions for a reason?"

"Yes." She bit her tongue against another fiery streak of pain racing across her shoulders. "You're not tall enough."

"Sorry, I'm doing my best." His tone was patient, confident; his grip steady and firm. "Come on, Sarah. You're doing fine. No more stalling. Let's go."

She was hanging by her fingers now, very aware of Tyler's

hands on her legs. Taking a long shaky breath, Sarah let go and felt Tyler stumble backward as he took her weight, then come up hard against the upright beam behind them. He stepped backward off the bale of hay with his arms tightly around her waist, pulling her with him, cushioning her descent. He landed with a grunt and slid sideways, coming to rest against another bale of hay, Sarah, more or less in his lap.

Tyler closed his eyes and fought to get his breathing under control. She was heavier than she looked, stronger; soft skin and sweet rounded curves in all the right places but with firm sleek muscles underneath.

Sarah Austin felt good in his arms. He'd like to keep her there, Tyler realized with a jolt that was damned near as unpleasant as having the wind knocked out of him. It had never occurred to him that someday, without any warning, he might once again be attracted to a woman. He wasn't sure he was prepared, or even capable, of dealing with those kinds of hard-to-control feelings again after so long a period of not allowing himself to feel anything at all.

"Are you all right?"

Tyler opened his eyes to find Sarah staring at him, violet blue eyes, framed by thick lashes, dark with concern.

"I think that's supposed to be my line." He still held her, even as David clambered down the ladder bellowing questions at the top of his lungs.

"I'm the nurse," she advised him brusquely. "I'll make the evaluations here." Tyler's tone was still gruff but no longer hostile, which Sarah took to be a good sign. "Nothing broken?"

"All in one piece. Are you okay?" He was almost grinning. Sarah remembered his reluctant smile from their first meeting and longed to see it again.

"No permanent damage. Just bumps and bruises and splinters." Tyler got to his knees and helped her to a seat on one of the bales. He was watching her very closely, almost as if he expected her to faint or have hysterics or something of that nature. Sarah shook her head. "It'll take Aunt Cam an hour to pick these all out of my hide."

"Ugh." David slid to a halt beside his father. "Your hands look gross!"

"David." Tyler Danielson pulled his son close for a quick hard hug. David buried his face in Tyler's neck and hung on for dear life. A moment later he raised his head to peer over his father's shoulder.

"It's gonna hurt like fury gettin' all those splinters out." He wiggled away from his father's embrace but not before Sarah saw the quick kiss Tyler dropped on the top of David's dusty, tousled head. She lowered her gaze to her hands, allowing him his private moment with David, knowing she had seen something rare and healing pass between father and son.

"I'll survive," Sarah assured him.

"You're not going to faint on me, are you?" Sarah looked up at Tyler, who was towering over her now that he'd risen to his feet.

"Good grief, no. Whatever gave you that idea?"

Tyler had the grace to flush. What indeed? Was he supposed to tell her that Allison would have been in hysterics, would have needed sedation to have that many wicked splinters removed from her hands? Even considering that she never would have gone up into the haymow in the first place?

And would his childlike and excitable wife have had the courage, the strength and stamina, to throw herself at David to stop his headlong plunge as Sarah had done?

No. He was being unfair to Allison with that last thought. She had been delicate physically and emotionally. She had leaned on him, relied on him to such an extent he'd felt suffocated and trapped in their marriage, but she'd always been a good mother to David. She would have done anything for her child, even if it endangered her own life. And today it had been his carelessness, not Allison's, that had allowed David to wander into danger.

"David." There was no warmth in the gruff voice this time. Sarah winced and David jumped to attention, having been engrossed in determining the extent of Sarah's injuries. "That was a foolish stunt to pull. You could have been badly hurt or even killed. As it is, your failure to obey nearly got Sarah hurt, too.''

David looked up at his father, stricken. Sarah longed to tell him that it was nothing. But that would have been making light of a dangerous situation. She had given birth to a child but she wasn't a parent. Yet she knew it was important that David realize his rash behavior could have similar or even more serious consequences in the future. She bit her lip and didn't say a word.

''I'm sorry, Sarah. I wouldn't want you to get hurt for anything, honest.''

''I know, David. It wasn't all your fault.'' Sarah couldn't resist the quivering lower lip, the hangdog expression in his big brown eyes. ''I shouldn't have swung on that rope, either. We were both wrong. I knew it was old, or at least I suspected as much.'' Sarah amended her statement when she saw the beginning of an angry frown crease Tyler's high forehead.

''You *are* a grown-up,'' David said quickly, sensing a chance to shift some of the blame onto older shoulders. ''You should have known better.''

''David,'' Tyler barked. ''That is not the point.'' The look he bestowed on Sarah said as plainly as words, *Give this one an inch and he'll take a mile.*

''I'm afraid it is.'' Sarah stood up, the rueful smile on her lips replaced by a grimace of pain. ''Oh, damn, my ankle.''

Her face was suddenly pasty white. Tyler had just been noticing, despite his determination not to, how well the peach color of her shirt complemented the thick chestnut waves of her hair and the pale creamy gold of her skin. Now her face looked pinched and strained. Her knees buckled and he swept her into his arms.

''What in heaven's name are you doing?'' Sarah's head jerked back so that she could look him straight in the eye.

''You looked like you were going to faint,'' Tyler informed her curtly. ''I've seen it before.''

''Well, I wasn't going to faint. My ankle's always giving out on me. I must have landed harder than I thought.'' Sarah took a deep breath as though preparing to confess a very unpleasant character trait. "It's an old softball injury, if you have to know the whole sordid truth."

"No kidding?"

"No kidding."

Sarah looked mutinous and wiggled to be set free. Tyler only pulled her more tightly against his chest. He wanted to laugh at her indignant expression. Did he really seem so formidable, so straitlaced that she was ashamed to tell him she liked to play softball? He grinned and although he didn't know it, the smile made Sarah catch her breath. He looked pleased and unshadowed by the demons that seemed to haunt him so much of the time.

Tyler hadn't felt like this in a long time. He couldn't remember the last time he'd enjoyed trading quips with a woman. Especially a woman as desirable and fascinating as Sarah Austin. "Just lean back and enjoy the ride."

For a moment he thought Sarah was going to protest further, but she surprised him by curling her arms around his neck and leaning her head against his shoulder. "Okay. But only as far as the back steps. I have to admit I'm a pretty sorry sight hobbling along on this thing." She kicked out her leg and eyed the already swollen ankle coldly. "Still, there's no way in the world I'm going to trust you to carry me up seven steep, narrow wooden steps, sore ankle or no sore ankle. And that's final."

"Don't you think I can manage to get you safely inside the house?" Tyler responded to the unknowing sensuality in her words, as much as to the spoken challenge to his manhood.

"Oh, I think you could manage all right," Sarah replied without a trace of guile. "But I don't trust those steps any more than I should have trusted that rope. If you fall and break *your* ankle, I'll feel responsible." Tyler started to protest but she placed two peach-tipped fingers against his lips. "I don't intend spending the rest of my vacation catering to a bad-tempered grown-up patient. My field of expertise lies with newborns. They are very much smaller, easier to handle and don't speak a word of English." Tyler looked as if he intended to respond in kind but Sarah never got the chance to hear his riposte.

"Dad. You didn't even ask me if I hurt myself," David said, jumping up and down beside Tyler, hanging on his arm. "All I got was a hug."

And a kiss, Sarah thought, the picture of that vulnerable spontaneous gesture popping unbidden into her thoughts.

"Are you hurt?" Tyler asked his son, one strongly arched black brow lifting toward his hairline.

"Of course not," David informed him. "But you should have asked."

"You're right, I should have asked. Now why don't you run and open the barn door all the way so I can get Sarah through without giving her any more splinters to deal with."

"Please do." Sarah looked up into Tyler's face, hoping to surprise him into smiling again, but as she did so the smile died in her own eyes. The closed shuttered look was back, as if the last few bantering moments had never occurred. He was silent all the way to the house.

Tyler set Sarah down on the third step and let her slide down to stand with his arms around her waist for a moment as she steadied herself on the weakened ankle. "Are you sure you can make it inside all right?"

"Yes. It hurts like the devil when this happens. Then in an hour it's almost like new. Really, I'm fine." If she could have thought of anything more intelligent to say she would have. But the truth of the matter was that his hard, lean body was too close to hers; his dark, watchful eyes, level with her own, almost took her breath away. She was lucky to be able to speak at all.

"Thank you for saving my son's life." Tyler knew the words were mechanical. Yet he stopped himself from saying everything that was on his mind. He had the suspicion that Sarah Austin would be a very sympathetic auditor of all his sins, and, God help him, all his hopes and dreams if he should blurt them out.

No matter how appealing he found her independent spirit and simple joy of living, no matter how good she felt in his arms, he wasn't ready to think beyond the moment, to think of his own wants and needs. He owed Allison that much loyalty—to concentrate all his energy on her son, and to see to it that David came first in his life.

He owed Allison that much for his part in her death.

"You don't have to thank me." Sarah was watching him, seeing too far beneath the surface, he suspected.

"He's all I have left in this world to love." Tyler turned and walked away without a backward glance. He had no idea why he'd said those words to a woman he barely knew.

Except he felt she would understand.

CHAPTER FIVE

"HI, SARAH. HOW'S YOUR ANKLE? I didn't see you limping too badly when you came outside so I said to Dad, let's go visit Sarah and Aunt Cam."

It was surprising how soon a person got used to having a devastatingly frank and straightforward eight-year-old leap right into conversations, Tyler thought. Or at least how soon one became resigned to the phenomenon. "No ill effects, I hope?" he inquired more formally than his son. David owed his life to Sarah's intervention and yet Tyler found he couldn't express his gratitude in any but the most superficial way. He had never been a demonstrative man, and the events of the last two years had driven him further into himself. He realized what was happening to him but at the same time he was powerless to stop the process.

"Only assorted bumps and bruises, sore fingers and a stiff ankle, of course. Perfectly normal symptoms in every respect." Sarah cataloged her injuries and held up her hands to show they now sported one or two adhesive bandages, just as David's usually did. "I will definitely survive." She laughed and the sound was so carefree and bright that Tyler found it hard not to laugh in return. He caught himself thinking that Sarah's laughter could probably heal anything. Even a broken heart.

"And that is why Sarah is supervising. And I am on my hands and knees doing the gardening. Hello, Mr. Danielson. I'm Camilla Weaver, your neighbor and Sarah's aunt." The older woman kneeling among the flowers looked very much like Sarah, with the same slender build, chestnut brown hair and intelligent eyes, but at the same time she gave the impression of being far more polished and worldly than her niece.

"Please call me Tyler," he responded automatically, his mind still on Sarah and the very real and equally unwelcome sense of excitement and anticipation she stirred within him.

"Thank you. I will." Camilla had removed one of her gardening gloves and now held out a white, long-fingered hand. Tyler leaned forward and took her outstretched fingers, one of his rare smiles touching Sarah, too, with warmth as quick and hot as summer lightning.

"Is there something I can do to help you?" Tyler asked. Camilla smiled in return, clearly as dazzled as Sarah found herself by the subtle changes, the sudden devastating charm underlying Tyler's austere rough-cut features when he forgot himself enough to let it show.

"You might hand me that ball of twine." Upon closer inspection, Tyler found that Camilla was kneeling amid a straggling bed of anemic petunias and stunted geraniums clustered around a small ornate gazebo in the backyard.

Sarah watched Tyler looking down at her aunt with that benign, masculine superiority most men adopt when a woman asks them for help of any kind. Usually it rankled Sarah but today she could only take pity on Tyler's bemusement. In her flowered dirndl skirt and pale pink blouse, Camilla looked almost as young as Sarah, carefree and charmingly flustered. It was a masterful performance.

And simply by contrast, Camilla made Sarah feel dowdy and useless in her serviceable denim skirt and peach-colored cotton shirt. It wasn't a comfortable feeling because she sensed her sudden bout of self-doubt was caused by the presence of the man before her. Pushing the unwanted conclusion into a dusty corner of her mind, Sarah leaned both arms on the gazebo railing, watching her aunt set out to charm Tyler Danielson.

"Meecham, the handyman, remembered how much I always loved flowers so he put these poor things out when he learned I'd be here for the summer. I couldn't stand to see them suffer for another moment.'' She staked up a drooping geranium and leaned back on her heels to study her work.

"They would have been fine until tomorrow, Aunt Cam," Sarah scolded from her vantage point at the railing where she'd been joined by an interested David. "I would have been happy to transplant them for you."

"Not with all those terrible scratches on your hands." Camilla patted the soil around the roots of a petunia the same shade of pink as her blouse. "There—" she nodded in satisfaction "—they look much happier, don't you agree?"

"Yes," said Tyler dubiously. In reality they appeared to be almost beyond hope but he didn't say so. He lifted his gaze, caught Sarah's sparkling eyes on him and realized she shared his opinion. He looked down at the flowers again. He couldn't afford to become lost in the beckoning, seemingly bottomless pools of her eyes. They promised so much for some lucky man; friendship, caring, passion. For some very lucky man who deserved all she could give—but not for him.

"These scratches will be healed over by tomorrow," Sarah said and knew her voice was high and strained. Tyler Danielson had looked at her as if he found her wondrous and rare and at the same time dangerous. It was a heady, disorienting sensation, exciting, yet frightening, too.

"But not all of them," David inserted with an air of great wisdom. "You could get an infection from messin' around in the dirt and all. Then before you know it they'd have to cut off your whole arm..."

"Enough, David." Tyler said forcefully. He should have seen that one coming but he hadn't. He shook his head in rueful apology as he held out a lean brown hand to help Camilla to her feet.

"Dad and I took a tour of the island yesterday," David said by way of explanation. "The guide told us this story about a guy who got lost coming across the straits from the fort on the mainland in the winter and had to have his leg cut off because it got frozen solid. They didn't even put him to sleep," he related with ghoulish little-boy relish. "They just sawed it off with him screamin' and yellin'..." David clamped his hand over his mouth. "Well, you know what I mean." He shrugged. "Sorry."

Camilla laughed and pulled off her other glove. "That's okay, David. It was a very hard life for those early French voyageurs and British fur traders."

"I think it would have been totally awesome," David said with great conviction as he bounced down the steps of the gazebo. Sarah followed more sedately in his wake, her twisted ankle, supported by an elastic bandage, giving her only a twinge of discomfort now and then.

"I have the feeling you wouldn't have been averse to living in that day and age either, Tyler." Camilla tilted her head slightly to meet his enigmatic midnight gaze.

"I think I might have enjoyed the experience." He smiled again and Sarah's heart gave another unruly jerk that made her catch her breath and miss a step.

"Why don't you gentlemen join us for a glass of lemonade?" Camilla invited. "I think Mrs. Meecham sent some cookies along that David might enjoy. They're chocolate chip."

"Great! Can we stay a little while, Dad?"

"If you like." The reply was curt, the tone reluctant.

Once again Sarah had the impression that Tyler Danielson had sealed himself away. The polite give-and-take of social interchange wasn't something he excelled at. Sarah could see him living on Mackinac in the days of the voyageurs, when strength, hard work and a disregard for personal comfort could take a man far. But that time was past so Tyler appeased his sense of adventure, his restlessness, by building bridges in out-of-the-way corners of the world.

And he had obtained that sense of freedom and fulfillment at the price of his personal happiness.

"David tells me you're from Georgia." With sudden understanding Sarah realized why Camilla seemed so determined to draw Tyler out.

"David has been living there with his grandfather. My work takes me all over the world." Tyler chose his words carefully as though he might betray himself in some way if he did not.

He was out of practice in dealing with such delicate, subtle probings. Since the accident he'd gotten used to the cut and slash techniques employed by the media, but he wasn't sure how to handle an interrogation conducted with such charming yet almost surgical precision.

"How is it, then, that you came to acquire Lilac Time? Most cottage owners are from the Midwest."

Tyler stopped walking and Sarah did the same. She was a step or two behind her aunt and Tyler, yet the tension that suddenly tightened the sleek muscles of his neck and shoulders was evident beneath the thin woven material of his shirt.

"Allison, my late wife, spent several vacations here when she was a young girl. I bought the cottage for her two summers ago. The year before her death." It had been another attempt to make peace between them, another try at giving Allison some interest outside herself, an attempt to create some stability in their lives. But this scheme had failed like all the rest. All his failures, his omissions, piling one on top of another until Allison had died.

"She was a guest of Justin Delano?" Camilla could be relentless when she chose. It was important to her to learn if there was any connection between the Elliot Brandon she'd known so briefly and the man and boy in front of her.

"Yes, as a matter of fact. Justin Delano befriended my father-in-law when he was his commanding officer during World War II. Their friendship continued until Delano's death."

"I see." She could feel it all coming back, the remorse, the sense of helplessness. Camilla's hazel eyes clouded over with tears. She bent her head to hide the telltale signs of emotion. Her voice, thank heaven, didn't betray her. "And your wife's family name. Was it Brandon by any chance?" Her question was certainly not out of line, yet Camilla's hands were clenched so tightly around her cotton gloves that the knuckles showed white beneath the skin.

David streaked past them pulling Sarah along by the hand as he pounded toward the back steps. "Come on, Sarah. I'm dying of thirst." He clamped his hands around his throat and groaned in mock agony. They all smiled, but his clowning did nothing to lessen the tension.

"Yes, it was. May I ask how you know?" Tyler looked stern, withdrawn. His brows drew together in a fierce straight line that spoke more of pain than anger.

"David's name was my first clue. And the fact that he told my niece his grandfather is a minister was another." Her hazel eyes were focused on a time only she could remember. "A young divinity student, a second lieutenant from Georgia. His name was Elliot David Brandon. We knew each other briefly during the war." And he had kissed her and held her and told her he loved her. And she had run away. Because she'd had no other choice. She had already been pregnant with another man's child. A married man, another woman's husband. And the baby she bore him had never been hers, either. She, like Sarah so many years later, had never been able to hold her child, touch her, love her. "But that was a very long time ago."

"It sure was." David was miffed at being so long ignored. He hopped down the steps addressing his next question to Sarah. But she was intent on watching Camilla and missed what he said. "World War II was ages ago, Granddad told me so himself. How do you suppose Aunt Cam remembered his name after all that time?"

SARAH HAD A GREAT DEAL of solitude during the next few hours to mull over the happenings of that long, eventful day. The rest of the evening passed slowly and for the most part she spent it alone. Tyler made his excuses for not joining them for refreshments and they were no more insincere than her aunt's pretense of interest in seeing that David got all the lemonade and cookies he desired.

Camilla smiled and said the right things but her thoughts were far away. It seemed to Sarah that her aunt's memories weren't happy ones. Sarah wanted to help her but didn't know where to start, so she said nothing and was angry with herself for doing so. It was obvious that the source of Camilla's distraction centered around a single man: the Reverend Elliot

David Brandon. What had he meant to Camilla in those far-off days of her youth?

It was decided that David would stay at Gathering Place while Tyler attended to business in the village, the reason he had declined Camilla's invitation in the first place. David was easily enough entertained. A videocassette of an old John Wayne movie that Camilla had brought with her to the island along with a small television and VCR kept him occupied. The film made up in free-for-all fistfights and shoot-outs for the disappointment of its having been filmed in black and white.

When David was fully engrossed in the action Camilla excused herself and went upstairs to take a bath. She was gone for a long time and when she returned, wrapped in an old terry-cloth bathrobe, she was still moody and disinclined to talk.

Sarah was bored with the movie, restless and unsettled. She couldn't get the haunted look on Tyler's face out of her thoughts, no matter how hard she tried. Finally she wandered onto the veranda to watch the sunset fade from peach to lavender behind the soaring ivory-colored towers of the Mackinac Bridge.

Inside the cottage she heard the twangy western music of the movie sound track swell into a crescendo then fade away into the credits at the end. A few moments later David joined her on the shadowed porch.

"It's getting dark." He climbed onto the wicker settee and pressed his small snub nose against the screen. "My dad isn't back from town yet. I think I should go look for him."

Sarah glanced at the luminous dial of her watch. Twilight lingered a long time this far north and it was already a few minutes before nine o'clock. The sunset was a glory of gold and peach shading to purple as darkness spread across the evening sky. She was a little surprised at how late it actually was. "It's too close to dark for you to be out wandering the streets. Your father probably just got caught up in his... business...and forgot the time." She had no idea what Tyler Danielson was doing in the village nestled at the foot of the bluffs. The shops would all be closed by now, the last boats having left for the mainland hours ago.

"He's never gone out in the evening and left me alone." David looked tired and lonely and a little scared.

Outside, late-calling birds and the sighing of night wind in the cedars had replaced the busy daytime sounds of the island. Mackinac's nightlife, what there was of it, centered around the yachts in the marina and the hotels. If Sarah went looking, would she find David's father slumped on a bar stool somewhere? Had drinking been the cause of the accident that killed his wife and sent him to prison? If so, she didn't want David to see him that way. Sarah made her decision with characteristic swiftness.

"Why don't you stay here and keep watch over Aunt Cam? She hates to be alone at night." Sarah lied without a qualm of conscience. "I'll go look for your father."

"But your ankle..." David sounded unconvinced.

"The walk will do me good."

"I don't know." David hesitated again. "It's man's work to go out in the dark looking for someone who's lost." He peered up at her very earnestly, torn between inclination and duty.

"No, it's not man's work, David," Sarah said quietly, reaching out to smooth a wayward tuft of curly brown hair off his forehead. "It's grown-up's work and I'm the grown-up. It will be easier for me to find him. I know the island pretty well. Do you agree?"

His little-boy face was serious, sunburned and anxious above the collar of a clean blue and white striped polo shirt. "I think you're right," he finally said, relief not altogether hidden by his best imitation of his father's scowl. "Aunt Cam needs me here."

Sarah nodded. "I'll get a sweater and flashlight. It'll be dark going down the steps." If she'd guessed correctly she'd probably locate Tyler in one of the bars along the main street. There weren't that many, if she ruled out the lounges in the largest hotels. Somehow, remembering the look on Tyler's face, she didn't think he'd opt for bright lights and music.

Camilla was still sitting where Sarah had left her, her face hidden in the shadows, untouched by the jeweled glow of a Tiffany table lamp. "Tyler isn't back from town yet and David's getting anxious. I'm going to go down the bluff and see if I can locate him. David will stay and keep you company. I know how much you dislike being alone at night." The slight emphasis on the last sentence gave Camilla her clue.

The older woman glanced at the mantel clock and then back to the small boy scuffing the toe of his shoe on the antique Persian rug beneath his feet. She patted the couch cushion beside her. "That's very nice of you, David. I really do prefer not to be alone in this big old house." She studied Sarah closely. "Are you sure you should be going out yourself? We could make some phone calls..."

Sarah shook her head. "I need the exercise, Aunt Cam. I'll run up and get a jacket. It's chilly now that the sun's gone down."

Ten minutes later, still slightly breathless from descending the steep flight of wooden stairs anchored into the bluff, Sarah stepped out onto Huron Street, her shadow swallowed up by the larger darkness of the bulk of St. Anne's Catholic Church. She turned left, walking west toward the sunset, past the Island House—the island's oldest hotel. Then she passed Marquette Park, named for the famous French explorer, where the smell of lilacs from the huge bushes that dotted the lawn was heavy on the damp night air. Finally she arrived at the well-lighted and noisy stretch of the business district.

As always for Sarah it was like stepping into some kind of time warp. White clapboard buildings, some with the false fronts and canvas awnings of a bygone day, antique streetlights and the clip-clop of a horse-drawn taxi vied with neon signs, video games and amplified music.

During the day the contrast was even greater. On view were bicycles built for two, surreys complete with a fringe on top, the shiny lacquered coach and liveried coachman from the Grand Hotel picking up guests at the boat docks, and pedestrians of every shape and description. Walk into any candy shop and a person could hear visitors ordering the famous

island fudge in the accents of half a dozen foreign languages.
Mackinac attracted a mix of people: young Midwestern sin-
gles, honeymooners from all over the states, Canadians, and
Amish families from Pennsylvania and Ohio, soberly dressed
but enjoying a place where the bank actually had the need for
a drive-up window equipped to handle a horse and buggy and
the blacksmith wasn't a novelty but a valued and contributing
member of the community.

But at the moment nothing interested Sarah as much as finding Tyler Danielson and giving him a small piece of her mind.
As she walked the dull ache in her ankle increased and her ire
grew apace. He shouldn't have left David alone for so long,
she thought irritably. The child was among strangers and
needed the stability of having his father close by. Especially
at night.

Sarah set her jaw, squared her shoulders and decided, if she
hadn't found her quarry by the time she reached the Iroquois
Hotel at the western end of the street, she'd go home and call
the police to deal with Tyler Danielson.

She was wondering if she should detour onto one of the
short side streets that connected with Market Street, the island's second main thoroughfare, and check out the only year-
round bar, when she spied a tall familiar figure moving toward
the boardwalk that curved away along the shoreline. Sarah
quickened her steps. It might not be Tyler Danielson; she had
no intention of hailing a stranger. Her ankle throbbed from the
additional strain of walking so quickly. The man ahead of her
was lost to sight for a few moments behind some concealing
shrubbery. By the time he emerged again Sarah was only a
few yards behind. He stopped and turned just as Sarah, hesi-
tating a few seconds, stepped out of the shadows cast by those
same shrubs.

"You don't need to hurry, Sarah. I'll wait for you." His
voice sounded faintly amused, slightly slurred, but not as if
he were drunk. He moved very close, his hand reaching up to
touch her cheek, lightly, swiftly; the caress as fleeting as the
beat of a hummingbird's wing.

"David's beginning to worry about you. I thought..."

"You thought you'd come and peel me off a bar stool somewhere, pour a bucket of cold water over my head and march me home?"

"No, of course not..." Sarah let the words dwindle into silence. His touch had made her long for more contact. She laughed, at herself as much as anything, but it did little to ease the tension that shimmered between them like heat lightning on a hot summer evening. "Actually I was hoping it wouldn't come to that."

"It won't." Tyler softened the harsh words with a ghost of his marvelous smile and tucked a wisp of hair behind her ear. "As a matter of fact, it's been so long since I've had anything to drink at all that I found my third mug of beer to be one too many. I came out here to walk it off." He motioned her forward, back the way they had come, then shoved his hands into the pockets of his gray slacks as if he couldn't trust himself not to touch her again. They walked in silence for several minutes, passing by the brightly lighted hotels, the closed and silent souvenir and fudge shops, retracing her route along the low stone wall that bordered Marquette Park.

"I'm sorry..." Sarah was recalling her earlier angry thoughts. She'd been guilty of jumping to conclusions, too, although they were the obvious ones.

"So am I." Tyler was wearing the same pale green linen shirt she'd seen him in earlier. It was short-sleeved and open at the collar to reveal the tanned flesh of his throat and a sprinkling of dark curling hair on his chest. The cool night breeze didn't seem to affect him at all. He no longer appeared as tense and rigid as a too tightly strung bow, but there was no hint of softening in the ebony darkness of his eyes. His thoughts were still his own, hidden, like his emotions, from a prying, curious world.

"David said you'd never left him alone at night." Sarah wasn't going to justify her actions but she thought Tyler should be made aware of David's fears.

"It's the first time I've ever left him in the evening. Do you know why? Because we've been together so little. Doesn't say much for our family situation, does it?" The marina was on their right. Sarah watched the moonlight glance off the wave tops as they passed.

"Still, I had no valid reason for jumping to the conclusion that you were down here getting drunk." Sarah made her apology in a little rush that brought a flush to her cheeks. She was twenty-six years old. When would she ever learn to apologize with some semblance of style? *Never,* she decided with a glimpse of momentary self-knowledge. She would never be so uninvolved to not care strongly about her actions, right or wrong.

"Yes, you did," Tyler said abruptly. "It's what everyone thinks, whether they say so or not. The truth is I was stone-cold sober the night of the accident. I let the car get out of control and Allison died as a result." Tyler heard himself talking and wondered where the words were coming from. Sarah hadn't accused him of anything, yet he couldn't let her think any worse of him than she already did. "I went to prison for nine months. Vehicular homicide is a pretty broad term. It can get you anywhere from six months to ten years. I got off easy." *Lord, why had he said that?*

He hadn't even finished that third beer, but his system was having trouble dealing with the rush of alcohol to his brain and blood. He wanted Sarah to understand what had happened on that rainy night that would live forever in his memory. Tyler had never told anyone all the details, not even his lawyer. The truth would have made a great deal of difference to the outcome of his trial, but at the same time it would have dragged David even deeper into the nightmare. No, what had been between him and Allison—the doubts and lies that had driven them apart—was better buried along with her.

"I don't think that's the case at all." Sarah wasn't about to back down now, although the scowl on Tyler's face warned her that she was walking on very thin ice.

"How much do you know about me, Sarah?" Tyler stopped moving abruptly, planting himself on the sidewalk in front of her, hands still in his pockets, legs spread. He bent his head toward her, as if waiting for a blow.

Sarah lifted her chin. "All I know is what David told me

that first day in the barn. He's a very confused and hurting little boy.'' She put her hand on his arm and felt the muscles bunch rock hard beneath her fingertips. ''Have you discussed the matter of his mother's death with him?''

''He's too young to understand.'' Tyler didn't shrug off the touch of her hand although his battered heart warned him to. ''He's been with Elliot since the accident. His grandfather blames me for everything. Some of his attitude was bound to rub off on David. He isn't sure of me even now.''

Sarah continued to regard him soberly. Her large slightly tip-tilted eyes were unclouded by shadows. There was no censure in their clear sapphire depths. She was listening to him, only him, hearing with her heart as well as her brain. It was a heady feeling, this sense of empathy, of oneness, she aroused in him. He wanted to tell her everything; the whole long complicated story of his disastrous relationship with Allison. He wanted to tell Sarah of his doubts about David's birth, unburden himself of his own failing as a father and husband.

''You must tell him what really happened, and soon.''

''That's not possible.'' Tyler started walking again and she kept pace, not touching but close enough so that he could smell the faint light scent of her cologne and the woodsy fragrance of her shampoo when she turned toward him.

Tyler slowed his headlong pace. ''I'm sorry. I forgot about your ankle. Is it giving you a lot of pain?''

''Nothing I can't deal with.'' Already Tyler recognized the stubbornness in her. ''You're avoiding my question. Why isn't it possible to explain about the accident to David?''

''It's not that simple.'' Tyler found himself wanting to take her in his arms. It wasn't merely desire he felt for her. It was that and more; an excitement, an energy that coursed through him as though he'd awakened from a drugged sleep filled with nightmares into the bright light of a new day.

''I can accept that it's a complicated situation, but why keep punishing yourself this way? You weren't drinking. That must have come out at the trial. What other circumstances are you hiding from your son?'' She pulled the collar of her white sweater jacket higher around her neck.

"We were arguing. It was raining and slippery as hell. I was driving too damned fast. I was thrown free but Allison was trapped in the car for hours. She died five days later without ever regaining consciousness."

"You've paid." Sarah never finished her sentence. Tyler took her by the arms and gave her a shake.

"We were arguing about David." His voice was expressionless. He released her as suddenly as he'd reached out to take hold of her. "I'm sorry. Did I hurt you?"

"No. Why were you arguing about David?" A chilling, squeezing pain closed around her heart. How would she deal with Tyler's secrets if he chose to confide in her?

"David isn't my son." He said it bluntly, sharply, so that the words were as cutting as the pain in his soul.

"Are you certain?" Another woman might have backed off in confusion and embarrassment, but not Sarah. He was beginning to understand that she would never be only superficially involved in events that touched her heart and emotions. And David had obviously done just that.

"No. I was out of the country while Allison was pregnant and when he was born. I was always out of the country, you see. That was part of our problem. I tried to pretend at first. I tried as hard to deceive myself about David as I tried not to fall out of love with Allison." He slammed one fist into the palm of his other hand and the sound was sharp on the quiet night air. "I knew how fragile her hold on reality had become but that last night I pushed and pushed for answers." He snorted in self-derisive laughter. "I figured I was within my rights. I didn't care by then one way or the other who David's real father might be. I think I even told her I didn't believe she'd ever really been pregnant at all. I only wanted to be certain. Allison became hysterical, flew at me, jerked the wheel so hard I couldn't steer out of the swerve, and she died as a result. After that what good would it have done to tell everyone why we were arguing? And more to the point, what further harm would it have done to David?"

He began climbing the bluff steps two at a time at a pace that left Sarah behind in a matter of moments. "Tyler, wait," she called. Surprisingly, he did so, stopping at the first landing in the steep angled flight, both arms resting on the railing. He stared out over the rooftops of the sleeping town but Sarah guessed he saw nothing. She came to stand beside him, trying hard to keep her breathing even, but her heart was beating too wildly. Tyler held out his hand.

"Again, I'm sorry. I had no right to take this all out on you. I don't care if David isn't my natural child, do you understand that? It's just that I felt I had the right to know the truth. God knows I was never the best of husbands, Allison was no more to blame than I was if she found even a little happiness with someone else. But I was rough and angry and Allison died because of it. I'll have to live with that guilt the rest of my life."

"She wasn't like you, Sarah, strong, sure of herself." Now that he'd started to talk Tyler found it hard to stop. It had been bottled up inside him for so long. "Allison was fragile both physically and mentally. She was afraid of so many things and it made me impatient. She clung to me like a little girl. At first I was flattered. We were both so young and I felt protective and far older than I had a right to feel. But as time went on and she grew more dependent, it made me impatient. I knew she needed help but I wasn't mature enough to accept the responsibility of being there for her every day and night of my life. So I ran away, in an acceptable way, and buried myself in my work. It was a great excuse for covering up what a real jackass I was."

Tyler turned his back to the view and stared up at the next flight of steps, his face mostly in shadow, the cords and tendons of his forearms standing out rigid in the diffused light of the moon. "I went to Brazil on assignment. Allison went to Chicago to study art for a year. She was talented but, as in everything, so insecure and unsure of herself. I thought it would help her self-esteem. She lived with Justin Delano and came here for a few weeks before David was born."

Sarah's throat was so dry she had to swallow twice before she could speak. "Were you with her when David was born?"

"No. He was a week or two premature. He was born in

Chicago while she was still living with Delano. At a private clinic whose name I can't remember.''

Sarah curled her fingernails into her palms, letting the salutary little pain clear her brain. She had been a patient in a private hospital in Chicago when her son was born. David had been an early baby, like her son. He was very close in age to the child she'd given up for adoption. Both families were connected to Justin Delano...

Sarah tore her thoughts away from her own private agony and found Tyler watching her, his face hidden in shadow. "You may have been wrong." Why was she defending a dead woman who, whether she could help herself or not, had hurt Tyler so desperately that he might never be whole again?

"She wasn't pregnant when I left the country, no matter how well she deceived herself into believing she was by the time I returned. For a long time I blamed every man she ever knew, including my own best friend. But there was never anyone... It was almost as if she wanted a baby so badly..." Tyler shook his head, at a loss to explain what he meant. "I don't know...it's almost as if she wished him out of thin air or something.''

No. Sarah wanted to clamp her hands over her ears to block out his words. It was all nothing but coincidence and conjecture. She had to stop twisting every word Tyler said so that she could come up with parallels that almost certainly had no validity anywhere but in her own longing heart and mind.

It was true that David had stirred something in her from the moment they'd first met. But only because he was a lovable child who was lonely and confused. *Nothing more.*

"I don't know what to say." Sarah spoke the simple unadorned truth.

Tyler lifted his hand and touched her cheek, lightly, softly, tracing a line to the corner of her mouth. "There isn't anything else to be said, Sarah." He came very close and took her hands. "You've listened to thoughts and feelings I've never revealed to anyone else. Thank you." For an instant she thought he might lean down and kiss her and she held her breath but the moment passed. Tyler kept her hand in his and started to climb again but more slowly, keeping her close to his side.

"Everything I've done since Allison's death, including not fighting to keep from being sent to prison, I've done to protect David's memory of his mother. I owe her that much."

They were at the top of the bluff. A freighter, lights riding high above the water, could be seen heading beneath the twin spires of the great suspension bridge in the distance. "I'll find my way with David again," Tyler said, more to himself than to Sarah. "We'll start a new life together, just the two of us." But he wasn't at all certain of the future himself and he was afraid the doubt was evident in his tone.

"You love David despite any question you have about his paternity. That's all that matters now, or ever." Sarah was remembering the quick, hard hug and kiss after David came down from the haymow. Was it only that afternoon? It seemed centuries ago, not merely hours. "Love him, tell him so. All the rest will work itself out in its own good time."

Tyler didn't stop to question the urge to take her into his arms this time. She came with only the slightest hesitation, as though she, too, were fighting some need stronger than her own will. "You say it so simply, make it sound so easy."

Lord, she felt good in his arms, as though she belonged there and always had.

"I never said it would be easy. Most things that are worthwhile never are." Sarah linked her arms around his neck and looked up at him in all seriousness. "Sometimes things sound simple only because they're so right."

"You make me want to believe again, Sarah, and that's a very dangerous thing to do to a man." The hard set of Tyler's jaw hadn't relaxed but the rest of him was molded along her body like pliant steel.

"Believing can accomplish wondrous things." A breeze sighed through the leaves of the huge old copper beech tree near the gate. It was dark beneath its sheltering canopy. Sarah could see nothing of Tyler's expression, only the silhouette of his rugged profile and the chiseled line of his jaw. She reached out a tentative finger to smooth away the tenseness.

Tyler lowered his head to kiss her and Sarah saw nothing more at all except a cascade of colored light behind her closed eyelids. His kiss was gentle at first, asking, searching. Sarah opened her lips to the questing invasion of his tongue and found he tasted of salt and mint and slightly of beer. She rose on her tiptoes to better savor the essence of him, pressing herself against him with an abandon foreign to her usual cautious approach to intimacy of any kind.

"Sarah." Tyler pulled her tightly against him, leaving no doubt as to the extent of his arousal. Sarah stiffened as he deepened the kiss, unaware until she gave a protesting little moan that what had started out as a gentle exploration had turned into something so needful that he was hurting her. Sensing her confusion and sudden unease Tyler forced himself to back away. Cupping her head between his hands, he tasted the corner of her mouth, the high sweep of her cheekbones and the curve of her throat and chin. "I'm sorry, Sarah, I didn't mean to hurt you."

"I'll blame it on the moonlight," she said but there was a quaver in her voice that wouldn't go away.

"Sarah..." Tyler never finished the sentence.

"Dad! Sarah! Are you out there?" David's voice was shrill and sleepy sounding. The screen door to the veranda opened and his son was outlined by the light from the main room behind him.

"David." Sarah stepped away as Tyler spoke, releasing her hand from his, moving back so that he could go to his son. She was right in believing he had to show David more openly how important he was to him. "I'm here. I've been talking to Sarah."

"You must have been doin' all kinds of talkin'. I don't like you to be gone so long," David said in a choked voice.

"I know. I'm sorry I worried you." Tyler lifted David down from the steps and stood him on the ground. He hunkered down on his heels so that they were eye to eye.

"Aunt Cam says sometimes grown-ups just have to go talk to other grown-ups." He stood rigid, his hands pushed deep into the pockets of his windbreaker.

"That's right, but it's no excuse for leaving you alone so long. I won't do it again." Tyler lifted a hand to ruffle David's hair but the boy ducked away. For a second or two Sarah thought he was going to turn away from Tyler's halting, touchingly sincere attempt to explain and apologize. Instead, David launched himself into his father's arms. "Let's go home as soon as I say good-night to Aunt Cam. She won't come out because she's wearing this ratty old bathrobe." In a flash, David disappeared inside the cottage.

Tyler stood and turned to her. "Sarah." Regardless of his doubts about being David's biological father, his love for the child was plain to see. There was also a frown between his dark brows that Sarah didn't need any more light to interpret. He obviously regretted the kiss they had shared just moments before.

"It was only the moonlight, Tyler, nothing more." She laughed a little. "Who can resist it?"

"It wasn't the moonlight, Sarah, and we both know it."

"It's too soon, Tyler." Sarah held up her hand as though to ward off his touch. She spoke bluntly because she knew as well as he did they only had a few moments to be alone.

"It is too soon." He shrugged and looked down at his hands. "I've told you things tonight I've never told another living soul. I'm not using you, Sarah. Whatever is between us is exciting and frightening and something I've never experienced before in my life."

"I feel it, too." She stood on tiptoe and dropped a kiss on the downturned corner of his mouth. "I'm not sure what to do next."

"It's been a long day. I suggest we call it a night."

"Umm." Sarah smiled in a way that caused Tyler's pulse to speed up again. "A very long day." Behind them David's piping little-boy voice could be heard bidding Camilla goodnight. Sarah listened for a moment, her head tilted a little to the side, then smiled again. She was regaining her equilibrium now that Tyler no longer held her so closely she could feel each slow drumming beat of his heart.

"Sarah, tonight..."

"Your first responsibility is to David." She turned away and started to climb the steps. David flew out the door and streaked past her like a small tornado.

"'Night, Sarah. Let's go, Dad." Tyler wanted to say something to keep her with him a little longer but remained silent. Sarah waved from the doorway and turned to go inside.

With a small corner of his mind Tyler listened and responded to David's questions on the way home, but most of his thoughts were taken up with Sarah. The kiss they'd shared had been many things but inconsequential wasn't one of them. He had no business becoming involved with Sarah Austin or any woman. He wasn't ready for the responsibility of building a new relationship. He wasn't even sure he was capable of loving anyone again. It was far safer to center the rest of his life around David and his child's needs than to risk his heart at love again. Safer, but cowardly, and in the long run very lonely, too.

CHAPTER SIX

"SARAH?" DAVID SOUNDED exasperated. "You aren't going to waste another afternoon poking through more old boxes of junk, are you?"

Sarah looked up from the still unopened box of her mother's mementos to see David Danielson's earnest sunburned face pressed against the screen door. "I really should get at it. It's been sitting here for almost a week now. Aunt Cam and I have all the rest of Grandmother's things sorted through." She eyed the box resolutely.

"It can wait for one more day, can't it?" David asked in a wheedling tone. "I've got a surprise for you." There was an edge of excitement in his voice. He hopped from one sneakered foot to another. Sarah felt herself weakening.

"I suppose that means you want to go riding again this afternoon and your father is too busy with another project." For the past several days Sugar and Spice had been pressed into service as mounts for the Danielson men. Sarah had given David his first riding lesson on the placid mares. She'd gone out with him once or twice since, but from the beginning, she'd made it clear that due to her lack of practice, teaching him to ride should be Tyler's responsibility.

Tyler had been reluctant at first, declaring, in his turn, that his riding skills were even rustier than Sarah's. She'd laughed and told him that with Sugar and Spice's decided lack of fiery temperament, that was no excuse at all.

"Sure, I want to go riding, but later. Guess what we're going to do now?"

"What?" Sarah asked, tugging her pink cotton sweater

down over her jeans as she rose and walked toward the screen door.

"Dad's taking a day off from fixing up things over there," David said, gesturing over his shoulder with his thumb. "We're going to the fort. We want you to come with us."

"I don't know, David." For days she'd been telling herself it was better that she avoid spending too much time in the company of the Danielson men. Each day that passed strengthened the recognition and longing that had drawn her to David at their first meeting.

"I'd like to second David's invitation to tour the fort." Tyler appeared on the steps behind his son. His hair was tousled from the brisk lake breeze. He looked good, dressed in a pale blue sport shirt and faded denims. "Please, Sarah, come with us."

Sarah gave up a little more ground in her solitary battle to keep her distance from Tyler Danielson and his son. "I think my box can wait one more day. I'll leave Aunt Cam a note to tell her where I am. She's playing golf with some friends this afternoon."

"Great." David scooted past his father, missed his footing and half jumped, half rolled off the last two steps. Sarah held her breath until he got up, apparently unharmed. "I'll get my bike."

"Is he always that…"

"Clumsy?" Tyler asked with a rueful smile that curved his mouth and crinkled the corners of his midnight dark eyes. "I'm beginning to believe he is."

"I was going to say, 'Is he always that much of a daredevil?'" Sarah improvised quickly. She laughed, sliding a note into the frame of the screen door where Aunt Cam couldn't miss seeing it. "He isn't afraid of anything. I envy him."

"You should be sympathizing with me." Tyler opened the screen and held it for her. "Daredevils can bankrupt their fathers, who have to buy bandages for their scrapes and bruises." It no longer felt so strange to be speaking of the trials and tribulations of parenting. Even the guilt was beginning to fade away. He loved David; he'd be the best father he could and he'd make up to his son for his mother's death in every possible way.

"Buy stock in a bandage company," Sarah advised, laughing, "earn back some of your investment." She grabbed a sweater off the bentwood coatrack by the door. She looked bright and pretty, like a strawberry parfait. Good enough to eat, Tyler decided as she knotted the sweater around her shoulders. The sun was warm overhead. It was almost hot in sheltered spots but the breeze off the lake was cool.

"I might break even." Tyler shook his head. Sarah laughed and he laughed, too, because he liked the sound so much.

"He's a great kid." Her smile twisted something deep inside him. He ran his hand over the back of his neck to ease the sudden tension. Was this what it was like, falling in love a second time? Maybe if it was he'd better back off before it was too late.

Tyler hesitated a moment then held out his hand to help her down the steps. He was tired of running scared, running from everything and everybody who might make him feel again, who might make him commit himself again. He smiled, too.

"I know he is."

IT WAS STILL EARLY in the season. There weren't a lot of tourists crowding the interior of the restored fort so Sarah, Tyler and David took their time wandering from one whitewashed building and its exhibits to the next. Fife and drum corps, in authentic uniforms of the War of 1812, entertained on the grassy expanse of the parade grounds. Muskets were fired in shot-and-powder demonstrations that made Sarah want to clap her hands over her ears. At regular intervals cannon fire roared out over the harbor. A reenactment of a court-martial was dramatically staged, all of which helped keep David occupied and less inclined to grow impatient with the more static exhibits.

David was still full of questions and enthusiasm when they decided to take a break and order refreshments on the patio of the building known as the Officers' Stone Quarters, a fortification in its own right and the oldest building on the island.

He seemed to have inhaled his Coke almost before Sarah had taken her first sip. He poked his straw up and down and slurped at the ice in the bottom of his paper cup with so much gusto that Tyler had to tell him firmly to stop. For a few moments peace reigned over their table as they discussed what they'd seen, then admired the view. Then David started to fidget in his seat once more.

"Hey, Sarah. What're you daydreaming about?" David had both elbows on the metal table. He was looking at her intently, his face screwed into a comical frown that somehow, irrationally, reminded her of her stern and dignified father. David folded his hands under his chin and kept staring with the kind of single-minded rudeness that's acceptable only in a small child. He snapped his fingers in front of her nose. "Did you hear me?"

Sarah reached out and squeezed his hand, making a comical grimace of her own. It wasn't his frown that reminded her of her father—it was his headstrong, headlong approach to life. "Yes, I heard you."

"Well, tell me," he demanded, resuming his hand-under-chin position.

For a moment she was afraid she was going to blush. What had she been thinking when David interrupted her contemplation of the view over the straits? What had been the last thought in her mind? *That she could very easily fall in love with his father.* That would certainly be an interesting little bombshell to drop among them. She caught Tyler's frown from the corner of her eye and knew instinctively that he felt it necessary to scold David for his lack of manners.

"Actually, I was thinking about your father."

"My dad?" She'd surprised Tyler, too, she noticed.

"Umm." Sarah nodded wisely. "I was thinking how much he looked like a voyageur."

"Voyageur?" David looked at his father consideringly. "You mean one of those French guys from a long time ago who went exploring in canoes?" He cocked his head to one side as if trying to picture his father in leather breeches and a wool cap. "He does sort of look like the picture we saw."

And Tyler did. He was tall and straight as a white pine tree, with coal dark hair and eyes. Beyond the physical resemblance, he had something she couldn't capture with pen and ink, Sarah decided whimsically. It was that same spark of adventure, of discovery, that had sent those long-ago voyageurs out to explore an untamed continent in flimsy birchbark canoes.

Tyler stood. "Except for the difference in your ages, the pair of you could have been twins. You have two of the most overactive imaginations I've ever encountered." He was laughing and David was skipping around the table so no one noticed the sudden uncontrollable trembling of Sarah's hands as she knotted her sweater around her shoulders.

Not twins, of course that was only a figure of speech. But mother and son. Was she wrong to wish it so?

David held out his hand to her, his other hand already enfolded in Tyler's strong grip. He was swinging his father's arm enthusiastically. "Come on, Sarah. Let's take the bikes down the hill and get some ice cream and fudge before we go home. We can ride like the wind."

"It's only downhill one way," Sarah reminded him. "Walking these bikes uphill is a lot more work and a lot less fun."

"Who cares about going back uphill?" David asked dismissingly. "It's a breeze."

They walked quietly toward the back entrance of the fort, where they'd parked their bikes. "Dad." David sounded thoughtful all of a sudden. His arms stopped swinging and he slowed his bouncing steps. They had just passed the building holding the exhibit recreating the fort's stockade. David shuffled to a halt. He squeezed Sarah's hand tighter but he was looking up into his father's face. His profile was solemn, his eyes wide and apprehensive.

Tyler's expression was guarded, as usual, so that if Sarah hadn't been watching so closely, she would never have seen the flicker of pain that crossed his features with David's next question. "Was the place where you were in prison like that?"

He turned to look over his shoulder. "That hole in the ground where they put people to punish them?"

Sarah wanted to cry. It had never occurred to her that David would associate his father's imprisonment with the dugout, a windowless cell used to hold miscreants over a century before. Tyler looked at her helplessly, then knelt before the child.

"It was nothing like that, David."

"Honest?" His voice trembled and the words poured out, stumbling over each other. "You wouldn't let me come and see you but I never thought it might be like that place in there." David's voice had sunk to a whisper by the time he finished speaking.

"The prison was a big gray building with a high wire fence and locks on the doors." Tyler chose his words carefully. He didn't want to frighten David any more. Why hadn't he realized that his son's active imagination might paint an even grimmer picture of prison life than was actually the case?

"Granddad said it was just a big building that you couldn't get out of, too. And Michael said there were locks and guards because other people might try and get out. But I knew you wouldn't. You never tried to escape, did you, Dad?"

"No." And he hadn't tried to escape from the prison cell of his own mind, either. Until he'd kissed Sarah that night on the bluff stairs. He ruffled David's hair. "I didn't like being in prison but we all have to have rules. Society, people and countries like ours." David nodded his understanding but his hand was still clenched tightly around Sarah's. "When the car crashed and your mother died, the judge decided I'd broken the law. I had to make up for my...mistake. It's all over now. We don't ever have to think about prison again."

"I'm glad." David smiled at his father and Tyler pulled the boy into his arms, dark hair and curly brown hair close together. He held the child tightly for the space of a long heartbeat before standing up again. David dropped Sarah's hand, his little-boy world restored to happiness once again. He danced away from both adults then ran back to urge his father to his feet.

Tyler stood quietly a moment, staring over the top of David's head at the whitewashed, stone and frame building that housed the exhibit. He didn't say anything for a moment, as David ran circles around them both, then he switched his dark, unreadable gaze to Sarah and shook his head. "I never thought about little-boy nightmares."

"He'll be fine." Sarah linked her arm through his before she'd considered the intimacy of her action. "You said all the right things."

"Did I? It's so hard to know what's right. He's had such a tough life the last couple of years." Sarah felt good tucked against his side. He closed his hand over hers, holding her a little tighter when she moved to pull away.

"Everything will be fine as long as you meant your words for yourself, as well." Sarah stopped trying to pull away from his touch. She reached up with her free hand and touched his cheek, making him look directly at her.

"Are you wondering whether I've forgotten? No. I never will. But if you mean, am I trying to put it all behind me, yes, I am."

Sarah let her fingertip glide over the slight roughness of his beard and the smoothness of his lips. "It is all behind you, both of you. Tomorrow is the only thing that matters. I know. I've been there, too."

Tyler kissed the tip of her finger very lightly but Sarah felt the shock of his touch all the way to her toes. He covered her hand with his own. "Someday will you tell me about it?"

"I...don't know." Panic welled up in her suddenly. How could she tell him that she wanted to believe David was her son when she hadn't a shred of proof?

"I'll wait." He spoke very quietly but there were strength and patience behind the simple words. He'd sensed the sadness in her from the beginning even through his own pain. She had given him so much already, hope and the ability to look beyond the past. He wanted to do the same for her. "Thank you, Sarah."

"For what?" She looked at him quizzically and he longed to stop, then and there, and kiss her; tell her all the things in his heart.

"For giving me back the future." Tyler knew he was on the verge of falling in love with her. She'd brought him back to life; he didn't know any other way to express how he felt. She cared for David, that was plain to see; she could come to care for him also; her response to his kiss that night on the bluff was proof.

"You're welcome." She closed her eyes, gold-tipped lashes laying thick and heavy against her cheek. She swayed toward him very slightly. Was there really a second chance for love? She didn't want to spend the rest of her life alone. You couldn't live in a vacuum, turn off your heart and feelings forever, or eventually you'd lose your soul. With a man like Tyler to love and cherish, she'd be strong enough to take on the world. But right now she wished the world would go away long enough for her to tell him so.

David had already wheeled his bike out of the rack when Sarah and Tyler passed through the gateway in the thick walls surrounding the fort. Time hadn't stood still for longer than that magic moment Tyler had held her in his arms, so she'd said nothing about anything at all. Now David made any kind of intimate conversation almost impossible. He bounced up and down in front of them, making roaring noises in his throat as though the bike were a high-powered sports car.

"I'm Magnum, the PI, and this is my red Ferrari," he yelled over his shoulder. "Watch how we take this curve."

"David!" Tyler raised his voice to warn David to slow down as they approached the steep downhill turn onto Fort Street. His son paid no attention. "David Brandon Danielson, I said slow down." David merely waved over his shoulder, already beginning to pick up speed on the steep pavement.

Tyler cursed under his breath, then speeded up his bike, Sarah close behind. But by the time they reached the street, David was already well ahead of them, gaining momentum with each turn of his wheels. "Slow down." Sarah knew David couldn't hear her but she yelled to him anyway.

Sarah's bike was old and heavy. She soon found herself falling behind. David had leaned forward over his handlebars, fighting to keep control of his bike, but every time he tried to apply his brakes, spurts of gravel flew up behind him and he fishtailed back and forth.

"Dad! I can't stop!" The faint plea for help was barely audible to Sarah over the pounding of blood in her ears. David skidded by a tour wagon lumbering along the roadway, his front wheel wobbling as he took the lead over the slow-moving vehicle. The wagon moved over to let Tyler and Sarah pass, blocking their view of the boy for an instant. Cyclists and people on horseback swerved to avoid colliding with the runaway bike.

Tyler raced after his son, avoiding pedestrians and cyclists sometimes only by inches. David dragged his foot, slowing his headlong pace a little, but not enough. Sarah knew that if he fell from the bike or hit some obstacle in the road, he'd be seriously injured.

Even as the thought crossed her mind, Tyler caught up with David, grabbing the handlebars of the boy's bike to slow his son's descent. They were almost at the bottom of the hill, where the street converged with the heavy traffic of Huron and Market streets. Marquette Park was on their left. "Get off the road, David." Tyler kept one hand on his own handlebars, one on David's, slowing him even more, heading him off the pavement. For a few yards into the park, David kept his machine under control. Then he panicked as tree trunks and sunbathers loomed on all sides. He wrenched his bike from Tyler's grasp.

Sarah skidded to a halt, sliding off her bike, almost running with it in her haste to catch up.

Tyler yelled. "David, jump!" David was heading directly for a huge, low-hanging lilac bush. *Hell*, Tyler thought distractedly, *that's no bush, it's a goddamned tree.*

"I can't." The scared little voice was so breathless he could barely hear it.

"Yes you can, Son. Jump!" Tyler put every ounce of command he possessed into the order. "Now!"

David swung a leg over the bar. The bicycle hit a tree root and bounced into the air. With a scream that echoed in Tyler's mind for a long time after, David flipped forward, rolling over and over in the soft grass. The bike tipped onto its side and skidded into a tree trunk.

"David? My God! David, are you all right?" Tyler jumped from his cycle and rushed to the motionless child lying in a heap on the grass.

Sarah ran, too, her heart pounding with fear and exertion. Tyler held David in his arms, staring up at her, fear darkening his eyes to charcoal. Sarah's hand flew to her mouth, images of permanent injuries and even more unspeakable horrors flashing through her mind.

Suddenly David moved; the arm that was hanging limply at his side pushed imperiously against Tyler's shoulder.

"I can't breathe," he groaned, his face ashen, brown eyes wide with shock and pain. He clung to his father for a long quiet moment, then pulled air noisily into his lungs.

"You're all right, David." Tyler's voice was hoarse with relief. "You just had the wind knocked out of you, that's all. Take it easy, okay, sport?" He cradled the child higher in his arms.

David was already breathing easier by the time Sarah knelt beside him to run her hands quickly along arms and legs, searching for injuries. He had scrapes on elbows and hands. His clothes were grass-stained and torn. Both knees were bruised and abraded. There was a jagged cut on the left one. Tyler pulled a snowy white handkerchief out of his back pocket and Sarah held it firmly over the cut.

"You may need stitches, David." Sarah took a second look at the injured knee and motioned toward the medical clinic down the street. She had no idea what sharp object had caused the laceration.

"No," David howled. He was definitely on the road to full recovery. "No stitches. No shots."

"Okay." Sarah couldn't hold back a tremulous smile. "If your father agrees, I'll take care of your knee at the cottage."

"How are we going to get home?" Tyler's face was pale beneath his tan. He still held David tightly in his arms but he, too, was regaining his equilibrium. He looked around. They had attracted quite a crowd.

"I'll give you a ride, mister." A young boy in a low-sided wagon, half-full of baled hay, pulled up at the edge of the street. "Where you going?"

"East bluff," Tyler said, not wasting words. Effortlessly he rose from his knees, David cradled securely in his arms. Sarah rose, too, with a helping hand from a park ranger who'd been attracted by the noise and the gathering crowd.

More helping hands loaded their bikes onto the flatbed wagon. Sarah stepped up to sit beside the young driver. Tyler climbed over the wheel and settled into the back of the wagon after handing David over to the ranger. When he was seated against a bale of hay he reached out for the child, folding him protectively in his arms once again.

The crowd began to drift away as the wagon moved up the hill. David's tears had been reduced to sniffles and hiccups. Sarah turned in her seat to hand Tyler a tissue she'd found in her sweater pocket to wipe the tears from David's cheeks, when someone in the dwindling group still watching them said loudly and clearly, "People who can't handle their kids any better than that shouldn't be allowed to raise them."

It was a thoughtless, cruel remark. For a moment Sarah hoped she was the only one to hear it but she knew she was mistaken when she saw Tyler's hand falter and stop as he smoothed David's tousled brown hair. Sarah scooted around in her seat, ready to give the speaker a piece of her mind, but it was impossible to tell his identity. She satisfied herself with glaring at all of them before the wagon moved past.

"If we stop by my place before you take David home, I can pick up the first-aid kit," she said, pitching her voice to carry over the clip-clop of metal horseshoes ringing on the pavement. "We'll have him fixed up in no time."

Tyler's voice, when he answered, was cold and distant, as it had been that first day in the barn. "Thanks, I appreciate your help."

Sarah sat quietly for the rest of the ride. It occurred to her to wonder what else—other than the fact that David's knee might still need stitches despite his objections—could possibly go wrong with what had started out as a very happy day.

CHAPTER SEVEN

SARAH'S PREMONITION of more trouble came true even sooner than she'd expected. The ride back up the bluff was long and tedious, with the sun beating down on their heads and any hint of a breeze cut off by the trees growing along the rim. David started crying again from reaction and pain. He refused to hold his knee still, bending it now and then to see for himself the extent of his injury. Each time he did, the wound started bleeding once more, bringing a fresh bout of exhausted tears in its wake. Sarah had a headache of her own by the time they arrived at the cottage. Tyler looked like a thundercloud, his eyes dark with remembered fear for his son; but his face was set and stern. David was in for a well-deserved scolding, Sarah deduced, no matter how gently his father still held him in his arms.

The wagon driver refused to accept any payment for his help, although they'd taken him out of his way. With a cheerful wave, he drove out of sight around the curve of the bluff. Sarah led the way into the cottage, holding the veranda door open for Tyler to enter with David held high in his arms. He stopped dead in his tracks, just inside the main room of the cottage.

"Damn it, Elliot, what are you doing here?"

Sarah turned, bewildered, trying to focus her sun-dazzled eyes on the occupants of the overcrowded, antique-filled room. Camilla's slight form was hunched unattractively in an overstuffed armchair near the marble-topped table by the door. Two men were standing, silhouetted against the sunlight pouring through the filmy lace curtains covering the bay window behind them.

"Sarah." Camilla jumped up, her movements jerky and so without her usual assured grace that Sarah felt a stab of alarm. "I'm so glad you're home." Her aunt's voice was rough with what almost sounded like tears. Her face was chalky white, her rouge standing out like clown's paint against the pallor of her skin.

"Aunt Cam, what's wrong?" Sarah moved out of the doorway to take her aunt's cold, trembling hands.

"These gentlemen are here to see..." Her voice halted when she noticed David's injuries for the first time. "Oh, dear, there's been an accident."

"What? Blast. I know I should never have allowed the boy to go with you, Tyler. I shouldn't have stayed away this long." The words were cold and as sharp as a knife blade. "You're not fit to care for him." The older of the two men moved out of the glare of sunlight. He was well past middle age, tall and broad-shouldered with just a hint of a paunch and a mane of wavy white hair. His face was square and intelligent, his nose both prominent and dignified. He looked like an Old Testament prophet, except that he lacked a suitable long white beard. It didn't take more than a quick glance at his dark shirt and clerical collar for Sarah to realize she was staring, rather rudely, at David's grandfather, the Reverend Elliot Brandon.

"Granddad." David gave a heartbroken little sob. He sat up straighter in his father's arm. "I crashed my bike and hurt my knee. Look." He held out his leg to show his grandfather a bright trickle of blood seeping from beneath the makeshift bandage. "I'm bleeding." He started to cry again.

Tyler tightened his arms around David's sturdy little body but the child resisted, squirming to be taken by his grandfather. It wasn't rational, he knew, that he should resent David wanting to be held by Elliot, but he did; damn it, he did. Elliot had always spoiled the youngster. With typical little-boy shrewdness, David probably hoped to postpone a scolding for his disobedience by playing on his grandfather's sympathies. That, or avoid it altogether. Tyler accepted the insight with his mind but not with his heart.

His heart felt only the wrench of his son's rejection, the cut of first a stranger's and then his father-in-law's insistence that he wasn't a fit guardian. A carelessly spoken word by a person he'd never seen before could be dismissed. But not Elliot's condemnation. Didn't he know how important it was for Tyler to reestablish his relationship with the boy? David belonged with his father. Didn't they all recognize that?

Sarah's hand on his arm cut off his angry bewildered train of thought. "David." She said the boy's name softly but her blue eyes met and locked with his. "Give your grandfather a hug, but then you'll have to come sit on a chair so that I can look at the cut on your knee."

She smiled at David, then looked back at Tyler. He could feel her willing him back from the dark corners of his mind where his thoughts had taken him. Sarah was asking, silently, for his cooperation. He wondered why it was so hard to give it. Elliot spoke again and the reason became very plain indeed.

"Give the boy to me." It was a command, not a request.

Tyler glared at Elliot, ignoring the demand. David started crying again.

Sarah had had enough. David was not going to suffer any longer while two stubborn men argued over his head.

"Tyler. Reverend Brandon." Both men turned at the sound of the unexpected command in her words. "It's important for David's leg to be treated as soon as possible." It was Sarah Austin, RN, who spoke and both men heard and accepted her authority.

"My apologies," Elliot Brandon said stiffly. "Of course, I want what's best for my grandson." Beneath the surface anger she saw pain and sorrow etched deeply into the older man's features. She wondered if it would ever be possible to heal the breech Allison's death had caused between these two proud men. If she should try, would she, too, be caught up in the bitterness? It was almost certain that she would.

"Tyler?" Sarah softened her tone but still neither man moved from where he stood, almost as though doing so would be an admission of defeat in their ongoing private war. It was the second stranger in the room who broke the impasse. He stepped forward and held out his arms. Sarah realized he must be Michael Parker, Elliot's assistant pastor.

"Come on, David. I'll carry you over to the chair. I've missed you. How've you been, sport?"

"Hi, Mike." David grinned through his tears. "I wrecked my bike racing down the hill. I hurt my knee," he repeated solemnly for effect. "Sarah says I might need stitches."

"Wow. Let me take a look." Mike was about the same age as Tyler Danielson, shorter, less broad in the shoulders, with honey-blond hair and laughing dark brown eyes. Sarah liked him on sight. He looked like a little boy, grown up in every way but his smile and his eyes. "Come on, Ty. Hand him over." He made his words seem like the ordinary, friend-of-the-family request they should be.

Sarah saw the muscles bunch in Tyler's forearms, knew he was considering telling his friend to go to hell; that he'd take care of David's injuries himself. She also saw him think better of the notion, saw the dark shadow of defeat touch his features for an instant as David held out his hands and Michael lifted him into his own strong arms.

Michael saw it, too. He gave Tyler a long level glance. "Don't you know 'almost' uncles are the best ones to call on for cut knees, Ty, old man? Good for sprained ankles, too, and broken collarbones. All life's little emergencies. Parents always faint, or cry, or otherwise get in the way. Don't they..." He hesitated, turning a thoroughly charming smile on Sarah. "I'm sorry, Ty hasn't introduced us."

Sarah wondered briefly if Michael was married. And if he wasn't how he'd stayed single so long with a smile like that. She smiled back. "I'm Sarah Austin. Camilla's great-niece."

"Pleased to meet you, Sarah Austin. I'm Michael Parker."

"Welcome to Mackinac, Reverend Parker." She inclined her head politely and motioned toward the oak pedestal table in the breakfast nook. "Over here, please."

"Look, let's get one thing straight. It's only Reverend Parker on Sundays and at weddings and funerals. I'm on vacation now so it's just Mike." He grimaced, glancing down as though reaffirming the subdued gray of his shirt and slacks. "I only wear the collar to get a discount on the bus." He didn't have little-boy eyes at all, Sarah decided suddenly. His words were casual but his eyes belied them. He was a man who had made a commitment to his God and to his fellow man. That would always be a part of him, she suspected, but his private life was his own.

"Thanks for offering to help, Mike."

"All in a day's work for 'almost' uncles. I've known this hell-raising, manipulative little brat since the day he was born." His voice sounded slightly hollow as he spoke the last words. He half glanced over his shoulder as if expecting some kind of response from Tyler, or perhaps from Elliot.

"I think you'd all better leave." Camilla spoke for the first time, diverting Sarah's attention as well as the men's. "Elliot, if you have anything to discuss with your son-in-law, it's best done in private." Sarah stared at her aunt openmouthed. It wasn't like Camilla to be so curt or abrasive.

"We don't have anything to discuss." Tyler's arms hung at his sides. He shoved his hands into his pockets and as he did so his hands balled into fists, pulling the soft, worn denim tight against his thighs. "David is my son. He stays with me."

"Legally he's still in my custody." Elliot Brandon looked remote and determined. "I'll take any steps necessary to get him back in court if you don't let me see him now, while we're on the island, Tyler."

"The hell you will." Tyler stepped forward menacingly. Sarah moved too, almost involuntarily, drawn forward by the waves of hostility radiating between the two men, ready to do whatever she could to avoid an all-out confrontation in front of David. Too many harsh words had been exchanged in the child's presence already. Those spoken unthinkingly in the past had caused him great anguish. She didn't intend to let the same thing happen again, not while he was under her roof.

Michael Parker spoke from behind her. "Ty, go home and cool down. I'll bring David over when Sarah is done working on his knee."

Tyler pivoted on the ball of his foot, half facing his friend. *Michael, the man he'd once believed might be David's true father.* Sarah felt the certainty of that conclusion course through her brain like a jolt of electricity. Had Michael Parker betrayed his best friend with Allison? She looked for something of Michael in David's tear-reddened eyes, the shape of his nose and mouth. She saw nothing.

"Damn it, Mike. Always the voice of reason." Tyler's tone was rueful. Michael sat David on a high-backed oak chair. Sarah hurried to place another to support his injured leg. She caught the tag end of Michael's grin as he stared up at Tyler's dark troubled face from where he knelt beside David on the floor.

"Always. Now get out of here. David's fine. Aren't you, sport?" No, Sarah decided suddenly and without any doubt. Michael Parker wasn't David's natural father. He wasn't a man to betray his friends, his God or himself, even if he'd loved Allison Danielson as much as he loved her son.

"Sure." David grinned back. It wasn't Michael's grin. It wasn't Tyler's or Ryan's or anyone's. And it was still adorable and, as always, hauntingly familiar. She couldn't deny that, but even teary and a little ragged around the edges, the smile was still unique to David. "I'm gettin' hungry, though."

All the heat and animosity seemed to drain out of Tyler as he gazed at his son. "How about a snack when Mike brings you home?"

"Swell, Dad. Tomato soup and a grilled-cheese sandwich," David announced with gusto. "I'm starved. And remember…"

"Make sure the butter is all the way out to the edge of the bread."

"Yeah. That's the way I like it."

"Coming up." Tyler turned and walked out of the cottage without a backward glance, ignoring Elliot Brandon as if he didn't exist.

"I'm going back down to the hotel." Elliot's voice was low and deep, soft with the accents of his native Georgia, smooth with the practice of half a lifetime of guiding his flock from the pulpit. He leaned over the back of David's chair to ruffle his hair with a big, strong-fingered hand. "You be a brave lad for Miss Austin."

"I will." David looked troubled. "Will I be able to go riding again, Sarah? I'm learning to ride horses, Granddad. Dad's teaching me, but the horses belong to Sarah."

"I'm afraid you're going to be out of the saddle for a few days at least, pardner." Sarah's heart turned over at the look of disappointment that settled over his face.

"That long?"

"You should have thought of that before you took off on your bike like a bat out of hell," Michael informed him bluntly.

David hung his head. "I know."

"I'll be by to visit you this evening and we'll think up some things to do until you're able to ride again." Elliot's voice was gruff with restrained emotion.

"I missed you, Granddad. I'm glad you came up here." David reached up to touch his grandfather's shoulder as if to reassure himself the man was really there. "It's a long way from Georgia." A thought evidently occurred to him. "Do you know where we live? It's just next door. A place called Lilac Time." He wrinkled his nose. "That's such a dumb name for a house."

"Lilacs are one of my favorite flowers." Elliot didn't look at Camilla but Sarah heard her aunt's quick indrawn breath. "I know where the cottage is. I've been there before. And I've been here, at the Gathering Place, before, too, but that was a very long time ago."

"I know," David said triumphantly. "That's when you met Aunt Cam, back in World War II." He may as well have said the Middle Ages. The look on Elliot Brandon's teak-brown face made the meeting seem like yesterday.

"Aunt Cam?" Elliot turned his head, looking at Sarah's aunt long and consideringly. Straightening to his full height, he smiled at her. Camilla didn't smile back. Her face retained its mask of stony calm, her hands clasped tightly in front of her. She didn't say a word. "I'm looking forward to talking about those days with…Camilla." His voice made the word almost a caress.

"Elliot, go, please." Camilla turned and fled up the stairs without another word.

The screen door slammed shut behind Elliot Brandon only seconds later.

"What the…blazes?" Michael curtailed whatever he'd been going to say when he glanced over to see David's avidly interested expression.

"I haven't the faintest idea," Sarah admitted with a determined look on her face. "But I'm sure as blazes going to find out just as soon as David's all patched up." As abruptly as everyone else, she disappeared through the swinging door into the kitchen in search of the first-aid kit.

"AUNT CAMILLA?" Sarah's whisper came from the doorway behind her.

The shadows were long and heavy across the wall of her bedroom. They moved like ripples of dark water over the cream-and-gold striped wallpaper as a steady breeze played among the branches of the maple tree outside the window. Camilla wondered if it was too late to pretend to be asleep. Her back was to the door; Sarah couldn't have seen her face. The chair she was sitting in, had been sitting in for so many hours, was a big old thing, high-backed, wide-armed, upholstered in a dreary dark green plush like the color of her thoughts.

"I brought you some tea and toast. It's getting late. You should eat something." Her great-niece had always been a stubborn little thing. Camilla smiled a little to herself.

"I'm not hungry, Sarah." Heaven knew that was the truth. Her stomach was so tied up in knots she couldn't even begin to think of food. "But thank you for remembering me." She wondered how much longer she'd be able to keep her past a secret from Sarah. Did she even want to anymore?

Except that it wasn't entirely a question of wanting. It wasn't that simple. Camilla's past sins affected Sarah's life, too. Deeply and forever. And she didn't want to contemplate more years of lonely half estrangement from someone she loved like a daughter.

"Are you ill?" Again, Camilla had to smile a little at the mother-hen tone in Sarah's voice.

"No. I've just got a rotten headache, that's all. Too much excitement today for an old lady like me."

"You're not old, Aunt Cam," Sarah said fiercely. Her voice was loud in the quiet room. The windows were open to the night air but the road outside the house was empty of traffic and none of the sounds of revelry from town carried this high up the bluff. Tonight Mackinac seemed to have returned to its past just as her thoughts were doing.

"I feel ancient." Camilla couldn't keep a hint of tears out of her voice. She'd always cried too easily. Sarah moved across the room and set the untouched tray firmly on the walnut dressing table against the wall. "I'm so glad you came to help me get this place set to rights. Have you any suggestions as to what we should do with the cottage?" She was grasping at straws, changing the subject, and they both knew it.

"I don't want to sell." Sarah went along with the switch of topic but Camilla knew it was a reprieve, not a victory.

"No. It's been in the family for too many years."

"Tyler and David must be making an early night of it. I see light in their bedroom windows." Sarah made a little conversational detour of her own. It couldn't be easy for her greatniece, either, this strange, stilted relationship they were trying so hard to maintain. Camilla knew it could never be right between them until she told Sarah all the truth. But not tonight. The ghosts were too close tonight, the ache in her heart too strong.

"I always liked to see lights in the windows at Lilac Time when I was a child. It was homey and comforting to know there were other people close by." Later, as a young woman, knowing who slept in one of those lighted rooms had been exciting for her, as well.

Camilla wondered if Elliot Brandon and Michael Parker were making an early night of it, too. She wished she had the courage to ask Sarah if they were staying at the Grand, as all her friends had used to do, or the Island House. Perhaps they were at the Iroquois? Camilla let her head rest against the back of the chair. The silence wove itself into its own patterns between them.

Sarah walked quietly across the big drafty bedroom with its heavy Eastlake-style furniture, her footsteps falling lightly on the creaky pine floor. Camilla heard her pull up the footstool that matched her chair. She opened her eyes. Sarah sat down, her expressive face shadowed with fatigue and anxiety, her blue eyes dark with compassion. "I wish you'd tell me what has upset you so."

"Ghosts," Camilla said obscurely and this time a tear seeped out and rolled down her cheek. She'd kept her secret so long, guarded it so well for so many years, that it should have been second nature to her now to hide her feelings. Usually it was, especially around Sarah. But not today. Today was different.

"Elliot Brandon is very far from being a ghost." Sarah's tone was crisp. She'd slipped into her professional role as care giver and didn't even know it, Camilla suspected. Perhaps it was easier for her niece to deal with pain from that slight distance. Camilla understood, or thought she did. How many years had she hid her longing for another child by being slightly flip and offhand about motherhood?

"Yes, he is very much alive, isn't he? I'm glad. I never knew if he'd survived the war... He's matured into a very handsome, dynamic man." Camilla couldn't keep the hint of possessive pride out of her voice. She hadn't thought of Elliot in years, not consciously, at least, but the moment she'd opened the door to his knock this afternoon, she'd known who he was. The shock of recognition had set her mind reeling into the past with all its hurtful memories.

Had it really been almost half a century? Impossible but true. So much of her life had been spent searching for the love she might have found with Elliot Brandon if she hadn't turned away from him after that long-ago summer. The revelation this afternoon had been instantaneous and devastating. She didn't think she was ever going to get over the shock.

"I wish you'd tell me about it, Aunt Cam." Sarah took a deep breath, waiting.

If she told Sarah the whole rather ordinary but still tragic story, would it bridge the distance between them? Or add to it? Sarah and her father were the only family Camilla had left. What if she lost them, too? The way she'd lost her baby, the way she'd lost Elliot's love and regard. "It was a long time ago. It shouldn't matter anymore," she answered, evasively. The words came out sounding hard and cold, like the lump of sorrow in her heart.

"It does matter. Your happiness matters to me and tonight you're very unhappy, we both know that." Sarah reached out and captured her hands. Camilla hadn't even realized she was twisting them together in her lap until the younger woman's comforting gesture.

"I've never told anybody about Elliot Brandon, Sarah." Camilla was pleading, begging almost. She was aware of it and for some reason didn't care. How could Sarah possibly know how difficult it was to find the right words after so many silent years?

"No one?" Sarah couldn't hide her dismay. They were both aware of it. "You never even confided in Grandmother?"

"No." Her sister had known she was pregnant. Helped make all the arrangements to give the baby a good home—with Justin Delano's help. But her feelings for Elliot Brandon had been her own. She'd never told anyone.

"I wish you'd tell me." Sarah got up, pacing the floor. She looked like her mother tonight, Camilla thought with a little start of surprise. Camilla had loved her niece by marriage. She'd promised her on her deathbed to look after Sarah. She'd failed in that trust, also.

"I ran away from Elliot Brandon just the way I ran away from you when you needed me, Sarah. It's as simple as that."

"You didn't run away from me, Aunt Cam." Sarah sounded confused.

"Yes, I did. I let you shoulder the responsibility of deciding what to do about your baby all alone. No. Worse yet, I let my sister bully you into doing what she thought best. The only difference with Elliot was that I made the decision myself.''

"Aunt Cam, I don't think I understand..."

Camilla looked down at her niece. "I'm getting things all mixed-up, aren't I? That's how my mind feels right now, all mixed-up. It's been such a long day." As if to counterpoint her words, the amplified sounds of a military bugle playing taps echoed over the bluff from the direction of the fort. "Ten o'clock already?" Camilla hoped Sarah would let the painful subject of the past fade away, like the sound of the recorded bugle notes on the quiet night air.

"Tell me, Aunt Cam," Sarah urged softly.

Camilla sighed and tried to order her thoughts. "I met Elliot here and fell in love with him the summer of 1942. He asked me to marry him before he went overseas. I said yes. Later I got cold feet and changed my mind." She was rushing her words a little and took a deep breath to steady her voice. "I wrote him a letter...just like in all those awful old World War II movies you see on the late show. A Dear John letter. Then I just disappeared out of his life. It was a cowardly, uncaring thing to do but I couldn't help myself."

"But that's only part of the story, isn't it?"

"Yes." Camilla wanted to cry and refused to do so. The sting of tears behind her eyes and in her throat was hot and painful. "I don't want to talk about it anymore."

"I understand." Sarah didn't sound as if she did, not really, but she didn't hesitate to say the words and Camilla loved her for her loyalty. "I still wish you'd tell me everything." Sarah's voice wasn't professionally distant any longer. She was on the verge of crying, too, Camilla could tell, although Sarah didn't allow her tears to fall, either.

"I never wanted to hurt Elliot. I never wanted to hurt you. I'm sorry I left you alone to face your father and my sister as I did. I promised your mother I'd look after you. I failed." It was funny how you thought that parts of your life were over, done with, dead and buried, Camilla thought. And then they resurrected themselves, in the middle of a bright June day, and your world turned upside down in a matter of hours.

"I'm old enough to understand now, Aunt Cam. I'm a woman, too. I won't judge you. I love you. Please tell me."

She was too tired to delve any deeper into memories so painful that even the edges of them hurt after so many years. She was too tired to sift through them any further in the privacy of her thoughts. "It's late." Camilla wanted and needed to be alone.

"All right. But you'll tell me soon?" Sarah's voice was gentle but very firm.

"Soon. Sarah, I promise I'll answer all your questions. But first I have to find some of the answers myself."

MICHAEL PARKER'S ROOM on the third floor of the Iroquois Hotel was high enough to see lights on the east bluff of the island. Yet there was only darkness where he thought the two cottages he'd visited today should be located. They were probably only hidden by the trees, he decided, turning away from the window, closing the wooden shutters that screened the view of the town and fort beyond. He left the window slightly ajar, listening to the rush of waves and the unfamiliar rhythmic clatter of horses' hooves on the street fronting the hotel.

The hotel was quietly luxurious, the walls thick and sound-deadening. He wondered if Elliot, in the room next door, was still awake. Was the older man pacing restlessly back and forth as he'd done for so many sleepless nights since Allison's death? Michael wanted to go to his friend, talk through the sorrow and anger that had kept Elliot at a distance for so many months, but he'd tried before and failed. Tonight would be no different.

He wanted Elliot to find the peace and acceptance his faith had provided him with in the past, the same faith and tranquillity of spirit he'd helped Michael himself to find when he'd dedicated his life to God and his fellow man. But even with the best intentions in the world, a man could only do so much to bring peace to another's soul. Elliot had to find his own way back.

Michael would do anything he could to help his friend and mentor come to terms with his sorrow for Allison and his animosity toward the man who'd caused her death. He intended to do his damnedest to try to bring about some kind of understanding between Elliot and Tyler, for their own sakes.

But mostly for David.

Sarah Austin wanted that, also. He'd realized that almost immediately while watching her. He saw the play of emotions across her expressive features this afternoon. She had an arresting face. Not beautiful, not even pretty in the usual sense of the word, but compelling nonetheless, with her thick wavy brown hair and fascinating blue eyes. It was almost as if... Michael shook his head, rubbing his hand across the back of his neck to loosen the tight muscles there.

He'd never seen Sarah Austin before in his life, as far as he knew. There was no use staying awake, teasing his memory, trying to come up with a time or place to satisfy the nagging sense of familiarity she'd saddled him with.

Still, she was part, now, of what had brought them all to the island: their love for David. A little boy's fragile happiness was the shining strand that bound them all together. He was a child they all loved: Allison, Tyler, Elliot, himself and now possibly Sarah.

David, the child they all loved, but who, in reality, belonged to none of them.

CHAPTER EIGHT

"I'M BORED," DAVID COMPLAINED peevishly. "How long do I have to hobble around with a stiff knee like this?"

"About a week," Sarah replied, unwinding the elastic bandage she'd put on him the day before.

"What am I supposed to do for a whole week?" he wailed. "We haven't even got a TV over there."

They were sitting in Sarah and Camilla's kitchen. Sarah had planned to go to Tyler's cottage to rebandage David's knee but fifteen minutes ago they'd shown up on the doorstep. Tyler looked a little frazzled. David, on the other hand, looked positively mutinous as he pulled himself up the back steps, refusing any help.

"Bad morning?" Sarah had asked conversationally.

"The worst," David's father admitted. "I ran out of ideas an hour before lunch."

Now Sarah was the one racking her brain for something to do. "You can always watch a movie on the VCR over here." David scowled at the suggestion. "I know, do you like jigsaw puzzles?" Sarah asked, applying salve to the edges of the laceration.

"No, I don't like sissy jigsaw puzzles."

"I do," Tyler said without thinking, as he watched Sarah's ministrations over the back of David's chair. The knee was red and swollen a little. He wondered if they should have it X-rayed. He wasn't sure what to do. Sarah had even had to ask Michael if David's tetanus booster was current when Tyler confessed he didn't know. Luckily, it was. Sarah caught his inquiring gaze and shook her head. She was smiling so he smiled back. "Okay?"

"This looks great." Tyler thought she looked great, too, in a pale lavender blouse and cream-colored slacks. Her hair was pulled up high on her head, held back by a couple of combs. She looked young and happy, only the slightest of blue shadows under her eyes betraying the tension that might still linger after a sleepless night.

"Are you kidding?" David asked, interrupting his wandering thoughts. "It looks gross, doesn't it, Dad?" His son squirmed around on the hard wooden chair in order to face him.

Once more, for only a moment, Tyler caught and held Sarah's sapphire-blue gaze. "It's going to be fine," she assured the child. A hint of mischief lightened her next words. "Of course a stitch here or there would make a lot prettier scar."

"Prettier scar?" David's tone was indignant.

Sarah looked up from replacing the gauze pad over the cut to find both Danielson men staring at her. She laughed, although Tyler's dark hooded gaze was as disturbing as always. "Sorry. Shoptalk."

"Scars aren't pretty." David was adamant. "I'd rather not have one." He looked at her as though she might be able to do something about it.

"No can do."

"Rats."

"If you don't like doctors and stitches and scars," Tyler began, unable to resist the opportunity for an object lesson.

"And shots," David interjected with a shudder.

"And shots. You'd better quit acting like Evel Knievel."

"Who's Evel Knievel?" David demanded, wrinkling up his nose at the unfamiliar name, derailing Tyler's lecture on obedience before he'd even got started on it.

"He's a professional daredevil," Sarah said with a remarkably straight face. Did Tyler remember their teasing conversation about David's penchant for rash behavior? "He tried to jump the Grand Canyon or something on a rocket-powered motorcycle."

"Did he make it?" David asked with more interest.

"I don't remember." Sarah frowned and shrugged, her face suffused with a tint of color.

"Did he make it, Dad?"

Tyler laughed. The laugh sounded rusty and out of practice but Sarah felt a tingle of excitement go through her just the same. "I don't remember, either, to tell you the truth, sport."

"I still never heard of him." David put a period to the subject. "Are you about finished?" he asked Sarah, pushing the long sleeves of his brand-new yellow Mackinac Island sweatshirt up to his elbows. Although it was a cool, overcast day, David had opted for denim shorts to save having to struggle in and out of jeans with his injured knee.

Tyler was still smiling faintly at his son. "Your age is showing, Tyler." Sarah couldn't resist the pointed rejoinder. He looked far more approachable today in a red and black checked flannel shirt and jeans, every inch the rugged voyageur she'd compared him to yesterday afternoon at the fort. Had David's accident only been twenty-four hours ago? So much had happened, it seemed much further in the past.

"Don't remind me," he growled, "living with this hellion is aging me by the minute." He frowned comically and ran his hand through the thick black waves of his hair. "I'll be as gray as Rip Van Winkle by Tuesday."

"That's better than being bald like our principal, Mr. Felson," David said.

Sarah couldn't think of anything to match that devastatingly candid remark.

Apparently neither could David's father.

Silence reigned in the big dark old kitchen for a minute or two while Sarah replaced supplies in the first-aid kit and tried not to break into a fit of giggles.

"I guess," David announced with a martyred sigh, "I could help you work on a jigsaw puzzle if there isn't anything else to do."

THE SOUND OF VOICES and laughter had been drifting up the stairs to Camilla's room for the past forty minutes. She'd tried to ignore them, tired and dispirited as she was from a long sleepless night. But Sarah's light caroling laughter beckoned. Tyler's more hesitant, deeper chuckles and David's shrill giggles piqued her curiosity, making her long to be included in their happy activity.

She was weary of her own company, yet afraid to face the questions that Sarah had every right to ask. She'd spent all her adult life running away from painful realities. It was very hard to change the habits of a lifetime in a matter of hours. Still, she could make a start, taking things one step at a time. Getting out of her too-quiet, lonely bedroom was a beginning.

Camilla moved to her dressing table and set about skillfully repairing the traces of tears and heartaches. She looked her age today, she discovered ruefully, and applied just a little more blusher than usual. In defiance of her sad thoughts, she dressed in a swingy flowered skirt and rose-pink blouse. As a gesture of bravado, she tied a matching pink scarf around the loosely pinned swirl of hair on her head. Taking one last look in the wavy mirror atop the walnut dresser next to the door, she was satisfied.

The world really hadn't stopped turning on its axis just because Elliot Brandon had walked back into her life after more than forty years. She might as well keep that fact in mind. With any luck she wouldn't have to see him alone; he had responsibilities to his church and his congregation. He couldn't stay on the island forever. She would wait him out. Everything would be all right.

Camilla made a sour little face at herself in the mirror. Of course, by all right, she meant everything would go back to being the way it had been before.

Halfway down the stairs that branched right and left into the main room of the cottage, Camilla realized the happy sounds of laughter and conversation from below had ceased. The change in the atmosphere was tangible. She knew what she would find—who she would find—even before she descended the last short angled flight. Elliot was standing just inside the door to the main room, glaring at his son-in-law. She almost turned and fled upstairs to the sanctuary of her lonely bedroom, but instead, made herself continue putting one foot in front of the other.

"Good afternoon, everyone." Camilla tried a smile, felt it stretch the corners of her mouth awry and gave up the attempt.

"Hi, Aunt Cam," David called from the porch where he was sitting on the wicker settee. The boy was propped up with pillows so that he could look down at the village with a small pair of opera glasses she and Sarah had unearthed from one of her sister's boxes of mementos.

"Feeling better?" Sarah asked. If her smile looked as stiff as her niece's, Camilla thought, she was better off without it. Unconsciously, Camilla squared her shoulders and moved into the big overfurnished room.

"Much. I'm afraid I'm guilty of being a terrible lazybones today." She directed an impartial smile at them all. This time it was easier. "I can't remember the last time I stayed in my room past luncheon." She couldn't keep on babbling inanities like a mindless fool. She shut her mouth with a snap. Then opened it again. Good manners insisted she acknowledge Elliot Brandon's presence.

"Good day, Elliot. I hope they gave you a comfortable room at your hotel?" She couldn't ignore him, she couldn't disappear in a puff of smoke like a magician's rabbit. Instead she smiled blindly and made small talk. Years of practice at playing the gracious hostess to her ex-husbands' European relatives and business associates made the ordinary pleasantry sound normal and unaffected.

"The Iroquois is a very good hotel. I slept like a rock. I assume Michael did, too. He's been out on his own exploring the island since breakfast."

"I'm glad you're comfortable." He had answered one of her questions, at least. She knew where he was staying, what part of town to avoid. The Iroquois was a lovely hotel, quietly elegant. Yet Elliot didn't look as if he'd spent any more restful a night than she had. The lines between his nose and mouth were etched deeply into his tanned skin. There were blue shadows under his gray eyes.

"I hope you slept well, also, Camilla." His accent was soft

and cultured, washing over her skin like a warm summer breeze. His gaze slipped over her, too, his eyes lingering an extra moment on her face. The look he gave her wasn't soft or warm; it was sharp, inquisitive, challenging. Camilla looked at the floor, unable to suffer the scrutiny without losing some of her hard-won composure. The silence stretched out a heartbeat too long before she raised her eyes to his.

"I always sleep well on the island." The lie came easily to her lips. "It's the cool night air, I believe."

"Undoubtedly." Were there still flecks of silver and ebony swimming in the irises of his gray eyes? Eyes whose sharpness hadn't faded with the passing of the years. She remembered the way he used to look at her and shivered. He was looking at her that way now. "But Sarah mentioned that you weren't feelin' well?"

"A touch of indigestion, that's all." He was still very quick to catch the faintest nuance of hidden meaning in a spoken word. She dismissed her sleepless night with an airy wave of her hand. Sunlight fractured on the surface of her diamond rings, dancing over the pine-paneled walls in rainbows of light.

"I see."

She was very much afraid that he did. Camilla walked out onto the porch, stealing a glance at Elliot's profile from the corner of her eye as she passed. He was a very dynamic man, a very sexy man, despite the fact that he was well into his sixties. Camilla wished he'd worn another dark suit and his clerical collar again today instead of the casual blue plaid shirt and gray slacks he had on. It was much easier to deny the fact that he still had the ability to make her breath catch in her throat and her heart speed up when he looked like a man of God—and not just a man.

"Granddad came to take me for a ride in his buggy," David piped up, resting the opera glasses on the windowsill as he focused on the livery-stable horse and buggy outside. "Dad doesn't think I should go."

Camilla didn't need David's forlorn little speech to explain the tension in the room. Tyler and Sarah had been seated at a folding table set up just inside the wide-open French doors that connected the big main room and the enclosed porch. Sunlight poured in, surrounding them all, covering the scattered pieces of jigsaw puzzle on the table with a tint of gold. David's father had risen stiffly at her entrance. He was still standing beside his chair, one hand on the back, the knuckles showing white beneath the skin. Elliot had his hands stuffed into the pockets of his slacks but the tendons on his forearms stood out below the rolled-up sleeves of his shirt, belying his nonchalance.

It was obvious that the two men were in disagreement about David. Suddenly Camilla was angry and impatient with both of them. David was trying very hard not to be frightened by the friction between the two people he loved most in the world but it had to be confusing and upsetting for the little boy.

Men. Camilla felt her ruthlessly buried maternal instinct forcing itself to the forefront. Sometimes they were such selfish, foolish creatures.

"I think a buggy ride is a lovely idea, David. We used to go for carriage rides around the island all the time when I was a girl."

"Come here and look at the neat red horse Granddad rented to pull it." He gestured out the window, pulling himself up by his elbows to look down onto the street at the base of the low stone wall surrounding the property.

"I'll take him for a ride if he wants to go." Tyler's tone was as stiff and unyielding as his body.

"I don't know..." David looked up at Camilla, bewilderment and confusion mirrored in his brown eyes. "Maybe I'd better just stay home. I don't want to make anyone mad," he whispered, looking to Camilla for help with his sad little quandary. "It's just that I haven't seen Granddad for weeks and," he finished in a defiant rush, "I'm bored stiffer than my knee."

Camilla hid a smile at the perfectly understandable aggravation in David's last remark. She turned slightly. Sarah had laid her hand on Tyler's arm. He moved as if to shrug it off, then thought better of it, reached down and gently laid her hand back on the table. Their eyes met and held for the space of several heartbeats. The stiffness and anger seemed to drain out of Tyler's stance and the expression on his dark, haunted face grew less fierce.

"You don't have to wait around for me to take you driving, sport. Your Granddad's here and all ready to go."

"You mean it, Dad?" Excitement replaced the confusion in David's eyes. He broke into a relieved lopsided grin. Camilla knew then why that smile had touched Sarah so. David looked like Tom Sawyer and Huck Finn all rolled into one small, sturdy package. His pleasure was infectious. "You come with us, too, Aunt Cam."

Camilla felt weak in the knees; her mind whirled in panic. She couldn't possibly spend that much time virtually alone with Elliot Brandon. "I...can't," she almost stuttered in her haste to voice the refusal.

"The fresh air will do you good," Sarah agreed, not helping matters at all.

"Please come with us, Camilla. We can talk over old times."

"No." She couldn't help the vehemence in her tone. One word was a small explosion of sound.

"All right," Elliot said smoothly. "David and I won't force you to accompany us." But his eyes held hers, filled with another challenge that Camilla was unwilling and unable to meet. She looked down at the painted wood floor under her feet. "But it would be a lot more fun for the boy. And for me, if we had a guide who knew the island as well as you do. Please say you'll reconsider and come along with us."

She was lost. Camilla raised her hazel eyes, bright with unshed tears. She'd never been able to refuse Elliot anything he asked when they were together all those years ago. She'd only acquired the courage to cut him out of her life when he was thousands of miles away. She hadn't gained much in strength of will even though decades had passed; he had lost none of his fascination for her. The mere sound of his voice still sent shivers cascading up and down her spine.

"Please, Camilla, come with us." Elliot held out his hand. He had included his grandson in the invitation each time he asked. It wasn't fair and he knew it. She didn't want to disappoint the child. If Elliot had said *come with me* she would have refused, immediately and adamantly. But he had not.

"I will, Elliot." It was all very simple, really; she didn't have any other choice.

FIFTEEN MINUTES LATER Sarah and Tyler watched the buggy and its three occupants move out of sight around the bend in the road that led toward Arch Rock and the southern side of the island. The silence stretched out between them. Tyler was staring out at the blue and gold glory of the June day, his back to the room and to her. Sarah stood by a fan-backed wicker chair, leaning her shoulder against its high rolled edge, watching him.

"You're going to have to get used to it, Tyler." Her voice was soft and full of understanding but her words were firm. How did you help someone so stubborn and hurting find acceptance for what he couldn't change?

"The hell I do." He ached with frustration. He wanted to punch something, lash out at everyone and everything that stood between him and David. "Elliot is David's rightful guardian until the courts say differently. I couldn't even bring him up here, legally, without Elliot's permission."

"Have you spoken to your lawyer about the matter?" Tyler wasn't interested in hearing the voice of reason, even when it was so pleasant a one as Sarah's.

"He thinks it would be better for all of us—"

"Better for David?"

"Yes. If we settle it amicably. Out of court. Damn it, he's right. But Elliot will never agree to my taking David out of the country. It's going to come down to a court battle anyway, so I might as well not waste the time and money to do it peacefully."

"Take David out of the country?" Sarah's voice was sharp with dismay she couldn't quite disguise.

Tyler swung away from the window. The back of his neck was stiff with tension. He rubbed his hand over the knotted muscles, trying to soothe away the ache with little success.

"I'm not a rich man, Sarah. I have to get back to work. I can't expect my firm to hold my job forever." He reached out, resting his left hand against the window frame at shoulder level. He shoved his right hand into the pocket of his slacks.

"You intend to go back to South America and take David with you?"

Tyler let the edges of a smile curve his mouth. "You make it sound like the dark side of the moon. Brazil's a beautiful country."

"I'm sure it is. I've always wanted to go there." Sarah blurted out the truth before she could stop herself. "I mean, I've always wanted to travel."

"Of course." Tyler looked at her over his shoulder for a long heart-stopping second, then went back to staring out the window. What would she say if he asked her to go to South America with him? Run away with him, live with him. Marry him?

"For David's sake you should try to come to some agreement..." Sarah moved away from the chair and picked up a piece of the neglected jigsaw puzzle, trying at random to fit it into the whole. She'd never allowed herself to think past the time they'd all be together on the island. She'd miss David, but far more thought-provoking was the utter certainty of how much more she'd miss his father.

"I'm not going to give David back to Elliot. Not even for a little while. He's my son." The words were sharp enough to cut.

Sarah didn't turn around. The pain in her heart was like a steel band wrapped around her chest. They were going to leave her, go back to their own lives, and she was angry at herself for caring too much too quickly. She was angry with Tyler for so easily shredding her hard-earned peace of mind. She was angry with fate for not allowing her to know for certain if David was her son. She looked down at the puzzle piece in her hand with tear-blinded eyes. If David wasn't Tyler's son he might, however slim the possibility, be hers. She had a right to know. She took a deep shaking breath, still with her back to Tyler. "The other night you told me you were certain David wasn't your child."

Tyler took three long steps across the porch. Grabbing her by the arm, he spun Sarah around. "Why did you say that?"

"I don't know," Sarah whispered, honestly bewildered. It had been a mistake to speak out. Tears pushed hotly at the corners of her eyes. She couldn't let them fall. "I'm sorry, I shouldn't have brought it up again."

"I don't *think* David isn't my natural son, Sarah, I'm almost positive he isn't."

Sarah realized she had hurt him and she was sorry. Why had she allowed her feelings to put her in such an untenable position? She couldn't confide her suspicions to Tyler. He wouldn't understand; he probably wouldn't believe her if he did. And worst of all, he'd never trust her again.

"I don't believe Allison was his mother, either, although I haven't any proof. He was a small baby; there aren't always any lasting physical changes in a woman's body. You're a nurse, you must know that."

Sarah nodded dumbly. His hands were strong and warm on the cold flesh of her arms. He held her tightly but not enough to cause her pain.

"Why are you asking me now, Sarah?" His dark eyes were wary, his body coiled to strike, to lash out at anyone or anything that stood between him and David.

"I don't like to hear you speak so callously of taking David away…" Sarah stood straighter. He could feel her muscles tighten beneath his hands as she squared her shoulders. He saw her breasts push against the soft cotton fabric of her blouse. Her chin came up. She looked lovely and determined and at the same time very sad and vulnerable. He wanted to pull her into his arms, stroke the soft shining waves of her hair, tell her everything would be all right from that moment on.

"You think I'm being unreasonable?" His voice was dark and dangerous. Sarah shivered but didn't back down.

"I think Elliot and Michael love him every bit as much as you do. I can see it, even if you can't."

"Sarah, you've never had a child. You can't understand how much it hurts to be separated, whatever the reason. I know I wasn't an ideal father to David before...before the accident but it's all going to be different now. If you've never had a child taken from you..."

Sarah wrenched away from his grasp. "But I have." The words came out like a hiss of steam, taking all her defenses with them. "But I have."

"Sarah?" She looked so fragile that a strong wind might blow her away. Tyler took her into his arms without a second thought.

"I had a child. I had to give him away." His arms were strong and warm and so comforting. She could tell him a little of what she believed in her heart and he'd never know what she suspected. "I gave my baby to someone like you and Allison. I have no idea who they were, no clue as to where he was taken. I can't be sure of his happiness, not today, not ever. But I can do something to make sure David is as happy as he can be."

Once more he sensed the strength within her but also the vulnerability. "Oh, Sarah, why didn't you tell me this before?" Tyler felt like kicking something, maybe himself. How many times had he ranted and raved in front of her, pouring out his anger and misery when she was hurting just as badly and keeping it all bottled up inside?

"I never tell anybody," she said simply. Yet she still ached to know the truth about David's parentage, the reality behind Tyler's doubts about Allison's pregnancy, the verifiable facts about David's birth. She couldn't stop relating what Tyler had already told her to her own experiences. She'd told herself over and over these last days that it was all only coincidence and conjecture. But still, she couldn't stop hoping and dreaming that David might be her son. "It's all over and done with," she said to remind herself as much as anything. "Over and done with." Tears slipped down her cheeks and dripped onto her hands. "I want David to be happy," she repeated, in a forlorn little voice.

"I never doubted that for a moment." Tyler's voice was

low and rough and warm. She liked to hear him use that tone. It made her feel desirable and cherished. It pushed the despair away. "Won't you tell me why you gave your baby away?"

"No."

"Sarah. You wouldn't let me shut myself away with my pain that night on the bluff stairs. Today I'm not going to let you do the same thing." He held her hands tightly between them. She could feel the slow steady thud of his heart against her palms. He meant what he said.

"It was the most expedient thing to do." She spoke so softly Tyler almost didn't catch the icy edge of betrayal hidden deep in her voice.

"Expedient?"

"Yes." Sarah swallowed a lump of bitterness that had lodged in her throat. "That was one of Grandmother's favorite words." But the bitterness included others, her father, Aunt Cam, Ryan and old Justin Delano who made all the arrangements, took care of all the details and covered all his tracks, leaving her with no clue as to her child's whereabouts.

"Tell me," Tyler ordered. She looked up into his dark concerned face and knew he had no intention of allowing her to turn away from him.

"It isn't a very original story. I was seventeen, unmarried and scared to death."

"The baby's father?"

"Seventeen and even more scared than I was. I haven't seen him in years."

"In other words, you didn't have any other choice." Tyler couldn't control the rough edge to his voice. "Damn it, Sarah. I'm more sorry than you'll ever know. But believe me when I tell you this. Wherever your baby is, if his adoptive parents love him one-tenth as much as I love David, he's one lucky little kid."

"I know he is." Again her voice was whisper soft, mist soft, but it sent a current of longing jolting through his body. Tyler leaned forward. She smelled sweet and clean like lemons and summer flowers all mixed together.

"What did you say, Sarah?" He lifted her chin with gentle

fingers. "Open your eyes." He fought the impulse to kiss the fragile, almost transparent skin of her eyelids, the curve of her cheekbone, the arch of her brow.

"No. I don't want to talk about it anymore. It's over and done with, just as I said. It can't be changed." He was relieved to hear a faint return of her usual spirit in the words.

"No more probing into the past, I promise. But, Sarah…" Tyler watched, intrigued, as she tilted her head in response to the hint of challenge he let seep into his words. "If you don't open your eyes right now I won't kiss you."

"What?" Sarah's eyes flew open. They were still bright with tears, like the deepest blue of Lake Michigan's waters, but with a trace of a smile in their depths. Tyler relaxed a little.

"You must want a kiss very badly."

"Don't be ridiculous." Sarah wrinkled her nose and sniffed in disdain. "I don't want a kiss. It's just impossible to stand around all day with my eyes closed, that's all."

"I see the matter differently."

"Oh, you do, do you?" Tyler reached up to circle her long slender neck with both hands. He could feel her pulse beat fast and light against his palm. He increased the pressure of his hands ever so slightly and felt the beat accelerate erratically. Gold-tipped lashes fluttered down onto her cheeks. She pulled her lower lip between her teeth and Tyler felt his own heartbeat quicken with a sudden rush of blood through his veins that tightened his muscles and burned its way into his brain.

"Your eyes are closed again."

"I know." She opened them, staring boldly into his. Her arms moved to rest on his shoulders. Her lips were smiling but her eyes were apprehensive and still a little sad. "You tricked me."

He pulled her close, wishing he could find the right words to make her forget all the painful memories, wishing he could find the words to give both of them that blessed oblivion. He couldn't, so he went on talking in the light teasing way she seemed to enjoy. "Did not."

"Did, too." Sarah's voice caught on the words. She faltered and swallowed hard as he pulled her close against his aching, hardening body.

"Did not." He lowered his mouth to hers before she could voice another protest. She didn't pull away. She melted against him with a sigh that went straight to his heart and lodged there like a small sleek arrow of pleasure.

"You're a very special woman, Sarah Austin," Tyler said when the kiss ended. Now wasn't the time for any rash statements of eternal devotion. She was too vulnerable and he was too unsure of himself, of his ability to accept the responsibility of another's happiness. "Everything will work itself out for the best. Everything."

Tyler was falling in love with her. Sarah knew it. She could see it in his eyes, his posture; feel it in the way he held her in his arms. It was an intoxicating, frightening realization. He was no more ready to believe in happily ever after than she was. This was apparent, too, in his uncertainty and reluctance to acknowledge his feelings openly. "I want to take this one day at a time."

"Sound advice." Tyler smiled reluctantly, then frowned. "Sarah..."

"Shh, don't try to explain how you feel. I'm mixed up, too."

"I don't think I can explain right now," Tyler admitted with resignation. "But we're not kids rushing to meet the future. We know even love can wait until tomorrow."

"You're a very special man, Tyler Danielson." She stood on tiptoe to kiss his beard-roughened cheek.

He pulled her close once more, then set her firmly away. "I think I'd better go before I forget my own good intentions." He still held her hands, refusing to let her go entirely.

"I think you should go, too." She smiled at him again. "I'll send Elliot over with David when they get back. Try to be civil."

"I promise." He would try, she knew. He had integrity and strength of purpose, despite past errors in judgment. He'd come to terms with Elliot's role in David's life.

Tyler looked down at their joined hands, then up to catch her eyes, holding her blue gaze captive. "If there's anything I can do to help you find..." He left the rest of the sentence unspoken.

Sarah took a deep breath. "Oh, Tyler." She was quiet a moment longer, trying and failing to keep a tiny quaver from creeping into her words. "I've followed every lead there was. My baby is gone. But, Tyler, I thank you with all my heart for offering your help."

He couldn't know how much it meant to her that he had made the gesture. She already loved David, his son by heart-bond, if not by blood. And now she was very much afraid she was falling in love with Tyler, as well.

CHAPTER NINE

"ARE YOU GOING OUT DRIVING with Elliot again this afternoon?" Sarah couldn't keep herself from asking the question.

"You're sounding more and more like your grandmother these days," Camilla replied with a smile that took most of the sting from her words. She brushed at toast crumbs that had fallen onto the leg of her beige slacks. She was wearing them with a man-styled forest green shirt belted at the waist. She looked comfortable, sophisticated and happy.

"I'm beginning to look like her, too," Sarah retorted, with a self-mocking smile. "Especially in this old kimono of hers."

"It suits you, my dear," Camilla said with an approving nod. "Makes you look slightly mysterious and exotic. Turquoise is a good color for you."

"Frankly, I don't know why I even wasted my breath asking about your plans," Sarah continued, taking her aunt's lighthearted reprimand as permission to pursue the subject. "You two have been together every afternoon for the last three days."

The two women were sharing a late morning cup of coffee on the veranda. Sarah had finally begun going through the box of her mother's things the evening before, but she was making small progress. The weather had been glorious, far too beautiful to spend time indoors, or to spend time in the past when the present was so inviting, the future so full of possibilities. The days were warm and breezy, the nights cool and still. She'd spent a lot of time with Tyler, helping him as he worked around the cottage, talking about everything and nothing, laughing, sharing long comfortable silences and kisses that warmed her heart more readily than the bright June sun.

"I'm doing what I can to help make things as easy as possible for David." Camilla wasn't teasing anymore. She set her china cup down on the glass tabletop with a chiming ring that emphasized her words. Blue eyes and hazel met and held across the width of the table. The look they exchanged was full of age-old feminine wisdom.

"I know…" Sarah didn't complete the sentence. After all, Camilla's personal life was her own business.

"Tyler seems to accept Elliot spending time with David far more readily if I'm along." Camilla stared at her hands, clasped lightly in her lap.

"That really isn't the point of this conversation, is it?" Camilla fidgeted with her belt. Sarah took a deep breath and went on speaking. "I appreciate what you're doing for all of them, but…" She was finding it hard to put her misgivings into words. Her aunt saved her the effort.

"But is it wise to spend this much time with a man who had me acting like a basket case a mere seventy-two hours ago?"

"Well," Sarah said and smiled a bit sheepishly. "I meant to phrase it a bit more diplomatically. But since you brought the subject up, yes, I am worried about you."

"Thank you, Sarah, dear." Camilla rose from the settee with her usual elegant grace. She patted Sarah on her silk-covered shoulder as she passed. "Let's just say I'm holding my own and leave it at that, okay?"

Camilla looked much more like her old—or did Sarah mean young?—self today. Her eyes were clear and sparkling and the bruised-looking shadows underneath had faded away. There was a delicate peachy blush on her cheeks that Sarah didn't think had come from Camilla's cosmetic table. She looked very much like a woman on the verge of falling in love…with a man who, once upon a time, she'd felt she couldn't marry at all…for reasons she still refused to reveal even after forty-five years.

Sarah frowned down into her half-empty cup of cold coffee. She knew as well as anybody that times changed and circumstances changed. Only in Camilla's case, she was more than

a little afraid those old issues were still alive. Perhaps they'd
been buried under the weight of years, but they were still
strong enough, immediate enough, even after all this time, to
cause her aunt a great deal of pain.

"And what about you, Sarah?" Camilla had been staring
out the screen door but now she turned to face her niece,
catching Sarah off guard, jolting her out of her thoughts.

"I'm holding my own, too, Aunt Cam."

Camilla wasn't about to be put off by having her words
deflected back at her. "You've been spending as much time
with Tyler as I have with Elliot and David."

"I'm aware of that." Sarah set her cup down. Pulling her
knees up to her chin, she smoothed the skirt of the heavily
embroidered dressing gown over her legs until only the toes
of her bare feet peeked out over the edge of the wicker chair
seat.

"I don't want you to be hurt, Sarah."

"I know that." Sarah rested her chin on her knees, following with her gaze the line on the horizon where the blue-green
waters of the straits met the even more brilliant blue of the
sky. She'd spent a lot of years avoiding being hurt, protecting
her emotions, sidestepping any kind of relationship that involved giving more of herself than mere friendship required.
It was a safe, but selfish, way to live. Her soul was beginning
to shrivel up inside her.

"Sarah? Why do you still believe David is the child you
gave away? Have you discovered some definite proof?" Camilla surprised her with the directness of her question. They
hadn't spoken of the matter for some time. The older woman's
voice was tight with strain. "Or is it only that you see Ryan
McKenzie in his smile still?"

"No." Sarah lowered her voice. "I don't see Ryan in his
smile anymore, Aunt Cam. And you're right, I don't have a
lot of proof, either, but in my heart..." She shrugged helplessly. Sarah wasn't sure how much of Tyler's confidences to
disclose.

"Sarah, there must be something more."

Sarah made her decision. "David isn't Tyler's son."

"I see." Sarah could hear the rustle of her aunt's clothing as she turned from the doorway to stare at her niece. Camilla didn't ask for details to flesh out Sarah's last terse statement and Sarah was grateful for the forbearance. "So, you've made your own deductions about Allison Danielson not being his mother?"

"Yes." Sarah's voice sounded unnaturally harsh even to her own ears.

"Is there any way you can prove it?" Camilla's question was unexpectedly gentle.

"Not conclusively." Sarah didn't want to think of the overwhelming odds against her ever finding proof of her child's identity—David's identity.

"Everyone who knew where your baby might be today is dead: my sister, Justin Delano, even, if what you say is true, Tyler Danielson's wife. You do have to accept those facts."

"But what I have discovered so far all adds up," Sarah said, unable to contain all her hope and excitement. "My baby was born at the private clinic Grandmother chose for me in Chicago. Allison's baby was born at a private clinic in Chicago, also. While Tyler was out of the country." Sarah kept her voice level and as unemotional as possible. "He can't remember the name of the institution but he said Allison was staying with Justin Delano at the time. Is it such a leap in logic for me to believe Allison and the woman who took my baby are one and the same?"

"No, I don't think so," Camilla was forced to agree reluctantly. She'd moved to stand behind Sarah. She couldn't see her aunt's face but felt her comforting nearness and was thankful for it. "My sister and Justin lived in the same neighborhood, attended the same church, moved in the same social circles. No, that isn't too farfetched an assumption." She halted a moment, as though gathering her own arguments. "What you haven't told me, though, is why you believe David isn't Allison's child any more than he is Tyler's?"

She should have known Camilla would ask that question. What was the best way to answer it? "Tyler believes Allison never gave birth to a child of her own. He doesn't know any details, doesn't have any proof. But it was that they were arguing about the night…Allison died.''

Camilla's breath hissed through her teeth. ''I see. Poor Allison. I imagine that would account, in part, for their unhappy marriage. Keeping secrets from loved ones is always very hard to do. How sad for all of them. Elliot loved her so very much.'' The last words were almost a whisper, spoken more for her own benefit than for Sarah's.

Sarah didn't want to feel sympathy for the dead woman but she couldn't seem to help herself. Allison's life had evidently been so full of fears and anxieties that she'd tried, desperately and with tragic consequences, to create a more happy and secure world for herself on a foundation of lies and fantasies.

''Yes, poor Allison,'' Sarah whispered.

''Sarah.'' Camilla hesitated, as if choosing her words very carefully. ''Your deductions may or may not be correct so far. But if memory serves, your baby was born on January sixth. David told me, just yesterday, that his birthday is January nineteenth. How do you account for the difference?''

January nineteenth. Somehow she'd never found the courage to bring the subject up in conversation, to ask David, or Tyler, outright what his birth date was. She hugged her arms more tightly around her knees, crushing the folds of cold heavy silk beneath her fingertips. She squeezed her eyes tightly shut against a painful rush of tears.

''January nineteenth is the day Justin took my son away from the clinic. I know because I was still a patient there. I was very run-down and depressed after the baby was born. The doctors recommended I stay. Grandmother agreed. That day I disobeyed the doctors, Grandmother and Justin. I went to the nursery and saw my baby.'' It had been the only time; and then only from across the room, and only for a moment before a vigilant nurse had spotted her and escorted her back to her room in another wing of the hospital. ''He was dressed in a little blue outfit. One of the nurses was putting a hat on his head, wrapping him in a big fleecy white blanket…''

''Sarah.'' Camilla let her hands rest lightly, consolingly on Sarah's shoulders.

"That's probably also the day the birth certificate disappeared from the clinic's business office. When I hired the private detective, he told me they don't file birth certificates with the authorities on a daily basis in a small hospital like that. Sometimes only once a week or so, if that often. Justin Delano was a very important, powerful man in a city where political clout can make a lot more than an unregistered birth certificate disappear. He could have had the original destroyed easily."

"He was probably doing what he thought was best for all of us." Camilla spoke so quietly, Sarah might not have heard her if she hadn't been standing nearby.

"Then you agree it might have happened as I've told you?" Sarah turned her head, lifting her hand to cover Camilla's where it still rested on her shoulder. They hadn't touched, except casually, for many years. For a moment Camilla's hand stiffened beneath her own. Then she turned it palm upward to grasp Sarah's fingers in a tight grip. Camilla was staring into the middle distance as though she'd seen a ghost, her thoughts caught up in the memory of some time and place only she could see.

"I believe it's possible, Sarah. But we have to admit that it's also unlikely. I'm sorry to hurt you, but the odds against David..." Camilla's attention was once again focused on her niece.

"I know. But it's still what I believe happened to my baby. There isn't any way I can ever know for certain, I suppose." Sarah gave a little sigh, half defiant, half sad. "It's all so complicated and so impossible to sort out. In my heart I know everything I've told you is the truth. But there isn't any way I can prove it, just as you've said. That's why I'll never say anything to Tyler. Or to David. No matter how much I've come to love them both."

"HI, SARAH." David was enthroned on a metal glider covered in a brilliant red, blue and purple paisley print. The glider sat in the side yard of Tyler's cottage beneath a lacy fretwork trellis that looked like the old-fashioned red climbing rose growing over it was the only thing still holding it upright. The boy had a plastic bucket of water by his side and a high-powered water pistol in his hand, which he was using to shoot the puffy white heads off dandelions going to seed.

"Watch this," he boasted, taking aim at a nearby plant. It exploded into a satisfying swirl of wet fluff. "Bull's-eye."

"Not bad shootin', pardner." Michael Parker was stretched out on the grass in front of the glider, his back to Sarah. He rolled over onto his stomach to bid her good day.

"Hello, Michael." Sarah wondered if she was blushing and felt like a fool. She really wasn't in the mood to make small talk; the unsettling conversation she'd shared with Camilla that morning was still too fresh in her mind. What if she said something now that would bring her suspicions about David into the open without meaning to?

"Did you come to help poor old Ty, or are you going to be a sidewalk supervisor like my pardner and me?" Michael was wearing baggy shorts in a boisterous Hawaiian print, running shoes and a white tank top that set off his tan and accented the width of his shoulders. His shorts, mostly green and yellow, clashed horribly with the paisley print on the glider. Sarah tried very hard to hide her smile as she stared at the kaleidoscopic contrast of colors.

"I could use some help, Sarah," Tyler called down by way of a greeting. She was smiling, he noticed, as she shielded her eyes from the dazzle of sunlight slicing through the trees. She spotted him and waved. He was balanced on the very top of Mr. Meecham's brand-new aluminum extension ladder, scraping old leaves and pine needles out of the eaves trough.

"I have a terrible fear of heights," she said, shaking her head so hard her hair swung forward along her cheeks. "You be careful up there." The warning slipped out before she could stop herself. Tyler grinned and wiped the back of his hand across his brow, leaving a smudge of dirt on his forehead. She looked cool and comfortable in a pale pink sundress and strappy rope-soled sandals, her hair hanging loose and free, catching stray winks of sunlight in its auburn depths.

"That's not what David's been telling me," Michael broke

in. "According to his account, you've got a great future as a trapeze artist in the circus."

"David has been known to exaggerate on occasion," Sarah reminded him dryly.

"Like about every other time he opens his mouth," Tyler added from his perch on the ladder.

"What does exaggerate mean?" David asked suspiciously, one eye closed against the sun as he looked to Michael for enlightenment.

"Stretching the truth," Michael informed him.

"Lying? I don't lie." David was adamant. "It's a sin, you know that," he added with a self-righteous look on his face.

"Adding extra details to make the truth more interesting is what he means, I think. Right, Michael?" Sarah prompted.

"Umm. She's right, pardner."

"I do like to make things interesting," David said, subsiding against the cushion of the glider with a pained look on his face when Michael and Sarah both burst out laughing.

"Peacemaker," Michael teased, with a grin.

Sarah laughed again. Tyler caught the echo of her laughter carried by the breeze as he gathered up his tools and prepared to descend the ladder. He thought he'd carry the memory of her laughter with him forever and realized suddenly that he didn't want just memories of Sarah to cherish. He wanted the woman herself in his life.

"What am I missing?" he asked, walking over to them.

His jeans were old and faded from dozens of washings. They fit his lean rangy body without a wrinkle. He'd rolled the sleeves of his thin green plaid cotton shirt high above his elbows. The day was warm and he'd left the garment unbuttoned halfway down his chest. Sarah found herself remembering what it felt like to be held against him and closed her eyes briefly against the wave of awakening desire that washed over her. "I was just telling Michael I learned my lesson that day in the hayloft, even if Master Danielson here didn't." She hoped her tone of voice was more normal than the unusually erotic train of her thoughts. "From now on, I never fly without a net."

"You must be talking about Dad," David piped up innocently. "He caught you that day. Is he going to be your net from now on?"

"I can think of worse occupations." Michael's quip kept the silence from stretching out too long. Tyler stared down at the wire brush in his hand. Sarah didn't know where to look.

"It wouldn't be too bad," David said consideringly. "How much do you weigh, Sarah?"

She laughed and shook her head, grateful for his devastating little-boy candor. "That is a question, young man, that you'd better learn never to ask a lady."

"Why?" David looked genuinely puzzled. "You aren't fat. Is she, Dad? I'd never ask you that if you were big and fat. It's not polite, is it?"

"No, sport, it isn't." Tyler cleared his throat, his words sounding choked with hidden laughter.

"Watch." David took aim at another dandelion head, satisfied that he'd made his point.

"Are you going cycling?" Michael had risen from his lounging position in the grass, brushing bits and pieces of twigs and leaves from his shorts as he did so.

"As a matter of fact, I'm on my way to the post office to pick up our mail. It's quicker to use the bluff stairs and walk." She didn't want Tyler to think she'd dropped by just to see what he and David were up to, although she had.

"Mind if I come with you?" Michael asked. "I promised my pardner here I'd get him some real food down in the village."

"I'm starved," David announced. "Dad can't cook anything but eggs."

"Hey." Tyler sounded more aggrieved than angry. "I'm getting pretty good at grilled-cheese sandwiches, don't forget."

"I want pizza."

"Sarah can show me the best place to buy pizza." Michael smiled again. "If it isn't too inconvenient?"

Sarah smiled back. "I'd be happy to."

"I wish I could come along." David sighed loudly to add more impact to his already broad hint.

"Let's not try such a long walk your first day back on your feet," Sarah cautioned.

"How does my knee look?" Diverted, David stuck out his leg to give Sarah a better view of the new scar.

"Looks fine. Just don't get too rowdy for another day or so, okay?"

"I'd still like to come with you. Mike could give me a ride on his back."

Michael held up his hand in self-defense. "Down those steps? No way."

"Well then..." David put his chin in his hand, trying to devise another plan.

"Be patient today and if the weather cooperates, I'll take you swimming in the pool at the Grand Hotel tomorrow." Sarah glanced at Tyler for permission. "If your father agrees."

"I thought perhaps we might rent a boat and go sailing tomorrow, sport."

"Swimming!" David yelled. "I saw that pool when I was out riding with Granddad and Aunt Cam. It's radical, all squiggly like a snake." He made swimming motions through the air with his hands.

"That sounds great. Mind if I invite myself along?" Michael asked, resting both hands on the back of David's glider.

"The more the merrier." Tyler would rather have had Sarah all to himself but he didn't say so.

"That's what I always say." Michael looked at Tyler, then at Sarah. "Are you ready, Miss Sarah?" he asked with an exaggerated bow and flourish of his hand toward the bluff stairs.

"Thank you, kind sir." Sarah batted her eyelashes in a terrible imitation of some remembered silent film star. The cannon went off at the fort, rattling the windowpanes on the porch and startling them all.

"Wow! Kaboom!" David added his own sound effects to the ones provided for the tourists.

"Ma'am." Michael offered his arm with another courtly bow.

"I ought to warn you, Sarah," Tyler said, watching them with just a shadow of a frown between his thick dark brows. "Mike suffers from the delusion of thinking he's Rhett Butler come back to life."

"Frankly, my dear, I don't give a darn what Tyler thinks," Michael misquoted in a drawl so thick that Sarah could barely understand him.

"Don't worry, Tyler." She looked him straight in the eye, instantly losing her bravado and the thread of her thoughts.

"Yes, Sarah?" He took a step toward her, his voice low and dark, challenging and exciting.

"I...I'm not Scarlett O'Hara," she said breathlessly, taking Michael's arm to steady herself.

"And anyway, Ty, old pal, you know the ladies generally compare me to Robert Redford, not Clark Gable."

"That's right. I forgot." Tyler waved him off.

"Don't forget my pizza," David reminded them loudly. "And no onions or little fishes on it, either."

"Yes, sir." Michael gave a half salute from across the gravel road. Sarah looked back once from the top of the bluff then turned and started down the steps.

"I wish Mike had gone to get the pizza and left Sarah here with us." David swung his legs over the side of the glider, testing his healing knee by swinging his foot up and down, back and forth. "Michael has too many girlfriends back home already."

"He does?" Tyler sounded skeptical. David was still frowning. He looked as forlorn and deserted as Tyler felt.

"Well, one or two, anyway. I guess I exaggerated a little," David admitted, preparing to reload his water pistol. "Sarah is our friend. I wanted her to stay with us, not go off with Mike. Why didn't you ask her to stay with us, Dad?" He turned his head to look up at Tyler, who was still standing behind the glider.

"I wish I had, sport." He leaned both forearms on the rolled metal back of the swing, looking at the spot where Sarah and Michael had disappeared. "I wish I had."

"I THINK I RUFFLED old Ty's feathers up there," Michael announced as they left the stairway and started down the steep narrow little street alongside St. Anne's Church.

"It doesn't take much sometimes," Sarah said before she could consider how revealing the statement sounded. "I mean..."

Michael stuck his hands in his pockets and sidestepped several elderly, blue-haired ladies on their way into the church's museum. "It's better than seeing him sit there day after day like some kind of mindless robot. Anger at least is a healthy sign." He grinned over at her roguishly. "Sorry, that's the psych major in me coming out. He's had a rough couple of years."

"I know," Sarah said very softly. "He's told me." She looked at Michael and knew intuitively that he read a great deal of meaning into her words. "You're Elliot's associate?" The question came out sounding loud and abrupt.

"Elliot is the reason I entered the ministry," Michael said matter-of-factly. "Religion wasn't too fashionable in the seventies so I got my degree in psychology. That's where I met Ty, by the way. I went up north to school. University of Michigan. But when I got back home...well, God called me and I answered."

"You've known Elliot Brandon all your life?" She left Allison's name unspoken, but Michael answered as if she had not.

"Since I was five and my parents moved to Columbus and joined St. Matthew's. Allison and I went to school together. I introduced her to Tyler."

"So you feel responsible for David, too?"

"You're a very savvy lady. Yes, I do. That's why I'm here with Elliot, I guess. Luckily St. Matthew's sponsors a two-week retreat and old-fashioned tent-meeting series every summer. The visiting evangelist also takes over the pulpit, so I could make the trip up here. Maybe pour some oil on troubled waters." He shrugged. "I'm playing it by ear."

"I see." Sarah wasn't sure exactly what else to say. She made the heavy pedestrian traffic on the sidewalk her excuse not to continue the discussion. They walked in silence until they'd passed Marquette Park and angled across Fort Street. The post office was on Market Street. Sarah picked up her aunt's mail and slipped it into the pocket of her skirt. The street outside was crowded and noisy as always on a sunny afternoon at the height of the tourist season. They walked back through the narrow landscaped oasis of City Park and emerged once more into the noise and bustle of Huron Street.

Michael came to a halt in front of a display of candy in a shop window. "You don't think..." He glanced over at Sarah, looking just exactly like any ten-year-old male in the same circumstances.

"No," Sarah said, taking his arm and steering him toward the bar and deli that made the best pizza on the island. "My figure can't stand any more samplings."

"Just one slice of the chocolate peanut butter. Or how about some peanut brittle or saltwater taffy? David..." Michael gave it one last shot.

"David's energy level is just about more than we can handle as it is."

"Yeah," Michael admitted. "But the smell is driving me crazy."

"Why do you think every fudge shop on Mackinac has an exhaust fan blowing onto the street? The natives even call the tourists 'fudgies.' They're easy to spot."

"How can you tell?" Michael asking obligingly.

"They're usually found standing in front of a fudge-shop window with the same glassy-eyed stare you're wearing."

"I can even smell it at night, up in my hotel room, if the wind is right." He looked over his shoulder with melodramatic longing but allowed Sarah to lead him away from the window.

She laughed, lifting her hand to her lips when heads turned to stare in her direction. "I can see where David gets his flair for the dramatic." Sarah stopped laughing.

Michael saw the change come over her, the look of indecision, and realized he'd been staring. She was probably wondering if she'd grown horns, or wings, or something. He
couldn't help it. It had hit him again, out of a clear blue sky,
that feeling of knowing, somewhere, he'd seen this woman
before.

"I'm sorry, Michael. Did I say something wrong?"

He pulled himself together. "No, of course not. Whatever
made you think that?" He started walking again, taking her
arm, tugging her out of the way of a group boarding a tour
wagon at the curb. He held open the screen door of the restaurant she indicated. "Outside of onions and little fishes, how
do you want your pizza?"

"Any way you like." Sarah gave him the best smile she
could manage. She'd been thinking of Tyler's admission that
at one time he'd suspected Michael of being David's father
and she'd let that guilty knowledge color her interpretation of
Michael's reaction to her innocent observation. She had to stop
letting her inner turmoil become apparent to those around her.

"I'll surprise you." Michael squeezed them into a small
table near the window. "How about something to drink while
we're waiting?"

"Anything as long as it comes in a frosted mug." Sarah
propped her elbows on the cool surface of the butcher-block
table and rested her chin on her hands, watching Michael walk
away from her into the crowd around the bar.

She couldn't see any easy way out of the situation she'd
gotten herself into. She had no concrete answers to the questions that had become so important to her since she'd met
David and his father. And worst of all, she was falling in love
with Tyler Danielson. How would the secrets she kept locked
in her heart affect their relationship? Was loving someone
worth the risk, the responsibility for all their happiness? She
thought that perhaps, if she was lucky, it just might be.

Michael made his way through the crowded, noisy tables
toward the window. He held two foamy mugs of beer high
above his head. Suddenly he stopped, almost tripping over a

harried waitress with a loaded tray of plates and mugs. She frowned. He smiled, mumbling an absent apology.

Sarah was sitting quietly where he'd left her, staring out the window with a sad pensive look on her face. Suddenly he knew where he'd seen her before. She'd been a girl then. She was a woman now, but the face was the same.

Thank God she'd never seen him that day nine years ago. She had been too wrapped up in her observation of the newborn in the clinic nursery. A baby boy.

The child Allison had named David Brandon when he was placed in her arms only a few minutes after the distraught young woman who'd given birth to him had been hustled away from the nursery.

Sarah was David's mother.

For all these years he'd kept Allison's secret because he loved her and was her friend as well as her spiritual adviser. After her death he'd thought her secret was safe with him forever, that his evasions and half-truths would be a thing of the past. Now he knew he'd been wrong. He was going to have to go on lying: to Tyler, to Elliot, to Sarah if she should learn the truth. All to protect the well-intentioned tissue of lies surrounding Allison's son.

CHAPTER TEN

"HI." TYLER HAD HIS HAND lifted to knock on the frame of the screen door. It wasn't necessary. Sarah was sitting curled into the corner of the settee, the box of her mother's mementos at her side. She had on a blue oxford-cloth shirt and a long-sleeved pullover sweater of a heathery darker blue that, even from across the room, enhanced and amplified the blue of her eyes.

"Hi, yourself. Come on in." Her voice was low and inviting. She waved him toward a chair.

Tyler hesitated when he saw the papers and photo albums scattered across the table. "Am I interrupting you?" Blue and white argyle socks peeked out below the hem of her jeans. Her shoes were on the floor in front of her, kicked off, no doubt, when she'd curled her legs under her. A small electric heater purred comfortably in a corner, its warm breath counteracting the chill and damp lingering on in the old house after three days of wind and rain.

"No. I still haven't really gotten started going through this box of my mother's things. Actually I'm just enjoying the sunshine." It had turned cold and cloudy late in the day after they'd taken David to swim in the Grand's pool. It had started to rain that evening and continued all weekend. Today it was still cool but the sun was shining bright and hot in sheltered spots.

"Makes Monday morning a lot easier to face when it isn't raining."

"It does." Sarah sighed and dropped what appeared to be several programs from old high-school football games onto the table. "My father's a very methodical man. He put the most recent things on top. The deeper I dig, the harder it is to put names and faces to the pictures, to decide whether or not to keep something. I think I'll wait till this winter and take everything down to the Keys with me.''

''The Keys?''

''Dad's retired from the Air Force. He's got a charter boat he runs out of Key West,'' Sarah explained.

''Sounds like a great place to retire,'' Tyler admitted.

''He thinks so. He grew a beard and all the tourists think he looks like Ernest Hemingway.'' Sarah fanned out the old football programs and stared at them, undecided as to their fate.

''Is this the way you want to spend the first nice afternoon we've had in days?''

Sarah looked up, intrigued by the low rough edge to his words. There were no shadows, no anger or pain darkening his midnight-blue eyes. What she did see reflected there upset her even more—no, not upset her—excited her. ''If I'd taken care of this when the weather wasn't nice, I wouldn't be in this predicament now.''

''We're alone today, or hadn't you noticed?'' Tyler asked.

''Alone?'' Sarah scooped up the football programs, hesitated, then dropped them into the box.

Tyler watched her, stood and moved across the room. He shifted the box away from the settee and sat down beside her. The hard-muscled length of his denim-clad thigh brushed against the bottom of her foot. Sensation flooded her. Sarah scooted a fraction of an inch farther into the curve of the settee. After that, pride, as much as running out of room, held her still. Tyler's green and gold plaid shirt was open at the throat to reveal a triangle of dazzling white T-shirt. The sleeves were rolled almost to his elbows, baring lightly muscled forearms dusted with curly dark hair. Those intriguing muscles tensed, then contracted, as he leaned slightly closer. ''Alone.'' He repeated the word. ''Your aunt's spending the day with friends?'' It was just barely a question and Sarah knew he was as much aware of the answer as she was.

She nodded.

"They took the first boat out this morning. They're driving down to Traverse City to shop. They'll be gone all day." Now why had she added that unnecessary detail?

"Michael took David to Sault Ste. Marie to watch the ore boats go through the locks. They'll be gone all day, too."

"And Elliot?" Sarah hesitated only a moment before asking the question.

"He's off island." Tyler's mouth tightened, deepening the lines between his nose and chin. "Visiting friends who've retired up here. A little place called Curtis, about sixty miles west of the straits."

"You're glad he's gone, aren't you?" Sarah spoke her thoughts aloud. She hated seeing the signs of renewed tension in him, the anger and bitterness return.

"I don't want to be available to Elliot. Sooner or later he's going to start talking about taking David back to Georgia with him."

"Are you certain of that?"

"Yes." Tyler looked as if he wasn't going to say anything more, then spoke. "Nothing's changed between us, Sarah. I'd be fooling myself if I thought it had. This is a cease-fire, a lull in hostilities, nothing more. Sooner or later, Elliot is going to demand that David go back to Columbus. With or without me. Until I have legal custody of my son again, I haven't got a leg to stand on."

"I was hoping..." Sarah looked down.

Tyler reached out before he could think twice and stop himself, folding her hands between his own. "You're hoping for a miracle, Sarah. I gave up hope of one a long time ago. I killed Allison." He did nothing to soften the blow of the blunt words. "Elliot loved her more than anything else in the world. David's all he has left of her. Every time he sees me, it reminds him of what he's lost."

"You don't hate him anymore?" Sarah's voice was whisper light, a thread of sound barely audible above the rush of wind worrying the leaves of the copper beech outside. She'd heard more than the surface emotions in his voice. She'd heard the resignation. Her blue eyes sought and held his gaze, demanding his answer, demanding the truth.

"I never hated him, Sarah. I don't think he really hates me. But he resents me, he blames me, and that will never change."

"Time…" Sarah twisted her hands beneath his to clutch at his fingers. What could she say that wasn't advice he'd heard countless times before? She gave up and spoke only what she felt. "Try, for David's sake."

"For David's sake…for your sake…I'll try anything. But not today." He rose decisively and pulled her up with him. She seemed younger, more vulnerable somehow, standing in her stocking feet, her hair lying loose and free on her shoulders, her blue eyes still locked to his. "Today is for us."

"For us?" Sarah felt silly but strangely elated, parroting his words back at him.

"Umm. I'm tired of sharing you with David and Michael and Aunt Cam. Don't turn me down, Sarah. It took most of the morning for me to get up the nerve to ask you at all."

"Ask me what?" Sarah couldn't help laughing up into the inky darkness of his eyes.

"To go on a picnic. I've already got poor old Spice hitched to the buggy. The hamper's packed and ready to go. All I need is a pretty girl at my side."

"And what if I say no?" Sarah couldn't help teasing him. She wanted to go. At least most of her wanted to go. That tiny, cowardly, selfish part of her wanted to stay right where she was, safe and insulated, and only half-alive, not risking taking the future into her own two hands.

"Then I'll go alone and Spice will get half a great stacked ham sandwich and…"

"I don't think stacked ham sandwiches are good for horses," Sarah broke in, frowning a little.

"You didn't let me finish," Tyler admonished with a scowl that was negated by the sparks of laughter in his eyes. "She'll also fall heir to your share of the dessert. Chocolate-covered strawberries."

"When you put it that way…" Sarah lifted her chin with

great dignity. "I accept your gracious invitation, Mr. Danielson."

"I'd rather put it like this." Before she could object, Tyler pulled her into his arms. His hands on her shoulders were light and compelling. His mouth hovered a fraction of an inch from hers. For a long moment they remained that way, his breath warm and moist on her cheek, the scent of his after-shave woodsy and fresh in her nostrils. Sarah closed her eyes when his lips brushed hers, swiftly, lightly, gone in the skip of a heartbeat. "We'd better not keep the horse waiting."

"Oh." Sarah was more than a little disappointed. "No, I suppose not. Am I dressed okay?" She looked down at her feet, wiggled her toes and giggled. "Except for my footwear?"

"You look great...for now." Tyler grinned and pushed her back into the cushions on the settee. "Here are your shoes," he said, handing them to her one at a time.

"What do you mean for now?" Sarah gave up being annoyed at having to ask such elementary questions. Tyler was enjoying himself and she didn't have the heart to spoil his fun. She'd only seen him this way now and then, when they'd been playing a game with David or, on occasion, when he traded friendly insults with Michael.

This is the way our life together could always be. Together with Tyler. Together with his son. My son. Our son. The thought sent a trill of joyful longing singing through her heart.

"I made reservations for dinner tonight at the Grand Hotel. I hope you brought something suitable to wear."

"Dinner at the Grand? I haven't been inside the hotel in...years and years."

"Then you'll go?"

Sarah thought of the silver and cream silk shirtwaist in her closet. She'd brought it with her only because she assumed at some point during her stay she'd be invited to a dinner party with Aunt Cam and her friends. It was a lovely feminine dress, far too expensive to justify its purchase for the quiet life Sarah led, but she hadn't been able to resist its allure. Now she was very glad she'd succumbed to temptation. She wanted Tyler to see her in it, to see her at her best.

"I wouldn't miss it." She smiled up at him in the way that never failed to set his heart pounding against his ribs. She didn't see him smile back, as though she were just as special and as wonderful as she wanted him to think her. Instead, she bent to tie her shoe.

The island had never seemed so beautiful: birds sang, tree branches danced in the breeze, sunlight glistened off leaves. Tyler and Sarah bypassed Arch Rock and Sugar Loaf, two of the island's most famous natural attractions, because Sarah was to have taken David there before he hurt his knee and Tyler decided he wanted them all to see the sites together. The words he used to tell her so were conventional enough. It was the way he said them that curled Sarah's toes inside her shoes, first with pleasure, then with a sting of discomfort as she thought again of all she had learned, all she now believed and all she was keeping to herself.

"How about taking in Fort Holmes?" Tyler asked, breaking into her uncomfortable reverie. They'd passed the Protestant cemetery, pausing to allow Spice to catch her breath where the road branched to the right, rising uphill once again.

"I haven't got the heart to sit in this buggy while Spice toils uphill any further," Sarah declared with a wave of her hand. "We'll probably have to carry her up the bluff when we get back to town as it is. Let's head down British Landing Road and picnic on the beach. I know a spot. It's posted, but the owners are friends of the family. It's lovely and sheltered."

"Sounds great." Tyler didn't lace the words with any hidden meaning and Sarah was glad. She was afraid she'd already given away too much of her desire to be alone with him.

Going downhill seemed to be just as much work for Spice as traveling in the opposite direction. When they reached the junction of State Road and Leslie Avenue, Sarah motioned them off to the right. "It's not quite so well traveled and we'll end up in the same place." She made a comical little grimace. "I think. It's been a while. Anyway, we can't get lost too badly. If we stay on this road Spice is liable to be spooked by cyclists on the downhill run. Some of the fudgies tend to get a little out of control from here on.''

"Want to tell me why they call it British Landing Road? I'm driving and providing the food and drink, so you might as well earn your keep as travel guide,'' Tyler suggested with a roguish grin.

"No fair. It's my horse and buggy,'' Sarah reminded him. "I could insist you walk back.''

"But could you make me?''

Sarah didn't know what to say to the lightly veiled challenge so she retreated into the safety of historical trivia. "I'm rusty on the facts but I know the gist of the story.'' She gave what she hoped was a saucy shake of her head, willing herself not to respond to the sensual undercurrent in his words. "During the War of 1812 the British landed on the north shore of the island, took the Americans at Fork Mackinac by surprise and captured the island. In 1814 the Americans returned, tried the same thing and failed, resulting in the death of a young officer, Major—I think—Holmes.'' Sarah folded her hands in her lap, pleased she'd remembered that much of the story.

"Ah, so that's where Fort Holmes got its name,'' Tyler said as though she'd shed new light on an age-old mystery.

"Yes,'' she replied primly. "The British called it... something else.''

"What?'' Again that hidden challenge, that undercurrent of sensuality had crept into his voice.

"I don't know. Anyway, we didn't get the island back until the peace treaty was signed in 1815.''

"And?''

Sarah took a deep steadying breath. "What fascinates me,'' she said in her best no-nonsense voice, "is that the British hauled their cannons all this way, miles and miles...''

"I think it's only about two and a half,'' Tyler said in the interest of accuracy.

"Uphill. In the dark. Without horses.''

"The American commander was never told war had been declared. He was completely unprepared for an attack,'' Tyler told her.

Sarah's eyes snapped blue fire. "I don't care. And I don't care what the guidebook says about it being a 'gentle, gradual incline,' either. It must have been sheer torture. The middle of July, all the mosquitoes and blackflies. The British deserved to win that one, if you ask me."

"Traitor." He made the word a caress and Sarah was struck dumb once again. "Are you always such a neck or nothing advocate of the underdog?"

"The British Army was hardly what you'd call an underdog, but yes, I'm afraid I am." Sarah made the admission with difficulty. Spice seemed to have gotten her second wind. She broke into a trot. Sarah wound her left hand around the struts holding the buggy roof and steadied herself against the bouncing motion of the seat. They were heading sharply downhill once more. The water was close by. Spice could smell it. So could Sarah.

Tyler saved the silence from growing awkwardly prolonged. "I didn't know you were such a history buff."

"Wait till you hear my spiel on the fur trade and Dr. Beaumont's contribution to medicine that quite simply made that poor voyageur Alexis St. Martin's life miserable." Sarah motioned to the right as they turned onto Lake Shore Road. A group of teens on ten-speed bikes passed them as if they were standing still.

"I can't wait." His eyes found hers again, midnight blue, sapphire blue, heated blue.

They were standing still for certain now. Sarah cleared her throat. "We'd better keep Spice moving."

Tyler made a clicking motion with his tongue and the placid mare started reluctantly forward.

"I think some of Michael's history lectures to David have rubbed off on me," Sarah admitted, more for something to say than anything else. The warmth of his eyes still teased her skin; Sarah slipped out of her sweater, knotting the sleeves around her neck. "Michael's only been on the island for a week and knows far more about things that have happened here, their true cause and effect, than I ever knew or even suspected. And I spent a lot of summers at the Gathering Place as a child." She ran her fingers through her hair, pushing feathery wisps behind the combs that held it off her face. A small lane appeared along the shoreline, bright red No Trespassing signs on either side of the narrow turn. "This is it."

Tyler guided Spice into the turn. He let the reference to Michael and the time he'd been spending with Sarah and David pass without comment. "The things we experience as children stay with us forever." His hands tightened on the reins as he pulled Spice to a halt. Tyler swung a long leg over the side and hopped down. Sarah jumped out from her side of the buggy before he could come around to help her alight.

"The good things stay with us, too, Tyler." She pulled a Hudson's Bay blanket with its familiar pattern of colorful stripes and a thermos from under the seat. Tyler made no comment as he tied Spice's reins to a willow bush after unhitching her from the cart.

He took the wicker picnic hamper and followed Sarah toward a deserted stretch of boulder-strewn beach. "The good things stay with us far longer than the bad." What she said might sound simplistic, she knew, but it was the truth nonetheless. More and more often lately, when she thought of the past, she was recalling the good times, the happy times. Perhaps it was because no matter what the future might hold, she'd found new hope with which to face the unknown.

Sarah spread the blanket with a flick of her wrist that sent it snapping in the breeze. The spot they'd chosen was sheltered and sunny, warm and private and very, very lovely.

Lake Huron rolled toward them in long blue-green swells that broke into swirls of white foam only a few feet away. Spice stood quietly in the shade of a big old pine, nibbling on willow leaves, the tree's shadow a dark contrast to the sun-warmed yellow sand beyond.

Tyler unwrapped the sandwiches, pickles and cheese and they ate in silence. Sarah was just finishing the juicy chocolate-dipped strawberry he'd promised her for dessert when he spoke again.

"You truly believe what you said about children remembering the good times, don't you, Sarah?"

She looked at him without guile or coyness. "Yes." She licked the strawberry juice and chocolate from her fingers while she watched his hand tighten around the plastic thermos cup of lemonade he held. He was stretched out beside her, propped on his elbow. He looked lean and vigorous, the thin, soft·cotton of his plaid shirt pulled taut across his shoulders and the breadth of his chest. He was a very masculine man, relaxed and at ease with himself, with his body, in a way Sarah had never been with her own, or her own femininity.

Except for his hands. She watched as his fingers tightened around the plastic thermos cup, watched the knuckles showing white through the skin.

"Despite what psychologists and psychiatrists tell us, bombard us with every day from newspapers, magazines, television?"

Sarah's heart contracted within her breast. He was afraid: afraid his tragic mistake had not only killed Allison but scarred David for life, also. "Love heals best of all," Sarah said quietly, her words carried to him on a puff of wind.

Tyler stared down at the cup of lemonade in his hand. "I used to believe that. I don't know anymore." He lifted his head, his expression troubled. His almost black eyes looked wary, a little sad. His vulnerability called out to Sarah's emotions, her compassion, her heart. She leaned forward instinctively to comfort him, both arms outstretched to take her weight.

"I still believe." Sarah didn't stop to allow herself to consider the possible outcome of her next action. She leaned closer still. She kissed him lightly, gently, their lips barely touching.

"Sarah, I told you once before that you were a dangerous woman to be around," Tyler said softly. He held her, his hand behind her neck.

"Why is that?" Was he going to say he was falling in love with her? Did they even need to speak the words aloud?

"Because you make me want to believe again, to live again. Really live, not just exist." He dropped his hand, freeing her from the gentle bondage of his touch, lowering his head, avoiding her eyes. Sarah had to stop herself from raising her hand to thread her fingers through the thick sable layers of his hair. He traced the narrow span of her wrist and forearm, the skin softly golden against the bright stripes of the wool blanket. "You make me want to feel again and that's the most frightening part of all."

"I know." Her lips were dry. She moistened them with the tip of her tongue.

For Tyler, looking up at the uncertainty he detected in her voice, the simple gesture was intensely erotic. He pushed the wicker hamper that held the remnants of their food to the side. It tumbled open, spilling its contents onto the sand, and neither one of them paid it a moment's heed. Tyler pulled Sarah into his arms. She came willingly, eagerly. He cradled her head on his shoulder, their legs tangling together on the cushioning sand.

He held her that way for a long time. Sarah felt the rise and fall of his chest under her cheek, the slow steady thud of his heartbeat under her palm, the quickening rhythm when she lifted her mouth to trace the hard, slightly beard-roughened line of his jaw with her lips. Tyler's arms tightened around her.

"Tyler?" Her voice was liquid crystal, sharp and sweet in his ear, in his heart.

"Umm?" He was trying to decide the best way to tell her he loved her but his body kept interfering with his thought processes. He felt like a kid again, all hormones and frustrated clumsy desire.

"Are we falling in love?" Sarah's voice dwindled away to a reedy whisper.

"What?" Tyler propped himself on one elbow. Sarah was still cradled in the curve of his arm but she wasn't looking at him. She was staring straight up at the sky.

"I said, am I falling in love with you?" She continued to stare wide-eyed at several fleecy white clouds pushed along by the energetic lake breeze.

"That's not what you said." His heart beat so hard against

the wall of his chest he thought it was going to burst. "I want you to repeat it word for word."

She turned her head slightly. Her eyes were clear and guileless. "Are we falling in love with each other? It's been so long. I was so young." She bit her lip. "I don't know how I feel."

It was very easy to say, after all. "We are falling in love, together. With each other, Sarah. And it's very different from anything I've ever known before, either, if that makes you feel any better."

"It does, a little." She smiled then, a crooked, funny little smile that made his heart flip-flop in his chest.

"Damn it, Sarah. I don't want to love you." The touch of his lips on her cheek made the roughly spoken words a lie. "I never wanted to love anyone again but I can't help myself. And suddenly I don't even want to."

His hand caressed her breast; his lips tasted the skin of her throat. She wound her arms around his neck, accepted his weight as he moved over her, gladly, exultantly. Her legs opened for him. The brush of denim against denim, the roughness of a metal zipper and the hardness of flesh that lay beneath it pressed into her stomach, sending quivers of desire all through her body.

Time slowed to a crawl, then almost ceased to exist. For Sarah reality was only a hazy darkness curling around the edges of paradise. A darkness that she tried desperately to ignore but that refused to be banished completely. She had never felt so loved and adored. She didn't want the experience to be marred by anything: memories or the tag end of common sense and its cautionary reminders. She had never, since her first passionate, untutored experience with Ryan McKenzie, allowed herself to come close to giving in to desire with no heed to the consequences of doing so. She wanted very much to be that spontaneous now. She could, almost, if only Tyler would go on kissing her, touching her, moving over her in age-old rhythms that were as new and intriguing as dreams of tomorrow for her, for them.

But she could not, because he didn't go on working his

sensual magic. He stopped, pulling her close against the heated warmth of his chest, stroking her hair, asking her what was wrong. "Sarah?" He made her name sound like a prayer of joy and thanksgiving.

"Tyler, I think we should stop." The words were hard to say but the lessons she'd learned of caution and the agony of loving unwisely were too deeply ingrained to be ignored completely.

"Yes, love, if that's what you want." Tyler had felt her misgivings, too, almost at the same moment they had first intruded on her pleasure. It was, for him, as if the sun had gone behind a small cloud and wouldn't show itself again. He wanted her more than he'd ever wanted a woman in his life, yet he couldn't be so selfish as to ask her to make love to him unprotected, unprepared. She had suffered enough already from the tragic outcome of giving of herself too fully, too unselfishly.

"I'm sorry. It's just all so sudden." He felt the warm moistness of her breath on his skin as he held her tighter against him, shielding her from the cool breeze that swirled around them, now, in reality as well as in his thoughts.

"I want making love with you to be the most perfect time of our lives. I want it to be special. I don't want any memories to interfere."

"Tyler." She didn't know how to respond. It was what she wanted, too, but she simply had no words to tell him why she felt that way. Her heart was too full. He was a wonderful caring man who loved her enough to put her wants and needs before his own.

Yet did he, too, harbor some few niggling doubts? Doubts that circled like small stinging insects disturbing her peace? Commitment was such a big step. It meant giving up hard-won serenity, opening herself to another's happiness and pain, tearing down defenses built up over long lonely years. She wanted to say something, do something to make it easier for both of them. But she could not.

There were secrets she must keep. Questions she alone had to answer. What was best for Tyler? For David? For herself?

She didn't want to think of all the lies and half-truths yet to be spoken, the truth left untold. It made her blood run cold with fear. "We'd better be getting back." Her thoughts elsewhere, Sarah said the first words that came to mind. "I...I have to press my dress for tonight..."

Tyler chuckled unexpectedly, delighting her as always with the deep rough edges of his laugh. "Was that prosaic utterance calculated to bring my raging libido back under control?" He pressed himself against her once more. "It didn't work."

"Sorry." Sarah took her cue from his response. She trusted him enough to be able to join in his gentle, sensual teasing even though her body still sang with desire, and her heart was heavy with silence. She moved her hand between them, caressing him with a boldness she didn't know she was capable of.

Tyler sucked in his breath and grabbed her hand, bringing it to his lips. "I don't think you're sorry at all."

"I couldn't help myself." She lifted her head and gave him a quick light kiss on the strong square ridge of his chin. "Maybe I should push you into the lake. It would be quicker than a cold shower."

"It would be the death of me. Don't even think of trying it, lady." Tyler rolled onto her once more, his lips inches from hers. Sarah held her breath, but his kiss was as quick as summer lightning, over in the flick of an eye, a promise of more to come. He levered himself up and away. Sarah loved him all the more for making the awkward moment more comfortable for both of them.

Sarah sat up. When the heavy satisfying weight of his body left her, she felt a deep and aching pain knife through her heart. She almost cried out. *If you lose him now this is how empty and alone you'll feel for the rest of your life.* She watched in silence as Tyler gathered up the remains of their lunch, then held out his hand to help her rise from the blanket.

"Come on, Sarah. Our reservations at the Grand are for seven. I think it will probably take me an hour to remember how to put on a necktie. I haven't worn one of the damn things in ages."

Sarah laughed and held out her hands for him to help her rise from the sand. Their happiness might be clouded by the secrets she harbored in her heart but it was still very real and very precious. "Poor Tyler."

"Yes, poor Tyler," he said with a doleful shake of his head. He untied Spice in order to rehitch her to the buggy. "Will you help me if I need it?"

"Always." Once again she hoped he didn't hear the emotion that made her voice catch in her throat. If she kept her secret she could have everything she'd ever wanted from life. Was that the answer after all? Tyler would love her. David would love her.

Only she would hate herself.

CHAPTER ELEVEN

"ARE YOU CERTAIN you'll be all right here alone?" Camilla stood at the foot of the stairway, watching as her great-niece hobbled painfully down the steps.

"I'll be fine." Sarah rested a hand on the newel post and stared hard at her aunt. "Stop worrying."

Camilla ignored the warning flash from Sarah's blue eyes. "I don't have to go with David and Elliot, you know." She adjusted the angle of her straw hat before the mirror by the door. Sarah's reflection frowned back at her. Camilla let her words trail off into silence. She was looking for excuses not to go and they both knew it.

"Aunt Cam, I twisted my ankle again. I didn't break my neck." She limped onto the veranda and lowered herself onto the settee with a sigh.

"I'm sorry it spoiled your evening with Tyler." Camilla brushed at an imaginary spot on her lime-green skirt. Out of the corner of her eye she noticed a pale rosy blush spread across Sarah's high cheekbones.

"If I can't manage to get in and out of a buggy without stepping on a loose stone and spraining my ankle, I deserve to have to cancel plans for a marvelous dinner, and be stuck inside alone on such a beautiful day." She laughed and spread her hands in a self-mocking gesture. "I'm hopeless." Sarah pushed the wide loose sleeves of her yellow cotton pullover above her elbows, her slim golden arms darkened to honey against the bright lemony yellow of the fabric.

"Why don't you ride along with us this afternoon?" Camilla was clutching at straws. David's presence was no longer enough to protect her from Elliot's appeal to her senses. In the days they'd spent together over the past week, she'd grown more comfortable with him, but she could still never completely let down her guard. It was only a matter of time until he brought up the past. Then what would she say? What would she do? Only her fear of being alone with her memories kept her from shutting herself into her room and hiding behind locked doors until he left the island. Except that should she do so, Elliot would probably come storming up the stairs after her and demand an explanation, an explanation she wouldn't be able to give.

"Thanks for asking, Aunt Cam." Sarah's voice was suddenly very gentle and Camilla realized her thoughts, her uncertainty, must be evident. "It'll be crowded at Arch Rock. And it's hot. I'd rather be here. Anyway, I'm going to finish going through my mother's box today. At least I can do away with the things I know are of no value. That way, if I go visit Dad this winter, it won't cost me a fortune to ship this stuff down to Florida." Sarah looked at her and smiled, a sad little lopsided smile that caught at Camilla's heart. "Besides, I need the time alone."

"And Tyler will most likely be back from his errand before we are." Camilla couldn't stop herself from making the observation. Her niece was acting very much like a young woman in love.

"Am I being that obvious?" A tiny frown appeared between Sarah's brows.

"No, dear. I know you better than most people and I love you very much. I wish for your happiness more than anything else in the world. You're like the daughter I...never had." The irony of the statement was that Camilla meant every word, even though the facts of her life made a lie of the statement itself.

"Thank you," Sarah whispered. "I hope your wish for me comes true."

"Sarah." Camilla spoke briskly to hide her own feelings as well as her reluctance to broach the subject at all. "Are you going to tell Tyler of your suspicion about David...and who his real mother is?"

"That's the sixty-four-thousand-dollar question, isn't it?" Sarah looked down at her hands. They were trembling. "Allison deceived Tyler for years. That hurt him so badly." Sarah faltered, then spoke again, her voice steady. "He needs to relearn trust and I'm deceiving him just like she did. I don't know what to do. I need to be alone, think it through..."

"Then, by all means, stay here and rest your ankle." Camilla decided not to probe further into Sarah's feelings. She wasn't able to propose a solution, no matter how much she wished she could. "You'll come to the right decision, Sarah, I know you will."

"I hope you're right, Aunt Cam."

There was real distress in her blue eyes as she dropped her gaze to stare at the cardboard box at her feet.

"Sarah. Aunt Cam. I'm ready to go." David banged on the frame of the screen door in a perfunctory knock. He bounced inside, knobby, scarred knees jutting out from beneath khaki shorts. His orange T-shirt brought out auburn highlights in his curly brown hair. "Granddad's coming up the hill with the buggy. I saw him." He held the opera glasses he'd appropriated after his bicycle accident to his eyes. "Your ankle's big as a grapefruit," he observed with interest, focusing on Sarah's bandaged foot, now propped up on the glass-topped table.

"Isn't it a beaut?"

Camilla felt her niece's mixture of pain and joy like twin arrows in her own heart. She still didn't see any of Ryan McKenzie in David's features or actions, but then she'd only seen him a few times ten years ago when she'd been staying with Sarah one summer. For the most part she'd tried, successfully, to blot that time from her memory. Now she wished she could recall Ryan's features and help Sarah fulfill her lonely quest.

"How about unwinding that bandage so I can see if it's all black and blue like my knee?" David stuck out one skinny leg to better show off the last fading yellows and greens of the bruise around the newly healed scar.

"Sorry, sport. No bruise, just pink, puffy skin."

"Boring." David lost interest. "Are you coming to Arch Rock with us?"

"No, I'm too busy here."

"Rats. Dad's gone to Mackinaw City to get something to fix the toilet. It won't flush and he says it was old before the flood."

"That old?"

"He's exaggerating," David said, obviously proud that he'd remembered the word. "It can't be that old."

"No, I suppose not." Sarah couldn't stop herself from laughing out loud.

"Anyway, he's bringing back some Big Macs and fries from McDonald's. What's so funny?"

"Nothing."

"Want to eat lunch with us?" The invitation was accompanied by a grin as big and wide as the love in Sarah's heart.

"I wouldn't miss it."

"Good. Here's Granddad."

Elliot Brandon stood just outside the door, looking tan and fit in a pale gray shirt and dark blue slacks. "Good mornin', Sarah. Have you hurt your ankle?"

"Yes." Sarah explained with an embarrassed laugh. "It's an old war wound. I stepped on a loose stone yesterday and twisted it. Again."

"I'm sorry to hear that." His smile was grave and charming. Sarah could imagine how he had looked in his uniform, serious and handsome. He would have appealed to Camilla, even then, fun-loving and heedless as she might have been. Why had she turned down his proposal of marriage? Sarah wondered if she would ever learn the whole story.

"Elliot, I'm ready."

"Mornin', Camilla. You look lovely, as always." The chemistry was still there. Sarah could feel it all the way across the room. Yet, if you looked closely, you could also see the wariness, the anxiety in Camilla's hazel eyes. Sarah had come to understand the older woman much better over the past two weeks. Her relative was balancing on a very thin emotional ledge, torn between wanting to be with Elliot Brandon and chancing exposure of something very fragile and carefully guarded within. Sarah hoped with all her heart that Camilla wouldn't get hurt.

"Our carriage awaits." Elliot held the screen door open. David darted past him as he extended his hand to assist Camilla down the steps.

"I'm driving," the youngster hollered. "Let's go." He bounded into the driver's seat, Camilla following more sedately to sit beside him. Elliot took the far seat, his hand outstretched behind her back.

"Goodbye, Sarah." Camilla waved at the dim form on the other side of the screened window.

"Have fun."

Sarah's words floated across the yard. *Have fun?* Camilla thought. She was alone with Elliot once more and she really shouldn't be. Spending time with him wasn't getting easier; it was getting harder. But it had also become necessary to her existence, like eating and breathing. *Lord, why hadn't somebody warned me I could still feel like this at my age?* Giddy and excited and frightened to death all at the same time. It wasn't fair. Her life should be settled now, sedate, the laughter and the tears subdued. She shouldn't be full of old doubts and new, exciting promises.

"David. Don't flap the reins like that. That animal isn't going to go any faster than he already is." Elliot's smoothly modulated voice broke into her chaotic thoughts.

"He's a slug," David replied, obeying his grandfather's directive with some reluctance.

"Now you're an expert on horseflesh, are you?"

Camilla wished Tyler Danielson could hear the love and pride in Elliot's voice when he talked to his grandson. She knew Sarah understood something of the older man's feelings. Camilla suspected that sensitivity might have some bearing on her niece's decision to keep her questions about David's true parentage to herself.

How would Elliot react if he learned David wasn't his grandson? He'd loved Allison so much; he mourned her death so deeply. Would his faith and trust in God be equal to the task?

Camilla wasn't a religious woman; at least not in the same way Elliot was. She just didn't believe that God had time to spend worrying over each and every action one made in a lifetime. It was up to the individual to manage his own existence as best he could with the brains and heart and soul God bestowed.

"Arch Rock, dead ahead," David announced with another unnecessary flap of the reins.

Two tourist wagons with their distinctive three-horse hitches and several rented bicycles were parked in the lot behind the great natural stone arch. People milled around, cameras in hand or hanging from straps around their necks, climbing the metal steps to the observation deck, staring at the fish visible in the clear blue-green water of the lake over a hundred feet below. "Is it always this crowded?" Elliot asked, frowning.

"I'm afraid so, at least during the peak season. Have you been here at all since the war?" Camilla found herself apologizing for the number of tourists and she didn't know exactly why. Perhaps because she felt a special affinity for this place, so steeped in legend as it was. She hated to see it become just a five-minute stopover for the tour guides. For centuries the Indians had considered the arch sacred ground, the gateway to heaven. And there were love stories associated with it, too; a lovely Indian maiden chained to the rock by her wicked father, her tears washing away the stone to form the arch before she was rescued by her godlike lover.

"Do you remember the story they used to tell of the lady who supposedly rode her horse over the arch?" Elliot's words proved that he, too, was affected by the beauty and history of the great rock mass, although the legend he recalled was of much later vintage than the ones that had occupied Camilla's thoughts.

She nodded. "I always imagine her, whoever she might have been, sitting on the porch of the Grand, surrounded by gentlemen admirers, accepting the dare. She would have worn a severe gray habit, a hat with no veil to obscure her vision or endanger her mount because she was truly a horsewoman and not a fashion plate like so many women of her era. Her mare was sturdy, I think, fine-boned and full of heart. She trusted her mistress enough to carry her anywhere. Good Lord, listen to me ramble on.'' She blushed and laughed and wished she had kept her musings to herself.

"You're still a romantic, Camilla.'' Elliot's eyes were warm, the touch of his gaze almost a caress.

Camilla shrugged off the power of his spell but it took all the strength she possessed. "I'm just a silly old woman who's probably headed for her second childhood.'' A tingling, almost forgotten wave of sensual awareness prickled across her skin. She hadn't felt so young, so alive, in years. It was one of the reasons she found it hard to stay away from Elliot. He made her feel as if life wasn't just passing her by; that she could still be part of it—if only she had the courage to be. And that was the problem, of course. She lacked the courage.

"This place is great. I wish Dad and Sarah had come with us. They really wanted us to all see it together and now they're missing it.'' David had dropped the reins into Camilla's hands as soon as the buggy rolled to a halt. He'd already circled the metal observation platform by the time Elliot and Camilla exited the buggy. Now he was back, demanding to know what lay at the top of a steep flight of wooden steps to the left of the arch.

"If memory serves, it's another great view of the lake,'' his grandfather explained, looking to Camilla for confirmation.

"Nicolet's Watchtower.'' Camilla supplied the information from memory and a bronze plaque nearby.

"Somebody else I never heard of,'' David complained.

"You will someday. He was a French explorer.''

"They're all over the place around here.'' David made a beeline for the stairs.

"He's so full of energy.'' Camilla didn't have to pretend with Elliot in one respect. He didn't know she'd spent all her adult life feigning disinterest in children. She could indulge her delight and wonder in David's company as she'd never allowed herself to do before.

"He's all I have left of Allison and her mother."

For a long moment Camilla said nothing; then she couldn't seem to stop the words from pouring out. "Elliot, I know it isn't any of my business. But please, for David's sake, don't allow your animosity toward Tyler to cause him any more distress. He's still just a little boy. He can't understand why the two people he loves most in the world are fighting over him."

"Tyler Danielson killed my daughter." Elliot's eyes were no longer warm and exciting. They were as cold and gray as lake ice in winter. "He isn't a fit parent to raise a child. Now that he's out of prison, he'll want to take David back to Brazil or some other godforsaken jungle somewhere. I won't allow it."

Camilla put her hand on his arm, feeling muscles stiff with tension beneath the warm hair-roughened skin. She smiled beguilingly up into his angry face, hoping to minimize the damage she might unwittingly have done to Tyler's cause. "You told me once that no place was godforsaken, it was only that the men who were there were too blind and arrogant to sense His presence. Don't be blind and arrogant, Elliot."

Elliot stopped walking, pausing at the foot of the steps. "You don't know what you're askin'."

"I'm asking for David's sake. I'm concerned about him."

"Don't be. It's between his father and me. I have legal custody of the boy. I won't press the issue but I want it known that he goes nowhere without my permission."

"Granddad." David's insistent voice interrupted before Camilla could press her argument. "Get up here. It's neat."

They climbed the rest of the way in silence.

When Camilla topped the bluff, David was bouncing away from her along the treacherous stone and root-filled path, leaning out over the rail fence to study the sheer drop to the shore road below. "Wow! Look at the big Navy ship. I didn't know they had those anywhere but the ocean."

"It's a destroyer, I think," Elliot informed his grandson, squinting his eyes against the glare of sun on water. "Probably on its way to Chicago."

"Sarah lives in Chicago," David said.

"You were born there."

"Yeah? I'm thirsty. I saw a drinking fountain down there." David changed the subject without a wasted breath. Pointing toward the parking lot, he streaked off down the steps.

"Be careful." Camilla felt her color rise as Elliot turned to stare at her overloud warning. "He's so impetuous."

"You used to be very impetuous, too."

"I got over it." Her words were more bitter than she had intended them to be. Camilla shifted the subject away from herself. "Elliot, do you remember the little cave that used to be here, along the edge of the cliff?"

"The one I climbed down to explore for Indian artifacts that summer?" He shook his head. "I doubt if the opening's even visible anymore."

"I'm not so sure. Look." Camilla leaned over the railing, much as David had done. "See? Over there. That oddly shaped boulder. Do you remember it?" She recalled with mixed emotions the afternoon so long ago when they'd come exploring with a group of other young people. Their gaiety had been slightly forced; the war news was bad and no one could predict what tomorrow might bring. She had begun to suspect she might be pregnant. But still, her memories of that day were happy ones, although the happiness had been brief and bittersweet. It was the day she'd admitted to herself that she was falling in love with Elliot Brandon.

"Come on." Elliot held out his hand. The turmoil of those far-off days came back to Camilla with a strength that she hadn't thought it possible to feel after so many years. "Camilla, let's try to find it again." Camilla felt his big strong fingers close over hers. She felt the warmth and the pulse beat of life and drew strength from his touch to banish the ache of the past.

"Why not?" If her smile was a little crooked he didn't seem to notice.

David was back beside them, water splashes darkening the front of his orange shirt. "What's goin' on? Are we goin' exploring?"

"I guess we are, a little." Camilla held out her other hand. They had the upper path to themselves. In the distance she heard the tour drivers urging their charges back into the wagons. It would be a few more minutes until the next batch descended on the site.

"What are we looking for?" David demanded, skipping alongside the older couple.

"There used to be a cave here, along the edge of the bluff."

"Like the one with skulls in it where the English guy stayed after the Indian massacre?" David's voice rose. "Were there skulls, Granddad?"

"No skulls, no bones at all. It was a very small cave," Elliot apologized, looking over at Camilla with a chuckle that said, "I wanted to find a skull, too."

David looked up at Camilla. "Michael told me about that guy who didn't get scalped when the Indians pretended to be friendly and then attacked the fort on the mainland. Dad took me to see Skull Cave the next day. It was an Indian burial ground but there weren't any bones left." He sighed, spreading his hands in disappointment. "I'd sure like to have a real Indian skull for a souvenir."

"We're not even sure the cave's where we remembered it, David," Camilla said. "It was a long time ago."

"Back in World War II." David nodded sagely. His attention focused on his grandfather. "Did you find it, Granddad?" His voice was thin and high, filled with excitement. "A real cave that no one else knows about?"

"It's been a long time...Camilla?" Elliot was standing at the edge of the bluff, or more nearly a cliff, although it was covered with ferns and brush and trees growing out of the thin rocky soil at strange and precarious angles. He was hanging on to the trunk of a sturdy maple sapling, studying the ledge below him. "Do you suppose that's the cave mouth? There've been some rock slides over the years and the trees are all different. But that boulder does seem familiar." He had a streak of leaf stain on his gray shirt and a smudge of dirt on his cheek.

"Elliot, come back up here." Camilla laughed; she couldn't

help herself. "You're too old for this kind of thing and so am I. You'll slip and fall and we'll have to call the rescue squad, or the fire department, or someone, to haul you back up. What will your parishioners think of that?"

"Let's make sure that's the cave, Granddad. I'll come with you." David started toward the edge. "It would be a fantastic place to hide. No one would ever find me. Not Indians or trappers or anyone." Camilla reached out and caught him by the collar of his shirt.

"Not so fast, young man."

"Granddad." David appealed to what he considered a higher power. "Tell Aunt Cam to let me go. I want to see the cave, too."

"Stay there, David," Elliot ordered. Camilla saw the excitement leave Elliot's face to be replaced by the knowledge of his responsibility for David's safety. "I'm not even sure this is the right place. And the ledge isn't safe. I could feel it shiftin' under me just while I was standin' there."

"I can't go down to the cave?" David stared wistfully up at Camilla.

"No, the bluff is very steep."

"Not even if Michael comes along? He's even a better climber than my dad."

"Not even if Michael comes along." Camilla felt her heart contract at the disappointment that showed plainly in David's brown eyes. Already he'd learned to substitute Michael for his father in Elliot's presence.

Elliot scrambled over the edge of the bluff in time to catch David's last remark. "Michael will be the first one to tell you not to try climbing down there without the proper equipment and safety devices. I was foolish to have gone as far as I did."

"I'd be careful." David made one last attempt.

"No."

"Okay. I can't wait to tell Michael and Dad about this place. And Sarah, too. I'll surprise them." He frowned down at his shoes. "What next?"

"Sugar Loaf?" Camilla suggested, wondering how long it

would be until David had his fill of natural attractions. She got her answer almost at once.

"Another pile of stone?" he said, tilting his head to look up at her as he asked.

"I'm afraid so."

"I'm gettin' hungry, you know."

"It's only ten o'clock, David." Elliot shook his head in disbelief. "We had breakfast less than two hours ago."

"That doesn't make any difference. I'm still hungry."

"Then I say let's save Sugar Loaf for another day and go back and get a snack. Mrs. Meecham sent over another batch of cookies this morning."

"Fantastic," David announced, drawing each and every syllable out to enormous lengths. "Let's go. I'll help Sarah look through her box." He set off for the buggy at a trot. "You think of the best things to do, Aunt Cam."

"The quickest way to a man's heart is still through his stomach," Camilla said with a wry grin.

"I do believe you're right." Elliot held out his hand to help her over a tricky spot in the path. "What kind of cookies might they be?" The path widened, and Camilla tugged to free her hand. Elliot ignored her. "Sugar or oatmeal raisin?"

"Double chocolate chip." Camilla quit struggling and left her hand where it was, although the steps down to the parking lot were wide and dry and the railing sturdy.

"Hallelujah," David said and Elliot grinned. "My favorite."

DAVID SWIPED AT THE MILK RING his glass left on the tabletop and only managed to streak it more. "Use a dry napkin," Sarah ordered absently. Her mind wasn't really on David's table manners or even his rambling account of the morning's adventure at Arch Rock. She was far too interested in the old black-and-white snapshots of her mother and uncle she'd finally unearthed from the depths of the cardboard box. The album of birthday and Christmas shots was her reward for a morning of viewing dusty report cards, faded valentines and school yearbooks where she had had a hard time picking her mother and uncle out of rows of stiffly posed adolescents.

"How's that?"

Sarah barely glanced at the streaky glass tabletop. "Fine."

"Want another cookie?" David asked hopefully, scooting across the settee cushions to peer over her shoulder.

"No, thanks." Baby pictures had given way to the first day of school. Sarah turned the page. One of the snapshots, fastened to the page with only two of those stiff little cardboard corners, fell onto her lap.

"I do." David sucked in his breath. "Dad," he hollered so close to Sarah's ear it made her jump. "Sorry." He grinned sheepishly.

"What?" Tyler's voice came from the kitchen, muffled by distance and the heavy swinging door. He'd offered to do the dishes after lunch, by which he meant disposing of the plastic foam containers that had, until a few minutes ago, held Big Macs and fries. Sarah, David and Tyler had eaten on the veranda. Camilla and Elliot had opted for omelets and ate them in the kitchen.

"I need another cookie. Bring me one, okay?" David lowered his voice a decibel or two.

"You've already had three." Tyler's voice was clearer and closer.

"I'm still hungry. Hey, who's that?"

Sarah didn't move a muscle. She couldn't. David leaned farther over her shoulder. He smelled of chocolate and slightly of horses and earthy little-boy smells. Sarah closed her eyes against a surging tide of emotion. "Who is that kid?" he demanded again.

"My uncle," Sarah said automatically. "It's his ninth birthday picture." David plucked the small black-and-white photo out of her fingers.

"I'll be nine my next birthday. Wow, this is old." He studied the snapshot for a second or two. "He's wearing funny clothes. Sissy short pants and knee socks. I like his hat, though. It's neat." He squinted down at the faded photograph. "Is it the girl's birthday, too? They have two cakes."

"Yes." Sarah couldn't make herself reach for the picture. It was the proof she'd prayed for. It was also the last thing in the world she wanted Tyler and David to see. At least not now, this moment, when she didn't have the words to explain. Would David see the resemblance she recognized? "That's my mother and my uncle. They were twins." She moved her hand to take back the photo. Everything seemed to be happening in slow motion.

David frowned down at the picture once more. "If he didn't have those weird old clothes on he'd look just like me." Sarah bit her lips so hard she tasted blood. With a direct effort of will, she reached across his arm to reclaim the picture. David catapulted himself off the settee. "Fantastic. I have to show this to my dad."

"David, no!" Sarah didn't move quickly enough. How could she when her body and brain were encased in sheets of ice? "Wait." The word was more a plea than a command.

"What's going on, sport?" Tyler appeared in the doorway, short-sleeved red shirt open at the throat, his hair dark and shiny as a raven's wing against the upturned collar. Sarah swallowed against the strength of her longing for him. He was carrying a plate of Mrs. Meecham's chocolate-chip cookies in his hand, smiling in that special way that never failed to set her blood drumming through her veins.

"Look at this old picture Sarah found in her box. It's her mom and her uncle. He looks just like me. Does he have brown hair and brown eyes, too? I wish this old thing was in color." Sarah didn't answer. She couldn't. David looked at her. "Sarah, did you hear me?"

"He has brown hair and brown eyes...just like you." Her voice thinned to a mere edge of sound on the last three words.

Tyler, looking curious, held the snapshot beyond the reach of David's grasping fingers. She saw the moment he made the connection, saw the moment he realized the truth. He handed David the plate of cookies, his hand steady as a rock. Sarah was shaking all over. He looked at her for a long silent moment, his face hard and expressionless. Sarah felt the ice that encased her seep into her heart.

"Go see if Aunt Cam and your grandfather want some more cookies." Tyler's voice was as expressionless as his face. "They're out by the gazebo checking on Aunt Cam's geraniums."

"Okay." David took the plate. He looked at his father with wide, anxious brown eyes. "Did I do something wrong?"

"No, sport." Tyler looked at his son and the stone mask melted away. "Just run along. I want to talk to Sarah a minute."

"Okay."

Sarah didn't move, Tyler didn't speak, until they heard the slam of the kitchen screen.

"How long have you known that David is your son?"

CHAPTER TWELVE

TYLER DIDN'T KNOW whether to start yelling curses or put his fist through the wall or both. What he really wanted to do was to grab David and start running, keep running, never stop until they were so far from everything and everyone they'd ever known that it would be impossible to find them. But he couldn't do that. There was too much at stake: David's future happiness and well-being, if not his own sanity.

Everything Sarah had told him about the baby she'd been forced to give away at birth fit the scenario he'd built up in his mind. Too many details dovetailed into place. Justin Delano, Allison and Sarah's grandmother had all had a hand in shaping this moment. Each had followed his or her own inclinations, fulfilled his or her own dreams or duties, all together weaving a web of deception, half-truths and lies, that still entangled the living from beyond the grave. Suddenly he hated all of them for what they'd done to him, to Sarah, and most of all to David.

"He's your son, isn't he, Sarah."

It was a statement, not a question. She answered it as such. "I think so." Even though fear squeezed her heart she could feel a faint stirring of joy, as well. She couldn't stop the smile that played at the corners of her mouth. It disappeared as quickly as the small flicker of hope that he would understand, its fragile life snuffed out by Tyler's next words.

"Have you known all along? Was that your plan from the beginning? To get to David through me?" His questions didn't make a lot of sense but how could he be sensible when his mind was a swirling mass of pain and anger? Logically he knew there was no way Sarah could have been aware of his presence on the island. It was all just one big coincidence, some sort of lousy cosmic joke.

"No." Sarah was too numb to feel the full force of the blow his words delivered. Her worst nightmares were coming true and she had no defense ready, just as she'd feared. "I wouldn't. Tyler, I..." *I love you.* It should have been so easy to say. They were the three magic words that should make everything right between them. But even magic words could be frozen into silence when faced down by the icy, dark-blue void of his stare.

"How long have you known?" His tone demanded an answer, commanded the truth.

"I...only guessed." Sarah spread her hands helplessly. "So many things added up, and he looked...he seemed so familiar, somehow. But I never dared to hope, until that night on the bluff steps when you told me about Allison and what you believed."

"You have no proof." God, he hurt inside. At least he was making her hurt, too. He could see it in the tension of her neck and shoulders, in the bruised expression in her sapphire eyes. They were swimming with tears that she wouldn't let fall. Tyler admired Sarah for that strength of character. She would stand and fight, even though her back was to the wall. She wouldn't collapse in a quivering mass of nerves and hysterics as Allison had always done.

He still didn't want to believe Sarah could be as deceitful as Allison, but she was. He held the evidence in his hand. He stared down at the photo, trying to deny the obvious. The picture was decades old, but the girl looked very much like Sarah must have at that age. *And the boy could have been David.*

"You have no proof." His voice grated on the words as if they might prove a talisman of some sort.

Sarah gestured toward the photograph, her hand trembling. "That's my proof. One snapshot and all I feel in my heart. That's all the proof I'll ever have but it's enough."

"I'll fight you all the way if you try and take him from me." The tone of his voice, the look on his face, told Sarah even more plainly than words that Tyler wouldn't be reasoned with. He was thinking with his heart, not with his brain. He'd shut her out, sealed himself away from her so completely, she knew she wouldn't get through to him now no matter how hard she tried. The realization burned like acid through her veins.

"I wouldn't do that, Tyler." Was it only yesterday that he'd told her he was falling in love with her?

"How can I be sure?" He tried to soften the rough edges of his words when he saw the effect his anger was having on her. He wasn't being rational and he knew it; yet he couldn't seem to help himself. How could this be happening now, when he'd finally started to get his life back in order, when he'd started to believe in the future again?

"Because I love him." *And I love you.*

Tyler felt some of the panic recede into the darkness from which it had sprung. It wasn't so much what Sarah said as how she said it that placated the demon inside him. "I know," he answered very quietly. "We both do."

"I won't say anything, or do anything, without consulting you, Tyler." Sarah stood up in her haste to make him understand. Photos and other bits and pieces of the past scattered in all directions. She'd been sitting so long she'd forgotten about her injured ankle. A sharp pain streaked through her instep as she rose. She ignored it, biting back a cry, swaying a little to catch her balance, but there was nothing for her to hold on to. Tyler was across the room in two long strides, his hands hard and sure on her upper arms.

"Okay?" His eyes were so dark a blue they were almost black, still devoid of expression. The look he gave her was frighteningly emotionless, as though he'd retreated even farther into himself than when they'd first met.

"I'm fine. I forgot about this blasted ankle." Sarah tried desperately to get the conversation out of treacherous waters. "Tyler, we can work this out. I care for you and David so much."

"I don't want David's life disrupted any more than it already has been. There's no way I can explain you, or your place in his life, without telling him the whole truth. I can't do that. I won't do that." Tyler's words were no longer spoken in the heat of anger. He sounded resigned.

"I won't say anything." Sarah tried for reassurance, missed, and realized she only sounded frightened and forlorn. She took a deep breath to still the panicked beat of her heart, so high in her throat it almost choked her. "I'm concerned about his welfare, too. But Tyler, don't take him away." She was grateful to hear the words come out clear and even, if not very strong. It was the hardest thing she'd ever done, not allowing herself to plead with him, not allowing her tears to fall.

"I'm not going anywhere." Tyler snorted in disgust. Releasing her, he swung away, staring out across the straits. It was a surprise to see the sun still shining in the sky. He was certain it had grown dark as midnight outside, as well as in his heart. "I haven't got anywhere else to go right now. My apartment's sublet. I'd have to move into the parsonage with Elliot. David and I...we're better off here."

"Do you want me to go? Leave the island?" Sarah honestly didn't know how she found the courage to speak. She would go, if that was what Tyler thought David needed right now.

"No." He didn't want her to go. He wanted her to stay with him, let him learn to trust her again. But could he risk that? He took the easy way out. "David wouldn't understand if you were to leave before you'd planned to return to Chicago."

"I'll be very careful around him, Tyler." He still held the photo in his hand. Sarah moved toward him, limping slightly. She held out her hand for the small rectangular image that had changed her world. "He'll forget the picture in a matter of days if we don't mention it again."

"Yes."

He sounded distant, as if he'd already erased her from his life. New pain knifed through her heart. David would forget about her, too, after he left Mackinac and went back to his familiar life in Georgia, or to a new life with Tyler someplace far away, strange and exciting and full of adventure. "Tyler,

I'm not going to try to replace Allison in David's life. I'll do whatever is best for him.''

"I know that, Sarah." Tyler let his breath out in a long soundless whistle. He did know that about her; although he wasn't sure why he could be so certain. No matter how much this discovery had thrown him for a loop, he still believed she wouldn't do anything to hurt his son. It was his own feelings, his own heart, that were so unreliable. "As far as David is concerned, nothing's changed."

"Thank you. I'm sorry you've been hurt, Tyler. I never meant you to find out this way."

"But I did." He shoved his hands in his pockets and balled them into fists.

"You did," she agreed very quietly. "Tyler, as far as we—you and I—are concerned..." Sarah let her words drift into silence, knowing the answer before he spoke.

Tyler turned to face her, not letting himself respond to the suffering in her blue eyes. "I think it will be better if we don't see each other for a while. I have to think this whole thing through, review my options."

He was telling her she had no right to plan anything for David, or for their future, either. Sarah absorbed the blow, deferring the pain as she'd done the rest, until later, when she was alone and the tears could fall.

"Tyler, my feelings for you are separate from my feelings for David." She wasn't expressing herself very well but she couldn't come up with a polished and logical explanation and she couldn't tell him simply that she ached with desire for him, for she loved him—as a man, not as a child.

He stared right through her. It didn't help to see he was as miserable as she was. "Are they, Sarah? How can you be sure? I think that's a question we can't afford not to find the answer to, for all our sakes."

CAMILLA WONDERED JUST HOW MUCH longer she should allow Sarah to remain shut away in her room. A day and a night seemed long enough. It was cold and damp this morning. The upstairs of the cottage wasn't heated. The kitchen, on the other hand, was cozy and warm and redolent with the smells of chicken broth and celery, parsley and rosemary. Camilla couldn't recall the last time she'd made chicken-noodle soup but she hadn't lost the knack. It looked delicious, smelled delicious and tasted delicious, if she did say so herself. It was time Sarah rejoined the living and shared a bowl with her.

She'd heard Sarah pacing the floor at intervals during the night. She didn't think her great-niece was sleeping now, since it was almost noon. Whatever had passed between Sarah and Tyler Danielson yesterday had been devastating to Sarah's peace of mind. That it concerned more than the discovery of David's true parentage was a foregone conclusion in Camilla's mind. She walked purposefully through the dining alcove and main room and started up the stairs.

Yesterday she'd been with Elliot, admiring the progress of her plants around the base of the gazebo, when David had joined them, a plate of cookies in his hand, questions in his brown eyes. Elliot hadn't grasped the significance of his grandson's rambling account of having found a picture of a boy who looked just like him, but Camilla did. She'd never seen a childhood picture of Rebecca Austin or her twin brother but there was no doubt in her mind that Sarah's maternal uncle was who David was talking about.

So Sarah had found another slim strand of evidence to weave into her tapestry of hope and faith. And perhaps a fuse to set off a charge to further damage the fragile framework of the relationship between David, Tyler and Elliot?

Camilla had stared helplessly at the reviving pink geraniums at her feet, waiting for the storm to break around them. But nothing had happened. Elliot listened to David's description of the old-fashioned clothes the boy had worn and his neat, funny cap. He said, "Isn't that interesting?" Then he accepted another one of Mrs. Meecham's cookies with a sheepish grin.

Camilla hadn't been able to muster much of a smile in return. Opportunely, Spice chose that moment to stick her head over the fence and whinny a greeting. Diverted, David shoved the empty cookie plate into Camilla's hands and switched subjects, wheedling his grandfather into saddling the two mares for a ride. Camilla had seconded the suggestion, relieved to have David's interest in the old snapshot replaced.

She'd been standing in the same spot, still holding the empty plate, when Tyler left the cottage. Her heart sank when she saw the darkness in his face, the frustration and misery. He knew. And he wasn't going to accept Sarah's part in David's life easily.

Is that how the adoptive parents of her daughter would have felt if she'd ever had the courage to search them out? She'd never tried to find her child but from what she'd learned of Sarah's experience in trying to trace David she was beginning to believe that looking would have been futile. Justin Delano had been a thorough and methodical man. It wasn't out of line to assume that he would have handled her daughter's adoption any differently than David's. If anything, that long ago, it would have been even easier to destroy any proof of the baby's real identity.

But Camilla would never know because she'd lacked the courage to find out. And that was what made the past so hard to accept, today.

David waved at his father as the two reluctant steeds ambled out onto the street. "Dad, I put the bridle and bit on Spice all by myself. Granddad had to saddle her, though." He sat tall and straight in the saddle. In his eyes, Spice was the fiery charger of every little boy's dreams.

Elliot reined in his mount. "We won't go far, Tyler." He spoke stiffly, formally.

"Granddad says he hasn't been on a horse in years," David volunteered, already urging Spice forward. "We'll just go a little way. Maybe back to Arch Rock. I know the way now."

Tyler nodded. "Be careful," he added automatically. He ran a hand distractedly through the sable dark layers of his hair. "Send David over to our place when he gets back, will you?" He didn't really seem to be looking at Camilla, although his midnight-blue eyes bored into her face.

"Tyler, I'm sorry you had to find out this way."

He didn't pretend to misunderstand her. "So am I, Aunt Cam." His tone warned her off. "Don't let David talk you into any more cookies. It will spoil his dinner." He turned his back and walked away. If she'd had any thought of trying to reason with him, the stiff, unyielding set of his broad shoulders disabused her of the notion, then and there.

"Of course." She knew her words were cowardly and appeasing. If he'd turned that frighteningly cold and unemotional stare on Sarah, it was no wonder her great-niece had retreated upstairs and shut herself into her room. Camilla could still feel the ice of his stony gaze twenty-four hours later.

She shivered but the chill she felt now, standing outside Sarah's closed bedroom door, was physical, not mental. She was uncertain about what to do. She'd come this far and was sorely tempted to turn around and go back to the warmth and comfortable loneliness of the kitchen. How could she presume to advise and comfort Sarah when her whole life had been based on lies? When the greatest lie had been a denial so personal and so agonizing that not one living soul had ever been allowed to share her grief?

And that was why she couldn't turn back now. Because if she could spare Sarah, or share with her, even a very small portion of her pain, it would be worth the cost to her own soul.

"Sarah?" She knocked softly, tentatively. No answer. Camilla considered retreating from the confrontation as she'd done so often before but rejected the idea. She knocked again, louder this time. "Sarah." She repeated her niece's name with more force. "Are you all right?"

"Yes." The answer came reluctantly. "I'm all right."

"I wish you'd let me in."

"I'd rather be alone."

"I know you would but that doesn't change the fact that you'll have to come out of that room sooner or later." Camilla's tone softened a little. "I made chicken soup. It's the universal remedy for what ails you." She smiled. "Especially if you have it with one or two glasses of the very nice Chardonnay I bought when I went down below with Madge and the girls last week."

"No, thanks."

Camilla ignored Sarah's refusal and the nervous flutter of her own heart. She turned the knob. The door wasn't locked, probably because most of the heavy skeleton keys to the old-fashioned locks had been lost years before. "Sarah, we need to talk."

"Why?" Sarah was huddled in a big walnut rocking chair, wrapped in a quilt of faded greens and pinks. Her face was pale and set, her eyes red-rimmed from weeping and bruised with sadness. She'd pulled her hair back from her face and tied it with a scarf, accenting the curve of her cheekbones and the angle of her small, determined chin.

Camilla sighed. It was going to be more difficult than she'd thought to break through Sarah's defenses. "Because I'm worried about you and I want to be of help if I can."

Sarah didn't look at her. Instead, she studied the carved finial on top of the four-poster bed directly above Camilla's head. "I found a picture of my mother and her brother. It's on the dressing table." Her voice sounded as tired as she looked. Camilla moved to the oak table, seeing herself reflected darkly in the wavy glass of the mirror above it. She looked her age again today, despite her best efforts with hair and makeup. She ignored her unflattering double and picked up the photo.

Sarah, she discovered, had looked very much like her mother at that young age. And David was the image of Rebecca's brother. Yet there were differences, too. David's nose was bolder, his cheekbones more defined. Still, there was no denying the relationship. "This is what you've been searching for."

"David was there when I came across it. He showed it to Tyler."

"I guessed as much." Camilla laid the snapshot down where she'd found it. "I'm sorry the timing was so unfortunate."

"It can't be helped now." Sarah sounded anything but resigned.

Camilla stared at the wallpaper, pink cabbage roses entwined with ivy tendrils on a cream-colored background. It had been fairly hideous when it was new. Now it had faded to an almost watercolor softness that lent it charm, if not beauty. Would telling Sarah that railing against fate didn't make its burdens any easier to bear help her at all? The silence stretched out between them. Camilla slid the snapshot a little farther toward the back of the dressing table.

"I gave Tyler my word that I wouldn't tell David what I've learned."

"I think that's wise." Camilla wasn't prepared for the animosity or the agony of Sarah's reaction.

"How can you stand there and tell me what's wise, Aunt Camilla? You've never lost a child, had him taken from you because you were too young and too confused to fight to keep him."

"Be that as it may." Camilla began to feel the room close in around her. It had never been so hard to play the part she'd created for herself. She'd been a fool to come up here and force the issue with Sarah. She couldn't help her niece. She couldn't even help herself.

Sarah erupted out of the rocking chair, sending it skittering backward across the wooden floor. "Be that as it may. Is that all you can say?"

"No, it's not." Camilla pulled her shoulders back and faced Sarah head-on. "You were blessed with the good fortune to find convincing enough evidence of your relationship to David to end your search. The odds of your ever doing that were beyond calculation. You've met him, you've established a relationship with him. That makes your good fortune more nearly a miracle." Her voice threatened to crack on the last words. Camilla swallowed hard to rid her throat of the burning sting of tears.

"But it isn't enough, Aunt Cam." Sarah let the old quilt fall to the floor. Her blouse was wrinkled, the collar askew, the tail hanging outside her jeans. "You just can't know how much it hurts."

"I can." The words almost choked her in their effort to be allowed to leave her tongue.

"That's impossible," Sarah said, holding out her hand in a

helpless gesture. "How can you know how much it hurts to lose a child?" There was bewilderment and pity in her niece's blue eyes. Suddenly it was too much hurt to keep inside another moment.

"I gave up a baby, too." Camilla's legs refused to hold her. She sat down on the lumpy mattress of Sarah's bed, her hands digging into the covers like claws.

"Your baby?" Sarah's tone was disbelieving. Camilla was equally shocked at what she'd done. She'd kept her secret so long. From so many people. Why had she blurted out the truth now?

"My baby. My daughter." She shut her mouth with a snap, holding back a sob.

"Oh, God." Sarah's plea to the Almighty came from her heart. "Aunt Cam, why didn't you ever tell me?"

"I never told anyone. Your grandmother insisted on it. Sarah, you have to try to understand what it was like all those years ago. I was pregnant, unmarried. The baby's father was a married man with other children and a very prominent wife." Camilla lifted her hand, trying to find all the right words and failing. Instead, she stuck to the facts, her voice low and whispery with tears. "He had a terrible reputation with women but I was naive enough, flattered enough, even silly enough, to think he really loved me." The pressure of tears behind her eyes was too much. They began to slip silently down her cheeks. Camilla made an effort to pull herself together. "It would have been a terrible scandal and I've never been very brave. I didn't even learn I was pregnant until after I came here to spend the summer with your grandmother."

"And that was the summer you met Elliot Brandon?" Sarah knelt beside the bed. She took Camilla's cold hands between her own. The older woman clung to her, seeking reassurance and finding it in her niece's gentle touch.

"Yes." There was an echo of wonder still to be heard in the simple affirmative. "But I couldn't tell him, you see. He was a minister, or soon would be, a man of God. And I, well, I thought I was no better than a magdalen."

"No." Sarah's voice was firm. "You were young and innocent. The victim of a selfish and uncaring man and a double standard that gave you almost no other choice than the one you made.''

"I didn't understand that then. Maybe I never have, until today." Camilla took a deep shuddering breath. "Most of all, I didn't want to see Elliot turn away from me when he learned the truth of my condition. And having him stay with me—out of pity—would have been even harder to bear than not having his love at all."

"That's why you sent him the letter telling him you couldn't marry him."

Camilla nodded sadly. "I couldn't tell him the truth. I couldn't go to him carrying another man's child. I went to Florida with your grandmother. Gasoline rationing made traveling difficult, so no one was likely to come all that way to visit us and learn about the baby. Justin Delano arranged for me to go to a little town near Sarasota for the birth."

"And Justin Delano orchestrated your baby's adoption, too." Sarah let the sharp edges of her words slice away at the familiar bitterness she still felt toward the dead man. Camilla merely nodded in response, looking down at their intertwined hands.

"Let go of the past, Sarah." As she spoke she felt a weight lift within her own heart. She smiled. The pain of it had been with her so long she'd learned to ignore its existence. Now she rejoiced that the dull ache was finally gone.

"Finding David is making it easier." Sarah smiled, too, and the magnitude of her discovery shone in her eyes.

"I never saw my daughter but I do know the child was a little girl," Camilla revealed, eager to talk now that the taboo subject had been broached. "I bribed one of the nurses to tell me so when I left the hospital." More tears formed in her eyes and slid silently down her cheeks. "I never made an attempt to find her."

"You would most likely have run into the same dead ends that I did. Justin Delano was a very thorough man. Even in Florida he had probably managed to make everything that could connect you to the child disappear. I wonder how many other quiet, private adoptions he arranged over the years?"

Camilla shuddered, shaking her head, her eyes closed against the past. "I don't want to know. I just pray that my daughter and any other children he might have placed found families that love them as much as Elliot and Tyler love David."

"I'm sure your daughter is well and happy wherever she is." Sarah stood up, wincing slightly when she put weight on her injured ankle. "You've kept this secret for so long." She frowned in disbelief.

"So very long," Camilla agreed sadly. "Do you understand now why I was so little help to you when you were carrying David?" Camilla held her breath. It was all out in the open and the earth hadn't split wide to swallow her. She'd been young and innocent and manipulated, just like Sarah. Did that help to justify her failure years later?

"I wish I'd known. I wish you could have told me." Sarah stopped speaking. So many hard feelings could have been avoided.

"The important thing is that you know now." Camilla smiled hopefully through her tears.

"And that I understand now," Sarah added softly. "Do you think Grandmother was trying to make it up to us just a little by leaving us the Gathering Place?"

Camilla squeezed Sarah's hands, then released her. They'd turned the corner. Everything would be all right now. "I don't know. She did love this place very much. She acted according to her principles and the dictates of her generation. She must have thought she failed us, too. You're all the family I have left. It must have hurt her to see us estranged."

"Her legacy has given us an opportunity to come face-to-face with the past. And if I hadn't come here this summer, I would never have found my child." Sarah closed her eyes against the stark finality of that statement.

"Being here has given you a miracle but it's also given the past an opportunity to intrude into the present." Camilla tilted her head and frowned thoughtfully.

"You mean Elliot's being here?" Sarah asked, wiping tears from her cheeks with the tips of her fingers. So many separate strands of all their lives were being interwoven on this tiny island, set into new patterns that would have bearing on the rest of their lives.

"He must never know." Camilla dried her own eyes with a tissue from the pocket of her skirt. "I want you to promise me that, Sarah. I've kept my secret for over forty years. Please forget I ever told you."

Sarah took her aunt's hand as the older woman rose from the bed. "Don't ask me to forget. I'll keep your confidence, that goes without saying, but if you still have feelings for Elliot, don't let your past stand in the way. Promise me."

"I don't know if I can do that." Camilla linked her arm through Sarah's as they started downstairs. "The past is sometimes very much part of the present. It's causing you and Tyler a great deal of anguish." She was silent a moment, gathering her thoughts. "I'm still not a brave woman, Sarah. After so many years of avoiding meeting life head-on, in all its pain and glory, I may be too old to even find love again, let alone summon the strength to make it last."

CHAPTER THIRTEEN

TYLER MOVED ASIDE the lace curtain covering his bedroom window and held it anchored against the frame with the palm of his hand. He looked out into the clear quiet night. There was a light on in Sarah's bedroom. Branches screened the view so that only the shadows of her figure passing back and forth were visible from time to time, but he knew. Aunt Cam had gone to sleep hours ago. Her window was only a dark rectangle against the paler bulk of the cottage. It was Sarah's room he watched; it was Sarah's body that he saw in tantalizing glimpses. He knew because it was two-fifteen in the morning and she was still awake, just as he was.

Tyler lifted his free hand and rubbed the tight muscles at the back of his neck. It had been a very long five days; the longest days of his life. He'd kept David close at first, manufacturing excuses not to allow him to accompany Aunt Cam or Elliot on any of their excursions. Camilla had come to him at the end of the second day, gardening gloves and trowel still in hand, and told him in no uncertain terms that he was only punishing David for his own misery. Reluctantly, Tyler had had to agree.

Camilla knew that David was Sarah's son; she had said nothing directly but he could read the knowledge in her eyes. He also saw compassion and integrity reflected there. She would keep Sarah's confidence; she would tell no one, not even Elliot. He trusted Sarah's great-aunt, regardless of the fact that his father-in-law was part of her past and very much a part of her present. She loved David; they all did. Camilla would do her best to see that he came to no harm.

It was getting cold in his bedroom and he picked up his

shirt from the chair where he'd tossed it hours ago. He dragged it across the broad width of his shoulders, letting it hang outside his jeans, not bothering to button it as he silently crossed the floor, moving into the hall as he headed for David's room. Soft little-boy snores greeted him as he stuck his head around the half-open door. David was a rounded hump beneath the white chenille bedspread. He was sound asleep, one arm flung out onto the pillow. The black band of his brand-new digital wristwatch, bought with this week's entire allowance, was dark against the white linen.

Tyler envied the child his sound sleep. He hadn't slept much at all for the past five nights. He couldn't get Sarah out of his mind, waking or sleeping. But at least awake he wasn't prey to his dreams. He could censor his thoughts, filter out the sweet memories of her touch, her kisses, the way she felt so right in his arms. Asleep he had no such defenses. He couldn't erase her from his brain or his heart but neither could he face her with what they both now accepted as the truth.

Sarah Austin was David's mother.

And he was falling in love with her. *Hell, I probably already am in love with her.* But that didn't alter reality. He needed time to sort out his thoughts, consider his options. He needed to get back to Georgia, talk to his lawyer, make arrangements to regain custody of David first and foremost.

His fear of losing control of his life as had happened when he went to prison, his fear of losing David to Elliot permanently, wasn't entirely rational, but it was very, very real. Deep inside him, now, at this moment, it was what mattered most. Everything took second place to that terrifying possibility. Everything, including his unresolved relationship with Sarah.

David twisted and rolled onto his side, muttering in his sleep, sending the cowboy hat and red bandanna scarf Michael had bought him sliding from the pillow to the floor. Tyler retrieved them and put them on the chair by the bed. David was turning into an avid horseman. A crooked half smile twisted his lips. His son's dreams were probably filled with

Indian braves, daring escapes and caves full of Indian artifacts and hidden trappers' wealth.

His dreams, if he should allow himself to fall so deeply asleep, would be filled with images of Sarah: scents and sights and sounds of her soft and pliant beneath him, strong and supportive at his side. Tyler pulled the blanket over his son's bony shoulders, no longer smiling.

He frowned, trying to see something of Sarah in David's round unfinished features, but the resemblance escaped him. What he did see of Sarah in his son was her headlong rush to experience life and learn its secrets. He bent and kissed David lightly on the forehead, then lifted his hand to push back a curly wave of brown hair from his brow. Perhaps, deep down, he didn't want to see a physical resemblance to Sarah in the boy's features. Probably because he'd tried so hard all these years to see something of himself in David and failed.

Tyler straightened abruptly and started back to his room. He hadn't told anyone yet but he was planning to leave the island. Elliot and Michael were due to return to Georgia in three or four days' time. He and David would have a day or two after that. He needed time to be alone. He needed to sort out his feelings. He hadn't talked to Sarah at length since the day he'd learned the truth about David's parentage but he couldn't go on avoiding her forever.

Yet he hadn't been able to make himself go to her, either. He needed to come to terms with her new place in David's life and deal with his feelings of betrayal, as well. Because, damn it, he did feel betrayed and it was tearing him apart inside. But first he had to get through the rest of the night, sleep, and still hold his dreams at bay because in the morning he would have to face Sarah whether he was ready to or not.

They were going sailing and Sarah was coming along. David had invited her yesterday when they'd returned from a short trip along the coastline. David had enjoyed the afternoon so much he'd run outside to tell Sarah and Aunt Cam all about it the moment they'd returned home from an outing with Elliot and Michael.

He'd launched into an account of the boat Tyler had rented

at the marina and outlined his great plan to sail under the Mackinac Bridge the following morning so that he could look up at all the cars and trucks passing by high overhead. Then, before Tyler could do anything to stop him, he'd invited Sarah along.

She had looked to him first for guidance, or perhaps a clue to his reaction. He'd stared at a point somewhere beyond her left shoulder and mumbled a polite second to his son's invitation. He'd already made arrangements to rent the boat for another day. He hadn't been able to think of any good reason for her not to come—at least not any reason he could bring up in front of the others. She'd smiled down at David, her sapphire-blue eyes dark with hidden pain, and accepted, thereby ensuring another sleepless night for both of them.

THE SUN HAD BEEN PEEPING over the horizon, the sky turning from dawn gray to summer blue before Sarah went to sleep. Now it was almost eleven. Ten fifty-six, to be exact. She ought to know; she'd looked at the clock often enough in the past hour. She couldn't find anything else to do. She'd buffed her nails, washed her hair, made her bed. She'd gone downstairs for coffee twice; she'd studied the high fleecy clouds long and seriously for any sign of rain. Nothing. It was a lovely day, a crisp breeze blowing out of the west, warm and sunny and perfect for sailing.

She wondered if it was too late to back out of the trip with Tyler and David. She didn't want to go. She'd been existing in a kind of emotional limbo for almost a week and she was afraid to break out of its safe and comforting shell.

Coming out would mean having to deal with the issues between Tyler and herself and she didn't want to do that. Not yet. This way she had hope, even if she did nothing to act on it. If she met him face-to-face and he rejected her outright, she'd have nothing left to cling to. Emptiness, she was coming to believe, was the most frightening prospect of all.

"Sarah." She closed her eyes against a rush of bittersweet happiness. She didn't care if David was never able to call her "Mother." Just knowing that happy, excited voice belonged to her child, her son, was miracle enough. She crossed the big drafty bedroom and raised one of the side-by-side double-hung windows.

"Are you ready to go so soon?" she asked, hanging out of the screenless opening to see David astride his beater on the street outside the cottage.

"You're late. You said you'd be ready at eleven." He proudly displayed a new wristwatch Sarah had never seen before. "It's eleven-o-two."

"Heavens. I'll have to fly."

"Step on it," David called back. "We have to walk the bikes down the long way."

At least he seemed to have learned a little prudence when it came to cycling on the island's steep hills.

"I'll be down as soon as I find a scarf for my hair." She shut the window with a bang, pulled open the chest of drawers and twisted a sunny peach and yellow striped scarf through the knot on top of her head. She didn't intend to spend the day brushing strands of damp hair out of her mouth and eyes.

"I'm leaving, Aunt Cam," she called as she passed the bathroom door. She could hear Camilla humming as she splashed in the huge cast-iron tub.

"Have fun, dear."

"I will." Sarah sounded more optimistic than she felt. She still had a lot of doubts about spending the afternoon with Tyler. They hadn't been alone together since the day she'd found the picture.

They had to talk, about David and, even more importantly, about themselves. But neither had been brave enough yet to broach either subject. Time was running out for all of them. Once they left the island it would be too late. Circumstances, just the problems of commitments, distance and day-to-day living, would help reinforce the barriers that already existed between them. She wanted to be part of David's life. But even more, she wanted to be part of Tyler's.

Perhaps that was why she'd agreed to have dinner with Michael Parker tonight. He knew Tyler Danielson better than anyone else. He might offer some solution, give her some piece of advice that would move her relationship with Tyler forward in some small way.

But even as she yearned for wise counsel, was she free to tell Michael what she'd learned about David's parentage? What loyalty did she owe a dead woman she'd never met?

Tyler, walking his bicycle through the gate, heard the last exchange between Sarah and David. "While we're waiting for Sarah to come down, why don't you go around to the stable and get her bike, sport? It will save some time."

"Okay." David didn't look overly pleased to be asked to run the errand. He walked off, scuffing sneakered toes in the dust, slamming the gate with more force than was necessary.

Tyler frowned after the departing figure of his son. Was it his imagination or was David becoming somewhat spoiled by all the attention he'd been getting these past few weeks? It seemed he was always coming up against these riddles of parenting. What was too much authority? How much was too little?

Sarah came out the front door just as David drew even with the cottage. As Tyler watched David told her of his errand, gesturing and waving his hands. Sarah thanked him and moved on down the path. She looked bright and pretty and very, very sexy in drawstring pants that were the color of peach sherbet and a sleeveless white cotton top. A white windbreaker lay across her arm; gold studs winked like sunbeams in her ears. Her hair was piled on top of her head and held in place with a scarf.

Only her eyes betrayed her. They were soft and dark as a twilight sky. Sadness lurked in their sapphire depths. Tyler wanted to make the sadness go away. But he could not. He was the cause of her sadness now, not the cure.

"You look as if you're pondering one of the mysteries of the universe." Sarah was determined to act as if this were just an ordinary day.

"Almost that important. The mysteries of parenting."

"Oh."

Sarah looked down at her rubber-soled deck shoes. Tyler realized his mistake almost immediately. She probably thought he was warning her off any discussion of David. And perhaps, honestly, he was. She lifted her head proudly, taking his cue. She looked into the distance and pronounced it a perfect day for sailing.

"You're right." Tyler also chose the safer subject of the weather. "At least as far as the rest of this morning goes. There's a possibility of squalls and thunderstorms later in the day. In fact, for the next few days."

"I must have been listening to the wrong radio station meteorologist." Sarah smiled but it took a lot of work. Tyler looked good, tan and sleek, the bright white cotton of his T-shirt setting off the dark sable waves of his hair. He was wearing red shorts and the silk-screened design of sailboats and clouds and bold slashing letters spelling out Mackinac across the front of his T-shirt were predominantly that color, too.

Tyler nodded sagely. "Probably one of those stations geared to the tourist trade. Always overly optimistic. Partly sunny instead of cloudy, a chance of showers when it's already starting to rain. I, on the other hand, have been listening directly to the Coast Guard updates." He gave her a wicked and very superior grin.

"Good. Then I'm not putting myself into the hands of a novice."

"No." Tyler's voice dropped in pitch. Sarah felt the familiar exciting tingle of the rough dark words skitter across her nerve endings. "Not a novice. Just a little rusty and out of practice." He watched her closely but Sarah held her ground.

"I haven't been sailing in years. Let's not get too brave, or foolish, the first time out." Her tone was superficially bright. It didn't fool Tyler. He knew he'd hurt her badly with his reaction to what they had learned of David's true parentage. If he felt betrayed by what had happened, so must she have been betrayed by the way he'd reacted.

"Here's your bike, Sarah. Let's go." Sarah dropped her gaze, grateful to be released from the beckoning pull of Tyler's eyes. David was miffed about something. His eyebrows, bleached almost blond by the sun, were pulled together in a fairly good imitation of Tyler's scowl.

"Thank you for bringing my bike to me. What's wrong?" She wanted to reach out and touch him but did nothing of the sort.

"You're welcome," he said grudgingly, glancing at his father. "All I get to do around here anymore is run errands and do chores. Make your bed, David. Dry the dishes, David. Go get Sarah's bike, David. It's a pain."

"It's called growing up," Tyler said. "Come on. I can't wait to see the boat." The boy brightened at the reminder of what the day had to offer and, all in all, it was a quick, uneventful trip down to the marina.

The sailboat Tyler had rented was a pretty little Sunbird with a rainbow-colored mainsail and a bright yellow jib. The cabin was tiny, only big enough to store the gear and get out of the rain. David thought it was fantastic. They parked their bikes and loaded the picnic lunch Tyler had ordered from a small deli near the marina.

With a minimum of fuss, considering the lack of recent sailing experience for both Tyler and Sarah, they puttered out of the harbor with the help of a small auxiliary motor and raised the sails. Soon they were running swiftly before the wind.

The remainder of the morning passed quickly. David was suitably impressed as they sailed under the mighty suspension bridge that spanned the narrowest portion of the straits. One of the longest suspension bridges in the world, its ivory-colored towers rose hundreds of feet into the air above them.

"What do you think of it, David?" Sarah asked, leaning back against the molded seat of the cockpit to watch cars and trucks pass overhead through the gridwork of suspension joints.

"Wow! I thought it was great to drive over it but this is..."

"Fantastic," Tyler and Sarah chorused in unison.

"Well, it is." David looked peeved. "I'm hungry, let's eat." He glanced pointedly at his new wristwatch. Obligingly, Tyler turned the sailboat toward the southern shoreline.

"No, Dad," David shouted over the slap of waves and the rush of wind in the sails. "That way." He pointed to the hills west of St. Ignace. "There must be a place to park this thing over there. See the sign? McDonald's. I'm starved for a Big Mac and fries." Set on stilts sixty feet high, the familiar golden arches were plainly visible in the distance.

"No way, sport." Tyler grinned down at David's scowling face. "The air's so clear up here it fools your eyes. It's six or seven miles from here to there and the wind's against us. You'll have to make do with the stuff in the picnic basket."

"I don't want that junk." David folded his hands over his chest. As he was wearing a bright orange life vest over his green and blue striped polo shirt, his hands barely met at the wrist, giving him the look of a colorful and dissatisfied circus fat man. "Is there a McDonald's here?" he asked shrewdly, gesturing toward Mackinaw City, behind and beyond Fort Michilimackinac, which was directly in front of them.

"Yes, there is." Tyler set his jaw. It looked as if this was going to be one of those increasingly frequent occasions where David pushed him to the limits of his patience. "It's starting to cloud up. The weather's changing. I don't want to waste a lot of time docking the boat just to walk into town and get junk food you can eat any day of the week. Some other time but not today." He thought he'd handled David pretty well, all things considered.

Sarah had been sitting quietly, sorting through the foil-wrapped sandwiches and pieces of fruit in the plastic-foam hamper. She handed him a ham sandwich. Tyler took it with a curt nod. She offered David half a turkey club sandwich.

"I hate tomatoes," he informed her belligerently. "You should know that by now."

"David, that's enough." Tyler pointed his finger at a section of the molded seat. "Sit down and eat. If you don't want turkey or ham, there's peanut butter and jelly."

"I want a Big Mac and fries," David repeated.

"Well, you're not going to get them." He was beginning to sound like an eight-year-old himself, Tyler thought disgustedly.

"Then I'll starve and it will be your fault," David announced and launched himself down the steps into the cabin.

Tyler stared at his uneaten sandwich. Sarah took a small bite of the rejected turkey club. She was trying very hard not to smile. The sandwich almost stuck in her throat. Poor Tyler, he was finally learning what it was really like to parent a child. So was she and she liked it very much. Sarah popped the tab on a can of soda, took a swallow and offered the container to Tyler.

He took it and shook his head, the bewildered look on his face touching something deep and caring inside Sarah's heart. "I've got to be doing something wrong."

"You're not doing anything wrong," she assured him from a fount of feminine wisdom she hadn't known she previously possessed. "David's testing you. All kids do it. They're always pushing to see how far they can go, what they can get away with."

"I suppose that's true." He propped his foot along the seat, one arm resting on the steering board. He took a bite of the ham sandwich and stared at the restored wooden stockade on the beach. "The point is, how far do you let them go?"

"As far as necessary to help them grow and mature but not so far as to put them at risk." Did he know how much this meant to her, to be consulted in the ordering of David's life this way?

Tyler squinted at the sun, fast disappearing behind a cloud. Sarah looked up, too, needing the pause in the conversation to gain control over her emotions. The clouds above were no longer fleecy white but ragged and gray, growing heavy with rain and the threat of storms.

"In other words, you're telling me that this is a very minor skirmish in an ongoing war, and not a major battle."

"Something like that." Sarah smiled and laid her sandwich on the seat beside her. She held the can of soda in her left hand and wiped at the beads of condensation with her thumb.

"It's been happening a lot lately," Tyler confessed. He liked having Sarah here to discuss things with.

"That's because David is learning to trust you."

"Trust me?" Tyler motioned with his sandwich toward the cabin, where pointed and pained silence reigned.

"What was David like when he first came here with you, Tyler?" She could see his thoughts turn back to those first tense days on the island.

"Polite, too serious, quiet."

"And now?"

"It's like living with a tornado on legs," Tyler admitted frankly.

"And what were you like those first few days together?" She leaned forward, drawn toward the strength and power of his body, the warmth of the half smile playing along the chiseled corners of his mouth, the promise of his touch.

"Too polite, too serious, quiet." He smiled fully then and reached over his bent knee to touch her cheek. The caress was as light and fleeting as the kiss of sea spray on her skin. "I get your point. David and I are developing a healthy father and son relationship. He pushes and pulls and I give him space, but not too much space."

"And you're always there when he wants to come home, when he wants to feel safe and loved because the world out there is too big and scary some days." Sarah settled back into the hard curve of the seat. She didn't want him to touch her again. It just made it harder to keep her distance. It hurt to be so close physically, and yet so far apart in every other respect.

"Sarah, I've been thinking."

"Yes?" There was something in his voice she couldn't quite identify. Sarah wrapped her hands around her knees, holding her breath, waiting for what he had to say. David chose that inopportune moment to stalk out of the cabin. Sarah bit her lip in frustration.

"I guess if there's nothing but peanut butter and jelly, I'll have to eat that."

"'Fraid so." Tyler looked sympathetic but slightly off balance.

"The next time anyone goes into town, I get to go along and get a Big Mac and fries," David insisted. "Please," he added with a sheepish but still slightly defiant grin.

"It's a deal." Tyler handed him half a peanut butter and jelly sandwich and a can of orange soda.

"Geez," David complained a few moments later. "It's get-tin' cold out here." He looked up at the sky, the second half of the peanut butter sandwich brandished toward the clouds. "It's gonna rain, I bet."

Tyler turned and faced toward the southwest. "Looks like the Coast Guard was a little optimistic, too. That squall line is headed our way."

"Can we outrun it?"

"We can try." He began to make preparations to set sail. "Sarah, a few minutes ago, before David came out…"

"Yes?" Sarah was busy stowing remnants of the lunch in the hamper.

"I wanted to ask you…"

A sudden unexpected gust of wind caught the little boat, laying the boom hard over, catching Sarah unaware, sending her and the hamper sprawling. Apples, bananas and two peaches landed on the deck and began to roll around. Sarah was luckier; she landed in Tyler's lap.

He held her close against him for a long, heart-stopping moment. What if she'd been hurt? He held her tightly a second longer then turned her in his arms. "Are you okay? Did the boom hit you?"

Sarah tried out her voice. It was breathless but steady enough. "I'm fine. I ducked. I just wasn't ready for that."

"Neither was I. How's the ankle?"

"Not a twinge." Sarah wiggled her foot to prove her point. She knew she shouldn't let Tyler hold her like this but she couldn't seem to help herself. David was scrambling around on hands and knees, retrieving the fruit, pitching it into the hamper helter-skelter. It wouldn't be fit for anything but fruit salad by the time they got back to the island but Sarah didn't even care.

"Good." Tyler found it hard to break eye contact. He couldn't seem to take his hands from the soft curve of her waist, either. Should he ask her to have dinner with him this evening? Was that a good way to start over again with her?

"You were going to ask me a question," Sarah prompted, her eyes sparkling.

"I was? I mean, I was." Another gust of wind rattled the sails and reminded Tyler the weather was deteriorating as fast as his common sense. Maybe she didn't even want to have dinner with him tonight after what had passed between them. He'd never know if he didn't take the first step and ask her. "I thought we might have dinner this evening at the Grand Hotel. We never made it the night you twisted your ankle, remember?"

Sarah sighed and he found he liked the sound very much. Her breath was moist and sweet where it touched his cheek. Her hands rested on his shoulders and suddenly he recalled how good, how right, she had felt lying beneath him on the beach.

"I'm sorry, Tyler. I can't have dinner with you tonight. I've promised Michael I'd have dinner with him."

"Michael?" When she moved away from him the day turned chilly and dark. Only the darkness wasn't all inside him. The sun had gone behind a bank of swiftly moving black clouds. "Where's he taking you?"

"To the Grand. He asked me the day before yesterday, when we took David to see *Crocodile Dundee* at the Mackinac Hotel's theater."

"I see. Perhaps another day."

"Another day." Sarah wondered if he'd even bother to ask again.

"We'd better be getting back. That squall line's getting closer by the minute." Tyler changed the subject as abruptly as he'd raised it.

With Sarah's help they were soon under way. It was a long rough trip back to the island. The wind was no longer steady but gusting from several points. Tyler was hard-pressed to keep them on course and steady in the water.

Once out of the lee of the mainland, the waves pushed and shoved the little craft from every direction. The lake was a roiling confusion of wind and waves but no more chaotic than his thoughts. He'd kept Sarah at a distance on purpose. Now he wasn't sure he wanted to continue that way.

But what did he want? Only the safe lonely responsibility of raising his son, putting his emotional life on automatic pilot so that no one or nothing could hurt him as Allison had done? Or did he want to take a chance on loving and living again with a woman like Sarah? Another sheering gust of wind caught the sail and sent them hard over. Tyler decided it was time to get his mind back on sailing.

Sarah was a good sailor, ready, whenever he asked, to lend a hand with line or sail. David sat quietly for the most part, huddled into a corner of the cockpit, trying to stay out of the spray and quick hard sprinkles of rain. After twenty minutes or so of being buffeted back and forth by wind and waves, he began to turn decidedly green.

"Dad," he wailed as if it were somehow Tyler's fault. "I'm going to be sick."

"Sarah." Tyler looked at her helplessly. David hiccupped and turned from green to white. Sarah gave up her place near the steering board, correctly reading the warning signals of an approaching crisis.

"Here, I'll help you lean over the side." She wasn't a moment too soon. David was wretchedly, chokingly ill.

Minutes later, his face wiped with a wet paper towel, the front of his shiny orange life vest damp with spray, David cuddled against her breast and whimpered in distress. "I still feel awful. I'm going to be sick again." But this time there was nothing left in his stomach to bring up. When the spasms passed he began to cry fitfully. "I want to go home."

"We're almost there, sport." Tyler's face was set, tense. He had jokingly referred to his sailing skills as being merely adequate but Sarah was glad to let him be in charge of the small craft. The waves hissed and streamed around them, racing past as quickly as the storm clouds overhead. She'd wedged herself and David into a corner to keep from being pitched onto the floor. Her windbreaker, even with the hood up, wasn't much protection from the rain. They were all soaking wet and David was miserable but he wasn't scared. That was due only to Tyler's skill.

Sarah was never so glad in her life as when they rounded the breakwater and made for the marina under auxiliary power. The wind had veered yet again, making headway slow and difficult. It was raining hard. Thunder and lightning cracked and roared in the distance, moving closer with each crashing peal.

Tyler was busy securing the sails but he turned to look as Sarah pointed toward the marina office. He swore under his breath, running his hand across his face. Two men and a woman stood under the shelter of the building's overhung roof. Behind them, on the nearly deserted street, stood a familiar buggy with a bedraggled Spice between the traces.

"Damn it, there's Elliot." Tyler looked at the pale, crying child in Sarah's arms. "He'll be furious, seeing David like this."

"He's only seasick, Tyler. He'll be all right in an hour or two." Sarah patted David on the head. She didn't want to let him go. She'd never had the opportunity to hold him in her arms this way before. She might never be able to do so again.

The little boat nosed into the slip. Elliot was there in three angry steps, pushing aside the yellow-slickered teenager who came out of the tiny marina building to help Tyler tie up the lines.

"David." Elliot's gray hair was plastered to his head, showing where it had thinned a little on top. His knit shirt, dark with rain, was pulled tightly across still muscular shoulders. His eyes were as cold and gray as the waves beyond the breakwater.

"Granddad. I'm sick. I feel awful." David started crying again. "Dad made me eat peanut butter and jelly and I barfed all over. And my stomach hurts," he finished and dissolved into a fresh rush of tears.

Elliot went down on one knee. He took David from Sarah's reluctant arms and cradled him against his chest, soiled life vest and all. His eyes fastened on Tyler and Sarah could almost feel the clash of wills. "I've told you time and again, you're not fit to raise the boy, Tyler."

Michael stepped forward, repeating Sarah's words. "He's only seasick, Elliot."

The older man waved him off. "I know he's only seasick. But he could have been drowned. He's all I have left of family in this world now that his mother is gone." His eyes had never left Tyler's set, angry face. Sarah was only now beginning to realize how hard it must have been for Tyler all these months, how much control Tyler had exerted over himself to keep from speaking out. "You had no business out in a boat that size in this kind of weather," Elliot continued angrily. "I'm going to talk to my lawyer about permanent custody when we get back to Georgia."

"Elliot, that is enough." Camilla was wearing a raincoat, one of those thin clear plastic ones. She took it off and spread it around David's shoulders. She shivered as the cold steady rain quickly penetrated the thin lilac cotton of her dress and matching short-sleeved jacket. "I'm tired of all of you. Can't you once put David's welfare before your own? Look at him. He's cold and miserable and you just go on fighting over his head as if he had no eyes and ears of his own. Shame on you. All of you."

No one said a word. Sarah stared at her great-aunt in amazement, seeing for the first time the steel underlying the softness. Elliot was as dumbfounded as the rest of them. "Camilla, I'm sorry," he began with some hesitancy.

Camilla sniffed. "I don't want to hear it, Elliot." She cut him off with a wave of her hand. "Bring David over to the buggy. We'll take him home and get him warm and dry. If you're bound and determined to argue with David's father, do it here where the rain might keep you both from losing your fool heads." She started toward the buggy. Elliot, still carrying David, followed. Sarah also obeyed.

Michael stepped into Sarah's path as she moved out of the meager shelter of the building's overhang. "We can postpone our dinner plans for tonight if you wish."

Sarah glanced at Tyler, saw him watching Elliot with his

son, saw the anger and uncertainty still burning inside him and shook her head. She was fooling herself if she believed they were any closer to an understanding than they'd been this morning, or yesterday, or the day before that. "Of course I want to have dinner with you." She hoped none of her disappointment was obvious. "I'll be ready at eight."

"Michael. Tyler." Once more Camilla voiced her commands. "You can pick David up when the rain stops. Please see to it that the bicycles all get back to the cottages. Maybe a walk in the rain will clear your heads, even if it can't instill a little sense into them."

CHAPTER FOURTEEN

"I THINK," MICHAEL SAID with his winning smile, "that this
hotel is even more impressive inside than it is outside." He
stared around him at the jewellike hues of the large, ornately
furnished lobby. The Georgian theme of the hotel's exterior
Greek revival architecture had been carried out in the dark
walls, pristine white woodwork, fanlighted doors and windows
and Sheraton chairs bracketing ruby, emerald and sapphire velvet sofas. Underfoot, huge scarlet geraniums, the hotel's floral
symbol, embellished a specially woven wool carpet. Outside,
along the almost nine-hundred-foot length of the white-
columned, clapboard-sided edifice, thousands of the red plants
bloomed in profusion with other colorful summer flowers.

"If it weren't for so many people in modern clothes, you
might almost believe we've stepped back in time." Sarah
smiled, too. The setting in which she found herself was elegant
and gracious in a way almost never encountered anymore. It
belonged to the world her grandmother and her mother before
her had known; a world Sarah could only read about and then
try to imagine.

Michael offered her his arm. Sarah placed her hand on the
dark sleeve of his suit jacket and they moved across the lobby
in the direction of the dining room. They'd arrived by horse-
drawn taxi a few minutes earlier and strolled along the famous
porch where millionaires, movie stars, royalty and U.S. pres-
idents had walked before them. A hundred years of history,
of life's little triumphs and tragedies had been played out on
that famous veranda and within these walls. Tonight Sarah was
part of the grandeur and tradition.

The maître d' led them to a table with a view of the straits.

Sunset from this vantage point would be magnificent but to-night there was no sunset. There wasn't even much of a view. It was still raining in fitful starts and spurts while mist lay thick and heavy on the water and moved slowly toward them up the hill.

"Sorry I can't deliver a gorgeous sunset," Michael said, his thoughts evidently following the same path as her own.

"The lack of a sunset is a very minor disappointment." The waiter held Sarah's chair, then presented them with menus, took Michael's order for what Sarah recognized as a very nice white wine and left them alone to choose their meals.

Sarah decided on braised chicken in wine sauce. Michael settled for a steak. "I'm not too imaginative when it comes to food," he admitted with another of his infectious grins. "I like to be able to identify what I'm eating."

Sarah smiled in return. "I'm glad we came here tonight," she said and she meant it. It was good to be with someone as open and friendly as Michael Parker. She needed his balance and serenity to counteract some of the upheaval in her life. She could talk to him; he would listen, understand, advise her if she asked. And he would allow her to voice thoughts and apprehensions if she did not.

The waiter returned with their wine, took their orders with a minimum of fuss and discreetly disappeared. Sarah stared at the pale straw-colored wine in her glass for a long moment. Light from crystal chandeliers reflected off the delicate china and heavy silver flatware as she lightly touched each piece of her table service, tracing the deep engraved pattern of the sterling. She wasn't really aware of how far away her musings had carried her until her companion spoke.

"A penny for your thoughts." Michael realized his approach wasn't very original but it seemed to work.

"I was thinking about David," she replied, not sidestepping the leading question.

"We all are." Michael took a sip of his wine. It was very good. Wine was one of his hobbies. But his thoughts now were not of clarity and bouquet but of promises kept and promises broken. How much could he reveal to Sarah of what he knew?

How should he handle this meeting? As a friend? Or as Allison's minister? Where did his loyalties lie? With the living or the dead?

"Is it possible that Elliot will be able to keep David in his custody, deny Tyler his son?" Sarah stumbled over the last word and felt the hot stain of color rise to her cheeks. She took a hasty sip of her wine.

"Sarah." Michael's voice was soft, his Southern accent very pronounced, as he slipped over the syllables of her name. "I'm aware of Tyler's uncertainty about David not being his natural child. You don't need to watch every word you say around me." His brown eyes reflected the overhead lights but the sincerity in their depths held a warming light of their own.

But she did have to watch every word she said. Her secrets were far more complicated than Michael could imagine. "Have you always known?"

"I've been aware of Tyler's misgivings for a long time." Michael chose his words carefully.

"I see." Sarah switched the focus of the discussion before she could change her mind or lose her nerve. "Tell me about Allison, please, Michael."

The waiter arrived with their soup before he could begin, giving him time to collect his thoughts. *She knows that David is her son.* He could see the certainty of it in the gemstone blue of her eyes, in the taut line of her shoulders beneath the soft silvery material of her dress. She was trying to decide whether or not to confide her knowledge to him.

"Allison loved David very much." He watched her hesitate as she lowered her spoon into her soup.

"I know." She smiled at him and there was a mist of tears in her eyes. "Even Tyler, as bitter as he is about some aspects of their marriage, has never denied that."

"In some ways David was Allison's last hold on reality. She did try very hard to stay well and happy for his sake but in the end her fears defeated her."

"I'd like to know whatever you can tell me about her." She didn't have to reveal her feelings for Tyler to Michael, either. He must have seen them growing closer. But how could she explain their sudden estrangement if he should ask? Again uncertainty assailed her. Was she risking too much by speaking to Michael of Allison, and of other things better left alone?

Sarah continued eating her soup as Michael gave her bits and pieces of Allison's past. He had no easy way to describe Tyler's wife. He had loved her, too, perhaps more than Tyler, because his love had lasted and Tyler's had not. But he had known Allison when she was growing up, before her fears of life and living had begun to overwhelm her. He'd tried to save her from herself but he'd failed. In all respects but one. He'd kept her secret about the events surrounding David's birth for all these years.

Michael's reminiscences about Allison lasted through the main course. Sarah listened quietly, letting him talk, trying to understand, to learn all she could about the woman who had taken her baby for her own. In her mind's eye she saw a lovely, sheltered and fragile girl, adored by her parents, devastated by her mother's death, dependent on her doting father. Through Michael's words Sarah saw Allison grow into a beautiful young woman who captivated both Michael and his tall, handsome Yankee friend with her Southern charm, delicate beauty and femininity.

For Michael Parker had loved her, too. It was plain to see in the way he brought out each memory of her, gave it life and substance for Sarah to share. How different might things have been if Allison had loved Michael as he loved her? He might have saved her from her own destruction. He was infinitely patient, gentle and caring, as strong and masculine as Tyler but in a very different way.

Tragically Allison had fallen in love with Tyler, a man she wasn't emotionally equipped to partner through life.

In those days, Sarah realized, Tyler would have been impatient, intense and unable to deal effectively with Allison's violent mood swings and lack of direction. No wonder Allison, who must have known she'd never have a child of her own, had been desperate to give her love to Sarah's son.

If Allison's life had turned out differently, she, Sarah, might never have had the opportunity to meet her son, to fall in love with Tyler. She felt nothing save compassion for the other woman.

Michael stopped talking. They were silent for several moments, each occupied with private thoughts. The dining room filled up around them and bits and pieces of a dozen different conversations floated by on the warm air, fragrant with the scents of rich food and vintage wine.

"Allison and Tyler should never have married." Sarah meant the statement with all her heart.

"It would seem that way. But they were very happy and very much in love at the beginning. Tyler will remember that someday, too, and it will help to ease his pain." Michael laid several bills on the silver tray the waiter had placed discreetly at his elbow. "Unfortunately, their love wasn't strong enough to stand the stress fate placed on their marriage. Some loves, like some people, are more fragile than others. But that doesn't make them any less real or less sacred."

"It does make that love very, very hard to sustain." The love she'd experienced with Ryan McKenzie had been both fragile and fleeting. The love she felt for Tyler, no matter what the outcome of their relationship, would never fade away.

"Yes." What a remarkable woman Sarah Austin was. She must be tempted to tell him the truth. Did Tyler suspect the truth also? His friend had never confided in him but Michael had always believed that something had occurred to bring Tyler and Allison's shaky union to its ultimate state of crisis. Now that he was making himself think about those dark days, Michael was almost sure that David's true parentage must have been the cause of those last tragic arguments.

Were they arguing the night Allison had died? Was that why Tyler had said nothing to defend himself at his trial? Was it that beyond his own remorse and guilt, he had been trying to protect David's memory of his mother? And in doing so he'd lost his freedom and the custody of his son.

"Is David much like her?" He could see the effort Sarah made to keep her composure when she talked of her son. Michael forced his own new doubts and conjectures to the back of his mind and answered as truthfully as he could.

"He has her love of animals and music. Have you heard him sing?" They walked out onto the porch. Michael briefly entertained the idea of having an after-dinner drink seated outside at one of the wicker tables. He saw Sarah shiver in the damp chill air and regretfully rejected the notion.

"No." Sarah's voice trembled a bit and she cleared her throat.

"He's very good. He's been singing solos with the church choir since he was five."

"And he played second base for his Little League team." She longed to ask him more questions. She wanted to know about David when he was a baby, a toddler, things she hadn't found the courage to ask Tyler. Michael seemed to understand her need. He told anecdotes about David as they walked along the great porch. Sarah listened and stored each and every morsel of information, of observation, away in her mother's heart.

"I think I should call a taxi, it's getting late."

"It isn't raining. Would you like to walk me home instead? It's quicker, really. I'll only ask you to go as far as the bluff stairs." She gestured across the beautifully landscaped grounds of the hotel, then down the hill toward the village.

"It's a deal." Almost as if they'd spoken the words aloud, they seemed to agree it was time to talk of other things. Sarah let Michael help her arrange the silver and black paisley silk shawl she'd found in one of the village boutiques around her shoulders and they started down the hill.

Sarah told him of her work with premature babies, the frustrations and the successes and the love and caring that went into sustaining each tiny life. Michael talked of his trials and tribulations as a Youth League basketball coach and of his duties at St. Matthew's. As always, his faith and trust in God were understated by ever-present realities in his life. Sarah envied him his serenity.

They walked slowly along the almost-deserted streets, studying the displays in darkened shop windows, catching glimpses of noisy revelers at the open doors of bars and restaurants along the way. If not for the mist and heavy wet air, it would have been much like the night she'd gone in search of Tyler. When she thought too long and too hard about all the problems in their relationship now, she almost wished that night had never happened.

All too soon they reached the opening of the narrow dead-end street that ended at the foot of the bluff steps. Sarah turned to face Michael. "You don't need to come any farther. It's late…"

"I always see my date safely to her front door." He threaded his fingers through hers and started up the street. The climb was steep, the footing on the wooden steps treacherous in the fitful light. When they reached the top, Sarah was breathless. They stopped beneath the branches of the huge copper beech near her house. Michael lifted his hand to touch her cheek in the same way Tyler had so often done. Sarah shut her eyes against a sudden surge of longing and regret that dear, gentle Michael wasn't the man who could fill the emptiness inside her heart. "Good night, Sarah."

"Good night, Michael." She continued to watch him from eyes that were more ebony than blue in the misty gloom. She had a very kissable mouth. He bent his head slightly, testing her reaction. Sarah closed her eyes, not moving away. Michael kissed her, slowly, tenderly.

Her eyelids fluttered open. "I'm sorry…" Sarah started to apologize but Michael placed his finger on the soft coral silkiness of her lips.

"Shh. No apology necessary. It was a good-night kiss between friends. Nothing more."

"No." Sarah reached up on tiptoe to touch his lips with a fleeting butterfly caress, the light from a nearby street lamp catching stray glints of auburn in her brown hair. "It was nothing less than a very special kiss between friends. Thank you for everything you told me tonight, Michael. It makes it easier. It helps." She moved away toward the pale rectangle of light shining behind the door of the cottage.

"Sarah." Michael didn't release her hand immediately. "Everything will come right in the end. You only need to have faith. In yourself and in the Lord."

"I'll do my best, Michael." She gave a funny, self-mocking

little laugh. "But I'd be very grateful if you'd say a prayer for me."

"Of course." And he'd say one for himself, too. He still didn't know how to resolve the issue of David, his inner conflict between inclination and duty. Michael started down the bluff steps, resigned to a long, sleepless night. He'd pray for guidance but in his experience, the good Lord in His infinite wisdom usually left one to work these things out.

CHAPTER FIFTEEN

"SARAH," CAMILLA CALLED through the heavy walnut panel of the bedroom door. "Sarah, are you awake?"

"Barely," came the sleepy reply. "What time is it? I forgot to wind my clock last night."

"It's nearly ten."

Sarah rubbed the sleep out of her eyes and climbed off the high mattress of her bed. She was beginning to make a habit of sleeping in in the morning. Grabbing a robe, she belted it tightly around her waist and opened the door. Camilla smiled brightly from the other side of the threshold.

"Good morning, Aunt Cam," she said, not quite so brightly.

"Good morning, dear. Did you have a nice evening with Michael?" Camilla handed her a cup of steaming black coffee. Sarah took it with heartfelt thanks. "I'm sorry I didn't wait up for you, but I just couldn't keep my eyes open a moment after eleven."

"Yesterday was a tiring day for all of us," Sarah said ruefully. Cradling the coffee cup between her hands, she moved across the room to her dressing table. "I did have a very nice evening with Michael," she went on, belatedly answering Camilla's first question.

"I'm glad. I like that young man very much." Camilla tilted her head to one side and regarded Sarah through narrowed eyes. "Did you tell him the truth about David?"

Sarah set the coffee cup on the tabletop. She had her back to her aunt but Camilla's reflection in the wavy mirror was clear enough that Sarah could read the concern in Camilla's hazel eyes. So many things had changed between them over the past few weeks. Camilla would never have asked such a question of her before their stay on the island. And if she had done something so out of character, Sarah would have resented the invasion of her privacy very much. Now she was grateful for the chance to put some of her chaotic thoughts into words.

"No, I didn't." She shook her head as she picked up the hairbrush and ran it through the tangles of her brown hair, coaxing it into a series of shining auburn-tinted waves. "We talked mostly of Allison and what she was like. How much she loved David." She put the brush down beside its matching comb very carefully, then turned to face her aunt. "But I said nothing of what I've learned. I don't have the right, not yet." She thought of Tyler and the barriers between them. "Perhaps I never will have that right. It's up to Tyler to explain to Elliot and to Michael. I'm not sure if he'll ever be ready to do that."

"You just have to believe he will," Camilla responded with a great deal of conviction. "And believe in your love. That's what makes it strong. That's what makes it last."

Sarah smiled. It was a little sad and a little lopsided, but a smile nonetheless. "Michael said something very similar last night. He said some loves are more fragile than others but if you work hard at them they can survive and grow. I don't want a fragile love, Aunt Cam. I want one that's strong and secure and capable of lasting a lifetime."

"Then you're going to have to go after that kind of love, in order to make it work, make it last."

"I can't make Tyler love me," Sarah insisted, leaning her forehead against the smooth cool wood of the carved bedpost.

"You can show him you love him. He'll come around." Camilla sounded very sure of herself.

Sarah voiced some of her frustration. "I can't convince him of anything when we never have a minute alone together."

"I can help you there, I think." Camilla ran her fingers over one of the pleats in her rose-pink linen skirt.

"In what way?" Sarah looked intrigued. Camilla couldn't help the smile of satisfaction that curved her lips.

"Elliot and I are taking David off the island for the rest of the day."

"You and Elliot?" Sarah raised a delicately curved eyebrow.

Camilla blushed and felt like an idiot for doing so. "You heard me correctly," she said somewhat testily.

"Is that wise?" Sarah was suddenly very serious.

"Probably not," Camilla admitted with more of her new-found candor. "I don't know where I stand with the man, Sarah, and that is the absolute truth. I don't want him to know the real reason I turned down his proposal of marriage all those years ago. I'm coming to terms with all those old hurtful memories and feelings but I don't think I'm ready to share them with anyone else but you." She smiled and lifted her shoulders in an elegant shrug. "Am I making any sense at all?"

"Yes, you are."

"Still, I can't seem to find the strength of will to say no to spending time with Elliot. And maybe in some small way I'll be able to help him overcome his animosity toward Tyler. At least I can try." She folded her hands in front of her, a determined look on her face. "Matters are at an impasse between them, Sarah. There's no other way to describe it. They're both acting out of love for David but he is the one suffering. If I hadn't been standing there earlier this morning when David asked Tyler to let him go with Elliot today, there would have been another argument for the child to witness. I'm sure of it." She shook her head sadly. "Possibly, that argument would have come to blows."

"I've been afraid that might happen, too," Sarah acknowledged reluctantly. "But I wish I had your confidence in my own abilities as a peacemaker." Sarah perched on the edge of the mattress, resting her forehead on her left hand, which was wrapped around the carved bedpost. What could she do to heal the breech between Tyler and Elliot without revealing the truth about David's parentage? The answer was nothing at all. She studied her bare toes sticking out from beneath the folds of her robe but saw nothing except the smooth high walls of the quandary that surrounded them all.

"It's not so much your abilities as a peacemaker that I'm relying on," Camilla revealed, as she turned to leave the room.

Sarah lifted her head, a little surprised at the whimsical tone of her aunt's reply. "It's that lately I've started to realize that there is a great deal of power in loving another human being. A great deal of power in simply being in love."

"IS HE ASLEEP?" Elliot spoke quietly, his voice barely carrying over the whir of the car's defroster, the mechanical swish of the windshield wipers gliding over wet glass.

Camilla turned slightly to peer into the back seat, her hazel eyes softening, a smile curving her lips, as she gazed at David's sleeping form. He was curled into a ball, one foot dangling over the seat, one leg tucked under him. He was still wearing the baseball cap emblazoned with a very large walleye he'd bought as a souvenir after catching one of the wary game fish that afternoon.

"Sound asleep. He's had a busy day. It was good for him to be with children his own age for a while."

"He did seem to enjoy playing with Wilbur and Mabel's grandchildren."

"Umm." Camilla thought back over the long happy afternoon they'd shared with Elliot's friends and their three energetic grandchildren at a small inland lake. She'd enjoyed the company of a couple who were her contemporaries in age and experience; she'd enjoyed the peace and quiet of their small lakeside retirement home; she'd been able to show her interest and pleasure in their hosts' grandchildren without inviting comment. But most of all she'd enjoyed spending time with Elliot away from the stress, the divided loyalties they all felt on the island.

She reached over the seat to lift the cap off David's head. He sighed, shifted a little to make himself more comfortable, but didn't waken. Straightening in her seat, Camilla turned to face forward again.

The fog outside the car windows seemed thicker with every mile they traveled along the lakeshore. It had never occurred to her during the long hazy but sunny afternoon they'd spent with Elliot's friends that they might be seriously delayed on their return trip. They'd accepted the couple's invitation to dinner. They'd lingered over coffee and dessert and leisurely farewells, unconcerned as the sun melted away into a cloud bank growing high and menacing in the west. There was mist in the bogs and low-lying swampland along the country highway as they headed back toward St. Ignace. When they turned onto U.S. 2 and came closer to Lake Michigan, an occasional mare's tail of fog crossed the road; the patches of mist grew steadily thicker as they approached the water. When they began to parallel the shoreline more closely, the fog surrounded them like cotton candy.

Camilla glanced at the clock on the dashboard. It had taken them over an hour to go twenty-five miles. She was almost certain now they would miss the last boat back to the island. The daylight was nearly gone, replaced by a gloomy dusk. Some of her contentment began to slip away. On her right, slow breakers rolled sullenly in, splashing on the huge rocks piled along the eroding shoreline in an attempt to stop Lake Michigan's assault on the roadway. The fog appeared thicker than ever in the looming darkness. "Is that the correct time?" she asked, indicating the clock on the dashboard.

"I'm afraid so." Elliot's eyes never left the pale glow of the white line at the edge of the pavement. "Have we missed the last boat?"

There were several ferry lines serving the island but their schedules were fairly synchronized. "We will, unless you can get us to the docks within the next twenty minutes." Camilla checked her own slender gold wristwatch. The luminous dial showed exactly the same time as the car's digital clock.

"We're still fifteen or twenty miles from St. Ignace. I'm sorry, Camilla. What do you suggest we do?"

"Find a place to stay for the night and catch the first boat over in the morning." She almost giggled but caught herself in time, turning the lapse into a half smile. "Don't look so stern, Elliot. We're very well chaperoned. I do think we might do better to find a small motel here on the highway, away from St. Ignace. We'll have a much better chance of finding one with two vacant rooms this far out. Thank heavens for credit cards. I have very little cash with me."

"I'll pay for the rooms, Camilla. It's my fault we're stranded." Elliot's tone was gentle but uncompromising. He was every inch the true Southern gentleman. Camilla decided not to press the issue at the moment.

"I think I remember a very nice-looking motel up ahead with a small restaurant attached. David might want a snack before bedtime."

"I'll call Sarah as soon as we're settled and tell her what's happened. She'll be worried when she realizes we're not on the last boat in."

"I'd better give the hotel a ring, too," Elliot said, searching ahead with his eyes for the glow of a neon sign announcing the rustic motel they'd been discussing. "I'll let Michael know what's going on."

"And Tyler?" Camilla felt no urge to smile now. At her question, Elliot's face became a stern, set mask.

He took his eyes off the road for a moment and glanced her way. "I'm not an ogre, Cam. Of course Tyler has to be told what's happened." He lifted his hand from the steering wheel in a gesture of frustration and aggravation. "It's just that I'm not sure of the best way to go about it."

"Lilac Time isn't equipped with a telephone," Camilla reminded him, beginning to understand how hard it was for Elliot to be put in the position where Tyler could fault his guardianship of David. "I think it would be best if Sarah tells him what's occurred."

"I think so, too. We can't seem to communicate at all without it deteriorating into a shouting match." A muscle jumped along the firm line of his jaw. "I think this is the motel we were speaking of."

"Yes, I believe it is." Camilla experienced a momentary surge of relief. Soon they'd be off the road, free of the danger of unseen obstacles and other drivers, those both overly cautious and overly brave about driving a curving, busy highway in this kind of weather.

"Good, the vacancy sign is lighted and the restaurant is still open. I could use a cup of coffee, or maybe hot chocolate. It's chilly and I do believe it's starting to rain again." Nerves were making her talkative. Camilla shut her mouth with a snap.

Elliot got out of the car. "Thunder," he said succinctly as a low rumble echoed over the lake just beyond the fringe of trees that sheltered the small motel from the worst of Lake Michigan's wrath. "Maybe the rain will wash away the fog so we can get an early start in the morning."

"I hope so," Camilla said very quietly as she watched him walking, still tall and straight, toward the motel's brightly lit office. "I hope so." Her relief had been replaced by apprehension. It was not very late in the evening, after all. She was going to be alone with Elliot once again. David wasn't just napping. He was sound asleep and would probably stay that way. There would be no human buffer between her and Elliot tonight.

She felt tired and vulnerable and unable to cope, wondering if Elliot would take this opportunity to press her about the past. Once again she found herself wondering what he would say if she told him everything that had happened to her that long-ago summer. How would he react? Could she take the chance? Or should she keep her secret, never reveal how very much she had loved him then? Or how very close she was coming to falling in love with him once again.

"CAMILLA?" ELLIOT'S KNOCK on the door that connected their rooms was very light. She wondered for a moment if she could pretend to be asleep, then decided better of it. He'd surely heard her moving around in the small room for the last twenty minutes or so. Feigning sleep was the coward's way out. She was becoming immensely tired of being a coward.

"Come in," she said in what she hoped was a normal tone of voice.

"Are you comfortable?" Elliot asked, looking around the small, simply furnished room.

"Yes. It's clean and warm and dry. What more could I ask on a night like this?" As if to give credence to her words, thunder grumbled and moaned in the distance. The trees crowding close to the little motel on three sides hid whatever flash of lightning might have accompanied the thunder.

"Cable TV," Elliot informed her with a rueful grin that just missed crinkling the edges of his gray eyes. "David is very disappointed. At least for the first five minutes or so he was. I barely got him out of his clothes before he fell asleep again. Sleeping in his underwear in the middle of the north woods is something of a treat, I gather."

"I wish I felt that sleeping in my slip was such an adventure. I'm afraid all it brings to mind is the fact that I'll probably need an extra blanket in the middle of the night." Camilla heard herself say the words and immediately wished she could have bitten off her tongue. Did the comment sound as provocative to Elliot's ears as it did to hers? Thank heaven she was too old to blush or her cheeks would be a far brighter pink then her skirt and blouse.

"Would you like something hot to drink? The restaurant is open all night, believe it or not. I don't think David will awaken again."

"That sounds very nice. Just let me get my sweater." Bright lights, perhaps music and other people; that's what they'd find in the café, and it was far safer than being alone, here, with Elliot in her room. "Did you get a message through to Michael the last time you called the hotel?"

"Yes. He'd been sheltering in one of the shops on his way back from dinner. It's raining cats and dogs on the island, he says."

They stepped outside to make the short dash across the gravel parking lot. The sullen muted roar of breakers foaming over rocks on the beach was a deep, continuous background to the patter of rain and the sigh of wind in the dark stand of pines surrounding them. It made the short hairs at the nape of Camilla's neck stand on end. Beyond the small brave rectangle of light from the restaurant it was pitch-black. It was not the kind of night to linger out of doors. She lifted her white cashmere cardigan over her head to keep off the rain and started walking.

Once inside the restaurant, it took a moment for Camilla's

eyes to adjust to the harsh overhead lighting. What she saw made her heart skip a beat. There were no other customers seated at the half-dozen or so square Formica-covered tables, no truck drivers lounging on the stools before the low counter at the front of the room. They were alone with the sleepy-eyed waitress who took their order for hot chocolate and disappeared into the kitchen.

Camilla stared at her reflection in the big plate-glass window that faced the beach. She saw a woman in her later middle years whose eyes mirrored too clearly the apprehension she felt in her heart. She shivered and looked away. Elliot caught the movement.

"Chilly?"

"Yes." Camilla hunched her shoulders into the warm folds of her sweater. "It's hard to believe it's almost July on a night like this." Beyond the small patch of light outside the window, the fog still swirled among the serrated tops of the pines. Lightning flickered ghostlike through the trees and thunder rolled and boomed over the water.

"The rain doesn't show any signs of letting up soon," Elliot observed, folding his hands on the tabletop.

"Is David afraid of storms?" Camilla asked as the waitress returned with two heavy earthenware mugs of steaming cocoa, each topped with a dollop of whipped cream.

"No, not particularly. He was sleeping very soundly when we left."

"He had a long busy day." Camilla folded her hands around the cup, letting the warmth of the coarse china seep into her chilled fingers. She took a sip. "Mmm, that's just what I needed."

"I'm glad." Elliot took a swallow of his cocoa and set the mug down with great precision in the matching saucer. "Do you know this is almost the first time I've been alone with you?" He tapped his finger on the edge of the mug. Camilla followed his hands with her eyes, head lowered, avoiding his gaze. "I think it's time we talked."

Camilla felt her blood congeal in her veins. She grasped at conversational straws. "Sarah doesn't like storms, you know.

She was very nervous when I called her after we arrived here. She promised to get my message to Tyler, regardless of the storm, but I know she'll be nervous in that big old house by herself tonight."

"She's a grown woman." Elliot wasn't about to be side-tracked.

"Yes, of course," Camilla admitted faintly. "I'm being silly."

"Have you been happy, Cam?" Elliot reached out to cover her hand with his but she drew it back so quickly she almost knocked her cup of cocoa over the edge of the table.

"It's been a lovely day." She steadied her cocoa and looked at her hands. They were trembling uncontrollably.

"I wasn't talking about today," he replied patiently. "Have you been happy in your life?"

Her head came up proudly. "Yes, why do you ask?"

"I've thought about you often over the years." He wasn't looking directly at her now. Absently, he swirled the melted whipped cream in his chocolate with the tip of his spoon. "I never tried to get in touch with you because I assumed that's what you wanted."

"It was." Camilla nearly choked on the words. If she hadn't had the heavy mug to hold in her hands, she would have been twisting them together in her lap.

"I think as fate or chance or providence has thrown us together again after so many years that you owe me an explanation." He looked up suddenly, his gray eyes catching hers. He held her captive with the forcefulness of his seeking gaze.

"Elliot," Camilla said gently. This time she reached out and touched his hand, lightly, fleetingly, retreating before he could turn his palm upward and imprison her fingers in his. "This isn't going to get us anywhere."

"I was very happy with my marriage. I grew to love Allison's mother very much. But I didn't marry for many years after the war. I was hurt, bitter, angry. I wanted an explanation of why you broke our engagement and you never gave me one. I'm not bitter or angry any longer. But a little bit of the pain has always stayed with me, inside me. Why, Camilla? That's all I want to know. Why?"

"I...I told you in my letter. I wasn't ready to get married, to give up my freedom."

"That wasn't a sufficient explanation then. It still isn't today. You were so full of life that summer. You were everything I'd ever dreamed of: bright and lovely and good."

"Elliot, don't..." Camilla bit back a sob.

"Was it because of my vocation? Or the difference in our social background?"

"No." Camilla spoke too loudly. She lowered her voice as the sleepy-eyed waitress looked up from the small TV set behind the counter. She was watching the *Tonight Show*; the familiar theme music drifted out across the room as the show broke for a commercial. Camilla heard the music, saw the flickering images as she glanced that way but paid them no heed. "It was all so long ago," she said hopelessly.

"Yes. And it's all so immediate tonight."

Camilla turned her head toward the doorway, unable to deny the truth of his words. She closed her eyes, hoping to find the strength inside herself to lie to him one more time. It was no use; the strength, the will to go on deceiving him wasn't there. She opened her eyes again, blinked, then looked across the parking lot at the motel. "Elliot?" Her thoughts were momentarily diverted from the subject at hand. "Did you leave the light on in your room?"

"Only the bathroom light." He, too, looked across, toward the motel. "You're right, the lights are on. David must be awake." He stood up, signaling the inattentive waitress.

"Go on," Camilla urged. "I'll take care of the bill. You don't want David to be awake alone in a strange place."

"No." His jaw was clenched and he hurried out the door without another word. Camilla paid the waitress, left a tip and followed him out of the restaurant, moving slowly despite the chill of the rain.

She let herself into her room quietly. The door between the two rooms was still ajar, just as Elliot had left it. She could hear him talking to David in a low soothing manner that made her long to be the one held safe and securely in his arms. Curiosity, envy, love drew her toward the sound of their voices. He was seated on the edge of the hard narrow bed, tucking David back under the covers. Sleepy little-boy eyes watched him; sleepy little-boy fingers curled trustingly into his hand.

"Don't worry, Granddad," David said, the edges of his words blurred and indistinct with fatigue, "I'll tell Dad it wasn't your fault we missed the boat. He won't get mad then. You won't have to fight with him over me again." He snuggled down into the covers. "I'll make sure everything's all right."

Elliot smoothed his hand over the tousled waves of his grandson's brown hair. *No, not his grandson,* Camilla realized with a dart of pain that lodged directly in her heart. *My great-great-nephew. My blood, not Elliot's.* Yet she knew he loved the child every bit as dearly as she ever could.

"Did you say your prayers, sport?" Elliot asked, his voice cracked and rough around the edges.

"Mmm, ages ago. Say good-night to Aunt Cam for me." He pulled the blanket up to his chin.

"I'm right here. Good night, David." She spoke softly. Elliot turned to acknowledge her presence. His eyes were bleak.

"Is it still raining?" David's brown eyes drifted closed then opened to focus on her briefly.

"Yes."

"Rats. I hope it's nice tomorrow."

"We'll just have to wait and see. Go to sleep, David."

"Wait and see." The last word trailed off into a yawn. In only seconds he was asleep again. Elliot got up from the bed and came toward her. His eyes were still troubled.

"He woke up, wanted a drink of water and couldn't find us. He was getting dressed to come over to the restaurant." He smiled suddenly. "He told me over and over that he wasn't scared of being alone."

"Only hungry," Camilla anticipated his next words with a smile of her own.

"How did you guess? I gave him a cookie from the packet

of goodies he had stowed away in the back seat. It seemed to do the trick.''

"You're a very good grandfather, Elliot.''

"Am I? Did you hear what he said to me a little while ago?''

Camilla didn't pretend to misunderstand. "Yes.''

"I can't go on accusing his father of not being fit to care for him when I'm not any more responsible than he is, getting us stranded like this.''

"You're overreacting, I think,'' Camilla said quietly, moving into the room. "We only missed the ferry, after all.''

"I know that.'' Elliot sighed and held out his hands. Camilla lifted hers to be folded inside. He drew her closer and she came with only the slightest hesitation. "It's only a small incident, I agree, but it proves a point. I've been making Tyler's life miserable because I've been so miserable myself. Grief is a terrible, blinding emotion. I've prayed and ranted and raved at God. I've blamed Tyler. I've cut myself off from everyone I care about. David is all I have left of his mother and Tyler killed her...'' He shook his head and took a deep breath as though ridding himself of some long-carried burden. "No, for my grandson's sake, I must never say that again.''

"Surely your faith in God has helped you?'' Camilla looked up into his face, so close, so dear. There had been changes over the years but beneath the added lines of age and wisdom, suffering and remembered happiness, she could still see the serious young minister, the brave warrior who had stolen her heart so long ago.

"It has kept me from despair, but I haven't allowed Him to heal my pain. Until tonight.''

"And tonight,'' she prompted gently, knowing from experience that he needed to speak the words aloud. She was in his arms now and had no idea how she had come to be there. She didn't care; she was only glad to be held in the safe, warm circle of his embrace.

"He spoke to me with a child's voice, through a child's words. David told me not to be sad, not to worry. He'd talk to Tyler and make sure he didn't get mad about our missing the boat. He was afraid, Camilla," Elliot said, working it out in his own mind. "Afraid his father and I would come to blows over him. Why have I let my own sorrow and anger blind me to his fears?"

"Because you're human and flawed, just like all the rest of us. For David's sake, for the sake of Allison's memory, you must try to come to terms with Tyler and the animosity you feel for him."

"I will try, Cam. For all those reasons and because you ask it of me." He led her through the open doorway to her room. There was only a single chair and the bed. Camilla didn't feel uncertain anymore. This was not the serious, untried youth of forty-five years ago. This was a mature and wise man, a caring, loving man who would understand the frightened and uncertain girl she'd been.

"Stay with me a little while. Stay and talk...of the old days."

His eyes held hers, looking deep into her soul, as if searching for something, then he nodded and kissed her gently on the forehead. "If you wish, I'll stay a while."

Camilla propped the pillows against the headboard of the bed and sat back against them. Elliot kicked off his shoes and stretched out beside her, pulling the bedspread over their knees to ward off the chilly dampness. He put his arm around her shoulders and Camilla allowed herself the luxury of cuddling close.

It felt right and good and the words she had to find within herself came almost easily to her tongue. She held nothing back, not even the tears. And when it was over, when she'd poured out her sorrow and regrets, Elliot pulled her head down onto his shoulder, kissed her gently and started to talk of love and living, dying and finding the faith and courage to go on, to grow and become a better person for the pain.

Camilla listened and understood and began to heal.

Elliot talked and listened and began to heal.

When he left her in the dark hour before dawn, he bent and kissed her again. It was a kiss of shared friendship, shared experience, of love lost and love, perhaps, to be found again.

Something had changed; something lacking had been restored within them both. And for the first time in a very long time, Camilla found she wasn't afraid to contemplate changes in her life.

CHAPTER SIXTEEN

SARAH REPLACED THE TELEPHONE receiver in its cradle and stared down at the instrument thoughtfully. They were safe and well; for that she was grateful. Aunt Cam had talked of fog and rain and hazardous driving conditions, but she had sounded strangely forlorn. Sarah guessed the reason.

Her aunt was alone with Elliot Brandon in a small motel with only a sleeping child to shield her from having to come face-to-face with her past. It was the situation Sarah knew Camilla wanted to avoid above all others. Sarah hoped everything would turn out all right, but now her attention, her own anxiety, was focused on Tyler and the message she had to deliver.

He wasn't going to be pleased. Sarah frowned and walked onto the veranda to watch the rain beat against the window she'd closed against the approaching storm. She was reluctant to find a raincoat and go out into the gathering darkness. There was a great deal of static tension in the air; there was a great deal of tension within her body and soul. She didn't want to speak to Tyler again. She didn't want to endure any more of the strained politeness they'd shared at lunch, the remoteness he'd displayed when they'd talked, in fits and spurts, of making plans for the afternoon and evening.

In the end, heartsick and dispirited, Sarah had invented the weak excuse of having to package up the remainder of her box of mementos and take it to the post office to mail to her father in Key West.

Tyler had accepted her spur-of-the-moment excuse so readily that Sarah could feel the hurt of it even now, hours later. When she'd returned from the village in the middle of the afternoon, he was nowhere to be found. She hadn't seen him again, didn't know he'd even returned to Lilac Time, until lights blossomed within the cottage as clouds rolled in and cut short the long June day.

She'd had such hopes for today, so many dreams, so many barriers she'd intended to see demolished. She'd planned on happily ever after and she'd gotten harsh reality. Sarah shivered and rubbed her hands along her bare arms, stroking away the gooseflesh below the short sleeves of her fleecy pink sweatshirt. Rain beat against the glass as though determined to break in and soak everything it touched. Prickles of apprehension spread across the back of her neck as a mighty bolt of lightning came to ground somewhere nearby.

She didn't like storms, never had, never would. Yet she couldn't delay her errand much longer. The last boat had docked twenty minutes ago. Plenty of time for the three travelers to have hailed a taxi and made their way up the bluff. Tyler would be worried. She had to tell him what had happened.

Fifteen minutes later she finally unearthed an old yellow slicker and slouch hat from the closet under the stairs. It was obvious Tyler wasn't coming over to inquire if she knew why his son was so late returning from the outing with his grandfather. She would have to go over to Lilac Time.

The waterproof material of the coat was stiff and musty-smelling. It was also cold to the touch. Sarah shivered as she wiggled her way inside. Beneath her fleecy pullover she felt her nipples contract against the chill. The slicker came to below her knees; the hat kept sliding over one eye. She caught a glimpse of herself in the entry mirror and stifled a giggle. She looked like a clown in a nursery-rhyme circus. Her pink drawstring sweatpants and pink running shoes contrasted wildly with the dull yellow slicker and ridiculous hat. It was too late to go change her clothes now. That would be nothing more than a delaying tactic, just as hunting the raincoat had been. She'd known all along Aunt Cam had a lightweight raincoat somewhere in her bedroom closet. It would only have taken a moment to bring it down from upstairs.

Glancing across the room, Sarah made sure the small cheery fire she'd kindled in the fireplace, for companionship as much as warmth, was in no danger of going out. She closed the mesh screen across the fireplace opening and placed an old-fashioned standing screen on the marble hearth just to be on the safe side.

The island possessed a very competent volunteer fire department and modern emergency equipment, including a fire truck, ambulance and police cruiser, which the tourists rarely saw. But many of the furnishings in the cottage were one-of-a-kind antiques. In a house the age of the Gathering Place, fire was always a worry.

Taking one last deep breath, Sarah stepped outside into the needle-sharp sting of cold rain being flung into her face and made her way resolutely toward Tyler's cottage. She banged on the door for what seemed like a very long time before she realized there was no one inside to answer. Making a cup of her hands, she peered through the screen door. The red and purple paisley cushions from the glider were piled against one wall. Two wicker rockers and a rickety wooden table were the only other furniture to be seen.

Most of the contents of Lilac Time had been sold at auction after Justin Delano's death. The huge cottage was furnished with only the fewest of secondhand necessities. What happy plans had Allison and Tyler worked out for its restoration? What innovative ideas to make this a gracious and comfortable summer home? Through the uncurtained window she could see into the almost empty main room. It looked stark and bare and cold. No wonder David spent all the time he could at Gathering Place.

Lightning streaked across the sky just a few feet overhead. At least that's how the brilliant flash affected Sarah's nerves. She shivered and blamed the frisson of icy sensation on a trickle of cold rain that had found its way down the back of her neck. She'd have to come back later, try again, screw up her courage to face the weather and Tyler's abstraction once more.

Or could she leave a note? Sarah tried the door. It was

locked. She gave the door frame a solid, satisfying bad
tempered whack with the heel of her hand. It didn't budge
Nothing had gone according to plan today, so why shoul
Tyler have cooperated by leaving his house unlocked while h
was away?

Sarah turned and started home. Her pants and shoes wer
soaking by the time she made it to the front gate. The rest o
her was more than a little damp, too. The ancient slicke
leaked from myriad tiny cracks and broken seams. She wa
wet, lonely and miserable. She didn't know whether to scream
in fury or burst into tears.

If she allowed her emotions to get the better of her, Sarah
suspected she would cry. Behind her angry bravado lay des
olation and despair. She'd lost her chance for happiness. She'
lost the man she loved to his own insecurity, the child she'
searched for all these years, without being given a chance to
explain her actions, to prove how much she loved them both
She'd gambled on having it all, on happily ever after, and lost
It wasn't fair.

Sarah wiped at a traitorous tear that had seeped from be
neath tightly shut eyelids. Nobody, she reminded herself with
ruthless honesty, had ever said that life was fair.

TYLER WAS SOAKING WET by the time he topped the bluff
steps. He hunched his shoulders against the buffeting wind of
the straits, paying little attention to his physical discomfor
Inside his head his thoughts were still squirreling around in
his brain, giving him no peace. Perhaps it was the brandie
that he'd shared with Michael at the hotel that kept him from
being able to bring coherence to his thoughts.

Perhaps it was the niggling, unreasoning, ever-present fea
that Elliot could just as easily have taken David anywhere in
the world instead of merely a few miles along the coastline o
Lake Michigan. He might never have brought his son back a
all. Was that why his blood ran slow and heavy with fear?

Or was it the recurring, terrifying sensation of events spi
raling out of his control, as they had the night of Allison'

death, that made him want to take his son and barricade them
both somewhere until he could sort it all out?

He'd settled some things in his mind over the last hour or
so. Talking to Michael had helped. His old friend had spotted
him—come looking for him, he suspected—at the ferry dock
nearest the Iroquois and called him over to explain that deteriorating weather conditions on the mainland had caused Elliot
to miss the last boat.

Tyler had pretended to understand but inside, in the bleak
lonely places in his heart and soul, he did not. He wanted
custody of David returned to him, legally and forever. Nothing
was more important than that. He simply wasn't free to work
productively, to love completely, in short, to be sane and
happy, until he could be certain that David would never be
taken from him again.

It all boiled down to one simple fact: until that happened,
he was no more in control of his life than the day he'd walked
inside the bleak stone walls of a Georgia prison.

SARAH SPUN ON HER HEEL when she heard steps on the gravel
roadway behind her. "Tyler?" His name came out someplace
between a prayer and a curse. Lightning flashed behind him;
thunder pealed overhead. The wind moaned and shrieked in
the branches of the copper beech and a few storm-tossed
leaves scuttled past her feet. "Where the devil have you
been?" It was a measure of her anxiety that she spoke so
harshly. Tyler, however, was in no mood to analyze her speech
patterns or body language.

"I was out looking for my son." His words were rough,
but he caught himself thinking how young and innocent she
looked in the absurd getup she was wearing. The raincoat she
had on was at least as old as she was.

"They missed the last boat." Sarah let her explanation trail
off into silence. He was standing so close she had to tip her
head to see his face. It was the face of a stranger, the face of
the sorrowing, bitter man she'd first encountered in the barn.
"They're well and safe."

Sarah's voice was so low he had to bend closer to hear her

speak over the noise of the storm. "And you were coming to find me, to tell me so?"

"Yes." Had she only imagined his words were less rough, that they held an echo of the dark warmth she found so compelling?

"Thank you, Sarah." He wanted suddenly to take her in his arms, hold her close, pour out all his hopes and fears and half-glimpsed dreams of the future.

"I knew you'd be worried." She smiled a little. "I was going to leave a note." Was he going to take her in his arms as she so desperately wanted him to do? Sarah looked at Tyler from beneath the brim of her hat. His expression was veiled by the shadows of dancing tree limbs and the sparkles of color before her eyes, the aftermath of looking almost directly at the last great flare of lightning.

"Michael saw me asking questions at the ferry dock. He told me what happened. I'd been prowling up and down the sidewalk like a caged tiger. All I could think of was that Elliot had taken David away, just as he has every legal right to do. I must have been a pretty grim sight. I'm surprised somebody didn't turn me over to the cops as some kind of nut case." The ghost of a smile slipped over his lips and disappeared as quickly as it came. "I think Michael dragged me into the hotel as much to get me out of sight as to buy me a drink."

"You're soaked," Sarah said matter-of-factly. "Were you this wet when Michael took you into the restaurant at the Iroquois?" She did her best to keep her voice even, resting the tips of her fingers on the slick wet material of his black leather jacket.

Water dripped from the thick layers of his hair until it glistened like ebony in the fitful light. She raised her hand and touched it, lightly, hesitantly. She took a deep breath. "Come inside and get warm." He didn't need a weeping, clinging woman now. He needed someone strong; someone to listen, to be a sounding board to drain away the misery of loss and failure that still haunted him. He needed a woman who was sure of her own ability to love and nurture, who could stand up to those demons and banish them from his heart.

Tyler pretended not to hear her last remark. If he went with her, let himself get warm and dry, let the brandy fumes swirling through his head dictate his actions, he'd never be able to leave her. "Believe it or not, I was almost this wet." He chose instead to answer her question. "The hostess never batted an eye, though, just waved us on through to a seat at the bar."

She reached up on tiptoe and sniffed his breath. "Brandy?" Sarah asked, inhaling the scent of good liquor, cold rain and something warm and vital and very, very male; something of Tyler himself.

"Yes. Two." Tyler could feel the anticipation, the sweet aching pulse of desire building inside him. He needed her; he wanted her.

"Come inside with me," Sarah said, her voice not quite steady. She hadn't imagined the hint of sensual excitement in his voice. It frightened her just a little bit but it pleased her a great deal more. "I could use a little brandy myself. It's freezing out here." Lightning seemed to be everywhere she looked. The storm was all around them and even the beckoning warmth she now sensed in his words wasn't enough to block out her nervousness. "Please come inside. I...I don't like storms."

"Are you afraid of them?" He couldn't help teasing her just a little. She always rose to the bait so enticingly.

"Yes, I am." She lifted her chin and stared straight into his eyes. She saw need and uncertainty reflected in the midnight depths, but it was the desire, the wanting, which underlay both those emotions, that took her breath away. He put his hands on her shoulders.

"I don't want to be alone tonight, Sarah." She was light and warmth and goodness. He loved her even if he hadn't yet found the courage to tell her so.

"I don't want to be without you tonight, either." Heedless of the rain, he lifted her chin with his fingers, tipping her head back to receive his kiss. Sarah's hat tumbled to the gravel, releasing the shining brown waves of her hair. Tyler buried his fingers in the silkiness and felt her arms go around his waist as she melted into his embrace. They stayed that way, raindrops mixing with the taste of brandy and passion, until a spectacular display of aerial fireworks and the thunder that accompanied the lightning exploded all around them. Sarah buried her face against the hard comfort of his chest. Her fingers curled like claws around the fabric of his jacket.

"Damn it, I hate thunderstorms," she muttered against him. Tyler couldn't help but laugh.

"It isn't funny." She stared up at him defiantly. "Aren't you afraid of anything?"

"I'm afraid of more things than you can know." He smiled down at her. Her face was wet, her nose tipped red with cold, but her lips were swollen and sweetly pink from his kisses and her eyes held the promise of marvelous things to come.

"So am I." Sarah's words were a mere whisper of sound in the noisy darkness. "Let's go inside and keep the night away for each other."

Sarah made a little production of hanging the raincoat and her hastily retrieved hat on the coat tree just inside the main room. Tyler stripped off his jacket and hung it over the back of a chair near the fireplace. His wet shoes and socks followed as Sarah went in search of towels to dry their hair. She came back not only with towels but with glasses and a bottle of excellent brandy, as well. Tyler poured while she took off her own wet shoes and socks.

She accepted her glass of brandy while Tyler rubbed the dampness from his hair. He watched silently as Sarah bolted her drink. Water dripped onto the shoulders of her sweatshirt from her still wet hair. Tyler took a single swallow of his brandy and set the glass aside. He dropped to his knees, gently removed the empty glass from Sarah's hand and began to towel the moisture from her hair.

The fire had burned to embers. Tyler looked at Sarah, saw her shiver as a cold draft swirled through the room in the wake of another storm-driven gust of wind outside the cottage. It would take a while to bring the fire back to life. Tyler made up his mind, crossed the invisible line between choice and inevitability.

"Sarah, where is your bedroom?"

She'd been staring into the dark red embers of the fire. It took her a moment to focus her vision on him and her thoughts on what he'd said.

"My room?"

Tyler nodded his dark head patiently. "Your room. Show me where it is. The fire is almost out. You're never going to get warm or dry sitting down here." He stood up, taking her hands, drawing her up with him. The wooden floor was indeed icy under her bare feet. Sarah winced.

"Your ankle again?" Tyler asked at once.

"My toes," she confessed with a tiny giggle as the brandy spiraled down into her stomach and sent a wave of giddiness circling through her body. "They're frozen."

"We'll have to see what can be done to alleviate the condition." Tyler looked down at her. Sarah tilted her head a little to one side and looked thoughtful.

"A hot water bottle would work." She frowned up at him adorably. "I don't know if we have one, though." Tyler found himself wanting to laugh again. She could always manage to do that, take him out of himself, make him see life in lighter colors, less serious patterns.

"I thought perhaps a kiss?" He smiled and Sarah decided the teasing hint of wickedness she detected in his coal-black eyes was the most erotic thing she'd ever encountered.

"A kiss," she repeated with a sigh. "Yes, that would do very nicely." He obliged her then and there. Not only did warmth curl into her toes and fingers, but a small white-hot ember began to burn low in her middle. Sarah wound her hands around Tyler's neck and didn't even make a token objection when he swept her high into his arms and started for the stairs.

"Aren't you going to tell me to put you down?" he asked, arching one brow so that it almost met the wave of black hair that had fallen onto his forehead.

"I wouldn't think of it," Sarah whispered demurely against the curve of his neck, but the warm touch of her lips on his skin was anything but demure. "Male egos are very fragile, or so I've been told. I wouldn't want to damage yours."

"What about my male back?" Tyler asked, stopping on the small landing for another quick kiss.

Sarah pulled her mouth away from his so quickly Tyler regretted the facetious inquiry almost immediately. "I didn't think of that. Tyler, put me down," she insisted, her sapphire eyes wide with alarm. "You'll hurt yourself." She was suddenly very serious, wiggling in his arms. Tyler ignored her directive, tightened his grip and continued climbing.

"My back," he said, not sounding even the smallest bit out of breath, "is a lot stronger than my ego. Hold still."

Sarah decided that discretion was the better part of valor. She subsided quietly and let herself enjoy the strength of his arms, the heat of his body, the play of muscles under her hands. By the time he set her down beside the bed, her heart was beating so quickly she could scarcely breathe.

They didn't speak again. Sarah seemed to understand that the touch of his hands, of his lips, was all the commitment he could make to her this night.

He skimmed the damp fleecy sweatshirt up and over her head. She wore no bra and her breasts were small and golden, fitting the curve of his hand perfectly, smooth as satin against the roughness of his palm. He finished undressing her quickly, tugging at the knot that held her drawstring pants around her slender waist, sliding them down over rounded hips, taking her panties with them.

She was very beautiful, her body outlined softly by the glow of the single light fixture in the hall. The storm was moving away, out over the lake, but the rain still fell, cocooning them in a small pool of twilight and silence. He continued to watch her until Sarah shivered, breaking the spell that held him immobile.

Tyler pulled back the blanket on her bed and pushed her down onto the sheets, covering her for the few moments it took to strip off his clothes and hang them over the back of a rocking chair near the bed.

Sarah lifted the bedclothes and he slid in beside her. He was silhouetted against the hall light for a moment and she shut her eyes against the surge of purely feminine delight she felt at the sight of his lean, rangy body. He was strong and gentle and caring, everything she dreamed she would find in the man she loved. She came to him without hesitation, lifting her arms to circle his neck, fitting her body alongside his as naturally as if they had lain together every night of their lives.

"Tyler, love me," Sarah whispered. She didn't stop to question the bubbling fountain of desire that sprang deep within her, providing the courage she needed to put aside the inhibitions that had so long held her in thrall.

She opened her heart and her body without hesitation because he had whispered his promise to protect her, had done so already. He cared for her; he had made himself responsible for the consequences of their lovemaking, assuring her pleasure and peace of mind. She loved him; now she knew he loved her, even if he couldn't say the words.

Tyler entered her slowly, carefully, moving with her, adjusting his rhythm to allow her to find her way along the glittering pathway to ecstasy. Her body adjusted quickly to the unfamiliarity of his. The first slight discomfort passed; the almost pain became heady pleasure. She pulled him closer, urged him on and soon was meeting every thrust of his body with her own.

Sarah lost her breath as her body tightened and contracted around his. Tiny starbursts of pleasure danced and swirled in the darkness behind her eyelids. The pleasure-pain grew more intense. Her eyes flew open. She wanted to tell Tyler to stop and let her catch her breath but she couldn't seem to say anything but his name. It sifted out from between her lips in astonishment, as all the electricity of the just-passed thunderstorm seemed to lodge itself in her lower body.

"Stay with me, Sarah." Tyler wasn't sure she heard him or understood him until her hands dug into his shoulders, her nails making tiny half-moon crescents in his skin. "Stay with me." He could feel his own pleasure demanding to be released. He felt the blood surging through his veins. She clung to him, murmuring his name again and again. He lifted his hand to caress her cheek. "Now, Sarah." He covered her mouth with his, lowered his hand between them and touched her.

Sarah exploded into a million glittering pieces, atoms scattered to the edges of the universe. The tiny delicate convulsions seemed to go on forever, leaving her floating anchorless in a great starry void. She wondered briefly if she would ever be whole again. Then Tyler surged into her once, twice, a third time, following her into the very private paradise spent lovers find in each other's arms.

She felt his weight, heavy and satisfying; she felt his arms, strong and comforting; she felt his lips on hers and knew what it was to be a woman, whole and complete.

They made love again in the cold dark hour before dawn, silently, without speaking, as though even endearing words would diminish what had passed between them. Tyler was relentless, his kisses deep and searching, his caresses insistent, his body on her, in her, demanding and exciting, allowing her to hold nothing of herself in reserve.

In the aftermath of passion, Tyler slept in her arms, but his rest was troubled and uneasy. Sarah lay awake and stared into the rainy darkness beyond her window. Nothing had changed because of this night. Nothing had been settled between them. But for the moment, she held the man she loved in her arms and that was enough. She stroked his tousled black hair and the strong beard-rough line of his jaw. She kissed him very lightly and settled herself to sleep.

When she wakened again she was alone in the bed. The room was filled with murky gray morning light. It was still raining but lightly, more mist than downpour. Tyler was half dressed. He looked over at her but didn't smile. Sarah felt her breath tighten in her chest. Reality was intruding already and she hadn't even had a chance to say good morning.

"I didn't mean to wake you, Sarah."

"It's all right." She was naked and it was chilly. She pulled the sheet up to her chin. "I...what would you like for breakfast?" She wasn't certain of the proper early-morning etiquette between first-time lovers. Tyler picked up his shirt and slid his arms into the sleeves. It was wrinkled but looked dry enough. His jeans, however, appeared to be slightly damp and they clung to his thighs like a second skin when he put them on.

"Nothing for me, thanks. I want to get back to our place, shower and shave before the first boat gets in." He seemed to be looking for something.

"You left your shoes downstairs," Sarah supplied. She wondered how she could reach her robe, for it was hanging on a hook behind the door a good ten feet from the bed. She didn't think she could nonchalantly slip out from under the sheet and walk over to get it. She felt too vulnerable, too exposed, as though the signs of their lovemaking and her intense response would be visible on her skin. She swallowed her pride. "Would you hand me my robe, please?" Suddenly she felt like crying. It couldn't just be over like this, as quickly as it had begun.

"Of course." Tyler walked around the foot of the bed, retrieved the robe and handed it to Sarah, never once directly meeting her eyes. She struggled into the cotton robe with one hand, trying not too successfully to hold the sheet to her breast with the other. When she was done with the humiliating maneuver, she belted it tightly, defiantly, around her waist. For a moment she wished she had her grandmother's antique turquoise kimono. It did suit her. She would feel more confident, better able to deal with the taciturn stranger standing beside her bed, if she were wearing the elegant, flamboyant robe.

Tyler buttoned his shirt, stuffing it into the waistband of his jeans. He kept his eyes fixed on the fringed end of the cream-colored bedspread where it dangled just above the floor. He'd have to look at her again sooner or later. He wasn't sure what was more upsetting to his peace of mind: the tantalizing glimpse of a golden breast as she slipped into her robe or the hint of tears in her brilliant sapphire eyes.

God, he loved her. But he wasn't free to tell her so, not yet, not while his life, his future, remained so uncertain.

"Sarah..."

"Don't say you're sorry, please, Tyler." She laced her fingers together and squeezed until the knuckles showed white beneath her skin.

"What made you think I'd say something like that?" Tyler sat on the edge of the bed. He pried her twisting fingers apart and took her hands between his own.

Sarah lifted her shoulders in a wordless little gesture that spoke volumes about the unsettled state of her feelings. "It seemed logical. You are leaving me, aren't you?"

Tyler sucked in his breath to deny the statement, then stopped. What had he been going to say a moment ago? *I love you, Sarah, but I have to leave you.* Wasn't that almost as bad as telling her he was sorry she'd given him her love, shared with him the most meaningful physical and emotional experience of his life?

"I love you, Sarah." It was imperative that he make her understand. "I love you but I'm not free...of myself." He frowned at their entwined hands, trying to make sense of his own jumbled thoughts. Sarah watched him for the space of a dozen heartbeats, then lowered her lashes so that he couldn't read the expression in her clear, honest eyes. "I have to get my life back in order."

She lifted her head proudly, spoke what she believed to be the truth. "You don't want to share David." Her words were barely more than a whisper, rough with unshed tears, but her gaze met his squarely, unflinchingly.

"Sarah, no. That's not it, damn it." He didn't sound as convincing as he needed to, because deep in his heart, he knew there was some truth in what she said. But more than that, it was that he wanted everything to be right. He wanted his career back on course, his life going smoothly, before he asked her to marry him. "I need time to bring everything into perspective." He stumbled to a halt, stopped speaking. Couldn't she understand what he was telling her?

"I think you had better go now." Sarah tugged her hands free of his grasp. "I want to get dressed."

"Sarah, I love you." He said it again, but it was evident she didn't believe him.

"Do you, Tyler? Or are you only hedging your bets where

David is concerned?'' It was the closest they'd come to speaking openly of David's parentage. "Do you think that if you love me I won't pose a threat to your relationship in the future?''

Tyler's words exploded from his mouth. "No, damn it, Sarah.'' Sarah flinched despite her determination not to. He took her by the upper arms and shook her. "You've got it all wrong.''

"Have I?'' She shook her head helplessly. "I think you'd better go.'' Sarah felt herself retreating inward to a small cool place deep inside where pain and heartache didn't exist. "Aunt Cam will probably offer to make breakfast for David and Elliot when they get back. You don't want them to find you here.''

"We'll talk about this later.'' He stood up, his expression bewildered but determined. Sarah continued to stare at her hands, folded on the creamy tufts of the candlewick bedspread.

"Before you leave?'' She closed her eyes against the stinging rush of tears that pushed against the back of her throat. The door closed very softly behind him. The sound of it echoed in the quiet room, almost as loudly as if he'd slammed it. Sarah sat quietly for a few moments, not allowing herself to think of anything at all.

Then unbidden came the memory of his words. *I love you.* He had said it; he meant it. But he wouldn't act on the words until he could get past the need, almost the obsession, to get David back legally. Tyler was so insecure about the child, about their relationship as father and son, that he couldn't commit himself to her—David's biological mother—until that need was realized. Sarah understood his actions with her logical mind, but not with her woman's heart.

A solitary tear slid down her cheek, and then another. She couldn't come this close to winning Tyler's love and David's and then lose it all. She simply would not allow it to happen. Sarah sniffed and wiped her eyes with a corner of the sheet. She wasn't going to let Tyler go without doing her best to stop him.

Somewhere in the big old house she heard a door slam.

Sarah fought back another urge to break into tears. Crying only got you red eyes and a runny nose. It didn't get you the man you loved. She certainly wasn't going to win any battles sitting in her bed crying. Sarah slid out from under the covers and opened the door to go down the hall and start running water for a bath.

A faint rise and fall of voices carried up the stairwell. Sarah stopped with one bare foot in the hall and one still in her room. Camilla's gentle questioning tone was easily recognizable. Tyler's answer was a mere rumble of sound. So he hadn't made his getaway, she realized with a tiny smile. David's piping soprano was easy to understand even from a distance. His next statement answered the question of why the stranded trio should be back on the island a good twenty minutes before the first boat was scheduled to dock.

"Granddad hired this really neat seaplane that takes people on rides over the bridge and everything and the pilot brought us right up to the dock. Everyone came out to watch us. It was fantastic."

Tyler made some response to David's enthusiastic description of the return trip. Elliot's low, resonant voice replied. Sarah didn't wait to hear any more. Five minutes later she was dressed, her hair was combed, and she was halfway down the stairs.

Tyler saw Sarah on the landing from the corner of his eye. His hands tightened on David's shoulders, bony and fragile-feeling under the cotton weave of his shirt and jacket. He stood behind the boy facing Elliot head-on, watching the older man through narrowed eyes. Sarah stepped into the main room. She was wearing some kind of gauzy mint-green shirt and jeans. Her hair floated soft and shiny brown around her shoulders. A faint rosy blush tinted her cheeks, as if she sensed the awareness of their new physical relationship in Camilla's speculative gaze. He wanted to go to her, acknowledge his feelings in front of all of them, take her in his arms to protect and cherish her, but he couldn't, not yet. He must deal with the matter at hand first.

"Elliot, I've decided to leave the island as soon as possible. I'm taking David with me."

"Dad?" David twisted around to look up at him, his face unbelieving. "I want to stay here with Aunt Cam and Sarah."

Tyler knelt and met the child's gaze squarely with his own. "Since your mother died your grandfather has been your guardian. Do you understand what that means?"

David nodded. "He promised the judge to take care of me while you were in prison." His voice faded to a whisper.

"Yes. But now I'm free and I want you back. I want it to be just the two of us." He didn't dare look at Sarah. He was hurting her but he didn't see any other way to explain the complicated legal maneuvering involved in a custody suit to his son. "I want to go back to Georgia and talk to the judge and the lawyers right away. Today."

"I don't want to leave the island," David repeated stubbornly. He looked as if he wanted to cry.

"We'll come back. I promise." He said it as much for his own sake and for Sarah's as for David's.

"Soon?" David tilted his head—the same way Sarah so often did. Why hadn't he noticed that telling little mannerism before?

"Soon."

"Granddad, are you coming back home with us?"

"Certainly, sport." Elliot smiled down at the child but the gray eyes he turned on Tyler were granite hard and cold as ice. "Why don't you go outside and check to see if Michael is coming up the bluff steps? Remember, Aunt Cam invited him for breakfast when we called the hotel from the dock. It's stopped raining and I'm beginning to wonder why he isn't here yet."

David glanced uncertainly at his father. Tyler nodded. "Go ahead."

"I'll ask him how he wants his eggs. Aunt Cam, do you have bacon? Michael likes bacon. So do I."

"I'll start cooking as soon as you let me know he's coming," Camilla said somewhat absently, her attention, like Sarah's, focused on the two men. David left the French doors that separated the main room from the veranda slightly ajar. The front screen door slammed shut behind him with a crack like a pistol shot.

"Do you really intend to leave the island today? Take the boy without my permission?" Elliot was fighting hard for control. His face was red, the cords on his neck standing out in bold relief.

Camilla laid her hand on his arm. "Elliot, last night you promised..."

He turned his head, looked at her for a long moment, then shrugged off the touch of her hand. "I didn't promise to allow him to take David away from me."

Tyler's eyes never left his father-in-law's face. His rugged features showed no expression at all. "I've waited long enough. I want custody of David returned to me immediately. I want to get on with my life."

"Does that mean leaving the country for months on end?" Elliot shot back.

"Yes. If I can get my old job back. I'm an engineer. Building bridges is the only work I know. It's what I do."

"And you intend to take David with you?" Elliot took a step closer, as if daring Tyler to give him the answer.

"Yes." Tyler held his ground.

"I forbid it. Do you hear me? I'll fight you every inch of the way. David is my grandchild. My only grandchild. I want him near."

Something in Tyler's face changed then; some inner wall of control buckled and collapsed inside him. Sarah saw it happen; she suspected Camilla did, too, because her aunt stepped forward and put both hands on Elliot's arm. "David isn't your grandchild." Tyler's voice was harsh, grating, but the words were clear, dropping into the sudden silence with small explosions of sound. "He isn't my son. He wasn't Allison's child, either."

For a moment Sarah was certain they would come to blows. Elliot's hands balled into fists at his side. He moved forward menacingly. Camilla's hold on his arm was no more restraint than the single strand of a spider's web would have been. "You're lying."

"No." Tyler held up his hand. He had no intention of trading blows with his father-in-law. He'd never intended to tell Elliot the truth in the first place. Something had just snapped inside him and he'd had no control over the words. It was too late to undo the damage but he wasn't going to make it worse by decking a man thirty years his senior. "I'm telling the truth."

They all stood rooted to the spot like characters in a play waiting for the curtain to drop. Not one of them heard the screen door open and close, because, for one of the few times in his life, David remembered not to slam it. Not one of them saw David's shocked and uncomprehending face as he came into the room to announce Michael's arrival at the top of the bluff and heard Tyler's words. Not one of them saw him leave again as quietly as he'd entered, tears streaming down his face, as the safe, secure walls of his world, so newly rebuilt, tumbled around him once again.

CHAPTER SEVENTEEN

MICHAEL FLICKED OPEN THE GATE and started up the walk. "David," he called, his tone friendly. The boy didn't answer him, didn't even turn around, just kept running toward the barn. Michael opened his mouth to yell the child's name again but thought better of it. Maybe the rush of wind through the pines and the spatter of raindrops in the leaves overhead had prevented David from hearing him. Perhaps he'd just been in too much of a hurry to see Sugar and Spice to pay heed to anything else. Michael smiled. Whatever the reason, it seemed even breakfast was taking second place to the child's love of horses these days. Anyway, David would show up quickly enough when it was time to eat.

Ten seconds later Michael's indulgent smile faded, replaced by a grimace as a cold raindrop found its way inside the collar of his waterproof jacket. It was starting to rain again. He knocked on the door frame, being careful to stay out from under a leaky section of eaves trough. The good-natured grimace turned into a full-fledged frown as angry voices spilled out the open French doors leading to the main room. Michael didn't wait any longer for an invitation to enter the cottage. Something was very wrong. He opened the screen and sprinted across the veranda to find Elliot and Tyler within inches of being at each other's throats.

"I don't believe you," Elliot muttered through clenched teeth. "You'd say anything to get David back. Well, it won't work. Why would Allison have lied about being pregnant? She was troubled, I know, but not irrational. Why would she claim some other woman's child as her own?"

"Allison must have believed we would never have a child

together." Tyler's hands hung stiffly at his sides. Obviously, he intended to do nothing to defend himself from Elliot's wrath. His eyes flickered over Michael, acknowledging, accepting his presence. "She knew that with her problems it would be hard to adopt a child through normal channels."

"Get to the point," Elliot shouted.

"Allison adopted David privately, on her own." Tyler spoke evenly, clearly, without a hint of emotion tinging his words. *Tyler knew the truth.* Michael realized his long silence was no longer necessary.

"Justin Delano made all the arrangements," Tyler continued. "Allison told everyone she was pregnant to avoid answering questions. And, I think, because she wanted so desperately to believe it herself. She even thought she had to lie to me. I'll regret that every day for the rest of my life."

"You can't prove any of this." Elliot broke free of Camilla's grip on his arm. Sarah moved, too, as if to step between the two men, but Michael was quicker.

"Elliot, wait. Listen to me." He couldn't do anything for Allison anymore, but he could do something for the loved ones she'd left behind. "Tyler isn't lying. God help me, he's telling the truth." It had taken all of Michael's considerable strength to hold Elliot back. Now the older man stopped struggling and looked directly at him for the first time.

"He's telling the truth?" There was a world of bewildered pain and grief expressed in the simple question, but also the beginning of acceptance.

It was Camilla who answered Elliot, not Michael. She lifted her hand and touched his beard-roughened cheek, making him look at her, making him see her. "We believe—" She broke off, seeking Sarah's eyes with her own. Sarah nodded her consent, her face white and strained. Some communication passed between the two women that Michael couldn't decipher. "When Sarah was seventeen she gave a child up for adoption. Her baby was a little boy. Justin Delano handled the arrangements. Sarah believes—I believe—that David is that child."

Michael shut his eyes a moment to help clear his thoughts. *Sarah knew the truth, also.* His suspicions that night they'd had dinner at the Grand Hotel had been correct. His loyalty to Allison was no longer justified. He must start to think of the living, of the future, not of the dead and the past. Michael dropped his restraining hands from Elliot's arms.

"David is Sarah's child." His words fell into a pool of silence. "I was with Allison when Justin Delano gave her the baby. I promised then to keep her confidence because I was her spiritual adviser and her friend. I never suspected she intended to keep the truth from you and Ty, even though she wanted other people to believe she was really pregnant. I gave her my word. And I've kept it until today. I saw the baby's natural mother just once, for a moment." He held out a hand toward Sarah in a gesture of apology. "It was Sarah."

Michael saw her eyes widen, saw her seek and find Tyler's dark gaze. Michael's back was to his friend; he couldn't gauge Tyler's reactions but Sarah's joy was plain for all the world to see.

"Thank you, Michael," she said simply. Her voice trembled, faded, then held firm. "Thank you for telling me."

He smiled crookedly, sadly. "I kept silent for Allison's sake while she lived, for David's sake after her death. Perhaps today the good Lord answered my prayers by not giving me time to contemplate right or wrong any longer." He'd spoken the truth at last, providing an opening to lay the past to rest once and for all. He thought, somehow, that Allison would have approved.

"I'm sorry, Elliot. I honestly intended for you never to know. It won't change anything between you and David," Tyler said with quiet conviction. "But I still want custody of my son returned to me."

"David." Camilla's sharply indrawn breath focused all their attention on her. "Where is he?"

"I saw him running toward the barn just before I came in here." Michael made the same connection between David's absence and the scene he'd just been part of that Camilla had. "How long were you arguing before I came in?"

"Too damned long." Tyler was pushing his way through the swinging door to the kitchen before he'd finished speaking.

Sarah followed him, her legs stiff with apprehension. How much had David overheard? His happiness was so fragile, his world and his security in it so newly restored. *Oh, God, please don't let him know; not yet. Not until we can tell him together*.

Tyler was staring into Spice's empty stall when Sarah stepped into the damp gloom of the barn. The stall door was ajar, a bridle missing from its nail by the door. David hadn't even tried to lift one of the heavy saddles onto the horse's back. They were both still in their places. Sugar was watching Tyler with interest, whinnying now and then, as if expecting him to fill her manger with hay and oats.

"He's gone." Tyler spun on his heel to face Sarah. "He's run away."

"He can't be too far away," she pointed out, as much for her own reassurance as Tyler's. "It must have taken him several minutes to get Spice bridled and out of the stall."

The others had arrived and were standing in the open doorway, making it darker than ever inside the small barn. Even so, Sarah could plainly see the anguish in Tyler's eyes, the corded muscles of his neck and shoulders. She longed to go to him, comfort him, but because of what had passed between them earlier, she was afraid to try.

"I'll take one of the bikes and check some of the streets and roads around the fort," Michael volunteered. "David may just be trying to work out what he overheard in his head. He may not be trying to run away at all." He grabbed the first bicycle he put his hands on. It was Camilla's, recently spray-painted white with a blue seat. At any other time, Michael would have looked slightly ridiculous. Now he only looked as anxious as the rest of them.

"Check back here in half an hour if you're close to a phone," Elliot ordered, then looked at Tyler to second his plan. "Camilla and I will stay here to field any calls."

"Yes." Tyler nodded his head once in agreement. "That's a good idea. Let's make a few calls now. I'll start with the ferry offices and ask them to keep an eye out for a small boy on a horse. Thank heaven it's early. There won't be any tour-

ists on livery-stable nags out roaming the streets for another
hour or so.''

"Tyler?" Sarah put her hand out but didn't touch him.
"What about alerting the police?"

"I'd rather try to find him myself. I don't want him to be
frightened any more than he's already been." He walked out
into the rain without a backward glance. Elliot followed him
toward the house. Sarah wrapped the folds of the oversize
cardigan she'd grabbed off a peg by the kitchen door more
tightly around her, shivering in the damp chill.

"Where could he be?" The island wasn't big. However,
except for the village and its environs, most of the land was
still near wilderness, owned by the state of Michigan. There
were thousands of acres, all rough terrain, heavily wooded,
making it very difficult to find one lost little boy.

"Spice won't take him very far off a road or path," Camilla
said softly, as if reading Sarah's thoughts. "She hasn't
changed her habits overnight. She's still the same slow, lazy
beast she's always been."

"You're right." Sarah sniffed back a sob. "He can't be
very far away yet. If I were eight and a half where would I
go to be alone, to try to make sense of a grown-up's mixed-
up scary world?" She was talking aloud, mostly to bolster her
own flagging courage, but Camilla took the question seriously.

Her brow furrowed into a frown. "The cave." Her fingers
clutched Sarah's arm so painfully she winced. "Elliot and I
showed him a very small cave we once found near Arch Rock.
Up along the bluff at Nicolet's Watchtower. He still talks
about it all the time, even though we wouldn't allow him to
try to climb down to it."

Sarah nodded, recalling bits and pieces of David's recent
conversations herself. Lately, caves full of Indian relics and
trappers escaping from murderous savages had figured prom-
inently in his imaginative and rambunctious play.

"Michael is searching in the opposite direction." Hope
lightened her voice. "It isn't far. I'll take one of the bikes and
leave right away. You tell Tyler what you've remembered and
that I've gone ahead."

"Sarah." Camilla's tone held a note of caution. "It's only a long shot. David might not have gone there."

"I know." Sarah managed a smile. "I have to do something, Aunt Cam. I can't just sit here and twiddle my thumbs while my son is out there somewhere alone and confused."

"At least take time to put on some rain gear," Camilla urged as Sarah wheeled her bike toward the door.

"No time." Sarah was adamant. "Besides, I'm already wet."

The short ride to Arch Rock had never taken so long. The tree-lined path seemed to stretch on forever. The gravel roadway was soft and slippery after several days of rain, making pedaling difficult. Muddy water splashed Sarah's shoes and pant legs and the back of her sweater. Rain continued to fall, hampering her vision as it dripped into her eyes. Her fingers were stiff with cold, her breath coming in hard little gasps by the time she coasted down the last slope into the parking lot.

It was empty—except for Spice, miserable and wet, tethered to a bicycle rack near the rest rooms. Sarah looked around hurriedly for a park employee, a ranger, a tour-wagon driver. There was no one. It was the end of June, peak tourist season, but it was also eight-thirty on a chilly, rainy morning. The wagons didn't start running until nine. Most of the walking or riding day-trippers hadn't made it any farther than Market Street as yet.

Sarah took the steep flight of wooden steps to the top of the bluff as quickly as she dared. The last thing she wanted to happen was for her ankle to twist under her and send her sprawling. At the top of the steps she paused to catch her breath. The path ahead was as empty as the parking lot. She hurried along, keeping a wary eye on the tree roots and rocks that seemed to be everywhere.

Every few feet Sarah leaned over the rail fence that bordered the edge of the path. She couldn't see David through the low growth of brush and small trees but she could see the shore road far below, and beyond that, the restless gray waters of the lake. She'd forgotten how steep, how dangerous a drop it really was. Her heart contracted with fear and frustration.

Where was he? Then she heard the sobs, forlorn and very, very near.

Ducking under the fence, Sarah dropped to her knees at the edge of the bluff. David was huddled on a large flat boulder about thirty feet below her. His knees were drawn up to his chin, his head resting on folded arms. He looked as wet and miserable as his faithful steed.

"David," she called very softly. She didn't want to startle him. He was very close to the lip of the ledgelike outcropping that ran along the bluff for fifty or sixty feet at this point.

"Sarah?" He looked up, scrubbing at his eyes with his fist. "I found Aunt Cam and Granddad's cave." He sniffed, pointing at a small dark opening about eight feet above his head. "Only I guess he isn't really my granddad anymore, is he?" He was asking for reassurance. Sarah didn't hesitate a moment to give it to him.

"Of course he's still your granddad." She made her tone as brusque and matter-of-fact as she could manage, considering the lump of emotion that clogged her throat. "How did you get down there?"

David frowned and waved his hand toward a dip in the path about twenty feet past where Sarah knelt. "I came down there. But I don't know if I can get back up by myself. It's kinda' scary comin' down here."

"Sit still," Sarah ordered. "I'll be right there."

"Maybe you should wait—"

Sarah cut him short. "Just stay put."

"Okay." Relief was evident in his tone. David lifted his head from his knees and watched with interest as Sarah started her descent.

Climbing down the face of the bluff was an experience Sarah didn't want to ever have to repeat. David had found adequate handholds in the stunted trees and bushes that grew out of the thin rocky soil. Sarah wasn't as lucky. Several times branches under her hand snapped off and sent her sliding helplessly toward the edge. She was only able to slow the headlong skids by grabbing at anything in her path. She was scratched and bruised and completely out of breath by the time she scrambled onto David's shelf of rock. He reached over and gave her a hug.

"Is your ankle okay?" He asked and Sarah's heart cracked a little at the lost and frightened note in his voice.

"It's fine."

"I thought this would be a neat place to come and live by myself," David admitted with a touch of defiance that was spoiled as he sniffed back a sob. "I don't want to be adopted."

"Why not, David? You know that being adopted doesn't make any difference to your father or grandfather. They still love you very, very much."

David nodded. "I know." He was silent a moment, arranging his thoughts; then the words burst from him in an anguished flood. "This kid in my class, Bill Whitson. He's adopted. His mom and dad are great. He's got an adopted sister and brother, too, but they're just little pests and we never play with them."

"I see." Sarah cleared her throat and swallowed a smile.

"One day Bill was walkin' home from school and this woman came up to him and said she was his real mom. She tried to get him to be her kid again. Bill didn't like her. He was scared to walk home for a long time. His mom—his adopted mom," David explained, looking a little confused himself, "had to come to school every day and pick him up till the woman went away. Now she can come to see him once a month but he still doesn't like her very much." Tears welled up in his brown eyes but he blinked them back manfully. "I don't want somebody I never saw before come to try and take me away from Dad and Granddad and Michael." The tears won and he started to cry again.

"Oh, David, sweetheart, that won't happen." Sarah's voice broke and she stopped talking, pulling David into her arms, brushing a stray wave of wet curly brown hair off his forehead. "I promise you, no one will ever try to take you away from the people you love. Ever."

That much she could do for her son.

"Do you think so?" David looked up hopefully. His relieved smile was a precious memory for Sarah to store away in her heart.

"I know so." Sarah settled him on her lap and wrapped him inside the generous folds of her once-white oversize sweater. He relaxed against her, shivering in his thin wet jacket. Sarah shivered, too, wondering how much longer she should wait for help before risking the steep climb up the bluff.

"I wish Dad would come and help us climb back up." David echoed her thoughts, nestling his head against her breast.

"He will." Sarah twisted around so that her back was to the lake, trying to protect them from a wind-driven spray of rain.

"Why didn't he tell me I was adopted?" David lifted his head, his brown eyes troubled.

"If you ask him when we get off this rock, he'll tell you."

"Billy's mom and dad said they chose him over all the other babies at the adoption place because he was the most special one."

"So are you. Very special." Sarah closed her eyes and settled herself to wait.

"It's pretty wet out here," David complained a few moments later.

"I think that's because it's raining."

"No kidding." David's tone was ironic. "I found Granddad and Aunt Cam's cave." He snaked one grubby hand out from under Sarah's sweater and pointed to the dark opening almost screened by ferns. "It's wet and dark and it doesn't smell too good, either."

"I think we'd better stay out here so your father will be able to find us more easily."

"Yeah. I still wish there'd been at least some bones or something in there, though." David sounded more than a little disappointed at the lack of gruesome relics.

Sarah was considering her answer to that remark when she heard movement and voices at the top of the bluff.

"Sarah. David." It was Tyler's voice. Sarah's heart beat faster in recognition.

"Dad." David sat up straight. "We're stuck down here."

"I'm coming down to get you." Tyler looked over the edge, saw Sarah sitting calmly with her arms around David and knew he was looking at the two most precious beings in the universe.

"I don't think that's wise." Elliot's face was white with strain. Tyler looked away from Sarah and David to glare at his father-in-law, unwilling to accept any advice or counsel from the older man.

"Sarah and David are trapped on that damned slab of rock."

"Elliot tried going down the first time we brought David here." Camilla stepped between them, her face beneath a damp silk scarf, determined and stern. "There are almost no safe handholds for a grown man. Can't you two forget your hatred and animosity for one minute and work with each other? David and Sarah's lives may depend on it."

"Camilla's right, Tyler. Nothing's more important than David and Sarah's safety." Elliot pointed down the slope. "See that stunted maple about fifteen feet along?" Tyler nodded. "We can get that far without a problem."

"After that?" Tyler didn't try to keep the harshness out of his voice. Elliot didn't flinch, didn't even look at him; he was already on his way down the bluff. "We'll improvise. And I'll pray."

Sarah and David had moved away from the slab of rock at the cave mouth. She was standing with her hands on his shoulders, her face pale and wet with rain, her eyes big and scared-looking. Tyler stood for a moment, studying their predicament, one hand curled around the trunk of the sturdy little maple, both feet braced against the slope. He started the rest of the way down. Elliot grabbed his shoulder, holding him back.

"It's still too damn chancy without a rope."

As much as Tyler hated to admit it, Elliot was right about that one very important fact. Camilla and Elliot had spent precious minutes searching for a rope while he harnessed Sugar to the buggy. They hadn't been lucky enough to find one and Tyler had been too impatient to wait for one to be sent up from the village.

"What alternative do we have?"

Elliot held out his arm. "Grab hold."

"What?" Tyler glared at the older man's outstretched hand.

"Grab hold of my arm. We'll make ourselves a human rope. I'll anchor you. Sarah can boost David up from below." His gray eyes held Tyler's in a steady, unwavering stare. "Camilla's right. We have to do this together."

"It will work." The agreement came reluctantly to his lips but Tyler nodded and held out his hand. "We'll do this together."

Sarah saw what they were attempting immediately and gave David a shove on the seat of his pants. "Climb," she ordered. For once he did as he was told without an argument. She steadied him from behind for the first few slippery steps and then, with a rush and scramble that sent stones and twigs tumbling over the brink of the ledge, he was safe in Tyler's arms. Sarah blinked back tears of relief as Tyler pulled back up the slope to catch his breath, while Elliot pushed David over the top, into Camilla's waiting arms.

"You're next." Tyler's voice held all the confidence in the world.

Sarah opened her eyes, blinking rapidly to focus against another stinging rush of wind-driven rain. Again Tyler and Elliot had formed their human chain. Except that she weighed a great deal more than David. What if she overbalanced Tyler, placed too much strain on Elliot's hold on the small, fragile-looking tree trunk, sending them all over the edge? She half turned her head to look down at the roiling gray waters of the lake.

"Sarah, no. Look at me." Tyler's voice was insistent, commanding, cajoling. "Is something wrong with your ankle?"

"No," Sarah shot back. "My ankle's fine but I'll make it on my own."

"No. You're going to let me help you." The cajoling note in his voice disappeared. He knew exactly what she was thinking. She was very brave and very foolish. He made his next words an order. "Climb, Sarah."

She did. Twice she slipped back; the second time she was within inches of grasping his outstretched fingers.

"Take your time, Sarah. We have all day if necessary." It was Elliot's voice, deep and confident. It cut through the wave of panic that threatened to overtake her as she lay flat on the muddy incline, fighting to catch her breath. "Find a foothold, set yourself and then just start climbing. Tyler will catch you. And I won't let go of him, no matter what."

Sarah lifted her head, attempting a smile that she suspected was more than a little frayed around the edges. The panic receded and then faded away. "Promise?" She answered Elliot but her eyes were caught and held by Tyler's dark gaze.

"You have my word."

Tyler didn't say anything. He didn't have to. He just smiled and held out his hand.

"THE SUN IS FINALLY COMING out from behind the clouds. Believe it or not, there's going to be a beautiful sunset." Sarah spoke softly so as not to disturb David, curled up asleep on the sofa near the fireplace. It had been a long, exhausting day. She was tired also, but far too keyed up to make an early night of it.

Tyler came up behind her as she stood in the open French doors, looking out across the veranda at the view of the straits. He put his arms around her and kissed the nape of her neck very lightly. She leaned against the hard comforting wall of his chest, content and at peace with the world.

"Is that a good omen?" Tyler nuzzled her earlobe, his voice a low rough whisper. Sarah felt a slow spiral of warmth spread through her at the touch of his lips.

"Yes." She turned in his arms to accept his kiss.

"I love you, Sarah." There was no reservation in his eyes or in his voice as he said the words, only love, deep and true and lasting. The love Sarah had been searching for all her life.

"I love you." She touched her lips to his in a lover's pledge that was as old as time.

"And David loves you." Tyler smoothed his big gentle hands over her hair, imprisoning her face between his palms. "He told me what you said out there on that slab of rock this morning. That you'd never allow his 'real' parents to come and take him away from me. You are a very brave and unselfish woman." He watched her closely, searching her eyes, her expression, for any sign of regret.

"I only said what needed to be said." She smiled and there were no shadows darkening the gemstone blue of her eyes. "I told you once, David never has to know who I am, if that's what's best for him. Right now, today, and perhaps for some time to come, that is what's best."

Tyler's dark brows pulled together in a frown. "I want us to be a family but it's all so damned complicated I didn't know where to start. Did I say the right things to him?" He valued her opinion; he needed her advice today and always.

"You said all the right things." Sarah looked over her shoulder in the direction of the sleeping child. "He's going to have a lot more questions, Tyler, don't fool yourself about that. He's a bright kid. He'll want to understand everything that's happened, examine all your actions. He's confused and insecure right now but he'll be fine in the end."

"Michael's a psych major, remember. He'll be there to help me over the rough spots." Tyler paused for the space of a heartbeat, took a deep breath and went on. "And what about you, Sarah? Will you be there for me? For us?"

"Till the end of time." She laid her head against his chest so he wouldn't see how close she was to crying again. The slow steady thud of his heart beneath her ear was soothing and exciting at the same time. They stood quietly for a long while, savoring the solitude, the privacy, the sense of oneness.

The big old house was quiet. The sounds of harness bells and the clip-clop of metal horseshoes on the pavement drifted up the bluff on eddies of lake breeze. Far out on the lake a buoy clanged with monotonous regularity. Aunt Cam had gone off with Elliot and Michael to have dinner at the Iroquois. They were alone at last with their sleeping son.

No, Sarah thought with a tiny lingering pang of sadness, *not my son yet.*

"We'll be leaving soon." Tyler's cheek rested on the top of her bent head. Her arms were linked around his waist. She held him tighter. He sighed and tightened his arms around her, also. "Will you come with us?"

Sarah smiled against the front of his shirt but the curve of her lips was bittersweet. "I can't. Not yet. I have obligations, a career…" She hadn't really considered what would happen after she left the island.

"You have skills that will be very valuable in Brazil." Tyler straightened, lifting her chin with the tip of his finger so that she had to look directly at him. "I'm asking you to marry me, Sarah Austin."

"And I'm accepting." She kissed him again and wished they were alone. She wanted to laugh out loud with the joy of her discovery. That momentary irritation, too, was part of being a parent, of being a mother. It made the frustration a lot easier to bear.

"When will you marry me?"

"When the time is right. You and David still need time alone together, now more than ever. I need a little time, too. I just can't walk out on Holy Family. I have to find someone to sublet my apartment." She frowned in momentary confusion. "You don't have a place to live, either." She grinned at the sudden look of consternation that crossed his face.

"I hate it when you're so practical." He kissed her to soften the sting of his teasing words.

"The rest of the world is still out there," Sarah admitted with a sigh. "We still have to deal with all the ordinary, everyday aggravations that don't seem to exist in a never-never land like Mackinac." She was suddenly serious. "But most of all, I want David to have time to get used to having a stepmother." She smiled. "You told me once we weren't kids rushing to meet the future. That even love could wait until tomorrow, if necessary."

Tyler rested his hands on her shoulders. He looked at her long and compellingly. "I talk too much. But you're right.

I've got a lot of things to work out for David's sake, and Elliot's, too, I suppose. And for us. Just promise me one thing.''

"Anything at all.''

"Just wait until tomorrow. It's not so very far away.''

Sarah touched her finger to his lips, tracing the hard curve of his mouth, sliding her arms around the back of his neck to pull his head down to hers. "The time will go quickly, I guarantee it. After all, tomorrow is just around the corner.''

EPILOGUE

"MOM! DAD! WE'RE OVER HERE."

It wasn't hard to pick out David's noisy, energetic figure or hear his high piping voice, even over the roar of the ferry's diesel engines. Sarah slid her sunglasses to the top of her head to help hold flying tendrils of hair in place as the ferry maneuvered alongside the dock. Overhead fleecy white clouds raced across a sky so blue it hurt to look at it. Below the fort the lilac bushes in the park were heavy with clusters of dark purple and white buds.

David continued to wave, both arms flailing above his head in enthusiastic welcome. Camilla and Elliot stood at his side, looking happy and at ease with each other. Elliot had brought David to the island a week ago after the end of the school term. Although he had relinquished legal custody of David to Tyler as soon as he'd returned to Georgia last summer, the youngster still spent a great deal of time with his grandfather. Elliot had turned most of his pastoral duties over to Michael Parker and planned to retire officially at the end of the year. Sarah wondered if there were wedding bells in her aunt's future.

They were all staying at Gathering Place because Lilac Time had been sold to a wealthy auto dealer from Milwaukee in the spring. Sarah was looking forward to spending time with Camilla and to being on the island again. But it would also be very, very nice to have some time alone with her husband.

They'd been married quietly at Christmas and over the course of the winter they'd become a family. Tyler had regained his enthusiasm for his work and his confidence in loving and giving. At the end of April he'd decided to accept a

two-year assignment to head up a bridge project on a tributar
of the Amazon near Manaus.

Ten days later, Sarah had been contacted by an America
doctor who had dealings with Tyler's firm. He ran a maternit
clinic near where they would be living and he was in desperat
need of a nurse with Sarah's qualifications. Until then, she'
been so busy settling into her new life as Tyler's wife an
David's mother that she hadn't realized how much she misse
her work. Now she found that she was as excited about he
new position as Tyler was about his.

But nothing thrilled her as much as her son. Sarah foun
being a parent, a mother, the most rewarding, exasperating
challenging experience of her life. She had never been s
happy. Even the one thing she'd been dreading, the day whe
David discovered who she really was, hadn't been the ordea
she'd envisioned.

One rainy afternoon during an Easter visit to Sarah's fathe
in Key West, David came across the box of mementos she'
shipped from Mackinac. As he leafed through the photo a
bums Sarah had waited, her nerves stretched to the breakin
point. When once again David came across the snapshot c
the boy he so closely resembled, it was Tyler who had take
him on his lap and explained, simply and directly, the stor
behind his adoption. Tyler kept to the facts, emphasizing h
love and Allison's, explaining as best he could the reaso
Sarah had had to give him away, how very much like a mirac
it was that they had all found each other and become a famil

David listened quietly, slid off Tyler's lap and walked t
where Sarah had been sitting, her hands clasped tightly to
gether, her heart beating high and fast in her throat. "Doe
this mean I can call you Mom now, instead of just Sarah?"

"I guess it does." She held out her arms and he steppe
into her embrace. As easily as that David had become, trul
her son.

"Mom. Dad." Sarah moved out from under the covere
walkway that connected the dock with the street just as Davi
launched himself at her with the force of a small tornado. H
exuberant hug left her feeling breathless and very much love

and no longer interested in thoughts of the past. "I missed you." He transferred his bear hug to Tyler's waist. "We got Sugar and Spice back for the summer," he told his father joyfully. "I'm learning to drive the buggy all by myself."

"Way to go, sport." Tyler ruffled his brown hair.

"Aw, Dad, don't do that. That's for babies." David danced away in disgust then came back three seconds later to link his hand with Tyler's. "Have you told Mom about the surprise yet?" he asked in a stage whisper that carried halfway across the crowded street.

"What surprise?" Sarah asked, giving Camilla a hug. "You look great, Aunt Cam."

"So do you. Marriage suits you."

"Island life suits you." Sarah gave her aunt a very knowing and feminine smile. Camilla looked flustered and Sarah laughed delightedly.

"Hello, Elliot." She reached up and gave him a peck on the cheek.

"Hello, Sarah." He enfolded her hand in a viselike grip. "Hello, Tyler." Elliot released her and turned toward the younger man.

"Elliot." Tyler returned the handshake. The two men would never be close, Sarah suspected; the scars for both of them were deep and hard to ignore. But at least, now, they were in agreement as far as David's welfare was concerned. The shock of so nearly losing him that day on the bluff had assured co-operation between them, if not affection.

"Mom, don't you want to know about your surprise?" David was jumping up and down with excitement. "Dad called us the other day. I helped Aunt Cam and Granddad make all the plans."

"What is it?" Sarah asked, smiling at Tyler as he watched David bouncing around like a jackrabbit.

"See for yourself." Tyler pointed toward the street with a grin of his own.

Sarah found herself staring at a liveried driver on the box of a highly polished surrey complete with fringe on top. She watched in amazement as the last of their luggage was strapped on behind by an equally splendid footman.

"Your carriage awaits, madam," Tyler announced with a flourish. Sarah stood rooted to the sidewalk. Tyler gave her a little push.

David bounded forward and took her by the hand. "It's your surprise. You and Dad are going to the Grand Hotel for a honeymoon. I wanted to come along but Aunt Cam says kids aren't allowed on honeymoons. I think that stinks." He looked mutinous.

The footman came around the back of the buggy to stand at attention by the rear wheel. Sarah stooped to give David a hug. "This is a very wonderful surprise."

"I know," he answered with justifiable pride.

Tyler held out his hand to help her up the steps. "I'm not taking any chances on missing out on our dinner reservations tonight," he said so softly only Sarah could hear. "I'm having room service send it up." His tone was serious but his eyes were full of love and laughter and something dark and heated that caused Sarah's heart to skip a beat.

Tyler turned back to give David a quick hard hug. "Be a good boy."

"I will. We're going to order pizza as soon as you're gone."

"That's our son." Tyler laughed, settling back against the cream-colored velvet cushions. He took Sarah in his arms and kissed her, unmindful of the interested bystanders all around them.

"Where to, sir?" the driver asked, touching his whip to the brim of his black top hat as the footman climbed onto the front seat beside him.

"The Grand Hotel," Tyler replied with an expansive wave of his hand. "And don't spare the horses."

LOOK FOR OUR FOUR FABULOUS MEN!

Each month some of today's bestselling authors bring
four new fabulous men to Harlequin American Romance.
Whether they're rebel ranchers, millionaire power brokers
or sexy single dads, they're all gallant princes—and
they're all ready to sweep you into lighthearted fantasies
and contemporary fairy tales where anything is possible
and where all your dreams come true!

You don't even have to make a wish...
Harlequin American Romance will grant your every desire!

Look for Harlequin American Romance
wherever Harlequin books are sold!

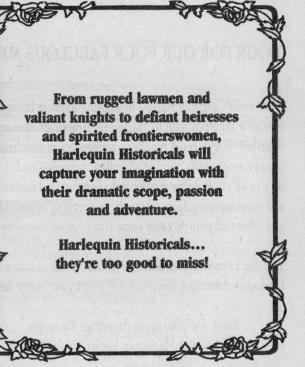

From rugged lawmen and
valiant knights to defiant heiresses
and spirited frontierswomen,
Harlequin Historicals will
capture your imagination with
their dramatic scope, passion
and adventure.

Harlequin Historicals...
they're too good to miss!

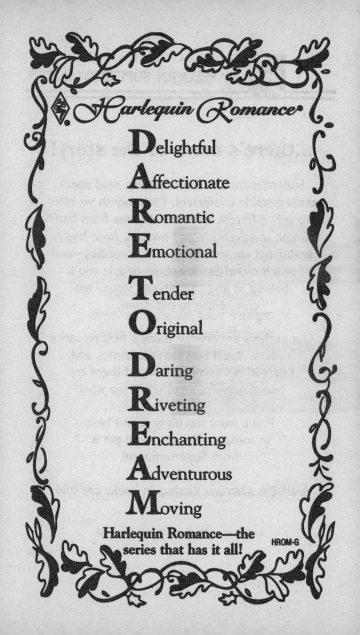

ℋarlequin Romance®

Delightful

Affectionate

Romantic

Emotional

Tender

Original

Daring

Riveting

Enchanting

Adventurous

Moving

Harlequin Romance—the
series that has it all!

HROM-G

HARLEQUIN SUPERROMANCE®

...there's more to the story!

Superromance. A *big* satisfying read about unforgettable characters. Each month we offer *four* very different stories that range from family drama to adventure and mystery, from highly emotional stories to romantic comedies—and much more! Stories about people you'll believe in and care about. Stories too compelling to put down....

Our authors are among today's *best* romance writers. You'll find familiar names and talented newcomers. Many of them are award winners—and you'll see why!

If you want the biggest and best in romance fiction, you'll get it from Superromance!

Available wherever Harlequin books are sold.

HARLEQUIN PRESENTS®

HARLEQUIN PRESENTS
men you won't be able to resist
falling in love with...

HARLEQUIN PRESENTS
women who have feelings
just like your own...

HARLEQUIN PRESENTS
powerful passion in
exotic international settings...

HARLEQUIN PRESENTS
intense, dramatic stories that will keep you
turning to the very last page...

HARLEQUIN PRESENTS
The world's bestselling romance series!

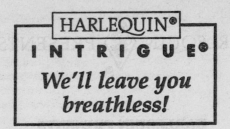